TIMOTHY K. CLARK

Rise of the Dragonwitch

We all come from warriors.
Otherwise, we wouldn't be here today.
So, stand up and fight
when your time comes.
Live to die well.

JÖTNARLAND
VALHALLA
VANAHEIMR
OCEANTIS
NIBURU
DIMIAN
HYPERBOREA
AGARTHA
OPONSKOYE
MAG MELL
RELNA THUNE
THE BLACK CITY
MANANNÁN
CASTLE LEVIATHAN
NIRVANA
IRKALLA
EYES OF THE GODS
SHANGRI-LA
KER-IS
PAN DÆMONIA
KUNLUN
VALLEY OF THE BLACK BONES
RIVER STYX
VULCA
HELL
SCHOLOMANCE ACADEMY
ELYSIUM
CAMELOT
OGUN
CIBOLA
QUIVIRA
SVARGA
CANELA
GODSRIBBON CASTLE
TRITON SEA
ATLANTIS
TIR NA

Prologue

My name is Finley Maguire, and I am dying.

If you happen to find my body, do me a favor: don't burn it. Seriously, I can't come back to life if I'm a crispy pile of ashes.

Oh, and please—don't bury me. There's no guarantee I'll be able to claw my way out of six feet of dirt, no matter how determined I am.

Here's the situation: I've been poisoned. By who? Good question. I've made a lot of enemies over the years—let's start with the Valhallans. They'd probably throw a parade if I dropped dead. And Atlantis? Yeah, the entire island wants me gone.

But let's focus on the story at hand. Pherric, the ever-optimistic mage (note the sarcasm), is currently throwing every ounce of his alchemy at the poison. He's... not hopeful. To be fair, he's *never* hopeful. His best estimate? Three weeks. Maybe four if he discovers a miracle at the bottom of one of his dusty potion bottles.

Which brings me to why I'm writing this. Pherric insisted that I jot down everything—my story, my fights, my mistakes—because I'll be "gone" for about a hundred years. Give or take. And, well, everyone I know will be dead by the time I wake up.

So, here we are. The final journal of Finley Maguire. Let's start at the beginning, shall we?

Because this is one hell of a story.

I

Part One

Chapter 1

R *un!*
The voice screaming at me was mine. From a distant, foggy, back corner of my mind.

Run, dammit!

But my body simply refused to listen. I stood there. And stared. With my mouth hanging open.

Now!

"Okay! Okay..." I said. Out loud. To myself.

I was a bit drunk. Well, actually I was a lot drunk. But I hiked up my dress and started walking on bare feet across the slick tiles.

Running was not my thing. I used to tell friends that if they saw me running, they'd better turn and run because they were about to die.

And running after a long night of partying? *Sooo* not the best idea.

But I had to get away from the creepy tall guy in the dark robe staring down at me. He stood between me and the rest of the people at the party. And no one was going to hear me yelling over the loud music.

Only bad part was that my boozy brain and feet were *not* on the same page. I stumbled a few times and completely fell on my face rushing to the fire escape. But I made it to the ladder and when I looked back, he was storming across the terrace after me.

I tried to get a good look at his face, but the hood on his robe was pulled down. And he was carrying my shoes and phone in his hand.

He wanted no trace of me left behind.

Taking a deep breath, I heaved myself over the low wall and onto the fire escape. My palms, slick with sweat, gripped the slippery metal ladder as I made my way down. The first landing wasn't far, but, of course, as a tall girl I just had to channel my inner klutz halfway there—my foot slipped, skidding off the rung. My fingers scrambled, gripping the metal bars like my life depended on it—because, well, it literally did.

And then, gravity said, "Not today." My hand slid, and I dropped like a sack of questionable decisions onto the landing grate and rolled toward the edge. The impact rattled me, and I barely managed to grab the rail before I went tumbling to the street below.

For a moment, I just held tight, doubled over, staring down at 110th Street. The bright lights of the Upper West Side blurred as a delivery truck rolled by. My breath came in frantic gasps, each one stabbing through the lingering haze of tequila and adrenaline clogging my brain.

"Get it together," I hissed to myself, trying to sound badass, even though my shaking knees and pounding heart gave off a completely different vibe. This wasn't the time to panic—I could have my meltdown later, preferably somewhere with fewer heights and more snacks.

At the next landing, I dared to look up. He stood there at the edge of the rooftop, a dark silhouette against the pre-dawn sky. I could not see his eyes but his stillness created a cold intensity that raised the hair on my neck, my arms.

I scanned the empty street below, searching desperately for anyone—a passing stranger, someone talking on their phone, a storefront light flickering on. But it was four in the morning, and the entire block lay silent and deserted, swallowed by the goddamn shadows.

Sweat burned as it ran into my eyes. I swiped at it with the back of my shaky hand before continuing my descent, each step feeling heavier than the last.

Okay, let me back up for a second. So, here's what started this *whole* mess.

Earlier that day, I should've let the call go to voicemail when my dad's number popped up. But I answered...

I was sitting at my dorm room desk, absently sketching out a cocktail dress on a notepad, the lines flowing easier than the hours I spent trying to focus on classes. My textbooks were stacked on the far corner of the desk, looming silent reminders of everything I was supposed to be doing. My junior year *should* have been winding down smoothly, but with barely enough credits to call myself a freshman, the gap was a pretty big canyon.

Fury overwhelmed me when my phone rang, cutting through the quiet. Everyone who really knew me knew the rule: don't call, just text. And then... don't text. But my father was the exception—the one person who ignored my rule completely.

I felt my shoulders tense as I rubbed at my forehead, bracing against the dull ache already creeping in, anticipating the familiar conversation that lay ahead.

I scooped up my phone. "What?"

"Is that any way to answer the phone, Finley?"

He called me Finley and not Fin—I was in trouble.

"What do you want, dad?"

"Well, your mother just forwarded me your midterm grades. And I do *not* like what I am seeing." I could hear him clacking away on his keyboard.

"Mom knows how to forward something? Wait! She was sober enough to check her email? Wow."

"Finley..."

"Dad..."

"I am paying a shitload of money for you to go to school and—" And he rambled on for a few minutes, but I ignored him. (Oh, and for your reference: a shitload is more than a buttload but less than a fuck-ton.)

"Finley? Finley?!"

I put the phone back to my ear.

"I know all this. I'm working on getting my grades up, dad. I really am."

"It's not the grades, Fin! So much as it is these *weird* classes! You started off Pre-Med and failed miserably... yet again. You've been kicked out of two schools! And you agreed to switch to a finance major, but... *none* of these goddamn classes make any sense!"

I always considered myself to be kind of smart, but you would not know it from my school progress so far. After being thrown out of my second *prestigious* school for piss-poor grades ("calculated mediocrity") and 'a lack of respect for the integrity of the academic process' as I recall one letter stating, my father demanded that I *get my act together* (a favorite phrase of his), start studying, and actually attend classes. The *right* classes.

"I don't... I'm not sure I want to be a finance... person," He had this way of making me feel like an eight-year-old caught eating cookies before dinner. "I-I don't think that's what I want to do."

"And what *do* you want to do? Be a loser your whole life?! Jesus, Fin!"

I held up my sketch of the dress, afraid to tell him the truth. "I don't know. I have no idea. Who does when they're twenty years old?"

"Most people have a pretty good goddamn idea by then, Fin! I did!"

"Well, I'm... I'm not most people. And I'm not you, so—"

"Look, you have a job waiting for you here at Ronin! *When* you graduate! But you gotta show your bona fides! You'll start low six figures, right out of school!"

"I know. But maybe it's not about money with me, you know. What if I want to—"

"You've got your accounting courses out of the way, barely... But what the hell is *Fashion Marketing*, *Textile Science*, and... *Drafting and Sewing*? Are these actual college classes?! You don't need any more electives! Oh, and everything is about money, Fin." He exhaled deeply. "Every. Thing."

You might've heard of my father—Sean Maguire? He's a big-shot hedge fund manager at Ronin Advisors in New York City, the kind of guy whose name gets dropped in glossy magazines and overpriced power lunches. And my mother? Well, let's just say her portfolio leans heavily into vodka futures. They live in a sprawling Greenwich mansion, complete with manicured lawns, a pool more decorative than practical, and just enough distance from the city so he can feel as though he belongs among the elite.

"I'm at the end of my rope with you, hon. You're a *girl*! Girls are supposed to be *good* at school! You don't want to end up like your uncles, trust me..."

We come from stereotypical Boston Irish stock—the kind that's been woven into the fabric of Southie for generations. My dad's brothers, his father, and even his grandfather wore the blue with pride, serving as cops and trying to keep their neighborhoods in line. The kind of men who talked with their hands, drank whiskey straight, and carried a sense of duty much heavier than their guns.

But my father? He had other plans. The Irish temperament, if you're unfamiliar, is equal parts ego, hot temper, and mule-headed stubbornness, shaken up and poured into one tenacious human. My scrappy dad leaned into that cocktail, ditching the family tradition for something flashier. He traded the badge for a slick suit and a sleek briefcase, heading to NYC to carve out his fortune off the backs of the well-heeled and overpaid.

"You have the chance to be a successful advisor at one of the most prestigious firms in Manhattan! People would kill for this opportunity! And if you don't straighten up and fly right, I will cut you off. Do you understand me?"

"Yes. I do... but—"

"Get it right, Fin. Bye."

That's how most of our conversations went—massive disappointment was piled on and various threats were made—and, as always, I was too spooked to defend myself. What did I want to be when I grew up? I thought maybe a doctor. Or a fashion designer. Or a writer. Oh, or a fashion writer! But financial advisor? Hell no. But all I ever got was, *'Decide what you want to be—as long as I approve—or I'll take away your money!'*

So now that I was completely irate, I needed some revenge. I consider myself to be a recovering introvert. I love being alone. Mostly because I'm the only person who will put up with me. I dread being around people. But... I'm also kind of a smart ass. Even got voted Class Clown back in high school. And I was constantly getting in trouble, being sent to the principal's office at least once a week. So, passive aggression was my only outlet. I did what I always do... I took out my anger on him... passively.

Searching online for his landscaping company in Cos Cob, I called them up, using my mother's slurred Boston accent, and told them: *"Hi, this is Missus Maguire. Yes, on Putnam Avenue. I would like you to come to ah house and remove ah front lawn today. Yes, that is correct. Take out the enti-ah lawn. And it must be done by tonight! I'm going to install rocks tomorrow so I can plant my succulent garden. And don't bother me in the house—I feel a migraine coming on. Thank you so much, dear. Buh-bye!"*

My father's lawn was his pride and joy—lush, green, and obnoxiously perfect, something out of a country club brochure. Honestly, I'm pretty sure he cared more about that stupid patch of grass than he ever cared about me. And now? The landscape company was coming to rip it all out. Every last pristine blade.

I sat back in my chair, the corners of my mouth twitching as I tried to hide the satisfaction bubbling up. Grabbing my drawing pad, I started doodling, each stroke fueled by a glorious mental image of the chaos to come. By the time I finished, I was grinning like a kid with the keys to the candy store.

Oh, yeah... I was running. Let's get back to that.

I started across the fire escape landing but tripped on the grate. My knee got bruised up, but I felt nothing—the pain was swimming upstream against the booze. Apparently.

Frustrated, I shouted up at the penthouse party. "This is your fault, Genevieve! I'm going to die because of you!"

The creepy guy had vanished; he wasn't climbing down after me.

Had he given up? I wasn't about to wait and see. Heart still pounding, I plummeted down the metal stairs, refusing to slow down.

Chapter 2

So, the psycho killer was chasing me—let's blame my dad for starters. If he hadn't pissed me off, I wouldn't have agreed to go out that night. But Genevieve? Oh, she deserves some of the blame, too.

She was relentless. Like, *relentless*. That afternoon, she practically blew up my phone with an endless stream of texts, each one more desperate than the last. *"We're crashing a red-carpet premiere in the East Village—it's going to be epic!", "Come on, it'll be fun!", and "You have to come!"* And on and on.

Honestly, I don't know why Genevieve wanted to be my friend. Maybe she felt sorry for me? No idea. But she was always trying to get me to do something. Every. Single. Night. She dragged me out to the hottest parties, the poshest clubs, and even backstage at the coolest concerts. One time I asked why she wanted me to tag along, she said it was because I made her laugh. And that was enough for her.

Was I jealous of her? Well, she was gorgeous with golden brown eyes, flawless dark skin, and dramatically high cheekbones. She was fit because she worked out two or three hours *a day*. Who does that? And the worst part? She was *nice*! Infuriatingly nice. So, no, not jealous at all. I straight-up hated her—as only a best friend could.

After a dozen texts, I finally replied. Told her I didn't feel up to it. That led to her *cardinal* sin—the phone call.

"Girl! You are going to this premiere with us! I will get you in and you *will* have a great time! We'll meet the cute actors, the director, maybe the producer—"

"I don't want to go out! There are *people* out there," I whined. "I don't want to people."

"Put on that little black dress you made and get your booty over here!"

"That dress isn't done."

"Yes, it is... I saw you in it, remember?" She did. And it looked... okay on me.

"You're not going to let me say 'no', are you?"

"Damn straight! Get yourself all *did up*! Be at my place by nine! Bye, lovely!"

I threw my phone at the bed. With my textbooks glaring at me, and my dad totally pissing me off, I decided to go out and get wasted.

Then I caught a glimpse of myself in the dorm room mirror. Tall for a girl—something that had always made me self-conscious. At least it helped conceal the parts of me I didn't love, like my belly. My one redeeming feature was my long, curly red hair—once the bane of my childhood, now a crown of fiery curls that I simply loved. And my blue eyes, which had always seemed to draw compliments. I sucked in my gut, but it did little to change how I felt—that mirror refused to be kind.

After trying on half my wardrobe, I settled back on the black dress. A touch of makeup followed, and I dared to slip on a pair of killer, overpriced heels. For once, as I gave myself one last look, I felt... decent. Maybe even good. Something that didn't happen often.

By ten o'clock, our cab dropped us in the East Village. We got out ahead of the line of cars depositing people in front of an old theater. This was the premiere for some movie that had won a big award at Cannes.

Paparazzi cameras flashed constantly as the film stars emerged like gorgeous butterflies from their limo cocoons.

Genevieve stopped our little group on the sidewalk outside for a confab before trying to sneak into the theater. "Okay, we're going in through the back door for guests. Not the red carpet entrance, okay? It'll attract less attention. We good? Finley, you good?"

"This is not going to work. They're not going to let us in without invitations."

Genevieve held up her hand. "You walk into every situation as if you're not only *supposed* to be there, but you're the one *in charge*! Just follow me and don't slow down... for *any* reason."

Always in complete control, Genevieve sauntered slowly up to a broad-shouldered security guard standing stiff in his black blazer. He reached out his hand for her invite. Pretending to talk to her agent on the phone, she pointed to herself. "Talent."

Waving her hand and shaking her head, she swept past him and held the door open as the others rushed in.

But... I hesitated. Taking a moment to summon my courage cost me. As I started after her, the door had closed.

The security guy turned on me, holding out his arm.

"Invitation?" His deep voice rumbled in my chest.

I was sure he could see my heart beating through that stretch jersey dress.

"I... Well... I-I, um..." My mind was blank. Nothing funny or snarky came to me.

He stepped in close, with his smell of cheap cigars and musky body wash.

"No invitation, no entry."

I finally came up with a wise-ass remark, but it was too late. Sighing dramatically, I shuffled back to the safety of the sidewalk.

Standing there, surrounded by people, I was completely alone.

Onlookers crowded the block. Movie fans waved their head shot photos and autograph books. Photographers shouted at the celebs.

As I reached for my phone to order a cab, my fingers froze. The street was a hectic mess, overflowing with honking cars and sleek limos weaving through the theater gridlock like predators. Traffic was at a complete standstill, stretching endlessly down the avenue. The blaring horns seemed to be closing in on me, suffocating any chance of getting a ride. There was no way I'd catch a cab in this madness. The thought of braving the subway made my stomach twist—I wasn't ready for the crush of people, the noise, the dark tunnels.

So, I parked myself on the stone wall that surrounded the valet parking lot, a wave of self-loathing crashing over me. Why did I go out? Why didn't I have the balls to follow her and her friends through that damn door?!

Why couldn't I be more like Genevieve?

Brushing bits of gritty concrete from my black dress, I scanned the crowded street again. The East 8th Street subway station was only two blocks away, but might as well have been miles. I'd have to pass by a couple of homeless guys and a few creepy assholes hiding in the dark alcoves of the deserted storefronts. Deep breath. *Suck it up, buttercup,* as my dad used to say... every time I got scared.

I took one step onto the sidewalk and froze. I had never ridden on the subway by myself. A subway full of crazies, dirtbags and muggers—who would be all crazy, dirtbaggy and muggy to me! I had dug myself a nice, deep hole and fallen in—I was stranded in the city.

"Hold it right there!" Genevieve and her friends burst through the theater doors, marching in to save me from the oncoming panic attack.

"You gotta be quicker than that, girl!"

"I know. I know. Go have fun. I'll be fine."

"Hell, we can't get back in *now*!" Genevieve leaned in to whisper. "No invitations, remember?"

"I'm sorry," I whined. "I ruined your night."

"What?! The night is long that never finds the day, lovely! So, we'll go out and conquer the bitch!" Genevieve had quoted Macbeth, but I don't think she knew what that line truly meant.

She held open a cab door as a stylish couple emerged. Flashing her pearly whites, she pointed to our ride. "Let's go, girls! The party awaits!"

Genevieve ordered our cabbie to take us to *Keres*, a new club on the Upper West Side.

As I do, when we arrived, I headed straight to the bar, ordering a round of shots for everyone, desperate to distract myself. We tossed those back and hit the dance floor, the music thumping in time with my racing thoughts.

Guilt gnawed at me, so I kept buying Genevieve and the other girls costly drinks, one after another, hoping to drown their memories of the premiere in a haze of alcohol.

Around two in the morning, we fended off the drunken hornpuppies who had swarmed us—well, them—and took a cab over to 110th Street for a mellow *post-festum* at a bond trader's swank penthouse. He was, of course, infatuated with the amazing Genevieve.

By four, all the drinking had caught up with me. As I stumbled to my feet, the room spun wildly, and a wave of heat washed over me. Sweat poured down my back, soaking through my dress. I needed fresh air—fast—or I was about to redecorate the host's apartment. And not in a good way.

I slipped off my heels and tottered onto the large terrace overlooking the Hudson River. The temperature outside had dropped considerably, but I was still burning up. I tugged at my dress, but the stretchy fabric clung to me like a high school band geek on a first date.

I found a nice, secluded spot behind some potted plants... in case I had to hurl. The cold marble tiles felt so good on my bare feet.

Genevieve pulled herself away from this handsome *boho chic* artist, who was desperately chatting her up, to check on me.

She laughed at my predicament. "Fin? You okay? Need me to hold your hair?"

"I'm good. Just need... a minute... to clear my head."

"In that case, it's selfie time!" She squealed with delight.

"Oh, god... no."

Genevieve yanked me up to get a photo of us together. "Come on! If you're going to look like shit, you might as well have New Jersey in the background!"

I tried to laugh but immediately turned back to hug the glass deck rail for support, laying my face on the cool metal.

Genevieve couldn't resist snapping several pics of my sad, drunken display as I swayed back and forth. She'd use them for future blackmail to get me out of my dorm room.

"All right, girl. Wait here for a hot second. I'll find you a water." She patted my back. "Just don't fall over—it's a long way down."

I made the mistake of looking over the banister and it was, indeed, a long way down.

Genevieve let out a tipsy laugh, sauntering back to the after-party. When I heard a favorite song echoing from the penthouse, I started to sway a little. I loved that song. But the patio swirled under my feet, returning me to the safety of my handrail.

Keeping my eyes closed, I let the breeze cool me down.

From the far end of the patio, I heard a hard thud.

I glanced over my shoulder, and my heart did that weird, panicky skip thing. A tall guy sporting a dark green robe was moving toward me, his steps slow and deliberate—creepy enough to make my skin crawl. His face was hidden beneath a hood, but the black tattoos winding down his cheek and neck screamed, *I do not belong here.*

This was not your typical party crasher.

In an instant, I sobered up. Okay, mostly.

Then, as if it was the most normal thing in the world, he stopped, picked up my phone and my heels, and just... stared at me.

That's when I did the only logical thing. I ran.

When I got to the final landing of the fire escape, I checked one last time that he wasn't following me down. Releasing the drop ladder, I scrambled down to the alley.

No one was walking the street. A few cars sped by. When I saw a taxi, I screamed and waved my arms, but the cabbie had a fare.

I headed around the corner toward the building entrance—to take the elevator back up to the party. As the front door opened slowly, I slid to a halt. No doorman was in sight. Panic set in. Desperately scanning for somewhere to hide, I darted back to the alley, pressing myself against the cold brick.

Peeking out, I spotted two guys from the party. One was looking down at his phone! A wave of hope surged through me—he could call the police, he could help! But I had to act fast.

As I stepped out, two strong hands gripped my shoulders.

I was pulled back into the darkness.

Struggling to scream, I felt a rough cloth press against my mouth. A strong acidic smell drifted up as I inhaled.

And everything faded to black.

Chapter 3

I awakened with a crushing pain splitting through my skull. This wasn't the dull throb of a hangover I knew too well—this was sharper, more brutal, as if my head were trapped in the iron grip of some unseen giant. Every pulse sent a wave of nausea twisting through me. Something was wrong—terribly wrong.

Opening my eyes was no easy task. They were crusted over with sleep, as if I'd been unconscious for days. Had I been out for *days*? I reached to pry open my eyelids, but my arms were restrained.

The sudden realization made my head hurt even more—I had been kidnapped!

I bent forward, trying to sit up, but my stomach roiled. This wasn't queasiness; I felt as if I were floating. Except for the strap across my waist, nothing touched my body.

But my internal organs were jumbled up inside. The sensation was oddly familiar—as a kid, I loved the thrill of soaring high on the old, creaky swings at the park. No matter how much my mom begged me to stop, I'd wait until I reached the peak, then let go of the chains, slipping from the worn vinyl seat to hang in midair—weightless for just a heartbeat—before crashing back down to the grass.

But this time I was actually floating, frozen in time. The strap holding me down was attached to a shiny metal table—the only thing keeping me from drifting away.

At least I still wore my black dress. Relief washed over me, but my hands still trembled slightly.

The table stood in the center of a pristine but stark room, its sleek surface seamlessly blending with the ultra-modern design. Brilliantly reflective silver cabinets lined the walls, but there were no seams or handles, and it gave the room a sterile, unbroken flow. The slick, metallic walls gleamed under the soft, ambient light, casting faint reflections of the table in an otherworldly glow. One large, translucent window stretched across the entire far wall, but no light came in from outside. In fact, the window was darker than any night, except for a faint bluish glow in the left corner. No doors were visible. The smooth counters, void of tools or equipment, heightened the room's sterile perfection. As though I were in a doctor's office, stripped of the usual clutter and filled with the eerie promise of a not-too-distant future.

I took in every detail as fast as I could, to provide the police with a decent description. That is, if my creepy kidnapper were to ever let me go. He was probably demanding a ransom from my father at that very moment. Good luck getting hold of him though! I'd be stuck there for days while he left message after message, like I had to do. Most of the time, dear old dad usually added money to my bank account rather than taking the time to talk to me.

I shifted my focus back to the large window—or was it a picture frame? My vision remained blurred, making it hard to tell. It appeared to be a glowing hologram of Earth. As I blinked away the haze, details sharpened: dark blue oceans swirling with bright white clouds. Beyond the deep blackness of space was sprinkled with tiny, twinkling lights like distant stars. But what caught my eye, and let me know this was a fake, was the enormous metallic ring circling the planet—a vast, silvery band that hovered above the Earth's surface, rotating in perfect synchronization. The ring didn't touch the planet, yet it followed its curve, a mesmerizing structure too surreal to be real.

None of this made any sense. My kidnapper had obviously slipped me psilocybin or... some other hallucinogen. I had sampled enough of them in my day—and that was the only explanation.

And the whole floating thing? Shit, I was higher than the Central Park

Tower...

I had to get out—now.

But there was no door. A shiver coursed through me, not just from the cold in the room but from fear. The hair on my arms prickled. The vein in my neck throbbed violently, each pulse reminding me how close I was to losing control. Every second I stayed, the walls seemed to close in, amplifying my need to escape.

I tried to slide from underneath the black strap, but immediately froze. A section of the wall slid away. My kidnapper *floated* into the room. He used his hands to guide himself along the polished counters but bounced hard against the wall. He pushed his way to my table.

"Wh-what do you want?" Despite the metallic walls, there was no echo.

I started to memorize this face, then immediately looked away. If I got a good long look at this jerk, I'd be able to describe him to the police. Because, you know, all those crime shows I've binge-watched have taught me that's a foolproof plan! Right. That ever ends well for the victim. They always end up in a ditch because, surprise, they *could* identify the kidnapper. Yeah, no thanks. I squeezed my eyes shut: *Nope, not today!* If I can't describe him later, maybe I'd live to see another day...

His cold fingers touched my face. I flinched. He gently pried open one eyelid and then the other, checking my pupils. My plan was fucked. I could ID him. Which meant I was going to die a grisly death after he got his ransom money.

"Where... am I?"

No longer restricted by gravity, his thick black hair waved about his head. His dark brown eyes showed a considerable amount of worry and... care for a kidnapper who would probably murder me in the too damn near future. He still wore that dark green robe, which now floated down around his knees. He looked a lot like a Spanish soccer player I had dated for half a minute my freshman year. He had black tattoos that peeked out over the neckline of the tunic he wore under the robe. More tattoos covered his forearm and the backs of his hands. Prison tatts, maybe?

Don't look at him! Don't look at him! my brain screeched at me.

"What's going on?!"

He placed his other hand on my neck. I flinched again. His icy fingers checked my pulse.

"Who are you? Where am I?! Look, my father has a lot of money. He'll pay you! I promise! Please let me go!"

Tears rolled down my face. The shivering became uncontrollable.

He said nothing but reached into the leather belt at his waist, pulled out the small rag from a small pouch.

"No. No! Not again!"

I tried to struggle, pulling my face from his hand, but he was too strong. The smelly cloth went over my mouth again.

Everything faded as I drifted into unconsciousness.

And I dreamt I was falling.

When I came to, my heavy eyelids begged to stay closed. I was no longer floating—the tug of gravity was once again pulling on me. I had been placed on a hard floor, leaning against a wall. My back was killing me.

As I blinked hard to clear my vision, the room sharpened into focus. It was compact, sleek, and gleaming—every surface coated in glossy silver, similar to the futuristic medical office. The space had the same minimalist, sterile feel as that room. There were no doors, but I knew not to believe that. The window was mesmerizing, filled with a vibrant blue sky dotted with fluffy white clouds that seemed to drift... upwards.

We were going down. Slowly. As if in an elevator going down the side of a building.

The kidnapper stood nearby, staring out the window. His hand gripped the strap of a brown leather bag slung over his shoulder.

Noticing I was awake, he slid on a grin and started speaking. His voice was deep, but I couldn't place the language. He sounded like a Russian trying to speak English, but... with a Chinese accent. His tone wasn't angry or threatening.

I wiped the drool from my chin. When I looked down, I saw that he had changed me out of my black dress. Fear overtook me as I pushed myself against the wall. I inhaled over and over but could not exhale.

His hands held out, a worried look crossed his face. More strange words fell from his lips. He crouched down, then backed off when I recoiled. He wanted me to think he meant me no harm, but my panic wasn't paying attention. I shook my head furiously.

He huddled under the window, showing me his palms. Finally, he gave up, sitting cross-legged and waiting for me to catch my breath.

Carefully reaching into his worn leather bag, he pulled out a hefty, ancient book. Its faded blue cover was etched with intricate golden symbols, gleaming faintly despite its age. As he respectfully flipped through the brittle, tattered pages, the weight of its importance seemed to hang in the air.

He spoke more of his strange language, pointing at the book and smiling like an idiot.

"W-what... do... you... want?" I spoke loud and slow, because that is how you help foreigners understand English.

He pointed to the peculiar scribbling halfway down the page.

"I can't help you. I don't speak... whatever *this* is."

I had a great language translation app on my phone, but my phone was nowhere in sight.

With the old book in his lap, he edged closer to me until our knees almost touched. Still grinning, he put his huge hands in the air, then tapped his chest, pointing a long finger to his head and mine.

Apparently, it was time for charades. "Look, I don't know what you want or why you kidnapped me or when you're going to kill me, but I—"

His eyes went wide. He protested with a wagging long finger to me, as if to say 'No! No! No!' He pointed from his head to my head.

Tracing a finger along a page, he muttered to himself until he found the right passage. Chanting in an even stranger language, he closed his eyes. He repeated the chant. Carefully and slowly, he placed his fingers on my head. I tried to act chill, but my heart nearly shot out of my chest.

More creepy chanting.

My eyelids grew heavy. Dizzy, wanting to pull away, I sat there unable to move my head to either side.

He pressed hard on my temple and forehead.

My skin tingled where he made contact. My forehead ached, as though I'd pulled an all-nighter cramming for a math final. His chant buzzed in my ears. The tingling on my skin turned to sharp, electrical shocks. But I was a statue.

And at some point, I passed out.

Blinking a few times, I opened my eyes. If I had been asleep, I certainly wasn't resting.

We were still in the metal box. Still descending. If this was an elevator, we were on the tallest building in the world.

The man was rummaging through his bag.

Rain pelted the window. Night had fallen, at some point.

Lightning flashed outside the window. The clap thunder caused me to jump. I screamed, throwing myself against the metal wall and pulling my knees to my chin.

The man rushed to my side, placing his hands on my shoulders as if comforting a child.

"Shh. Shh. You are in no danger," he soothed.

Too scared to realize the guy was now speaking English, I hyperventilated. Tears ran down my cheeks. I had no idea what was going on or where I was. I knew I was going to die and had absolutely no control over anything. I had gotten used to living on my own, out from under my father's thumb, and needed that control. But that had all been ripped away.

Another lightning flash, more thunder.

I curled into a ball, sinking to the floor and sobbing.

The guy stood there, looking down on me. He exhaled deeply, ran his hands through his hair—he had no idea what to do with me.

I caught what seemed to be a look of regret on his face. He forced a fake smile but turned back to his precious window to stare out at the rain driving against the glass.

Chapter 4

Harsh, bright sunlight dragged me kicking and screaming to consciousness. I'd probably never slept more in my life, yet somehow felt like I'd been hit by an MTA express bus—twice. Outside our lone window, I could see mountaintops in the distance. We were *still* descending!

My kidnapper sat against the opposite wall, his knees up and head down.

I needed to pee. Badly. But I wasn't going to say anything. It wasn't as if there was a bathroom, or even a damn door, on this... box.

When his head popped up, he seemed to sense we were near the end of our journey. Grabbing his bag, he jumped to his sandaled feet and stretched his long arms.

After surveying the scene outside the window, he turned to me. "It is time. We must move, and move quickly. Do you understand?"

I nodded. Arriving at a destination meant that my situation would probably go from bad to worse. I began shivering again.

He held out his hand, but I shook my head—taking his hand implied consent.

"You are frightened. I know you do not trust me now, but everything will be explained," he said. "I simply need time."

Staring at his fierce dark eyes, looking for signs of hostility, I saw nothing but pity.

"Let me help you."

Our metal room went dark as we descended into a structure of some type. He implored me with his eyes, his hand still outstretched.

Against my better judgment, I took it. Pulling me to my feet, he led us toward a solid steel wall, which slid apart without a sound. Hand still gripping mine, he paused, peering into the pitch-black room beyond. Without hesitation, he tugged me through the doors. As we stepped inside, my eyes darted upward. Through a large rectangular opening in the ceiling, I saw a massive cable, thicker than a tree trunk, stretching endlessly into the sky. Whatever it was connected to—way up there—was completely out of sight, swallowed by the clouds.

"Let us hurry!"

We dashed into a vast hall, where the high, arched ceilings were supported by thick wooden beams that were dried and cracked. A massive, blackened fireplace dominated the far wall. Scattered chunks of stone and crumbling debris were scattered across the cold, bare stone floor. Our sudden arrival had stirred the dust, sending it swirling in lazy spirals through the sunlight filtering in from narrow, slit windows. The air was thick with the scent of decay—this place had clearly been abandoned for a long time.

As I took a few more steps into the empty chamber, I sensed something was off. Yes, my legs were wobbly from not standing for what seemed like days, but that wasn't it. As I took another step, it dawned on me that my body felt lighter. As if I had lost weight—which I would not have been mad about. How long had I been asleep? How many meals had I missed?

"Quickly now! Move!" More shouting. He was very shouty.

As we left the hall, we passed through a rusted iron gate. I caught a glimpse of the lock—it had been clearly melted from intense heat.

Gripping my wrist, we went through a maze of hallways and empty rooms. Despite my apparent weight loss, I had trouble keeping up. All that running wore me down. I gasped for breath and my legs were liquid. When I'd start to fall, he would easily haul me up and keep me racing along down the corridors of gray stonework.

After descending a wide spiraling staircase, he slid to a halt at a heavy set of wooden double doors. He held his ear up to the wood, listening for signs of danger. I panted hard as I looked around the room. Pools of blood had congealed on the cobblestone floor. But there were no bodies. The melted door lock, the blood, and his desperation to get out told me he had probably broken into the place. That gave me leverage. Should I start screaming? Refuse to go with him? But my brain locked up from fear.

Satisfied the coast was clear, he pulled the tall door open slightly. Rusty hinges echoed through the room. We silently slipped into bright sunlight. Ahead of us stood a massive stone wall, with weeds and long grass filling the gap.

"We do not have much time. The day is late and our descent took longer than expected."

Curious about our weird elevator, I looked to the top of the old building to get a better view of the giant cable that shot up through the roof—I really wanted to see where we had come down from. We were standing outside an old castle. Once-proud towers were now crumbling, their jagged tops silhouetted against a bright blue sky. Vines snaked up the weathered walls. The facade, once smooth and regal, was now mottled with lichen and moss, giving it a sickly green hue.

Hands on my hips, gasping for air, I backed up to get a better look. The thick tether up into the sky was gone. Had it been pulled back up? Or... was it ever there at all.

"Oh, my god!" I screamed.

My kidnapper reacted as though we were under attack, crouching down, fixing his eyes on the overgrown courtyard.

Then I laughed. "I know what this is! This is a prank, isn't it? Just a big... *seriously* elaborate hoax!"

"Keep quiet! Someone may hear us," he whisper-shouted.

"What are you? Some kind of hypnotist? Who put you up to this? Was it Genevieve?! Oh, my god, I'm going to kill her!"

His gaze darted around the courtyard. "*Please* be quiet!"

"That's what this is," I told him. "You guys pretended to kidnap me because I got white-girl wasted last night and this is... payback?!"

He begged. "Please."

Emboldened, I got even louder. "Seriously, how'd you do it? I mean I thought I was really up on some *space station*! And the super long fake elevator ride? That was a slick touch. Okay, where is everyone?"

I moved into the high grass of the yard, searching around every corner. "You can come out now!"

He placed his long hand over my mouth, dragging me to the wall of the castle. I struggled but was no match. He poked his head around the corner, scanned the courtyard for signs of life—he seemed genuinely scared.

When no one came rushing to attack us, he relaxed. A little. Then let me go.

"Where is my friend?" I whispered angrily. "Come on, the joke isn't funny anymore."

"Quiet. Or I will be forced to kill you..."

I hate when people dress up for a Halloween party and they stay 'in character' throughout the whole damn party. It's so annoying. I adjusted the sad, gray piece-of-crap tunic he had dressed me in, marching back to the courtyard.

"Seriously, Genevieve! You got me! Come on out!" I stopped my kidnapper by wagging my finger as a warning to keep him from snatching me again.

Something sharp cut my arm—pain raced through me. "Oww!"

Whatever hit me bounced off the stone wall near us. I screamed, grabbed at my shoulder. It was warm and wet; blood stained my hand.

I had been shot.

"You will do as I say now, yes?"

I nodded furiously. The pain was intense. Blood ran between my clenched fingers. I looked at the bloody arrow leaning against the stone wall.

"We are going to run."

I managed a curt nod, though my legs wobbled underneath me.

Gripping his robe with my bloody hand, I gasped, "I don't know if I can!"

"You have it within you... deep down. I believe in you. You are... the chosen one."

Wait, what? My mouth dropped, but he shoved me forward before I could respond.

Behind us, the sound of heavy footsteps tore through the tall weeds, growing closer. Whoever had shot me was coming to finish the job.

Chapter 5

We hurried along the wall toward a huge, rounded tower rising up from the far corner of the abandoned castle.

After only running a few short steps, I had exhausted the fear coursing through me. I couldn't keep going. My feet were killing me, the lack of oxygen was killing me, and mean people with goddamn arrows were *trying* to kill me.

We rounded the tower and my kidnapper hunkered us down.

"Stay quiet!"

I gulped air as fast as I could. Covered in sweat, I realized my twenty-four-hour deodorant gave out about twelve hours ago. At least we were out of the hot sun.

We heard someone shouting orders—men in boots trampled through the tall grass.

He closed his eyes, focusing on his breathing.

"Why are we stopping? Someone's trying to kill me!"

"Quiet... Please."

His head dropped lower, fingers pressing hard against his head.

I swallowed hard, my eyes darting around the stone courtyard.

He began a slow, soft chant as our pursuers closed in.

A flicker of movement caught my attention. Two shadows appeared on the far wall—they were running. One belonged to a tall, thin man in a flowing robe, his silhouette fluid and quick, while the other—a smaller figure—struggled to keep pace. My heart raced, but despite the shadows' frantic movements, no one appeared to be casting them on the wall.

He lifted his head, eyes snapping open, and yanked me back against the castle wall. Four large men sprinted past, bows in hand and quivers strapped across their backs, moving away from the tower. Their silver helmets gleamed under the sunlight, crowned with red plumes, and their white tunics—marked with a bold red X—fluttered over the silver mesh armor beneath. Black pants with red stripes completed their uniforms, making them an imposing sight as they headed away.

My eyes followed as they chased the shadow of the tall man and short woman further along the outer wall.

I started to speak, but my kidnapper placed his hand up. The guys with bows were racing after a couple that looked remarkably... like us.

Once they were far enough away, he pushed me in the opposite direction, and we dashed around the tower. At the outer wall, we veered toward a set of short, square towers. Between them stood a raised metal gate, its heavy chains clinking faintly in the breeze as we approached.

He skidded to a stop, throwing out an arm to keep me from rushing forward. Together, we watched as a team of the tall men in white tunics surged through the gateway.

We started to run but they surrounded us in no time, pointing swords and aiming arrows at our chests.

Both of us gasped for breath, our eyes locked on a slender, severe man striding through the open gateway. The same as my captor, he wore a dark green tunic, his neck and hands covered in black tattoos, even extending to the smooth surface of his bald head. Gravel crunched under his boot heels. The soldiers parted and he swept up to my kidnapper.

"There you are, Pherric!"

"Gerrod," said Pherric, which seemingly was his name.

"Tracking you down has not been an easy task." He ignored me entirely.

"That was my intention." He eyed Gerrod carefully.

Pherric placed his hand on his leather bag, gripping it tightly.

Another tall man, also in a green tunic, hurried up to the bald man's side. Where all these tall men came from, I had no idea. The new arrival had dark beady eyes, black scuzzy hair and needed a shave. I shuddered when I realized he might be turning me over to these jackholes.

"You hid your mind well, but... using the Godsribbon was a mistake," mused Gerrod, looking toward the top of the castle as though he was also searching for the missing elevator cable.

"I had no choice."

"I would love to say turn the book over and all will be forgiven, but you have gone too far, committed too many crimes against the Scholomance. However, I have always harbored an inexplicable fondness for you, Pherric. Your death shall be swift and painless. And such a shame that you have condemned this poor child to a similar fate."

At last, Gerrod glanced my way, his forced smile barely masking the disdain simmering beneath.

What on Earth was happening to me? This was a living nightmare. I'm not sure when I fell down the rabbit hole but this had to be rock bottom.

The bald guy turned to his minion, Captain Scuzzy. "Feed and water the beasts, Nerus. We ride within the hour."

"Does he have the book with him, preceptor?" hissed Nerus.

"I highly doubt Pherric would be so... bold... as to bring the book here with him, Nerus," Gerrod stated with contempt.

The knuckles on Pherric's hand turned white as he squeezed the leather bag.

"We should search him to make sure he—"

"Go feed... and water... the beasts," grumbled Gerrod, without looking at the scuzzy dude. He was not a happy camper.

"Aye, preceptor," whispered Nerus. He hustled off toward a small group of men wearing the white smocks.

Gerrod gave Pherric a sidelong glance. "I must say, I was sincerely impressed, Pherric. The stones on you to steal the *Arcanum Libellum* from under our noses! And you were only a sixth year?"

"Fifth," whispered Pherric.

"Fif*th*?! I highly underestimated you," pondered Gerrod. "Just a few short years away from being a mage to a king!"

"*That* was the problem, Gerrod."

I had had enough. "Okay! I'm over *whatever* this is! Can someone please give me a ride back to Manhattan?! I'm exhausted and I seriously need a shower to wash off—"

The backhand from Gerrod knocked me sideways and I dropped into the tall weeds. For the first time ever, I saw the stars people talk about when they get smacked upside the head.

"Let this one go," snarled Pherric. "She is not involved in my treach-ery."

He helped me up, shoving me behind him, to protect me, as I rubbed my sore jaw.

"Release this tiny woman? Into our world?" Gerrod scoffed. "Her execution will be a mercy compared to what she would face out there, alone. You involved her when you stole her away, Pherric. You are to blame for her death."

Pherric looked away—his plan in ruins.

"Now, hand over your bag. I will need our book and the cup back..."

A horn blared in the distance, sharp and urgent.

Both men snapped their heads toward the castle gate, eyes wide, before locking gazes.

It seemed both of their plans had just been ruined.

Chapter 6

The horn blared again, sharper and closer this time. Gerrod's face twisted with fury, as his snarl cut through the warm air. Without hesitation, he barked orders at his men, sending them scrambling up the walls like ants in a storm.

Stepping to Pherric, he leaned in to whisper, his eyes darting around. I strained to hear their conversation, but the sharp ringing in my ear from Gerrod's earlier blow muffled the words, leaving me in the dark.

Rubbing my cheek, I made a mental note that Baldy McAsswipe was going to hear from my father's attorney.

Nerus, the greasy-haired minion, slid to a stop at his boss's side. "Preceptor! The Irkallan king is here!"

"I know, fool! My hearing works still! Close the front gate!"

Gerrod exchanged a final look with Pherric, gave a curt nod, and swept away to the castle wall stairs.

Nerus sneered and shouted to Gerrod without looking away. "What of this... filth?!"

"Where can they go?!"

The slimy toad stared at Pherric's bag for half a second, then followed his master up the stone steps leading to a walkway along the outer wall.

"Will you please tell me what's going on?" I didn't know whether to be scared or angry. But confused? I had no problem with being confused.

"Now is not the time, Finley Maguire," Pherric said. "I will tell you all... *if* we survive this."

"Well, that's... depressing."

"Come!" He pulled hard on my wrist again, and my wrist was not happy about it.

On the wall, Gerrod's soldiers had their arrows in their bows, but stopped short at aiming them down at our new visitors.

Pherric yanked me into the gatehouse and we hurried through the dim stone corridor. Ahead, the massive iron gate groaned as it descended, its pointed teeth sinking into the earth with a dull thud. Sticking to the shadows, we crept along the walls, our steps muffled as we edged closer to the outside of the wall.

I cautiously peeked around Pherric, squinting through the iron bars. A broad, wooden bridge stretched over a murky moat, its water an unsettling mix of black and green. The castle was perched atop a small hill, with a sun-scorched field of brittle, yellowed grass that went on forever. To our right, a dense forest loomed, the thick trunks of ancient trees towering above, with their wide, circular leaves rustling carelessly in the wind.

Lining the field stood row upon row of soldiers, their polished armor gleaming under the harsh sun, mounted on massive, peculiar gray horses. Over the armor, they had black tunics lined with a blue trim. More soldiers filed in at the rear—enough to make up a small army. Their faces were slick with sweat and grime, their armor spattered with what appeared to be dried blood. With military precision, they lined up at the base of the small hill, fifty across and hundreds deep.

One man rode his monstrous gray horse forward, breaking ranks with the others. He pulled off his helmet, revealing a wild mane of dirty blond hair that caught the wind as he smiled toward the wall above us. Though covered in grime and blood, he looked regal. Impressive. But, deeply intimidating. His bright blue eyes gleamed across the yellow field. Broad-shouldered with powerful forearms and a lean waist. I have a thing for nice forearms—I might have drooled a bit at that moment.

"Damn," I whispered. "That's the king?"

"Yes. He is called Malek," Pherric said. "King of Irkalla."

I started to talk, but Pherric put his hand over my mouth—I was *this* close to biting his damn fingers.

My injured arm throbbed, reminding me that I had been shot. I held my hand to the wound to stem the flow of blood. And my cheek stung. All of which made me forget that I still had to pee. Almost.

Gerrod shouted from above us. "Your majesty!"

The king's mouth curled up into a devilish grin. "Preceptor Gerrod! Imagine my surprise seeing you *here*! In Cíbola, of all places," Malek yelled out, his voice a deep and stirring rumble.

"Likewise, majesty. You are quite a long way from home."

"I heard tell of a Prominan army that had gathered in this kingdom. The rumors proved to be true. We were, however, victorious! And the threat is... no more," Malek boasted.

"Ah, I see. Rousting a camp of exiled females and children must have been tiring work." Gerrod sounded as though he wanted to go a few rounds with this king.

Malek responded to his taunt. "We still have some fight left in us."

"What can I do for you, your majesty?"

Malek rattled a finger at Gerrod accusingly, laughing to himself. "Well, I also heard whispers there was... unusual activity at the Keep of the Godsribbon. A place that is off limits to all!"

"I am surprised you deal in as much gossip, majesty. I always thought that best left to the house maids and bicorn milkers."

Malek tensed up, his hand gripping the handle of a sword at his waist. But he looked away, clenching his jaw, and composed himself.

"Hearsay can be knowledge, Gerrod. And knowledge is power. I have even heard stories that there has been disorder and unrest brewing at the Scholomance." Malek lorded his insider info over Gerrod.

"The situation has been handled, Malek."

"As you say... but the gods have favored you with my presence this day. So, I am here to offer our services."

"Your services were neither requested, nor are they needed," said Gerrod. "I am in control here."

Malek sighed. "I find that the dead are rarely, if ever, in control..."

The sound of a knife slicing into a watermelon caused Pherric and I to look up.

I nearly screamed when Gerrod's headless body fell from the wall above us, landing on the grass outside the gate. His head followed, hitting the ground with a thunk.

I covered my mouth to keep from vomiting. "Oh, god. What... just happened?"

Pherric turned to me. "Nerus betrayed him, as Gerrod suspected. If you want to live, you will do exactly as I say. Do you hear me?"

I nodded furiously.

The big, black gate began to rise in front of us.

Malek and several soldiers kicked their beasts to start the short journey to the castle.

Pherric closed his eyes, murmuring his weird, foreign chant.

The two shadows appeared again—on the far wall of the corridor. They were the same shapes: a tall man in a robe and a short woman.

Keeping his eyes closed, he abruptly stopped his chant. "When I say run, you will follow me. We run toward that forest. Yes?"

He started his chant back up.

The shadows I had seen running earlier reappeared, swirling like smoke against the stone wall. My breath caught as they peeled away, shifting into fully-formed apparitions—blurry, dark figures with wisps of shadow trailing behind them. At times they were translucent, almost ghost-like, and at others, they appeared unnervingly solid. They looked similar to us... but they weren't us. Mesmerized, I watched the figures dart from the castle hallway into the sunlight, turning left and sprinting alongside the outer wall, moving with an eerie, unnatural grace.

"Run!" Pherric shouted.

And run I did.

Several of Malek's archers fired arrows at the two apparitions that had run off to the left, along the castle wall. The arrows went through them but clattered against the stones.

We dashed across the wooden bridge and swerved to the right, toward the ominous forest. Some of Malek's archers notched their arrows.

Looking over my shoulder, another set of apparitions ran from the gatehouse and across the drawbridge—sprinting directly toward the approaching king.

Malek held up his hand, staying his archers. "Ignore them! They are but Scholomance witchery!"

As I pumped my tired legs, I saw the two shadows run at Malek, then right through him, fading into nothingness.

I tried hard not to fall on my face as I raced toward the nearest trees. But they were more than a city block away. My legs screamed at me. My heart beat out of my chest. Sweat stung my eyes.

It was time to give up.

Pherric realized that I was falling behind and returned to my side, grabbing my good arm and dragging me along.

"Hurry!"

I shot a look back at the castle. Malek had stopped on the drawbridge. He was staring down at the wood surface. Did he see the trail of blood from my arm? His head snapped around, his eyes locked on us.

I fell into the thick grass. Pherric tried to pull me to my feet but I had nothing in the tank. Why couldn't he just let me lay down and die?

Hovering above me, Pherric stared at Malek with fear in his eyes.

"Please?"

He held his hand down to me. I'm sure I was a lovely sight, lying on my side, gasping for air. I saw the look of disappointment (see also: *pity, sadness, regret*) on his long face. My father had always given me that same look. Too many times—and that was all I needed.

I let out a loud grunt, pushing myself up on wobbly legs.

Pherric seemed genuinely shocked.

I walked past him, putting one foot in front of the other, over and over, until I was running again. I made it to those trees on nothing but anger.

The forest seemed to be a slightly better place to die.

Chapter 7

The wild grasses thinned out as we neared the dense forest, making it easier to run. Slightly. I mean... I still had to *run*.

Back at the castle, Malek had disappeared from sight. But four of his soldiers were galloping their thick, weird horses after us.

Under the cover of the trees, I stopped running and bent over to catch my breath.

But Pherric kept trying to drag me along.

"Are you kidding me?!"

We jumped over the prickly underbrush, veered left and crawled over a tree trunk, and then raced back and forth between the huge trees.

But we were on foot and those soldiers were gaining ground. I felt the vibrations of their fat hooves clomping on the forest floor.

It dawned on me that I maybe had a few seconds to live. I had always thought I'd go out while sipping a cocktail under a palm tree, beside a luxury pool, at 90 years of old age... not running through a stupid forest. This was some serious bullshit.

Ahead of us, several of the big gray horses burst through a patch of tall shrubs. We slid to a stop.

These new riders, wearing battle helmets and holding swords, rode hard directly at us.

Utterly exhausted, I fell to the ground to await death—I had no intention of dying on my aching feet.

Their horse hooves thumped the ground around my head. When no blade slashed into me, I realized they were headed after the soldiers chasing us. I wanted to turn, to see what was going on, but I stayed down on all fours, dry-heaving whatever was left in my stomach and gasping for air. And my bladder had decided it had had enough of my restraint.

I heard swords clashing, angry grunts, and finally... the screams of men. *Dying* men. This nightmare was never going to end!

By the time I caught my breath, their battle was over. At that point, I didn't care who had won, because I was done.

As the riders returned, Pherric took my face in his hands to look me in the eyes.

"I had hoped to prepare you first. But I wasn't expecting Gerrod. And I certainly did not expect Malek," he soothed.

"Prepare me for what?"

I tried to turn my head to look, but his hands kept my face still. When I pushed him away, I turned to our rescuers. Then I screamed. Loudly. I crab-walked backwards until I bumped into one of the bulbous trees.

What I thought were horses were not horses. Well, they were... *sort of* horses. If a horse mated with a rhinoceros, then maybe. They had long, strong legs. Instead of fine horsehair, they had a hard and leathery skin. They were thicker and taller than horses. Much heavier... and with long, wide snouts and teardrop-shaped nostrils that rose up to a sharp point.

The first rhino-horse carried the largest man I have ever seen. He removed his helmet and revealed a large head, broad and imposing, crowned with thick, bluish-black hair tied back into a taut ponytail. His brow stuck out, shadowing deep-set black eyes that burned with disdain. A nose like a flattened boulder sat between sharply angled cheekbones, giving him a look of severity. He had soccer balls for shoulders that pushed hard against the silvery chain mail top he wore. Long, muscular legs gripped his rhino-horse. Every inch of him radiated raw power, and his gaze pinned me in place, making me feel even smaller and more insignificant.

He cocked his head at Pherric. "*This* is what you return with?!"

On the second horse sat a creature that seemed caught between man and beast—an ape, but he sat taller and thinner than those you would see at a zoo. His low, sloping forehead and wide, grinning mouth gave him an almost playful air, but his eyes glinted with something sharper, more calculating. A short, broad nose sat above a face and body cloaked in dark brown hair, thick as a coat. Despite his animalistic features, he carried himself like a man, sitting upright in his leather shirt, covered by chain armor, and pants as though he'd been born to ride. He casually pushed back his metal helmet, revealing a mischievous grin that promised trouble, leaning forward as if ready to leap into battle at any moment.

Then... the ape talked. "So, she is your champion, eh? And she's a *firehair!*"

At that moment, I decided I had really lost my mind. Maybe I had fallen off the penthouse balcony and this was... Hell? No. I was most likely bat-shit crazy. That was the *only* explanation.

Pherric stood me up, my knees almost giving out from under me.

"This is Braylor." He pointed to the giant guy.

Then he pointed to the ape-man. "And this is Temurr."

Temurr's grin turned to a wide smile, and he tipped his helmet to me. I just stood there, a complete idiot.

He pointed to his chest, which was at my eye level. "And I... am Pherric."

"Yeah, I figured that out." I tried to sound tough but I couldn't stop trembling.

Chaos shattered our awkward introductions—annoyed shouts, snapping branches, and the unmistakable thunder of hooves crashing through the undergrowth. The sound of pursuit. My heart skipped a beat as I looked past Braylor's colossal frame. More of Malek's soldiers, their armor glinting between the trees, were charging relentlessly toward us, their beasts tearing through the thick brush.

Before I could fully process anything, Pherric grabbed my waist. Without a word, he hoisted me into the air as though I weighed nothing. My scream was lost in the confusion as the ape-like warrior surged forward on his horse. Pherric tossed me over his saddle, my stomach lurching with the sudden movement, and vaulted up behind Braylor in one fluid motion.

"Hold fast!" Temurr snarled, his voice sharp with urgency. He dug his heels into the sides of the gray beast, spurring it into a breakneck gallop. Branches whipped past, clawing at my arms and face. Temurr's grip on me was the only thing keeping me from being thrown to the forest floor.

Behind us, the roar of our pursuers grew louder, their shouted orders and pounding hooves a deafening drumbeat. Temurr's jaw was set in stone as he steered the animal with one hand, his gaze locked on the path ahead. The trees blurred into a chaotic, green tunnel, and the scent of crushed leaves and sweat filled the air.

Our enemy was closing in.

All I could do was lay there on my stomach, exposed and embarrassed, as we crashed through the forest. Branches cut my arms and legs. Thorns caught in my hair, nearly pulled it from the scalp. The beast would occasionally fall from beneath me, as we ran down and back up ravines, only to rise up and knock the air out of my lungs.

We rode for what was an hour of pure torture, but it was probably only twenty or thirty minutes. Charging through a stream and into tall grasses, we raced into a maze of thin trees and weeds and we even doubled back several times.

With the horse-beasts panting from exhaustion, we eventually stopped in a small open area surrounded by tall, orange grass. Yes, it was orange. And there were a half dozen of their weird horses tied up to wood stakes in the dirt. But no other people waited to greet us.

I looked up at Temurr, who was sniffing the air from his saddle. "Um, can I get down now? This hurts and—"

"Quiet, child!" the ape hissed.

Pherric hopped off the back of Braylor's creature, striding to the center of the clearing.

I heard a voice. A woman's voice. "We are being hunted! We must leave. At once."

Parting through the tall grass, *she* appeared—easily the tallest woman I had ever seen. Her long, golden hair fell in waves over her toned shoulders. Piercing blue eyes locked onto me, sharp and firm. She could see straight through every lie I'd ever told. My stomach twisted. She was stunning. So much that she could make you feel invisible just by existing in the same space.

I hated her instantly. Because something about her radiated raw power. Confidence. Danger. In other words, she was nothing like me.

Her dark red tunic, embroidered with symbols I couldn't begin to decipher, swung around her knees as she stepped into our clearing. It might've been beautiful if it weren't partially hidden beneath glinting chainmail, each link catching the sunlight as a brilliant diamond. And then there was the axe she held. Heavy, brutal, and balanced casually in her hand like it was nothing more than a shopping bag.

A chill shot down my spine. She could probably crush me without breaking a sweat, and the worst part? She *knew* it. Her every movement was deliberate, exuding a quiet, terrifying control that set off the fight-or-flight warning inside my head. Gorgeous and terrifying—quite a combo.

Pherric lifted my chin, pointing to her. "This one is called Gunnr." Of course her name was Gunnr. Perfect name for a kick-ass warrior chick.

Pherric lifted me off the saddle and set me down.

Another ape-man emerged from behind her, his broad frame pushing back the orange grass as he stepped forward. He moved with a slow, deliberate gait, the ground crunching under his heavy boots as he stood beside the Viking Barbie.

At first glance, he was a dead ringer for Temurr—same hulking build, same unnervingly long arms—but there was something different about him. His hands were clasped tightly in front of him, fingers twitching slightly, and his dark, deep-set eyes flicked between us with a kind of quiet unease. His expression was...worried? Could these guys even *feel* worry?

Like Temurr, he wore armor over his shirt. His black pants were stitched together with strips of leather that stretched across his muscular legs, looking both practical and intimidatingly cool. But what really caught my attention was the weapon slung over his broad shoulders: a long, polished bow, paired with a quiver full of sleek, deadly arrows. The sight of them made my injured arm sore again.

Unlike Temurr, who practically dripped with confidence and disdain, this guy gave off a strange mix of tension and caution.

"This is Frip," said Pherric. "Temurr's mate."

I looked up at the ape who had ridden me to this clearing. Temurr winked down at me with a silly grin still stuck to his face.

Shoving her way past Frip came someone—or something—that definitely wasn't fully human. She was shorter than me, but compact, built like she could snap a heavy tree branch in half with her bare hands. Her posture was slightly hunched, her thick, jutting brow giving her an intense, almost primal stare. Everything about her screamed fierce. I was starting to sense a theme with these people.

In one hand, she gripped a short sword menacingly. The blade was pocked and stained from years of use. Her tunic was a patchwork of vibrant, mismatched swatches, a chaotic contrast to the feral vibe she radiated. Wild, curly brown hair surrounded her face and shoulders, but it didn't stop there—thick tufts of hair sprouted on her hands and across the tops of her ridiculously large, muscular feet—bare and calloused, but clearly capable of covering ground quickly.

I couldn't help but stare, equal parts horrified and fascinated. If I made it out of this alive, one thing was certain: this girl and I were going to have a serious heart-to-heart about waxing. Assuming, of course, she didn't cut me in half first.

"And this is Cira."

I gave my best fake smile to her but she seemed shocked. Rushing forward, she grabbed onto my hair like I was a doll. She accosted Pherric, pointing at me.

"A *firehair*?! She will bring nothing but bad fortune on us!"

I pulled free, leaving only a few strands of my red hair in her fist.

"What is your problem, girl?!"

Pherric tried to soothe her. "She brings the best of fortune in her kingdom, where there are many like her. We will be fine."

Cira grunted, wiping the strands of hair from between her fingers as if she would catch a disease. She stormed off but never took her eyes off me.

He waited until she was clear, his eyes staring just beyond me.

"Finally, let me introduce... Kasuma."

Kasuma emerged from the brush like a spirit stepping out of a dream, and for a moment, I forgot to breathe. She was about my height but impossibly slender, her entire form encased in a seamless, skin-tight white suit that seemed to shimmer with the faintest suggestion of light. No belt, no visible weapons—just her.

Her hair wasn't blonde; it was pure, bright white, like the fresh snow in Central Park under a full moon. Her features were delicate and unmistakably Asian, but her skin had an otherworldly hue—a pale bluish-white that seemed to almost glow in the forest's dim light. Her eyes were a dark black ink, deep and unblinking, giving her an air of quiet but unnerving intensity.

Then I noticed the most striking part of her: the wings. They unfurled behind her, arching gracefully upward before trailing down to her hands, each feather impossibly fine and perfectly formed. The wings didn't flutter or twitch—they simply existed, a silent declaration of her otherworldly nature. She looked both fragile and unbreakable, serene and terrifying, a force that could either heal or destroy with a single thought.

And there I was, standing before her, feeling more human—and more vulnerable—than ever.

On his horse creature, Braylor gave a quick look behind, then leaned down to Pherric. "If we are quite done with the polite introductions, I suggest we keep going."

"Quite right," exhaled Pherric. "Everyone! Malek's men are close behind. We must put some distance between us and the Godsribbon Castle! Prepare your karkadanns!"

Temurr growled. "Eh, surely we've lost them. We can rest here for—"

"We leave now. Malek will not stop searching for us." Pherric placed a protective hand on his leather bag.

I pinched myself hard enough to leave a bruise, because that's what I heard you are supposed to do when you're caught up in a terrifying nightmare. But I did not wake up. And I was very much going insane.

I wanted to race off into the brush. Hide from everyone. I wanted to be back in my dorm room. I wanted to be back in my city. And I really wanted to stand in a hot shower for about an hour.

But fear gripped me and I had no fight left. No will to run, no energy to question or argue. Nothing. The only thing I could do was stand, a helpless child lost in a strange land.

Chapter 8

The rest of the group swung onto their gray beasts, and without a word, we plunged back into the endless labyrinth of the forest. The thick canopy overhead swallowed most of the light, casting shifting shadows over the ground. We rode fast for hours, the rhythmic pounding of hooves the only constant in the ever-changing but odd landscape.

I was never one for nature, but the whole forest seemed... off. Like I was in another country. It was a hot spring day, but I saw the golden-colored and red leaves of late fall. Even the twittering insects off in the distance sounded different. Almost alien.

We quickly twisted and turned, veering sharply through thick under-brush, scaling steep hills that left me clinging desperately to Temurr's saddle, then descending into valleys where the air grew damp and heavy. We crossed streams that gurgled in protest, the beasts barely breaking their stride as the water splashed against their thick legs. After a long while, the trees blended together into an indistinguishable blur.

Each time I thought I'd found some landmark—a crooked tree, a peculiar plant—it disappeared, swallowed by our endless journey. My sense of direction, usually quite fragile, was shattered completely. Every twist of our trail led us deeper into the unknown, and with every passing mile, the forest seemed to close in tighter, as if it too wanted to keep me lost. But then again, without the map app on my phone I doubt I would have been able to find my own elbow.

Hours later, when they felt safe enough, we eventually slowed to a trot.

Which was still ridiculously bouncy. Temurr finally let me sit up on the beast, in front of him, while he killed time by bandaging my arrow wound.

He sniffed at me as he applied a wrap. "The gods smiled upon you, child. I sense no poison in this wound."

Oh, I had questions—*so* many questions—but bit my tongue. The rush of everything that happened at the castle and our crazy escape had distracted me. But riding through this endless forest gave me the opportunity to remember that I had been kidnapped. I was still in danger. I had no idea where I was and what they wanted from me.

The only thing I could not wrap my mind around were these strange people who held my life in their hands. The talking apes, the short stocky girl with hair on her hands and feet, the massive Neanderthal dude, and— holy shit—the white-haired Asian lady with freaking *wings*! That was either some Hollywood-level makeup artistry, or this was all some kind of crazy hallucination created by my tired little brain. And nothing in my life had prepared me for this type of mental breakdown. It was going to take years of therapy to fix this shit.

Riding at the back of the group, I watched as they spoke to each other in hushed whispers. I even heard infrequent laughter—probably at my expense—and some quiet arguing—also about me, I'm sure—as they threw the occasional glance my way.

Temurr grew uncomfortable with our riding position and threw me like a slab of beef back over the saddle. I endured the rest of our bumpy ride on my stomach, stretched across the hard, wrinkled skin of the horse-like creature. Pherric had called them karkadanns. Such a strange and exotic word for such a hideous and stinky creature.

Beyond the pain of riding while stretched across the karkadann, it was that awful smell. But then... I had no idea if the stench came from the horse-thing or the ape man.

I eventually found out the answer to that.

The group dismounted near a sparkling river to let the rhino-horses drink and graze.

Temurr leapt from the karkadann, cursing loudly. "By the gods, I can take this no more!"

He was incredibly strong—I know because he easily picked me up and tossed me to the ground.

As I pushed myself from the mud, the motley team gathered around to inspect the prize Pherric had worked so hard to steal. I'm sure I was quite a sight. I hadn't showered for what had to be days and had also peed, perspired, and puked all over myself. And now, I was covered in filthy sludge after riding all day on the back of a beast. No filter was going to fix this selfie.

Each stared down on me and it was plain to see their hopes had been dashed. No one had a word of encouragement or a look of kindness or a sympathetic smile. All I saw was sadness. And maybe anger from two or three of them.

But Temurr had seen... and smelled enough. He threw me over his shoulder. I screamed and pounded on him to no effect as he stomped his way through the grass like I was a sack of potatoes.

"Stop that, Temurr!" yelled the other ape man, called Frip. "Put her down! She is the one from the prophecy!"

Temurr chortled, but marched straight ahead. At the river's edge, he threw me into the black water. It was freezing cold but, to be honest, it was the greatest feeling in the world—better than any treatment, facial, or massage from the finest spa in the city. If the water had been warm they would have had to drag me back out.

As I rinsed off my slimy face, Frip helped me out of the chilly river. He threw a dark blanket, smelling of karkadann, around my shoulders and guided me back to the strange group.

With Temurr done with me, I found myself parked on the back of Pherric's beast as we pushed through the enveloping darkness. The river had soaked me to the bone, and every shiver felt was a cruel reminder of my misery. My body screamed for warmth, for the steady heat radiating from Pherric's back. But there was no way I'd give him the satisfaction of knowing I felt even an ounce of comfort in his presence. I clenched my fists against the urge, keeping my distance as the beast's rhythmic strides carried us deeper into the night.

My mind forced me to relive the events of my day over and over. I had gone from fearing for my life at the hands of these people to depending on them for my safety. A million and one questions flashed through my brain. But I forced myself to be patient, even though patience was not my métier.

We rode for a few more hours, then finally stopped near the same river. I parked myself on a rock and watched my captors.

Pherric passed by, carrying a load of dried sticks. By that point, too tired to be afraid, I stood up in defiance—if I was stuck with them, I was going to be a big pain in the ass.

"Listen, your little camp is coming along nicely. Is my cabin nearby? I could really use a hot shower and bed with a decent mattress. Firm, but not too firm and—"

Pherric looked at me without expression.

"I'm guessing room service is out of the question?!"

Everyone hustling about the camp stared me down.

Pherric started to march back to his crew but paused. "You would improve your situation if you kept your mouth closed."

"Why? Because they would all think even *less* of me now?"

He looked at his disheartened team. "I doubt that would be possible."

In anger, I plopped back down on my rock and watched as the others worked hard to dig a hole deep enough to get a fire going, collect some edible berries, and water their beasts.

I nibbled at the strange berries and gulped down water of my own, despite the fact it tasted like wet dirt. The little group ignored me as they talked and laughed. One of the ape men got in a rather heated argument with the huge Braylor dude, which did not seem to be the smartest move if you ask me.

Above me, a low, rhythmic whooshing broke through the stillness of the forest. Flapping—massive and deliberate, like the wings of some colossal bird descending from the night sky. I dropped my cup, the sound of its fall barely registering as I slipped off and pressed myself against the rock.

Out of the shadows, she appeared. The woman with wings. Kasuma. She swept down with effortless grace, the air stirring briefly around her as she landed beside the campfire. For a moment, I couldn't breathe. She wasn't just some strange, ethereal figure—she could really fly! My mind struggled to comprehend what I was seeing.

She moved with the confidence of a seasoned predator, her piercing black eyes scanned the camp and then me. In her hands, she carried two creatures—rabbits, but unlike any I had ever seen. Tiny, dirty antlers crowned their sturdy heads, as if they belonged to some fairy tale book from when I was kid. She passed them to one of the ape-men without a word, and he set to work, skillfully skinning the odd creatures as the fire crackled in anticipation.

I remained frozen, staring in awe from my hiding place. Everything about her—her wings, her effortless movement, even the otherworldly prey she had brought back—seemed to defy the rules of nature. She was a living contradiction, and I couldn't look away.

Pherric saw my panicked expression—he stepped up to me, holding my shoulders and placing himself between me and the flying woman.

I pointed, tried to speak, but only gibberish poured out.

"I know you have questions. And I will provide some answers. Where shall we start?"

"I-I-I... uh," I stammered. I couldn't think of a single question. They were all jammed down in a bottleneck trying to race through all at once.

"I will start by welcoming you to Tir Na."

"Tir Na? That's the name of this country?" I pointed all around us as if he were a deaf person. "This is a different country, right?"

"Tir Na is my world," Pherric stated. "Terra is your world."

My mind went blank. "Um... what?"

He sat me down at the base of a nearby tree, drawing a round circle in the dirt between my feet. "Tir Na."

"Terra? Terra... that's another name for Earth, right?"

I was answered with a smile.

He drew a larger circle next to his original in the dirt. "Sol."

"Sol? Oh, um... *Sol!* That's the sun!" I foolishly pointed to the night sky.

Pherric nodded. Next, he drew another small circle on the other side of the sun. Then he pointed a long finger at me, then to his new dirt circle.

"Terra. Earth."

I was confused and kept staring at his diagram on the ground. The wheels spun in my head, trying to process everything.

"You are from Terra. I have brought you to Tir Na."

"I'm on another... *planet?*" I asked, probably already knowing the answer. "But... how? Wh-why?!"

I spoke loudly enough that all the other conversations around the fire stopped. They stared for a moment, then went back to the hushed whispers.

"How do I not know about this planet? How does *everyone* not know about this?"

Pherric drew orbits around the sun for both of the planets in the dirt. "In the forbidden books, I have read that Terra and Tir Na are on the same path in the night sky."

He motioned that both moved around at the same speed, with the sun always in between the two planets.

"So, you're saying that we never see each other because we're always on opposite sides of the sun? Of-of Sol?"

"Yes."

"Um... okay, that would probably have made sense for the last couple thousand years, bro... but, uh, *not* today. We've got satellites, probes, and missions to Venus and space telescopes and—"

He held up the long finger, wiping away his original drawing. His finger made another large circle in the dirt, then he drew a circle around that, pointing to the sky.

"Do you recall seeing the ring, through the window, when we were above our world?" When I nodded, he smiled. "That large metal beast surrounds us. Like a very long serpent, so long it can bite its own tail. The Scholomance calls the ring the World Serpent. Gunnr's people refer to it as Jörmungandr. I made sure you would see the ring before we left. Because I knew you would not believe my word."

"I... remember. I think," I stammered, completely unsure about anything at that moment.

"Eons ago, the gods... they seeded life here on Tir Na, as well as on Terra. Some believe they came back to see us, many times, to check on the progress of all of the species."

"Progress?"

"Yes. They wanted to make sure life on both worlds had continued and that we were thriving," he said, drawing another dirt circle again. "It is the belief of the Scholomance that Terra had more progress. We do not know why. But the gods knew they had to hide this world. And so, they used their magic to put the World Serpent around Tir Na."

"I thought the ring was just a... a space station with an elevator?" I made a circle with my thumb and finger and used my other hand to show Pherric a small elevator dropping down from my circle.

"The World Serpent uses special spells—ones that I do not understand— to shield our world from your view," he said. "This same spell also hides the Godsribbon."

"Godsribbon?"

He moved his thumb and finger down from his own hand circle. My mind immediately jumped back to the castle, when we had emerged and I had looked up for the space elevator cable but could see nothing above.

"And you might notice that you do not weigh as much now..."

"Yes," I said, thinking back to the feeling of taking my first steps out of the elevator.

His hand returned to the ground, drawing yet another circle followed by a slightly smaller one and pointed to both.

"I don't get it," I said.

"From what I have gathered in the texts, your world, Terra, is slightly larger. Tir Na is smaller," Pherric said, as if that explained everything. "It was difficult to walk on your world."

I could only shake my head. What did a smaller planet have to do with anything? But then I recalled old videos I had seen in school of the astronauts, bouncing around and slowly floating down, on the moon—the moon was smaller than the Earth.

Pherric watched the wheels continue to spin away in my head.

He smiled, patted my hand, and started to stand. "You have been through enough today. I will—"

"No!" I looked up and dragged him back down. "Why did you do this to me? Why am I here and... how quickly can you get me back?!"

"You cannot return. You are the chosen one."

My most recent horoscope had not mentioned *one damn thing* about me being the chosen one...

Chapter 9

"What the hell does that mean?" I asked. "*Chosen* one?"

Pherric could only provide a sly grin.

"Chosen for what?"

The giant Neanderthal, who had been brooding near their fire since his argument with one of the ape guys, could take no more. He tossed aside his mug, rose up like a mountain, and marched over to Pherric. With little effort, he pulled the thin man to his feet.

"You have made a grave error, Pherric," said Braylor. "She cannot be the one written about in your prophecy." He pointed at me, then jabbed Pherric in the chest. "You obviously captured the wrong female!"

I jumped off my rock to speak directly to Braylor. "Yes! You are one hundred percent correct! I am not your 'chosen one'! Whatever the hell that is! Do you understand me? Not. The. One."

The giant returned his harsh stare to Pherric. "This podgy, little waif will in no way aid our cause!"

Did he call me podgy? I had no idea what that meant but it sounded an awful lot like fat. I mean, I'll admit I had a bit of chonk going on, but... podgy? Braylor was now on my Hate List. Number One, with a bullet.

"The prophecy speaks of her, Braylor. I know this for a certainty," pleaded Pherric.

"Wait! What am I the *one* for? Because if it's some virgin sacrifice or something, that ship has sailed, man!"

Pherric, desperate to defuse the situation, walked Braylor back to his seat on the log near the fire. He stole an animal skin bag from Temurr, which probably contained some kind of alcohol, and gave it to Braylor. Temurr protested but the giant growled at him, sending the smaller ape back to sulk on his small boulder.

Pherric returned, inhaling deeply as if to prepare himself. "Allow me to explain?"

"Look, whatever this is about... whatever you need, I can't help you. Okay?"

"Please... listen?"

Frustrated, I sat back down and gave Pherric a quick nod. But I crossed my arms to let him know I was not happy.

"Good. I was a student at Scholomance, an academy for mages in the kingdom of Pandæmonia. The man who was beheaded? Gerrod? He was the preceptor who ran the school. I was born in a city called El Dorado, here in Cíbola, and sent off to the Scholomance when I was young, after I had shown a predisposition for alchemy—"

"Whoa. Whoa! Did you say *El Dorado?* As in... the 'City of Gold' El Dorado?"

"Gold? Yes. El Dorado is made mostly of gold. It is a lovely metal, but fairly common on Tir Na"

"Common? Really? It is extremely valuable on Earth... I mean Terra. Very rare..."

"We use it for ornamental objects, decorations. It is too soft for weapons. But not a bad replacement for teeth and—"

"Wow," I said. "So, it does exist. Sorry. Sorry, I'll stop talking."

He knew that would not be the case.

"I attended Scholomance for five years. I studied potions. As well as the mindforms I used to fool the Preceptor's guards and Malek back at the Castle of the Godsribbon—"

"Wait. What are *mindforms?*"

"While studying there, I learned of a prophecy... one that predicted—"

"And you think I'm part of this prophecy?"

He smiled the kind of smile a parent gives a child who asks if they have ice cream for breakfast. "First, I want to tell you about Tir Na. Our world is made of many realms. We are now in Cíbola."

"Yep, got that," I acknowledged. All these weird names were too much.

"Mag Mell is the home of Braylor's people."

Braylor arched an eyebrow in our direction at the mention of his homeland.

"Nibiru, on the island of Oceantis, is the home of Kasuma's people." She nodded and her wings ruffled slightly. "Gunnr hails from Valhalla. Frip and Temurr are from Kunlun, and Cira is from the cave kingdom of Agartha."

"Is this gonna be on the test? Because... I won't remember all these names."

Pherric shook his head. "And then... there is Irkalla. Malek's kingdom. There are many more domains but Irkalla is the largest and most prosperous. And Irkalla is the problem. Everyone's problem."

"And this is where the prophecy comes in?"

"Yes. For hundreds of years, our realms have known nothing but peace. Our greatest enemies have been the deadly monsters that inhabit Tir Na—"

"Monsters?" The hair on the back of my neck flew up.

"Vicious creatures that have fed on our flesh and destroyed entire cities. We have fought against them for generations, forcing us to develop weapons and techniques to end their rule. We have hunted these monsters to the point where there are few left. I don't want to give you the impression that Tir Na would be a peaceful place if it were not for those creatures. There have been border wars and clashes over resources—Braylor's people are always fighting with Temurr and Frip's people; Gunnr's kind fight with Cira's and so on—but this threat from Irkalla is new."

"Caused by the pretty boy on the horse-thing back there? The king?"

"According to the prophecy, we are entering into a dark and dreadful new age. It has been written that an emperor will arise, promising peace and prosperity but delivering only pain and death, who will rule for a thousand years. I believe Malek intends to fulfill that prophecy."

He rambled on for several more minutes, ranting his doom and gloom, but all I could think about were the monsters he had mentioned. Real, live, actual scary monsters. My eyes kept watch on the dark forest around us.

"Do you understand?"

"Should I be taking notes, professor?"

"Only in the past few years has our world grown darker. Before Malek, the Irkallans were a kind and giving people. His great, great grandmother gave us the Queen's Language; a language that many of us speak today. In the past, various rulers have sought out more power, more food or water, more land... but not the Irkallans; they sent out ambassadors of peace. Even Malek's mother, Queen Dirvilia, worked to help depleted kingdoms that had lost everything to the beasts of this world. But when Queen Dirvilia was killed, Malek became the new ruler at only ten years of age."

"And he's been kind of a dickhead ever since? Yeah, I could see that..."

"He was too young to lead at that age, but was crowned king when he reached seventeen. And his quest for resources and power has been insatiable ever since. Malek started by taxing his own people, even though his realm was the richest in all the world. He then turned to neighboring kingdoms to demand payments and—"

"And when they didn't pay, he attacked. Yeah, that's what the organized criminals on my world called 'nod and a wink' protection. My grandfather used to tell me stories about the mob guys who ran that racket in neighborhoods he patrolled," I said.

"Malek used his wealth to amass the largest army ever assembled. And he has them well-trained. The Irkallans have invaded many kingdoms for the purposes of protection, but they have killed their people and stolen their resources. Naturally, he has left garrisons behind to ensure obedience. He is slowly building his empire."

"Well, I hate to break it to you, Pherric, but I'm not a big time general who has commanded armies. I really can't help you here."

"He is doing far worse than invading other nations. He has been using his might to wipe out entire species. Anyone who is not Hominan."

"Hominan?" I asked.

"You and I are Hominans," Pherric explained. He turned to the others, who were pretending not to listen, over at their campfire. "The king wants to purge our world of anyone who is not like us. For the past few years, he has systematically eliminated hundreds of thousands of beings—like Temurr and Frip, Cira, Braylor, and Kasuma." He dropped his voice a notch lower, for effect. And it worked. "He is a bringer of death and destruction who has ushered in this dark new age. The age of Hominans."

"And... how am I supposed to help?"

"The prophecy describes these dark times but also mentions a hero who will lead us against the oppressor. Against Malek. A hero will incite an uprising to restore peace and balance—for all species—that will last a thousand years."

At first, I could only stare at him. My mouth might have fallen open at some point. Then I started to laugh. I laughed hard. So hard, I doubled over. The entire group stood, staring at me out of concern. They exchanged worried looks. Which, for some reason, made me laugh more. The emotions of the day had caught up with me; it was the only explanation for my reaction.

Frip approached Pherric to whisper in his ear, a worried look on his face. The ape man held out his arms, moving close as if to give me a hug.

Anger flashed through me and I pushed his hairy hands aside. My face burned hot. I ran away from them, embarrassed at my outburst and ridiculous display of laughter.

After a few minutes, I pulled myself together. "Pherric?"

He leaned against a tree, trying to project an air of calm, but his jawline was tense and his eyes uncertain.

"Look, I'm sorry but I am not your stupid *chosen One*, okay? Do you hear me? In the morning, you need to take me back to that castle and send me back up that elevator! You then beam me back to Earth or whatever the hell you did to get me here! Understand?!"

He crossed his arms, looking down at the ground, and waited.

"Well?"

"I cannot do that, Finley Maguire."

"Why?!"

"The castle is now guarded by Malek's soldiers. I had one chance to sneak in, collect you, and return. It would take an army to return you to Terra."

"So... I'm stuck here? For how long?!"

"Forever," he stated, with great certainty.

I moved closer. "I am not *any* kind of hero, Pherric. Not even close! I-I'm a spoiled rich girl who doesn't know how to cook, clean or... drive a car! What am I supposed to do? Learn how to fight with a sword and lead everyone into battle or something? That is so stupid! I probably can't even *pick up* a sword!"

"The prophecy says nothing about you fighting," he admitted. "But it does mention a girl from Terra who will bring every species together to defeat our oppressor. She will inspire us, unite us, and lead us to victory..."

Exhaustion took over. I was not some charismatic, political leader who could give inspirational speeches and lead the troops to glorious victory on a battlefield. Anxiety washed over me. I put my back against a tree, slid down to the roots, and buried my head—tears were forming but I wasn't about to let him see me cry.

He sat next to me, looking off into the dark night. "This has been too much, too fast, for one day. We'll talk more in the morning."

Tears rolled down my cheek as I stared into the completely indifferent darkness.

Chapter 10

Lying on the unforgiving ground, my back pressed against the rough bark of the tree, I tried—and failed—to make sense of everything. A new planet. Pherric's bizarre prophecy. Creatures straight out of a fever dream. My mind spun in dizzying loops, clinging desperately to any shred of logic. This was really happening. To *me*.

And yet, a nagging voice in my head wouldn't shut up: *What if you're already crazy?* I chimed in with, *What if you're not crazy now, but you'll drive yourself insane thinking about it?* I squeezed my eyes shut, trying to silence the voices, but they only got louder.

In a last-ditch effort to keep my sanity intact—or what was left of it—I clung to the one lifeline I had. *This is real. It has to be real.* I repeated it over and over, a simple mantra, until the words lost meaning. Finally, I surrendered to exhaustion, convincing myself—however tenuously—that accepting this madness was my only way out of it.

After light from the fire faded and the snores of the giant Braylor died down, and after much tossing and turning, I eventually found a few hours of sleep deep into my first night on Tir Na.

In the morning, a tickling sensation on my leg woke me. My back ached as I had rolled over to sleep on my stomach, using a tree root for a pillow. With my eyes closed, I felt something move lightly over my back. That woke me immediately. Panic set in when I sensed a furry finger glide across the back of my neck.

Taking a quick look behind me, Braylor hovered above. His huge hand reached toward my face. I screamed, tried to push off the ground, but

Braylor shoved me back down. I felt a tightening around my neck.

From the corner of my eye, Braylor grimaced—upset that his attempt to kill me in my sleep had been thwarted.

He placed his other giant hand around my neck. I could no longer scream.

Pherric sat up from his sleeping position on the other side of my tree, his eyes round and hands held out, but he did nothing to stop Braylor.

The tightening around my neck worsened, cutting off my air.

I tried desperately to pull his fingers from my throat but it was pointless; Braylor's hand was a block of marble. The giant grunted, as he strained to take my life. I would have thought just snapping my neck would be a breeze for him.

Before I passed out, a loud crack went off close to my ear. The pressure against my neck lessened. I could breathe again. I forced myself to sit up, holding my neck, gasping for air.

Braylor leaned back, turning a lifeless creature over in his massive hands, his expression unreadable. Then, without warning, he extended it toward me. The thing was long and thin like a snake, but its tiny front and back legs dangled awkwardly, their claws curved and sharp. Its fur was a deep, almost mossy green, slick with some unidentifiable muck.

The head resembled a weasel, but with unsettling tweaks—its nose replaced by a stubby, pig-like snout. Tiny bone tusks poked up from its jaw, giving it a strangely fierce look despite its small size. It was a bizarre mix of cute and grotesque; nature had played a cruel joke and no one was laughing.

Braylor grunted. "Ramidreju."

He tossed the dead creature into the forest, quickly noticing my fear was directed at him.

"Glad to be of service," he added, sarcastically.

"Braylor!" Pherric screamed. "Do you know how rare that is?!"

He ran after the discarded body.

Braylor wiped his mighty paws clean as he lumbered off.

Pherric returned with the Ramidreju carcass and squatted in the grass.

Removing a small knife from his brown leather bag, Pherric made a long slice along the belly, through the green fur, and let the guts fall out. I nearly vomited. After several swift cuts, he peeled back the fur and laid the pelt, skin side up, on a rock bathed in the sunlight.

When I could breathe again, I noticed he had tossed the remains to Frip to prepare breakfast.

"What is that... thing?"

Pherric wiped his hands in the wet grass. "Ramidreju. They are good diggers. They burrow in the ground for food. But, for some particular reason, they also love gold. They're drawn to it. This Ramidreju made the mistake of crawling over *you* to get at my gold."

He reached into his bag and pulled out thousands of dollars worth of gold nuggets. My eyes went round as saucers when he tossed the nuggets off into the high grass. It took every last ounce of willpower to not rush over, scoop them up.

"Very rare creatures. Their fur aids in healing," said Pherric. "Among other things."

"I have a question," I inspected the tree before leaning against it... in case anything else decided to crawl on me. I pulled a huge dead bug from my stringy hair and realized how badly I needed to go home.

"I am sure you have many."

"Up in the... Godsribbon, why did you pretend you didn't know my language?"

He shrugged. "I do not speak your language."

I laughed out loud. "Um, you're speaking it now..."

"Do you recall our time on the Godsribbon, when I read from my book and chanted? I know you were rather scared at the time, so—"

"No, I... remember."

"I used a mindform to... embed the Queen's Language in your head. So, now you are able to understand all of us."

"You *gave* me your language?" I rolled my eyes. I've always had a great grasp of languages. Back in high school, I took four years of Latin because *dear old dad* had it set in his mind that I was going to be a doctor and needed to learn it. He had no idea I also took four years of French—because *Hello!*—I thought I wanted to be a fashion designer *extraordinaire!* By my senior year, my teacher told me I had even developed a *North Paris* accent, whatever that means. Whenever people start learning a new language, they start with the most common useful phrases. But I like to learn their curse words first. Foreigners love it when you use their curse words.

"You speak the Queen's Language now."

"Uh, no... I'm speaking English. And so are you."

"I am not."

"Look, I don't know what mindforms are or how they work, but I do know you can't teach someone a language in... in just minutes." I doubted his sanity.

"Allow me to explain. We have a few moments." He turned to see that the others were busy eating the green furry ramalamadingdong creature they had cooked up.

"I'm not going anywhere. Unfortunately."

"I used a mindform to help you learn our language. Mindforms are... a sort of energy that we cannot see, hear, touch. They are everywhere, all around us, floating waves on the sea, constantly moving throughout our world and beyond." He pointed up to the morning sky. "Imagine that you have a strong and specific thought. Now imagine that you send out that thought on a string, from your mind, in the form of energy—"

"Energy wave strings? You're losing me... Because if I am right now speaking your language, that's straight-up magic, dude."

"People have learned it and spoken it for generations. It is out there, in the ether, waiting to be heard," Pherric said. "All I did was show it to you."

"Oh, right. Can you *show* me a thin waistline? I'd really like to drop about twenty pounds."

"What I do is not magic. There is nothing mystical associated with the Scholomance techniques. We simply tap into what exists yet cannot be seen by mortals."

The others began gathering their belongings, packing the karkadanns.

Temurr threw a pack over his hairy shoulder and marched over to us. "We must leave. Now. As you say, Malek will never stop looking for you. And his troops will be out there."

Pherric nodded to him, grabbing my shoulders. "We'll talk as we travel?"

I nodded.

Pherric scooped up his leather bag as the others mounted their rides. Part of me wanted to sneak off, run as far away from these weird people as I could. But the rational part of my brain told me that I'd most likely die a quick death in those woods. For once, I listened to the rational side.

Chapter 11

Our little tribe trotted out of thick forest and slowly climbed in a single file line up toward a pass sliced between a towering mountain.

Sitting on the back of Pherric's karkadann, I listened to the others talk about me like I wasn't even there.

"You heard the child, Temurr. She is not the one from the prophecy. And how do we know we can rely on the ancient ramblings, most likely written in sweeping generalities, of some long-dead shaman?" the massive giant asked.

"Braylor, please. The gods have spoken. Who are you to question their wisdom?" replied Temurr, the ape-like man.

"So, we are all at the mercy and whims of a sorcerer's interpretation of the will of your so-called *gods* then?" Braylor pointed a finger directly at Pherric. "Pherric's interpretation of that long-dead fellow's divination? Utter and complete drivel!"

"Ignore the prophecy at your peril. As well as the peril of your people," said Cira, she of the hairy hands and feet. "The creators know better than you..."

I was neither an optimist nor a pessimist. I thought of myself as a realist. I accepted what was real, what was possible. And ancient prophecies were meant for either the dreamers or the doom-mongers. Braylor was right—prophecies were just predictions, without supporting evidence, of some future outcome. They were purposely vague. If something similar occurred, they would be proven correct. And if they didn't, the prophecy was ahead of its time. However, my convictions crumbled as I watched Braylor, a living Neanderthal man, argue with Temurr, a talking ape. And the fact that I could understand what they were saying—a whole new language inserted into my head, just like that—was magical. What I thought was real and possible had been thrown out the window.

I decided to ignore them and whispered to Pherric riding in front of me. "So, about the whole 'giving me a language' thing?"

"Quomodo sentis?"

"Quomodo sentis? Uh, that means 'how are you feeling' in, um, Latin," I stuttered.

"Or would you prefer... comment allez vous?"

"Comme ci comme ca," I replied, out of habit. "Wait, you speak Latin and French, too?!"

"Using the power of the mindforms, I acquired the language thoughts in your head and interpreted them," said Pherric. "I liked to learn a few useful phrases. And some curse words. I learn their curse words first. Foreigners love it when you use their curse words."

To say I was shocked was a massive understatement. Had he read my mind? How did he know my thoughts? "What kind of creepy, hypnotistical... mindjack is this, Pherric?!"

"Not *mindjack*, Finley. Mindform."

"All right. I'll play along. How do these *mindforms* work?"

"Your mind is a powerful tool. The matter inside your head creates thoughts, and those thoughts are made up of energy. Not a great deal of energy. Very small. But energy nonetheless. And for some reason, that energy never seems to die out."

"Yes! I remember that! From a science class I took in high school. Energy can never be created or destroyed, only transformed into something else."

"That is a beautiful thought," he smiled as he said it. "In that case, your mind has turned a thought into a form of energy that exists, on a small scale, and that energy stays in the world. Just as that mountain ahead exists. You can touch the mountain, see it. And though the wind may one day whittle it down to a bump in the road, the specks of dust will live on in another form."

"Okay, that I can follow," I said.

"At Scholomance, we are trained to tap into the energy that makes up all of nature. Use it. Take advantage of it. Remember the strings I spoke of? Imagine being able to see those strings, for every thought anyone has ever had, spread out across the world. Most people are very passive, mentally. But when they are forced to think, to come up with an idea, their energy creates vibrations in those strings. If you know what you are looking for, you can sense the vibration and it becomes your own thought. Does that make sense?"

"Um, you kinda lost me."

"Have you ever heard of two people having the same idea, in different kingdoms, at exactly the same time? The first person who created the wheel, for instance... there was likely someone else who came up with that clever invention at a similar point in time."

"Wow. You guys actually have wheels on this planet? That's a relief."

"The magic on your world was impressively overwhelming to me. I will admit. But your advances pale in comparison to what the gods of our world created. Most of which was fashioned long before any of our species ever existed," said Pherric.

"Did they create any pharmacies? Because I forgot to pack my antidepressants."

He turned his head back to give me a smirk, even though I doubt he knew what I was talking about. "Think of a mindform as a sound. When you hear a loud sound, everyone nearby can hear it. But the sound dissipates as it moves through the trees and over the land; it becomes quieter and quieter until there is only silence. But our thoughts? They started out as matter but are transformed. They become energy. Unlike a loud sound, they start off very quietly, never dissipating, and people rarely seek them out. And really strong emotions and thoughts create an energy that cannot be ignored, even by the passive thinkers. Two people, in different parts of the world even, can be on the same string vibration and not even be aware.

It has always had different names; intuition would be an example of—"

"Or sixth sense! My dad calls it a 'gut feeling' all the time. He just knows something but he can't tell you why," I said.

"People pass down knowledge to their children. Do not eat the red plant but the orange plant is safe and nutritious," Pherric said. "However, we are also given an intuition that takes advantage of the collective memory of our ancestors. Their thoughts are now energy, riding the strings, waiting to be recognized. What I did was simply show you the language that has been created and thought about and taught to children for generations."

"Dude, you're veering into serious cult leader mumbo-jumbo. How does that explain being able to create those... people I saw?! The ones who looked like us?"

"Have you ever seen a spirit?"

"You mean a ghost? Um, no, not really. But, boy, have I been ghosted. Quite a few times."

"Your thoughts move outside of your mind, in those energy waves, and so the places you have been to and the objects you have touched have absorbed parts of your mindform energy. When people are mourning the loss of a loved one, their thoughts and emotions are heightened and they tap into that energy, effectively conjuring up the deceased. But they are not really there. It is merely a mental projection. It takes serious focus, and intensive training, but one can learn to project the images and even memories from one's mind into the physical world. That is what I invoked at the Godsribbon Castle. I can teach you these techniques."

"Okay, you can stop now," I whined. "My headache is back."

Gunnr pulled her karkadann back to us, letting the others pass. Her royal blue eyes burned holes through me. The woman had no laugh lines because she had probably never smiled in her life.

She glared at Pherric. "It is time for her to begin the training."

Pherric grunted approval.

Training? That sounded very tiring. But, in my mind, I instantly pictured my very own training montage! Swinging a sword, firing arrows, kicking Braylor in the crotch and laughing as he fell at my feet.

"Dismount the karkadann," Gunnr commanded.

"What?"

"Get down." She was not smiling. "Now."

I gripped Pherric tight, whispering, "Is she going to kill me now? And say it was a 'training accident'?"

He pulled my hands from his waist. "You will be fine, Finley."

Pherric gave me a nudge off the karkadann. My sore legs and feet gave out on me as I hit the ground, falling hard on the dirt path. I quickly tried to sit up, but that was impossible because my feet were flung above my head. After several attempts to do one sit-up, I rolled onto my belly and pushed myself up.

"For the rest of the day... you walk."

Gunnr galloped back to the group.

"Wait! You can't... I can't... No!"

Pherric shrugged—this was out of his hands. I staggered to my feet and crossed my arms. My blood boiled. I was not about to march on foot all day.

He watched my reaction, then trotted along after the others.

I refused to move. They continued up the road toward the mountain pass. I couldn't believe it—they seriously wanted me to walk!

Pherric glanced over his shoulder, his voice sharp and urgent. "Beware the hellhounds, Finley! They are known to haunt these mountains!"

The word slapped me. *Hellhounds?* My throat tightened.

"They've got a taste for Hominan flesh!" he yelled, his voice carrying over the rocky terrain.

My heart pounded like a drum. I spun wildly, scanning the far cliffs and shadowy trees for any sign of the beasts.

And then, as if the mountains themselves conspired against me, a low, haunting howl echoed in the distance—deep and guttural, like a wolf's but far more sinister.

"Pherric, was that—?" I stammered, my voice barely audible. But whether it was a real howl or one of his mindform illusions, I wasn't about to stick around and find out.

The slight breeze was suddenly a piercing windstorm, chilling my bones. My legs trembled, but the sheer terror of being left behind shot me forward.

With a desperate burst of energy, I scrambled up the path, my eyes darting back to the distant trees. Every second an eternity, each step an agonizing test of endurance.

Chapter 12

The chill left my body once I caught up with them. The relentless heat of the sun pressed against my back, amplifying the misery of trying to keep pace. Each step was wading through syrup as the dry, searing air clawed at my throat. Dust, churned up by the pounding hooves of the karkadanns, clung to the slick sheen of sweat on my skin, turning me into a gritty, gasping mess.

My legs screamed in protest, and my lungs burned with every shallow breath. I dared to glance back, hoping for some sign of progress. The trail stretched behind me, making fun of me, as I realized we'd barely covered the distance of two city blocks.

The running to catch up with them had already worn me out. I wasn't sure how long their little joke would go on, but I knew I was in trouble. Pherric had stuck me with some janky pair of homemade leather sandals, with *zero* support, and my ankles were killing me. If I had a decent pair of *Prada* sneakers then I probably could have... well, no. Nothing would have helped.

Before we headed into the mountain pass, I turned back for one last look. To the left, a deep blue sea stretched out, glinting under the sun like someone had tossed glitter on it. To the right, the spiky outline of Godsribbon Castle sat perched on a hill, its space elevator cable still annoyingly invisible from this far away.

I tried to lock it all in—every tree, every ripple of water—but deep down, I knew it was pointless. Even if I survived whatever was coming, I'd never find my way back here. Back to the only place that could get me home.

Ahead, one of the karkadanns pulled away from the group. The other ape man, Frip, rode back toward me. Gunnr gave him some wicked side-eye, so Frip held up his first two fingers at her—which I guessed was the equivalent of flipping her off, on this world—as he stopped at my side.

He pulled out a waterskin. "Drink."

"Oh, thank you!" I exclaimed. I drank too much, too fast, and spilled all over myself.

He turned the karkadann and slowly trotted up the path. I worked to keep up with him.

"I want you to be aware, dear, that they are going to demand much from you. Expectations are quite high."

"What do they want?"

"Some expect everything. While others... nothing. But that is the way of life."

"Well, th-that's not fair," I stammered.

"That is also the way of life."

His long, hairy arm grabbed the water bag from my hand. I couldn't resist giving him the same gesture he used to flip off Gunnr as he rode away. As if on command, Frip's karkadann dropped a huge, steaming turd directly in my path, forcing me to hop out of the way and exert even more energy that I did not have.

As I pushed through the tangled grass and weeds just off our dirt path, something caught my eye—a broken wagon wheel, half-buried in the overgrowth. It lay there, discarded and splintered, as if it had tumbled down from the mountain pass ahead.

I turned my gaze to the saddle gap in the mountains. One side loomed with a harsh rock face that climbed a hundred feet straight into the sky. The other sloped into a treacherous maze of ledges littered with fallen boulders, twisted trees, and thorny shrubs—each shadow seeming to breathe.

Braylor, Temurr, and Cira pulled their karkadanns to a halt. Their eyes darted to the cliffs, and though they didn't say a word, their tense whispers and exchanged glances said everything. Something was wrong.

Something was waiting.

At the back of the group, Pherric waited for me to catch up and then pulled me up onto his karkadann behind his back.

"Oh, thank god! I thought you guys were seriously—"

His head snapped back. "Quiet."

"What's going on?"

He nodded to the pass ahead. In the middle of the canyon stood a wooden coach, painted red with bright silver trim all around. One of the wagon wheels was missing. None of the animals that would pull a wagon were visible.

And a huge boulder lay in front of and just to the left of the wooden coach, obstructing our path.

We made our way slowly into the mountain pass. Cira slowly pulled a sword from her belt. Temurr and Frip slipped their bows off their shoulders. Pherric lightly snapped the reins and we caught up with the group and they slowly inched their way closer to the damaged coach.

"We came through this pass without incident several days ago," whispered Pherric. He reached down the side of his karkadann and pulled up his shield.

"It just looks like that boulder came down the hill and messed up the wagon. They probably went looking for help and—"

He kept scanning the higher elevations. "That is what it is meant to look like. This... is an ambush."

A slight snapping sound spooked Cira. She turned back to the rest of us. "Shields!"

Everyone raised the round, metal shields from their mounts, locking them over their shoulders like armor. Everyone except Kasuma. She spread her arms wide, her wings unfurling in streaks of brown, tan, and pale gray; a living canvas ready for battle.

The karkadanns plodded forward, hooves heavy on the dirt path, each step drawing us closer to the ominous carriage and boulder ahead. The air became hard to breathe.

Then came the *whoosh*—arrows and spears rained down from the cliffs above.

Cira moved with lightning speed, leaping from her beast. With a sharp slap to its flank, she sent the karkadann bolting past the wreckage, leaving us to face the storm.

"No, Cira! Wait!" Braylor screamed.

She raced to the slope of the mountain that ran up to the ledges, gripping her small sword in her teeth as she climbed.

Braylor grunted in exasperation. He fended off arrows with his shield as he pulled out his heavy sword.

Instead of fighting, Kasuma extended her wings and flapped several times as arrows fell all around her. She lifted off her saddle with each thrust and was soon floating in the air. It was amazing to watch her take off. She bolted straight up, turned in midair, then flew back out of the pass. Just like that, she was gone.

Pherric watched her go but did not take out a weapon. He held his shield high to protect us both. I wrapped my arms around him, whimpering and crying out as each arrow pinged off the metal.

Temurr and Frip dismounted and sprinted to the other side of the canyon, placing their backs against the sheer stone wall and launching arrow after arrow.

Gunnr and Braylor jumped down like warriors straight out of an action movie, each following right on Cira's heels as she stormed up the slope. Gunnr swung her axe onto her shoulder like it weighed nothing, while Braylor clenched his sword so tight I could almost hear the leather on the handle creak. They raised their shields and unleashed these primal, gut-wrenching war cries that forced me to duck down even lower.

An arrow struck our karkadann. The creature recoiled in pain, bucking and rearing up. I fell hard to the dirt while Pherric held tight to the reins, staying upright on the saddle.

I was exposed.

"Hide!"

"Where?!"

He pointed to a patch of bushes growing against the flat cliff face. I scrambled on all fours across the dirt. A makeshift spear sank into the ground directly in front of my face and I froze.

"Finley, run!" Pherric implored.

I sprang to my feet and bolted, dodging the spear like my life depended on it—which, of course, it did. I dove behind a hedge just as another spear ricocheted off the rock face above me with a sharp clang. My heart pounded, trying to escape my chest. The barrage stopped, and I realized they didn't see me as a threat. For now.

I scanned the first few ledges of the pass, my throat tight, fully expecting to lock eyes with Malek's soldiers in their terrifying blood-streaked armor. But instead, I saw gaunt, wild-eyed men with unkempt beards and tattered tunics, hurling spears and firing arrows with desperate ferocity. They didn't look like soldiers.

A shriek ripped through the canyon, sharp enough to make me flinch. Cira exploded onto the first ledge, her sword flashing in a deadly arc. She was a whirlwind of rage, slashing through two of the wild men like they were nothing more than practice dummies. Blood sprayed across her face and arms, but she didn't even blink.

Then an arrow thudded into her side. My breath caught—surely that would stop her. But no. Cira didn't fall; she didn't even hesitate. She snapped the arrow shaft with a grunt, the motion so fierce and fluid it was like breaking a branch. And then she was back in the fight, her sword carving a brutal path through the men.

I pressed deeper into the hedge, my pulse a drumbeat in my ears.

From directly above, the cry from an attacker startled me. The man who shot Cira fell from his ledge atop the sheer face of the mountain. He hit the hard dirt in front of me with a dull thump. The blood pouring out of the guy caused me to hurl on the hedges.

As I looked up from the dead man, Kasuma flew away from the cliff face and over the canyon. She had tossed the man off the cliff. Holding out her wings, catching as much air as she could, she flapped her wings hard to evade an onslaught of arrows, then disappeared behind the sheer rock face.

I dropped back into the itchy bushes as a ragtag team of men ran up the dirt path that we had come through. They let out a sad attempt at a war cry, with their swords held high, and cut off our only exit from the pass.

Gunnr broke away from Braylor's side, running back down to the path to take on the new arrivals, angering the enormous cave man.

"Gunnr! Stay in formation!" He turned to fend off an attack from behind.

Up on the widest ledge, Cira turned into a rabid dog as she charged another group of hapless raiders. Growling and barking, her sword bit into each of them.

Frip and Temurr hustled from the cliff wall to the broken carriage, taking turns popping out from behind cover to fire their arrows.

Braylor threw his back to the slope to take on a half dozen attackers. He deflected one blade as another struck his shield. The sword deflected off, but sliced into his upper arm, forcing him to drop the shield.

My heart pounded as I helplessly watched from the bushes. I wanted to do something in some way, in *any* way, but I also wanted to run for my life. And keep running until I reached that damned castle. Run until I was home. And safe again.

Gunnr rushed at the men guarding the pass, ducking under their sword strikes. She slid through the dirt and cut deep into the legs of two men with her ax. She leapt up to deflect a blow from another. Her eyes were wide with excitement and I thought I caught her smirking as her weapon slashed into the man's shoulder.

Braylor drove his sword into the chest of the man who cut his arm, then swung the lifeless body around to take the brunt of the blows from the others. He then kicked the dead man off his sword with his boot, knocking the body into them and pushing them back.

Another group of men charged the carriage. Temurr and Frip dropped their bows, drew their swords, and put their backs up against the wagon. They hissed and spat at their enemies as they slashed and stabbed with rapid blows.

Pherric had finally gained control of our karkadann. He jumped down and set the wounded animal loose. When a man attacked him, Pherric diverted a sword thrust with his shield and used it to crack the man in the side of the head.

Gunnr threw him a look. She parried a sword blow, then tossed Pherric her knife.

The shiny blade landed at his feet. But he only stared at it.

Frustrated, Gunnr rolled her eyes and resumed her offensive.

Holding the shield over his head, he stopped at the bushes. "Are you hurt?"

"No, I'm fine! But... shouldn't you... be helping them?!" I begged, pointing to the knife lying on the ground.

Pherric scanned the battlefield. "I cannot."

"What are you? Some kind of coward?"

He handed me his shield. "Take this. Protect yourself. At all costs."

I smiled—he had changed his mind.

But Pherric did not join the battle. Unbelievably, he raced down the path and out of the pass.

Chapter 13

I watched Pherric disappear in utter amazement. He couldn't just run off like that! We needed everyone to fight these guys, because I really did not want to die. *I hate dying*, I whined to myself.

Guttural and inhuman noises erupted from Cira from high on the ridge. She was a sight to behold. She fought with a blind rage. Her long, braided brown hair flailed about, as her face flushed a dark shade of crimson. Making no effort to defend herself, she ran directly at the last three men on the ledge, shrieking loudly as spit flew from her mouth.

Cira cut down the first attacker with her sword, then leapt on to another, her weight shoving the man to the ground. Grabbing his shield—with her teeth—she stabbed him over and over. The remaining attacker swung his sword at her back. Without taking her wild eyes from the dying man on the ground, she countered the blow with her blade, slashed across his thighs, and was rewarded with a spray of blood.

Wiping the spatter from her eyes, Cira jumped from the ledge, throwing herself down on the men surrounding Braylor.

While I watched her fight, a man lunged into my bushes, his filthy hand yanking my tunic and hauling me onto the dirt path. I screamed but was drowned out by the battle. I clawed at his arm, but he was stronger—his grip determined. He dragged me against him, his scraggly beard scraping my face, and his rancid, hot breath filled my nose, making my stomach churn. My mind screamed a thousand commands—kick, bite, stomp—but my body froze, trembling in useless panic.

Then I felt it—a cold, jagged knife pressed against my throat. My breath hitched as the blade bit into my skin. He muttered something, low and guttural, as he tightened his grip, his intent clear. I was his prize, his hostage. Each step he took pulled me toward the open pass. My vision blurred.

As quickly as he had taken me, he let go. I put my hands to my neck, turning to him.

Kasuma stood directly behind the man, her hand clutching his shoulder. She quietly slit the man's throat. Trying to stem the flow of blood, he fell dead at my feet.

I looked up, to thank Kasuma, but... she was gone.

"Get down, Gunnr!" I heard Pherric's voice.

Surrounded by attackers, Gunnr peered over their shoulders, nodding. The blonde warrior parried a strike, dropping to the blood-soaked dirt. The men turned to the canyon entrance. Pherric marched at them, his arms outstretched. He threw two small, round objects into the ground at their feet. A cloud of red smoke billowed up. Gunnr rolled across the dust as she sucked in as much air as she could, covering her mouth and nose. The slight wind gusting through the mountain pass delivered the misty red fog into the faces of the men.

Breathing hard from the battle, they quickly inhaled the vapor. Coughing and gasping, they fell to the ground.

Gunnr vaulted to her feet.

"No, Gunnr! Wait! Do not—"

With her ax, she ended every man lying unconscious on the ground.

"There was no cause for that!" he cried.

Gunnr crouched and used one of their tunics to wipe the blood from her axe blade. "Of course there was."

"They were incapacitated!"

"That made for easier work. And for that... I thank you." She winked at him, and ran off to help Temurr and Frip, who were fending off attackers with their short swords.

I heard a nauseous popping sound. Turning, Braylor released the body of a man whose brains were running down the side of the slope.

Standing beside him, Cira ran a man through with her sword. Still in her furious wild-eyed rage, she turned her sword on Braylor.

"Stop, Cira!" Braylor bellowed. "I am with you!"

Panting hard, screaming and frothing, she backed the giant up against the side of the cliff. She placed her sword on his chest, gasping for breath. I could only stand there, watching in terror—was Braylor going to have to kill her?

"Cira! I beg of you!"

Similar to a feral animal, her head snapped around and she pointed her sword at me. In a manic fit, her eyes darted all around the mountain pass—looking for another enemy to kill. Sweat blinded her as she grunted in anger. But there was no one left to kill. She gulped. Blinked furiously. And dropped her sword.

We waited, staring at her, unsure what to do next.

Cira began to convulse, eyes rolling in the back of her head. As if a switch had been flipped, she collapsed in Braylor's arms.

He gently lowered her to the tall grass as Pherric knelt beside her, tending to the broken arrow in her side.

Temurr and Frip plucked their arrows from several corpses, then met up on the dirt path.

"Well, that was fun, that was," said Temurr.

Frip slapped him. "Death is never fun, Temurr."

"And it required more effort than it should have. We needed to stay together!" Braylor held a hand to his bleeding shoulder wound.

A determined Gunnr wiped axe blood on her sleeve as she approached. Her disdain for me was evident—I had done absolutely nothing to help. Pherric glared at the warrior woman and she replied with a smirk.

Looking around in fear, I whispered, "So, um, who were those guys?"

"Bandits," assured Braylor. "They most likely attacked a merchant in this carriage earlier this morning, and we were an added prize."

I saw no other bodies. "What merchant?"

"I can smell the dead, further along the pass," Temurr said. "Dragged them off the road to lure us in, they did..."

"This is a common thing here? Are we going to get attacked everywhere we go?"

Frip threw a hairy arm around my shoulder. "These are difficult times, dear. Malek's deadly campaigns have exacted a heavy toll on nearly every realm."

I took a closer look at our weary band. "Wait... where is Kasuma?"

Gunnr nodded her head in my direction.

"I am here."

I nearly jumped out of my skin as I turned—she was standing there the whole time.

"Are you well?" She had a high, lyrical voice, and spoke with what sounded like a South African or Australian version of the Queen's Language.

I nodded.

"The Tengu are sneaky, they are." Temurr shivered as he peered over his shoulder. "Let us return to the road. This place makes me nervous."

Kasuma spread out her arms, launching up with three hard flaps. A breeze wafted over me, but there was no sound.

"Wow. How does she do that?"

"With her wings..." Braylor shook his head, shuffling away and nursing the wound.

He scooped up the unconscious Cira, placing her across a karkadann. Gunnr and Kasuma guided the remaining karkadanns to the carriage and they mounted up.

I approached Braylor. "Hey, I can, I don't know, ride with Cira. You know, make sure she... doesn't fall off."

"She will be fine."

He trotted off.

Once again, I was left in their dust.

"Come on, you guys!" I shouted after them. "Slow down!"

But they were on the move.

I started running after them. "You have no idea how much I hate you all right now!"

One of them replied with a laugh that echoed off the sheer canyon walls.

"Assholes!"

Tir Na was not my happy place.

Chapter 14

They rode on through the mountain pass and into a range of sand-colored hills covered with low grasses and sharp rocks. I managed to jog along behind them for about half a minute, then switching to a fast walk while pumping my arms high in the air—I had to at least look like I was trying.

We went up and down, back up and down again, hill after hill—at one point, I was convinced they were aiming for the damn hills on purpose—until we finally descended to the wide plain. The views were probably quite spectacular, but I was too busy dying a slow death. My blisters had blisters. I was covered in dust and sweat and sweaty dust. And smelled exactly the same as the inside of a boy's gym bag.

The group stopped around noon to eat some dried fruits and meat they had stored in saddle bags. After downing half a waterskin, I forced down a few hunks of the nasty leather that they called food... and instantly felt as though I was going to throw it all back up.

Pherric took some time to tend to me. He tore strips from the bottom of my tunic to bandage my feet—which meant they expected me to keep going at this awful pace.

"So, what happened back there?" I asked quietly, so Gunnr would not hear.

"Well, those bandits were either hungry or they were looking for coin to—"

"No, I mean... why didn't you fight back? And why are you super mad at Gunnr for killing the bad guys?"

Pherric paused for a moment, then went back to wrapping up my foot. "I have sworn to protect life. Never take it."

"Oh, so this Scholomance place trained you to be a doctor? 'Do no harm'?"

"No. They did not. At Scholomance we are taught to be mages and to serve the leaders of this world. The academy trains students in alchemy, healing, languages, and mindforms, of course, which we use for divination and conjuring. However, there was a heavy concentration on potions; a specialization of alchemy. In our world, Potionmasters are utilized to bring about death. I could not abide by that doctrine and, so... I had to leave the academy."

Pherric pulled a vial full of a red powder from his leather bag. He sprinkled it on the fabric and then covered the sores on the bottom of my foot.

"Had to leave? Or were you thrown out? And I'm not being judgy here. I've been thrown out of some of the best schools—"

"I escaped. Once selected for Scholomance, you are forced to stay until your training is complete. If you pass, you are auctioned off to the nobles, merchants, military commanders, and the best are sent off to aid the monarchs."

"And if you don't pass?"

"You become a slave," Pherric said. "And when they have enough slaves, you are fed to the livestock."

"Ouch."

"I want to heal people, not hurt them. So, I have always been drawn to alchemy," he admitted. His eyes turned to mine, knowing what I would ask next. "Alchemy is the transformation of matter; turning base metals—like lead, copper, nickel, tin—into a more perfect metal like silver, platinum—"

"And gold?"

"Well, more useful metals. At Scholomance, the greatest alchemancers were able to create the greatest of all the metals—kath. Kath is used to make the best swords, spear tips, and arrow points. It is the only known material that can penetrate the hide of a dragon."

I slid off the rock I sat on. "Say what?"

He lifted me back onto my seat so he could finish wrapping my foot.

"Dragon-dragons?" I looked up at the sky. "As in real, flying, fire-breathing dragons?"

"Ah, so you have heard of dragons?"

"Dude, they have been in our folklore for... well, forever! And they really exist here?!"

"They do indeed. Dragons ruled our world long before any of our species took their first steps. They have killed so many, destroyed whole towns and cities, ruined farms, and eaten our livestock. Once we discovered kath, we were finally able to fight them off. And their numbers have been reduced over the generations..."

I looked at the clouds above. Clouds that could be hiding a massive dragon. One that might swoop down at any second and sear me to juicy perfection.

"To my point... alchemy is mostly involved in healing. Highly skilled alchemancers can transform lead into platinum but they can also treat wounds and illnesses. Base metals and all the species of this world are made up of the same elements found in soil. Some alchemists have been able to cure the sick using the right combination of mindforms and potions. There are even ancient techniques known that can raise the dead..."

"Speaking of the dead, can you bring my feet back to life?"

"The process has already begun." He shook the red powder in the vial before placing it back in his leather bag.

"Enough with the sorcery, Pherric," announced Braylor, as he strode past us.

Gunnr, following along behind Braylor, stared down at me. "We are exposed on this grassland. It is time to ride." The fire in her eyes burned bright. "Well, not you..."

As she stormed off to her karkadann—when I was sure she couldn't see me—I flipped her off.

Pherric stared at my hand, processed what I was doing, and then flipped her off himself.

We shared a smile. My only smile on that horrific day.

Chapter 15

"Where... are we... headed?" I gasped, between breaths, as I jogged alongside Frip's karkadann.

"Pherric says we have allies in the city of Quivira," said Frip. "It is a Hominan enclave but we will be safe there. If we stay hidden."

"Wait. Hominan. I know that word." I had heard too many words lately.

"Like you," Frip explained. "Your kind."

"Oh, that's right. Hominan."

To distract myself from the pain in my sides and legs, I needed to process something, anything. I had heard of *hominids* in a science class, but I thought those were primates... similar to Frip and Temurr.

"Can I ask, um, what is your kind called?"

"Prominans, of course," said Frip, as though I should have known that. He handed me his waterskin. I took a quick drink. I had learned that drinking too much water would come back to haunt me.

In the distance, there was a line of tall trees. The beginning of a forest. I hoped our destination was nestled in there somewhere. Close.

"Okay. And what about the big guy up there?" I handed him the waterskin.

"Braylor? He is Fomorian." If there was a caring soul in this band of warriors, it was Frip. The only one to show any empathy toward me. With the exception of Pherric. And even then, the bastard had kidnapped me and brought me here for his delusional prophecy.

"Fomorian," I repeated, even though I doubted I'd remember it. If there was an Earth equivalent, my guess would be that Fomorians were similar to our Neanderthals. But he was nothing like those old *caveman* stereotypes. The black shirt and silver chainmail did nothing to conceal the hard line of muscle underneath. His shoulders were broad and heavy; his chest was massive. He reminded me of those egotistical bodybuilders back on Earth, with his thin waist and bulgy legs. But most of those Venice Beach types were short and stocky. Braylor had to be seven feet tall. Even riding the massive karkadann, he radiated coiled energy, a big cat ready to pounce on a mouse. Every movement, every shift in his posture, screamed controlled violence. His dark eyes, framed by full eyebrows and a heavy brow ridge, should have made him look brutish—but instead, they lent him a fierce, almost otherworldly allure. He was not a caveman. Not at all.

Before I could ask about Cira, movement from the corner of my eye caught my attention. It was coming from a clump of trees across the plain.

I stopped dead in my tracks.

"Holy shit," I mumbled.

Frip noticed, pulling back the reins and turning his ride to follow my eye line.

"What?"

"You don't see *that*?!"

"See what?"

"That!" I pointed out, rather obviously.

Less than a mile away, something massive stirred the treetops. My jaw dropped as a Brontosaurus—an actual, living Brontosaurus—stepped out from the dense line of trees.

"Oh, the thunder lizard?" Frip said casually, as if he had seen thousands of dinosaurs every day of his life.

Thrum. Thrum. Each of its colossal steps sent subtle tremors through the dirt path beneath my feet, reverberating up my legs and into my chest. I stood still, my eyes wide, as the prehistoric giant extended its impossibly long neck, delicately plucking leaves from a towering tree. Its four pillar-like legs supported a body so massive it looked like it could crush boulders without noticing. A whip-like tail swung lazily behind it, tapering to a sharp point that swayed with effortless grace.

But what really made my heart stutter wasn't its existence, or even the sheer size of something I'd only seen in books and movies—it was the horn. A single, razor-sharp spike extended from its forehead, glinting in the sunlight like nature's own spear. This wasn't just any Brontosaurus. It was something more dangerous, more surreal. A creature out of both history and nightmares.

"You have *dinosaurs* on this world?!"

"That is a species of torodan. We call them thunder lizards, because—"

Thrum. Thrum.

"Because the ground shakes. Yeah, I get it."

I reached for my phone so I could take a photo. Genevieve would totally not believe me without a pic. Of course, I had no phone. And I would never see her again.

Pherric noticed we had fallen behind. He turned his karkadann to us, a curious look on his face. I motioned with both arms at the impossible Brontosaurus. Pherric shrugged, spinning his ride on the path. "We must hurry."

Hands over my head to pull in as much air as I could, I watched the magnificent beast pull leaves from the tree and chew slowly like a cow. This creature could not exist. Should not exist. But it was real. And it was marvelous.

I never looked away as I stumbled along the path. Even more questions popped into my head, but the others had already entered the forest. I tore myself away and sprinted hard to catch up.

Everything on Tir Na was tall—towering, stretching, and defying belief. The trees in this alien forest were no exception. Their trunks were massive, like the columns of some ancient temple, their bark shimmering faintly with hues of deep emerald and obsidian. The canopy loomed impossibly high, reaching farther than any skyscraper in Manhattan.

Above me, leaves larger than sailboats overlapped, forming a dense, interlocking quilt that filtered the sun into scattered spotlights. The light that did reach the forest floor was tinted green and gold, creating an otherworldly glow that felt alive.

Everywhere I looked, massive ferns and thick, twisted vines wove their way around the towering trunks, pulsating softly, like veins in a living creature. The ground was a tapestry of mosses in colors I'd never seen—cobalt blues, fiery oranges, and pale silvers—that seemed to shimmer when stepped on, releasing a faint glow in my wake.

The air was humid and rich with the scents of alien blossoms, their petals unfurling like miniature galaxies. Above me, strange bird-like creatures with translucent wings glided silently, their iridescent feathers casting small, glittering rainbows as they passed. The forest pulsed with life, a quiet symphony of unfamiliar chirps and low hums, and that made my skin prickle.

This was Tir Na: beautiful, wild, and utterly otherworldly.

As I jogged along, I couldn't shake the feeling that I was the odd one of the bunch. The outlier. And it wasn't just about being shorter than nearly everyone. I was insignificant, pointless... I was unworthy to be among these proud, confident, strong warriors. I knew what the others had quickly realized—Pherric had made a huge mistake bringing me here. What frightened me the most was that they might soon abandon their little experiment, leaving me alone to die.

Their constant disapproving glares and snide remarks had one positive side effect—they sharpened my resolve. Aside from Pherric's magical medicine for my feet and the occasional drink of water, that resolve was the only thing that kept me going.

Nothing motivated me more than someone telling me I could *not* do something. When I was a freshman, a math professor said to me, "Maybe college isn't right for you", after I failed one of her ridiculously hard tests. And that lit a fire under me. When I aced her final at the end of the semester, I waved it in her face and marched out of the classroom laughing like a crazy person. My father was disappointed with the "C" I got in the class, but I wore that smile for days afterward.

"Hey, Terran! Try to keep up!"

Gunnr, parked comfortably on her karkadann, shouted at me from up ahead. I was so lost in thought that I had stopped jogging and started wandering the forest floor, staring aimlessly at the trees.

"The Arachne live in these woods!"

Arachne? I quickly realized that arachnophobia was *a fear of spiders* so that meant... spiders!

"They are quite large and often very hungry!"

She somehow knew I was scared to death of spiders. But then, who wasn't? I swallowed hard, the lump in my throat refusing to budge. Suddenly, the forest wasn't so beautiful—it was a predator lying in wait. The rustling leaves in the nearby bush sounded too deliberate, like something lurking just out of sight. Above me, a strange bird let out a piercing screech, its cry slicing through the heavy silence. Then, behind me—a twig snapped. My heart thundered in my chest, each beat loud and panicked.

I stumbled forward, the dirt path blurring beneath my feet. Every shadow between every tall tree seemed to shift. To crawl. I strained my eyes, half-blinded by fear, scanning for any sign of those giant, ravenous spiders. Were they above, hidden in the dark canopy? Or creeping along the ground, ready to strike?

The wind picked up, rustling the foliage around me, and I couldn't tell if it was real or my imagination conjuring threats from every direction. I raced to catch up, the growing sense that I wasn't alone tightening around my throat like a noose. I could almost feel the phantom legs of some unseen creature closing in.

Gunnr seemed to hate me the most. I assumed Gunnr was either a powerful woman in a warrior society, where women were equals in battle, or she had to work twice as hard as the men in her tribe in order to be accepted. In either case, to her, I represented weakness. And she despised me for that.

I stopped close enough for Gunnr to hear me, struggling to catch my breath.

"So, lots of dangerous arachne around here, huh?"

"Do not try to befriend me, child. I doubt you will survive the week..."

She snapped her reins, racing away.

I squinted and coughed, waving away the cloud of debris she kicked up, with a big grin on my face.

Challenge accepted.

Chapter 16

Around sunset, my torturers finally stopped to rest and water the animals, including me. After a painfully short break, Temurr and Braylor lit torches and we were back on the path. Frip had said we were headed to a city. So I found myself praying we would see this glorious destination around every turn and or just beyond another cluster of trees, but we only journeyed deeper and deeper into the pitch-black forest.

Whatever Pherric had done to heal my feet had worked wonders. But after walking and running all day, the muscles in my legs were ready to give out. I finally had to stop all together. I fell to my knees, promising myself I would only stop for a minute.

"Guys! Wait. I can't... I..."

When I looked up again, they were gone—swallowed by the suffocating darkness.

Forcing myself to my feet, trembling, I listened. And this time, the forest had really turned against me. There were no more noises. The birds had fallen silent. The wind that whispered through the canopy was gone. Even the trees seemed to hold their breath.

The faint glow of their torches had vanished, leaving me stranded in the oppressive gloom. I took a hesitant step forward, then another, my ears straining for any hint of movement. And then—snap. A branch breaking behind me.

I was afraid to move, whimpering. Without thinking, I bolted. My foot caught on an unseen root, sending me sprawling face-first into the dirt.

Another crack—closer this time. My head whipped around, but the darkness revealed nothing. I clawed my way forward, crawling through the cold, wet dirt and sharp underbrush.

Above me, something heavy scrambled onto a tree. The limb groaned under its weight, and I could feel a presence bearing down on me.

Further back, the sound of rapid footsteps—dead branches and leaves crunching in quick succession. Panic surged as I heard it: click-click-click. The sound came from my left, mechanical and alien. Were they communicating? Were there more than one?

Tears blurred my vision as I pushed myself forward on shredded palms and gashed knees. My breaths came in ragged gasps, and the forest seemed to close in tighter with every desperate crawl.

Something big crashed through bushes on my right. I lowered my head, curling myself into a ball, ready to die. I heard a *shlucking* noise, then a dull thud. A heavy weight hit the ground.

But no giant spider bit into me. Nothing dragged me off into the night.

I found a reserve of adrenaline, just enough to stand up and start running again. I focused on my wobbly legs, trying hard to keep them from collapsing underneath me. Stumbling, scrambling, I pushed off tree after tree until I was far away from where I had heard those frightening sounds.

Pain shot through my sides. My mouth bone dry. But when I saw the torch light ahead, I sighed in relief—I had caught up with them.

I burst into a small glade as they unpacked the karkadanns, setting up camp for the night. Utterly worn, I tripped over a log and nearly fell into the fire that Temurr was stoking to life.

"She lives!" he announced, chuckling to himself as he struck a piece of flint with his knife.

"Surprisingly," Braylor replied.

Frip and Pherric placed me on a damp log, handing me water.

Pherric opened a vial containing a green powder. "Take this."

"Oh, *please* let this be poison." I downed the contents, chasing it with water.

"What happened out there?"

I looked at their faces, full of pity. I forced myself to stand so that I could lie to them with confidence. "Thanks to you jerks, I had to fight off one of those Arachne things all by myself!"

"All by yourself," Braylor mused. "With no weapon?"

Gunnr and Frip exchanged grins. Temurr cocked his head to the side.

"Yes! I had no choice! You abandoned me! I–I kicked it hard. I probably killed it. And then I had to run all the way here!"

Temurr stared at my dirty knees. Braylor chuckled to himself.

"What?! You think that's funny?! To leave a defenseless person alone in these freaky woods with no protection?!"

"Oh," Braylor said. "You had plenty of protection..."

Kasuma silently slid up beside me, running the flat of her sharp knife across the arm of my tunic, wiping away the Arachne blood.

"It was the least I could do," she purred.

Of course, everyone had a great laugh at my expense. Infuriated, I clenched my fists and stormed off like a child threatening to run away from home. And I desperately wanted to run, but had nowhere to go. Creatures were moving about in the darkness beyond.

Utterly exhausted and embarrassed, I curled up behind a log and fell fast asleep. I have no idea how long I was out, but when I came to, it was still dark and the others were around the fire.

I tried to sit back up but my body said *nope*. Frip noticed me stir and came to my rescue. He threw me against a log in front of the fire.

"I'm beginning to think you like her more than me, that one," Temurr joked.

"You would do the same for me, dear," Frip responded, then paused. "On second thought, no... I doubt you would."

Temurr threw a bone he'd been gnawing on at his mate. Frip giggled along with him.

"Back to our plan?" Gunnr: life of the party, she was.

"*What* plan?" asked Braylor, taking a drink.

Pherric chastised him. "Braylor." I had a feeling he did that a lot.

"Am I wrong? Do we *have* a plan? Or even an idea for a plan?"

"I never claimed to have all the answers," replied Pherric.

"No. You are the promiser of hope! But hope will not defeat Malek's army."

"Malek is the king guy back at the castle, right?" I said out loud, to my regret.

Gunnr snorted. "The mind on this one. Heh. She is as sharp as a Chupacabra trap."

"Listen up, sister! I have had enough of your shit—"

Gunnr jumped to her feet, gripping the handle of the axe at her back.

"I'm sorry! I'm sorry! Please don't kill me!" I said, lowering my head, waiting for the death blow.

Pherric tried to bring it down a notch: "We are all on edge. These are trying times. Please... Gunnr?"

Gunnr plopped down on her log. Temurr grinned at her and she shoved him off the log, causing him to laugh hysterically as he rolled through the wet leaves.

Frip took on the referee role. "As it were, Pherric. We have no plan but we do know our goal... Kill Malek. Correct?"

Kasuma sat quietly on the ground, her legs crossed and her wings covering her back, silently tearing off pieces of meat, slipping them in her mouth.

"Kill him, remove him from power... whatever it takes," admitted Pherric.

"Um, because I'm, uh, new here... I have to ask. If you remove this *evil* king, won't someone just as bad take his place?"

Cira looked up from shoving meat in her face to shake her head.

Braylor held his hand up to her.

"It is a fair question," Braylor said. "For generations, every species has been plagued by the dragons and the flesh-eating torodan. We were united behind the cause of survival. We worked together to defeat these creatures. But we have been without a common enemy for while. And now—"

"And now you're turning on each other," I said.

Braylor nodded. "Malek has been using our differences to rally the Hominans against all other species. Creating a new foe. He started with Frip and Temurr's kind because they look and act so differently from his kind."

Temurr turned to Frip. "Did he just insult us? I think he insulted us. I am insulted, I am."

Braylor ignored him. "And it was easy to enlist my kind against them because we have been at each other's throats forever. Malek then turned his people against the Bànshēn Rén, because of their history with Gunnr's tribes in Val—"

"The who?" I blurted.

Cira, still in her feeding frenzy, waved to me with greasy fingers.

"The Bànshēn Rén—Cira's species," Pherric said.

"We believe Malek tricked the Valhallans into believing the Bànshēn rén were stealing livestock and farmed goods from them—"

"They were stealing from us!" shouted Gunnr.

Cira tossed her food aside. "Liar!"

Gunnr reached for her axe again but Braylor eased her down. Gunnr shoved his meaty paw away.

Pherric waited patiently for Cira to stop staring at Gunnr. "As you can see, he has created tension or taken advantage of what was already there. Malek plays on our petty disputes while he enriches his kingdom at the expense of everyone else. He wants nothing more than to exterminate all who are different from you and I. None of our leaders have seemingly pieced together this puzzle. And we feel it is now too late..."

"So, he's making it all a 'hominans against the world' kind of thing?" I asked. "Us versus them? No, I doubt he would want to just kill off everyone else."

My eyes went from Kasuma to Braylor, to the ape men, and then Cira. They were all so amazing and unique. But my error was immediately apparent. People always hate anyone different. My classmates always made fun of me because I was tall or that I had red hair. And I was only *slightly* different.

"We believe it to be so. However, not all hominans stand with him. There are those still siding with the other kinds," said Pherric.

I added up all the different species around the campfire. "There are four different species on your world? Do they outnumber the hominans?"

"There are five other species," said Pherric. "I could not convince the Atlanteans to join our cause."

"Atlanteans? Oh, right... the lost island of Atlantis?" I asked, knowing the answer. "Let me guess—they're mermaids? Right?"

I laughed—but they nodded in agreement.

Frip chimed in. "And mermen! Naturally."

"Naturally." I shook my head. They still had dinosaurs here and dragons were real. Why not throw in Atlantis, too?

"Atlanteans look similar to hominans, dear," said Frip. "But they have gills in their sides, so they can breathe underwater and—"

"Yeah, I get it. We're good," I patted his hairy hand.

Across the fire pit, I watched Cira steal a piece of Gunnr's meat.

Gunnr swiftly drove her dagger down into the log, landing the blade between Cira's fingers.

"See?! They are *all* thieves!" shouted Gunnr.

Cira pulled back her hand. "I am still hungry!"

I pointed at Pherric. "So, wait... *you* brought everyone together?"

"Once I learned of the prophecy, and escaped the Scholomance, I spent the next several months traveling to every realm enlisting help. Those here before you... are their representatives."

"What he means is that he got stuck with us, he did," said Temurr. "Because we were too stupid to say no."

"That's ridiculous, my love. *I'm* not stupid," said Frip.

"Oh, but I am?!"

"No, dear. Your simply find wisdom to be... challenging." With a loud monkey-scream, Temurr leapt on top of Frip, bowling them both off the log. They wrestled in the dense undergrowth while Frip giggled with glee.

"You can see the level of quality we are dealing with here," stated

Braylor.

"Back to your question," Pherric chimed back in. "Hominans outnumber the other species. But... if we were able to bring all our allies together, we might rival Malek's forces. My goal was to assemble a team to help me bring you to here and then—"

"And then *not* have a plan to do anything after that..." Gunnr said.

"No, I wanted us to *develop* a plan of attack," said Pherric. "As I have said, I do not have all the answers... but something needs to be done. Or we will not survive the dark times ahead."

Chapter 17

The sun eventually came up. Against my will. So, I stirred beside the smoldering embers of our fire, realizing a rough fur had been draped over me. I didn't even recall lying down. My body ached, every muscle stiff from the day before. As I sat up, my tunic crackled—dried sweat and mud turning the fabric into something closer to armor. Disgust twisted in my stomach. The thing deserved to be burned, but it's not like I had a travel-size wardrobe tucked away somewhere. For now, I was stuck with that walking biohazard.

Pherric rode up on his karkadann, handing me dried meat. I did not bother to ask what it was; I simply ate it all. Probably better not to know.

"Did you sleep well?"

I grunted at him. "Hey, whatever you put in that vial? It really helped heal my feet. Now they only smell really bad."

"Most of what you smell is the Arachne blood on your sleeve."

I sniffed my tunic. He was right. I gagged at the stench.

"Please tell me I don't have to run *all day* again."

"As you wish. I will not tell you that you have to run all day."

He got another grunt from me as I struggled to stand.

"We shall be in Quivira before nightfall."

"Great," I sighed. "You got anything in that bag that'll make me *not* want to run straight off a cliff?"

"You are improving."

"Are you kidding? Every part of my body is in pain! I hurt in places I didn't know I had places! Even my pain has pain. It takes weeks or months of training to get to where you can run all day!"

"What I meant to say is that your attitude is improving. You did not ask for a ride. You simply accepted the fact that you had to run."

"Wait, does that mean if I *had* asked... you would have given me a ride?!"

He snapped his reins, trotting his karkadann onto the path to follow the others.

"Can I have a ride?! Please?! Wait!" I shouted. Ignoring the pain, I raced out of the glade and back into the forest.

Our journey through the mighty forest took up most of the day. Strange bugs bothered and bit me as I stumbled and grumbled along the worn path. Lucky for me, the twisting and winding trail through dense underbrush slowed their karkadanns enough that I was able to keep up. Unlucky for me, our trek seemed to be mostly uphill.

At last, we broke free from the forest and found ourselves on the edge of a high cliff, staring down at a sprawling valley below. A flickering river wound through the vast basin like a silver ribbon. Beyond the valley, a jagged range of gray, mist-shrouded mountains loomed on the horizon, their peaks pushing up into the purplish and pink sky.

In the heart of the gorge stood a solitary mountain, its rugged slopes slowly being carved away by the defiant river, which was forced to split and curl around the base before reuniting on the far side.

Atop this island peak, the city of Quivira was perched like a yellow diamond on a ring, its walls catching the fading sunlight. Below the city, smooth terraces had been meticulously carved into the mountainside, each brimming with life—clusters of villages and small huts, patchworks of thinly-spaced farm fields, and groves of fruit trees. The terraces descended in orderly layers, a testament to generations of careful excavations, with a single road winding all the way around and down.

The only link to the outside world was a single, narrow guarded bridge that stretched precariously from the mountain to the distant valley wall, a lifeline between Quivira and the land beyond. The scene was both breathtaking but otherworldly–a painting from a fairy tale book.

What made me gasp for breath—besides all that running and climbing I had to do—were those high city walls and roofs. Nearly every one was covered in gold. I mean it really looked the same as real, actual gold. And the setting sun was hitting that gold on full blast, creating green and red halos over the golden domes, spires, cupolas and roof tiles.

I leaned against a cluster of massive rocks at the cliff's edge, my eyes drawn to the immaculate city below. Three colossal towers punctured the dusk sky, each one more imposing than the last, standing proudly at the heart of the bustling mountain metropolis. From that height, the city seemed flawless, its compact design a marvel of harmony and precision. But my admiration faltered when I noticed the rows of enormous, weathered panels scattered throughout. Made of corroded metal, these huge sheets perched atop poles and rooftops, angling skyward like frozen waves. Each panel, patched together with various iron squares and rectangles and scorched from fire, spanned hundreds of feet and stood nearly as tall, their curved tops and flat bases casting long shadows over the city. The sight of them, stark and industrial against the city's elegance, were a deliberate blemish on an otherwise perfect canvas.

"Welcome to Quivira," said Frip.

He took a quick drink from his waterskin, handing me the bag.

"It's stunning... but why do they have those big metal panels covering everything?"

"Ah, yes, the old fire barriers. Many cities still have them," Frip replied.

"Fire barriers? What for?"

"Dragon attacks..."

Dragon attacks. Because that's a thing.

"Pray to the gods you never encounter one."

"I think if I pray anymore, my god is gonna block and report me..."

Frip pulled his head back, a quizzical look on his face.

"You are a strange creature, Finley Maguire."

The man-sized talking gay monkey just called *me* a strange creature.

Temurr rode up to us. "It's almost dark. Time to move."

Frip patted me, dashing off to mount his karkadann.

"Try not to get us killed," warned Temurr.

I blew him a kiss and started my jog down the trail toward the city of gold, because... downhill.

Night settled in as we made our way across the lone bridge, its wooden planks creaking beneath us. The pale, white wall of the mountain city loomed ahead, glowing faintly in the moonlight. A cool mist rose from the river below, swirling around us and shrouding our movements in an eerie, shifting blue fog.

Our two ape men and the giant silently slipped away from us and vanished into the mist, their hulking shapes swallowed by the shadows. My pulse quickened—whatever lay behind those walls, we were getting closer. I had a brief thought of reporting my kidnappers to any law enforcement we might run across. But I shook that off. Too much was unknown.

Pherric and Gunnr took the lead as we approached the entrance. I rode behind on Temurr's beast; the joy of being off my feet nearly made me cry. Cira covered her humongous feet with ill-fitting boots from Braylor, tied back her wild long hair, and slipped on gloves to conceal those hairy hands. She then tied the two extra karkadanns to her saddle. Kasuma had to work a little harder—she borrowed a tunic from Frip, worked a thick cloak over her wings and white suit, and pulled up the hood to cover her bright, white hair. She rode with her head down, concealing those black eyes.

As we closed in on the tall iron gates, I whispered to Cira, "If the people in this city are cool with other species, why are we hiding?"

"According to Pherric, we have allies here. But not everyone is aligned with our cause. Malek has likely posted a garrison of Irkallan soldiers here—they are in almost every realm now. He claims it is for protection, but they do it to maintain control while they tax the people to death."

"Why doesn't anyone fight back?" I asked.

"Well, you were kidnapped, brought here against your will, and are working with your captors in order to stay alive, on a mission with no plan, that may well end with your death…"

"Touché." I couldn't argue with that.

"I assume that means 'you are absolutely correct'." I smiled to myself. She had a sense of humor.

Loaded merchant wagons and a line of people, carrying full sacks over their shoulders, exited the city. They glumly passed without acknowledging our presence.

Four tall guards stood sentry at the black gates, holding long spears next to their gold-plated armor. Their mustard-colored tunics were trimmed in royal blue trim and their shiny helmets had blue plumes on top.

"Are those guys from Irkalla?" I asked.

"They are Quiviran," Cira said. "The Irkallans would not waste men here. They are most likely stationed up at the main entrance. But we are not going in that way…"

"We're not?"

One of the guards let a couple of young men carrying freshly-caught fish past us and through the wide metal gates, and then he sauntered up to Pherric. He had dark hair and eyes, a full black beard, and the same Spanish complexion as Pherric.

"State your business!" bellowed the guard.

"We are here to sell our karkadanns."

He laughed. "May the goddess of luck be upon you then! You shall need it!"

"Why is that?" Pherric inquired.

The guard pointed to the wagons and people heading away from the city. "They were all trying to sell their wares here and had no luck. Why should you be any different? Except for the Families, there is naught a soul in the city who can afford to buy *anything*."

"That bad, is it?"

"Aye," admitted the guard. "Probably worse. Be on with ya then!"

He waved us through the gates, eyeing Cira and Kasuma with suspicion but too weary to take a closer look. We slowly marched our karkadanns inside the shelter of the outer wall, along the path that wound up and around the mountain to the glowing city above.

When Cira finally lifted her head, I leaned in. "What did he mean by *the families?*"

"We are in Cíbola, which is a sovereign nation, but there is no king or queen ruling this country. Instead, three families control everything. There are other rich and powerful houses in the city but the top three have held onto power for centuries. They are filled with weak and lazy nobles, who make as many foolish decisions as a ruler, but... having a group of three helps lessen the idiocy."

"I see." I didn't see.

The dirt path on the first terrace was dimly lit by a handful of flickering torches, their light barely cutting through the thick night air. We halted briefly at the edge of a small village, Pherric scanning the area to ensure no one took notice. Satisfied, he led us off the main road.

We passed a line of crumbling huts, their white plaster walls stained and roofs patched with brittle straw. Hollow-eyed villagers peered cautiously from cracked doors and shattered windows, their faces etched with fear and desperation. My chest tightened, and I averted my gaze as we slipped silently into the shadow of the white outer wall.

Chapter 18

We trotted along behind Pherric's karkadann, its heavy hooves pressing soft indentations into the brittle grass. The fruit trees surrounding us turned out to be barren, their empty branches reaching out like frozen fingers in the pale, bluish light of Tir Na's moon.

He kept us close to the main wall that ran along the first terrace. The city's distant hum hundreds of feet above cloaked the noise of our movements.

I glanced skyward, unsettled once again by the foreign moon. It loomed larger than Earth's, smooth as polished stone, and eerily unblemished. Was it even real? Of course, if this planet was smaller, maybe it needed a bigger moon to keep in an orbit aligned with Earth. Which meant that maybe their gods had built the moon? I had no idea.

Pherric guided us closer to the stone wall lining the first terrace. The air carried an uneasy stillness, like the world had paused to watch us. Shadows stretched long across the ground under the faint silvery-blue glow. Then, a sound—low and muffled—from beyond the wall. Pherric halted, raising his hand sharply. We all stopped.

I gripped the saddle tight, waiting for his signal. After an agonizing pause, he nodded to Gunnr. She slid off her mount, her movements fluid but deliberate. Cira and I dismounted too, our feet hitting the ground as softly as possible. Every nerve in my body screamed for action, but we stood motionless, staring at the wall, the shadows, the unknown.

Then came the laughter.

Pherric spun away from the wall and took steps toward a small cluster of the spindly fruit trees. Cira slid her sword from her belt—that high *shhiiinngg* sound of steel moving against metal.

Gunnr reached for her dagger handle—Pherric stayed her hand, shaking his head. He then pointed at Cira, giving her a stern look. She lowered the blade.

I looked all around us. Naturally, Kasuma had vanished. Like she always did.

More muffled laughter drifted from below the trees, bouncing off the barren trees and breaking apart in the quiet night. I squinted into the darkness and spotted two figures beneath the twisted branches—one leaning heavily against the other, their shapes swaying slightly.

Before I could signal to the others, Cira's karkadann let out a sharp snort, its hoof striking the dry grass with a hollow thud. The sound rippled through the stillness, and the two figures looked our way.

A male voice shouted out. "Who goes there?!"

A woman's voice called the man back to her. I grinned. They apparently had a little rendezvous in the woods planned for their evening.

Pherric led his beast into the open, wanting to meet the man before he got too close.

"Pardon us, sir. We were merely looking for a place to camp for the—"

"Who are you?" the soldier demanded, his hand at the sword in his gold belt. He wore the golden tunic trimmed in royal blue, with a blue plume on his helmet.

"I am Pherric of El Dorado," he soothed, holding his empty hands up. "We recently arrived in your fair city, sir."

Standing beside her karkadann, Cira tensed into a ball of energy. Ready to pop.

"This land belongs to the Barboza family of the First House," growled the soldier.

"We did not mean to trespass." Pherric tried desperately to diffuse the situation.

"And yet, trespass you have..."

The guard turned his head, placing hands to his mouth to sound the alarm—but a hand covered his face. Kasuma stepped from behind, placing her hands on the man's forehead.

"Kasuma, no!" begged Pherric.

With a quick turn of her hand, we heard the snap of bone. The soldier's body folded to the grass. The silent assassin stepped up to Pherric, wiping her hands together to rid them of the man's sweat.

"What?" She petted the long face of his karkadann.

"A missing guard will raise questions!" Pherric said.

"I am quite sure that the half-dressed maidservant back there was going to keep him occupied for a little while."

"You killed her, as well?"

"For the cause," said Kasuma. "You remember the cause, yes?"

"Yes, but they will come looking for him," he said, the frustration evident. "We cannot create more problems for ourselves that—"

Ooomph!

The loud grunt pulled our attention to the outer wall. A dark form sailed over the top, landing with a dull *thud* in thick grass.

"Well, that was not fun," groaned Temurr as he pushed himself up from the ground, dusting dried grass from his backside.

Another loud *oomphing* grunt from the other side of the wall—another dark figure flew into the air. The shape struck the top plate of the wall, tumbling over and over as it fell into prickly shrubs below.

Frip leapt out of the bushes, cursing and dancing about as he pulled small needles from his fur.

"You did that on purpose, you clumsy oaf!" Frip shouted at the top of the wall.

"What?! Your fat ass weighs more than your mate's!" bellowed Braylor from the other side.

Pherric furtively scanned the area. "Quiet, you dolts!"

Temurr went apeshit on Pherric. "I could have climbed that wall! But no! You told him to throw us over, did you not?!"

"You could not be seen scaling the wall, Temurr."

With a massive grunt, Braylor jumped up, grabbed the top of the wall, and pulled himself up to lay flat on the surface. He surveyed his surroundings, then lowered himself to the foot of the wall.

Cira handed me the reins to her karkadann. "Braylor, help me hide the bodies."

"Bodies? Did I miss the fun?" Temurr joked.

"No. Do not hide them," said Gunnr. She also handed me her reins; I was their new stable boy.

"What?!" Pherric questioned. Gunnr ignored him.

"Place them together," she commanded. "Under one of the trees. Put her hands on his neck, and tie his belt around her neck. This was a... lovers' quarrel. If we hide the bodies, it will look suspicious and the guards will investigate."

"Damn, girl. Remind me not to get on your bad side," I said.

She threw me an icy glare. "Too late."

Braylor and Cira dragged the bodies together and arranged them. Pherric and Kasuma slipped away to scout the area for more unwanted visitors.

Once again, I stood on the sidelines while others did the hard, gruesome work. I wanted to help—wanted to be more than just another pair of eyes watching the bodies pile up. But as I stood there, the weight of it all finally hit me: this wasn't some abstract cause or distant tragedy. This was real. People were dying. We could die. And yet, they believed it was worth it. They were fighting to stop a genocide, to save entire species from extinction. Somehow, I convinced myself that that made their actions justified. No matter what it cost.

Back on Earth, I had seen plenty of atrocities online. The kind of horrors that flood your feed with headlines, hashtags, and outrage. I played my part as the perfect armchair slactivist—firing off posts, sharing articles, and riding the wave of virtual indignation. It felt good, easy. It didn't demand anything of me beyond a few clicks. And the likes? They poured in, feeding my shallow sense of accomplishment.

But now, here I was, on a different world, caught in a fight that wasn't about performative outrage or hollow gestures. This was real action, led by people willing to sacrifice everything to stop some genocidal maniac from wiping out entire civilizations. And somehow, a few of them believed I could help. That I could make a difference.

Was that ridiculous? Absolutely. I didn't feel like a hero or a leader—hell, I barely felt competent. But for the first time, I wasn't just talking about change or liking it from a distance. I was standing in the thick of it. And for the first time in my life, I felt like I had a purpose. Even if it was borrowed, even if it was fleeting—it was something.

Everything was pulling at me, tearing at me from the inside out, to help in some way. But I stood there and watched them doing it all. Like a coward.

Chapter 19

With our team reunited, we mounted up and pressed deeper into the mountain terrace. With my legs shaking from overuse, and before I could protest, Pherric took pity on me and hauled my battered body onto the back of his ride with little effort.

The dirt path wound its way along the edge of the cliff, the drop-off growing more daunting with every step. We passed several outwardly deserted farmhouses, with empty fields and rows of bare vines, and darkened huts as we prowled along the road.

For fear of being detected, we avoided conversation. The warbling of strange insects provided the creepy soundtrack to our covert mission.

Up ahead, I could hear babbling water splashing against stone. As much as I used to complain about public restrooms, I would have killed for a filthy truck stop gas station bathroom on the Jersey turnpike at that point. The sound of that falling water did not help matters—but the leaves on nearby scraggly trees looked a bit too pointy for my needs. Pherric silently gestured at the two flickering lights ahead, piercing the darkness along the path, and that helped distract me from my agony.

As we rode up to a plain white hut with a thatched roof, the two small candles glowing in the windows were extinguished. I peeked around him to see an older Hominan woman emerge with a torch and dagger in her hands. Her fire illuminated the fountain, carved into the side of the mountain, that collected the water flowing from the cliff face.

She stood half a head taller than me, her wiry frame as thin and strong as the farm tools she likely used. Streaks of gray threaded through her long, dark hair, though she wasn't as old as the leathery, sun-baked orange of her skin initially suggested. Years of labor had etched hard lines into her face, but her sharp, hawk-like features were anything but frail.

Her dark eyes, fierce and unblinking, seemed to see right through us, their intensity magnified by the long, angular bridge of her nose. But with that candlelight, she couldn't see us clearly. She raised the torch higher, the flame flickering as she squinted, sizing us up with a wary precision.

"That's far enough!" she bellowed. "What do you want?! I have no food here!"

Pherric hopped down and stepped forward, palms held high. "Long live the three houses. I saw a cyclops on the journey from Atlantis."

"Long live the three houses. The road to Irkalla is full of dragons." She smirked. "Welcome..."

They must have been using some kind of code because she lowered her dagger and held her torch back, lighting the way to her hut.

"Ah, Pherric! It *is* you! It has been forever, child!" she scolded him.

Pherric reddened as they hugged. "Far too long, Runa."

"Everyone! Inside. Quickly," she urged.

Runa hurried to her door and stood back, letting everyone in as she inspected our crew.

"Hurry along! We do not have all night," said Runa.

She nodded to each of us. When Braylor stepped up, she threw him a huge grin. "Welcome, handsome!"

He grimaced at her as he bent low and turned his shoulders to fit through the doorway.

When I went to pass her, she grabbed me with her free hand, eyeing me with suspicion. "I have to ask, girl. Did you ride that karkadann here or did it ride you?"

She cackled out loud like it was the funniest thing she'd ever said. She got my best fake smile in return.

After everyone had entered her hut, she took a final look around and pushed the wood door closed.

"Well, this sure is interesting company you have gathered, Pherric."

Runa danced around everyone as they dropped their gear. She grabbed an empty pitcher, threw it into my hands. "Gather water from the fountain outside."

Tired, hungry, and desperate to pee, I wanted to toss the pitcher back at her and tell her to go get her own damn water. But... I didn't.

I had, however, taken too long to reply. Runa grabbed my tunic and pulled me close to her face. I learned more about her dental hygiene than I cared to at that moment.

"Look around this room, child. Are you not the youngest here?"

Pherric intervened, pushing his way between us. He handed me the empty pitcher.

"Finley, please fetch water for everyone? As is the custom here."

I glared at both of them but took the pitcher. Apparently I was supposed to automatically *know* how things worked. As I made my way to the door, I got a snarky smirk from Gunnr.

I returned to everyone seated in a circle. Runa motioned for me to pour water into cups set out on her small table.

"The situation here seems dire," Pherric said to Runa. "Is it like this across Cíbola?"

"It is like this across the entire continent, my boy." Runa sighed, slowly lowering herself on a stool across from him. "Every nation from here to Valhalla is hurting for resources. Fruits and vegetables were the first to run out. They have run low on grains. They can water the livestock, but barely feed the ones they have left. Prices are scandalous—for the cost of a loaf of bread you *should* buy a feast! Most have resorted to hunting and fishing but must go days away from the city to find prey. Malek has squeezed us dry. He has hidden huge stores of food here, but that is only to keep his soldiers and the Quiviran guards satisfied, while he steals the rest back to his kingdom."

"I was afraid it would come to this."

"Once a day, his men dole out slop to keep the city from uprising," she told him. "So, forgive my manners, but... I have nothing for your guests."

Pherric reached into his bag, handing her some dried fruits and meats.

"No! I could not!" she protested.

"You will. I insist," he told her, pressing everything into her thin hands. "And we will leave supplies for you."

Her shame was visible, but she took what he gave her.

"How can I help?" Runa happily changed the subject.

"We need to sneak into the city."

Runa laughed, slapped her knees, and turned to me. "Ha! That is not usually how it works around here!"

Confused, and scared of Runa, I whispered to Cira. "What does she mean?"

"Quivira used to have a diverse population," Cira said. "Before Malek, there were many of Frip and Temurr's kind living here. Some of my people, as well. Once he came to power and invaded this nation, most fled the city. But a few stubborn ones remained."

"And they were slaughtered!" Temurr shouted. He stood but Frip quickly pulled him back down, wrapping an arm around his shoulder and rubbing his back.

"Yes. They were," said Pherric. "But many Hominans objected and helped the others escape. Those like Runa here. They created passages, out of the city, through a series of natural caves and handmade tunnels. Those escape routes ended here, below this house. She has helped save many lives."

"That's so savage!" I said to Runa. "You were all *Harriet Tubman and the Underground Railroad* up in here! Nice."

As if I had eaten one of her children, Runa stared at me and then looked to Pherric. He held out his hands and shook his head, as if to say don't even bother.

"We must move quickly. If we are discovered here, you would be in danger," Pherric told her.

Runa nodded. She seemed to enjoy having company but knew what must be done. She slapped her knees again, and rushed to the corner of her small house. Pherric dragged a wood chair away as Runa pulled back a white woven rug. She grabbed a handle in the floor, pulling it up, revealing a door that led to a shallow storage space below.

I leaned in, squinting to make sense of the contents below—just a few round jars and some wooden boxes, nothing unusual. Before I could investigate further, Runa shoved me aside with a muttered curse. She dropped to her knees, her hands working swiftly as she pushed aside a false floor, revealing a hidden door.

With Pherric's help, she heaved open a second, heavier door. The air around us seemed to shift as we looked down a shaft stretching into the darkness below. Faintly, I could make out the rough rungs of a makeshift ladder clinging to the walls, disappearing into an unknown depth.

"What's that?"

"A passageway. We will be able to walk under this hut and into the mountain. Then we begin the long journey up," said Pherric, pointing up at the ceiling.

Braylor stepped between us to get a good look down the hole. "You expect me... to go down there?"

"We have no choice," Pherric explained. "It is our only way to smuggle you and the others into the city."

"No, no, no, no, no," Braylor mumbled. "I–I cannot... No. Absolutely not."

"You're not afraid, are you, handsome?" Runa teased him, flirting.

Braylor stood tall, backing away from the dark pit. His head scraped the plaster ceiling, sending dust flying about the room.

I raced to him, grabbing both his hands, and looked up into his eyes. "Hey, Braylor. Look at me, okay? We can do this."

I finally found a way to help...

"Easy for you, tiny one. I *will* get stuck down there." Braylor turned to Pherric. "No. Let me climb up the mountainside instead."

"That is not an option, Braylor."

I smiled at him, rubbing the backs of his hands. I looked to Runa. "He'll fit through the passage, right?"

"Well, we did not have many Fomorians trying to evacuate from the city, except for children and a few elderlies," she admitted.

"You see?!" he exclaimed. "I will not make it through!"

"You will do just fine... handsome," Runa added.

Braylor looked pleadingly at Pherric. "She wants to kill me. You know this, correct?"

"On the contrary. I would rather keep you here," smirked Runa. "With me..."

I glared at her. For some reason, and for the first time in forever, a fit of jealousy ran through me—the old beezy was getting a bit excessive with all the *handsomes*.

Pushing my way between them, I stared at him until we locked eyes. "Please, Braylor. Just try... for me."

I didn't know him and, as grumpy as he always was, I doubted that would work. But his massive shoulders dropped slightly. He lowered his head to avoid destroying more of the ceiling.

"I will... try," he said.

Chapter 20

I was *volunteered* to lead the way through the tunnel.

Pherric pulled me aside as the others scooped up their weapons and belongings. "I need you in that tunnel before Braylor. You will go first."

"And you will drop dead. There's no way I'm going down there alone!"

"Why?"

"Because I'm not fond of the idea of crawling into a pitch-black hole, on an alien planet, only to be eaten by some bizarre creature that lives down there—one that you *casually* forgot to mention!"

So, I went down into the tunnel first.

Braylor demanded the rest of the crew follow behind him, so they could pull him back out when he got stuck. Because he knew for certain he would.

Runa lit a small torch for me and I dropped it down the hole. The start of the tunnel was about twenty feet below. Rung by rung, I lowered myself. When hungry jaws didn't bite me in half on the way, I scooped up the torch and held the flame out—I could only see a short distance ahead. The tunnel stood about two feet above my head and was around six feet wide; not small for me, but...

Using the torch, I lit several dusty lanterns placed along the tunnel wall. When I returned to look up, Braylor's eyes were wide with fear.

"You got this," I said.

He sneered at me, the tunnel, life itself. But eventually, he descended the ladder. Dirt sprinkled down as his shoulders dragged along the narrow shaft.

"All right, you made it! Look at you go!" I told him as his giant boots touched the dirt floor.

Dusting himself off, he glared at me and took a deep breath. The tunnel wasn't as small as he had imagined. But he did have to bend down and turn his huge shoulders.

I slowly worked my way along, lighting sconces and returning to check on the big guy. He nearly filled the entire tunnel. His heavy plodding caused dirt to drop with each step, his arms widening the tunnel on every swing.

"This is madness," Braylor grumbled.

"For the cause," I said. "Remember?"

"Yes! Yes! How could I forget? The chattering Pherric never lets me forget! He is such the whiny snot!"

We made our way deeper into the burrow.

"You're doing great..."

"Is it me or... is this hole getting smaller?" asked Braylor.

It was.

"No, that's all in your head. Let's just keep moving."

Farther along, Braylor was forced to drop and crawl on his knees. Even I had to duck my head.

"The tunnel... is shrinking... not good," said Braylor.

"We're okay. You still fit."

As we crawled deeper, the space shrank down. His shoulders knocked lanterns off the shaft walls. All he could see was my face by torchlight.

"We must go back!"

"We're almost there," I soothed.

"How do you know?!"

I didn't.

"Hang on. I'll show you!"

That was a big mistake. I went deeper along the tunnel, lighting half a dozen candles. The walls turned from dirt to solid rock, which meant we were probably under the mountain. That also meant they must have had a harder time digging out the passage.

I raced back to Braylor. He had stopped crawling. A look of horror fell across his big face when he saw the rocky passageway tapering down.

"Everyone behind me! I am backing out! Move along or I will run you down!" he screamed.

"No! No!" I held my hands out, imploring him.

Sweat beading on his forehead, his eyes went wide with panic and his breath came in short gasps.

"It's okay," I said. "Just a little claustrophobia."

"I do not have that! I simply hate being confined in small, tight spaces!"

I dropped my torch, placing my hands on his cheeks. "Hey, listen to me. Okay? Just listen. Take a deep breath. And another. Good."

He gulped and closed his eyes, taking short and shallow breaths.

"I'm here with you. We can do this. It will not be easy but I am right here."

"I will die swinging my sword, not stuck in a tiny hole... do you hear me?!"

"I hear you."

He lifted his head to look in my eyes, knocking more dirt free from the top of the tunnel. The dirt poured off him—and in my face.

"Oh, shit! It's in my mouth!"

I spat out the dirt and wiped dust from my eyes. Braylor chuckled.

"Stop laughing!" I said, repeatedly spitting and trying to get all chalky, gritty dirt out.

He laughed a little more.

"It's not funny!" I demanded, playing it up a little; laughter was a useful distraction.

"Oh, that was funny."

"To *you*!"

When I got the dirt out of my eyes, we went back to work.

"Come with me. Let's do this," I said. "But I need you to crawl on your belly now, okay?"

With another heavy sigh, he laid on the dirt floor and squirmed forward on his elbows.

As I scrambled backward into the tunnel, my palms scraping against the cold, damp earth, the flickering firelight illuminated the scene above. Pherric stood just behind Braylor, his face partially lit by the dancing flames. And there it was—a smile. But not just any smile. It was one of quiet pride.

It stopped me cold. Pherric, the hardened, unflinching leader, actually *proud*? That wasn't something I'd seen in what felt like forever. It was jarring, almost out of place, but strangely reassuring.

The height of the underground passage lowered a bit more but, luckily for Braylor, remained the same width. He bitched and moaned the whole way and only had one or two more panic attacks. I kept talking him through it, making him laugh. The more I made the sour giant laugh, the better he was at handling our situation.

Once we were through the bedrock of the mountain, the shaft opened up and the floor climbed at a slight elevation. Eventually, we were all able to stand as we emerged into a natural cave.

Braylor stretched and groaned once he could stand. After wiping off the dirt, he snatched the torch from my hand and stepped into the cave.

"What! Not even a... thank you?" I asked.

He was baffled. "For what?"

As the others crawled from the tunnel, I stormed past Braylor.

"What?" he asked me, then looked at the rest of the team.

"Well, she did help you make it through," said Pherric.

"I did not need *any* help! That was merely a confining space. I am Braylor!" he blustered.

Arms crossed, I could only roll my eyes at him. Males—no matter the species—are *all* the same.

He grabbed Pherric by his tunic and loudly whispered. "But we are *not* going back out that way..."

Pherric nodded, trying hard not to smile, as Braylor stormed deeper into the cold, wet cave.

Chapter 21

We spent the rest of the night following Cira, the cave dweller, as she led us through the subterranean caves and tunnels. We scaled rock walls, waded through an underground river, dodged a few falling rocks, crawled through natural passageways, climbed shafts, inched our way along narrow ledges—basically spelunking the hell out of the mountain under a city.

In the early morning hours, Pherric shuffled us into a long handmade passageway that stretched nearly a city block. At the end of the tunnel, we stopped at a ladder that I hoped would take us to the surface, to whatever our objective was going to be—I was exhausted, freezing cold, and soaking wet.

Pherric scaled the ladder, listening intently at the wooden door above. When he heard nothing that gave him pause, he tapped out a secret code against the door. When the hatch opened, he climbed up the ladder.

I pulled myself through the opening until I was standing on a floor in the center of a library, filled with stacks of scrolls, maps, and gold-leafed books. Several guards, decked out in crimson and gold-trimmed shirts and black breeches, greeted us with swords drawn.

Pherric held out both hands, to show he was unarmed. "Long live the three houses. We are here at the command of Lord Diago. I am Pherric."

An imposing yet elegant figure strode into the library, his presence commanding attention with ease. His long silver hair, neatly tied back in a sleek ponytail, shimmered faintly in the warm glow of the room. A broad, confident smile spread across his face, exuding charm and self-assurance.

Every detail of his tailored attire, from the gleaming silver rings to the leather shoes, spoke of wealth and influence. He moved with the assured confidence of someone accustomed to power.

"Long live the three houses! Pherric, you have arrived!"

He hugged Pherric and stepped back to look him over. His shoulders were back and his head held high as he looked down his long hook nose at Pherric with a wry smile.

"Is that really you?" The man feigned concern. "The last time I saw you, you were but a thin little boy…"

"My lord," Pherric said, bowing his head slightly. "It is good to see you again."

His lord looked quite regal in his royal blue silk top and high-waisted black trousers. He hugged Pherric one last time, then put his arm around him as he turned to the rest of us.

"What have we here?" he said.

"Lord Diago," said Pherric. "Let me present Frip and Temurr, from Shangri-La in Kunlun. Braylor, who hails from Manannán in Mag Mell. Cira of Agartha. Gunnr Hallsdottir is from Vanaheimr in Valhalla. Kasuma from Nibiru. And—"

Lord Diago pushed by me and stepped up to Kasuma, bowing his head slightly and waving both hands away from his forehead. Kasuma grinned. Apparently Diago knew the appropriate greeting for her kind.

"As I draw breath, you are the first Tenguan I have had the pleasure to meet," said Diago. "Welcome to the House of Lascarus! In truth, a warm welcome to you all—!"

Pherric cut in. "Sir? If I may? Allow me to also introduce Finley Maguire."

Lord Diago turned toward me and then looked down. I'm sure I was quite a sight. And probably a stench, too.

He forced a half smile. "My apologies. Welcome, Finley Maguire. And from where do you hail?"

I started to say Manhattan but Pherric beat me to the punch. "She is… Atlantean, my lord."

His eyes narrowed as he inspected me. After a beat, he shared a forced smile with Pherric.

"I see." He knew that was complete bullshit.

Clasping his hands together, he addressed the group. "Well, I am sure you are all utterly fatigued from your perilous journey! My steward will escort you to your rooms, where you can freshen up."

Lord Diago looked at me. "As best you can..."

Have you ever felt so disgustingly gross that you knew taking two or three showers would still not get you clean enough? I felt that way the night we arrived at Diago's house. One of his chambermaids tried to help me but I had to push her out the door. No one was coming near my hot mess. But soak in the wood tub, I did. Until the water was cold.

I crawled into the small four poster bed and slept the entire day away.

While I was out cold, someone must have sneaked into the chamber and laid out clothing for me. I slipped on the linen chemise and then a sleeveless forest green velvet dress, with white embroidery at the neckline. Whoever picked out my clothes, and the marvelous pair of silk slippers, had judged my size well. After I fought to rid my curly red hair of the rat's nest, I went off in search of the others.

There are moments you never forget, and walking down Diago's marble staircase was one of mine. The sheer extravagance of the place made my lack of makeup or even decent hair feel like a crime. As I descended toward the secondary hall, just off the Great Hall, every head turned. To me.

The room was straight out of a period drama: dark hardwood floors, ridiculously high ceilings with thick, carved beams, and a wall of windows that framed the jagged black mountains like a painting. Multiple seating areas were scattered around, each more lavish than the next.

For once, I wasn't caked in dirt or sweat, and the difference wasn't lost on anyone. A few people actually stared, their mouths opening slightly. Frip elbowed Temurr, who promptly shoved him off the edge of their divan. Pherric and Braylor rose from their goth thrones like they were preparing for a royal audience. By the fireplace, Gunnr raised her wine glass, giving me a subtle nod—the equivalent of a standing ovation from her. Kasuma barely glanced up, more interested in fussing over her feathers.

I straightened my spine, let my shoulders drop back, and lifted my chin just a touch. For the first time, I wasn't just the mud-streaked outsider. And as I stepped into the hall, I made damn sure they noticed.

Most of the misfits sat back down, or turned back to the others to resume quiet conversations or drink their wine. They had all cleaned up nicely. Somehow, they had even found clothes that fit Braylor. And he looked quite good, but somewhat uncomfortable, all fancied up. More than once, I noticed him reaching for the scabbard that was not at his side.

Pherric took me in with his eyes. "You look beautiful, Finley."

"If you think this is beautiful, I must've looked like a skeezy trash panda before."

"Nonsense," said Braylor, stepping in and handing me a metal cup full of red wine. "You looked more like a drowned Hyperborean nandi."

I didn't know what that was, but it didn't sound good.

I started to speak but he winked at me. "But you are less of a nandi now."

He ambled away to chat up Gunnr by the fire.

"Come! Let me show you the city," said Pherric.

Earlier, a butler from the manor had set out a snack for me to munch on. But a ravenous hunger remained, so the wine went straight to my head. I could not wipe the smile off my face from coming down the staircase. I am *never* the center of attention. I'm the cute, funny, slightly—and I *mean* slightly—chubby sidekick to one of my gorgeous friends, like Genevieve. The perfect wingman. I was the girl that boys came to so they could get closer to her. So, my entrance was fun. I just wish I had done something with my hair.

Pherric showed me through some double doors out onto a large balcony.

"This is Quivira."

Lord Diago's keep loomed at the farthest edge of the mountain summit, like a sentinel guarding the end of the world. From our balcony, five stories above the ground, the city stretched out below—a dense, intricate tapestry of medieval life. Having grown up surrounded by New York's towering steel and glass monoliths, I couldn't help but think how small this city seemed in comparison. Yet, it held a power of its own.

Three massive towers dominated the center, undoubtedly home to the ruling families, while half a dozen sprawling manors, much like Diago's, dotted the mountain's plateau. The tightly packed houses were crisscrossed by narrow, unpaved streets, forming a labyrinth of cobblestones and clay. And yet, all of that faded in the face of what truly left me speechless: the gold. It glinted everywhere, adorning rooftops, arches, and even the intricate railings of the towers. Pherric had mentioned that this wasn't unique—there were more cities like this in Cíbola. El Dorado and the Seven Cities of Gold weren't just myths; they were real, glittering proof right in front of me.

"When I was last here, Quivira was alive," Pherric murmured, his voice low and rough. He leaned heavily on the stone railing, his gaze fixed on the city below. "Even in the dead of night, there was music in the air, laughter spilling from every corner. The people lived with joy, with hope. Now..." His words trailed off, his jaw tightening. "Now, all I feel from them is despair. Fear. The life of this place has faded."

The golden city below suddenly felt less like a dream and more like a fragile, crumbling relic.

"Hmm, speaking of fear... this kinda reminds me of when we were last together on a patio and you *kidnapped* me," I said with a snarky smile.

"For that, I am truly sorry. But you are an absolute necessity. My purpose was well-intended and my quest was one of honor," he said.

"But w-why...?"

"You? Believe it or not, you were described in great detail in the Scholomance prophecy. You were not difficult to find."

"I was in the prophecy? And it said 'Finley Maguire, an extremely cute, rich girl living on the Upper West Side with absolutely zero leadership or fighting skills, is going to save our planet'?"

"Not... in so many words," admitted Pherric. "The ancient texts spoke of an irascible young female—the descendant of a legendary warrior, mind you—with an astute mind and quick wit.”

“Well, *that* does sound like me,” I said, being sarcastic. “Wait! Except for the legendary warrior bit. I don’t know if I’d call my grandfather legendary. He was a hard drinking Irish cop who probably only became a cop so he wouldn’t get arrested.”

“Your ancestor was a powerful chieftain among a collection of tribes called the Celts.”

“That would make sense. I am Irish. Wait a second! You guys act like fire was your most recent big discovery... how can you know who I descended from?

“The energy waves from your ancestors remain in the aether, just waiting to be read. When I arrived, I ruminated for a full day in order to take advantage of the mindform energy on your world,” said Pherric. “I was able to sift through the strings, delving deep into your rather harsh history, and eventually find you through your forefather.”

I was skeptical. But impressed. And oh-so curious. “Go on.”

“And... you are descended from Fionn mac Cumhaill.”

“Never heard of him. Who is he?” I asked.

“Fionn’s warrior father, Cumhaill, was the leader of the Fianna tribe. His mother, Muirne was a druid. Cumhaill wanted Muirne for his own, asking her father if they could wed. However, Muirne’s father would not allow his daughter to be with a bloody barbarian. This led Cumhaill to abduct her—

“Sounds familiar...”

“And they formed a forbidden union—”

“Which is code for ‘they hooked up’, I’m guessing?” He gave me the look. “Sorry.”

“The expectant Muirne was exiled by her father. Cumhaill was killed in a battle by Goll mac Morna. When the child, Fionn, was born, the mother feared that Goll would try to kill him.”

“He figured Fionn would want some revenge once he grew up,” I surmised.

“Exactly. Muirne left the baby with the druid Bodhmall and her partner

Liath Luachra. They reared Fionn in the forests and mountains of ancient Ireland. When Liath was young, she was renowned for her fighting skills. It was her teachings of the child that I found most interesting; she taught the boy to not only survive, but thrive, on his own. Liath took Fionn into the forest to study life, to watch a particular creature and not stop until he had learned a vital skill. From the fish, he learned to remain still and be patient. From the insect, he learned to overcome obstacles ten times his size. From the bird, he learned to strike swiftly at the right moment. She taught him to run with the animals and hunt like them. Fionn went on to be a mighty warrior, killing Goll mac Morna, and taking over the Fianna clan."

"I see where this is going," I said.

"There's that sharp mind," said Pherric. "It is said that Liath took up a sharp stick, gave the boy one, and chased him around the forest, and poked him constantly. Painfully. This developed his speed and agility. And his will to succeed and overcome. Once Fionn could catch up with her and inflict his own painful blows... she set him loose on the world."

"Let me guess... you guys are going to teach me... just like my ancestor was taught?"

"Your training starts tomorrow," said Pherric.

Chapter 22

For the rest of my first night in Quivira, I crammed far too much food into my face and washed it down with way too much wine. By the time I staggered up my new favorite staircase to my bedchamber, a familiar phrase from my grandfather drifted through my alcohol-soaked brain—something he'd always say to grandma before a wild night with his buddies: *Eat, drink, and be merry, for tomorrow we may die.* And tomorrow? It was the bottom of the inning, two outs, bases loaded, and Death was up to bat.

I woke sprawled across an ornately carved, four-poster bed that was ridiculously high off the ground. My head dangled over the edge, hair sweeping toward the floor. As I cracked my eyes open, the world swam into focus—and so did a face. A pair of piercing royal blue eyes framed by long, golden hair stared back at me, uncomfortably close.

Gunnr crouched beside the bed, her expression a mixture of irritation and amusement. She sneered. "Wake up, child."

"No, not today... Not you," I whined. I tried sitting up in bed but my pounding head had other plans.

"Yes, me," Gunnr said, bouncing to her feet and throwing open the curtains. "Yes, today."

"You drink too much," she added.

"I was sober for a few years. Then my mom got me a keg for my eighth birthday party and it was all over from there—"

Gunnr grabbed the back of my linen chemise and literally dragged me from the room, down the stairs, and onto a huge courtyard that faced the surrounding mountains.

Shaking my head to stir my addled brain, I shuffled to the stone wall at the edge of the yard and peered over the edge—it was a straight shot down the mountain cliff to the river below.

She handed me a heavy chainmail shirt, made up of small interwoven metal rings. "Put this on."

I pulled the mail top over my head.

"Do you have this armor in anything a little more form-fitting?"

Gunnr exhaled. "Let's be over and done with this, as quickly as possible."

"Is this the part where you pretend to show me how to fight and then... *accidentally* hack me to death with your ax?" I asked, giving her air quotes knowing she had no idea what air quotes were.

"Why would I kill you?" she asked, then gave me back some air quotes of her own. "You are the *'Chosen One'*."

"Can we please stop calling me that?" I begged.

"Gladly."

"You don't believe Pherric either?"

"Why should I? A supposed ancient prophecy—that the rest of us have never seen—claiming that a singular, special girl will come along to save our world?"

Gunnr pulled out her ax, letting the sharp steel glimmer in the morning sunlight.

"I believe we have everything we need... right here."

"Then let's skip this little exercise, so I can go back to bed," I pleaded. "My head is killing me."

"Oh, I will not be training you to the point of *neardeath* because you are part of some mythical prophecy... I will be doing so because you are weak, spoiled, and pathetic."

"I love you, too, Gunnr."

"First, I want to see what I am working with."

Gunnr handed me a long thin knife, handle first. At nearly a foot in length, I thought it would weigh a ton but was light, nimble.

The thought of a knife fight scared me senseless. I decided to stall. "So, what's your story, morning glory?"

"How do you mean?"

"Where did you go to school? What's your major? Where do you see yourself in five years? I mean... who is Gunnr Headsbanger?"

"Hallsdottir!" she bellowed. With a flick of her axe handle, she knocked the knife from my hand and laid the blade against my neck.

"Touchy subject?" I was scared to death but couldn't let her know it.

Gunnr patted my face and withdrew her ax. "You are naive, but you are not stupid."

"I'll bet that's the nicest thing you'll *ever* say to me." I adjusted the hot and heavy chainmail anchor strapped to my chest.

"You got into my head, incited anger. That is a tactical skill that you should use to your advantage."

"Look, we both know I'm not going to turn into some ax-wielding badass... like you."

"Another wise strategy—pull me off-guard with flattery." Gunnr almost, barely, and kinda smiled. Then she slapped the knife back in my hand.

She set down her ax, pulled out a similar knife from her black boot.

"As you have noted, it would take years and years of training," she said, looking me up and down. "Or decades, in your case. But my goal is to help you learn to handle a blade. To do what you can, with what little you have, so you can hopefully stay alive. Understand?"

I nodded. As much as she seemed to hate me, she did seem to want to help me protect myself.

"Until we can build up your strength, you will need to focus on short, sharp, and swift movements. Going up against a strong, seasoned warrior would make no sense. You have to use their aggression, their strength, and their weight against them. You are smaller, lighter, and... seemingly smarter. Let us begin..."

And train we did. Without all the gory, painful details Gunnr actually worked me to *neardeath* that day. And every day for over a week. But there was no miraculous moment where, on my second day, I managed to disarm her and hold my knife at her neck until she tapped out. However, she did teach me how to hold the knife correctly, position my legs to maintain balance, and keep a proper distance.

Gunnr made me hack away at a wood post to build up the strength in my spaghetti-noodle arms. She showed me the importance of attacking an opponent's hands and fingers, not their bodies.

"If you can cut a tendon or muscle in their fighting hand, your adversary is rendered useless," she instructed.

After days of ridiculously hard work, she paused my training to ask a question. "What's the first thing you should do if someone comes after you with a dagger or sword?"

"Sweep the leg?" I asked.

Gunnr looked at me as if I were from another planet. Well... bad analogy. So, I hopped into the knife fighting stance we had worked on for days—keeping my blade near my midsection, my other arm vertical to defend against attack, and my body at an angle to hers.

Gunnr shook her head. "The first thing you should do is run."

"I hate to run."

"You will hate dying even more."

We spent days and days working on timing. She told me timing was everything. I needed to not only be able to hit an opponent, but hit them during or after they tried to stab me.

"A smaller, weaker opponent should be able to strike a stronger one four to five times before the opponent can attempt one... if they have perfect timing."

We practiced slashes, jabs, and counter strikes over and over.

Throughout my all-day training sessions with Gunnr, members of the team came out to the courtyard or looked down from a balcony to watch my progress. They never made comments or offered tips. Even Lord Diago monitored my feeble efforts.

When training first started, Gunnr used a stick dipped in red paint. As we sparred with each other, whenever I would make a mistake—lunging too hard, getting too close, losing my balance—her stick marked me with a red line or spot, letting me know how many times I had died. I ended most days looking like an idiot's marked-up term paper. By the time we finished, we sparred with real blades. I nearly always suffered cuts, but not as many as when we first began.

I put everything I had into my sessions with her. Of course, I begged to stop when I was utterly exhausted. I'd whine and complain about the cuts and bruises... but Gunnr never let me skate by. At the end of every day, I was completely worn out, with my muscles shaking so badly I could barely hold a utensil to eat my dinner.

On our final day together, we sat on the stone bench along the courtyard wall. Gunnr wrapped a strip of white cloth around a huge, bloody gash on my shoulder.

"You are still weak and pathetic, but you might live a few moments longer in a knife fight."

"I feel like I just got a gold star from my favorite teacher," I said, beaming with pride.

She flashed one of her scornful looks.

Her battle axe and a sharpening stone rested further along on the bench.

"How come you're not teaching me to use the ax?"

She shook her head. "That is a warrior's weapon. The others may teach you the sword, but you will never be ready for the ax."

"Well, that's not fair. If it's better than a sword, I want to know—"

"Better? It is far superior. If the axe handle breaks, you add a new one. Try *that* with a sword. The cost is much less. Parrying with an axe is difficult, but you can fight much closer and eliminate their advantage. And both the sword and axe can get dull with repeated use, but the weight of the sword is down at the handle while the axe carries all the weight at the top. So, you still cause damage or even death with a blunt ax. Then... there is the utility of the ax; you can cut your firewood with it."

"I see." I didn't really see. Had no idea what she was going on about.

As she tightened the dressing on my wound, I watched her grow distant.

She stared off into the valley beyond the courtyard.

"What's up?"

Gunnr looked up in the air.

"No, I mean… what's going through that head of yours?"

"It is nothing. A momentary weakness."

She stood up but I grabbed her hands. She pulled away in anger, but accepted my sincere smile.

"Sometimes, it's easier to talk to strangers than friends or family. Sit."

After a brief battle inside her head, Gunnr snarled. Her face reddened. She leapt onto the bench, straddling me and wrapping a hand around my neck. Her other hand lowered a knife point to my eye.

"You asked me who Gunnr Hallsdottir is?! This is who I am!"

In fear, I pushed against her wrist—her grip tightened.

"Gunnr… please!"

"My name tells you everything you need to know! I was not born into a prominent Valhallan family. Not raised by a caring mother or trained by a mighty father. I was abandoned as an infant! Left on the steps of the Great Hall in my city, Vanaheimr!"

As I struggled to get air, her fingers eased. A little.

"And?" I needed to keep her talking.

"That they did not immediately run a sword through me and feed me to the fenrir was shocking!"

I was finally able to gulp. I let go of her wrist. "But… you survived."

Tears welled up in her angry eyes. "Aye! At four years, I proved my usefulness as a slave to them! I cleaned their cesspits, fetched their food, learned to cook."

"So… you earned their respect?"

She laughed, using the back of her knife hand to wipe away tears.

"Hardly! All the great warriors in my land, after they have come of age and proven themselves in battle, are bestowed the surname of their fathers. Thor's son would become Thorson. Skard's daughter would be Skarddottir and the like—"

"And you became the daughter of… the Hall," I said.

Gunnr released my throat, keeping her free hand on my shoulder.

"Ha! Yes. It was their cruel joke! But what they did not know was that I spent what spare time I had working hard to be a great warrior. While they slept, I would steal away with an axe and train. While they ate their feasts, I trained. When they went on their raids, I trained. When they drank themselves to sleep, celebrating their victories, I trained."

"So... you trained a lot," I just let it slip out, regretting it immediately.

She snarled, raising her knife at my face again.

"I'm sorry. Tell me more..."

"When I challenged the greatest warrior in Vanaheimr, the Jarl's son, they laughed at me! Me! But when I killed him, their laughter stopped. And I was banished. And I no longer have a tribe. No longer have a home! I am an *útlaga*! An outlaw. Forever to be a *skogarnord.* A forest dweller."

As a tear streamed down, she slid off me to the stone bench and looked away. In shame.

"Why would they banish you?! Shouldn't you be rewarded for, I don't know, being able to kill *really* well... or something?"

"I did not have the right to make the challenge, as I had no family name. And they doubted my abilities; the Jarl's son probably thought he would smack me on the ass with the flat of his axe blade and send me back to the cesspits. When I defeated him... I became an outcast for my crime."

"That's terrible," I said.

"I want not your pity, child."

"Well, I simply meant that—"

"I know what you meant. But I have been thinking about what you asked me for quite some time."

She twirled the knife between her fingers. "When you asked... who I am."

I nodded. She held the blade up to my face until I could see my reflection. "This... is who I am. This is Gunnr Hallsdottir."

Gunnr sank into the bench, her shoulders sagging under the weight of her own frustration. She looked away, probably embarrassed by the crack in her armor. She had let feelings overcome her. She was raw. Exposed.

I had been there myself. And like her, I kept everything bottled up inside until I couldn't hold it back anymore. And I would explode, only to immediately regret everything that came pouring out.

We sat in silence, staring ahead, with Diago's manor looming in the background. But everything that we saw at that moment was many miles away. In my case, light years away.

But me being me, I couldn't resist adding to the conversation.

"Hey, since we're having *girl time* here, I've got to ask. Do you, um, well... have any sanitary products, for that time of the, uh, lunar cycle?" I asked.

Gunnr wrapped a strip of white bandaging around her knife and handed it to me.

"I hate you."

And she grinned at me. For the first time.

Chapter 23

I had fallen asleep standing up.

Pherric worked away in an alchemy lab he had set up in a store room in Diago's keep. After long days of training with Gunnr, he forced me to spend evenings studying his magic.

"Finley?"

It had been a semester or so since my last chemistry course, but he quickly reminded me why I hated it so much.

"Finley."

Pherric had scoured the manor for ancient manuscripts, piling them high on a long, scarred table that dominated his new workshop. Faded books with cracked spines and brittle pages were stacked precariously, some propped open to cryptic diagrams. Glass bottles and delicate vials, brimming with vibrant liquids and coarse powders, shimmered in the flickering candlelight. They were scattered across a chaotic array of aged maps and curling scrolls, their inks smudged from years of handling. The air was thick with the sharp tang of herbs, the metallic bite of unknown minerals, and a faint, underlying scent of something burnt and bitter.

"Wake up."

My eyes opened. "What?"

"You fell asleep. Again," he scolded.

"I did not." I wiped the drool off my chin. "Well... maybe I did. But what do you expect? I'm exhausted, Pherric. I can't keep this up!"

"You can and, in fact, will keep this up."

I skulked around his table, running my finger along a map and flipping through an old manuscript. When I picked up one of the vials and shook the powder around, he plucked it from my hand and set it down carefully.

"What good will it do? You can't cram everything that everyone knows into me in just a few months?"

He collected several bottles and consulted his thick blue book covered in gold symbols—only now, I could read the title: *Arcanum Libellum*.

"We do have limited time. But why not teach you as much as we can, while we can?"

"But what's the point?"

He collected a mixing bowl and pointed to a glass vial on a shelf. I handed the vial to him. He poured out the powder and began grinding it up.

"While studying at your academy on Terra, were you required to stand before a magister and other students and then demonstrate your knowledge?" Pherric asked. He combined his ingredients, filling the room with a rotten egg smell.

"What? Stand in front of the class and give a presentation? Oh, hell yeah. All the time. I hated it."

"Understandable. But was it easier when you were an authority on the subject and could speak to it?"

"Well, of course. Speaking publicly is scary enough, but my biggest fear was not knowing the answer. It's kinda what made me study harder all through school, because I couldn't stand that feeling of not knowing the right answer."

He concentrated on adding carefully measured dust to his concoction, then some more thick fluids. "Then consider that we are giving you the necessary knowledge, in measured amounts, should you ever need to present yourself."

"You mean... if I ever need to fight to save my life?"

Pherric reached across the table, grabbing a silvery pockmarked rock, tossing it into his mixing bowl. He stirred until smoke rose up. Sparks jumped from his crucible. I covered my nose at the horrid odor. He stirred the brew and poured in a small amount of water. The contents steamed up.

With my fingers jammed in my nostrils, I took a closer look. "What are you making?"

He pulled out a blackened rock and held it up for me to examine. He pulled the hardened skin off the rock, revealing a small chunk of gold. He handed it over to me for inspection.

I was beyond stunned. "You can make gold?!"

"The ingredients, by themselves, are common. But when you combine them, in the correct order, you make something truly unique and remarkable."

Pherric's analogy was not lost on me. He knew he could not make me a fighting expert overnight, but he and his little group could provide lessons that might save my life. Some day.

I continued my training the next morning with the two Prominans. While Temurr and Frip were fairly handy with the sharp and pointy handheld weapons, they were considered experts with a bow and arrow.

My expectations of training with a bow provided a temporary sense of relief. I thought there would be a lot of standing there, aiming at targets. I was wrong.

"This is a bow," Temurr said slowly, as if I were hard of hearing. "And this is an arrow."

I cocked my head to the side, just far enough that Frip punched Temurr hard in the shoulder.

"What?!" Temurr screamed.

"She knows that, you *bèn den*," Frip replied. Then, he remembered his manners. "That means he is a silly fool!"

"Bygods, how do I know what she knows?!" he shouted, shoving the bow into my hands.

The first time I tried to shoot an arrow was a total disaster. After what seemed like *forever* of them drilling me on how to stand, where my shoulders should go, and how to hold the bow just right, it was finally go time. I was pumped.

But as soon as I held the bow out, I completely underestimated how much tension was in that string. My wrist gave out, and the bow shot backward, smacking me square in the nose. Yep, I basically punched myself in the face with a medieval weapon.

After they stopped laughing hysterically, rolling around on the courtyard tiles, they helped stop the nose bleed.

When I *finally* figured out how to draw the bow without looking like a complete idiot, they handed me my first arrow. Big moment. I pulled the string back with everything I had, arms shaking like I'd just done a hundred push-ups. Frip looked like he was about to step in and stop me, but Temurr? Nah, he just held Frip back and gave me this smug little nod, like, *Go on, let's watch this trainwreck.*

The second I let the arrow fly, I learned the hard way that my forearm was right in the danger zone. The string whipped forward and took a chunk of skin with it. Temurr, of course, doubled over laughing while Frip played nurse, wrapping me up like I'd survived a battle.

What can I say? Day one was off to a *stellar* start.

Archery? Definitely not an easy 'A.' It was a crash course in pain, frustration, and—you guessed it—more pain. Frip and Temurr, my sadistically charming instructors, spent *weeks* drilling me on every little detail of fighting with a bow.

Sure, I spent time trying to hit targets (spoiler: I didn't), but that was just the tip of the iceberg. One day, Frip had some poor lackey haul in a tree branch, and I had to carve my own bow. From scratch. Then came making the string, stringing the bow, and—for some reason—learning how to forge arrowheads down in a creepy, dungeon-y basement. Don't even get me started on cutting nocks; I failed miserably until they explained I had to cut perpendicular to the wood's growth rings.

And fletching? Yeah, apparently, the bigger the feather, the straighter the arrow flies. But then it's heavier and you lose range, so, you know, pick your poison.

After a week or so of this torture, Temurr decided I was ready for a "challenge." He set up a hay bale *way* across the courtyard and handed me a quiver with forty arrows. The mission? Hit the target as fast as possible while he timed me with an hourglass, because of course he did.

I unleashed all forty arrows like my life depended on it—and missed the hay bale. Every. Single. Shot. Temurr's smug little grin grew wider with each miss. After that disaster, I collected what arrows I could find (RIP to the ones that flew off the cliff) and went again. First ten arrows? Whiff. The last thirty? Three hits total. I wanted to chuck my bow into the abyss and storm off, but I knew better. They'd probably have me running laps as punishment.

Temurr and Frip just stood there grinning, no doubt planning new ways to mock my amazing lack of talent.

The two ape men made me *run* around the courtyard, up and down steps, and all around the manor before I would fire arrows at my target. Then I had to sprint to retrieve the arrows, turn and run back, and fire another round. Rinse. Lather. Repeat. They'd usually let me rest by the time I would puke my guts out—that's how they knew I'd had enough. I was well on my way to an archery-bulimia disorder.

In my final week of working with the couple, I recalled what Pherric told me about Liath. She had instructed my ancestor, Fionn mac Cumhaill, to study the animals in his forest, watch them until he learned something valuable. I tried to do the same with Temurr and Frip. With the dark cloud hanging over everyone, from trying to depose a king and save their kind, tensions were high. And climbing higher by the day. But Frip and Temurr brought a sense of play and fun to nearly everything they did. Even under the stress of all that waiting, and having to teach an idiot like me, they were calm.

One afternoon, while eating a hard, gray meat for lunch, I paused and turned to Temurr. "Um, is this karkadann?"

Temurr looked closely at it. "It was."

I nearly hurled, throwing down the plate. "We're eating the karkadanns?!"

"Food supplies are dwindling, Finley. Even in Lord Diago's house,"

Temurr shrugged. "Runa most likely slaughtered our beasts to survive. She would have been able to help herself, her village and even send some up to us."

It felt like I was eating the funny-but-helpful horse sidekick from one of those animated movies.

"How can you eat the karkadann that probably brought you here?" I asked.

"With a little salt and some ground *blaska*," said Temurr.

Exhausted and a little loopy from a day of intense exercise, I actually laughed at that.

"How do you do it? How are you so chill? How can you find humor when everything around you is falling to pieces?"

"We make you run hard before you shoot. Teaches you to calm yourself before firing a single arrow, it does. When you breathe hard, your aim will be off. You must slow your breath, slow the heart, to be perfectly still," Temurr said. "Too much tension, worry, too much fear... and you will lose. I find humor, and peace, in anything, whenever I am able. When you do that, you win."

He picked up a chunk of his gray meat, handed it to me.

"So... chill," he said,

He took another nasty bite of karkadann.

When my training with the ape men was complete, I was able to shoot an arrow like a modern-day Robin Hood... if he were drunk, blindfolded, and missing an arm. Well, not really. I was finally able to hit the bale on two out of five shots. And a bullseye in one out of twenty. Okay, thirty. But there was only so much you could do with me in a short amount of time.

On my last day, as dark clouds rolled in overhead, Pherric and Braylor emerged from the manor. Braylor grabbed a bow and an arrow, shoved them into my tired hands.

"Show me," he demanded.

I looked at Temurr, who gave a quick nod.

A surge of panic shot through me like a bolt of lightning. My hands trembled as I made my way to the chalk mark etched on the terrace stones, each step heavier than the last. I fought to steady my breath, but my chest tightened. My face was red hot as I drew back the bowstring, my fingers barely holding steady.

I released. The arrow veered sharply to the right, missing the target by a mile. Braylor sighed, shaking his head, and trudged away. Deflated, I closed my eyes and rested the bow's smooth wood against my forehead, letting the weight of failure sink in.

Temurr cleared his throat. "Now, shoot five arrows as fast as you are able."

Standing beside me, he held up the quiver with five arrows.

"Now!"

I grabbed one, fired. Then another, without thinking or taking a breath. Thunk-thunk-thunk. The first two missed; the last three bobbed up and down in the bale of hay.

I turned to Braylor, hoping he had seen it. But he was gone.

Dejected, I sank to the stone bench.

"Impressive, Finley. Progress has been made, it has."

I stared at the empty doorway. "Not enough, it seems…"

Pherric patted my shoulder and wandered after Braylor.

Frip decided it was time to pull all the loose bits of target straw from my hair.

"What is your home like?" he asked.

"Oh, it would take days to tell you about that," I said.

"Probably best that I do not know. We only found out about your kingdom when Pherric recruited us." Had he decided not to tell everyone I was from another planet, but from some faraway land?

"He has not shared much of what he learned in the Scholomance. Said he wanted to protect us. For some reason. That is why he sailed off from the abandoned castle alone to retrieve you, I believe."

"Makes sense, I guess. My… kingdom is quite advanced. We have some tools that you might consider to be magic," I admitted, thinking of our phones and cars and every other gadget on Earth. "But, I can say this with certainty. We are in no way any smarter than the people of your lands."

"Can I ask? Are there other species in your kingdom?"

"Um, well... in the distant past, there were..."

"Like my kind?"

"Yes. But, uh... They all died out thousands of years ago. In our kingdom."

"Died out? Or were killed?" asked Frip.

I thought about it. I truly had no idea, but I knew what he wanted to know.

I turned to him. "Look, I don't really know what happened to them. I suppose the tribes of my people might have... well, probably killed off your species. But, it's different here, in these lands. Here, you've survived! For a lot longer than in my land. And you have evolved. Just like the Hominans. You now have a chance that all the other species in my kingdom never had."

"I worry that we are simply prolonging the inevitable," mused Frip.

I took his leathery hands in mine. "We're going to do everything we can to not let that happen. Okay?"

He nodded, but remained unconvinced.

Chapter 24

Pherric leaned forward, placing his elbows on the giant table. "So what is our strategy to remove Malek as king?"

We had gathered in the Great Hall for dinner, which led to a brainstorming session. Over the course of many weeks, they tried over and over to come up with a plot. Without much success. And those meetings quickly devolved into shouting matches with people storming off to lick their wounds or prevent a murder.

"Here we go again," Braylor muttered to himself.

I sank down in my chair at the table, quietly sipping my wine, to avoid the fray. And the glassware, if they started flying. Again.

"Yes, here we go. We need to act. And we need to do it *soon*," exclaimed Pherric, his deep frustration evident.

"Well, as I've stated—many times—we need to start gathering an army," said Temurr.

"And your suggestion has been noted, Temurr. But, as others have pointed out, that will take up to a year or more." Pherric said, gritting his teeth. "Time we do not have…"

Temurr pounded his thick ape hand on the table. "We would be farther along if we had started that process *months* ago!"

"But what of the logistics for such an operation?" asked Braylor. "How many troops are required? How will we feed them? Pay them? How long will they be away from their families and farms?"

Temurr lowered his head, speaking to the wood floor at his feet. "Their farms and families will be gone if they do nothing."

Frip gingerly held on to Temurr's wrist. He turned to his mate, sadness brimming in his dark eyes.

"Malek has successfully lured away all the best people, with good pay and the food that he has stolen from every kingdom," Frip said. "We cannot compete with his resources."

Lord Diago stepped into the room. "I have heard tell, through my sources, that Malek has amassed fifty thousand soldiers outside the Black City. Adding to the fifteen thousand Irkallan warriors he had on hand. He is at the point where he can turn away those not qualified or capable to fight."

"Great! So we are left with Malek's cast-offs?" said Braylor. "Ah! This is a waste of time!"

Temurr thumped his chest. "The great army of Kunlun would be all that is needed to wipe out his feeble Hominan horde!"

Frip gripped his arm again, utterly embarrassed. But Pherric chuckled and Gunnr rolled those blue eyes of hers.

Temurr sank into his chair. "Apologies."

Kasuma took her turn by standing up and spreading her wings. "If we recruit an army, my people could attack from above, surprise Malek, and—"

"From above?!" Braylor butted in. "Even with the protection of their godmagic, the Black City still bore the brunt of dragon attacks for generations! They are heavily fortified against an aerial assault. His archers would pick your people apart if you tried to get past his defenses."

Kasuma held her tongue, silently sitting and crossing her arm wings around her body.

Temurr crossed his own arms at Braylor. "Well, if we cannot raise an army, what is the alternative?!"

Braylor opened his mouth, but Kasuma stood up once and placed both hands on the table. "What if you send me, and only me, into the city. You know well my skills of stealth and deception, as well as gaining access to the inaccessible."

Braylor sighed. "Your skills are legendary, Kasuma. But you lack the ability to impersonate a Hominan. You cannot effectively hide your wings!"

"I was able to sneak into *this* city."

He rubbed his face with his massive hands. "We might be able to get you into the Black City, passed the untrained eyes of their outer wall guards, but not near his castle. And even on the darkest of nights, you would not be able to simply fly past his spotters. If this were the assassination of some noblemen or merchant traveling through the city, we would certainly call on you. But, unlike the Quiviran guards, his people are ready and waiting. They are assuredly preparing for the kingdoms to make an attempt on his life."

"Then we must raise an army!" Temurr demanded. "Bring all the species together and confront him directly. That is our only hope!"

"Yes, I can see it in my mind now," replied Braylor, sarcastically. "Fomorians fighting shoulder to shoulder with Prominans. The Vikings harmoniously battling away with the Bànshēn rén at their side. How glorious it shall be!"

"You're not helping, Braylor," Pherric scolded.

"As I said... waste of time," Braylor said, standing up as if to let everyone know his part of the conversation had ended.

"Then what would you have us *do*?!" asked Temurr, jumping into Braylor's rather large face. Which is not something I would recommend *ever* doing. "You big oaf!" Or that.

Braylor clenched his fists and his face got all snarly.

Gunnr stood. "We need to draw out Malek. Away from his city. In battle. He relishes a good fight. And if he leads his army to face us, we would have our chance to end his reign."

"What makes you think he will present himself to us like that?" Braylor challenged.

"He led a battalion of soldiers to the castle of the Godsribbon!" said Gunnr.

"He will not be so foolish again," said Pherric. "He claimed to be quelling a rebellion of Prominans in Cíbola but, in fact, he was secretly looking for something."

"Looking for what?" asked Braylor.

"That is inconsequential," said Pherric. "Because... he did not find it."

As I quietly sat there, sipping my wine, Pherric instinctively clutched his leather bag. Again. He was never without it.

"But Nerus revealed himself as a traitor to the Scholomance that day, when he assassinated Gerrod on the castle wall. I have heard from my spies that Nerus is now Mage to the Irkallan king. His duty is to ensure that Malek does not embark on any more foolish adventures. I can assure you of that. From now on, only Kane will lead Malek's forces."

"Kane? Who is Kane?" I asked. I found it so hard to keep track of all these names and places.

"Sir Kane of the Black Bones!" roared Braylor.

Pherric waited for Braylor to stop slapping his own knee. "Not many shake in fear at Braylor..."

Braylor snapped at Pherric. "Well... they should."

"Sir Kane is Malek's Knight Commander," Pherric told me. "They have been friends since Malek was a boy. His father counseled Malek's mother and Kane is now a confidant to the young king. Malek implicitly trusts the man."

Temurr rose. "Then, we have no other choice! We must raise an army, defeat his forces, and kill him as he cowers behind his throne!"

"Or die trying," added Cira. She had sat silently at the table but Temurr's excitement infected her—her face burned a bright crimson and her hairy fists balled with rage.

"I have an idea," said Lord Diago. "But... you will not like it."

I gulped down my wine as he made his way behind me at the table in his Great Hall.

"What about your prize pupil here?" Diago said. I looked back and forth at everyone, hoping he wasn't talking about me.

"What about her?" said Pherric defensively.

"She is learning quickly and doing quite well. She has a Hominan appearance; she is attractive, smart." I had *no* idea who this old guy was talking about. Attractive? "And she has a... quirky charm that might help her pull off a miracle—"

"Wait, wait, wait," interrupted Pherric. "There is no way we could use her to assassinate the king of Irkalla! I will not put her in that position!"

"Then let me ask... what choice do you have?" said Diago.

Pherric opened his mouth to say something, but had nothing.

"For the sake of argument—and that is all this is—how would we do it? I can tell you there is no way we would be able to introduce her as a new servant in his castle. We could never get her close enough to the king," said Braylor.

Lord Diago smiled. "While my house is not among the top three in Cíbola, I have many powerful connections and considerable pull within the Irkallan aristocracy. It will take time, fortune, and the calling in of a number of favors, but I might be able to get her on the guest list for an upcoming festivity or society function."

Braylor snorted. "Malek is preparing to wipe out our entire species! He has no time for parties!"

Diago pointed at Braylor. "You do not know the king as I do. He is vainglorious and self-absorbed. He lives for a good festival and will look for any excuse."

I whispered to myself. "Nero fiddles while Rome burns..."

"What was that, child?" asked Diago.

"Nothing." I hunched further down in my seat.

"I do not like this as an option. Not in the least," said Pherric, his face burning a bright red. "No. We will find another way."

You know all those big regrets you've had throughout your entire life? This was another one of mine. I was outside my body, watching someone else speak the words for me:

"Don't I have a say in this? I mean, you guys brought me here. And I want to help. If this is what you need me to do... I'll do it."

That was the wine talking. Not me. No way in hell.

Chapter 25

"You will die."

"Thanks for the vote of confidence, Pherric," I grumbled.

He strode with purpose down the quiet cobblestone street, his pace brisk and unrelenting. Every few steps, I had to break into a jog to keep up with his long, determined strides. His eyes darted over his shoulder now and then, sharp and watchful, scanning the shadows to ensure we weren't being tailed.

"This is not a game, Finley."

As the setting sun bathed Quivira's golden walls in a warm, amber glow, the city's narrow streets remained eerily quiet—unlike the usual hum of life that marked dusk in most places. Only a few beggars lingered in shadowed doorways, their hands outstretched in silent pleas. A dozen servants, their faces tense and eyes darting nervously, hurried past, clutching packages as they rushed toward unseen destinations. The shops we passed stood shuttered and silent, their wares hidden behind boarded windows. Apartment entrances loomed dark and lifeless, and abandoned warehouses lined the streets like empty husks. Finally, we turned onto a broader avenue, the silence lifting slightly with even more people going on about their business.

"This is the Vard. We will be less conspicuous here," he said.

"Hey! I know this isn't a game, okay?"

Once we reached the main thoroughfare, Pherric eased his pace, though his head remained low and his eyes sharp. Vibrant but weathered triangles of fabric crisscrossed above, marking the patchwork canopy of tattered tents. Beneath them, merchants peddled their goods with desperate fervor—offering everything from rotting produce to gleaming gold pots and intricately beaded necklaces. Their voices rose in a chaotic chorus, vying for the attention of the few passersby who drifted through the dusty street, casting quick glances at the goods on display.

"Lord Diago is suggesting that you pretend to be a member of noble society. It is not enough to simply dress like them—you need to know how to walk, talk, and act like them."

"Please. Do you have any idea how many parties and events I've crashed? This is my whole raison d'être, Pherric!"

"I did not acquire *that* much of your French language."

"If you brought me here for a reason, if there was something I was really meant to do here—it's this!"

"Even if you managed to measure up to highborn expectations, and nothing about that will be easy, you would not only be expected to get close enough to the king but... to kill him," he said. "Have you ever killed anyone, Finley? No. You have not."

"Oh... I didn't think that far ahead."

"And if you were able to summon the courage to execute a powerful warrior, you would need to escape without his personal guards running you through with their swords! That is certain death, Fin."

"Well, when you put it that way..."

"That is the way it is," sighed Pherric. "I forbid it!"

I stopped walking. He noted that my hands were on my hips, my lips were pursed, and steam was venting from my ears.

"You did not just say that," I warned.

"Say what?"

"My father tried to pull that whole 'I forbid it' shit with me and let me tell you right now that won't fly with me, buddy!"

"Finley, I am responsible for you! And I do forbid you to take part in any ridiculous scheme—one that will only get you killed!"

I hiked it back toward Lord Diago's manor.

It was Pherric's turn to keep up. "Finley, please! Will you please stop?

Listen to me!"

Nothing, and I mean nothing, sets me off more than when someone forbids me. My father used to say that all the time—*I forbid you to stay out late!* and *I forbid you from seeing any boys until you're eighteen!* and my favorite, *I forbid you from seeing* that *boy!*

Maybe it was the wine talking, or maybe my recent training gave me a false sense of my own abilities, but I made up my mind, as we trekked back to the manor, that I would actually be able to pull it off.

"Finley, you are here to light a fire under the others!" He was still talking. "Not throw yourself into the fire!"

I rounded a corner to face a squad of soldiers patrolling the middle of the street. They eyed me suspiciously when I froze in my tracks, like a thief caught *in flagrante delicto* with the stolen jewels. They weren't wearing the Quiviran royal blue and gold colors, but sported silver chainmail over black tunics with blue trim with no plumes on their metal helmets—they were Irkallans.

I twirled around to walk back the way I had come, making me look even more guilty.

"Halt!" shouted the stocky, bearded leader, his sword sliding from the sheath.

Pherric arrived at the corner, curiosity spreading across his face as to why I had turned and stood still. Heavy boots stomped along the cobblestones toward us.

"Run," I whispered.

Without a second's pause, Pherric seized my wrist and yanked me into a sprint. We hauled ass down the street, my feet barely skimming the cobblestones. His strides were long and purposeful, but my shorter legs struggled to keep up. My chest burned with every gasp, the sound of my ragged breath drowned out by the pounding of boots behind us.

The soldiers were gaining.

Pherric stole a quick glance over his shoulder, his face grim.

"Stay close!" he barked, his grip on my wrist tightening as if sheer force could drag me faster.

We barreled down the crowded street, dodging startled Quivirans and weaving between vendor tents. Pherric yanked me hard to the right, leading us onto a narrower street. His strides stretched farther with every step, while the Irkallans behind us closed in, their shouts growing louder. He veered left into an alley without hesitation.

I risked a glance over my shoulder—two of the fastest soldiers were on my heels. My heart slammed against my ribs as I followed Pherric around the corner. The alley threw us out onto a wider thoroughfare, where vendors shouted prices and pedestrians ambled through colorful stalls.

Suddenly, a vivid memory surfaced: my grandfather grumbling about suspects always splitting up during a chase. My pulse spiked, and before logic could stop me, I made a split-second decision. Pherric veered left into the crowd—I went right.

It was the dumbest move I'd ever made.

I zigzagged through clusters of people, using them as a makeshift shield. Behind me, the soldiers shouted for people to clear the way. I cursed under my breath. Of course they'd follow me, not Pherric. I was the slower, easier target. But at least I had one edge: no chainmail, no clunky helmets. Just me, a light tunic, and the adrenaline of impending doom.

I squeezed between two men arguing over a purchase and dove beneath a wooden pushcart. Pain tore through my knee as the rough cobblestones scraped it raw, but I bit back a scream and scrambled up, dashing into another alley. Behind me, the soldiers snarled as they crashed into the hagglers and struggled around the cart. It bought me a few precious seconds.

Halfway through the alley, regret hit me like a brick wall. Pherric could've conjured his mindform shadows, led them on a wild chase while we slipped away unnoticed—I was such an idiot.

Emerging from the alley, I glanced back. I'd gained some ground, but not enough. I pushed harder, my lungs on fire, taking random turns through the maze of narrow streets. Somehow, I ended up back where we started, Diago's manor looming in the distance.

The rhythmic clatter of boots echoed behind me. I spun onto another side street, hoping to outmaneuver them, only to skid to a stop. The street ended at a wide, open terrace. Beyond the stone railing, the mountains dropped sharply into a river far below. I was at the city's edge.

To my right, the imposing outer wall of Diago's estate stretched high. To the left, a three-story shear warehouse wall. I had nowhere to run.

The Irkallan soldiers rounded the corner behind me, their heavy footfalls thundering closer.

Without thinking, I vaulted over the railing and crouched low, pressing myself against the cool stone. Through the gaps between the balusters, I watched as the soldiers burst onto the terrace, their heads on swivels. My pulse pounded in my ears as I lowered myself down, gripping the underside of the railing with shaky fingers. My feet scrambled until they found a narrow, rounded lip of stone jutting out from the flat wall.

Their boots thundered above me. I clung to the edge, my breath ragged but silent, willing my rattled muscles to stay locked. Slowly, painstakingly, I began to edge sideways, working my way beneath the terrace overhang. My nails scraped against the stone as I fought to hold on. Above, the soldiers muttered and cursed, chainmail clinking as they paced.

The clink of metal on stone sent a shiver through me—a soldier was leaning over the railing. I flattened myself as much as I could, barely daring to breathe.

"She has to be close. Search everywhere!"

I made another big mistake—I looked down. The cliff plunged hundreds of feet to pointy rocks and the turbulent river. Only the precarious, decorative ledge supported my weight. Every gust of wind a taunt; a reminder that gravity was waiting to ruin my day.

Above, the scrape of boots grew fainter, but I couldn't relax. My fingers ached, and my legs burned from holding in that position. I swallowed hard, eyes flicking up to the stone lip and back down to the dizzying drop.

"Stay here! I will gather reinforcements," said one soldier. "Keep searching!"

From my precarious perch beneath the terrace, I spotted the corner of Diago's manor, where the outer wall met his estate. The slim ledge and railing extended all the way to his house. My fingers burned, and my calves shook with the strain—I couldn't hold on much longer. A part of me wanted to scream for help, to plead with the soldier above to save me—but I knew exactly what that would mean. My only hope was to inch my way toward the manor and hope I could find a way inside.

The soldier's heavy boots echoed as he paced above. When his steps receded, I seized my chance, sliding a hand forward, then a foot, keeping my body flat against the wall. Don't look down. Don't think about the drop. Just move.

Sweat slicked my grip, and every inch seemed to be a lifetime. But I pushed past the edge of the outer wall. At last, I reached the foundation of Diago's house. Stone tiles stuck out just above me. I reached up, my fingertips brushing their smooth surface. My first attempt slipped, leaving me dangling for a heartbeat for an eternity. My other hand clung to the ledge, trembling with the effort. A frantic glance back at the terrace revealed the soldier still missing in action, and I exhaled.

Steadying myself and reaching again, I locked my fingers over the edge. With great care, I shuffled along the ledge, my eyes fixed on the manor's stonework.

When I reached the first window, frustration hit—there was no hand-hold, no way to climb up. The second window loomed ahead, but it offered the same grim reality. Beyond that was my training courtyard. But my ledge didn't stretch that far.

I pressed on, inching closer to the second window. Then disaster struck—a fingernail snapped. I hissed in pain, clutching the ledge tighter as blood trickled down my finger. The red smear on the stone sent a chill through me. The slick surface would drop me like a rock if I wasn't careful.

"Hey, there," came a deep voice from above.

I strained to look up. Braylor stood at the first window, grinning at me.

"Pull me up," I whispered.

"Do you... hang around here often?"

"Pull me up now!"

I worked my way back to the first window as Braylor leaned out. As I reached him, he suddenly pulled himself back inside.

"What are you doing?!"

"An Irkallan soldier sits on the railing."

Braylor motioned with his head. I looked but saw no one.

"Don't care! I'm about to fall!"

He peeked out the window again. "If he sees me pull you up, he will know you are in here."

I adjusted my grip, my fingers sliding around in the blood. "Better than me being dead, dumbass!"

We heard shouting from the street. Braylor peered out his window again.

"He has gone."

My fingers finally let go, sliding off the bloody smooth ledge. Braylor's big hands grabbed my wrists and he hauled me through the window with no effort. The room looked like Diago's personal office, with a fancy desk sitting in the middle under a chandelier of gold and silver. Personal artifacts and weapons hung on the walls and thick red curtains surrounded each window.

He set me down, his strong hands holding my waist. And he didn't let go. We were close. Too close. Breathing hard from hanging off the side of the building, I tried to look away. But his hand reached down, pulled my chin up. I realized his eyes were not black but a deep, dark brown with tiny flecks of orange. My heart raced as his warm hands pulled me closer.

"You know... the house does have a *front* door," Braylor stated. "You could always use that."

Oh, if looks could kill...

I pushed away from him, crossed my arms, and turned to the open window.

He paused for a moment, then lumbered out of the room.

Men can be absolutely perfect at times, but then they open their mouths.

I heard shouting from within the house and people began running about.

Braylor popped his head back into the library.

"The Irkallan soldiers have found you!"

Chapter 26

The pounding at the manor's front doors sent a jolt through me, each bang was a hammer hit to my head. Voices clashed in panic—warning shouts, brash commands, hurried footsteps. I stumbled through Diago's office.

"What are you doing?"

"Looking for a place to hide!"

I didn't know where to start. The grand desk loomed in the center, but they'd check there first. The heavy drapes fluttered slightly in the draft, but I'd be seen in seconds.

"Think, think!" I whispered, my voice barely audible over the chaos outside. They were working their way through the house.

I pushed books on the shelf aside, looking for a hidden lever.

"Where's the secret passageway?! There's got to be one here!" I talk to myself occasionally. "Every castle has a secret passageway!" Because I'm the only one who ever listens.

Braylor snatched me by the arm, dragging me into the hallway. Maids and butlers threw themselves against the walls as we raced by.

"What's happening?!" I struggled to remain on my feet as he hauled me through the kitchen wing of the manor.

"One of the soldiers must have seen you disappear through the window!"

We startled the aging cook and her young kitchen staff as we bolted through the wide door. The smell of karkadann meat filled the room, as a blazing fire in the open hearth roasted skewers for our evening meal.

Braylor slid to a stop in front of the plump chef, who held her apron up to her face in shock.

"Is there an exit other than the main doors?!"

Staring up at him with eyes round, she shook her head.

"Buttery?"

She gulped. "Through there... under the pantry."

Braylor yanked me into the dim food storage room. Without a word, he shoved a heavy crate aside, revealing a hidden door cut into the wooden floor. He heaved it open and peered down, groaning.

"Why must I always be forced into the smallest spaces?"

Ignoring him, I scrambled down the narrow stairs into a cramped, icy cellar that reeked of fermenting wine and stale mead. Shadows danced on the stone walls as Braylor handed me a candle. His broad shoulders barely fit through the opening as he squeezed himself down, grumbling under his breath.

The floor door thudded shut above us, sealing us in darkness save for the frail circle of candlelight.

He rolled a barrel from the stone wall. "Build a partition!"

I rolled another to him as he stacked them on top of the row he had assembled. The poor guy had to hunch down, tilt his head to the side, to even move around the small cellar.

"What about the others?" I asked, ducking behind our makeshift partition.

He pulled several boxes in with him, huddling beside me.

"They hopefully found a place to hide. I should have planned for this but felt too at ease, too secure, here."

Braylor snuffed out the candle and we waited in silence. Well, for as long as I could.

"How long do—?"

"Quiet..."

"You're no fun."

"Indeed."

The muffled shouts above sharpened into commands. Heavy boots pounded through the kitchen, and the flickering shafts of candlelight streaming through the pantry floorboards were suddenly broken by shifting shadows. Soldiers were up there.

Braylor's hand settled on my shoulder—a gentle reminder to keep my fat mouth shut. Dust floated down between the cracks, and I clamped my lips together, my lungs screaming for air. I counted two, maybe three people pacing directly above us. Every creak was a prelude to disaster.

Then the pantry door burst open, slamming against the floor. I flinched but bit down on my lip to stifle a gasp. Boots clattered down the narrow stairs, and the buttery filled with the glow of a swinging lantern. Its harsh light swept over the casks and barrels, sending eerie shadows dancing on the walls.

I shrank deeper into the corner, hoping the casks would keep us hidden. But the soldier wasn't satisfied. His lantern swayed higher, the light briefly grazing my face. I squeezed my eyes shut, my heart thudding so loudly I was sure he could hear it.

He paused, rising on his toes to peer over the top of the partition. The edge of his helmet glinted as he leaned closer. My fingernails dug into the damp wood. Then, with agonizing slowness, he turned and started to climb the stairs.

A voice boomed out, stopping him on the first step. "Is she down there?"

The soldier held his lantern back out, took another look at our wall of casks and boxes.

"No, sir!"

As he bounded up the staircase, I let myself breathe again.

Another set of boots ran up into the pantry over our heads, sending more dust drifting down.

A raspy voice spoke. "Sir Kane, we have searched the manor! No sign of the thief!"

At the worst possible moment, the dust got to me. I felt a sneeze coming on. My body reacted involuntarily—I inhaled, my eyes shut and chest contracted. When the sneeze came, Braylor pinched my nose. Hard. My eardrums nearly popped.

I emitted a sharp *snorf* sound.

We immediately stared up at the floorboards. A pair of boots cautiously descended the wood steps.

Braylor whispered. "Stay hidden. I shall surrender."

I vigorously shook my head, which sent snot flying from my nose.

Boots scraped the gravel in the middle of the cellar. I peeked between mead barrels.

The Sir Kane guy held out a lantern, inspecting the buttery. The front of his sleeveless black surcoat, trimmed in royal blue, displayed a silver-stitched dragon. If I had to guess, he was in his early thirties, but a few gray hairs streaked through his well-behaved beard and thick brown hair.

His gaze fell on our partition. Even though he was spectacularly built, it was his thoughtful eyes that knocked me off balance. There was a confident intelligence behind those light brown eyes.

A faint expression crossed his lips, an almost stealthy grin. When Braylor realized the lantern light fell on my face, he pulled me back from the gap between the barrels.

Had he seen me?

Another pair of shoes fervently clomped down the cellar staircase.

"What is happening here!" I recognized that voice.

Kane reluctantly turned away from us. "Lord Diago, I presume?"

"Remove yourself and your soldiers from my keep! Immediately!"

Kane held out his hand. "I am Sir Kane, Knight Commander of the Royal Irkallan Army. A pleasure to meet you."

Lord Diago deflated like a balloon.

"Ah, I see. Lord Diago Candala, patriarch of the Tenth House of Cíbola. At your service... Sir."

"My men reported a thief entering your manor, my lord. My apologies for the intrusion."

Diago tried to regain his composure, crossing his arms and standing tall. "And the presence of a Knight Commander is required to root out a common thief?"

"In dangerous times such as these, the safety of the Cíbolan people is of the utmost importance, my lord. I am here to ensure these soldiers treat your staff and home with respect and care," assuaged Kane. This guy was good. Smooth and charming.

Diago stole a quick look at the wall of casks. "And have you found this... thief?"

"No, Lord Diago... We have not."

"Then I require you to leave this place. At once." Diago bristled, looking down his nose at the Knight Commander.

Kane threw a final glance our way. I pulled back from between the barrels again.

"As you wish, my lord."

Sir Kane made his way back up the steps. As I started to rise, Braylor pulled me down with a finger to his lips. Diago followed his uninvited guest up the stairs and out of the pantry.

"Thank the gods, you live!" Pherric exclaimed. "When you ran away from me, I feared the worst."

He swept into the sitting room off the Great Hall. When I rose up from the divan, he hugged me tight.

"How did you get away?" I let Frip return to his work, bandaging the leg I had scraped while sliding under the pushcart.

"I hid around a shop corner and engaged a mindform, projecting an image of a cloaked man running away, to send the soldiers on a wild Hamsa chase," he said. I *knew* it. "I've been searching the streets for you ever since. I thought it wise to return here... in case you made your way back. And you *did*!"

"You should have seen what I had to go through to—"

Temurr handed Pherric a mug of wine. "Sir Kane of the Black Bones was here. In this very keep."

Pherric stopped mid-sip of the wine. "What?"

He dropped to a chair as Temurr told the story, a dazed and bewildered look in his eyes. It turns out the others hid in the secret passageway under the library, where we had entered Diago's manor.

When the ape man finished, Pherric turned to Braylor. "Do you believe Kane knew you were hiding down there?"

"I doubt it. Or he would have revealed us." But Braylor did not seem convinced.

Pherric turned to Diago. "Why is Malek's Knight Commander in Quivira?"

Lord exhaled and then shrugged his shoulders. "It is not a good sign, Pherric."

Exhausted, Pherric stared at the ceiling before turning his attention to me. "Until we know more, you will continue your training. With Cira. In the morning."

"But I-I had to climb outside the building... and my... I-I almost fell," I whined. "And my... my..." I held up my bloodied finger, pointed to my scraped leg.

Cira reluctantly nodded.

"Get your rest," announced Pherric.

My best pouty face did nothing to change his mind, so I shuffled off to my room.

Chapter 27

orning training with Cira began as expected—grueling. Despite the fact that she knew I had almost been mortally wounded in my extremely brave escape from those fierce soldiers, she devoted the start of class to telling me everything I did wrong.

"Your mistake was in allowing yourself to be cornered. Try to keep moving, but take moments to evaluate every circumstance before committing," Cira said.

"I had no spare time to evaluate anything! Those guys had way longer legs than me! They were on top of me constantly! And they would've caught me sooner or later, so I had no choice."

Her feral eyes locked onto me from beneath a heavy brow. She wore a new tunic that she must have sewn together herself, pieced together from wildly mismatched fabrics, a riot of colors that clashed violently with her primal energy. Her hair had returned to a mane of untamed curls, spilling around her face and over her shoulders.

"No excuses. Ever," she admonished. "Do you understand? When someone is twice our size, *we* have an advantage. We are lower to the ground so we have better balance. If soldiers chase too closely, you change directions constantly. If they are upon you, lower yourself until they stumble over. Stay in constant motion because they are heavier and will tire more easily. Wear them down, Finley Maguire, but never stand and fight. And certainly do not hang yourself off the edge of a mountain."

I nodded. No more excuses.

"When confronted, your legs are as long as their arms. So you must use them. Low, swift kicks are effective as long as you stay away from their reach. Do not be afraid to use every opportunity given to inflict pain—pull, bite, kick, chop, gouge—if you want to survive. But don't put yourself in a position where you cannot fight back. Climbing over that railing was not a smart tactic," she admonished.

"I didn't think," I admitted. "I just reacted."

She stood me up and faced me.

"And you were favored by the Creators." Cira eyed me up and down, slightly shaking her head back and forth—she wanted to be anywhere but standing there with me. "Let us begin your training. Starting with close-quarter contact. If you cannot keep moving and do get trapped, make use of the sensitive areas."

"Nothing like a good knee to the family jewels," I said.

She smiled. "Yes, that technique is... a given. But keep in mind the eyes, ears, nose, and throat."

Cira used several fingers to jab my throat.

"Oww!"

Using her palms, she smacked my ears. When I reached for my ears, she punched my nose, knocking me back.

"I want you to remember those sensitive areas," she said. "And the groin area of course."

I put my knees together to keep her from kicking me there so she threw her foot across my knee cap, sending me to the courtyard tile.

"Double oww!" I bellowed.

"Kneecaps are sensitive, as are feet," she announced. I swung my legs to the side to keep her giant, hairy foot from stomping my ankle.

"You are learning," she said. "There may be hope for you..."

She held out her hand and I tentatively took it.

"Keep your elbows in to protect your sides. Feet are always balanced, without more weight on one or the other foot. Forearms up to protect your sides. And, until your wrists are stronger, keep your hands out straight and attack with your palms or the sides of your hands."

I imitated her stance, with my feet spread apart and my arms up. With a quick strike, the side of her hand flew over my fingertips and tapped my throat. Again. Not hard, but enough to slightly close my windpipe.

"Stay agile and crouch at your midsection to avoid direct hits."

I grabbed my throat, struggling to breathe.

"By dropping down, you lower the area your arms must protect."

"I see," I said, though it came out as a garbled, gravelly hiss. "Can you please stop... hitting and... kicking me now?"

I felt a sharp pain in my leg.

"What's wrong?"

"I think I pulled a muscle," I said, massaging the back of my thigh.

Cira pushed a finger hard against my leg. "You cannot pull what you do not have, Finley."

She got a harsh glare from me—and she cracked a smile.

"Oh, you've got jokes now, do you?" I said.

Cira let out a short self-conscious laugh, looking down and away from me. "Let us build up your strength, shall we?"

Training under Cira wasn't just intense—it was like fighting a storm and losing every time. Every morning, before the sun had a chance to warm the sky, she had me on my feet, dragging me through hand-to-hand drills that left me exhausted. And in pain. I had the bruises to prove it.

Then there was the contraption—a monstrous wooden stand bristling with stubby, outstretched arms. She made me strike it until my knuckles throbbed, each hit forcing me to refine my technique.

"Punch hard but do not throw yourself off-balance."

"But," I whined. "It hurts!"

She grabbed me by my tunic and pulled me in until we were eye to eye. "Pain is a choice."

"Except when it hurts!"

She sneered at me. "You are exactly like gold, Finley Maguire. Pretty but soft."

I rubbed at my swollen knuckles. "Aww, you think I'm pretty!"

The short sword became my closest companion—or my sworn enemy, depending on the day. Cira showed me how to wield it with precision, her own blade flashing in the light as she demonstrated deadly moves. My hands ached from gripping the hilt for hours, but I pushed through, desperate to match even a fraction of her skill.

She spent days teaching me to throw axes, daggers, and spears at small targets.

"When your opponent is larger, keep them at bay with a projectile weapon. But do not leave yourself unarmed," she commanded.

Despite her expertise and extensive tutelage, I never managed to get an axe or knife to stick in a target but I could occasionally hit the target. After eighty or so attempts.

One day, I slept in a little too long.

"You are late," she stated.

"You're only late if you show up," I snarled, too tired to open my eyes. "Next time, I won't show up."

Let's just say that by the end of that day, my body felt like it had been put through a grinder. I collapsed onto my cot, every muscle screaming, only to be woken at dawn for more.

Whenever possible, in my vain attempts to avoid as much physical punishment as possible, I would pepper Cira with questions. Where was she from? What were her people like? Of course, she'd still make me do push-ups while she told her stories.

"My people are called the Bànshēn rén. We are a species that mostly originated in the Kingdom of Agartha, well north of Quivira. Our kingdom is made up entirely of a huge range of mountains hundreds of axims across," Cira told me.

"Axims?" Most words translated immediately for me, after Pherric used his mindforms to implant the Queen's Language in my head, but not all. Someone might say the word *bargd*, for instance, and I would hear that word being spoken, but my mind instantly translated it to *house*. By this point in my journey, I dreamed in the Queen's Language.

"Axims. A measurement of distance. Five thousand footfalls equal one axim." Since most people's feet here were longer than mine, an axim was probably equivalent to a mile.

"My people live within this range, in an extensive subterranean system of caves." That might explain why they're not as tall as the other races in this world, as well as their crazy long, hairy feet which must help with climbing. But I didn't want to ask.

Cira stared off the edge of our training terrace, talking to no one in particular. "We are great artists. Our ancestors painted the caverns with moments from decisive battles and great hunts. All of our history is being recorded in murals on the walls and ceilings of every grotto, tunnel, and cave—an epic gallery of stone that will outlive us all."

"That sounds amazing. I'd love to see it all some day. Are you a painter, too?"

She gave me a broken smile. "I try. But I am more drawn to song. I love music, love to dance wild and free in my tribe's music chamber, where the sounds bounce off the walls and surround you and carry you away. I have melodies of songs in my head but I never had time to learn an instrument. Food has been too scarce."

She had confided in me that her people have always been a passionate, untamed race and had only recently become unhinged once the Irkallan king cut off food they were importing.

Memories from seventh grade violin classes flooded my brain. "Why don't you write down your songs? You know, for later. Once this is all over."

"Write music? You cannot *write* music. That is like *talking* sculpture—describing a statue does not make it exist."

With that statement, our training turned that afternoon from ways to kill people to how to write music. I started her with singing out *do-re-mi-fa-so-la-ti-do* so that she could hear the various melodic pitches of the sounds. We found some old parchment and a coal pencil and I transposed those sounds into letters from the Queen's Language, similar to the C-D-E-F-G-A-B-C scale I had learned. I showed her how to write down notes—whole, half-quarter, and eighth along with rests—on the five parallel lines, but didn't get too crazy beyond that. Unlike my own ability to grasp her training, she took to my session and it just clicked. She ran with it, snatching up every piece of paper in Diago's manor she could get her hairy hands on and writing down her musical compositions. She peppered me with questions, wrote her sheet music, and sang her new melodies in the evenings and during our meals. Much to Braylor's delight. Cira was not a good singer. But she was passionately dedicated and you can't fault that.

During the days, Cira worked me hard. We constantly sparred with one another and I would occasionally get in a few good shots. And when I did, I expected her to go crazy on me like she did back at the mountain pass when those bandits attacked—her frenzy that day was a sight to behold. If you look up the word *berserker* in an online dictionary, there's probably a picture of Cira flaying someone alive with her short sword.

I decided to broach the subject on our last day. "So, when the shit gets real, you're a pretty fierce fighter."

"We have always fought with ferocity," Cira said. "Because we are not afraid to die."

"Like... not afraid at all?" I asked, doubting that anyone had no fear of death.

Pherric strolled onto the courtyard, squatting down next to us. I busied myself removing yet another fingernail that had been destroyed that week.

Pherric chimed in. "If someone says they are not afraid to die, they're either a liar or they are Bànshēn rén."

"Death before cowardice," Cira stated unemotionally.

"So, your life means nothing to you?" I asked.

"I serve my people. There is no greater honor than to die for the Bànshēn rén."

I held up my hands. "Right, I get the *rah-rah* fighting spirit. Defend your kingdom, and all that, but—"

"No, you do not understand. When you train, Finley Maguire, you do *just enough* to get by. You seek to survive the day, but not win. You serve yourself... not your people. And certainly not us," hissed Cira, rising up and pointing her long finger at me.

"What's wrong with surviving?" I replied, letting her get under my skin.

Pherric tried to move between us. "I do not think that we should—"

"Shut up!" we both yelled at him and he backed away.

"Animals *survive* but what have they accomplished?! Do animals elevate their species or do they just eat, mate, and sleep? We are meant for greater things than to merely exist!"

"How can you do greater things when you're *dead*!" I screamed.

"The farmers invent new ways to grow food while the warriors give them cover. The artists create culture while the warriors guard their backs. The healers develop new ways to save lives while warriors gather the ingredients they need. What have you done to improve the world, Finley? Are you a doer or are you a taker? From what I have seen, I believe you to be a coward who hides among the brave, eating their scraps and living off the hard work of others!"

"Ouch," I said, taken aback. I felt as though she had punched me in the chest and I couldn't inhale. "Look, I'll admit... I-I was a princess, skating through life and-and, no... I haven't done shit with my life. But... I'm here now. Isn't that worth something?"

"*Only* if you stop trying to survive. *Only* if you pour everything you have into everything you do here. *Only* if you make a difference," Cira said. "I need you to make a difference, Finley Maguire..."

She stormed off, angry with me.

I turned to Pherric. "What the hell did I do?"

"They are a passionate people, Finley."

"Well, I only wanted to find out more about her. Back in that mountain pass, with the bandits? She fought with a fury I have never seen before."

He walked us to the stone benches out at the edge of the courtyard to sit.

"And you have seen a lot of fighting in your day, have you?"

"Well, if you ever see a New York girl tie her hair back and tell her friend, 'Hold my phone'... just know you're about to die."

I inspected my jacked-up nails. No manicure in the world could fix that shit.

"Well, I do not know a great deal about them, but they call it *battlefury*. When they fight, the Bànshēn rén drift into this trance-like state where they become extremely savage," he said. "As you have witnessed."

"There's no drug involved? Nothing that gets them all worked up like that?"

"No. And once their frenzy begins, they do not stop until the enemy is defeated. That is why the Valhallans have had such difficulty dealing with them. They would chase them into their subterranean lairs and nearly all who dared go in after them... never returned," he sighed.

"Pherric?" I pleaded, my own frustrations welling up. "What am I doing here? I'm not a warrior and no matter how much training you put me through, I'm never going to be like Gunnr or Cira or... or any of you! I wasn't *born* into this!"

He grinned, placing his hand on mine. "You said you wanted to help and I believe you will. I am not happy about the plot to use you as an assassin, but I know that you are going to..."

When his voice trailed off, I looked up from my nails.

"I'm going to what?"

"Shh... listen," Pherric said. He stood on the stone bench, turning his head all around, to determine where a sound came from.

"What is it?"

He hopped off the bench, grabbed my hand, and pulled me toward the manor. "Come with me!"

We raced through Diago's manor, toward the front, and onto a small balcony that overlooked the city.

"What's wrong?" I asked again.

He lifted a long finger to my lips, silencing me with a look that could carve stone. His head tilted, every muscle in his wiry frame tense, as if he were straining to hear the faintest whisper of danger. I followed his gaze toward the heart of the city, and that's when the noise began to rise.

At first, it was a distant, low hum, like a brewing storm. Then it swelled:

voices shouting over one another. The rumble deepened, vibrating up from the streets like a restless beast stirring beneath the cobblestones. Was that a scream? No, several. And then, disturbingly, the unmistakable sound of laughter.

Quivira, which had been eerily subdued moments before, seemed to shudder awake, its quiet replaced by something raw and electric. The city was waking up.

"Finley, I have to go."

"Let me go with you!"

"No, I *cannot* risk you being seen on the streets again," he said. "Gather the others. I will return soon."

Chapter 28

Lord Diago's servants brought our dinner into the great hall while we waited for Pherric to return with news. Food supplies had dwindled significantly during the last few weeks. They called it stew but it would have been better described as broth.

The Lord of the 10th House of Cíbola took a seat next to me at the table as I slurped the sad soup.

"Allow me to apologize for the quality of your meals, as of late." It is rare to see someone smile as they apologize, but the elegant Diago pulled it off.

"Hey, your eminence. No, it's cool. Or should I call you 'your highness'?" I nervously avoided eye contact with him. "I'm sorry. I have no idea how these things work."

"The lords and ladies of Cíbola are not of noble birth. It is an honorary title given to the families of the Houses. Please... call me Diago," he said. With his tall frame sitting straight up in the high back chair, his legs crossed, and a long finger across his upper lip he sure looked like he was of noble birth.

"Got it. Diago. I can work with that." I pushed my bowl away because I was making embarrassing slurp noises.

"I must also apologize that I have not made time to get better acquainted, Finley Maguire... of Atlantis. However, I have been monitoring your progress and you seem to be adapting quite well to your training."

"If that's code for 'they haven't killed you yet' then yes, I'm doing well."

He smiled, leaning forward. His tanned hand slid the soup back under my face.

"You need your strength. Please eat. That is all I have to offer... at this point."

Not wanting to offend, I gave a slight nod and sipped more broth.

"I heard of your daring escape from the Irkallan guard," he continued. "I wanted to thank you for exposing a flaw in my security." He made it sound like I had discovered a backdoor hack into his online bank account.

"All part of the 'trying not to die' service that I provide."

"Of course, with our reduced reserves of food and wine, there is not much to steal. And prices are high enough that our currency is nearly worthless," he stated, mostly to himself. "My family has been in the business of trade for many generations, importing spices, dry goods, fine fabrics and furs, as well as exotic wines. At one point in our history, this House had taken up the Fifth position among the Families. In recent years, as the Irkallan king rose to power, we have fallen out of favor."

"Ah. I see." I had no idea what he was talking about. "So... that's the reason you're willing to take us in? Help us out?"

"The situation will only improve for my House when everything returns to normal. Again, I wanted to offer my apologies. And let us hope that young Pherric returns with good news," Diago said. "If you will excuse me..."

I nodded as he rose from the chair to make his rounds at the dining table. I picked up my cold soup and drank quickly from the bowl.

Later in the evening, I stood on the balcony that overlooked Quivira. All the things that Cira had told me kept running through my mind. *Stop trying to survive. Make a difference.*

I glanced through the doorway and into the manor. The others had gathered in the sitting room next to the great hall.

I had to get out of there and find Pherric. Starting for the door, I stopped in my tracks—they would never let me leave. I peeked over the balcony railing. Could I climb down and sneak out through the front gate?

Do not try to follow me, a faint voice instructed.

Confused, I looked high and low for the man behind that voice. "Hello?"

The surrounding windows were closed. No one stood inside the manor room behind me.

I will return soon. It was Pherric's voice. And it was inside my head!

"Pherric? Can you hear me? Pherric?" I said out loud, as if we were talking on the phone. "Come in, Pherric!"

Had he been reading my mind? Well, sort of. He caught my mindform. With my pulse pounding, as I considered an escape route, he had deciphered my wavelength. My string. I could only smile and shake my head. That was a trick that I needed to learn.

When I left the balcony to return to the others, they had moved out to the courtyard. Cira paced like a caged tiger. Gunnr sharpened her sword. Temurr kept flicking Frip's ear until he chased his mate across the terrace. Kasuma whispered secrets to Lord Diago.

They acknowledged me as I made my way across the stone tiles but said nothing. All I could do was stand there, my arms at my sides, and simply exist. That feeling was why I always hated going to parties—I would be surrounded by people and yet felt utterly alone.

The summer night was warm, but a chill ran down my back.

When everyone turned their attention toward the manor, I spun around. Pulling his hood back, Pherric flew onto the courtyard. The look of concern on his face thankfully pulled me out of my funk.

"I have grave news," he announced. The others crowded around him. I pushed my way between all the giants so I could hear.

"Discovered us, have they?" asked Temurr.

"Of course not," chided Frip. "Or they would be knocking down the front gate! Go on, Pherric."

"The Irkallan king has delivered large quantities of food to the city. Wagons began arriving this afternoon and have been pouring in since."

"And that's *not* a good thing?" I asked.

Braylor scoffed. "It is most certainly not good."

My stomach grumbled at the thought of food. "Why not?"

Pherric turned to me. "Malek's troops have been cutting off resources to this city for over a year now. His troops have stolen shipments from river boats and robbed merchant caravans coming into Quivira. They have destroyed their farms, poached livestock, and raided the city stores. They then shipped nearly everything off to Irkalla, leaving nothing behind for the people."

"Well... at least he's bringing it back, right?"

Braylor growled. "This action will make him appear the hero because he will be feeding his starving victims!"

"Oh." I shrank into the hole I had dug for myself. "Sorry."

"And a hero he has become. Most of the city has gathered to welcome his *gifts* to them," seethed Pherric. "They are shouting his name, cheering loudly, thanking his soldiers for returning only a small fraction of what he has taken *from* them. How can they be so blind?!"

My stomach growled. "Hunger makes you do crazy things. Did you happen to bring in samples back with you? I would kill Gunnr for some bread right now."

"You would try." Her hand grabbed the handle of her sword.

"It was a joke! Geez," I told her, half-jokingly.

Pherric ignored us. "Malek is most likely doing the same across all the Hominan kingdoms but will continue to starve and weaken the realms of other species. He is wiser than I gave him credit for."

Kasuma spoke up. "This explains why Malek's knight commander was here in Quivira."

"True. He most likely arrived in advance to make arrangements with the First Family. For their cooperation..."

Cira stepped forward. "Beyond the accolades he is receiving, why did Malek go to all this trouble?"

"He withheld food as a tool to recruit soldiers into his armies," said Kasuma, placing a hand on Cira's shoulder. "Since his was the only kingdom offering work, as well as resources, he was able to enlist quite a few. And by providing for the Hominan realms that side with him, he creates allies. In a sense, he is winning the war without firing a single arrow…"

"Let him!" said Cira. "This will not affect our plan."

Braylor turned to her. "This drastically alters the plan, Cira."

"So the people have some food again! What does that matter?"

Braylor was dejected. "For our plan to work, we must find safe passage through Cíbola, Elysium, and then Hell, to get to Irkalla, and—"

"And they are all *Hominan* kingdoms," Cira finished his thought.

"Aye. We did not have many friends in those realms to begin with," added Temurr. "We will have even fewer after Malek's… gesture of kindness."

"Wait, did you say we're going through Hell?" I stammered. They ignored me.

"Simply because Malek is passing out some food?" Cira asked. "How good were these supposed allies?"

"We were always going to avoid the cities, Cira. However, we had planned on help along the way. From people we *know* cannot stand the Irkallan king, but Malek's tactics will allow him to station more of his soldiers in their lands. He will be able to build a network of spies. And spread lies, incite fear throughout the kingdoms," said Pherric.

"We must abandon this scheme of yours," announced Braylor. "It was irresponsible to begin with and now it is simply imprudent."

Pherric got in Braylor's face, pointing a finger at his chest. "No! Our schedule has simply advanced. We leave tomorrow!"

Braylor stared at Pherric's finger on his chest until he pulled it away.

"We are not ready," snarled Braylor. "*She*… is not ready!"

When Braylor turned his eyes in my direction, everyone followed his gaze. I gulped.

"I'm… sorry?"

"We will hone her skills along the way to Irkalla," Pherric declared. "It was foolish for us not to have left already. We will make her ready. We have no choice."

II

Part Two

Chapter 29

The morning sun burned away the river mist, painting the valley in molten gold as Quivira stirred to life beneath us. The city's usual calm felt different today—charged, as if even the towers and walls knew we were about to flee. Lord Diago's plan was already in motion. He wasted no time, bringing me, Braylor, and Kasuma into his personal office. The weight of everything seemed to press down on me as we entered the room. Whatever final details Diago had to share, they would shape our survival—and there was no room for error.

"Your journey down the mountain should be easier than your climb up."

Braylor was doubtful, but intrigued. "How so?"

Diago laid out a city map across his long desk, pointing to the main gates.

"All the caravans that brought food in for the people will most likely be returning home today. Empty," he said. "From this Vard here."

"And no one will examine an empty wagon on the way out of town," confirmed Braylor.

"Exactly."

Diago was droning on, lost in the weeds of his master plan, but I had more important things to do. I casually roamed the office, my eyes scanning the shelves and running over the walls. This was a castle—there *had* to be a secret door somewhere. It was practically a requirement. I ran my fingers along the spines of dusty old tomes, knocked on suspicious-looking panels, even gave a few dramatic nudges to random candlesticks.

Nothing.

As we wrapped up, Diago leaned in, all serious, and pulled me aside. My heart raced—had he caught me snooping? He marched me to the far corner of the room and, with the flair of a magician revealing his greatest trick, pushed on a section of the wall. It bounced back and creaked open, revealing a narrow stone passageway cloaked in darkness.

I gasped, my grin spreading ear to ear.

"I *knew* it!" I whispered, triumphant.

The lord smiled, placed his hands on my shoulders. "You are a clever girl, Finley. May the gods smile upon your journey."

I bowed my head. "Long live the three houses."

"Long live the three houses."

Diago had already sent Gunnr and Pherric out of the manor in the early hours to steal a merchant wagon. Braylor wasn't happy about hiding in the back of the cramped and crowded carriage, but he knew anything was better than squeezing through the small caves and tunnels below Quivira. To clear some space in our getaway wagon, Kasuma decided to fly. I followed her to the courtyard. She handed me her concealment cloak and a small kit bag.

"I shall meet you along the north road, on the other side of the river, once you are safely away. Then we will begin your training."

"Is it safe for you to fly out of here? What if someone—"

Kasuma winked. "I doubt anyone will see me."

Without a sound, Kasuma climbed onto the stone railing and stepped off like it was no big deal. My heart nearly leapt out of my chest. I bolted to the edge, practically tripping over my own feet, and looked down.

She plummeted, free-falling hundreds of feet like a rock—until her wings snapped open. With the grace of someone who'd done this a million times (and probably had), she caught the air, veered north, and skimmed just above the rushing river.

The mist swallowed her up, leaving only the faintest ripple in her wake. Show-off.

I joined Pherric and Gunnr on the high-back seat on the front of the covered merchant wagon. Temurr, Frip, Cira and Braylor had stuffed themselves in the back, hidden under a canvas tarp. A chill whipped through me as Pherric snapped the reins of the karkadanns and we set off.

Gunnr flashed me a dirty look. "Try not to look like you are doing something illegal."

I plastered on a fake smile.

"And try not to look like you are mentally disturbed," she added. "Simply imagine the long, difficult journey ahead of us. And then act like that. Or... I will run you through with my sword." And just like that, my anxiety returned. But she nudged me hard in the side, gave me a sly smirk.

With four karkadanns lumbering ahead, their hooves thudding like distant drums, Pherric expertly merged our wagon into the bustling caravan snaking toward the city gate. I sat awkwardly, unsure of where to look or what to do, so I settled on staring at the weathered boards beneath my feet.

Then the smells hit me—warm, intoxicating, and utterly unfair. Fresh bread baking in a stone oven, eggs sizzling in fat, and nuts roasting over an open flame wafted through the morning air, each more tantalizing than the last. My stomach let out a growl so fierce it startled even me.

Gunnr glared at me, unimpressed, and shook her head.

The Irkallan soldiers barely gave us a second glance as we rolled through the gate. No inspections, no questions, not even a grumble of suspicion. I guess we didn't scream *threat*.

We wound our way down the mountain until Pherric suddenly veered off the main road before the outer wall. He wanted to check on Runa.

When we got to her place, though, it was empty. No sign of life, not even the karkadanns we rode in on. Those poor beasts were probably halfway digested in our guts by now, which made me feel horrible all over again. Pherric scanned the empty house and his face darkened.

"She's gone," he muttered, voice tight. "Probably fled weeks ago."

His worry hung in the air like storm clouds. But we didn't have the luxury of time to linger or hope for answers.

We slipped back into the caravan line like we belonged there, rolling through the front gates and over the bridge to the mainland. The city faded behind us, but my nerves didn't. I kept glancing over my shoulder, half-expecting a squad of Irkallan soldiers to barrel down the road after us.

Pherric and Gunnr chatted like we were on a casual road trip. They swapped boring travel facts—distances, landmarks, blah blah blah—but I couldn't tune out the uneasy itch between my shoulder blades. Someone was watching. I could feel it.

I scanned the road ahead, the forest to our left, and the river rushing to our right. The trees, thick and shadowy, tugged at my attention. Too many dark places to hide. I squinted up the hill, and there—just for a second—I caught a dark shape darting between the trunks. My stomach dropped.

As we clattered along the dusty road, my eyes stayed glued to the treeline. Then I saw it: a face, pale and unfamiliar, peeking from behind a tree. The moment our gazes locked, he yanked himself back into the shadows. Panicked, I wanted to warn Pherric, but what if he overreacted? A chase could alert the caravan—or worse, the soldiers.

I played it cool, or tried to. My heart thundered in my chest as I stole quick glances at the woods. After a tense stretch of road, Pherric veered the wagon off to the side. Gunnr hopped down and started fiddling with a wheel, all fake concern and muttered curses. No one in the caravan stopped. No one cared.

Once there was a gap in the traffic, Pherric guided the karkadanns off into the tall grass. We climbed a small hill, tucking ourselves behind a thicket of shrubs, and finally came to a stop. They untied the harnesses, their movements quick and quiet. Something was coming, and they knew it too.

Braylor and the others emerged from under the tarp.

"That took entirely too long, wizard!" grumbled Braylor.

Pherric held the reins for Gunnr to mount one of the beasts. "At least you did not have to crawl through small tunnels to flee the city."

Braylor flipped him off and rode away. Temurr and Frip mounted another karkadann. Pherric joined Gunnr and they galloped off. I hoped Cira would let me ride with her, but she took off on her own.

"You noticed the spy in the forest."

I jumped out of my skin. Kasuma appeared before me. Again. From out of nowhere.

"Will you stop doing that?!" I screeched at her, clutching my chest and panting hard.

She snatched her cloak from my hands and pulled it on, concealing her wings, then strapped her kit bag around her waist.

"Yeah, I did see the spy," I replied, catching my breath.

"That is good. Your training has begun. However, your first mistake was in staring too long—letting him know you know he was there. When a spy is aware he has been observed, he doubles his effort to conceal. Or that spy might be replaced, and the next one may be better than the first. It is best to let them think they are being clever."

I looked into the dark forest and pointed. "So, it's okay to let the spy just keep spying?"

Her eyes twinkled. The corners of her mouth twitched. "He has been... discharged from his duties."

She patted my shoulder ever so lightly and started walking up the hill after the group.

I tagged along. "I've got to ask... how do you move so damn quietly? I sound like a herd of stampeding karkadanns compared to you."

"Ah, yes. Being very lightweight is helpful," said Kasuma.

"You calling me fat?" I gripped my belly.

Kasuma laughed. "You will never be as light as me, Hominan. My bones are hollow. This helps me fly. However... I am a terrible ally in battle. I will be teaching you methods to advance with stealth *and* become invisible in the shadows."

"Ah, well, I've always been the wingman to a hotspice, so I know plenty about being invisible," I said.

She cocked her head and stared at me as if I'd just thrown a rock at her head.

"Any help you can give me is appreciated," I added.

"Then we will begin with how you walk," Kasuma commanded. "Starting now."

"Well, we don't have to start now, I-I just meant that—"

"Straighten your back. Your lower back must never move. Keep it firm no matter what action you take." Her delicate but strong hand pushed against me and pulled my shoulders back. "Keep your feet wider, for continual balance, and bend slightly at the knees. People get careless when they walk but once we build up your leg muscles, they will support and absorb your weight and reduce the noises you make."

I nodded gravely, but my awkward lumbering through the grass made me look like a zombie in search of brains.

"You must assess the terrain before you take a step, looking for the most quiet path to your destination. Then you set your toes down, and then the ball of your foot, but do not shift your weight yet. Once you know the step will be silent, you add your weight and lower your heel."

Following her directions, I shifted from zombie mode to walking like a weird robot.

"Bend your knees. Absorb your weight before transferring any weight," she said.

As their karkadanns disappeared over the crest, we heard a sharp whistle.

"We will continue your training later," she said. "Catch up with the others."

She spread out her wings and began flapping. I watched her rise up and then zoom away over the hill. I took a deep breath, mentally preparing myself to chase after their karkadanns. After all my conditioning and training in Quivira, I had the strength to keep up, but.... I still hated to run.

I spent the next several days jogging along behind them. The trail twisted through dense forests, where the air was so thick with moisture I was swimming through soup. Massive ferns and bright, waxy leaves slapped at my face, and vines tried to trip me up at every turn.

We skirted around a colossal mountain of rock, with a dark peak tucked away in the clouds. Our path wound up and down hills that burned my calves and left me gasping for air. Then came the open grasslands, where the sun beat down mercilessly and every step I was trudging through thick mud.

By the time we set up camp each night, my legs were beyond sore, and I was practically crawling. Twice, I twisted my ankle on loose rocks. The first time, I bit my lip and kept going, but the second time I hit the dirt hard, cursing the mountain and everything on it. Frip huffed but knelt beside me, expertly bandaging my swollen ankle with hands that were surprisingly gentle.

Pherric wasn't far behind with his alchemancy potions (Alchemancery?) Basically, his magic concoctions worked wonders—cooling, numbing, and setting me back on my feet in no time. "You will live," he grunted, tossing the empty vial back into his pack.

Even with the bruises and blisters, something about the ever-changing landscapes lifted my spirits. The wildness, the constant motion, and the little victories—like making it up a steep hill without falling on my face— kept me moving. I grew stronger every day and my endurance continually improved. I eventually found a gait that allowed me to keep my breath and not let the others get too far ahead.

To make things worse, Kasuma insisted I run alongside the karkadann she shared with Cira, all so she could drill her stealth techniques into me.

During our breaks, she corrected my posture and balance with an almost obsessive precision. The stealth exercises were maddening. I spent half an hour on a single step, starting with the pinky toe and gradually shifting weight through each toe until my foot was fully planted. Every movement had to be deliberate: arms positioned just so, momentum perfectly aligned, and weight distributed with surgical care. Even breathing wasn't spared—each inhale and exhale had to be controlled.

"Breathing must be quiet but consistent. Holding your air will lead to stronger, louder exhalation," Kasuma always warned. "Always through the nose."

While we were on the move, she helped me walk and even run quietly. Well, more quietly than I ever had before. And that's not saying much.

Every evening, after Kasuma would finish with me, poor Pherric was stuck trying to teach me the ways of Tir Na society folks. What I really wanted to do was to learn how he could read my thoughts and do that mindform fuckery, but he was all focused on the Auntie Etiquette lessons.

We crossed from Cíbola into a kingdom called Elysium, steering clear of cities and bypassing every small town along the main roads. As we journeyed north, the shimmering blue-green waters of the Triton Sea stretched alongside us. For days, we followed a wide golden beach, where Temurr and Frip couldn't resist splashing each other in the frothing waves. Braylor, ever the grump, glared at their antics while Pherric hurried them along.

When the coast gave way to towering cliffs, rising hundreds of feet, we veered inland, climbing into rolling hills dotted with massive rock formations. Tired from the long journey, we made the mistake of following a path filled with wagon wheel ruts.

After the sun had set, the skies decided to open up. An angry rain pelted us as we slogged along through the mud. Lightning danced across the field in the distance. Running behind the group, I turned my face to storm to let it wash away the dust and sweat of the day.

Riding at the head, Temurr held up his hand. They stopped as I quietly caught up. Their eyes darted about as they listened intently.

"Someone is coming," he whispered.

Frip sniffed the damp air. "I smell them."

Braylor motioned for me. I squished through the mud up to his karkadann and he easily lifted me onto the back.

"Should we hide?" asked Cira.

Gunnr gripped her axe handle, pulling the handle partially free.

"Too late, it is," Temurr exhaled, pulling his bow off his back. "Damned rain."

Pherric snapped his reins. "Put away your weapons and let us act as if we are meant to be on this road!"

He trotted ahead as we exchanged looks. Temurr held his bow to the side of his beast and Gunnr slid her axe down. We drew our cloaked hoods down to hide our features. For Braylor, that was like trying to hide an elephant behind a light pole.

To get a better look, I peered around the big guy as we rounded a slight bend. Several men in light cloaks, using their spears as walking sticks, led two lanky karkadanns struggling to pull a covered carriage through the muddy ruts. A half dozen more men and women followed, along with several children.

Pherric nodded to the men we passed. "Gods be with you, travelers."

"And with you," said the one closest to him. Obviously the leader. He was lean, handsome, with a short brown beard and sharp eyes.

We veered our rides off the roadway to let them pass. As wariness set in, their men stood a little straighter but they kept walking. Almost all of them stared suspiciously at Braylor's massive frame as they marched by. I spotted several more women and some young kids riding inside the carriage. I exhaled in relief—these were not soldiers.

A wiry young man, barely old enough to grow a scraggly beard, took a few steps off the road. His fiery brown eyes lit up when he caught a better glimpse of Frip.

"Satyrus!" his high-pitched voice squeaked. I couldn't translate the word, but it sounded like an insult.

The travelers jumped back, women screamed, and nearly all drew a weapon.

Braylor reached for his blade.

Temurr threw his hood back, baring his teeth.

"Another one!" shouted a child.

Fear washed across every face. The men held out weapons as the women hid the kids.

Pherric turned his karkadann about. "We mean you no harm! We are simply passing through—"

"No harm?!" shouted the leader, holding out his spear. "And yet, you consort with these monsters!"

"Monsters?!" Braylor tossed his hood back.

Another gasp. Cries of fear. The travelers jumped further away.

"Braylor, stop." I grabbed at his arm but he brushed me off.

A round woman with a bright red nose pointed at us from the carriage. "They will take the children! And they will eat them!"

The travelers summoned their courage—armed to the teeth, they took tentative steps toward us.

Gunnr and Braylor slipped off the karkadanns, pulling out their swords. Temurr reached for an arrow. Cira sprang onto the back of her ride. Frip held his shield.

"Wait!" I screamed. I jumped down, running between everyone with my arms raised. "Just wait!"

"Finley, get away!" shouted Pherric, trying to control his karkadann.

"Please, stop this!" I had no idea what I was doing. "There's no need for violence. Please?"

The wiry youngster aimed his sword at me. "She lays with Satyri! Been defiled by them! Ignore her!"

Pherric reached out a hand for me. "Withdraw, Fin! Now!"

Lightning flashed overhead, causing the already tense travelers to recoil in fear.

Braylor and Gunnr marched up behind me.

"Step aside," growled Braylor.

I turned to him, placing my hands against his chest. "No! Don't do this."

"Braylor!" I heard Pherric yell.

"There are children..." Over my shoulder, the travelers advanced in the rain.

"Let us ride! Now!" insisted Pherric.

A huge chunk of brown wet lettuce grazed Braylor's shoulder, breaking into shards. His dark eyes narrowed as he pushed me aside, his sword deflecting a ball of thrown fruit.

I ducked under his arm, placing myself between him and the travelers.

"Don't become the monster they fear! Rise above it! Show them you're better than they are! And... you *are* better than them!"

The women and children in the carriage continued to hurl food.

"Jesus, I'm trying to save your life, lady!" I screamed at one of the women. I flipped back to him. "Let's just leave!"

Braylor growled low in his throat, straightening to his full height as he shoved me behind him. His eyes never left the crowd, but even he took a cautious step back, nodding first to Pherric, then to Gunnr. The air reeked of damp rot as chunks of spoiled food rained down, mixing with the relentless downpour. A flash of lightning turned the angry faces into ghastly masks, their shouts lost for a moment in the deafening crack of thunder.

The mob surged forward, waving rusty swords and rickety spears. Their curses cut through the storm.

"Ride!" Pherric shouted, his voice sharp with urgency.

We scrambled onto our mounts. A spear sailed through the air toward Frip, but he deflected it effortlessly with his shield. Temurr twisted in his saddle, fury blazing in his eyes, but Frip slammed his hand down on their reins.

The mob's chants rose to a fever pitch as we kicked our beasts into motion. More spears zipped past, some missing by inches. The sickening thud of rotten vegetables and scraps against our backs and heads barely registered over the pounding of hooves and the roar of the storm.

Their insults echoed after us, swallowed by the darkness as we vanished into the night, the storm our only cover.

Chapter 30

We rode hard, pushing deeper into the countryside as the night stretched on. The storm finally gave up all it had, and we stopped beneath a grove of twisted trees, their gnarled branches dripping with the last remnants of rain. Exhausted, we slid off our karkadanns, who immediately began drinking from the puddles scattered across the field. The only light came from distant flashes of lightning, illuminating the storm's retreat in short, creepy bursts.

We exchanged uneasy glances. There was some serious tension hanging over our camp. And the dark, open fields offered zero comfort.

Temurr stooped to gather firewood, but Braylor's low growl stopped him.

"No fire," he said, his voice firm. "Out here, it will be a beacon. Too easy to spot."

The ape man ran a hand down his arm, swabbing off a pint of water from his hair. "We are soaked to the bones, Braylor. We need to—"

"We need to survive, Temurr! Those Hominans will report our presence at their first opportunity."

Pherric, walking the edges of our makeshift campsite, turned to Temurr. "You are sure we are safe here?"

I parked myself on the cold, wet ground with my knees up to my chest for warmth.

"According to my calculations," said Temurr, his dark eyes scanning the terrain and nostrils flaring to breathe in the air. "We are axims away from the nearest city."

Temurr appeared to be a living map app for our ragtag crew. How anyone could navigate their way through a pitch-black rainy night was beyond me. Of course, almost everything on this world seemed beyond me. Except for the bigotry and intolerance. The people of Tir Na had the same prejudices and fears as those back on Earth. Anyone who was different was, at best, an object of contempt or, at worst, an enemy. But I so desperately wanted those travelers to meet Frip, Temurr and—well, maybe not Braylor— and just talk to them so they could see that they were not monsters, not something to fear.

"Here," muttered Braylor.

I looked up at the blanket he held out for me. "Is that your way of saying thank you?"

He stared at the clouds above. Unfolding the blanket, he shuffled around me, laying the smelly thing on my shoulders.

"It is."

"I see. You're welcome."

He squatted in front of me, pulling the blanket tight around me. "I am welcome to what?"

"Oh, it's a phrase we use where I'm from whenever someone thanks us." It dawned on me that I had no idea why people said "you're welcome".

"It is a stupid phrase." Braylor. Always on point. "But I did lose my temper and did not consider the presence of children. You were wise to point them out."

"And extremely dangerous to put yourself in that situation," admonished Pherric. He crouched down next to Braylor, his eyes inspecting me for any signs of injury.

Braylor snorted. "She kept a bad situation from becoming very bloody, wizard."

"And could have been met with the tip of a spear in her side!"

Pherric rose up, but Braylor rose higher. "She is normally quiet as an ankou and when she *finally* holds firm on something, you condemn her for it?!"

"I am responsible for her safety!"

"Well, then you should not have brought her here, wizard!"

"She is vital to our plan!"

Braylor grinned as the gears spun away inside his thick skull. "But, she is your... chosen one. Part of your precious prophecy, correct? She is destined to lead us to victory! She is our champion. Therefore nothing can happen to her. Or do you doubt your ancient texts and soothsayers?"

Pherric's cheeks burned bright as I pulled myself up from the mud.

"I will not leave anything to chance. And we will not tempt fate, Braylor. By your reasoning, we could throw her off a cliff and the gods would gently lower her to the ground!"

"Let's try, shall we?!" Braylor barked out a laugh, turning his massive frame toward me.

I immediately jumped back. "Whoa, whoa! Hold on a minute!"

"He is being flippant, Finley," Pherric assured.

"Am I?"

Pherric placed his slender hand against Braylor's shoulder. "She is not suited for this, my friend. And she may never be. However, we will do all that we can to... see this through. Do I make myself clear?"

Still grinning, Braylor simply shook his head in disappointment. At Pherric. He waved his hand—dismissing us—as he plodded off.

I had nothing.

Like she always did, Kasuma appeared behind me, motioning for me to follow her. I wanted to defend myself to Pherric, but I quietly tagged along behind Kasuma like a good little girl.

"You will concentrate on refining your stealth techniques."

"Now? Here?" I sighed. Kasuma gave me that look a mother gives to her child the first time they say no to her. I heard the lingering sound of my whining floating in the air, so I stood straight, nodding. I was ready.

As it turned out, practicing Kasuma's techniques of hiding and staying motionless still required a buttload of effort. I thought it was simply a matter of concealing yourself behind a tree or curtain. I was wrong.

"Every single time you enter someplace new, you must first locate potential hiding places. And the moment you hear someone approach, you silently move to a spot. And more is required than remaining perfectly still—you need to eliminate your height, your silhouette, and your color."

"Um, I'd have to be invisible to do that…"

"In order to survive, every species will first look for movement as a sign of danger. So, ceasing that movement is your first step. But many seek out danger at their eye level. Rarely do we look above or below. So, if possible, you will remove yourself from their line of vision. We are all highly skilled at recognizing shapes, so you must distort yours to become more difficult to see. If you cannot hide behind an object, hide in front of it or on either side to eliminate the outline of your body."

"Okay, that makes sense, but how do I change my color?"

"Light is your enemy. And color is only found in light. Lose yourself in darkness whenever you can. Keep your pale skin covered as much as possible. And, most importantly, keep your eyes shut. My own eyes are as black as night, but I still must keep them closed because my enemy might see reflections from them."

"But what if someone spots me? Comes after me? If my eyes are closed, I'll have no way of knowing!"

"No. You will have no fear. You cannot worry you will be seen. Since you are not looking at them, you will remain still and silent—even if your mind tells you someone has discovered you. Even after you have been sliced open by your enemy, you will never react," she demanded. "Because you are made of stone."

"I'm sorry, but if someone stabs me I'll probably at least say 'oww' or something."

Through the night, as the others rested, I stayed awake, drilling the lessons Kasuma had hammered into me. I practiced standing on one foot, as motionless as a statue, until even the slightest sway felt like failure. I worked on disappearing into the shadows, keeping low and silent. Again and again, she made me scale a tree, nestling myself into the branches like a predator lying in wait. Each time I climbed down, she'd silently motion for me to do it again. Balance, crouch, climb, repeat—until my muscles burned and my hands were raw.

"Once again, the Adarna-gakur pose," she ordered.

I squatted on the wet ground with my head down and arms wrapped around my body. Struggling to keep my balance, I focused on my breathing.

"Soothe your mind," said Kasuma.

I repeated her command, in my head, over and over.

"I can still hear you breathe."

I stopped breathing.

"Now I hear you not breathing."

I looked up. "Oh, come on! How can you hear me *not* breathing?!"

"Your heart quickens from fear. Your mind knows you are holding your breath and so... it fights for survival. I can hear the throbbing in your neck, Finley."

I shot her a dirty look over the arm resting in front of my face.

"In through the nose. Quietly. Evenly. Slow your heart. One beat... then another. Until you are the stone."

A sense of calm came over me. I felt my heartbeat—thump, thump... thump—as it actually slowed down. I counted the seconds between each inhale and exhale. One, two, three.

"There. *That* is Adarna-gakur," she announced.

I fell back on the ground, relaxing in the mud. "What the hell does that even mean?"

Pherric sat with his back against the tree, watching the whole process. "The adarna is a beautiful bird with long white tail feathers. Old mages say the adarna has healing powers, can make people fall asleep, and can even turn one to stone."

"And gakur is 'to hide' in the tongue of the Tengu," said Kasuma.

Eager to avoid another strenuous pose, I pushed myself up from the mud. "I've heard a lot about the other species on this world but very little about yours. Tell me more."

"We have no time, Finley. Azeban-gakur," she commanded.

"I better be getting paid overtime for this."

With all the strength I had left, I used Pherric's shoulder to climb up the tree and onto a large branch.

"I can still see your silhouette," Kasuma warned, ruffling her wings.

Gripping the wet branch, I dropped my hips off the side and held on tight.

"Better."

I inhaled and let it out silently and then focused my mind, ignoring the pain in my hands as I held on to the tree. In through my nose and out through my mouth. My heart rate slowed. A hush fell across our small grove of trees.

And then Braylor snored.

Kasuma, Pherric and I shouted in unison: "Braylor!"

He quickly sat up, grabbing for his sword. "What?!"

Delirious and utterly exhausted from my ninja instruction, I laughed so hard that I snorted. Even the well-comported Kasuma covered her mouth with her feathered hand, chuckling lightly. Pherric peered around the tree, laughing at the confused Braylor.

I was all fun and games until my fingers slipped off the wet branch and I fell with a heavy thud in the muddy grass below.

Then it was their turn to laugh at me.

Chapter 31

Kasuma finally stopped torturing me sometime during the night. I collapsed onto a patch of high grass, barely registering the folded blanket Braylor had handed me, before sleep swallowed me whole.

I dreamed of standing at the back of a classroom during the final exam. I hadn't attended a single class in months, yet somehow, I had to pass. Frantically flipping through the exam pages, I realized the questions were written in a language I didn't know. The weight of failure crushed my chest, and I woke with a start, gasping for air, my heart pounding against the wet Elysium grass.

The morning sun fought a losing battle against the heavy gray fog that held stubbornly to the field. As the others mounted up, I tossed the damp blanket into Braylor's saddlebag and fell into step beside them. Cira handed me a strip of dried kark meat, her usual wordless offering. Chewing on the leathery snack, I followed as we headed toward a gentle rise, hoping for a clearer view of what lay ahead.

Temurr and Frip were the first to reach the top of the small hill. Temurr pulled on the reins to keep his beast still. He seemed bewildered. I ran to see what he was looking at but Pherric and Gunnr flew by me.

"Temurr..." Pherric dropped his head in disappointment.

"My calculations were not correct," Temurr admitted. Frip reached out, punched him hard in the arm.

I hit the rise, and the sight before me stole my breath. A sprawling city, its walls built from deep red stone, stretched out beneath the cloudy

"

morning sky. And those walls loomed tall, with their edges softened by the bluish mist. Four round towers anchored each corner, their proud, timeworn faces staring rebelliously at the foggy sky. Green and yellow banners snapped in the cool breeze, their vibrant colors a stark contrast to the reddened stone.

Outside the protection of the walls, a rural village bustled with life.

A towering white castle, at the city's heart, gleamed brightly despite the hazy mist. Its walls were impossibly smooth, as if carved from a single block of marble, and its towers poked the sky, capped with golden spires that caught what little light the sun could push through. The main keep rose in the center, crowned by a banner bearing a proud symbol—a golden dragon intertwined with a radiant star.

The fog shifted and thinned, revealing glimpses of stained-glass windows that sparkled like fine jewels. Despite the distance, I could almost hear the faint echo of bustling courtyards, the clang of swords on shields, and the hum of a city that, like me, barely slept.

Braylor arrived on the hill. Cira and Kasuma brought up the rear.

I felt a steady reverberation through my sandals. "Uh… guys."

"We camped that close to Camelot?" seethed Braylor. "We could have been slaughtered in our sleep, Temurr!"

Wait… Camelot? As in *the* Camelot? Arthur and the round table and all that? I strained to ask too many questions all at once.

"I know. Well… I know now." Temurr shrugged.

The ground shook beneath me. "I think something is coming."

"We must leave before we are spotted," said Gunnr.

I dashed out to the edge of the hill, pointing at the city. "Too late!"

Six knights exploded through a swirling white cloud that covered the wide-open field, their green and yellow surcoats snapping over their shiny plate armor. The rhythmic clanging of their armored karkadanns filled the air, the beasts' snouts and chests plated in iron, their breath fogging in the cool air. Their lances gleamed, lowered, ready.

"Ride! Now!" Pherric barked, his voice high with urgency.

Pherric yanked his karkadann around, its hooves skidding in the damp grass before it lunged forward. Gunnr was holding on to him tight as their beast tore into the ground with desperate power.

"Climb on!" Braylor moved forward on the saddle, holding out his big hand. I reached out and he snatched me up behind him, cranked on the reins, and our karkadann began racing after the others. I gripped him tight to keep from flying off.

I risked a glance back, and my stomach twisted. The knights were closing the distance.

Peering around the massive giant blocking my view, I saw Pherric kick his kark hard, the jolt causing his leather bag to thump rhythmically against the saddle between them.

A sudden whoosh pierced the air, a spear slicing past my ear close enough to move my hair.

With both Braylor and me crammed on the poor karkadann's back, we were lagging behind the others. Yet, somehow, we were still outpacing the knights. They had probably been pushing their mounts at full speed since leaving the city, which meant we might actually have a chance to outrun them.

Ahead, Pherric's precious bag bounced loose from its perch. It rebounded off the saddle, then launched into the air. Gunnr lunged for it, her hand closing on nothing but air. The bag hit the ground, rolling and tumbling wildly through the tall grass.

Without thinking—or fearing the obvious consequences—and like an absolute fool, I leapt off the karkadann's back. All for that stupid bag. My father would've disowned me on the spot.

"Finley! No!" Braylor screamed.

I tumbled past the leather bag, the rough ground scraping against my arms. Scrambling back, I seized the strap and clutched it tightly.

When I looked up, my stomach dropped. The knights had closed and were right on top of me.

A spear slammed into the mud between my legs, quivering ominously.

Before I could react, two knights dismounted, their boots hitting the ground with heavy thuds. They seized my shoulders and shoved me into the mud, the impact driving the air from my lungs.

The remaining knights thundered past, chasing the others without a second glance.

"Easy, boys! We haven't established a safe word yet..." These things just fall out of my mouth.

As I struggled to break free, they pushed my face down to keep me motionless.

"At least buy me a drink first!"

I realized, instantly, that all the training had been wasted on me. I wracked my brain, desperately searching for a fighting technique to get me out of my mess. But nothing came to mind... when it counted.

In the distance, I heard high-pitched screeches from karkadanns, war cries, and heavy hooves pounding the ground. Then swords clashed and men screamed. Finally, the thunderous gallop of an approaching kark.

I managed to twist my head to see Pherric, riding alone, drive his shield into one of the knights holding me down. Sliding off the saddle, he threw the shield into the other knight with a loud clang. He pulled me up off the grass as I scooped up his leather bag.

As Pherric helped me onto his karkadann, the first knight appeared behind him.

"Look out!" I shouted.

As the knight slashed down, Pherric spun away but the blade cut into his forearm—his shield fell to the ground. The knight lifted the sword to finish the job while the second one rushed to help. Before either could strike, they were trampled by Braylor's karkadann.

Braylor shouted at me. "Help him up!"

I stood Pherric upright as he held his bloody arm. I threw his boot in the stirrup and tried as best I could to push him onto the saddle. He slumped over, moaning in pain, but did grab the reins with his good arm.

"Be off!" commanded Braylor.

Pherric kicked his boot into the side of the karkadann and raced off alone across the field.

One of the knights staggered to his feet. Braylor spun his beast around, kicked the knight in the chest with his boot, and sent him flying.

"That... was simple-minded, Finley!"

He easily dragged me onto the back of his karkadann.

"I know! I know... my calculations were not correct either."

Using his mount, he chased away their rides. Digging his boots into the kark, we charged across the wet grass and away from the injured knights on the ground.

We quickly caught up with Pherric to ride alongside him.

"Will you live, man?!" shouted Braylor.

Pherric leaned back in his saddle. "Aye. If we can get away."

Holding tight to Braylor, I leaned out so Pherric could hear me. "Can you mindform these assholes? Throw them off the scent?"

Pherric had lost a lot of blood and the pain clouded his mind. He shook his head.

"Then we will do it without your magic!" Braylor bellowed, pulling out his sword.

He rode the karkadann hard as we pulled away from Pherric.

Our team fought for their lives on the open field. Gunnr and Frip clashed with the knights on foot, while Temurr and Cira defended themselves from the backs of their beasts. Kasuma flew above the fray, unable to fight in hand-to-hand combat.

Gunnr deflected a blow and slashed her axe into the side of a knight, but caused no damage—his armor protecting him. Cira struck the shoulder of another knight and then tried to drive the point into his chest without effect. Nothing could penetrate the thick, smooth plates covering the knights.

"The biggest drawback of full plate armor?!" Braylor shouted back to me.

"Yeah?"

Braylor lifted his broad sword straight out, turning the blade. He swung hard as we rode past the knight attacking Temurr. The flat part struck the knight's helmet, caving it into the man's head.

"They dent easily!"

Braylor pivoted and trampled Gunnr's assailant. When a mounted knight took the fight to Braylor, he parried his swinging blade. Like an alley cat, he launched off our ride and toppled the knight. With a few smashes of his thick fist and the hilt of his sword, the knight's helmet was crushed.

"Braylor, stop!" Pherric pleaded, riding up to our group.

Deciding to cut and run, the remaining knight stopped his attack on Frip and raced his karkadann back toward the city. Gunnr started after him.

"Let him go," said Pherric, looking down at the dead knights on the ground. "Let him go, please."

Gunnr turned on him. "He will bring reinforcements!"

"They are most likely on the way," Temurr surmised, panting hard and staring at the city in the distance.

"Then we must ride!" shouted Cira. Her face burned red but she had not yet given over to the frenzy.

Frip nodded, riding up next to her. "Sage advice, dear." He patted and rubbed Cira's shoulder, trying to calm her.

Gunnr wrapped Pherric's wound and jumped up behind him. Frip helped Temurr onto his saddle. Kasuma hovered above, staring off in through the mist.

Gripping his shoulder, Pherric steered his karkadann to Braylor.

"What?" Braylor panted.

"We cannot keep killing people who are not our enemy!"

Braylor pointed at the bodies in the dirt. "They attacked us!"

"Because we invaded their territory," said Pherric very slowly to make his point. "They are protecting their lands, as you would, and we ran from them. And gave them no choice."

"They were going to capture her, Pherric. What would you have me do?!"

"Not kill them, to start with!" Pherric said.

"They wore fully plated armor, you cur! We could not defeat that without a longbow at close range or a halberd... and I am quite sure those would have killed them as well," sneered Braylor. "What does it matter whether these fools live or die?!"

"Because then it makes us no better than Malek, Braylor," he replied.

"Maybe we should have settled it by rolling hoops or playing a card game!" A wry smile cut through Braylor's broad jaw.

"We do not need to act like savages," said Pherric.

He regretted the words as they fell from his mouth.

Braylor leaned back, crossing his arms. Temurr flashed a glare at Pherric as well.

"Ah, I see…" said Braylor.

"I did not mean—"

"Let us not become the very thing that Malek proclaims that we are! Is that it?" Braylor asked mockingly. "We must rise above our feral and beastly natures, everyone! And be more Hominan! Like the godly Pherric here!"

"Braylor, I—"

"Oh, I know what you meant, man. I have heard the propaganda from Irkalla. I have heard the whispers from the dark alleys that I walk by in your cities. We have listened to our elders go on about how much you fear us *savages*," he hissed. "For generations, Hominans have avoided the other species… until you needed us for something."

"I am not like that… not one of those people," said Pherric. "You *know* that."

Braylor ignored him. "Oh, but you need us now! Do you not, little man?"

"Braylor, please. We are fighting against Malek's propaganda. We must avoid killing when we absolutely do not have to kill. If the Irkallans are saying you are bad and to be feared, we must not reinforce their notions! I am not trying to make some grand condemnation of your kind. I am trying to let you know that I abhor the death of any species—yours included! That is the sole reason I am here! Do you understand?"

"Do you know why I joined your little quest, Pherric? Do you know the reason?"

Pherric obviously had never asked. "You want to stop Malek from wiping out your kind. And all the other species."

"While the males from my village were away at a mating ritual for another clan leader, a raiding party of Irkallans attacked," said Braylor. "Our females fought hard, sending over half of the Irkallans to be with their gods. But they were not prepared for battle, Pherric. Those Irkallans killed my mother and two sisters... The only family I had left."

Everyone lowered their heads. My heart broke for him and tears welled up.

"I am sorry, Braylor. I had no idea," said Pherric.

"Despite their treachery, despite what Malek's men took from me... I do not wish to kill all Hominans. But I do plan on killing Malek. Hopefully with my own hands. And I will tear out his heart and eat it like the savage that your kind thinks that I am... And to do this, I will kill anyone and *everyone* who stands in the way of my vengeance. *That...* is why I am here. Those men lying there? They stood in my way and they put your *chosen one* in danger. I have no remorse. And that knight that you let get away? He will return to his people and share the story of the vicious creatures that slaughtered his comrades. Your appeasement has only put us in more danger. And when Malek finally rises up against us, the people in this city will join the fight for their own vengeance. Violence and death are a means to an end. And you are only making it worse, Pherric. Do *you* understand?"

Without waiting for a response, Braylor trotted us away. While still within reach, I tossed Pherric his leather bag.

I heard Gunnr whisper to Pherric. "We must leave. At once..."

Braylor guided our sullen group away from the city at full gallop.

Chapter 32

We rode hard all day, the relentless pace driven more by unease than strategy, putting as much distance as we could between ourselves and what was—against all logic—apparently Camelot. I couldn't shake the surreal realization that the myths I'd once dismissed as bedtime stories or half-forgotten legends were, in this world, disturbingly real. Dragons, hellhounds, Camelot itself—it was all here, tangible and dangerous, not confined to the pages of old books.

What I couldn't wrap my head around was how. How did two worlds—mine and this one—share such eerily similar folklore? Was it pure coincidence, some strange cosmic parallel, or something more deliberate? Did these gods—if you could call them that, because everything sounded to me like they were some kind of alien space travelers—use both planets as their personal playgrounds, toying with real lives for amusement? Had they snatched people from one world and deposited them in the other, scattering knowledge like breadcrumbs through the ages?

I had no answers, and the questions churned endlessly in my mind. Yet, no matter how hard I tried to focus on solving this mystery, my thoughts kept drifting back to Braylor.

The stunning sky—thick clouds playing across a bright teal backdrop—offered little comfort, the beauty a harsh contrast to our sulky silence. Aside from a few arguments over directions, we continued north with a wordless tension.

Guilt gnawed at me, and the quiet only fueled my torment. Braylor's grief weighed heavily; he had lost everything in the brutal attack he described. Yet, I also saw Pherric's point—avoiding a trail of blood was crucial if we hoped to unseat Malek. Still, I couldn't shake the horror of what I'd done.

Braylor's family had been stolen from him, and my rash actions had added more innocent lives to the tally. Every time I tried to justify it— reminding myself we were on a mission for good—the image of mourning families shattered my resolve. Sons, husbands, fathers... all gone because I tried to save some stupid ancient book, further splintering our fragile group. Once again, my well-intentioned help had caused only harm.

That night, the silence persisted. Frip dressed Pherric's wound without a word. We ate in isolation, feigned sleep, and resumed our march before dawn. The oppressive weight of sorrow and anger followed us, heavy as ever.

The next evening after we camped, I decided to break the silence. I approached Braylor, who sat staring at his own personal fire. As he tossed twigs into the flame, I sat close to him.

"Hey, listen. I'm really sorry to hear about what happened to your family. If you ever want to talk about—"

"I suppose we have finally come to your training time with me," said Braylor, his eyes glued to the fire. "I have watched the others waste their time with you, trying desperately to endow you with abilities, in a matter of months, that we all started learning as babes. I have been holding this sword since before I was able to stand."

He stood up, his hand resting on the sword hilt sticking out of the scabbard at his belt.

"Well, it hasn't been a complete waste—"

"First, I must give you a gift. This weapon shall be yours. For the rest of your life."

The gravity in his voice made the air feel heavier, like the whole world was holding its breath for this moment. I stood there, frozen, as he solemnly retrieved a leather sheath from the karkadann's saddle. With an almost religious reverence, he slid the blade out and presented the handle to me like it was Excalibur itself.

"This… is your sword."

I took the weapon, its sharp edge glinting in the light, and turned it over in my hands. "So, what's the deal? Is this some kind of ancient relic? Does it have mystical powers? Talks to me in riddles?"

"No," he replied flatly. "It is a sword."

"Okay, but does it have a name?"

"Yes," he said without hesitation. "Sword."

Braylor ruined *everything.*

"My plan for you is this—you will actually do something useful. Educational. Something that will force you to learn a real skill."

"Okay… and what is that?" I feared the worst.

"From now on, if you want to eat… you will catch your own food," he announced.

"Wait, what?!" It was the worst.

"Tonight, you may eat plenty from our supplies. Then, you eat only the food you provide for yourself," said Braylor, mesmerized by the flames.

"I'm not a hunter! I don't know how to kill anything, or… or cook it!"

The closest I ever came to hunting was tracking food delivery order statuses on my phone.

"And that is why *my* training will be your most effective. The others have taught you to fire a bow, swing a knife, and be nimble on your feet… so you will now apply those skills."

"Oh my god, why do you hate me so much?"

Finally looking at me, he placed his massive fingers on my chin, lifting my face up to his.

"I need you to be able to survive on your own. This is how I learned as a child. And this is how you will learn."

He held my gaze, his hand resting gently under my chin. I fell into those delicate orange flecks scattered like embers in the depths of his dark chocolate eyes. They drew me in, as if I could dive headfirst, and lose myself entirely, and—and then remembered how much I love food. "But, I can't!"

"Go fill your belly now, girl. You have many hungry nights ahead of you."

He sat down to stare at his fire.

"This is because you think I'm fat, isn't it?!" I protested.

"I do not think you are fat—"

"Well, podgy then."

Braylor sighed. "When you first arrived, you were soft. Weak."

"And now?"

"You are... less soft. Less weak."

Like a petulant toddler, I stomped off, kicking at the dirt like it owed me money. Why was he always such a colossal jerk?! Off in the shadows, I crossed my arms, teeth grinding in fury—not at him, but at myself. Of course, I wanted him to sweep me up in some ridiculous, dramatic gesture. Stupid brain. Stupid hormones. Why did my knees have to turn into jelly for *him* of all people? The brooding, self-satisfied idiot.

But then my stomach growled, loud and traitorous. Ugh, fine! He was right—I needed to eat. Before I got hangry enough to make things really awkward.

I woke the next morning to the sound of conversation. My heart lifted as I wiped away the crusty buddies caked on my eyelids. Small conversations were taking place around our little camp as the group ate their meals. The recriminations and anger from several nights ago seemed to have somewhat faded.

I plopped down next to Pherric as he chatted with Gunnr.

"Morning," I whispered, trying not to break the spell.

Both he and Gunnr nodded at me and continued to discuss our travels for the day. I grabbed a slice of the dried meat out of his hand.

"Oy!" The massive man jumped over the fire and snatched the meat from my hand. "If you're hungry... go hunt!" he shouted at me. "You must earn your keep."

And the spell broke. Everyone stopped talking, looking away. After an awkward silence, they split up and gathered their belongings.

I had no idea what to do. I gazed around the wide open plain surrounding our camp. All I could see were small green bushes and tufts of long grass.

Handing me a bow and a quiver full of arrows, Frip gave a curt nod. "I assume you'll be needing these," said the adorable ape man. His kindness knew no bounds.

I hugged the stuffing out of him. Temurr gave me a stern look from atop his karkadann. I stuck my tongue out at him and blew him a raspberry—phttthhh!

That made Temurr giggle. But the thought of raspberries made me even more hungry.

Chapter 33

For several days, I flailed around with my sword while jogging behind the karkadanns, swinging, thrusting, and trying not to stab myself. My arms and back constantly burned with the effort but, after my embarrassing failure against the knights, I was determined to be at least marginally useful with a blade—or at the very least, less embarrassing.

Braylor gave me his grudging approval. Temurr, on the other hand, seemed convinced that these exercises would end with me chopping off a leg or maybe a foot. Honestly, given my technique, I couldn't entirely disagree with him.

As I hacked at the air like an overenthusiastic toddler with a toy sword, we crossed into new terrain. The wide, endless plains dissolved into a harsher, more desolate landscape—rocky hills bristling with scraggly trees and stubborn bushes. The ground itself was bizarre: a salty, greenish-blue dirt that sparkled in the sunlight, as if the world had decided to sprinkle glitter over its apocalypse. I'd heard of blue grass, but blue dirt? That was a new one.

By day four, I was running on fumes—literally. With no food to be found, my stomach decided to declare war on me. Back on the plains, I'd failed spectacularly at catching the tiny, quick rodents that darted across the grass. Now, in this unforgiving landscape, it seemed like even those critters had given up and moved somewhere less bleak.

One afternoon, mid-run, my body had enough. I collapsed in a graceless heap, panting and cursing the universe.

"You look terrible," Braylor observed, ever the charmer.

"Great," I wheezed. "Just what every girl wants to hear."

"I will feed you. But you must stop this nonsense of trying to be a warrior. We can lead you to a nearby city, give you some coin, and you will adapt to living on your own—"

"No! I will not give up."

"The life of a warrior will only lead to your untimely death."

"Really? I thought not eating would lead to my *untimely* death."

Just beyond Braylor, I spotted a red lizard sunning himself on a rock. I pulled my bow from my back and sprinted toward a potential source of food. I crouched, drew my bow, notched an arrow—and missed by a mile.

I plodded back to Braylor. He started to say something, but placed his huge hand on my tiny shoulder. "You will ride with me—conserve your energy."

That seemed like a test. But my willpower faded fast and I reluctantly joined him on the karkadann.

From the higher vantage point, I scanned the area for any sign of life. I'd hop down to fire off arrows. I chased after every strange, inedible creature I saw. When I couldn't see any live animals, I found myself searching for poop piles or sniffing the air for new scents. But nothing ever came from my efforts.

The team kept offering hunting tips and reminders, as any of it helped.

"You must be silent and patient."

"Hunt only one type of animal."

"Stay within a small area and wait."

"Remain still and watch for movement."

I started off replying with thank-yous or smiles but, after a while, my *hangriness* took over and I would simply grunt at them or flip them off.

After two more days of nothing to eat, I had trouble focusing. Eventually, and oddly, I completely lost my appetite. And I was so tired... all the time. The only thing that kept me going were the looks of pity from Braylor. Or he would smirk and do a slight shake of his head, which drove me crazy. I simply *had* to prove him wrong, show him I could do it, without anyone's help.

"You have been working hard, Finley," he would tease. "How about one little piece of meat? Give up and you can eat all you want." More testing.

I doubted he would have even given me anything to eat; he just wanted me to beg.

On the seventh day with no food, I was so hungry that white stars constantly flashed before my eyes. As we trotted along through the morning, I saw what looked like a massive line of low, black clouds ahead of us and I refused to ask anyone if they were real, for fear that they'd force me to eat.

By the afternoon, I was beyond exhausted. I let my eyes close... just for a moment, and I only snapped out of it when I started to slip off the karkadann. As I hauled myself upright, my eyes locked onto a looming range of serrated, smoke-black mountains. The same dark clouds twisted above them, churning like a slow, deliberate hurricane. A twisted sense of relief flooded through me—at least I wasn't hallucinating from hunger.

We rode toward a narrow fissure in the sheer black cliffs, flanked by massive stone doors etched directly into the mountain's face. The portal yawned, perpetually open, exuding an ominous stillness that dared anyone to enter.

On either side of the gateway, two monstrous hellhounds loomed, carved from the obsidian stone. Each stood a hundred feet tall, their long snouts and sharp ears frozen in a perpetual snarl. Eyes burned a deep, blood-red, and their gaping jaws, lined with gnarled, uneven teeth, seemed ready to unleash a sound that would tear my fragile psyche apart. They bayed silently at the angry sky, sentinels of a world that welcomed nothing but despair.

"This place looks... fun."

Braylor kicked the kark, wanting to be the first to enter that ghoulish place.

"Wait! We're going in there?"

"Yes."

"On purpose?" Shocked, I was.

"Welcome to Hell," he said.

"Nice," I said, more than a little afraid. "Do they have a food court?"

"Must everything be in jest?" He looked back at me, one eyebrow raised.

I shrugged. "As my father used to tell me, it's my coping mechanism. Don't worry—it drove him crazy, too."

"I do find it annoying."

"Go to Hell," I replied.

"As you wish…" He kicked his boots again, speeding our journey toward the gates of Hell.

We crept through the enormous doorway, the sharp stone edges looking like a mouth about to swallow us whole. The black sky loomed overhead, the craggy cliffs seemed to lean in closer with every step. Our shields were up, weapons tight in hand. If ever there was a place for an ambush, this was it. All we needed was a slow, menacing drumbeat and a few shadowy figures lurking around the crevices. But no dramatic standoff happened. No spears. No arrows. Not even a demonic cackle to spice things up. Just silence. Awkward, unsettling silence.

Inside the mountain pass, the world went from a cheerful sunny afternoon to full-on midnight in record time. The dark clouds? Nope, just layers of thick, swirling smoke, belching from a distant volcano that looked ready to blow its top. The air smelled like someone had been hoarding rotten eggs since the dawn of time. Lovely.

Every crunch of our karkadanns' hooves on the blood-red dirt echoed around us. Gnarled black rocks jutted up like giant tombstones, daring us to come closer. And the ash—big, fat flakes of it—fell lazily from the sky, landing in our hair, our clothes, our mouths if we weren't careful. My throat was sandpaper after a few breaths, but hey, who needs clean air in literal Hell? Oh, and did I mention the heat? It was like someone left the oven door open, but instead of cookies, all you got was the distinct impression that your skin might melt off your face.

It was the perfect vacation spot if you hated yourself and wanted a scenic view of the apocalypse.

"Okay, this is kinda scary," I admitted to Braylor.

"Some believe life in our world started here. The fools thought that our ancestors lived here, with their gods, in the Underworld. Before time began. The story states that we were lazy, selfish and took our lives for granted. So the gods spat us out onto the ground. They want us to know hardship, pain, and loss. They understood that suffering would teach us to better appreciate the Underworld upon our deaths."

"And what do you believe?"

"I believe that Hell is a dead and lifeless kingdom containing a black mountain that spews fire and ash and smoke. But I do love what Hell provides to me. That mountain is a mighty forge that creates kath," he said, pulling his sword halfway out of the scabbard. "Kath is a gift from the land. And kath makes me happy. Therefore, Hell brings me joy."

"Not a phrase you hear every day. On my world, Hell is supposed to be this supernatural place where you go when you die—a lake of fire that they burn in for eternity. If they've been *bad* during life."

"So, telling someone to go to Hell is a curse?"

"Yep."

"Interesting. Do not share this information with Gunnr. The Valhallan elders have been known to venture down from the north, to sojourn in Hell, during their harsh winters. They love the dry heat."

"Wow. Hell is a lot like Arizona..."

We set up camp for the night in what could generously be called an alcove, tucked under the edge of a massive black rock formation. The overhang was just enough to keep the worst of the ashfall off us, which was basically the one and only perk. The red dirt around us was riddled with tiny holes, each one hissing steam like the mountain itself was breathing. One larger vent nearby caught my eye, so of course, like an idiot, I leaned in for a closer look. Yep, just as I thought—bubbling molten lava, simmering away like the world's deadliest soup. And it smelled like death, if death had eaten a lot of sulfur.

The heat was next-level awful, the kind that made every breath feel like swallowing fire. No way anyone was sleeping that night. Every time the so-called breeze stirred, it brought with it a blast of scorching air. Honestly, it was like someone had turned on a pair of industrial-strength hair dryers and aimed them directly at my eyeballs. My eyes watered constantly, but evaporated immediately.

Meanwhile, the karkadanns shuffled and huffed, clearly as over it as I was. I lay back against the rock, sweat trickling down my neck, wondering if we'd all just cook in our sleep. If not for the soul-crushing heat and the literal lava pits around us, this could've been downright cozy.... to a snowman.

Cira went off to hunt food for everyone. Except me. Which meant I had to make the same lame effort, even though I knew I'd come up empty-handed.

But I grabbed a waterskin and my bow and quiver and set out. Temurr tagged along on my adventure. He knew I was at my limit. Before we left, Braylor warned him not to make any effort to gather food on my behalf. The ape man stared at him, wiped the sweat from his hairy brow, and flicked it at the giant.

We meandered around the rocky terrain before climbing onto a harsh, black hill on which nothing grew.

"This is a real time-waster," I moaned.

"Hunting is our most important task, child. Now, whining on the other hand... is a true waste of—"

"But there's nothing here!"

"Game is plentiful, it is. Wherever you may be. You only need know *where* to look," Temurr assured. "Wait... someone approaches. Hide."

As I searched for a hiding spot, he yanked me behind an uneven row of gray boulders, the rough stone digging into my back. We peered out just in time to see a rickety, ash-caked wagon trundling along the uneven ground below. The creaking wheels sounded like they might give out at any second. Two hulking, bald goons sat on the buckboard, their scarred faces locked in scowls as they urged a pair of karkadanns forward. The beasts looked half-dead—gaunt, ribs showing, their leathery skin cracked and faded. The whole grim parade crawled steadily toward the looming black volcano in the distance.

Temurr gave a slight nod; we were clear to resume our hunt.

When I came across a pale, spiky vine entwined among slabs of rock, I plucked off one of a half dozen dark berries and held it up.

He shook his head. "The berries will not kill you, but... make you wish they had."

After an eternity, we navigated narrow ledges that clung to the rock face, scrambled down into a glassy gully carved by ancient lava flows, and trudged over a series of unforgiving hills. The oppressive heat pressed down on us like a smothering blanket, and the gnawing hunger clawed at me. Each step felt heavier than the last, and despite his usual stubbornness, he finally made me stop every so often to catch my breath. Not out of kindness, of course—more like he didn't want to deal with the drama of me collapsing on the spot.

"So, where is all this plentiful game?"

I passed him the waterskin. He drank a small sip.

"It might make sense for us to climb up a ways and travel along one of these crags."

He pointed to a massive rock mountain, full of steep cliffs and rows of rocky ledges, directly ahead of us. The thought of using up all my strength to climb seemed incredibly dumb.

"Really?"

He raised his eyebrows and repeatedly jabbed his head toward the bleak peak.

Then it hit me—the poor guy was giving me a clue and I was too addled to see it.

Without saying a word, we marched to the steep hill. He easily scaled the side of the cliff while I slipped and stumbled my way up the sharp rubble. Temurr pitied me at one point, reaching out a hairy hand to help, but I pushed it away. I was going make it on my own, dammit. That garnered me a prideful smirk from the ape man.

When we were halfway up the steep incline, we veered off onto a precarious overhang, its edge crumbling slightly under our weight. Crawling along, hands scraping the rock, we eventually came to a pockmarked boulder stubbornly blocking our path. Before I could curse the stupid thing, a flicker of movement below caught my eye. I stopped dead, peering down at a ledge about fifty feet away.

There, nestled among a tangled bed of dry twigs, was a creature about the size of a large dog. Its crimson, leathery skin gleamed faintly in the dim light, and it stretched out two thin, sinewy wings with an almost lazy grace. Its smooth, pointed tail curled and uncurled like a cat's, the tip twitching. It gave a few lazy flaps, settling deeper into its nest.

I leaned closer, heart pounding. "Wait...is that a baby dragon?"

Temurr snorted quietly. "Wyvern. Fully grown, that one is."

Great. A snack-sized monster with a Napoleon complex.

"Can I eat that? I mean... it's not some revered creature or something, is it?"

"They are pests that kill small livestock." A sly grin curled across his thin lips. "Fire away."

I slowly, quietly removed my bow and selected an arrow. I kept my eyes locked on the creature. I knew I only had one shot at this; I couldn't go another day without food. I tried to notch the arrow but my hands were shaking. I tried to swallow but my mouth was dry as dirt. I tried to focus but sweat ran into my eyes.

But I took aim anyway.

Temurr watched the tip of the arrow vibrate back and forth. "A suggestion?"

I exhaled and nodded, lowering my bow.

"Do not aim. Do not fire a single arrow."

"Um, that would take my chances of eating tonight from slim to none."

He pulled two more arrows from my quiver and handed them to me.

Three arrows. He wanted me to fire *three* arrows. I shrugged and silently stuck them in the red sand at my knee while watching the Wyvern over on the ledge.

He placed the two extra arrows up on the flat part of the boulder. I looked at him and then the arrows, unsure of what to do.

"Fire as fast as you are able."

After a deep breath, I closed my eyes. I let my mind see myself rapidly firing three arrows as fast as I could.

I was ready.

I pulled back the string. My arm still shook, but not as bad.

Before I released an arrow, Temurr reached out and pulled my bow gently away from the target.

"Now. Fire your first arrow."

My aim was completely off. I wouldn't even hit the side of the mountain.

"But... I'm not aiming at it."

"I know," purred Temurr. "You always miss your first shot."

Confused, I tried to reset myself. Deep breath. Imagine firing three arrows. In a row. Slow my heart.

I fired my arrow off into the dusty landscape below.

The Wyvern flapped its wings, two feet lifting off the rock.

I fired arrow number two, striking the cliff face behind the creature as it took flight.

Arrow number three struck the Wyvern at the base of the left wing, sending it tumbling to the ground below.

"I did it!"

"You did," agreed Temurr, staring over the edge of our boulder. "Excellent."

"How did you know I would be able to hit the thing?"

"A decent archer can fire twelve arrows in a single minute. A great one about twenty. As a novice, we noticed you could fire ten. Which is impressive. Accuracy is not your ally, but speed is."

I hugged him tight, then we hurried down the hill. The creature struggled, trying to right itself and take off again.

"End her misery."

"Her?" My heart sank. He wanted me to kill the thing.

"There is no triangle shape at the end of the tail. The Wyvern is female."

I gulped again, taking out the sword from my belt.

"I-I've never... killed anything before."

"Then today will be your first, it will."

I took several deep breaths and then held it in. The Wyvern stared straight at me, eyes filled with fear. I didn't know if I should stab it or slice down on it. So I did both. I screamed out a sad version of a war-cry and poked her hard skin, then slammed the blade down, partially cutting her body in half. Blood poured from the Wyvern as she slowly died.

Temurr winced. "Well, I suppose that will work, as well. Next time, remove the head. Causes less pain."

Regret washed over me. I had killed something *and* caused it pain. But my hunger screamed at me: stop bitching and start walking.

We raced back to camp and I held up my prize to the team, jumping up and down like an elementary school kid with her first participation trophy.

"I did it! I did it!"

Braylor gave Temurr a stern look.

"Mind your temper, Braylor. She did it all on her own," he soothed.

The giant remained unconvinced, but stood to inspect my catch. "She is rather... small. But it will serve the purpose. Cook it up and feast, girl."

"I need the tinderbox."

I looked around our little camp and spotted Temurr's sack. He had a small wood box that contained the items needed to start a fire. I grabbed the kit and set to work.

Clutching the flint in one hand, I struck it repeatedly with my knife, mimicking Temurr's nightly ritual. Sparks flew, but the stubborn little pile of dried brush refused to catch. The others sat back, grinning like idiots, clearly enjoying the show. I could hear their snickers, the occasional pointed comment followed by stifled laughter.

Minutes dragged on, and my arms grew heavy, my hands numb from the relentless effort. Meanwhile, hunger twisted my stomach into knots.

Blinking away the sweat that burned my eyes, I threw a glare over my shoulder. They didn't even try to hide their amusement. Jerks. Teeth clenched, I redoubled my effort, striking faster, harder.

Finally, just as I was about to snap, a thick finger tapped my shoulder.

I turned on Braylor. "What?!"

He pointed to one of the holes in the ground, filled with piping hot molten lava bubbling up from the ground. He handed me a long branch that had been whittled down to a stick... perfect for skewering meat.

"Hell hath no fury like a woman embarrassed..." I seethed.

His laughter echoed through the miserably hot, dark canyon.

To show me up, Cira returned triumphantly with two large Wyverns, and a few lizards thrown in for good measure.

I gave her my best fake smile.

After desperately butchering the carcass with a knife, I had my first meal in a week. It was the most disgusting, foul-tasting, painfully dry meat I have ever had and quite possibly the best thing I've ever eaten in my life.

Chapter 34

We slogged deeper into the fiery armpit of Hell, steering clear of Dis and Tartarus—two charming little towns built far enough from the volcano to avoid choking on ash, but still in the neighborhood of despair. Instead, we aimed straight for the black volcano itself.

In no time, we were a serious mess. The relentless heat turned our tempers into ticking time bombs. No one could sleep, and food became a rare commodity. The air thickened with sulfur and ash, reducing every breath to a bitter gag. With every mile, the world around us grew more hostile.

At one point, we stumbled upon an old hag who looked like she had crawled out of a soot-covered grave. She gleefully fleeced Pherric for her overpriced water—water she dispensed from a wagon that seemed held together by sheer spite. But desperate times and all that. Our karkadanns were practically keeling over from heat exhaustion.

At least I had the luxury of riding those poor beasts. Not that it made things much better. Half the time, I was stuck behind Braylor, my new least favorite person in the world. I spent most of the time boring metaphorical holes into the back of his head, replaying every moment he had been a smug, insufferable jerk. Let's not forget how he let me starve for a week, only to scoff when I finally managed to hunt down my own meal. Did he congratulate me? Nope.

He wasn't just a bully—he was a self-righteous, egotistical prick who seemed hell-bent on booting me from the group. And yet, in some twisted way, it made me wonder: was he the only one who gave a damn? I doubted it. He wanted me gone. Out of his hair for good.

The worst part? I couldn't stop staring at him. Braylor, the living storm cloud, with his perpetual scowl, condescending glare, and doom-and-gloom outlook that sucked the life out of everyone around him. His pessimism was like a slow-acting poison, seeping into the cracks of our already fragile group. And yet, there I was, hopelessly fixated.

Why? Because deep down, I envied him. The way he carried himself, like the world couldn't touch him. It wasn't the puffed-up bravado I'd seen a hundred times before. Braylor didn't need to strut around, barking like the big dog in the yard. No, he was pure smoldering energy, a predator biding its time. There was something terrifyingly real about him—he wouldn't run from a fight. He wouldn't even flinch.

And damn it, I wanted that. Just an ounce of that raw, unshakable confidence.

"Why," I muttered, shaking my head, "am I always attracted to assholes?"

Apparently, I said that out loud.

Frip looked over his hairy shoulder at me. "I am cursed with the same affliction."

I couldn't tell if he was being literal or not.

He nodded at Braylor. "He would make a good mate. Although bearing his children might rip you in half."

"Mate? Children?! No, no, no! That's not... I mean, I didn't mean that—"

Frip chuckled. "I am teasing you, dear."

As we approached the mile-wide plume of greasy, black smoke coiling up from the crater, the terrain morphed into a geological nightmare. Massive plates of volcanic rock poked skyward, like the earth's bones had been violently shoved to the surface by the roiling magma below.

We picked our way along knife-thin ridges and plunging valleys, the sharp remains of lava flows long since turned to stone but still looking like they'd like to ruin your day. The peaks around us were downright menacing, like some cosmic dentist had yanked out a giant's rotting teeth and left them to claw at the smoke above in defiance.

The ground underfoot wasn't much better. It radiated heat, like the earth itself was sweating and annoyed we were even here. The whole place screamed "land born of fire," and we were the idiots trespassing on its turf.

Pherric and Cira slowed and made their way alongside Frip's karkadann.

"Interested in seeing a lake of fire?"

Flashbacks to when my grandparents had dragged me to Sunday School in the summer popped into my head. I recalled the teachers reminding us that every sinner would burn for all eternity in a fiery pit in Hell.

I reluctantly nodded.

We dismounted and scrambled up the slope of the crater. Heat blazed down on us. Sulfur burned the inside of my nose. Embers drifted up and the thick ash made it hard to breathe. We pulled up our tunics, covering our mouths. All across the rim of the plateau, flames leapt up and dropped down in.

"I knew I should've taken that gap year in Paris. Or Tijuana. But Hell? Wasn't even in the top three."

Sweat slicked my back as we clawed our way to the crater's edge, every movement dragging more heat into my lungs. When I finally peered over, my jaw dropped. Below us stretched an immense, churning cauldron of molten lava, a hellish sea of fire. The surface bubbled and hissed, sending plumes of searing gas skyward. Occasionally, a jet of lava erupted, arching high before crashing back into the roiling inferno, folding in on itself like molten serpents swallowing their tails.

The heat was suffocating, baking my face until my skin might crack. We flattened ourselves on the ground, trying to stay away from the worst of the rising flames. I squinted across the glowing expanse, but the crater was so vast that the opposite rim seemed to blur into the shimmering haze. It was as though the planet had opened its jaws wide and decided never to close them again.

"Shouldn't I be throwing a ring in here, or something?" I mumbled.

The lava belched up in streams of hot liquid. I started seeing those shapes as the arms of people, reaching up to the heavens, as they burned alive. I saw heads and full torsos pop up, writhing in agony, in those lava formations. If this were ancient times and I saw this display? Well... it was easy to see how someone might believe that souls were burning in a hellfire of eternal damnation.

"Holy Hell." A sudden realization hit me like a ton of bricks. "Pherric?"

He squinted from the fiery heat as he watched the cauldron below. "Yes?"

"I'm not the only person from Earth to have been brought to Tir Na, am I?"

He held up his hand to block the blaze. "We must leave now."

We scrambled back down the side of the mountain.

"To answer your question," Pherric said, helping me jump over a small river of lava. "You are likely not the only Terran to be brought to our world."

"So, there are people from Earth here now?"

"That, I doubt. Use of the Godsribbon has been banned for hundreds of years. But there are records within the Scholomance of people being conducted back and forth. Why do you ask?"

"Well, I don't know. It's just that... well, seeing the things that I've seen so far... So much of our myths and folklore," I stammered, looking back up at the crater. "And even our religions are based on things that seemed too crazy back on Earth. But.. they're actually *real* here! I mean being in Hell and seeing a lake of fire? And the Wyverns?! And–and even Kasuma! She's a woman in white who can fly! That would be the very definition of an angel on my world. Put a bow and arrow in her hand and she's Cupid! What if, a thousand years ago, someone was dragged to Tir Na and saw all these things? And... and they were sent back to Earth? The stories they could tell! And all of this could have been the basis for the legends that got passed down, generation after generation..."

He picked up whatever mindform was firing off from my head. "I believe you have made an important connection for your species. And your world.

Just as we still have many questions about the origins of the gods who made this world and left so much of their magic behind."

I hustled to keep up with Pherric, as he bounded down the slope to escape the heat and fumes.

"The *gods*... Who were they?" I wondered, trying to corral all the wild thoughts racing around in my head.

"I did not have time to explore the subject in the Scholomance archives. However, most references to them were purposely vague and highly reverential."

"Kind of like your *prophecy?*" I pulled my tunic down from my mouth, flashed him a grin.

He glared at me with deadly serious eyes.

A sharp crack echoed through the air, followed by the muffled din of distant voices. Pherric went rigid mid-step, his head snapping toward the sound. Without a word, he veered off course, scrambling along the steep incline. I hesitated, glancing back toward the relative safety of our path, then cursed under my breath and took off after him. My boots slipped on the loose gravel as I raced to catch up.

We dropped behind a mound of reddish lava rock, pressing ourselves flat against the scorching surface. Carefully, we peeked over the top. Below us lay a sprawling valley, carved long ago by the relentless flow of burning rock. Over time, human hands had reshaped the terrain, transforming the ancient river of fire into a hive of brutal industry.

Dirt roads snaked down the steep ravine, zigzagging like veins feeding a diseased heart. Yawning magma vents had been hollowed out into caves, their mouths propped open with weathered wooden beams. Makeshift cranes, fashioned from rough timber, groaned under the weight of ropes, buckets, and pulleys used to haul up who-knew-what from the depths below. The whole place pulsed with a grim rhythm, a bleak symphony of creaking wood and faint, tortured cries.

"The kath mines of Vulca," Pherric muttered, his voice tight with dread. His eyes darted frantically across the valley, scanning every movement like a cornered animal.

Thousands of people, of nearly every species, trudged down the paths carrying heavy loads. Shirtless guards cracked thick whips and screamed at the workers. Giant men pushed loaded mining carts out of the valley.

"And?"

Gunnr and the rest rushed up to join us on our overhang. Frip gasped and Braylor let out an angry growl.

"What's going on?" I asked, staring at their horrified faces. "What's wrong?"

Kasuma popped up over my shoulder, startling me. "The Kath Guild, made up of alchemancers, controls this mine. They are nowhere to be seen. And there has never been this much activity."

"They are depleting the kath, they are!" Temurr raged.

"So, who are all those people?" I asked.

"Slaves..." said Braylor, through gritted teeth.

One of the workers, a Hominan, carrying a heavy bucket, slipped on the path and spilled his load of gray dirt. A bald guard snapped his whip, striking the man. A dark, bloody cut spread across his shoulder and back. As the poor guy struggled to scoop the dirt into the pail, the guard whipped him again.

"I'm so confused."

Kasuma patiently grasped my shoulders. "Those are Irkallan soldiers. Malek has taken control of this mine from the guild, and—"

"And he uses slaves to over-mine the kath!" Braylor pushed up from the edge.

Pherric leapt to his feet, grabbing Braylor's arm. "No, Braylor! We can do nothing! We will be exposed!"

Braylor easily shook off Pherric's grip. "Those are my brothers and sisters down there!"

"You cannot save them!" shouted Gunnr.

Braylor withdrew his massive long sword. "Then I will die trying..."

The giant spun on a heel and sprinted down the side of the volcano.

We all looked at each other, wondering if we should abandon him or go after him.

Frip exhaled. "Why does Braylor have to be such a...a—"

"Such a Braylor?" I snarked.

He squeezed my hand.

"We need him," I pleaded with Pherric.

A snarl passed his lips, but he nodded.

"We shall try to stop him from doing something foolish."

With that, we darted down the steep hill toward our karkadanns.

Chapter 35

Braylor vaulted onto his karkadann and raced ahead, charging toward the base of the looming volcano. We scrambled after him, struggling to keep up, the oppressive ash dragging at our heels. At the edge of the valley, we concealed our beasts behind a black formation of cooled lava, its warped surface resembling a frozen cascade of thick oil.

With our heads low and crouching down deep, Gunnr and I slipped into the valley of the Kath Guild's mining operation. Hundreds of canvas tents sprawled across the valley floor, each sheltering a blacksmith drenched in sweat. We heard the rhythmic clanging of massive hammers against raw metal, the sound ricocheting off the steep ravine walls like a chaotic symphony.

Closer to the towering stone forges, the true lifeblood of the operation, slaves heaved carts filled with ingots of raw metal. Their blistered hands and bowed backs told the story of an endless toil. From deep within the mines, more laborers emerged, straining under the weight of freshly unearthed ore, eyes hollow from exhaustion.

The massive forges blazed like the very heart of the volcano, feeding on the ore used to churn out sword blades, spear and arrowheads. Irkallan guards prowled the area, ensuring the relentless production line never faltered, their cold eyes scanning for the faintest hint of disobedience.

I spotted Braylor bent down behind a stack of wooden crates. "There he is!"

Gunnr pulled me back behind an ash-stained tent with her strong grip. She pointed to the bloody body of a soldier, lying next to another tent—

Braylor had already introduced himself.

"Retrieve him. Now," she commanded.

"Why me?"

"Because he listens to you—you got him through the narrow tunnel under Quivira. And because... you are small."

I rolled my eyes so hard at the Amazon warrior that I think I saw my brain. But she was right. And I knew it wasn't going to be easy. I needed a new approach. One of my father's old tactics, when trying to deal with me, popped into my head.

After waiting for a patrolling Irkallan to pass, I dropped low and raced over to Braylor, hiding behind his massive frame.

"Do not attempt to deter me, little one," he warned.

"Oh, I wouldn't think of it."

"There are Fomorians being held..." He turned to look at me with his surprised face. "Truly?"

"Try to stop you? Are you kidding me? You're as stubborn and difficult as I am. So I know there's no changing your mind."

Perplexed, he shifted his gaze back to the slaves. "Good."

"So, do we have a plan?"

He swiveled around, grinding the red dirt under his boots. "Yes, the plan is for you to rejoin the others and remain safe."

"Oh. Well. That's a stupid plan. You see... if you're going to die, I'll have to die as well. So, where do we start? Do we just run out there with our swords and start slashing away until the Irkallans kill us? Or, and I really like this, do we get captured and put in chains... and we die slowly doing all this slave work?"

"Finley..."

"It'll be kind of neat dying in Hell. Save them the effort of having to drag my sinful soul here later."

"Leave this place at once!"

Braylor actually growled at me. I didn't flinch. But I did have to spit out a huge ash flake that fell in my mouth.

"So, if you're going to let these guys kill me," I stated. "Let's get it over with. Right now, big guy."

The creak of wooden wheels cut through my half-baked attempt at reverse psychology. We craned our necks around the stack of crates, drawn by the harsh clanking of chains. A towering Fomorian emerged, his every step a sluggish, reluctant march as he pushed a cart overloaded with raw metal blades toward a swordsmith's tent.

Like Braylor, he bore the telltale features of his kind—heavy brow, high cheekbones—but this one stood well over eight feet tall, his immense frame radiating brute strength. The resemblance ended there. His scalp was scorched clean, and his back and shoulders were a brutal canvas of whip scars. Worst of all was his expression: a hollow, dead-eyed stare that spoke of a spirit long since broken, crushed beneath the unrelenting weight of hard work and suffering.

"Brother," Braylor hissed as loudly as he dared. "Brother!"

The Fomorian finally looked in our direction but turned away when he saw us, as if he couldn't be bothered by our existence.

Braylor edged around the stack of crates. He noticed the chains binding the giant's legs and arms.

"I shall free you!"

Braylor lowered himself as much as he could and started toward the cart. The giant suddenly realized we were there. His eyes widened.

"Get back!" He held up his thick hand.

Braylor drew his broadsword. "You are coming with us!"

Still in a stupor, the Fomorian watched as Braylor's blade cut through the chain between his wrists.

"No..." whispered the giant.

Braylor leapt behind the captive and shattered the chain holding his huge legs.

"I cannot." Utter defeat in those words.

Braylor dragged the giant behind the wood boxes.

"You will," Braylor announced. "We must cut free as many as we can. And I need your help. But I am alone here..."

He held out his sword. The downtrodden giant pulled back his massive shoulders, standing upright for the first time.

He turned to look down on Braylor. "Do you not believe I could have attempted escape by now? Little one?"

Braylor lowered his sword.

"That I would not have willingly died in battle... rather than slave away under their whip?" His dark eyes sparkled at the thought of a glorious death.

"You wish to... stay?" Braylor was way past confused.

"I must stay."

"Why?"

"These troggs hold captive my mate and children. If I do not do as they wish, they will kill my family."

Braylor looked away from the giant towering over him.

Lakes formed in my eyes.

"Please leave with us. Now," he begged.

"I must stay. For them."

Anger flashed across Braylor's face and he offered up his broadsword again.

"This slime would not waste the resources to house your families! You know that! You know your family is gone!"

The giant grabbed Braylor's tunic and jerked him in close.

"Do not, little one! Do not take away the only thing I have left!"

Braylor attempted to look around at the miserable camp. "What?! What do you have left?"

"I have hope, mongrel. Do not steal that from me!"

He released Braylor and his face went blank. He plodded back to his cart. We watched in pain as he willfully went back to his grind, with his broken chains dangling, as if nothing had happened.

I seized the moment, grabbing Braylor's arm, and pulled on him as he stood there in shock.

"We gotta go. Now. Or we'll end up just like him!"

I watched him struggle as his eyes darted around the compound. He wanted to reach out to the others of his kind, and even took a step towards them, but must have quickly realized that those who wanted to leave were already dead.

"Braylor. Please?"

He shook my hand from his arm and marched off, forcing me to hunch over and scamper after him.

We managed to slip out of the mining camp—barely. Braylor, of course, needed constant reminding that stealth involves *not* acting like you're itching for a fight. We had to shove him into hiding more times than I could count whenever Irkallan soldiers strolled by, and let me tell you, he wasn't exactly cooperative about it.

As for escaping Hell? Yeah, that was a whole saga. Pherric's "quick getaway" turned into days of dodging patrols, sneaking past busy roads, and skirting sketchy little villages where every shadow looked like it had a sword. By the time we finally rode out of those cursed, smoke-choked black mountains, I nearly cried when fresh air hit my face.

The desert stretched out before us, a gorgeous spread of dark red sands, bright orange rock formations, and a sky so blue it almost hurt. And suddenly, all I wanted was to run—like, *really* run, just to remind myself that we were finally free.

I hopped off Braylor's karkadann and jogged alongside for as long as I could. It felt good to show off to the others a little—that I would choose to run rather than be forced to—but I had also become somewhat *addicted* to the feeling. Considering my mom was a lush and I came from a line of hard-drinking cops, that sounded about right. I could no longer avoid the urge to sprint and jump on the rocks and dash ahead of the others.

And it didn't hurt that I had started developing those lines in my legs, as my muscles got stronger. I had never had *any* kind of definition like that before and I wanted more of that. But I would have killed for a decent body lotion—the skin on my legs was as leathery as that damned Wyvern I had to eat.

After a week of riding, we traveled up from the low valley and dry barren land and into a woodland region. I jumped into the first small pond we encountered and soaked in the warm, beautiful water the way anyone would lounge in a luxurious bathtub.

I watched Braylor cup his hand and take distracted sips of the fresh water. He had kept even more quiet than usual after we left that slave camp, as if his own bit of remaining hope had been crushed under a swordsmith's hammer. I wanted desperately to hold him, let him know I was there for him... but knew he would never allow it.

I kicked myself for being drawn to him. I have always felt a strong connection to the slightly damaged. The disaffected. Maybe not the bad boys, but... the more rebellious ones. Like me. Not that I had a ton of those annoying college boys constantly throwing themselves at me. As the slightly chunky monkey, I was always the sidekick. On most nights out, I only had to deal with the random chubby-chaser or fight off an end-of-the-party drunken frat boy. For me, alone in my dorm, my lovers were usually named Ben and Jerry. Single as a Pringle, that was me.

But having seen a more emotional side of him, I found myself watching him in a more... longing way. His every move intrigued me. That black hair of his had grown out a little over the last few months and I wanted to run my fingers through that mane. And, yes, I wanted him to kiss me. Fiercely. I could feel his arms wrapped around me, pulling me in close.

Sitting in the pond water, I realized I had fallen into one of my thousand-yard stares and I quickly snapped out of it.

Gunnr laughed at me. She had caught me scoping out Braylor.

Embarrassed, I dragged myself out of the perfect pond and stormed off.

Chapter 36

I avoided eye contact with Gunnr for most of the day. That night, I cooked up a jackalope that required seven arrows to take down. And that was after I trapped it against a fallen tree. The others feasted on a white deer with a gold horn on its head, unironically called a Goldenhorn, that Temurr had hunted. Their meal smelled delicious, while my skinny rabbit with antlers tasted like rancid turkey that had been left out to rot on the kitchen counter of a crack house.

While we ate, Gunnr fawned over Braylor. She laughed whenever he mumbled, randomly touched his arm, and even placed her hand on his leg. She'd then glance at me and smirk, causing rage to burn inside me—and I really wanted to cut the bitch.

"Finley."

The whole Gunnr thing was weird because I'm not the jealous type. But I was forced to deal with the fact that Tir Na might have turned me slightly feral.

"Finley!"

I was thousand-yard-staring again.

"What?"

Everyone around the fire was looking at me, grinning.

"Join us please?" asked Pherric.

I shuffled over to sit next to Frip.

"As I was saying, we are dangerously close to Irkalla. We must find a way to cross the river Styx. With all the weapons being transported into their kingdom, we have to assume that taking any of the ferries across is no longer an option."

"I refuse to swim, wizard," announced Braylor.

Gunnr laughed uproariously, touched his arm. Again. The damn old hag.

Pherric drew two long, wavy lines in the dirt. He loved drawing lines in the dirt.

"For the most part, the Styx is wide and the current strong. The narrowest crossing point would be several axims to the east, here," he said, pointing to his lines. "But Lord Diago warned me that Malek is reinforcing the weakest points along his border. So... we may meet some resistance."

Frip, sitting beside me, explained as though I were a child. "He means we will have to kill some Irkallans."

"Yeah, I got that. Thanks," I patted his hairy hand.

"I did not say kill, Frip," Pherric corrected.

Frip covered his mouth.

"But, in this instance... it may be necessary," Pherric added. "If we are to have any chance of success, we cannot be seen crossing the border."

"This would be a good opportunity," said Kasuma. "For Finley and I to train on our Nonshi techniques."

Part of my sessions with the winged lady involved this next-level kung fu movie shit she called Nonshi. Kasuma said the translation to the Queen's Language was *silent warrior*. But it sounded an awful lot like ninja. We practiced throwing knives and sharp metal stars, using thin ropes to strangle opponents, and dropping metal spikes to hobble pursuers. She even helped me put together my own Nonshi tool kit.

Pherric sat up straight. "Well, this is not the appropriate time to—"

"To kill her first Irkallan? Why not?" challenged Kasuma. "If she is to be involved in the attempt to assassinate Malek, she will need the experience."

Holy shit. All of my training and preparation had seemed like play time. None of it seemed real until that moment. We were almost in Irkalla. And I was part of their plan. To be involved in the death of a king. I gulped hard.

Pherric stared at me, sensing my fear.

He turned to Kasuma to object, but he had no argument. He lowered his head, nodding.

The mighty rush of a river echoed somewhere ahead, weaving through the trees. A soft breeze whispered through the leaves above, insects chirped their nightly tunes, and all those lovely forest sounds did their best to mask my constant screw-ups.

I stepped on a branch, creating a loud crack that reverberated through the forest. *CRACK.* The sound exploded through like a gunshot. I locked up, heart hammering, straining to hear if anyone else had noticed. Only Kasuma, of course.

I spotted her twenty feet away, gliding around a thin tree as if she were made of shadows. Normally, Kasuma wore white—something about blending in with the sky when she flew. But tonight, she was all sleek black: a sleeveless cloak that clung to her like a second skin, her wings free and ready for action. She'd even made me dress the part, shoving me into a heavy, dark cloak with the hood up, and wrapping my face in thin black fabric until only my eyes peeked out. It was suffocating in the warm night air, but complaining wasn't an option.

Kasuma pointed at the narrow path ahead. No guards. The riverbank was ours.

We crept forward and crawled onto a large, flat rock that projected out over the Styx. An evening mist clung to the water, swirling above its churning surface. We lay still, watching the opposite shore. Nothing but trees and shadows. The coast was literally clear.

My eyes drifted to the water below, where the river's frothy current surged past, fast and unforgiving. Swimming across? Not an option unless you wanted to end up miles downstream—or worse.

A cold knot of dread coiled in my stomach. This was real. This was *happening.* And despite Kasuma's presence, I felt utterly, crushingly alone. My chest tightened, and nausea crept in. I shut my eyes, forcing myself to take slow, steady breaths. *In, out, focus.*

Then Kasuma's head tilted slightly, motioning toward a darker patch of forest across the river. The signal was clear. It was time.

"There. Soldiers," she whispered, over the roar of the river.

"How do you know?"

She carefully pointed her forehead at the woods again. I noticed a thin column of smoke rising from the top of the trees—a campfire.

"Listen."

At first, only the sound of the water... and then insects filled my ears. I focused, trying to sift through the ambient noise, until I heard what she had heard—the low rumble of men talking. Several of them laughed.

"Remove your kit."

I slipped the rolled-up cloth from my belt and unfurled the dark fabric to reveal my tools—several thin ropes with knots, a knife, two smooth rocks, two metal spikes, four sharp metal throwing stars, and a hollow stick.

Kasuma pointed to the stick. I removed it and slid the kit under my belt.

"I will take you as far as I can but they may hear the splash. Stay under the water and wait, breathing through your stick."

The fear inside me bubbled over again. She was going to fly me over the water, drop me in, and I was supposed to breathe through a tiny stick. I could feel the blood drain from my face.

Swallowing back the bile that had wormed its way up my throat, I nodded.

Kasuma stood, her wings unfurling like a flag stretching over the rock. I clenched the hollow tube between my teeth, biting down hard enough to leave marks, and got to my feet behind her. My arms slipped around her waist, careful but firm.

She exhaled slowly, glancing back at me. "Run."

No time to second-guess. I bolted alongside her, our feet slamming against the rock in perfect rhythm.

"Jump."

We leapt together. Her wings snapped open, catching the night air as they pounded down, over and over, with all the force she could muster. My stomach flipped as the rock fell away beneath us. For a glorious second, we soared.

But gravity wasn't going to make it easy. Each heavy beat of her wings bought us less and less altitude. The river rushed below, dangerously close. By the time we reached the halfway point, our feet were practically skimming the churning water.

"Now!" Kasuma barked.

I let go, rolling off her and plummeting toward the Styx. She shot upward, wings suddenly free of my weight, disappearing into the dark.

I wasn't so lucky. The river slapped into me like a wall of ice, pulling the breath from my lungs. My scream turned into a bubbling mess underwater.

I rolled over, kicking hard toward the surface, but the current yanked me downstream. My limbs flailed as I fought to stay afloat, panic rising with every second. Just when my lungs felt ready to burst, my hand slammed into something solid—a rock.

I latched onto it, clutching tight with both arms as the river tried to tear me away. *Not today.* Dragging myself inch by inch, I reached a tree limb jutting from the bank and hauled my body onto the shallows.

Water streamed off me as I stayed low, keeping my head barely above the surface, heels digging into the muddy riverbed. I lay there, gasping quietly, every muscle trembling, waiting for the pounding of my heart to settle.

When I looked up, a soldier stood on the beach, his gaze fixed on the churning river.

My lungs screamed for air. Slowly, I raised the hollow tube clamped between my teeth from the muddy water. Carefully, I blew it clean and took a shallow, desperate drag. The sharp taste of river mud hit the back of my throat, but I didn't care—I could breathe.

The soldier paced the riverbank, his boots crunching on the gravel, stopping occasionally to peer into the Styx. The narrow tube could barely deliver enough air to keep me steady, and panic slithered into my thoughts.

The soldier stopped. Right above me.

Breathe, Finley. Just breathe. I clung to Kasuma's mantra. Air in. Air out. Slow the heart. *In... out...* My grip tightened on the stick as I focused on counting. One, two, three in. One, two, three out.

When I finally opened my eyes, the soldier was gone. But I didn't move. Not yet. I took several more cautious breaths, each one steadier than the last. Then, inch by inch, I started to rise. First my nose broke the surface, then my eyes. Water dripped down, but I didn't flinch.

The beach was clear.

Keeping just my eyes above the sloshing current, I flipped onto my stomach and waited, straining my ears for any sign of the soldier. Nothing but the rush of the Styx.

Following Kasuma's instructions, I inched out of the water like a ghost, trying not to make a sound. Every droplet sliding off my cloak echoed in the quiet night. Five agonizing minutes later, I was free of the river, slinking low on my hands and toes across the muddy bank.

I darted into the cover of the trees, where Kasuma waited, crouched behind a thicket of leaves. She gave me a curt nod, her expression unreadable, and without a word, we slipped deeper into the shadowy embrace of the Irkallan forest.

Chapter 37

We worked our way through the dense woods, heading toward the Irkallan soldiers clustered around their campfire. Kasuma moved like a light fog, drifting over the forest floor without so much as rustling a leaf. Meanwhile, I sounded like a bull stomping through a luxury tableware shop on Park Avenue.

Neither of us heard the soldier returning from the riverbank.

Focused on Kasuma's progress, I cautiously stepped over twigs and avoided dried leaves, watching as she suddenly froze mid-step. Her wings folded tightly around her, and she melted into the darkness. My stomach clenched. She'd spotted something.

A crunch of boots on stone hit my ears, coming from the path behind me. My breath stopped. I turned, catching a glimpse of the soldier's silhouette through the trees. Moving quickly but quietly, I backed up to a thick trunk, pressing myself against the rough bark. I slid down into a crouch, tucking my chin to my chest.

Breathe. Slow your heart. The words pounded in my head as I fought to control the rising panic. I counted my breaths, willing my body to be still. A statue. A lifeless stone.

The soldier's footsteps halted.

He was close. Too close. My ears strained, every nerve in my body screaming for escape. Had he heard me?

Crunch. Another step. Slow, deliberate. His boot snapped a twig, the sound impossibly loud.

My pulse thundered in my ears. He shifted again, quieter this time, stepping off the path. The faint swish of his pant leg brushing against low branches sent my panic into overdrive.

I dared to glance up.

Big mistake.

The soldier's eyes locked on mine, and his hand flew to his sword. The unmistakable *shing* of metal echoed through the trees.

I stood up straight, turning to run.

Over my shoulder, I heard a gurgling noise.

I looked back to see Kasuma grab the soldier's body and lower him to the forest floor. She extracted a bloody knife from his back.

She pointed at him. I quietly stepped in and helped her lift the dead body. I wanted to take him deeper into the woods but she shook her head and pointed to her ears—it would make too much noise.

As Kasuma wiped her knife clean on her cloak, she glared at me. I hated that look. I had let her down. Again.

Kasuma placed her lips impossibly close to my ear and whispered. "Three men. Around the fire. Kill the one on our left. Work fast or they will come looking for *him*."

When I looked up, she was gone.

I pulled my knife from the kit in my belt.

I started to process everything. If these men were sitting around a fire, they'd be facing each other. Because she was so silent and quick, she was most likely already in place... waiting for me—to go first.

My throat dried up. My heart thumped. Beads of sweat ran down my face.

I had to kill a man...

I stepped cautiously onto the path, each step deliberate and soundless. The orange glow of the campfire flickered ahead, casting dull shadows that danced like restless ghosts. My pulse quickened as I drew closer, the low murmur of voices threading through the still night.

Sliding behind a cluster of trees at the edge of the campfire, I peered around a wide trunk. A group of Irkallan soldiers, sitting in a loose circle.

One soldier sat on a log no more than five feet in front of me, close enough for me to see the soot smudged across his jaw. His gaze was fixed on another soldier, who stood gesturing wildly as he spun a tale of a brutal war battle.

These men were no ordinary grunts. They sat with an air of casual confidence, but their hands never strayed far from the hilts of their swords. They had seen some things.

I swallowed hard, my fingers brushing the dagger at my side. *What the hell am I doing here?*

I crawled on all fours until I was at the edge of the clearing. I dropped to my belly and crawled up behind the target with my knife gripped in my teeth. Red dirt stuck to my clammy hands, but I grabbed the blade. I was too scared to exhale.

Convinced the soldier could hear my pulse pounding in my neck, he shocked me by laughing at the guy telling the story.

Time was running out. I pushed myself up, then onto my feet while staying in the soldier's shadow.

One of the men spoke. "Where's Tello? He should have returned by now."

My guy looked over toward the path. If he moved in either direction, the others would see me—it was now or never.

I leapt from my crouched position, grabbed his forehead with my hand, and put the knife to his throat and...

I couldn't do it. I was paralyzed.

Kasuma darted from the darkness, slicing her knife across the neck of a soldier. A string of blood spurted into their campfire. She lunged after the other man, driving her knife into his chest.

My soldier stood and swatted me with his long arm, sending me flying against a tree at the edge of their clearing. He towered over me, drawing his sword from his scabbard.

For a brief moment, I expected Kasuma's blade to slice his neck or stab him in the chest—but she did not rescue me this time. The soldier snarled at me, raising his sword to drive it through my chest. Without thinking, I leaned forward and slashed my knife across his shin. When the blade caught bone, I shoved it deep into his calf.

The soldier bellowed, doubling over in pain, and fell back against the log. I rolled away, bounced to my feet, and rushed him with my knife. He batted me away with one hand and gripped his injured leg with the other.

I started to slash him but he raised his arm to block me. Halfway through my swing, I dropped my arm with the knife down and stabbed at him.

My knife plunged through his black tunic and into his heart. He gasped as his eyes went wide and mouth fell open. Like a falling tree, he slowly dropped backward into the fire.

I had just... killed someone. To death.

Panting hard, hands shaking, I let go of the bloody knife. When my whole body began to shake, I dropped to the forest floor. Tears flowed as I rocked back and forth.

Kasuma, arms crossed, was probably mad that I didn't kill the guy faster. Looking for other soldiers, she dashed off into the darkness.

I screamed when I looked at the soldier's boots dangling in the air. I looked down, only to see the blood splatter on my hands. When I caught a whiff of his burning flesh that had fallen onto the fire... I turned away and blew chunks.

Several minutes passed by. Or maybe hours. Kasuma returned to the camp. She scooped up my knife, wiped the blood off on the pant leg of the dead soldier, and handed it to me.

"Never leave a weapon behind."

She pulled me to my feet.

"I–I... I–I—"

"Yes, you have killed a man. It does get easier. This will not be the last death at your hand, Finley. Now, we must let the others know so they can cross the river. We need to get away from the border."

"Oh... okay," I stammered. I avoided looking at the body as she guided me away from the campfire.

"Move!"

In a daze, my body shaking uncontrollably, she marched me through the forest toward the River Styx.

Chapter 38

I remember nothing from meeting up with the others or helping everyone across the river. I was in shock, shivering uncontrollably. When the hero blows away a bad guy on TV, everything seems effortless—there are no consequences. Everything about the killing looks.... easy. Too damn easy. But there was *nothing* easy about it. I ended someone.

I felt raw and exposed. Scared. But the numbness that followed was horrifying, as if I were the one who died. I existed but was no longer alive, merely going through the motions. Kasuma had told me that it gets easier. But I could not see it, how murdering someone could ever possibly become normal. Well, not for any *sane* person. The look of sheer terror on that Irkallan's face was permanently etched in my memory.

At some point that night, in the dark woods, Pherric gave me a hug. And my knees gave out and I fell apart, sobbing uncontrollably.

"I am so sorry, Finley. I thank the gods you are unharmed, but I never should have put you through that."

"No, no. It's not your fault. I need to grow up eventually," I said, wiping my nose on his tunic. "This is the world I live in now, I guess."

He held my head to his chest. "I am sad that you had to kill. But subduing a warrior requires skill you do not yet possess."

I pushed away from him, wiping away the tears. "I'm sorry if I let you down."

Pherric looked me in the eyes and gave me a fatherly smile.

"I want you to know that you make me very proud. You have made amazing progress, Finley Maguire."

Tears flowed I threw myself against him, more from his kind words than the anxiety from killing the soldier. Words I doubted I had ever heard from my family.

We rode north through the Irkallan wilderness during the day, and the dead soldier visited my dreams every night. When I managed to fall asleep, my mind kept conjuring up the soldier. He would rise from the campfire flames, grinning down at me mercilessly. Or he'd chase me through the dark woods. I woke from nearly every nightmare screaming, flailing, sweating. Poor Frip would be there to hold me and soothe me back to sleep, only to have it all start over again.

On a rainy afternoon, Temurr rode alongside the karkadann I shared with Braylor. To lift my spirits, he tried a more unorthodox approach.

"Are you busy, Finley? Or just... *killing* time?"

I stayed quiet.

"Most likely you are plotting your next assassination..."

He got my harshest glare.

"Whoa. If a look could *kill*, that one might do it," he said, trying not to laugh.

I stared off in the distance.

"Still, I wonder how you will *execute* your plot. You see, if it were me, I'd *dispatch* several schemes and... *do away* with the mediocre ideas. Simply... cut them to pieces. Then *put down*... well, *eliminate* the ones that—"

"Fuck off, Temurr."

The adorable ape man feigned shock and surprise. And he received a faint, ever-so-slight smirk in return.

Temurr started galloping away. "Well, then... *fuck off*, I shall."

During rest periods, I caught Braylor looking my way, but he had no words of comfort. Nothing to offer to try to cheer me up. Only a look of disdain; a look he wore frequently.

Our group maintained our routine of steering clear of roads, cities, and towns. We scavenged food from nearby farms and hunted creatures drawn to the streams snaking through Irkalla's dense woodlands.

As the sun dipped below another horizon, casting long shadows over our weary group, we trudged through a forest of spindly, skeletal trees. Frip had assured me that these woods would shield us from prying eyes near the bustling trading city of Ker-Is, keeping the Irkallans off our trail.

The quiet was broken by Cira, crashing through the underbrush on her bare, hairy feet. She skidded to a stop in front of Pherric, chest heaving, her eyes wide with alarm.

"We've got a problem!" She pointed a shaky finger toward the path ahead.

Braylor and Gunnr pulled blades from scabbards. Pherric tried to calm his nervous kark as it hopped around in fear of the feral Cira.

"Are we in danger?" he asked, his eyes darting around the woods.

Rather than answer she grabbed his leg.

"Something is wrong here," she whispered. "Head north."

"But the main road is—"

"North. Yes."

He pulled her onto the saddle in front of him, handing her the reins.

By the time the sun dropped below the trees, we emerged from the cover of our forest. At the bottom of our low hill, a cobblestone road snaked through a vast open field of tall grasses and around groves of trees.

"Cira, this is not a good idea," said Braylor. "We could be spotted. Malek has spies everywhere."

"You think I do not know this, Braylor?" asked Cira. "But do you not see it?"

Braylor grunted. "I see nothing."

"That is the problem. This road north leads to Agartha." She pointed off to our right. "Only an axim east is the Great Crossroads of Irkalla, containing all their trade routes. They run to the Black City, over to Mag Mell and Pandæmonia, and back down to Hell."

Braylor "We are aware, Cira. But what does—"

"This road goes on to Agartha, but also provides trade for northern Irkalla, Hyperborea and on to Kunlun to the east. And *no one* travels on it?!"

"The hour is late, girl. What of it?" scoffed the giant. "Since Malek's reign began, all trade has diminished. I am sure all roads are lightly traveled these—"

She hustled up to his side. "But not empty. Not during the day. When I scouted ahead, the sun yet stood high in the sky and no caravans were about. Ker-Is sits right at the Crossroads. One of the most populous trade centers in the kingdom. This makes little sense!"

Pherric lowered his head. "Something is, indeed, wrong then."

Her face turned bright red. She kicked the karkadann and raced down the small hill we stood on, with Pherric barely hanging on to her.

"Cira! No! It's too dangerous!" The giant growled, snapped his own reins, and we all chased after her.

Temurr shouted ahead to everyone. "If you see any Irkallans, turn and run! We have come too far to have it all end here!"

No one seemed to have a problem with that, but I couldn't see us leaving Cira behind. For any reason.

We struggled to keep up as Pherric and Cira bolted ahead, her bare feet kicking the karkadann hard in the sides, before veering sharply toward the Great Crossroads. The city loomed in the distance—a once-proud fortress with white walls, now smudged and stained by smoke. No massive dragon shields overhead, just four round towers anchored at each corner, crowned with charred white spires.

Rows of scorched fruit trees lined the path leading to the city. The iron gates stood wide open, and the air hung thick with eerie silence. No bustling crowds. No guards. The only sign of life was a lone, tattered flag fluttering weakly atop one of the soot-darkened towers. It looked less like a city and more like a ghost of one.

Cira and Pherric disappeared through the gaping gates. The rest of us slowed, shields up. Braylor, Gunnr, and Temurr scanned the walls and towers, searching for any hint of danger. Kasuma slipped off the back of Gunnr's kark and, with a snap of her wings, vanished into the black sky, a shadow against the ruins of the pale walls.

We walked our karkadanns up to the main gate, past hundreds of wooden spears supporting decapitated heads, their eyes and tongues long gone.

"Oh, dear god," I muttered. "Whose... heads were those?"

"Bànshēn rén." Frip covered his eyes. "They are Cira's people." I could feel his heart breaking along with mine.

We passed through the gate towers and into Ker-Is. After a massive half-circle courtyard, a wide main street cut through the center of the city with narrower side streets branching off to the sides like a wagon wheel. Debris from burned merchant tents and booths clogged the roads. Small smoked-stained stone buildings stood alongside the charred remains of wood and plaster houses. Fire had destroyed everything.

Bodies of the men, women, and children littered the streets and doorways and stone steps. As we journeyed deeper into the courtyard, the smell of dead and rotting flesh hit us.

Pherric and Cira rode back into the courtyard from a side street, her fist holding the reins was as bright red as her face. Tears began to roll, staining her dusty cheeks. She seemed very close to her *berserker* mode as she panted hard and her eyes danced all about, looking for someone to kill.

Blood from the dead had soaked into the dirt, creating dried pools of dark burgundy. Spatter stood out in sharp contrast against the white walls. I turned away when I saw a woman's body whose stomach had been sliced open and she had died trying to hold it all in.

I took a deep breath and whispered at Frip to take my mind off that sight. "So, wait. The Bànshēn rén did this?" I pulled my tunic up over my nose.

"No!" Cira snapped her head in my direction, her teeth bared.

"Why not?" Gunnr's contempt was clear. "Your people are more than capable of it."

"This is not the time," warned Temurr.

Cira focused her rage on Gunnr.

Temurr injected himself. "They would not do this. The Bànshēn rén did extensive trade with the merchants of Ker-Is. They cannot farm in their underground cities. And they do not trade with the Valhallans."

"No," Gunnr spat. "They only steal from us."

Cira dismounted her kark, pulling out her sword. Temurr held up at hand, then looked at the Viking warrior.

"Gunnr? I am warning you. I will help her, if you continue your attack..."

Gunnr snort-laughed, waving them off.

Temurr turned back to Cira. "It would not be uncommon for your people to be in this city. And if they were hungry and angry enough... and refused to pay exorbitant prices... There may have been an altercation that led to a fight."

"That is impossible!" protested Cira. "The Bànshēn rén have been banned from Irkalla! We would have only been close to Ker-Is as part of an invasion!"

Braylor dismounted and walked the courtyard like a detective at a crime scene. He eyed the city walls, stepped over several decaying bodies, and picked up a burnt arrow shaft from the ashes. Finally, he lumbered over to an Irkallan corpse and kicked it over with his boot. He swatted away buzzing insects as he knelt to inspect the wounds.

Kasuma swooped down from the night sky and nodded to Pherric—the city was empty.

"This was made to look like an attack by the Bànshēn rén," Braylor surmised. "But they did not do this..."

Pherric smirked slightly, as if he had waited quietly until this moment to let Braylor see the evidence for himself.

"How do you know, Braylor?"

"Cira is right. Her people would not have been in this city after Malek banned the other races from Irkalla. Even if some had slipped in, wearing disguises, they could not have killed *this* many. Which means they would have had to assault the city. From the outside. And there are no siege towers, ladders, rams or catapults sitting out there. And the walls show no signs of a battle. The gate is still intact. And, the Irkallans have left all the dead here, but... there are no Bànshēn rén bodies," said Braylor.

"But what of the heads on the pikes outside the gate?" asked Gunnr. "Irkallans reinforcements arrived and there is your result."

Cira grunted and furiously shook her head. "We did not do this. We would never... No. Not us. No.”

“There are only a dozen heads out there. Which could have been from anywhere, from any time,” said Braylor. “If you look closely at these dead... their injuries were not caused by the short bow of the Bànshēn rén. Or their short swords.” Braylor held up a long arrow shaft. “These people were killed by long arrows.” He rolled the body over with his boot. “And by long swords. Weapons of the Irkallans...”

Cira sulked. But she slid her sword into the sheath, working to control her breathing. Her anger subsided—it was not her people’s fault.

Gunnr laughed. “Surely you do not think that Malek destroyed one of his own cities, do you?”

Pherric came to Braylor’s aid. “Why do you think it strange? What better way to incite your own people against others than to have a supposed enemy destroy one of your cities and kill its people? It is actually quite genius—I doubted Malek wise enough for such a tactic.”

Gunnr remained unconvinced. “I have seen them in battle, Pherric. You know her race is certainly capable of... this.”

Cira’s face flashed red again—she reached for her sword.

“The Bànshēn rén did not do this, Gunnr,” concluded Pherric.

Gunnr rolled her eyes, but rode off to Braylor for a closer look at the bodies.

Kasuma whispered to Pherric. “We have to leave. At once.”

Pherric looked around the dead city. “We cannot be caught here... or we will share the fate of these people.”

Braylor patted Cira’s shoulder, trying to console her, but she pushed his thick hand away.

“Let us ride!” shouted Pherric. We headed out through the gate.

Kasuma flapped her wings and soared up to the dark clouds looming over Ker-Is to watch over our retreat.

Chapter 39

"What ails you, dear?" Frip surprised me, whispering into my ear from behind.

I grabbed at my exploding heart.

"You people have got to stop sneaking up on me!"

The talking ape man sat next to me as I tossed pebbles into the small stream flowing by our camp for the night.

"The more quiet you are in this land, the longer you live, child. It is our way," he purred. "However, I was quite noisy in my approach and, yet... you did not hear. I believe your mind to be quite far from here. You are worried, I assume?"

"Worried? Me? Ha. What could I possibly be worried about?"

"Being the chosen one is a tremendous burden."

After leaving the desolate ruins of Ker-Is, we melted back into the safety of the forest, heading north toward Biringan City. Tensions simmered, every step of the way. Sniping comments turned into heated bickering, but mostly, we trudged on in heavy silence.

At each campsite, unease lingered like smoke. We built fires in shallow pits, carefully hidden to keep the flames from being spotted. Once the flames were extinguished, we sat in oppressive darkness, the shadows around us feeling more alive than the people beside me.

Anxiety clawed at me, ever-present and relentless. I tried to drown it out—focusing on hunting for food or stepping in to break up fights between Braylor and the Prominans or Gunnr and Cira. But the deeper we pressed into Irkalla, the harder it became to escape my own thoughts. They always circled back to the plot they had devised. Each mile we traveled only made it feel more inevitable. While the prospect seemed exciting—assassinating an evil ruler bent on the destruction of all these remarkable species in this world—it also scared the shit out of me.

"For the last time..." I growled, balling up my fists. "I'm not... the chosen one."

I looked Frip in his soulful eyes and quickly realized he truly believed I was predestined to save the world. "Look. I... You need to be ready for the fact that I am not good. At anything. And that I'll most likely let you down."

I could not tell him prophecies weren't real and don't come true.

"You could not let me down, dear. There is something special about you. What you may lack in abilities, you make up for in spirit. The gods, not an ancient prophecy, have chosen you."

"Thanks, but... I'm not special. But it is... nice to feel needed. To have a purpose. Even if it's a purpose that gets me killed. Back in New York," I said. He cocked his head at me. "I mean, back in my land I had an easy life. But I had no purpose. Nothing to look forward to. I had no idea who I wanted to be. But I doubt many girls my age—in my land, anyway—know who they are or what they want to do. So, to be able to help you all out? Wow. If I could do something, even in just a *tiny* way, that helps prevent all this killing going on? That would be very cool, you know? But I'm also... frightened. You know? Dying just doesn't seem like it would be all that much fun."

"You fear death."

"Um, yeah! Who doesn't?"

"I do not," he muttered.

And just like that, I figured I had probably opened the can of worms marked *Religion*. Frip believed in his gods, so I steeled myself for the ape man to start on me about the everlasting life that I had waiting for me after death. My grandparents were hardcore Catholics, always trying to convert me, but I could never really buy into it.

"I have always been and always will be," he started. "My spirit, that is. Whenever it pleases the gods, I am born into this world so that I may know joy and suffering. When I die, they return me to my natural state. Throughout the ages, my spirit may have been placed into a bonnacon, or a Hominan, or even a chimera. Who knows? And when I am gone as Frip, I will return into another form. And then I will go searching for Temurr's spirit... because we are meant to be together."

"So, you believe in reincarnation?"

That word mystified him so I continued. "It means that after you die, you are reborn as another person."

Frip pondered my definition. "But... why a person? Why not a rock?"

He looked at the oval river rock in my hand, gently scooping it up.

"A rock?"

"Or a tree? Or a mountain? Or a cloud! A cloud would be nice," he examined the smooth pebble. "You see, this rock may contain the spirit of one of our ancestors. And the gods placed their spirit here so he could enjoy the bright light of Sol in the day, the fish swimming by, and the cool water. Water that will slowly, over many generations, wear the rock down to a piece of sand. And then the gods will take the spirit up and place it somewhere new."

I smiled. "That... sounds nice. A very peaceful way to spend a thousand years."

"So, be not afraid," Temurr said, gently tossing the rock back into the flowing stream. "When you focus on your fear, you miss out on those tranquil and joyful moments. You are who you are, until you are not. Then you are you again. As something else."

"I like that."

"And I would like to return... as a bird. I envy Kasuma, her flight."

"And I envy her small boobs. Trying to run without a decent sports bra is seriously not fun."

And, yeah, I had to run again. As we got closer to the capital city—and Malek—I spent a lot of time running alongside the group. The pain, agony and downright torture of running easily took my mind off what lay ahead.

And, if I somehow managed to get away with killing the king, I knew I would need to run for my life.... so working on my conditioning made sense.

The deeper we ventured into Irkalla, the closer we came to a menacing range of soaring black mountains that seemed to pierce the sky like the tip of a spear. Their steep, angular faces were etched with sharp ridges, exuding an unwelcoming, almost predatory aura. They loomed high enough overhead that patches of snow still held on to them, defying the late summer heat and adding an eerie contrast to the obsidian stone. Each step closer felt as though the mountains themselves were warning us away, their imposing silhouettes casting long shadows over the dark green world below.

I jogged through a vibrant evergreen forest, weaving along narrow rivers that sparkled in the dappled sunlight. A brief shower under a small waterfall rolling over smooth, flat rocks was a rare moment of peace. Irkalla's breathtaking beauty surrounded me—trees ablaze with brilliant orange and red leaves, wildflowers painting the landscape, and vibrant alien-to-me birds sailing through the canopy. This kingdom was a paradise, a lush Eden in every direction. Yet for a certain king, even paradise wasn't enough. The rich always want more.

As the sun dipped below the treeline, casting gold streaks through the forest, the others carefully guided their karkadanns down a steep hill. I sprinted ahead into an open clearing—and froze. The blackened ground crunched under my boots, and the charred remains of massive trees stood like skeletal guardians. An eerie silence hung over the burnt glade, broken only by my shallow breaths. At the far end, a massive lump loomed in the shadows, unmoving yet unmistakably ominous.

I crouched low, my eyes scanning for any hint of breathing. Whatever it was, it appeared to be dead. I exhaled and stood up, curiosity chewing on my better judgment. Step by cautious step, I moved forward, the crunch of branches and brittle brush beneath me unsettling in the silence.

As I approached, the shadowy form began to take shape—a massive skeleton. The blackened bones glistened faintly, their charred edges harsh against the pale sky. Could this have been one of their dinosaurs, killed in a fiery inferno? I slid nearer, standing beneath the colossal rib cage, its sharp arches reaching up to the tree tops like a monument to destruction.

"Finley, wait!" Pherric cried out behind me.

I turned back as he bolted across the burnt glade.

"We must leave here! Now!"

His long tattooed fingers reached for me as he ran.

"What? Why?"

Pherric grabbed my shoulders, his eyes darting around, scanning the skies.

"Sometimes... they come back!"

When I struggled to pull free, he effortlessly tossed me over his shoulder like I weighed nothing. My protests were muffled by the tension crackling in the air.

At the edge of the clearing, the rest of the group stood motionless, their wide eyes scanning the skies. Their fear was palpable, a rare and unnerving sight. Kasuma's sharp hand gesture cut through the silence, urging Pherric to move faster. Braylor's knuckles turned white as he clenched the hilt of his sword, a bead of sweat slipping down his temple.

Gunnr, usually unshakable, took deliberate, cautious steps backward, disappearing into the shadows. The unspoken threat seemed to loom overhead, pressing down on them like an invisible weight.

"Who comes back?" I asked.

"Dragons."

Laying on his shoulder, I returned my gaze to the giant skeleton.

"That's... a dragon?"

"Yes."

His boots crunched on the burnt grass as he ran me under the trees. As soon as he set me down, I bolted off through the trees.

"No, Finley!" Pherric yelled.

Avoiding the opening in the woods, I circled around to get as close as I could to the dragon bones. The others grumbled and shouted and stomped through the underbrush, trying to keep up.

"Stop, child!" I heard Frip over my shoulder.

My jaw dropped as I crept closer to the massive skeleton, still hidden beneath the cover of the trees. Every bone gleamed a deep, unnatural black, as if charred by some ancient inferno. The dragon's colossal skull lay heavy against the ground, its long snout lined with serrated teeth—each one as long as my forearm. Rows of razor-sharp horns protruded from the back of its skull, adding to its menacing silhouette.

The skeletal wings stretched outward, their thinner bones resembling elongated arms, branching and eerie, tree-like fingers. The rib cage loomed before me, its immense, arching bones wider than my legs. The back legs were monstrous, their thick, black bones larger than my entire body. The spine coiled from the back of its skull, winding over the burnt grass like a dark river of bone, ending in a barbed tail tipped with thick, menacing spikes standing at attention. The sheer size of the beast was staggering—and deeply scary.

Pherric caught up with me, panting hard. "That is close enough."

"What do you mean *they come back*?"

"The dragons... many times, they return for their dead."

"Why?"

"There is a legend that the dragons collect the bones of the dead and take them to an ancient burial ground, somewhere far to the east... perhaps in Kunlun. It is known as the Valley of the Black Bones. Although no one has seen it and lived to tell the tale. Many believe the dragons gather the remains of their kind and carry them to their final resting place," said Pherric. "To honor them."

"That would imply... an intelligence, wouldn't it?"

"Do not glorify these dreadful beasts, Finley. They have plagued all of Tir Na for thousands of years. The dragons not only steal livestock and destroy crops, they have razed cities and annihilated more people than Malek could ever hope to achieve. Only in the past few decades have we created the weapons we need to defend ourselves and fight them off. Their numbers are greatly reduced. But their reign of terror is far from over—we must leave here at once."

I took a quick look at the empty sky above. A shiver ran down my spine and goosebumps rose up to conceal the freckles on my arms. As if in a trance, the image of streaming fire— from the mouth of a dragon, blowing right at me and enveloping me—raced through my mind.

That was all the incentive I needed to quickly move on.

Chapter 40

"Welcome to Biringan," announced Braylor.

Under the cover of darkness, we slipped down a series of low hills, emerging into a sprawling valley at the foot of those ominous dark mountains. Across the valley stretched fields of crops, ripe for harvest and shimmering faintly under the moonlight. Beyond the fields, a sea of tents sprawled out like a patchwork quilt, punctuated by the flicker of hundreds of campfires. Soldiers, little more than restless shadows, moved in clusters, their shapes blending with the eerie darkness. Behind them, a wide river glinted like a blade in the night.

If this was supposed to be the legendary capital of Irkalla, the seat of the mighty kingdom everyone was so terrified of, I couldn't help but roll my eyes.

"The Black City."

Yeah, there was no city. No imposing towers, no sprawling walls—just tents, soldiers, and farmland.

Leaning over Pherric's shoulder, I jabbed a thumb toward the obvious void where the supposed "city" should be. "So, uh... who wants to tell him?"

Pherric's lips curled into a wry smile, his eyes flicking toward the empty space beyond the fields and the bloated army camp. I couldn't decide if he was amused or horrified.

"The city is there."

Pherric dismounted our karkadann, allowing it to feed on the grasses at the forest edge.

"Is it inside those scary mountains?"

"No," he said. "Do you remember the magic the gods used to hide the Godsribbon at the castle?"

"Uh, yeah, but... wait! Are you telling me there's an actual city—right *there*?! You're kidding me?!"

"I kid you not, Finley. If you look closely, to the west, you can see caravans and people traveling the main road in and out of the city."

He pointed to the left side of the tall mountain range. Above the crops and the tents, I could make out the tops of wagons, a few shiny helmets, and tops of spears moving to and from.... nothing.

"The Irkallans have an invisible city?! That is so not fair!"

"No one knows the intentions of the gods. But I doubt it was intended exclusively for Irkallans. The gods likely hid this area from view for their own divine purposes. And when discovered by the Irkallans, a city was built within."

"The... Black City."

"You cannot see Biringan, but it is there nonetheless. By far, the largest city on Tir Na."

Gunnr poked her head between us. "Tell me you have a plan for getting in there?"

"I do indeed."

Braylor stomped over to Pherric, a thick finger on his chest. "Do not tell me I need to crawl through a tiny tunnel!"

Pherric smacked the giant's massive shoulder. "There is a tunnel."

Braylor groaned.

"But it is quite large!"

Gunnr laughed. "And how far away is this tunnel?"

"Quite near, actually. Supposedly, there are seven entrances to Biringan, including the main gate... but I know of an eighth."

"And how do you know of this secret entrance? How do we know it is not a trap?" Gunnr asked.

Pherric walked among the trees, in search of something. "In Quivira, Lord Diago let it be known that his importing and exporting endeavors included dealings in forbidden goods."

Everyone followed Pherric as he worked his way through the trees.

"He runs a black market?" I asked, not really shocked.

"A fair phrase to use, I suppose," said Pherric, as he inspected the tree trunks. "He told me they make use of a hidden underground passage to smuggle their illicit wares into the city."

"A *big* passage?"

"Yes, Braylor," assured Pherric. "And I believe our way in is... there."

He pointed to a hardwood tree that rose a hundred feet above the evergreens, with a trunk three times as wide as Braylor's shoulders. The giant exhaled.

Gunnr pulled on Pherric's tunic until they stood face to face. "And Malek does not know of this passage?"

"Lord Diago recently smuggled the wine we drank through this very tunnel. He assured me it remains safe, Gunnr."

"As safe as it can be," she sneered.

Temurr searched along the base of the tree until he found a hidden handle under the bark. He pulled and a door appeared.

We looked around the woods for signs of soldiers. Braylor returned to the karkadanns, slapping their rumps and shooing them off into the forest. Frip grabbed a handful of pine needles to cover our tracks around the base of the tree.

I cautiously stepped through the opening onto a small ledge. Most of the insides of the tree remained, to keep it alive, but the space seemed just large enough for Braylor. A winch had been attached above my head with ropes leading down. A makeshift ladder had been nailed to the roots.

Temurr used his tinder kit to light a small candle on the wall of the tree as I climbed down the ladder.

My boots touched the hard dirt floor and I took out my sword.

Temurr smirked from above. "If they find you down there, I doubt that will help."

"I'll feel better."

"That is the spirit!" he chuckled, joining me in the tunnel.

He lit candle after candle as we journeyed slowly along the passageway. Braylor, looking quite panicked, fit easily into the passageway (only needing to bend his head down and twist his shoulders.) Frip brought up the rear, blowing out the candles as we worked our way through the secret tunnel.

An hour later, we came to the end of the tunnel. Another ladder greeted us, leading up to a wooden hatch.

"After you?" Temurr said.

"Me? Why me?"

"Well, my dear, because you look *slightly* more Irkallan than I do."

I stared at the others. Getting someone else to the front of the line would have been a huge hassle.

Staring at the trap door above, I drew in a deep breath. And began to climb.

Chapter 41

The hatch above my head was locked. Of course it was. I pushed on it again, because apparently I believe in miracles. Surprise! Still locked.

I glanced down the ladder at Temurr and Pherric. Temurr winked, like this was some sort of joke. Not helpful.

With a sigh, I knocked lightly on the wooden door, hoping nobody would hear. Naturally, footsteps creaked overhead.

The hatch opened up, and suddenly, a knife dangled in front of my nose. I stared at the blade's tip with crossed eyes. Holding it was a young guy with a patchy beard, skin that looked like it had lost a fight with a rake, and breath that could ferment grapes.

He squinted past me, holding a candle out to inspect the ladder below, then flicked a glance into his room like he was checking for backup. He swung the hatch fully open, and I climbed into a cramped, windowless room with stone walls, a single open doorway, and more wood crates than a dockyard. My hand stayed firmly on my sword hilt.

The guy backed up, wiping his nose on his sleeve while shooting nervous looks at the doorway. Yeah, definitely a picture of trustworthiness.

Behind me, the others scrambled into the room, their boots thumping on the floorboards. If this was a trap, it wasn't subtle. I gave Temurr a pointed look, but he just grinned like he was having the time of his life. Perfect.

Pherric stepped forward. "Long live King Malek. The ride from Hell was disappointing."

His secret code phrases were cute.

"The road to Irkalla is full of bandits," said Bearded Boy, wiping his nose again with the back of his hand. "Welcome."

He kept fidgeting, eyeing the door, and that made me more nervous.

"I am Pherric and this is—"

The bearded man held up his snotty hand. "I do not care."

"We need to get safely to Lady Anisha's quarters, across the city in the Trade District."

He inspected Braylor, the Prominans, and a girl with wings. "Would not do to be runnin' a storehouse wagon through a rich quarter at night."

Pherric pulled several coins from his leather bag, placing them in the young man's hand.

"Why should we not use the finest wagon in the Warehouse District?" Pherric suggested.

The greedy young man hefted the coins and dashed out the door.

A companion of our bearded friend heaved open the massive warehouse doors, revealing a bustling cobblestone street alive with motion. The yellow and orange glow of street torches spilled over our gray wooden wagon, giving it a ghostly sheen.

I hopped up next to Gunnr, who was already seated beside our driver, Bearded Guy. She threw me a sharp glare, her eyes flicking toward the wagon bed. I got the message and slid behind the bench, crouching low. Gunnr tugged her cloak's hood tighter over her head and adjusted her crimson tunic, ensuring it concealed the chainmail underneath.

Temurr, Frip, and Braylor were buried beneath a worn tarp at the center of the wagon, unmoving. Meanwhile, the others leaned casually against the back gate, their faces shadowed by deep hoods. We looked like a mismatched group of outlaws—or the sort of cargo no one wanted to inspect too closely. Hopefully.

"Onward!" shouted Bearded Guy. He cracked the reins and his team of large karkadanns pulled the heavy wagon away from the storehouse.

"Please keep your hands, arms and legs inside the vehicle at all times,"

I said.

Gunnr sneered.

I smiled back. "In the event of a water landing, your seat cushion can be used as a flotation device."

"And to think, the fate of the world depends on... you."

I opened my mouth to say something else dumb, but my brain short-circuited as the city came into view. Beyond the warehouses, the firelight from lanterns and torches revealed hundreds of towering, white spires. Most were round, some tapered elegantly as they climbed higher, their sections adorned with lush green vines and small trees spilling over the edges. At the very tips, blue and black banners snapped in the breeze, marking the city with its signature colors.

Unlike the eerie silence of Quivira, Biringan was alive—every wall, every tower, every street was lit with torches flickering against the night. The noise hit me like a tidal wave: voices shouting and laughing, tavern singers weaving melodies to the tavern goers, vendors barking out deals, and karkadanns clopping steadily along the cobblestones. It reminded me of those late Manhattan nights, where the city seemed to hum and breathe with its own energy.

As we left the warehouse district, I caught sight of the royal citadel of Irkalla. Rising at the far end of the city, Malek's palace looming above it all. It wasn't just a single castle—it was a fortress layered into the hills, each tier protected by white walls, culminating in a monstrous twenty-story keep with round corner towers that made the rest of the city look tiny.

Wonder turned to dread as the wagon rolled through the wide streets of the Merchant District. I was in the Black City, but it was nothing like I expected. White, brilliant, alive, and overwhelmingly his. This was Malek's stronghold, the very heart of his kingdom. And here, surrounded by his power, he held all the cards.

My grandfather once told me that every sane person always has to deal with some kind of fear. He said you can do one of two things when you get scared, "Forget everything and run, or fuck everyone off and rise."

But, he drank a lot, so...

Normally, in a moment like that, I would want to desperately jump off that wagon, sprint back to the warehouse, and run screaming through the tunnel under the city. But this time, it was different. Maybe I was ready to rise?

It was time to kill Malek or die trying.

I needed a drink.

Chapter 42

"**I** will not have Finley attempt to assassinate Malek," Pherric announced.

I slammed my small fist on the wood table. "No way! That's such bullshit!"

I was *so* relieved!

After we arrived safely at her manor in the Trade District, we gathered around the long dining table dominating Lady Anisha's Great Hall. Her residence, though narrow, exuded an understated elegance, tucked neatly among a row of similar stone homes in a posh neighborhood. Decorative trees lined the manicured street, their leaves whispering in the gentle winds. Tall iron fences framed each property, offering just the right balance of privacy and opulence.

The cobblestones outside gleamed under the soft glow of beeswax lanterns, which cast warm, flickering light across the quiet street. It felt worlds away from the chaos we had left behind, a bubble of tranquility that almost made me forget why we were there.

"What?!" said Braylor.

"I only went along with your scheme in order to keep us together until we arrived safely in the Black City. And we know, after her experience at the River Styx—she is not prepared for this."

Temurr leaned across the table. "Then why is she here? What of the prophecy?"

"The prophecy does not suggest Finley is the one to execute an emperor. She is to be a uniting force, her presence an inspiration—"

"Her presence?!" Braylor bellowed. "Inspiration? What is she, Pherric? A talisman for good fortune?!"

I stared at the roaring fire in the hearth of the Great Hall.

"Who will then be the assassin, wizard?" asked Frip, staring down at the table. "You?"

"After much consideration, Gunnr would be the wisest choice—"

"Gunnr?!" cried Braylor. "She is a barbarian!"

He turned his head toward her—Gunnr arched an eyebrow.

"Not meaning to offend."

"No offense taken," she said. "But he has made a point, Pherric. I would gladly kill the man where he stands, but I am not... refined."

"If Malek hosts a party in his stronghold, the three of us will receive invitations. And you are the only experienced warrior, Gunnr. It must be you."

"I would be wise choice for a personal guard, but to be a Lady of the Court—"

"Lady Anisha can instruct you both on court etiquette—"

"Etiquette?! Me?" Gunnr protested.

Braylor stood from the table. "We have no time for this foolish nonsense!"

"We must leave this foul city!" shouted Temurr. "And raise an army!"

As they argued, I shuffled off the corner of the hall to pour myself another cup of wine. I was truly relieved—I'm no warrior or trained killer. Not like Gunnr or Kasuma. And Pherric confirmed as much. I was their inspiration. Which basically made me a cheerleader for the home team. I was nothing more than a living St. Christopher statue to protect weary travelers from sudden death.

The back-and-forth devolved into a shouting match. I half-expected a chair to be thrown at some point.

Normally the quiet one during their arguments, Kasuma stood and whistled loudly—ending all the bickering.

"I want to know something. Now, please. What expectations did everyone have for this alliance?"

"Of what do you speak, bird woman?!" grumbled Braylor.

"In your mind, you must have expected our group to fail... and fail spectacularly."

Each person in the room was taken by surprise. They exchanged dumbfounded looks.

Pherric spoke first. "Kasuma, now is not the time for—"

"It is very much the time for this," she said, slowly walking her way around the others at the table. "Think this over for a moment. A young Scholomance student," she gestured at Pherric. "He escapes from his academy, with a vague prophecy in mind, and sets out to round up a variety of representatives to aid in his cause to stop an evil king."

Temurr exhaled. "That much is clear, Kasuma. I do not understand—"

"He spent many months traveling to our kingdoms to enlist help," she said, touching Pherric's shoulder as she passed by. "And look at what he was given. The Bànshēn rén gave us a child—"

"I am not a child!" Cira seethed. "I am a warrior!"

Kasuma ignored her. "The Prominans gave us two outcasts, guilty of a love that is forbidden in their kingdom... because they are unable to procreate."

Temurr put his head down and squeezed Frip's hand, as if to silently apologize.

"And a Fomorian, bent on revenge for the great loss of his family, who would have accompanied a meandering bicorn if it meant he could kill Malek."

Braylor, deflated, looked away as she strolled by.

"Finally, we have a Valhallan who was cast out by her people for the death of the chief's son."

Gunnr threw her shoulders back. "And what about you?"

Kasuma locked eyes with Gunnr. "I was sent along by our king to spy on you. My mission was to report on your progress, if there was any."

"You... are a spy?!" Temurr leaned on the table, ready to pounce.

"Of everyone in our ensemble, I was the only one able to convince a ruler to act. The only one who knew that action needed to be taken. Before it is too late."

I made my way back to the table, curious about where she was going with this.

"What is your expectation, Kasuma? To tear us down?" asked Cira.

"Mine is that we are meant to fail. All of our rulers? They expected us to fail. Even we, as a team, do not believe we will be victorious."

Temurr threw back his head to growl at the high ceiling above. "So, you are saying we should give up?!"

"That is the last thing we should do," said Kasuma. She placed both hands on the table, spread her wings, and looked at each one of us. "Because we have already defeated their expectations!"

"I do not understand," said Pherric.

"We are here! Pherric, you have successfully gathered a band of warriors together, representing nearly all the peoples of Tir Na. You have brought the chosen one from her land. We have infiltrated the Black City—the very home of the would-be emperor—and are now refining the tactics needed to end his reign! Do you not see? No one, not one single ruler or even any of us—thought we could get this far! And do *this* much! Yet—"

"Here we are," said Gunnr.

"Yes!" Kasuma exclaimed. "People live in fear now, thinking nothing can be done and that the time to act has passed us by. If we are to somehow make an attempt on Malek's life and fail, we will still have won! We were able to *try*. And that will show our leaders that if a ragged and motley crew such as ours can attempt to kill Malek... then they will know that it can be done."

"We... will give them hope," Frip said, letting Kasuma's speech sink in.

"Hope that Malek's reign can be ended," said Cira.

"Aye. Whatever we manage to do from this point on will be... a triumph. Let us continue to plan and perhaps—the gods will smile upon us."

Our team needed a name. Like *The Hopeless Hopefuls* or something. Out of pure excitement, I stuck my hand out over the table.

Everyone stared at it. Then me.

"What do you want us to do?" asked Braylor.

"Well, on my world... when we band together to... do something great, we all put our hands together."

Tentatively, each warrior placed a hand on mine.

"Now what?" Braylor. Again. "Do we sing a song?"

As official team cheerleader, I gave him my best fake smile. "On the count of three, we all shout 'Lex talionis'! One, two, three!"

Everyone shouted "Lex talionis!"

Well, they sort of half-mumbled it—but it was a start.

"So, now you will tell us..." said Braylor.

"What?"

"What is 'lex talionis'."

"Oh. It's from an old, dead language in my land. Translated, it means the 'law of retaliation'. Whatever has been done to the victim is done right back to the bad guy, as payback. An eye for an eye."

Braylor nodded. "I approve of this. Lex talionis..."

Chapter 43

"Oh, yes!" Lady Anisha purred to Pherric, her eyes sparkling with approval as she studied Gunnr. "She is a beauty indeed."

Gunnr stood before them, clearly uncomfortable in the role she had been thrust into. She shifted awkwardly, tugging at the hem of the light blue, silky dress that clung to her muscular frame in a way armor never did. The fabric shimmered like water, its off-the-shoulder design leaving her strong arms exposed. Her blonde hair, usually tied back in a no-nonsense braid, had been freed, trimmed, and artfully styled into soft waves that framed her face. The result was striking. She looked elegant and confident—or at least, that's how she appeared to everyone else.

But Gunnr's expression betrayed her discomfort. She crossed her arms, then uncrossed them, trying to find a pose that didn't feel ridiculous. Her steel-blue eyes darted toward Pherric, silently demanding an explanation for why she had been subjected to this transformation.

"Can we be done with this?" she muttered under her breath, her fingers brushing the hilt of the dagger strapped inconspicuously to her thigh beneath the flowy fabric. She might look the part of a noblewoman tonight, but she was still Gunnr. Always prepared. Always ready.

Anisha tapped her bottom lip with her finger. "Hmm."

Only slightly taller than me, Lady Anisha's body was round from wine and shapeless from age. She had to be pushing fifty, but she was pushing back twice as hard. Her hair and makeup were always perfect, dresses stylish and sexy, and her infectious laugh always made me smile, if not laugh, along with the *grande dame.*

"Walk for me, my love!"

I peaked my head around the scarlet tapestry to watch Gunnr stomp across Anisha's parlor without grace, style, or even a hint that she might be a woman.

"Well... that is unfortunate," sighed the Lady.

Gunnr grunted. "What?"

"Let me simply say that you, my love, will be my greatest triumph!"

The Viking's eyes lit up, as if it were a compliment. Pherric tried not to laugh.

"Bring me the other one!"

I hesitated for a moment, adjusting the dark green strapless gown that clung to me like an awkward second skin. Its deep hue had been chosen to highlight my red hair and blue eyes—an ensemble carefully crafted, yet wholly foreign to me. My bare shoulders felt exposed, vulnerable. Still, I stepped out from behind the tapestry, forcing confidence I didn't feel.

Her sharp eyes landed on me immediately, lighting up with predatory glee. "A firehair!" she exclaimed, gripping Pherric's arm like a delighted child spotting a rare toy. "Walk to me, my pet!"

I took a deep breath and began to walk, trying to mimic the grace of how I thought a noblewoman should walk. Shoulders back, head high—I had this. Or so I thought. Halfway through the sitting room, I realized I was overdoing it. The swing of my hips felt exaggerated, forced, and my confidence started to falter. My pace slowed awkwardly, and I shuffled the rest of the way to her, cheeks burning with embarrassment.

She cackled, a sound that was both amused and cutting. "Like many a lover, dear," she drawled, her lips curling into a smirk, "you started strong and gave up on the pace a might too quick."

Pherric coughed to stifle a laugh, his shoulders shaking just enough to make me want to slap him.

I straightened, folding my hands demurely in front of me, and gave her my best icy glare. "Perhaps I'm simply saving my strength for the finale."

Her laughter rang out, full-throated and genuine this time. "Oh, I do like this one!" she declared, clapping her hands as if I were a prized mare she had just purchased.

"I could do it again," I tried to apologize.

Before she could say anything, I exhaled. Channeling my friend Genevieve, I lifted my chin, pulled my shoulders back, and strutted across the room and back to the Lady.

Anisha stared at me, tapping her lower lip.

"Tell me again, Pherric," she said. "Why we are *not* adorning Malek's arm with this lovely jewel?"

"Finley is not an option. Gunnr has the skills necessary to—"

"To neuter the royal pup?"

"Precisely. Can you teach her the ways of the Irkallan court?"

She gave Gunnr a second appraisal.

"Show her how to walk, talk, eat, sit, and speak like a member of our high society? Not in a thousand years..."

Pherric collapsed in his chair. "But—"

"But why should we do that?" queried Lady Anisha. "Why not have her represent *her* kingdom? She could be the daughter of a Jarl, Pherric. Valhallan royalty, as it were. We will have to soften a few sharp edges, here and there. But she is most likely aware of the customs of her people."

"That... would certainly work to our advantage," admitted Pherric. He shared a hopeful smile with Gunnr.

She turned to me. "This one, however, will be more of a challenge."

"Why's that?" I asked.

Anisha ignored me. "You say you have told others she is Atlantean?"

"Yes," admitted Pherric. "With so little being known about them, I thought that would be the best approach."

"Allowing us to use her skin color and height to our advantage. Yes, I see it. However, if we are going to have her pass for an Atlantean, I need to make some changes."

"Wait, what do they look like?"

Anisha stood up to examine me. She grunted as she bent forward over her tummy rolls to fluff my hair.

"Well, my pet, I dare say there has never been an Atlantean with such a lush fiery tangle, nor has there been one a mane so long.”

I loved my hair and it had taken forever to grow it out. The thought of a cut and dye absolutely killed me.

“And my seamstress should be able to approximate an Atlantean gown for you and a strap dress worthy of the Jarl class for our Valhallan. But that is not our biggest concern with fire-mane here.”

My anxiety ramped up again. “What? What’s our concern?”

Pherric looked me in the eye. “Gills.”

I gulped. “People from Atlantis really do have… gills?”

Anisha twirled away from me, inspecting my body from afar, to tap her lip.

“They do. And they like to show them off. Or maybe it is so they can breathe. I have no idea.”

“Are we talking a sleeveless tunic, cut down to the waist, or more of a backless halter dress?” We were in my element now. “We could still expose the sides, but cover the slits with a mesh fabric that… teases the existence of gills.”

“I like her, Pherric.” She smirked and her eyes twinkled. “And I would have plenty of work for you, my dearest… if you survive this ordeal.”

I had learned earlier that Lady Anisha owned more than a few of the classier brothels scattered throughout the Black City. Some of her *working* women had loaned me their clothes, helped me dress, and applied my makeup. And they were talkers. The three helping me had gossiped about the indiscretions of the knights and nobles, the lords and the ladies, and especially the king.

“Let us begin with her hair!” announced Lady Anisha. Her *Ladies of the Night*, as she called them, scurried from behind the parlor tapestries and hurried me away.

As someone who’d spent plenty of time at high-end spas back on Earth, my standards weren’t just high—they were skyscraper-level. But credit where it’s due: Anisha’s girls went all in on the noblewoman makeover. First, I finally got to drown my desert-dry lizard skin in lotion that actually worked, leaving me softer than a baby karkadann. While I basked in that tiny victory, one of her ladies tackled my absolute disaster of a manicure with the poise of someone chiseling granite.

Then came my hair. I specifically asked for a trim—just a few inches to tidy things up, right? Wrong. This lady went full Ed Scissorhands, hacking away until I was left with a pixie cut so short my forehead looked like it was hosting a minimalist art exhibit.

Then came the dye—a black ink that smelled like rotten fish and despair. She slathered it on with zero mercy and informed me it had to stay in for what for an hour. She plucked the shit out of all the unruly eyebrow strays and dyed those, as well.

By the end of it, I probably looked like a rebellious pageboy from a medieval drama. Fabulous.

One of Anisha's ladies took on the Herculean task of teaching me how to properly apply their medieval-level makeup. With my freshly dyed black hair, she went for a bold cat-eye look—the kind I'd tried a million times after bingeing beauty tutorials back home but never managed to nail. This woman? She made it seem effortless.

Instead of the usual pink blush I would've used, she opted for some kind of bronzer-like powder that gave my face a sun-kissed golden glow. She even dusted it over the scars from all my various wounds, like it was no big deal. The pièce de résistance? A paste of bluish-black lipstick that she carefully applied, would give my lips a rich, striking look. Or so she said.

I hadn't seen my reflection since Quivira, and let's just say my expectations weren't high. When she led me to a mirror, I braced for disappointment.

What I saw stopped me cold.

I didn't recognize the young woman staring back at me. Her face was angular, with cheekbones sharp enough to cut glass. Short, jet-black hair framed her features, and her thin, dark brows gave her an almost regal edge. The glowing blackberry lips completed the transformation. Only a pair of blue eyes offered a trace of familiarity.

I just... stared. Mouth in an oval, brain not computing. Who was this fierce, polished stranger? Because it sure as hell wasn't me. Or at least, not the me I thought I was.

Chapter 44

Weeks of waiting for the king to host a party turned Lady Anisha's manor into a pressure cooker of tension. Braylor and Temurr couldn't go two hours without clashing over something trivial, escalating their arguments to full-on shouting matches. Meanwhile, Cira's frustration simmered dangerously—still furious over her people being blamed for the carnage in Ker-Is, she lashed out at anyone who dared come within range.

The most explosive fights, however, came courtesy of Kasuma and Pherric, who went at it like wildcats over his reckless plot to assassinate Malek. After one particularly heated argument, Kasuma's patience snapped. She stormed outside, wings flaring, ready to fly to the castle and take a shot at the king herself. Pherric wasn't about to let her go rogue—he had Anisha's guards restrain her, the winged wonder spitting curses and threats at him the entire time.

Gunnr had her own struggles. She got her own glowup, with a slight trim to that gorgeous blonde hair, a decent mani-pedi, and a skin regimen to heal years of damage from the cold, wind, and sun. She basically raised herself and had only known the hard life of a slave. Society was as foreign to her as Tir Na was to me. She would reluctantly practice putting on makeup, only to apply way too much in a ham-fisted way. She'd don a beautiful tunic, but she'd walk with her feet wide apart and shoulders hunched. She was absolutely breathtaking and yet utterly uncomfortable and without confidence, no matter how many compliments were paid.

So, we spent a lot of time together. I worked on helping her be a little more refined and she tortured me with sword fighting skills. The most difficult thing for me was getting her to not stomp around like a caveman. The hardest for her was probably not giving in to her instincts and chopping my head off with her ax.

One evening, after dinner, I decided to focus on teaching her how to walk gracefully with poise and confidence.

"Remember, Gunner," I said, standing up straight as I talked to her. "Keep your shoulders back. Place one foot in front of the other."

She began her stroll through the Great Hall with her head up, but her eyes immediately returned to her boots.

"No! Eyes up!"

She looked straight ahead but then spread her feet apart, walking flat-footed again with heavy stomps.

"Not like that. Pretend you're walking on a tree branch—one foot in front of the other."

Gunnr turned on me. "If I were walking on a branch, I would have to look down or else I would fall off."

"Okay, bad example. Just walk towards me, head up, eyes on me, shoulders back..."

She stood taller, exhaled, and moved her feet correctly. But she took giant strides and started swinging her shoulders back and forth.

"Keep those shoulders still!"

Gunnr screamed furiously, turning away, and sulked with her hands on her hips.

"This is useless!"

"One more try?"

"Why?"

"Because you need to pass for a noble woman, not a soldier marching off into battle."

In anger, she whipped around and sprinted towards me. "I *am* a soldier!"

She grabbed my tunic and lifted me off the floor.

"Killing is all I know!"

I held her forearm as my feet dangled. "And I don't know killing. But that hasn't stopped you from trying to change *me*."

In frustration, she dropped me hard onto the dining table. She leaned against the edge and stared at the floor, as regret replaced anger.

"We both have to do things we're not comfortable with. And it's not going to be easy. At all. But we have to try. Or all that we've done? It's been for nothing."

Gunnr started to reply, but her instincts kicked in—she stood and stared at a doorway, as her hand reached for a knife.

Pherric rushed into the Hall.

His face was pale and his eyes red, as if he'd been crying.

"I have terrible news," he said, his voice haltering. "However... we may now have our opportunity."

Gunnr sprinted from the room.

"What is it?" I asked. "What's going on?"

"Let us wait for everyone," he said.

Pherric stood at the head of the dining table in the Great Hall. He held a small handwritten note in one hand, and that hand was trembling. Sweat formed on his upper lip.

Gunnr raced back into the room with the others falling in behind.

Braylor sat on the table, causing it to creak loudly. "We are all here, Pherric. What news do you have?"

Pherric waited for the squeaking of chair legs on the stone floor to stop. He exhaled, quickly looking at Cira and then down at the table.

"Well, go on, man!" Braylor. Again.

He was unsure how to proceed. "Lady Anisha's spy has informed her that a great battle has taken place in the north." Pherric looked at Cira again. "Malek's army invaded Agartha."

"Ha! Not a wise move on his part!" added Cira.

Pherric stared at the handwritten note. "After a minor skirmish, the Irkallans stole away with several Bànshēn rén children. When the Agarthans did not immediately pursue... the children were executed."

"What?!" Cira jumped up, knocking back her chair.

"The children's heads were delivered to the leaders of the Bànshēn rén. They became enraged and killed the messengers. They then swarmed the Irkallan army in a valley south of the Agartha mountains."

Frip stood next to Cira and reached out, but she pushed him away and paced the room, her face burning hot.

"Making every effort, the Bànshēn rén fought against Malek's troops, slaughtering an entire legion of his men."

"Good!" A maniacal grin crossed her face.

"The battle lasted... for several hours," Pherric said slowly.

Her grin faded and shoulders slumped.

"It was an effective ruse, to draw them out and wear them down," added Pherric. "Malek sent in several more legions after the Bànshēn rén were exhausted. They... killed them all."

Confusion swept over me. "Killed who? The Irkallans?"

Braylor walked away, hands on his head. Cira fell hard to the floor, wailing and pounding her fists on the stone floor. Pherric looked up from his note in tears.

"Malek killed the Bànshēn rén, Finley. All of them. At least all who joined the battle. The spy claimed that over thirty thousand are gone. Males, females, children. All had come out of the caves to fight the Irkallan army."

My own tears flowed. As I turned to comfort Cira, Pherric held me back.

"No, Finley. She might kill you in a fit of rage."

Some fell into chairs and cried, while others walked back and forth or stared at the walls in a state of shock. Gunnr lowered her head, out of respect. Lady Anisha slid quietly into the room. She waved her fingers and servants carefully passed out mugs of wine. I grabbed two. Braylor took a mug but shattered it by squeezing too hard. Cira wept as we drank in silence.

After a time, Cira exhausted herself. Frip and Temurr scooped her off the floor and whisked her out of the hall.

The servants continued to bring wine as Pherric pulled up a chair and sat at the dining table. Braylor scooped up the chair Cira had thrown back and gave a nod to Gunnr and Kasuma and they moved in close.

"You had said we have... an opportunity?" Gunnr whispered.

"According to Lady Anisha," said Pherric. "The news of the slaughter is several days old. Malek may soon send out announcements to all of Irkalla of his great victory over the Bànshēn rén—that was in retaliation for their supposed attack on the city of Kel-Is. The king is planning a feast to welcome home Sir Kane and the conquering heroes."

"This will be our only chance," said Braylor.

"Chance to what?" I asked, completely forgetting about our plot.

"To kill Malek. At his own party," Braylor sneered.

"Can Lord Diago ensure we are on the guest list?" asked Kasuma.

"I believe he can. I will send a messenger tonight." Pherric hurried from the Great Hall.

Braylor eyed Gunnr. "Are you ready?"

She replied with a smirk.

Kasuma placed her hands on my shoulders. "Lex talionis..."

"An eye for an eye," I said.

Chapter 45

The invitations arrived by messenger five days later, on the morning of Malek's celebratory feast.

Those extra days gave Gunnr and I time to prepare for the party. We worked with Anisha on the protocols of polite society, we learned the greetings and customs of noble Irkallans, Gunnr brushed up on Valhallan traditions, and I soaked up any details they had on the Atlanteans—which was not much.

Anisha's ladies pulled out all the stops for our gala outfits, turning us into something resembling nobility—or at least trying to. For me, she whipped up a stunning royal blue dress with silvery flecks that caught the light like stars. The fabric was smoother than silk and clung to me in all the right places. The sides were cleverly filled in with fine mesh to disguise my inconvenient lack of gills. My one gripe? The length. Down to my ankles. And, not to brag, but I kind of wanted to show off my "new" legs. For the first time ever, I *liked* my legs!

Pherric wasn't so lucky. He had to settle for a shiny red robe, a crisp white jacket, and black stockings borrowed from Lady Anisha's steward. The ladies worked overtime concealing his black tattoos with makeup on his neck and hands, and the result was passable. I guess the fact that he didn't stand out was kind of the point.

According to Gunnr, her ensemble was straight out of Valhalla—a tunic paired with a lime-green apron adorned with ornate brooches. She tried to accessorize with a sword (classic Gunnr), but Anisha somehow talked her down from that cliff.

When the fancy white carriage rolled up to Anisha's manor, we said our goodbyes in style. Gunnr waved off Temurr and Braylor's attempts to give her advice. Kasuma, ever the perfectionist, fussed over Pherric's lapels, wiped a smudge of lipstick from my face, and tightened Gunnr's leather belt like a mom sending her kids off to prom.

Cira hugged me and Pherric, but when she got to Gunnr she gave her a deadly serious look.

"Yes?" queried Gunnr.

Cira snarled, "Make him die slowly. Very slowly."

Gunnr walked quickly away from the manor, climbing aboard the carriage.

Before I joined her, I looked around. Braylor stood behind the others, his arms crossed. I walked over to him.

"No last-minute guidance?"

I wanted to throw myself against him, hold him. I wanted those big strong arms around me, consoling me, as he kissed the top of my head and told me I would be all right. I was terrified, shaking in my brocade fabric short boots, and needed his embrace. But the big idiot just stood there.

"Do not die."

"That's it?"

He stared out over my head. "Do not let the others die."

I could not storm off in anger. In fact, I couldn't move. My hands began to shake. My heart jumped into my throat. Cold sweat formed on my forehead. I felt close to passing out. And he noticed. His huge hands grabbed my shoulders and he looked into my eyes as he held me up.

"This is a terrible idea." He shook his head.

Struggling not to cry, I stared around and took a few deep breaths. "I can do this. I can."

Braylor reluctantly pulled me in, gave me a stiff hug, and patted my back like he was burping a baby. "Good. Oh, and you do not smell... horrible."

His sad attempt to comfort me made me laugh. I looked into his dark brown eyes one last time. And what I saw broke my heart. There was no worry in his look, only pity. The face my mother would make when she drunkenly spilled an expensive drink. There's nothing worse than liking someone who doesn't like you back.

Before the tears could flow, I pushed away and rushed from the house.

Pherric helped me into the carriage. "We will succeed."

I started to say that I hoped so, but only offered an awkward smile. I knew we were going to die.

According to Lord Diago's handwritten note accompanying the wax-sealed envelope, the invitation was addressed to Hervor, daughter of the chieftain of Kvenland in Valhalla. As for me? I was her plus-one, and Pherric was her steward. And no one ever asked for a steward's name, they had told me.

The carriage creaked as it rolled through the torch-lit streets, the weight of silence heavier than the threat of danger outside. Pherric sat rigid, his sharp eyes darting to every shadow as if waiting for an ambush. Gunnr sat across from me, lips moving soundlessly, rehearsing her new name and role over and over as though she could will it into truth.

I clung to the sound of the horses' hooves on the cobblestones, forcing myself not to give in to the panic clawing at my chest. Instead, I focused on Cira's rage, her seething hatred for Malek. I let her fury fill the space inside me, drowning out the trembling fear threatening to take control. My heart raced as if it were my own anger driving it, my hands shook as though readying for battle. But beneath it all, fear festered, whispering that this night would end in blood.

Pherric broke the uncomfortable silence. "Your name is Kelaino."

I was lost in the city outside the carriage window. "What?"

"The name is Atlantean. Kelaino means 'the dark one'."

I reached up, touched my new black hair—but I bet he had something more sinister in mind.

"Do not drink at the feast, Finley."

I cocked my head to the side. "No shit, Captain Buzzkill."

"It's just that we are under a lot of stress and—"

My anger flared. "I get it, Pherric! And, yes, I'd love nothing more than to down a gallon of vino and smoke a fat J, but... we have work to do."

"As long as we are in agreement."

"You're like the brother I never wanted, Pherric."

"And... Hervor?" He grinned at her. "As a steward, they may not let me through the gates. You must insist because you'll likely need our help to escape. But please do not pull out their eyeballs if they say no."

Gunnr snorted. "I promise you nothing."

"Please bear in mind that you are nobility. Daughter to the Jarl of Kvenland. You're used to getting everything you want," he told Gunnr.

For a young guy, Pherric was quite wise. And not just on matters such as this, which was impressive because I doubted he had ever been to a party full of lords and ladies and kings. I appreciated that he was smart enough to bring me along for more than support. I was his Plan B. He needed backup and why not have a completely different woman along? One tall and the other short. One with short dark hair and a blonde with long hair. He had hedged his bet. Very wise indeed.

I smiled as Pherric peppered her with more tips. He really was like a brother to me. He was handsome, a bit mysterious, and obviously smart, but... he wasn't Braylor. As I looked at him, I could sense strong emotions. Coming in light, vibrant waves. A bit of fear, which was natural. But I picked up on something else. Self-doubt, maybe? A lack of confidence... that we would pull this off. Was his mindform training finally starting to pay off?

Our carriage rolled through the imposing main gates, the towering stone walls casting long shadows in the fading light. The path wound its way steadily uphill, flanked by carefully pruned hedges and torch-lit statues that seemed to watch us go by. At the second gate, the guards barely glanced at our invitation before waving us through, their armor gleaming dully in the dying sunlight.

By the time we passed through the third wall—each layer more intimidating than the last—a queue of carriages had formed ahead of us. We settled into the line, waiting our turn as the last rays of the sun slipped below the horizon. The awkward realization hit me: we weren't fashionably late. We were pathetically, embarrassingly early. Perfect. Exactly how you want to make your grand entrance into a royal gala.

I concentrated on my breathing, working hard to calm myself, until a guard opened our carriage door. Pherric rushed out of the carriage and held out his long arm. As we climbed down, Pherric helped us off the step. Gunnr and I went toward the castle first as he bowed his head, following closely behind.

The massive white keep blazed against the twilight sky, illuminated by thousands of torches strategically placed along the inner wall, their flickering flames casting orange highlights on the polished stone. Long black banners, adorned with the intricate blue crest of Malek's family draped dramatically down the towering walls, their sharp contrast emphasizing the keep's stark grandeur.

Soldiers clad in black tunics with striking blue accents and gleaming mail armor stood at rigid attention, stationed in pairs around the castle grounds and lining the imposing staircases. Their polished helmets reflected the torchlight, giving them an almost spiritual appearance. The weight of their silent, watchful presence was enough to keep even the boldest guests on edge.

At the base of the smooth stone steps, a long black carpet unfurled like a shadow, guiding arrivals toward the grand entrance. A collection of nobles and dignitaries, dressed in vibrant silks and brocades in every imaginable color, gathered in small, tight-knit clusters. Their hushed conversations carried an air of restrained excitement and intrigue, punctuated by the occasional glance toward the gates to see who else might arrive. Some walked with measured grace, their heads held high, as they ascended toward the towering double doors of the palace.

The air buzzed with a mixture of opulence and unease. This was no ordinary gathering; it was a showcase of wealth, but mostly the power in the heart of Irkalla. Above it all loomed the keep itself, an unspoken reminder of Malek's dominance over the city—and everyone in it.

"Fancy digs." I stared up at the white castle and scanned the dark mountains enclosing the estate.

"Not now, Finley," scolded Gunnr.

We began a slow, careful climb up the stone steps. As if taking our time would prevent the inevitable.

I stole a quick glance over my shoulder as we climbed the hill. From this vantage point, the Black City sprawled out like a shimmering tapestry of light and shadow. Tall, pale towers pierced the sky, their smooth stone facades catching the warm, amber light of the setting sun.

The bustling streets below wove between the towering structures, alive with movement that seemed to ripple like waves. In the heart of the city, a colossal stadium loomed, its grand arches and tiered walls dominating the skyline.

The faint echoes of life—vendors calling out their wares, karkadann hooves clattering against cobblestones, and the hum of countless voices— rose faintly to the hill, creating an intoxicating music that blended vitality with a dash of tension. They were a people at war, but life continued on.

"Taking in your last sunset, Finley?" mocked Gunnr.

"Yeah. I probably am."

She grabbed a handful of her Valhallan tunic. "Everyone dies eventually. Even you."

Abandoning all pretense of style or grace, she started stomping the rest of the way up the stairs.

"Well, hopefully not in my lifetime."

Chapter 46

Bowing his head, Pherric handed the sealed invitation to the senior official after he waved a pair of guests through the open doors of the castle. The wire-thin man, regal in his fine black robe, greeted us with a nod and a blink as he accepted the envelope. He handed it to a younger version of himself to open, stroking his wire-thin mustache and sizing us up as he waited.

Gunnr held her head high and I pretended to look bored.

The subordinate whispered in the official's ear, handing him the invitation to inspect.

He exhaled deeply. "I must apologize deeply, Lady Hervor of Kvenland. Due to concerns for security, all of the... tertiary guests invited to the gathering have been excised from our list and I—"

"I do not understand," interrupted Gunnr. "What are you saying?"

"I was attempting to offer my apologies for—"

She stepped in and the official took a step back.

"Am I to understand that I will not be allowed entry?" She struggled to control her temper. "Will I miss out on celebrating the annihilation of those filthy creatures?!" Her hatred showing for the Bànshēn rén was kind of frighteningly real.

"Lady Hervor, I assure you—"

"I have an invitation!" Gunnr shook with rage.

"We dispatched messengers in an attempt to contact all our esteemed guests who would be inconvenienced by—"

"You did not contact me." Gunnr balled her fists up. "I got dressed up in this ridiculous outfit and came all the way up here!"

Two soldiers guarding the doors stepped towards us.

Pherric knew she was terribly close to going off on the guy. He put his hand on her arm. Gunnr shook him off—she was going full Karen.

"I demand to speak to the palace steward!"

With the soldiers at his side, the official looked down his long nose at us. "Once again, you have my sincerest apology for the misunderstanding, Lady Hervor."

Pherric shook head at Gunnr—this was not the time or place. Her jaw clenched tighter. He nodded to the official. "Long live King Malek."

"Long live the king," the official replied.

Gunnr marched down the steps. Pherric waved to a page to fetch our carriage.

"What's going on?"

"I do not know. It is possible Nerus, Malek's mage, feared someone would try to take advantage of the feast. And when he could not discourage the king, he culled down the list. Or, they are aware of our plot and our presence in the Black City. However, if they did know, I highly doubt they would let us walk away."

"So, what do we do now?"

He was shaken. Lost. "We must regroup. Come up with an alternative scheme."

"But... Cira!" My anger got the better of me and Pherric held up his hand. "What about her people? We must do something—now—before he wipes away more people!"

He stopped me before we reached the base of the stairs, before arriving guests could hear him. "What would you have me do, Finley? What recourse do we have?"

If Genevieve were there, she would have known what to do. My mind jumped back to when she tried to sneak us into the movie premiere. We needed a "back way" in, away from the attention. I scanned the grounds surrounding the castle.

"Is there another entrance? Like a servants' entrance? Or... for the kitchen staff?”

"Yes. But they have enhanced their security. Any point of entry will be difficult.”

"Difficult, but not impossible.” I had no plan, but knew Genevieve would not give up if she didn’t make it through security on the first try. "Trust me, okay?”

We joined Gunnr in the coach. My mind raced as I tried to come up with a plan. Three of us attracted too much scrutiny. I doubted Gunnr could charm her way in. Pherric might be able to get in, but he couldn’t kill the king—I was at a loss.

Pherric directed our driver to take us back to Lady Anisha’s manor.

What would Genevieve do?

"Anyone have a small dagger?” I asked.

Gunnr whipped out three small knives in a matter of seconds.

I took the shortest one and handed it to Pherric.

"Get us to a back entrance to the castle. Please?”

He sighed, then shouted new directions to the carriage driver. I stripped off my beautiful long blue dress, turned it inside out.

"Finley, what are you doing?!” said Pherric.

I pulled the bottom hem of the dress all the way up to the waist.

"Pins!” I demanded.

Gunnr removed a few pins that the ladies had placed strategically in her hair, handing them to me. I used the pins to hold the hem up tight to the waist on both the side seams.

"Did anyone give you makeup?”

She grabbed a small clutch that she had left on the seat, handing it to me. I pulled the dress on and applied fresh lipstick. I opened a tin of dark powder and applied it for more of a smokey-eye look.

Without a mirror, I looked at Gunnr for approval.

"Well, you look like one of Anisha’s Ladies of the Night.”

"Perfect,” I said.

I took Gunnr’s small dagger and hid it under the belt behind my back.

Pherric held up his hand and started to speak.

"Before you freak out, I'm going to try to get in. But I have to do this…
alone."

"Alone?! I forbid it—"

"Stop right there. This will only work if I go in alone."

"Finley…"

"I know. But this is the only way."

My heart was trying to break free from my chest.

Gunnr sneered at me. "She will be fine."

She dabbed away the perspiration on my upper lip. "You are ready for
this…"

"Let's hope."

"Remember to kill him slowly. For Cira."

I exhaled and nodded.

Pherric grabbed my wrist. "Finley… tread carefully. Please?"

"If I was going to be careful, I wouldn't get out of this damn carriage."

When the coach rolled to a stop, I threw the door open and ran away.

Chapter 47

Once clear of the carriage, I scrambled across a lush yard to a grove of skinny trees with bright yellow leaves. Standing in the cool shade, I made an effort to pull myself together. I needed to come up with an idea to help get me backstage. But all I could think about was how much I wanted Genevieve standing there beside me.

My face lit up as I imagined her whispering voice in my ear. *Act like you're supposed to be here! Remember... you're the one in charge!*

Deep breath.

You got this, girl!

Beyond the grove stood a two-story stone building, distinctly separate from the main castle—this was the palace kitchen. It looked more of a fortress than a workspace, and for good reason: it was the lifeblood of the castle's grand feasts. I hovered at a low wall that circled the building, trying to summon the guts to approach. Finally, I slipped in behind a group of workers hauling crates of fresh supplies, blending into their hurried pace.

Inside, the kitchen was an orchestrated symphony of activity, a blur of sights, smells, and sounds. The rich aroma of seafood dominated the air, mingling with the earthy scent of roasted vegetables and the sweet tang of freshly baked bread. Fires blazed in three massive hearths, their glow casting flickering shadows on the walls.

Two enormous tables stretched the length of the room, piled with ingredients in various states of preparation. Young girls hurriedly unloaded crates of vegetables, their arms laden with vibrant greens and roots. The cooks moved with practiced precision, their knives flashing as they chopped, diced, and minced whatever was placed in front of them. A sauce chef stirred a bubbling cauldron of something rich and savory, sprinkling in pinches of spices with the precision of a magician.

Across the room, boys tended to enormous, skewered fish—some nearly as long as the boys were tall—rotating them carefully over the glowing embers of the hearths. Baskets of bread emerged from hot ovens, golden and steaming, only to be immediately sliced and whisked away by servers rushing to keep pace with the kitchen's frenetic rhythm.

It was chaos, perfectly choreographed, but more from fear than the joy of hard work.

The head cook, a plump old woman with a red face, oversaw the whole dizzying operation. She shouted out orders, inspected outgoing dishes, and sampled work in progress.

The server ahead of me picked up a tray of food, so I grabbed the very next one from the table.

The head cook squinted at me. "Oy! You there! Who are you?!"

I put the food tray back on the table and raced out of the kitchen.

As a line of servers marched toward the keep, I rushed up beside one and began speaking in French to him. He recoiled in fear as I talked in a strange language but he kept walking. So, I kept speaking French, patted his arm, and fake-laughed.

"Comment allez-vous, monsieur. Je suis l'organisateur de la fête! Ne fais pas attention à moi!"

From the corner of my eye, I spied two guards at the door standing at attention as I approached. But I kept chatting with the horrified server, pointing to the keep and at the food on his tray.

"Rappelles toi! Servir la nourriture sur le côté gauche, monsieur!"

The soldiers, dressed in the sleeveless blue and black tunics over their chain armor, started towards me.

"Stop right there!" shouted the older guard with a scraggly beard.

I ignored him and marched between them... as though I *owned* the place.

The old guard grabbed my shoulder and pulled me back as the frightened server continued through the doorway. The younger, pale-faced guard stayed quiet while the older one leered down. "Where do you think you're headed, young lady?"

"Excusez-moi, y a-t-il un problème?"

Frustrated, he bent to my level so I could see his lips move. "Do you speak the Queen's Language?"

"Of course I do," I said, switching to his language. "But I am running late and have no time for this!"

Despite my attitude, the fear in my eyes had to be giving me away.

"This is the servants' entrance. All guests are to use the front—"

"I'm no guest, you fool!" I put my hands on my hips, glared at him. "I am Kelaino! Of Atlantis! The official party planner for tonight's banquet!"

"Party... planner? What is a party planner?" he sneered.

Sweat poured down my back. "Is it not obvious?! The *planner* of the *party*?! Mon Dieu! The steward of the castle sought out my services for the feast!" I was losing what little bravery I had stored up and could not stop talking. "I am here to orchestrate tonight's festivities! I have come all the way from Atlantis for tonight's *Under the Enchanted Sea* celebration. Do you not see all the... seafood?!"

The older guard smirked at his comrade, turning back to me and crossing his arms.

"Well, then it seems as though your work is done here... Kelaino of Atlantis. The celebration has already started."

"And... and I am here to make sure everything goes according to plan, espèce d'idiot! Now step aside, I have work to do!"

The older guard removed his sword. "What is the steward's name? The one who pays you... for your services?"

Another soldier noticed my interrogation and started towards us.

I gulped as the house of cards fell all around me.

"Well?" he said, as he prepared to fish-kabab me.

I let the fear wash over me. My eyes went wide and I looked furtively around us. I waved at him to lean down.

"Can we talk?" I whispered.

"We are talking."

"Privately! You're already in danger and I don't want these other soldiers to get killed!"

I carefully grabbed his arm and held firm. Confused, he let me lead him toward the wall of the keep, holding up a hand to the other soldiers.

"Killed? What are you going on—"

"Shh!" I held my finger to my lips, looking all around to make sure we were alone. "All right, you figured me out. I'm not really the party planner."

"Of that, I am quite aware—"

"Quiet, please," I said, secretively peering around him which caused him to look around with me. "Do you know who Nerus is?"

The old guard winced.

"Nerus," he said, as more of a statement than a question.

"Creepy guy. Cold eyes. Greasy hair."

"The king's mage... Aye. I know of him."

"Yes!" I tried not to smile when I saw a flicker of fear in his eyes. "He's a powerful sorcerer. And, if he knew I was talking to you, he might cast a spell on us both!"

The soldier's jaw clenched as he swallowed hard.

"I was sent here... by Lady Anisha."

I let that sink in—he knew of her services.

"I was supposed to gain entrance... discreetly. I am here because he has a... a weakness for Atlantean women, if you get my meaning."

He grunted his disgust.

"But now I am scared!" I pulled him close. "And if he finds out that *you* know about his... fetish? Well, he might use his magic on both of us! Turn us into... into—"

"Hydras!" he yelled, pulling away the tunic at his neck. Sweat beads ran down his temples.

"Quiet!" I said, glancing around us. "And, yes! Hydras. Or worse! So, you cannot tell the others. But you are in danger now. From Nerus. He can read minds!"

"What should we do?"

"Well, I... must go to him. Now. And lie with him. Even though I'm really, really afraid. Because if I don't, then... *poof*!" I exploded my fingers in his face. "I'm doomed! But you can save yourself. You must try hard to not think about Nerus, or me, and maybe—just maybe—you will be spared."

The guard stood up straight, exhaled, and cleared his throat. I tried to read his reaction. Has he seen through my bullshit?

He turned to the younger guard. "The party planner is here on important business!"

His buddy looked from the guard to me. "But—"

"Stand aside!"

He placed his big hand behind my back, guiding me through the doorway into the castle. I stumbled across the marble floor. When I looked back, he had wrapped his arm around the young guard, escorting him away from the doors.

I hustled out of view before he had a chance to change his mind.

Venturing along a wide hallway, unsure of what to do next or where to go, I pretended to stare at a tapestry on the wall as servants, carrying casks of wine, passed by. When they were out of range, I detoured down a small hall. Hiding behind a golden vase as tall as me, I dropped the hem of my dress. I used my reflection in the gold pot to wipe away the excess makeup, fix my hair.

When I was satisfied, I took a huge breath and let it out slowly.

"You can do this, girl," I told my reflection. "You got this..."

I held my head high, plastered a smile on my anxious face, and headed farther into Malek's castle.

Chapter 48

I wandered aimlessly through the endless corridors of the Irkallan palace, acting like I had a purpose. Workers dashed around, shuttling through doors and up and down the halls, too busy to care about the "noblewoman" strutting confidently on her way to a royal banquet. My heels clicked on the polished flagstones with authority—fake it till you make it, Fin. They ignored me, and I ignored them, both parties perfectly content with the arrangement.

As I neared the Great Hall, the murmur of a crowd grew louder, pulling me from my thoughts. The palace was stunning—bright white walls adorned with colorful tapestries and ornate portraits. High windows welcomed the dark orange glow of the setting sun, while massive pots held exotic trees and cascading greenery. Hanging baskets spilled over with lush plants, and flickering flames from wall lanterns bathed the space in warm, golden light. It felt less like the castle of a mad king and more like a luxury retreat. Except, you know, for the whole evil, tyrannical overlord vibe—and that little detail dampened the ambiance.

I slowed my pace as I neared the Great Hall's entrance. Eyes down, I avoided contact with anyone who might mistake me for someone who wanted to chat. A quick smile here, a polite nod there, and I busied myself admiring the mosaics on the ceilings and the tapestries on the walls.

A portrait of an Irkallan queen caught my attention. She stood tall and poised, wearing a flowing white robe and a smile that reached her eyes. Long silver hair framed her face, cascading over her shoulders. Instead of sitting on the throne beside her, she stood confidently next to it. Was this Queen Dirvilia, Malek's mother? Her happiness seemed real, almost radiating from the canvas. Hard to imagine she birthed the nightmare currently ruling Irkalla.

When a loud, drunken group barreled past me toward the Great Hall, I fell into step behind them, letting their chaos shield me from unwanted attention.

As I stepped into the hall, I couldn't help but stare. The room was massive—three stories tall, lined with thick white columns, and lit by hundreds of flickering candles. It could have fit five hundred people easily, though only about three hundred were seated at the long wooden tables that stretched across the space. Statues of kings and queens, carved from gleaming white stone, stood at the base of each column, their silent gazes watching over the partygoers.

At the far end of the hall, on a raised platform, was the main table. Ornate and commanding, it was reserved for the king's most loyal lords— a place of honor I'd be happy to avoid. The grandeur was overwhelming.

I veered off to the side of the hall, making my way close to the main table on the dais. As soon as I sat down, a servant placed a metal goblet full of wine in front of me.

I could hear Pherric in my ear—*Don't drink at the feast, Finley.*

Fuck you, Pherric—and took a long sip of seriously-needed wine.

Watching people was my thing. I scanned the room over the rim of my goblet. Couples danced in the wide gap between the four table rows. Musicians, sitting in chairs behind the columns, played a light and fluffy melody with oddly-shaped stringed instruments and horns. Clustered into their little cliques, the lords and ladies seemingly whispered court intrigues, judged those who were less affluent, and shared catty gossip. So, basically... it was a typical party.

After a bell was rung, servants began rushing out the first course of food and the guests took to the tables. The murmuring turned to a dull roar as wine was drunk, toasts were made, and stories were told. An older lady in a stuffy smock-like red dress thankfully dominated the conversation at my end of the table, complaining about her servants and the lack of high society feasts over the past year.

More wine was served after the first course. The first cup I deserved, but the second through fifth? Probably not.

Worry set in. I feared Malek would be a no-show for his own party. Then I freaked out that he would *actually* show up. Could I do it? Did I have the nerve to try to kill the king?

Lost in thought, I noticed that the crowd had quieted down. The musicians played a loud fanfare with their horns.

Everyone stood.

On the dais, a few of the king's knights stepped from behind a lush blue curtain, pulling it all the way back.

The people moved away from their chairs and bowed. I struggled to keep up, nearly tripping over the leg of my chair.

The horns blared louder. The king stepped through the curtains, a big smile on his face and his hands in the air. The people rose up and cheered. Many lifted their wine goblets.

"Long live the king!" shouted one man across the Great Hall. And everyone repeated him in unison.

Malek nodded, waved, and pointed at a few lucky ones as the crowd hooted and clapped. The last time I saw him, all dirty and grimy from battle, had been at a distance from the Godsribbon keep. All those many months ago. Now, he was freshly scrubbed and very handsome, with a modest gold crown arrogantly tilted to the side, resting on his clean blond hair. His deep-blue eyes smiled in triumph. He adjusted his black leather tunic as a steward removed his gold robe, and he then took his seat at the center of the table.

The horn section wrapped up their tribute and people returned to their seats. Servants ran out with our next course. Too nervous to eat, I picked at my plate and stole quick glances at the king. The lords at his table fawned all over him, each trying to laugh the loudest or tell the most engaging story. Between sips of my wine, I noticed Nerus slip out from behind the curtain. A steward slid a chair under as he sat just over Malek's shoulder.

I turned away from the main table on the dais—I did not want the sleazy mage to recognize me. Without thinking I pulled on my dyed and shortened black hair. I stared down my tanned arms, my thinner waist. And I smiled to myself. He wouldn't be able to spot me in this crowd.

Though my wine cup kept magically filling itself, it had also filled me with courage. I had worked hard to get into this room. As I felt the cold steel blade hidden at my back, I was reminded that I knew how to use it. But my fear still held a tight grip. My palms were sticky and my pulse raced. Could I actually try this? I mean... I could barely kill the guy out in the woods near the river.

I sat up straighter in my chair and focused my mind. Malek needed to die. And I was the only one who could do the deed. The task was mine. And I might be full of fear but I was now someone to be feared.

But would I be able to make it out of the room alive?

I studied the possible exits. Guards manned the doors that the guests had used. I now knew there was a doorway behind the curtains on the dais, but the soldiers and lords that would await me made that a risky option. The servants had two entrances on either side of the dais. And they might be reluctant to stop me. Since I had come in from the kitchen, I might be able to find my way back out. I had a plan!

I smiled to myself. Now I just needed to get close enough to the king to stab him in the heart.

Behind the main table, a servant whispered into Nerus' ear. He conveyed the message to Malek. The king rose from his chair. Everyone in the Hall followed his lead and bowed their heads.

"I wish to thank all of you who have gathered here tonight to celebrate our triumph over the filth that invaded Ker-Is and paid for that transgression with their lives!" His voice was deep, commanding. He was magnetic, powerful... with an air of strength hidden behind that charming smile and those sparkling eyes.

My fists balled in anger as the people in the hall clapped.

"I would love to have led the charge against those vile creatures myself!" He side-eyed Nerus. "But I have been advised against taking my rightful place on the battlefield!"

The crowd moaned and jeered.

"However, on this night, let us celebrate the victorious heroes who were brave enough to have saved our kingdom from the marauding horde of Bànshēn rén!" shouted Malek to thunderous applause.

He pointed to the back of the room. Everyone turned.

Soldiers pulled open the two mighty doors leading into the Great Hall. Women gasped, men hooted, and I crossed my arms.

"Our army has, only now, returned from their triumph!" continued Malek. "Lead by the dramatically late—as he always is..." Everyone laughed. "Sir Kane, Knight Commander of the Royal Irkallan Army!"

They went wild as Kane stormed into the room, along with ten of his top knights. And they looked like they had just walked off the field of battle and rode for days straight back to the capital. Blood and dried mud caked their chain armor, covered by their black and royal blue tunics.

Kane and his men bowed to their king.

His face was hidden behind gore and dirt, shaggy brown hair, and growth of beard, but I could still make out those bright, thoughtful eyes from across the Hall. The same light brown eyes that had stared at me as I hid behind the crates in the buttery under Diago's manor. Eyes that—well, I hated to admit it—I wanted to see again.

He nodded to his king and shared an embarrassed smile with the adoring crowd. I sensed a thoughtful but tortured soul behind those eyes.

Like a wave crashing down, I was engulfed in shame. That filthy asshole had been the one leading the charge against Cira's people. He was responsible for the deaths of tens of thousands! And there I was, mooning over him like some freshman girl crushing on the handsome professor in English Lit.

Kane kept his head lowered until the clapping and cheering died down.

A servant brought him a horn filled with wine. He faced the people and took a huge swallow, garnering more cheers. He swept his arm across the row of knights standing at attention, passing on their accolades to his men.

"And tonight, while we celebrate the end of one of our enemies!" shouted Malek. "We must remain vigilant! Many of the vile beasts of this world envy Irkalla and will try to take what belongs to us! The fight is not over... it has only begun!"

The people shouted, pumping fists in the air.

"Enjoy the feast and make merry!" Malek raised his goblet to those in the Great Hall and then again as he smiled directly at Kane.

I watched the Knight Commander's reaction. Kane gave a weak smile and finished his horn of wine. Then he steeled himself, as if preparing to go back into battle. He walked up to the dais, leaped onto the platform, and they grabbed each other's forearms. Malek patted the man's grimy face.

The exuberant crowd resumed their conversations.

Kane bowed to Malek and quickly excused himself to go get cleaned up, jumping from the dais and landing near my table. I stood there and stared. Kane studied me, his head cocking slightly to the side, for a long moment, as if he were trying to place me. But he tossed out a polite grin, a courtesy nod, then ran off to his room.

As I returned to my seat to await my chance to kill the king, I caught sight of Nerus standing off to the side of the platform. He was scanning the mass of people scattered throughout the Great Hall.

I flinched when he closed his eyes.

Nerus was searching for a threat. As a mage, with more training than Pherric, he must have been sensing my anger. My strong desire to assassinate Malek. My mindform. I knew what I needed to do. To keep him from detecting my presence, I needed to gain control of my emotions, focus my thoughts, and calm my nerves.

Instead, I held up my empty goblet to a passing servant and asked for more wine.

Chapter 49

After all the food had been brought out and the desserts served, it was time for the entertainment.

Singers tormented my ears.

A jester told jokes at nearly everyone's expense, except for the king. "You, my good sir, what a long and lovely nose you have! Should you ever be bored with living the life of a lord, you could catch fish with that hook!"

The contortionists that came out next were... creepy. Human bodies should not be able to bend like that.

I waited patiently, biding my time, for a chance to drive my knife into Malek's chest. At the same time, I hoped he would simply slip out the back and disappear.

As the chamberlain began to announce the next act, Malek intervened. "Enough of the show! Let the musicians earn their keep! It is time to dance!"

The guests clapped as the band started playing a rhythmic tune.

I perked up. This was my shot; a chance to take down the king. My time had come. At last. The only problem—I was shit-faced.

One of the lords rushed up, asking me to dance. I turned him down.

Malek stood behind the main table, whispering to a friend. They were judging the women in the crowd, picking out their next conquest. I staggered to my feet, hoping to catch his eye. He ignored me.

I turned my attention to the guests. I had danced at my fair share of weddings and knew that the knife hidden at my back would be a problem. I slid the blade around to my right hip, hoping that the handle didn't stick out too far.

Malek sauntered down to the dance floor. A shapely blonde hurried up to the king and bowed. The cocky creep inspected her, flashed a wry smile, and held out his arms. The guests oohed and aahed as they spun across the floor.

"Would you care to dance?" said a deep voice, over my shoulder.

I knew Kane was standing behind me before I turned around.

"I am not much to look at... but I am a respectable dancer."

I exhaled, summoned my best smile, and spun about. He had cleaned up nicely. His hair was combed but the beard was still wet. The muddy armor and tunic had been replaced by a midnight blue buttoned jacket, white shirt, and tight black pants. Simple and elegant.

"Well, that is a lie. I am a terrible dancer."

I stared up into those damned eyes of his.

"By the gods, I hoped that would have gotten a smile from you. I'm apparently not funny either. Are you sure you still want to dance?"

"Yes. Of course." I lied.

He led me to the dance floor, placed his arm around my back, and pulled me in close.

"My name is Kane."

The wine refused to let my brain cooperate. "Good."

Kane spun me away, drew me back in.

"And you are?"

"I am... Kelaino." At least I remembered the name. "Kelaino, of—"

"Ah! Let me guess... Atlantis?"

"Well done, Sir Kane," I said, with a forced bravado and an uncomfortable laugh.

I was nervous. But I was also angry.

"Please, Kane will do."

"Yes. Kane *will* do... whatever his king commands." I couldn't believe I said that out loud. But having this butcher touch me made me want to hurl. "Apparently."

He was taken aback. At first. But a smile crept across his face as we danced among the other couples.

"So, you do not approve of retaliation against the Bànshēn rén for their attack on Kel-Is?"

Alarm bells finally went off in my head.

"No, I... You see, I—"

"Interesting. And is that the official consensus among the Atlanteans?"

"Oh. No. Opinions expressed are solely my own and do not express the views or opinions of my employer."

Kane went from taken aback to downright confused, so he laughed.

"The gods have truly smiled upon me this night."

"What do you mean?"

"You, Kelaino of Atlantis, are quite fascinating."

We twirled and swirled around the floor. "I've been called worse..."

We danced closer and closer to Malek and his partner.

"Have we met before?"

I turned my attention back to him.

"Huh?"

"You look familiar," he said. "I have seen your face, these eyes, before."

I looked away as he tried to place me. "Oh, I bet you use that line on all the hot young ladies in Irkalla."

"Line?"

"Yeah, you know, like a fishing line—cute little phrases men use to *reel in* the women?"

"Ah." He grinned again. God, it was hard to hate that grin. "You are indeed fascinating."

Malek found another blonde babe to dance with. Kane spun me out and pulled me back to him.

"I must make it a point to visit Atlantis."

My anger surfaced again. "Yes! You could come see the sights, taste the food, and kill our people."

The king and his new dance partner glided closer to us.

"Speaking of killing," said Kane, pulling me in tight. "What did you have planned for the feast?"

"Wait, um... I don't understand—"

Kane placed the palm of his hand against my hip, pushing on the knife under my belt.

"I think you do..."

He shot a quick look over at the king, grabbed my wrist.

"Let us get some fresh air."

Sir Kane, Knight Commander of the royal Irkallan army, led me off the floor.

I took one last look over my shoulder. Malek continued to dance. And my only hope of killing him faded away.

Chapter 50

He yanked me through a set of doors and out of the Great Hall before I even had time to process what had just happened.

I had nothing. No clever excuses, no witty deflections, no charming lies. My brain was an empty void of panic. I'd blown my one chance, caught red-handed by Malek's right-hand man. And now? Well, now I was going to die.

As we walked down a long corridor, Kane finally released his iron grip on my wrist. His strides shortened, making it easier for me to keep up. At the end of the hallway, he shoved open a stained-glass door that led to a balcony.

I stepped out onto the cool flagstones, the crisp night air slapping my overheated body. My gaze drifted upward, past the high walls of the city, to the heavy black peaks looming ominously in the distance. The breeze tried to soothe my frayed nerves, but my heart raced too fast, my face burned too hot.

Kane stood there, watching me like I was some kind of riddle he was determined to solve. Arms crossed, his expression was unreadable—cool, calculating. My knees wobbled slightly under the weight of his silent judgment.

The sound of the door creaking behind us broke the silence. A servant stepped onto the balcony, carrying a carafe of wine and two hollowed-out animal horns. Kane gave a brief nod, took one of the horns, and let the server fill it.

He held the other out to me, and I hesitated before taking it. My fingers brushed his briefly as I accepted the drink, the smooth surface of the horn cool against my trembling hand.

"Who are you?" he asked, his voice sharp and cutting through the still night like a blade.

"Um, I'm... well, I'm me," I stuttered. "Kelaino of Atlantis."

"Who are you really?"

I knew he had felt the knife hidden in my dress. I turned on him, crossing my own arms—if I was going to go down, I would go down with an attitude.

"Your prisoner... apparently."

He leaned against the stone railing, shaking his head. "Are you?"

I exhaled. No one had prepared me for what to say or do in case things went badly.

"Well, if I am... and I think I am... I'm surprised you brought me out onto this beautiful balcony. Don't you usually drag your prisoners down to the dungeon?"

"The... dungeon?"

I walked closer to him to see beyond the railing. We were only about one story high—I might be able to survive the jump and run away.

"Yep. And usually you put them on a torture rack to get information out of them."

"What is a torture rack?" Rather than angry, he seemed amused by me.

"Um, I think you tie chains to the prisoner's ankles and wrists and use rollers to stretch them out until they confess."

"That sounds quite effective."

I cocked my head at him. "Oh, yeah. And then there's thumb screws." What was his game?

"Thumb screws? Like screwing metal into the thumb?" He did a twisty motion with his finger.

"I don't know. I think it's like a vice that crushes fingers and toes."

"I should be writing these down," he said. "All very good ideas."

He finished off his wine, poured more for me.

I watched him over the rim of the horn as I sipped. My elbow brushed against the knife handle at my side.

"Okay, I'm confused," I admitted.

"About?"

"Well, you rushed me out of the party. I think I know why... But I'm seriously not sure why I haven't been... arrested."

"I do have some questions for you."

Kane tapped his wine horn against mine—we both drank up and he poured more.

"Do you agree with the king's plan to create an empire for all Hominans?"

My mouth dropped open. "Um, well, I..."

"Of course you do not."

"Uh, I-I don't know," I stammered. "What do I know of politics and warfare and conquest and all that? I'm just a girl..."

Kane sat back against the stone railing to be on my eye level. He quickly looked beyond me to make sure no one could hear him.

"You have no position on Malek slaughtering millions in his quest to eradicate all other species? Including Atlanteans? And, yes, he will come for your people eventually," Kane whispered.

"Um, pardon my ignorance, but aren't you the one doing all his dirty work?"

Kane stared at the flagstone on our balcony. "I am loyal to the crown. I serve the kingdom."

"But are you loyal to Malek?"

His wounded eyes looked up at me, but he said nothing. He didn't shake or nod his head.

I drank my wine to get through the silence.

Still looking down he finally spoke. "Do you know how I got the *black bones* moniker?"

"Sir Kane of the Black Bones? Nope, never heard you called that before. Not once." He gave me a stern look. "Go on."

"One morning, back when I was a young man, I was sword training with the castle weapons master. In the courtyard below us."

"Wait. You grew up in the castle?" I needed to keep him talking, so he wouldn't lock me up in the dungeon.

"Yes," Kane said, rubbing his sculpted jaw. "My father was the royal council to Malek's mother, Queen Dirvilia. I was raised, from an early age, to become the Knight Commander within the walls of this keep."

"Wow. And I still have no idea what I want to be when I grow up…"

He laughed again. He was a great audience for my stupid comments.

"Well, that morning the Queen herself brought her oldest son, Laran, out to the courtyard to watch me train.

"Malek has a brother?"

"He… did. Laran and I were best friends. I grew up with him. However, Laran was not handy with a blade. Or *any* weapon. He was more of a statesman, like his mother. Even little Malek could best him when they sparred."

He gulped down half his wine and then stared into the black sky.

"As they ventured out onto the courtyard, a dragon attacked from above. The beast killed the weapons master with his dragonfire, but I managed to leap out of the way. Then he went after Laran and Queen Dirvilia. I tried to protect them, only… I was but nineteen years old. The only real experience I had was hunting game with my father. Staring at that dragon… fear gripped me and I did… nothing. I simply stood there with my lips trembling, trying not to soil my breeches. The dragon perched on the courtyard wall and swept me away with his tail. The vicious creature launched himself at the queen and Laran and tore them to shreds with his sharp fangs."

"Oh, my god! That's horrible," I gasped.

"Without thinking, I cried out and ran directly at the dragon with my kath sword in front of me. The dragon lurched his weight around, drew back to breathe his fire on me, and—purely by accident—my sword found its way between his scales. And into his heart. No skill was involved but… the gods blessed me in that one moment."

"Hey, you did all you could!"

"I couldn't save my queen. Or my friend. I failed."

"Killing a dragon seems like a pretty big deal, Kane."

"Years later, I even managed to capture a dragon."

"You *captured* a dragon?! Get outta here!"

"It was the last dragon to attack the Black City. Armed with kath arrows and swords, we fought fiercely to defend what was ours. I lost a hundred men trying to bring down that monster. While he burned my soldiers, I shot an arrow into his underbelly and wounded him. When I went to sever his head, Malek stopped me. He wanted to keep the dragon as a... pet."

"A pet?" I said. "Was it the same dragon?"

"I do not know. Perhaps." He gazed at his boots. "After the funerals for the queen and Prince Laran, they made me a hero. There was a procession, in my honor, through the city. They even knighted me. And... that is how I became known among the Sir Kane of the Black Bones."

"And that's how Malek became king?"

"Eventually. He was only nine or ten at the time. Dirvilia's mate, the Prince Consort, took over the duties until he came of age."

"And you have been by his side ever since..."

He exhaled deeply. "Before my father passed, he made me swear to remain loyal to the crown. To provide counsel. To protect the kingdom. But the burden has been... demanding."

"Sounds to me like you and Malek are not exactly on the same page," I said.

"I do not believe we are even looking at the same book."

Chapter 51

Empathy crept in, unwelcome and annoying, like an itch I couldn't scratch. And let's be real—that was not good. Kane was still my captor, after all. No matter how often he poured wine or how tragic his story sounded, he wasn't suddenly my buddy.

This guy was clever, and I wasn't about to forget it. Getting me tipsy on wine and tossing out a heart-wrenching tale was all part of the game—his game. The strategy was clear: lower my guard, earn my sympathy, and get me to spill everything about the others and our plan.

Well, joke's on him. My lips were sealed tighter than Lady Anisha's corsets.

"Is something wrong?" he asked.

"I don't think you're going to have to worry about being called Sir Kane of the Black Bones anymore. I think your new moniker will be the Butcher of the Bànshēn rén ... Oh, or better yet—the Assassin of Agartha." I downed my wine, knowing that might be my last drink ever.

He clenched his fist, staring down at the flagstones. "That is not fair."

"But nearly wiping out an entire species *is* fair?!" I wanted to reach for my knife. And use it. Repeatedly.

Kane leapt to his feet, gripping my shoulders. Frightened, I tried to step back but he held me in place as he shook with rage.

"I did not do this!"

"What do you mean? Of course you did!" My hand reached up to my belt where my knife rested. "You were leading the army."

His hands tightened on my shoulders. "Malek sent an envoy to Agartha without my knowledge on the pretense of negotiating peace after their attack on Ker-Is—"

"Which they didn't do! You slaughtered some of your own people and made it look like the Bànshēn rén did it!"

He seemed genuinely shocked. "What do you mean?"

"I was there! In Ker-Is!" I said, sharing too many details yet again. "The city was probably evacuated and you killed a small number of Irkallans and left their bodies! Your weapons were used! We... I found long arrows among the dead. The Bànshēn rén live in caves and shoot short arrows. It was staged to look like they did it. And you know that!"

Kane let go of me and turned back to the balcony wall.

"I was... I was not aware of this," he stammered.

"Bullshit! If you're the so-called Knight Commander, you would have to know!"

He sat on the wall and stared off into the black night.

"I have fought against his plans every step of the way. The king obviously does not trust me."

"What do you mean? You've been with him his whole life. How could he not trust you?"

"I was trying to explain," he said, as he collapsed in on himself. "His emissaries left Agartha and stole away with some children. When the Bànshēn rén did not follow after them, they killed them."

"And that wasn't your idea?!"

"I could never have done such a thing... I swear to you. On my father's honor. This all took place as I was conducting training exercises with the army remaining. I received word the envoy had been attacked by them, which surprised none of us. Not after Ker-Is. I rode out immediately with several regiments. After a day of riding, we arrived to find that the legion that accompanied the envoy had been decimated. When the Agarthans attacked us, we fought back. And you know the rest of the tale. I did not have all the details until our journey home. Events have escalated quickly in the last few months, ever since the arrival of the king's mage," he said. "He now has the king's ear."

"You're lying," I told him, not entirely sure that was true.

"What would I hope to gain by lying? As you said, you believe yourself to be my prisoner."

"So, I can just walk outta here? And you wouldn't stop me?"

Kane held his long arm out toward the door as he stared at his boots. "I would have one of my knights escort you out—one that I trust. But you must not try to return to the feast."

I took a step toward the exit. Instead, I turned to him. "What will you do?"

He turned his sad eyes to me. "I shall get blind, stinking drunk."

He staggered to his feet.

Run, Finley! Get out of there! My brain screamed at my heart. But my heart refused to listen.

"Want some company?" I asked.

Kane offered me his arm and, like a fool, I took it.

"I have got a bottle of spiced Ardarian rum in my quarters."

"Oh, I'm not falling for the old 'spiced Ardarian rum in my quarters' line! No way, no day!" I drunkenly hiccuped.

He smiled, for the first time in a while. "You are quite intriguing."

We stumbled up some stone staircases and through a maze of hallways to his chambers.

As Kane tried to fill my glass with more of the strong liquor, he continually leaned forward until he missed the glass, pouring it onto the table, then the floor.

I tried to drag my glass along with the bottle to catch as much as I could.

He bent so far that he lost his balance and fell face first onto the patterned rug.

We laughed so hard we couldn't breathe.

Kane occupied a huge, luxurious room high in the castle. A four post bed with curtains at one end, with a table and cushioned chairs in the middle, and a wardrobe with his own personal bathtub at the other end. Several tall windows stared down on the bright city below. Lit candles filled the room and a fire raged in the hearth.

He staggered to his feet, taking a couple of steps to catch his balance. Aiming for his chair, he missed and hit the table, then fell into my lap.

Our howls echoed through the chamber.

When he pushed himself upright, my nose filled with the smell of alcohol.

"Oh, wow," I said. "You smell just like my mom."

"You are a curious woman, Kelaino of Atlantis." He laughed at me, lurching toward the fireplace.

"Oh, if I were you, I would not walk near an open flame!"

Kane chuckled and took another long drink from the bottle. He splashed some liquor into the fireplace and flames blasted from the hearth.

"Boom!" I said.

We fell out again, convulsing with laughter.

He plopped into his chair, pushing a bowl of dark fruits over to me. I picked one up and stared at it. It looked like a large, brown raisin.

"Are these dates?"

"They are gorlas!"

I ate one. "Well, it tastes like a date to me."

A melancholy washed over him. He fell back in his chair, staring at the bottle. "You mentioned your mother. Do you miss your family back in Atlantis?"

"My family is dead—"

"I am sorry."

"—to me. They're dead *to me*."

That cracked us both up. Kane doubled over and tumbled off his chair.

I remembered that Malek was still down in the Great Hall—enjoying his feast—and that I needed to stab him. But the entire room was fuzzy.

"Oh, shit!" I said.

"What?" He poked his head above the table.

"I gotta go back to the party!"

"The party? What... No, you cannot go to the... Wait!"

I rose up, adjusted my dress, and tried to focus on the door across the room. I lined up my path so that I could walk as straight as possible in that direction.

Kane pulled himself from the floor. "Kelaino! Wait!"

I marched toward the door, but veered to the right and ran into the wall. I held my hand against the cold stones and worked my way to the door.

Kane cut me off. "Kelaino. Please. Stay here this evening."

"I can't! I have to go kill the king!" Yes. I said that. Out loud.

"You will be the one killed if you return to the Hall. However, I have a plan..."

I don't remember anything after that.

Chapter 52

I woke in pitch black darkness. The hangover headache hit me next. Hit me hard.

Closing my eyes, I groaned and pushed at the pain in my temples with the palms of my hands.

As the previous night played back in my mind, I finally sat up. Why was it dark? Had Kane put me in the dungeon for admitting I wanted to kill Malek?

I was sitting on a soft surface and the material felt silky. I threw out my hands and grasped more plush fabric. Pulling back the curtains, I found myself on Kane's four poster bed. He had not had me locked up.

I peeked into the chamber. On the other side of the room, Kane rose out of his bathtub and grabbed a towel. I hid back behind the bed curtains. Damn, he was hot. And I could *not* unsee that.

I poked my head out again. Kane dabbed the bath towel across his wet skin, over the matted hair on his chest and stomach. And what a beautiful stomach it was—his abs had abs!

When he caught me gawking at him, I hid behind the curtains.

"Come, eat!" he called out. "I had them bring you plenty of eggs and sausages. Some bread. And some wine."

The word wine made me throw up a little in my mouth.

Still wearing my gown from last night, I stepped down from his bed. My legs ached and my head had been squished by a karkadann. I dragged myself across the room, slipping into a chair. Bright light shone through the windows, forcing me to cover my eyes.

Between my fingers, I watched him wolf down breakfast. He had slid on a silk robe, but those magnificent chest hairs were calling to me, begging for my fingers to run through them.

"How are you still functioning?"

"You started drinking before me." Prick.

I flipped him off. "In Atlantis, this means good morning..."

He flipped me off. "Good morning to you!"

I stole a piece of his sausage while staring directly at him.

"I saved your life last night."

"You did. I think. Did we do... anything else last night?"

"Such as?"

"You know what I mean."

More grinning. "I was a gentleman. You passed out. I let you sleep on my bed, Kelaino of Atlantis."

"Stop calling me that," he said.

"Shall I call you by another name?" I locked eyes with him. "How about Kel?"

"That works. Geez, I wish you guys had coffee."

"Coffee?"

"Morning drink. In Atlantis. Wakes you right the fuck up."

He slid over a mug full of wine, along with that handsome smirk of his.

"No 'hair of the dog' for me." I pushed the mug away.

"I must visit your island! The way you talk is fascinating!"

Kane reached beside his chair, picking up my knife. He showed it to me and then set it on the table.

I stared at the blade, then I looked at him. "Um..."

"Do not worry. That was intended for Malek, no doubt."

"You're... okay with that?"

He sat back in his chair, taking a drink of the wine from the mug.

"Were you sent here, by the Atlanteans, to assassinate him?" he asked. Then he shook his head, held up his hands. "No, it does not matter. What matters is that you were here to kill him. And that is enough for me."

"I don't get it. You... th-this doesn't bother you?"

He gulped more wine.

"Kane, why don't you mind that I tried to kill your king?"

"Because I want you to end his reign."

"What?!"

He whispered. "My father was a great man. My respect for him immeasurable. However, as I have explained, I am a man of honor and I have sworn my loyalty—"

"To the kingdom. But not to Malek," I exclaimed. Hope swelled in me. "And last night, you said you had a plan."

"Yes. While I cannot dishonor my father's memory and disregard my oath to him, I must do something to stop Malek! If he desired to build an empire and subjugate the other races, that *might* be acceptable. But his plot to turn his people against all of them and wipe every other species from existence? That is not the way of Irkalla! And not the will of his ancestors, who worked so hard to help all the peoples of Tir Na."

"But?"

"But... I cannot kill him."

"So, you can bend the rules but not break them?"

"You are one to easily disobey the wishes of your father then?"

That one hit me hard. I stared out the window, avoiding the look that was probably in his eyes.

"No. I'm a bend-don't-break kinda girl, too. My dad is not quite as great as yours... but I never stood up to him when I should have. So... mad respect to you. You are my kind of not-quite-right in the head."

I grabbed the knife, twirling it around in my hand.

"I'm guessing you want *me* to take him out? Because that would ease your conscience? Get rid of the asshole and keep your hands clean?"

"It shames me to admit it, but... yes."

I leaned across the table and pointed the knife at him. "There's no shame here, Kane. None at all. You want to do what's right and you want to honor your pops. Have your cake and eat it, too. I get that. But I lost the only chance I had to end that ditch pig last night."

Kane laughed to himself. "That was not your only chance. Your plan was naive and dangerous. You had no chance."

"Why? A crowded hall. The king dancing among his people. I could have stabbed him and disappeared in the chaos. And it would have worked if you hadn't dragged me off."

"You would not have succeeded, and you would have been captured or killed. Nerus, the king's mage, had a premonition before the feast and feared for him. At his urging, Malek wore a chainmail shirt under his shirt last night."

I had not thought of that. I could have gotten myself killed for no reason at all. Epic fail.

"So, this was all just a big, fat waste!"

Kane stood, holding out his hand. He helped me to my feet and pulled me close to him.

"It was anything but a waste," he said with a deep, almost hungry, tone.

I stared at his chest hair far too long, then looked into his eyes.

Kane kissed me, softly at first. Teasing. Tempting. My tongue met his as my legs melted. He placed his hands on my cheeks and kissed me, harder and longer.

His robe fell open and I pressed against him. Kane groaned and I almost gave in completely.

With my hands against his chest, I pushed away.

"Whoa. Oh, I never do that on a first date," I said.

He reached down into the bowl of dried-up brown fruits—handed me two dates.

I burst out laughing and returned to those strong lips.

A knock at the door.

I rushed behind the table as he pulled his robe tight and marched to the door, opening it wide.

A chamber maid stood in the doorway. "Begging your pardon, Sir."

She handed him a stack of folded clothes, towels, a bowl, and a bottle.

"My thanks," he said.

I stepped further out of sight before the maid spotted me.

Kane closed the door.

"What's that?"

He held up the clothes and supplies, placing them on the table.

"This is part of my plan."

Chapter 53

"The king has a regular routine after every one of his festivals. And we will take advantage of that predictability."

Kane had dressed himself in blank pants, white shirt, and tight dark blue waistcoat.

"After a night of celebrating, Malek likes to spar with swords in the courtyard. Get the blood going. He then bathes and eats a heavy luncheon."

"I could do it then! Serve his food with a side dish of steel!" I waved my knife in the air.

"That would not be wise. There can be quite a bit of traffic in the Great Hall at meal times. After last night, your look is known. If a woman from Atlantis is thought to be the assassin, there would certainly be a retaliation against your people. Now... remove your clothing."

"Um..."

He smirked. "I am a gentleman. Remember?"

Kane held up the bottle and shook the liquid inside.

"We need to dye your hair, to effectively change your appearance," he added.

"No need!" I said.

I picked up the bowl of water from the table and dragged Kane to his bathtub.

"Run that water over my hair," I said.

I leaned over the edge of the tub as he poured the bowl over my head. I scrubbed my hair and drops of black liquid fell into his bath water.

"Bygods, you have firehair!"

I sat up, pointing to a pitcher of water, and he rushed over to retrieve it. I leaned back over the tub, and he poured more water onto my head.

"Why does everyone have a problem with red hair?" I wrapped a towel around my head after I was sure all the black dye was out.

Kane reached out and felt several strands sticking out from my towel.

"It was thought that those with red hair were enchanters and brought bad luck. Many believed they were responsible for dragons attacking our cities."

I looked up at him, in alarm. Was I putting the mission in danger?

"But that was long ago. You are more of a curiosity these days. You simply do not see many with firehair these days."

I picked up the plain brown tunic that the maid had delivered.

"Turn around?" I asked.

Kane spun his head, walking over to the table to drink from his wine mug.

I wiggled out of my gown, splashed water on my face and body from the tub.

"I see that you do not have the... gills of an Atlantean," he said.

My eyes shot up to a mirror on the other side of the tub. Kane stared at me through the reflection.

I motioned for him to turn away. He winked and nodded as he walked to the windows overlooking the Black City.

"So, yeah. I'm not really from Atlantis," I said as I put on the tunic.

"That does explain a few oddities."

"Okay, so I'm not going to stab him at lunch. What am I doing?"

"After a big function, he will likely rest in his chambers. However, he will first have a healer's apprentice come to him to administer a massage."

"If you can get me into Malek's chambers before the apprentice shows, I might have a chance to skewer the bastard and run off before anyone discovers his body?"

I understood his plan. "Precisely!"

"But how am I gonna pass myself off as this apprentice? Won't they be worried about letting a stranger in, to give this asshat a happy ending?"

He looked at me like he had no idea what I was talking about, which was likely.

"If you are at his door, it means you already have passed numerous inspections. No one knows you are here with me. No one will suspect. I shall walk you to his chambers. But then—"

"Then it's up to me to do the deed," I said.

"Indeed."

A deep breath as I steadied myself.

"And you're sure he's going to want his massage? Today?"

He held my hands, staring into my eyes. "I have confirmed it, but we must hurry. You need to get in and… back out quickly. There can be *no* hesitation. I do not want to lose you, do you understand me?"

I nodded my head.

The realization that I would need to kill overwhelmed me. Again. I finished off the wine in his mug, trying to steady my nerves.

He handed me the clean towels and the bottle of oil.

"Are you able to go through with this?" he asked. "If not, please tell me now and I will escort you safely from the castle. I have grown to care for you a great deal. And this is a huge burden to place on your shoulders."

I was truly scared.

"No, I can do it. I can. I have to."

He slid my knife in between two of the towels and kissed my forehead softly.

I smiled to myself as I watched Kane march ahead of me through the halls of the castle. His confidence was infectious. Having an ally—a man we thought was the enemy—on the inside *inspired* me. I felt like I might actually be able to pull it off.

I kept my head bowed and my eyes down as I followed behind him. We encountered a handful of passing servants and a few soldiers standing guard, with none of them paying any attention to me.

We climbed several sets of stairs until we reached the top floor of the keep. Kane became more guarded. He peered around a corner and motioned me to stay close. We moved quietly along a corridor until we came to a large hallway open to the air on one side and decorated with a mural on the other.

Kane pulled me back into the dark corridor. "We are here. Simply walk up to the entrance to his chambers, bow your head, and wait. The guards will open the door for you. Do not say a word."

Deep breath and a short nod—I was ready. Kane held my shoulders, smiled down at me, and then kissed me.

"May the gods protect you." Kane hurried down the corridor.

I bolted toward the king's quarters, not wanting to think about anything that came next. The hall contained a series of arches, exposing an impressive view of the Black City beyond. I took a few brief glances of the golden sunlight in case they would be my last.

With the towels and bottle of oil in hand, I hurried up to the two ornate doors guarded by stoic Irkallan soldiers. True to Kane's word, they didn't say a thing, just opened the doors without so much as a glance in my direction.

I slipped inside, trying to be as invisible as possible. The layout wasn't straightforward—several smaller rooms branched off the main entry, so I followed the faint sound of muffled voices down a narrow hallway.

I paused at the threshold of a sprawling chamber. Except, curiously, there was no bed in sight. Massive wooden beams crisscrossed the ceiling, and a fire crackled in a grand hearth, casting flickering shadows across the room. Furniture was scattered throughout—wooden chairs, a sofa, and a settee near the tall windows. Toward the far end, a rectangular table was flanked by benches, and an intricately carved desk sat in one corner, littered with papers and what looked like maps.

Near the fire, Malek stood in a crimson silk robe, one hand resting on the mantel as he casually sipped wine from a horn. His demeanor was relaxed, but his sharp eyes hinted at constant calculation. Across from him, a dark-haired man in a black cloak listened intently. Their low conversation didn't carry, but the tension in the room was palpable.

I lingered in the shadows, gripping the towels like a lifeline, my pulse racing. Whatever I had just walked into, it was definitely above my pay grade.

"When will we perform the ceremony?" Malek asked the man.

"Now that I have the book, I can cast the spells at any time," said the man.

I stood there patiently waiting for him to notice me.

Malek patted the man's black cloak. "Immortality awaits, I suppose."

I took several steps forward; Malek finally turned his head.

"Ah, time for my treatment!"

When he walked toward me, the man in black turned around to reveal his dark rat eyes and weaselly features. I got worked up in a hurry—would he recognize me?

"Nerus, we shall continue our talk in a few hours!" Malek said over his shoulder.

The king of Irkalla was even more beautiful up close, even after a night of partying hard.

He inspected me for a moment. "Where is Hazida, firehair?"

Nerus moved closer, his eyes glued to me. I busied myself by setting down my bottle of oil and towels.

"Um, she has taken ill, your majesty," I stammered, my chin on my chest.

"Not a bother! Let us hope, for your sake, you have her talents!"

"Yes, your majesty."

Malek striped off his robe as he spun around to lay out on the cushioned settee.

"Your majesty," said Nerus.

I quickly covered the king's bare ass with a towel, avoiding eye contact with the slimy mage.

"Malek, sire?"

"Yes? What is it, Nerus?" Malek growled from his prone position.

"This woman. I am sensing a great fear in her."

"Wouldn't treating a king for the first time strike fear in any woman?"

"Great fear and... much anger," he warned.

"Ah, Nerus, you are such a worried old hag!" Malek laughed, adjusting himself on the settee.

I kept ducking down, turning my face away from the mage.

"She looks familiar to me! And rarely is fear mixed with such anger unless... she's here to kill you, sire!"

Chapter 54

I reached under the towel, gripping the knife handle hard.

"Guards!" I heard Nerus shout.

I threw my knee against Malek's back and lifted the blade above my head.

"There you are! We have been trying to find you," said Malek.

He shifted his weight, tossing me off balance and to the floor.

The king rolled off the settee, slipping on his blood-red robe.

I rushed at him, trying to remember the moves Cira had taught me—don't extend the shoulder too far, keep my balance, target the closest part of his body.

Malek beamed, standing with arms out wide.

I thrust the knife at his chest. He turned his torso sideways. I slashed to the right, knowing he was within range, and he ducked. Malek bounded upright. I turned the knife in my hand, to drive down at his collar bone. He deflected my blow with the back of his hand.

He punched at my side, thinking I would lose my balance when he pushed my arm away. I pivoted on the ball of my foot, carrying all the weight, and slashed across my body at his fist. My knife tip narrowly missed as he lowered his arm.

"Oh, she is quite good!" Malek cheerily announced to Nerus.

We circled each other as two guards rushed the room.

I lunged and missed. Knowing I was out of time, I sprinted at him, slashing at his shoulder. He pushed my arm away. Closer to him, I looked down at his belly but plunged my blade higher, at his neck.

The knife nicked his skin. He grabbed my arm, knocking the blade from my hand, and put his arm around my neck.

I had lost my only chance.

Malek laughed, shoving me to the floor.

The soldiers scooped me up.

"She is too good," Nerus observed.

Malek held out his hand from the cut on his neck, inspecting the amount of blood. Just a flesh wound.

I struggled against his soldiers, but they were too strong.

Breathing hard, I yanked back enough to put my face in front of his, before they could drag me away to be executed.

"What do you mean you've been trying to find me?!" I screamed.

Malek held a towel to his neck, taking a step closer.

"You are Finley Maguire, are you not?"

Shocked would have been an understatement. He knew my name.

"I knew all about your attempt to assassinate me at the feast last night," he said. He leered at me from toe to head. "Honestly, I was expecting a more formidable woman. Not a child."

I kicked at him with my leg, hoping to get at least one good shot in. Malek deftly spun to the side.

"But such a fiery spirit!" he said.

"I think it time to break that spirit," sneered Nerus. "Your majesty."

Malek inspected his red robe, wiping at the blood that had dripped on the material. He grabbed my face with his hand, forcing me to look down at his precious silk robe.

"Do you know how they dyed this robe?" said Malek. "They used the menstrual blood of thirty virgins. They said it was to protect me and grant me good fortune from the gods. A little of the king's own blood will only improve my odds—so, I thank you for that, little firehair."

I struggled against the men holding me back and growled at him. I wanted desperately to spit in his face but my hungover ass couldn't summon a thing.

"Sire," said Nerus.

His cold, dark eyes lingered on me. He licked his lips. The knuckles on his hand that gripped my knife glowed a bright white.

"Sire?"

He wanted to kill me right then and there. But the slithery voice of his mage pulled him back into the moment.

"What? Oh, yes," he replied.

He looked at the soldiers. "Take her to the Great Hall. I must get dressed."

The guards started to drag me from the chambers, but the king stopped them.

"But. first... let us bring her to heel."

Malek punched me hard on the side of my head, knocking me out cold.

Chapter 55

When I came around, everything was dark—a rough burlap sack had been placed over my head. I tried to lift my arms, but they were tied behind my back. I was lying on a wood floor on my side. And my head, already hurting from my hangover, throbbed even harder.

I struggled to push myself upright, but I could only rock back and forth.

"Ah, she wakes!" Malek's voice.

Someone from behind picked me up, setting me on my knees. I could sense other people on either side of me.

"Let us finish this quickly! I have an important matter to attend to this evening."

Hands ripped the dark hood off my head. As I let my eyes adjust to the brightness, I scanned the room. We were at the far end of the Great Hall, in front of the raised platform that held the king's dining table.

Malek, hands on his hips, grinned down at me from the dais. He wore a short silver jacket, with matching pants, and a royal blue shirt. He had also placed his crown on his head, in case I had forgotten.

Nerus hovered over the king's shoulder.

Kane was to the right of Malek, with a worried look on his face—his eyes begging me for forgiveness.

"Let us greet our other guests, shall we?!" shouted Malek.

Six other people, with hoods on their heads, sat on their knees in front of the platform.

The hood came off the one to my left to reveal Gunnr. She glared at me in anger, as she struggled against the ropes that held her arms.

Another guard ripped off Pherric's hood. He examined the room, then his grieving eyes fell on me.

Soldiers pulled off more hoods. Temurr, Frip, and Cira had been planted to the left of Gunnr. Braylor and Kasuma were on Pherric's right. They all looked as though they had been through a massive fight—cuts bled and bruises swelled and darkened.

"Looks like we have everyone!" said Malek.

Someone had turned us in. Was it Lady Anisha?

"Oh, everyone except for the patron of your doomed misadventure."

"We have no patron, Malek," avowed Pherric.

Two guards dragged in a body, letting it hit the floor with a thud. One of the soldiers dropped Lady Anisha's head into the middle of our group. I screamed. Braylor and Cira roared in anger. Pherric lowered his eyes.

"I beg to differ," Malek answered.

Pherric stared at the floor. "Our attempt to... end your reign was entirely my scheme. I gathered this group together for that sole purpose."

"Truly? It seems to me as though you are all delegates of your collective nations, no? Representatives of your rulers," challenged Malek. "And your actions speak in proxy for your leaders!"

"We did this of our own accord. No one sanctioned our quest."

"Quest! Did you hear that, Sir Kane? They were on a *quest* to kill the king!" He patted the shoulder of his right-hand man. Kane threw a half-smirk at his king.

"We acted alone," Pherric stated.

Braylor growled. "Do not explain yourself to this halfwit, Pherric! He is not worthy!"

It hit me like a crosstown bus—I was going to die in a matter of minutes. I began to sob as I crumpled to the floor.

"I am the halfwit?! And yet, here you are... on your knees before me like whipped hellhounds."

Braylor cried out and tried to stand. Three guards pounced on him, pushing him to his knees.

"Before I order your execution, I thought you would like to know how this halfwit made fools of you all!"

Boots marched across the hall floor. I peered over my shoulder. Soldiers escorted Lord Diago up the aisle between the rows of tables.

"My sincerest gratitude to you, Diago!" said Malek.

I gasped. Pherric's lip quivered as pools flooded his eyes.

"How?" he whispered. "How... could you do this?!"

Diago stared at him, beaming brightly, and clicked his tongue. "Dear boy, my family and the House of Lascarus has suffered far too long under the rule of the Three Houses. And our financial situation needed to be greatly improved. Thanks to the generosity of the king... those issues have, as of now, been solved."

"You betrayed me for coin?!" Pherric seethed.

"Boy, your parents sold you to the Scholomance to pay off their debts—you should be used to being chattel at this stage. As of today, we are the First House of Cíbola!"

"You traded our lives to be a servant in Malek's empire?!" Pherric turned away, crying out in anguish.

Gunnr spat on Diago's boots and cursed him.

Diago replied with a smug smile, then gave a curt nod to Malek. "If you will excuse me, your majesty. I have important business."

As Diago turned to leave, Kane stepped forward on the dais.

"No one gave you permission to leave," Kane snarled. He seemed seriously pissed that Diago had turned us over to the king.

The arrogant bastard stopped in his tracks.

"And you will bow to your emperor, Diago," added Kane.

When Diago failed to turn around, the Knight Commander drew his sword.

"Emperor?" queried Lord Diago.

"Let us remain calm, gentlemen, as we are on the same side," soothed Malek, holding his hand up and grinning ear-to-ear with pride in Kane.

"Lord Diago," he continued. "You will most certainly collect your reward before you depart. However, I am standing here today thanks to your valiant efforts! So, you will be witness to the punishment of these traitorous renegades for their attempt on my life."

Diago spun around, bowing deeply. "Yes, your majesty."

"It is good that you know your place," said Malek.

The Lord of the First House of Cíbola slithered off behind the guards to hide in the shadows.

"On to the matter before us," said Malek. "I hereby declare that you are to die for your crimes against Irkalla!"

Malek hopped off the dais and slowly walked past everyone.

"Now..." He tapped his finger on his lower lip. "Who will be the first?"

Chapter 56

"Let's start with the Prominans. Their smell bothers me..."

Malek laughed to himself. Nervous laughter followed from the guards in the room.

I pleaded with my eyes for Kane to do something. He looked away, in shame.

Nerus impatiently crossed his arms. "Just kill them already!"

Malek fired off an arched eyebrow at his mage.

"At your pleasure... your majesty," Nerus added.

I gulped hard. My heart pounded. Lines of blood ran down to my fingers as I pulled at the ropes on my wrists.

Kane hopped off the dais, strolled over to the king. "Would it not make more sense, your majesty, to make an example of these traitors?"

"What are you speaking of?"

"Why not take them to the Arena... for a public execution? Announce to the world that you, as Emperor, are more than capable of quashing any attempted insurrection."

I doubted Kane had a plan, but he was trying to delay my inevitable death.

"No," Malek said, tentatively. Then he stepped forward and pointed to a soldier. "No! I want to watch them die now!"

He looked back at Kane. "But we will hang their bodies from the castle walls and place their heads on pikes at the city gates!"

Malek's executioner, a bare-chested man with a helmet that covered his face, stood behind Temurr. A massive axe rested in his thick hands.

Kane whispered in Malek's ear.

The king laughed quietly. "Oh, an intriguing idea! Bygods, let us see what happens!"

Sir Kane held his hand out to a soldier. "Give me your coins."

He withdrew several coins of his own and grabbed a mug from a table.

Malek pulled the mug out of Kane's hand. "I will handle this!"

The knight commander's face turned bright red.

Malek wandered into our half-circle as we worked to free ourselves from the ropes.

"We are going to play a little game!" said Malek. "Does that not sound exciting?! I have... let me see, a few silver coins in this cup and a few gold coins. To let it be known that I am fair, I will permit you to draw your own coins. If you select a silver coin, your life will be spared. And if you select a gold coin, well, I am afraid my executioner will have to live up to his title."

Malek peered into the mug again, swishing the coins around.

"Looks to be fairly even odds!" he exclaimed. "We will start with the lovely Tengu maiden."

He held out the cup. Kasuma twisted herself around to show that her arms were bound.

"Unbind me and I shall choose," said Kasuma.

"I am a halfwit." Malek clucked his tongue. "But I am not a complete idiot."

The king walked behind her, bent over, and she plucked out a coin with her roped hands.

"Does this beast understand words?" the king asked Kane.

Kane nodded.

Malek spoke loudly, slowly, to Braylor. "Select a coin, creature!"

"I will not play your games, fool," Braylor cursed, spitting onto the floor.

"I see," said Malek. "Well, then I shall choose for you!"

He closed his eyes, dug out a coin, and placed it in Braylor's huge hand.

Pherric, still numb from the betrayal of Diago, grabbed a coin between his fingers.

Malek stepped behind me. "And now, we come to our feisty, but woefully inexperienced, assassin!"

Out of the corner of my eye, I caught Gunnr staring at my hands as I picked my coin.

The king stepped up behind her and whispered. "As a fellow Hominan, I am rooting for you. But... the company you keep? Such a shame." He tsk-tsked loudly for all to hear.

As the king handed out his coins, Gunnr leaned heavily against my side, nearly knocking me off balance. Before I could react, her fingers darted out and snatched the coin out of my hand, replacing hers with mine.

I whipped my head around to glare at her, my eyes blazing with shock and anger. But I didn't alert Malek. I couldn't. My mind spun as I clenched the new coin in my hand. She took my coin—my one chance of survival. Every shred of hope I'd clung to shattered in that moment, leaving me hollow and trembling.

I sank to the cold floor, tears slipping silently down my cheeks. I had nothing left. Nothing but the bitter realization that Gunnr's life was worth more than mine. She still had a purpose, a chance to make things right. Me? All I'd done was fail—over and over again. At everything.

Resignation settled over me like a heavy shroud. If my sacrifice meant she might live to fight another day, then so be it. Even if it meant giving up the last piece of hope I had.

"Reveal the verdicts! Did the gods look favorably upon you? We shall see..."

Malek motioned for the guard behind Kasuma to reveal her coin.

The guard held up a gold coin—she was marked for death. My stomach twisted.

Pherric's coin was silver, but his face remained stoic. No relief, no hope. Just dread.

Then it was my turn. The guard yanked my coin from my hand and displayed it for all to see.

Silver.

I had been spared. My breath caught as I glanced at Kane, but he only closed his eyes, his face an unreadable mask.

The guard pulled out Gunnr's coin next—and it was gold.

I stared at her, my heart sinking into disbelief and panic. Gunnr? She saw that I had a gold one and switched the coins... to spare my life.

She turned to me, her face calm and composed, offering that sly smirk.

"Why?" I whispered, barely able to speak.

Gunnr leaned in close, her voice low but firm. "The fate of our world depends on... you. Unfortunately." She followed her grim words with a quick, almost cheeky wink, leaving me reeling. "Lex talionis."

I gulped and nodded. She stared straight ahead, welcoming her fate.

Frip and Cira got gold coins.

Temurr's was silver. He would survive while his partner was sentenced to death.

He flipped out. "No. No, my love! No!"

The ape man thrashed about, savagely straining against his ropes and shaking his head.

Malek backed up as two guards subdued Temurr, shoving him hard on the floor.

"No! No, Frip! I cannot lose you!"

"I have accepted it, dear!" Frip tried hard to soothe him. "Please do not hurt yourself!" he cried.

"Bygods, I thought they were both male!" said Malek. He joked with a guard. "You never can tell with their kind!"

Braylor growled. "They are male, you stupid prat!"

Malek held a hand to his face. "Oh, that is most foul! Well, at least *one* of the deviant beasts will no longer infest my house," sneered Malek. "Kill the unfortunate ones!"

"You can't do this!" I screamed at Malek. "Please!"

Malek leapt to the dais to avoid the upcoming blood, waving nonchalantly at the executioner.

I watched the burly man take his place behind Frip, hauling his axe off to the side.

Temurr sobbed.

"I will find you, dear. In the next life. I will find you. I promise," Frip soothed.

Pherric whispered to Temurr. "Do not watch."

I wailed out as I threw myself over, burying my face on Pherric's shoulder.

Frip turned his head to me. "Do well, sweet girl. Do well, and take care of—"

The axe cut through him. And I will never forget the dull thud of his head striking the wooden floor.

Chapter 57

"No!" Braylor cried out. "You bastard!"

Temurr raged against his cords, thrashing about and roaring at Malek. A swarm of soldiers threw themselves on him, pinned him to the floor, waiting for his wailing to turn to whimpers.

Braylor strained to break free, without succeeding, from the three sets of chains they used to bind him.

As I sobbed on Pherric's shoulder, he tried to shush and calm me. I knew how much he worried and wanted to protect me, but I was gutted. As though I was bleeding out on that floor next to Frip.

I sat up and stared through the tears at my friend lying dead on the floor, burning it into my memory—his head lying at the knees of Temurr, those wide eyes full of dread, mouth hanging open.

I gasped at the realization that this was only the beginning of our torment.

Cira lurched back and forth, catching our attention.

She looked at Gunnr, then to me, and gave a slight nod.

"Make a difference, Finley."

She nodded to Kasuma—and she gave a nod back to Cira.

Cira only had one soldier standing guard behind her—what was she planning?

Her face turned that terrible bright red. Her eyes went wild. And she went into her trance. Her body shook. Spit flew from her lips.

Cira hopped from her knees and launched up into the air. She lowered her arms down, stepped through them, placing her hands in front of her body.

"Stop her!" shouted Malek.

The soldier left Temurr and grabbed her shoulders, dragging her to the floor. She threw her legs in the air, wrapping them around the guard's neck. Cira grunted and writhed. As she tightened her thighs, I heard a crack as she broke his jawbone.

"Guards! Kill her now!"

The man guarding Kasuma rushed to help. She silently pulled herself free from the ropes on her wrists.

Cira let out a violent scream, her thighs cracking the man's skull—his body fell to the floor.

"End that savage!" ordered Malek.

As the soldiers held her down, another wrapped his forearm around Cira's neck. She bit him, pulling away a chunk of flesh, and laughed hysterically.

He used his good arm to slit her throat open. Blood sprayed on me and Gunnr.

"No!" I screamed.

Cira's body pulsated, twitched as the guards threw her to the floor.

I heard the sound of ruffling feathers. Kasuma leapt to her feet, spread her wings, and jumped to the top of a long table.

"Kill that monstrosity!" Malek bellowed.

Kasuma darted down the table, leapt over a swinging sword, and dodged the thrust of another. She flapped hard, taking flight.

"Fools!"

He grabbed a dagger from a soldier's belt and threw it. After Kasuma beat her wings in the air, her elevation dropped enough to let the dagger sail over her head.

Men ran after her, but she floated through the doors of the Great Hall.

She was free. Cira had completed her final mission—saving one of us with her distraction.

Malek berated his guards, throwing a petulant tantrum.

My tears fell on the floor as I leaned over to Cira's body. "I will make a difference."

The king paced back and forth. The cowardly Nerus rose up from hiding behind the dais table. Kane stared down, avoiding eye contact, with hands on his hips.

"I grow weary of this," said Malek, composing himself.

He drew his sword, shouted out a war cry, and ran the blade through Gunnr's heart.

She gasped as life drained away from her.

"Gunnr!" I shouted.

Malek wrenched his blade from her chest and her body fell on my lap. I wanted to hold her, gently lower her down, but she dropped forward onto her face and rolled back. She would have been disappointed by my display of useless emotion, but I could not choke it back and more tears fell.

I snarled at Malek. "You worthless piece of shit!"

The king howled with fury. He swung his sword down at me and— stopped short. He laughed like a madman, wiping blood from his face with the back of his hand. His eyes danced as he placed the tip of the blade on my neck. Whipping it away, he sliced my skin. I recoiled in pain as the warm blood ran down to my shoulder.

"Mind your tongue, hellcat!" he shouted. "I am trying to be a man of honor, but you are making it most difficult!"

Braylor struggled yet again, but Malek's men took no chances—they rushed behind the survivors, placing blades against necks.

He wiped Gunnr's blood off his sword using my tunic.

I rocked back and forth on my knees. My vision blurred and, as if I were staring through a red tunnel, I could only see Gunnr's blood-stained blonde hair spread out on the floor at my knees.

"Take this rabble to the Arena. They shall die in a public execution... tomorrow, at midday!"

I heard the sound of his boots, and then those of his minions, march away on the creaking hardwood floor.

Lex talionis, bitch.

Chapter 58

The Irkallans stripped us of everything—our clothes, our dignity—and shackled us in heavy chains before tossing us into the back of a filthy prison wagon lined with iron bars.

Word must have spread throughout the Black City, because by the time we were paraded through its streets, hundreds of citizens had gathered to watch. They screamed curses, flung rotten food, small stones, and clumps of mud at us. The wagon driver, clearly enjoying the spectacle, kept the karkadanns' pace excruciatingly slow, ensuring we absorbed every insult, every humiliation.

The path ended at the rear entrance of the gargantuan stone stadium at the city center. Its towering six-story walls, lined with columns and wide arches, loomed above us. The sight made my stomach churn.

The guards yanked us from the wagon and dragged us down into the cold, oppressive dungeon beneath the arena. Shackles clanged as they were removed, only to be replaced by the dull ache of bruised wrists. Without ceremony, they shoved me, Temurr, Pherric, and Braylor into a dank cell that reeked of mold and decay.

No one spoke. We were too shattered, too consumed by the weight of our failure.

I stumbled to a corner, wrapping my arms around myself in a vain attempt to keep warm. My eyes fixed on the only distraction in the pitch-black cell: the relentless drip-drip-drip of water echoing from somewhere deep in the shadows.

At some point during that long, endless night, exhaustion won. I drifted off sitting up, the cold stone wall pressing against me as my mind mercifully dulled to the horror of what was coming.

We were startled awake by the heavy clang of boots against the stone floor, echoing down the dark, damp hallway outside our cell. A short, muscular man, his bald head gleaming under the dim torchlight, waddled toward us, dragging a bucket that sloshed with every step. He stopped in front of our cell, the sour stench of the bucket hitting us before he did. Using a cracked ladle, he scooped out four portions of thick, gray stew into chipped wooden bowls and placed them unceremoniously on the grimy floor, muttering something we couldn't understand.

I shivered uncontrollably as I staggered to the cell door, my teeth chattering with the cold that seemed to seep into my bones. Pherric was already there, his face set in a grim mask as he picked up a bowl and handed it to me. The stew quivered like sludge, and the rancid smell made my stomach churn. Despite this, he passed the other bowls to Braylor and Temurr with steady hands.

I hesitated, the foul food threatening to turn my stomach before it reached my mouth. But I had no choice. Gagging and grimacing, I forced down every slimy bit, each swallow a battle against my gag reflex. If I was going to meet death at noon, I wasn't doing it on an empty stomach. A fight was coming, and I'd need all my strength.

Pherric sat next to me on the stone floor. "Are you well? Considering?"

"Am I ready to die, you mean?"

Pherric gave me a weak smile. "As Kasuma so eloquently put it, we were meant to fail."

"Thanks for the awesome pep talk, bro."

He stared through the bars, a wistful grin on his face. "The Irkallans are most likely placing the heads of our friends on stakes outside the city walls."

"Really, you should go into motivational speaking. You've got a knack."

"Malek will undoubtedly display our heads as well."

My hand instinctively went to my throat. "You suck at this."

"But do you not see? We were dangerously close to killing the king. Our plan—the plan of a group of outcasts and misfits—almost worked. By putting our heads on view, our allies will know that we nearly succeeded."

"Yeah, yeah... we gave people some hope. Rah-rah. Yippee."

"We did our absolute best, Finley."

"I know. Really, I know. But I don't want to just die for the cause, you know? I was *this* close, Pherric. I managed to cut him with my knife! *This* close, you know? The only thing I'll have to show for it—a bloody death in front of a big crowd. I get it. I'm going to die now. With my head on a stick, apparently. But I kinda did want to be... the One. Well, the one *you* thought I was. Dying wouldn't be so bad if I had taken him out."

"You made every effort. And hopefully, your name will go down in history. Go to meet your gods with that in mind."

A tall, broad-shouldered gladiator with cropped hair strode confidently toward our cell, flanked by a group of thugs for support. One of them stepped forward and unlocked the door with a loud clunk.

From the back of the cage, Braylor shot toward the opening like a caged tiger. Before he could take two steps, guards leveled their swords at his face, the steel gleaming even in the dim torchlight. Two more soldiers, clad in Malek's signature black-and-blue tunics, emerged from the shadows, their blades drawn and ready. Outnumbered and outmatched, Braylor clenched his fists but retreated without a word, his chest heaving with suppressed fury.

Temurr remained slumped on the floor, staring blankly at nothing. The streaks of dried tears on his rugged, hairy cheeks were a painful reminder of his heartbreak. He'd lost the love of his life, and I could see he'd already surrendered to despair. My heart ached for him, though I hesitated, unsure if my presence would comfort or annoy him.

But when you have zero fucks to give, you stop caring about the little things. I marched over to Temurr and knelt beside him, pulling him away from the wall without hesitation. Wrapping my arms around him, I hugged him as tightly as I could. For a moment, he sat stiffly, but then his broad arms came up to hold me, gripping me as though he might fall apart without it. His silent tears mirrored my own, and we stayed there, clinging to each other, trying to draw strength from the only warmth left in this cold place.

The gladiator finally stepped into the cell, his massive hands planted on his hips, and scanned us like livestock at auction. With a curt motion, he signaled for the guards to bring in the fighting equipment.

The torches along the corridor sputtered weakly, their fuel nearly gone, casting uneven shadows that danced on the damp stone walls. The guards threw tattered canvas loincloths into our cell, one for each of the boys. When my turn came, they tossed me a matching loincloth and a dented, paper-thin piece of armor meant to cover my torso. I wondered, fleetingly, if Kane had intervened to make sure I'd have some better protection.

Helmets with full face coverings followed, clanging against the floor as they were unceremoniously dropped into the cell. Sandals, too, were handed out, their soles worn thin. Pherric traded his sword for a battered, wafer-thin shield, inspecting it grimly before tucking it under his arm. Braylor and Temurr barely glanced at the helmets or sandals before dumping them in a pile at the edge of the cell as the guards barked for us to move.

We were herded out in single file. The gladiator waited near the arena gate. His expression unreadable as he finally handed us weapons—if you could call them that. Each sword was a pitiful sight, rust pitting the blade and rough edges threatening to crumble at the first strike.

Temurr accepted his without protest, his fingers curling loosely around the hilt like it was a dead weight. His eyes were hollow, his spirit gone. He didn't even bother to adjust his grip. The sight made my throat tighten. It wasn't the sword he was holding—it was his surrender.

"Malek has changed his mind about executing us," Pherric said.

"What do you mean?" I asked.

Braylor waved his sword. "He wants a bit of a spectacle."

I realized the fact that we had gone from a public execution to fighting in the arena, which meant Kane must have influenced Malek again.

"We still have Kane on our side," I said hopefully.

Braylor turned in the dank, dark hallway under the arena, glaring at me. "What?"

"Sir Kane? He of the Black Bones? He's on our side."

"How do you mean?" Pherric asked.

"That's right! You guys don't know! Kane is on our side," I whispered. "He helped me. He kept me from trying to kill Malek at the feast. Apparently, they knew I was coming and he was wearing armor! Kane helped sneak me into Malek's chambers the next day, so I would have a better chance!"

Braylor laughed. Pherric shook his head.

"I highly doubt that Malek's Knight Commander is our ally," said Braylor.

"Well, he is!" I protested. "In fact, he's the reason we're not getting our heads chopped off right now. He's given us a fighting chance!"

"Well, little one. This one won't fight." Braylor nodded at Pherric. "And there's not much fight left in that one." Braylor threw a shoulder into Temurr. But the ape man ignored him. "So, you need to stay behind me. Do you understand? I plan to take some of these bastards with me!"

I grabbed his big forearm, turned him to face me. "No. I am going out fighting, too. I will make Cira, Frip and Gunnr proud of me."

Braylor held my chin up with his finger and thumb. He seemed to feel some pride. "I doubt I could stop you. Not anymore."

"Damn straight."

I pushed his hand off my face, marching up to the gate toward the light at the end of the tunnel.

Chapter 59

I clutched the cold iron bars, my breath shallow as I stared into the arena. A warm-up fight was underway, though it looked more like a massacre. The scene was surreal: several gladiators circled a towering, reptilian beast, its massive green-scaled body writhing in pain. Seven serpentine heads whipped and snapped furiously, their long necks swaying like deadly pendulums. Swords stuck grotesquely from its flanks, blood seeping out in streams and pooling on the sun-baked orange sand.

"What the hell is that?" I asked, my voice higher than I would've liked.

The creature staggered, its massive clawed feet gouging the sand as it lashed out at its attackers. One head lunged at a gladiator, missing by inches as the man shouted and struck back with his blade. The crowd roared, feeding off the chaos, their cheers and jeers drowning out the snarls of the beast and the warriors' war cries.

"That," Pherric said gravely, his voice low and steady, "is a hydra."

"Looks scary."

"They seem fierce but are mostly harmless. This is simply a spectacle... to get the crowd worked into a frenzy."

The hydra's many eyes were wide, full of fear. And pain. Desperate. I knew I'd be in the same situation soon. Too soon.

One gladiator smashed one of the heads with the flat of his blade then hacked it off at the base of the thin neck. The audience roared.

Another thrust a spear deep into the side of the hydra; the beast reeled in anguish, moaning loudly at the sky.

A third gladiator leapt on the hydra's back. He drove his sword down to the hilt. The hydra stumbled, falling hard to the sand. I felt so sorry for the creature as the rest quickly pounced, slicing off the remaining heads. More hooting and screaming.

We waited as a karkadann, hauling an iron sled, was brought in to carry away the hydra carcass.

I stepped back when I heard creaking metal. The huge iron gate lifted up. My head was spinning. My vision blurred. And I had a weird taste in my dry mouth—like I'd eaten a really old rat.

I knew I wouldn't walk out of that arena alive. But I stepped into the archway, determined to at least try to act like a badass. Marching out of the tunnel, I stood defiantly on the sand. My feet wide apart and my chin held high.

They mercilessly booed me.

With my sword gripped tightly in my hand, I turned slowly around in the sand, aggressively staring at the people on all three different levels. Thousands of men, women, and even children had gathered—they jumped to their feet, cursing and waving fists.

I smirked and flipped them off. That smirk wasn't real, but I was sure as hell going to put on a show.

On the far side of the arena, Malek stood on his platform smiling at me. The first tier—he was close. Jumping-distance close.

Nerus, Kane, and a host of royals were seated around him, dressed in their finest colorful robes.

Braylor and Pherric stood beside me. I peered over my shoulder. Temurr slouched there with his head down, shoulders sagged, hands clasped in front of him.

The iron gate lowered to the sand, locking us in.

Pherric bent down, pretending to wipe away bloody sand from his foot, and picked up a broken hydra tooth from the ground. He slid it into his loincloth. I grinned and shook my head—even when he was going to die, he was still collecting ingredients for his alchemy.

"And now, citizens of Irkalla!" Malek bellowed to the crowd. "I give you the main tournament of the day!"

Their cheer was deafening.

Malek held up his hand, waved, turning slowly and smiling that self-satisfying, shit-eating grin.

Pherric squinted in the bright sunlight. He stared at the upper deck of the stadium. "This used to be a renowned amphitheater... where they performed the plays of Jacek and Sandulf the Great—"

"Now is not the time, Pherric," Braylor growled. "You are about to die."

I grabbed Pherric's arm. "Please tell me you will fight?! To protect yourself?"

He shook his head.

"I admire your conviction," I told him. "It's stupid, but I admire it."

"I shall die a few seconds before you do. And no one will have suffered at my hand."

The audience hushed as the King held up his hand.

"I present to you," screamed Malek. "The traitors to the Irkallan Empire!"

Boos and hisses rained down.

"Would you believe... these fools tried to assassinate me?!"

They moaned. Rotten food fell at our feet.

"While I was able to personally kill their accomplices!"

Malek waited for the applause to slow.

"I saved the deaths of these four... for you!"

Cheers and whistles rang out.

Malek nodded to a guard at the far end of the arena, who opened a small metal gate.

Three Irkallan soldiers paraded the heads of Gunnr, Frip, and Cira around the arena on the end of long pikes. I had no more tears left for my friends—but my blood boiled.

I turned my attention to Temurr as Frip's decapitated head was walked by. He shed no tears either. His eyes narrowed. He bared his teeth. I flinched when he let out a frightening war cry. Temurr beat his chest in fury, spit flying from his lips.

Braylor smirked. "There he is..."

Panting hard through his nose, Temurr lifted his sword, closed in rank beside us. Beside his friends.

A large metal gate at the other end of the arena slid open. Twelve sweaty, muscular gladiators swaggered onto the sand. They wore nice metal helmets, shiny armor that covered their arms and legs, and held quality weapons.

I leaned over to Braylor. "Do you think you could throw me onto Malek's platform? I might be able to take him out?"

"Those archers would have something to say about it," Braylor said.

He nodded to men lining the stadium, holding longbows. With arrows notched.

"Couldn't hurt to try."

"It would, most likely, hurt a great deal."

"I really do hate you."

"You love me and you know it." Braylor smirked. "Oh, and when you get in trouble, take shelter behind me."

"*If* I get in trouble, you mean..."

"Finley Maguire, you are not the chosen one," laughed Braylor. "But you *are* certainly unique."

After a terse grunt, he stepped to the center of the arena. The twelve gladiators tried to circle us, so we slipped through their ranks and threw our backs to the arena wall, closest to Malek's platform.

The warriors closed in. Started to test us. They lunged with quick strikes—we parried away—and leapt back to safety.

The crowd goaded them on.

Malek leaned on the low stone railing, grinning and sipping wine. Kane stood over the king's shoulder, a worried look on his face.

Tired of waiting, a gladiator rushed me. He swung his blade down and was met by Braylor's crappy sword. The giant countered. And the battle was on.

Temurr drew first blood. He clashed with a guy carrying a net and short spear. The warrior's net caught on the Temurr's sword hilt, drawing him in. He tried to spear him, but Temurr rolled on the ground to the man's side. He popped up, driving his sword into his opponent's shoulder. Temurr kicked the warrior back and drove his blade into the guy's heart, scrambling back to us.

Pherric hid behind Braylor, trying to help by holding out his shield.

I fought with a warrior carrying a short sword. He slashed at me—I parried but my arms shook at the force of the blow.

I've watched a lot of TV shows—the ones with those big battle sword fights—and this was nothing near that. It was not coordinated. Not smooth. Fights with weapons are messy and awkward and ugly—kind of like sex for the first time. Skill is certainly involved, but many one-on-one battles are sometimes won with pure luck.

My adrenaline jumped into overdrive. I tried to focus on my lessons, from Gunnr, Cira and the others, but I pushed them to the back of my mind. I parried another blow from the warrior. He was too strong. On instinct, I sprang in close to him. Hit his nose with my sword handle. Kicked his nuts. And slashed his belly. He fell away. He might have died, but it was all a blur. I'll never know.

When another asshole attacked, he took a small slice out of my arm. I swung my blade back. But missed. He thrust his sword at me, and I turned to the side. I stabbed my blade at his lower torso, and he turned like I did—I missed. We locked swords. Got face to face. He growled, pulling his blade away to strike me but—I didn't pull mine back. Instead, I thrust mine down and slashed his hand. He was cut deep on the back of his fist. And dropped his sword in pain.

I rushed him, shoving my blade deep into his collar bone. Too deep.

My sword got stuck.

Chapter 60

I shoved my foot against the gladiator's chest, yanking hard to pull my sword from his shoulder. Another one came at me from the right side, slashing down with his blade. He grazed my old metal helmet, denting it up even more, and sent the sharp edge down into my shoulder, slicing up the last good one I had.

The new guy was off-balance, so I kicked my heel in his ribs. He fell at Braylor's feet. Braylor parried a thrust from his opponent and—without looking down—drove his sword through my guy on the ground.

A nice headband probably would have kept all that sweat from stinging my eyes, but you do what you can with what you have. I had a filthy wrist to backhand my sweaty face. And the blood spatter all over me didn't help. Grunts and screams, the tinging of metal clashing, deafened me. But all the smells were the absolute worst—blood and body odor and fear assaulted my nose.

Temurr had killed another warrior and Braylor had three lying at his bare feet. Thick blood pooled all around us, hovering and expanding away on top of the sand.

I glanced up at Malek. He was *not* a happy camper. The king waved his arm. Another group of warriors rushed from a tunnel.

Gobs of human muck ran down my chest, under the armor. My right shoulder was on fire, which had caused me to switch my sword to my left hand. I didn't have a whole lot left.

I backed against the wall, as a man with a spear rushed in. He had seen the others fall and wisely kept his distance. He prodded me once.

but I deflected the spear tip with my sword. But then he got tricky. The gladiator started to jab me. I lifted my sword to block but the spear wasn't there—he had duped me. He stabbed me with the spear point, sliding through the armor and deeply piercing my side.

"Oh, damn... That's gonna leave a mark..." I muttered.

The man cackled, giving me an opportunity. I pulled his spear out and slammed the tip into the wall. The gladiator lost his balance. I slashed down with my blade cutting his hand halfway off. I shoved the blade edge into his neck. Bleeding severely, he dropped to the sand and crawled away.

I staggered behind Braylor, putting my back to the wall for support.

"Had enough, hellcat?!" Braylor teased.

"Yeah. For today. I'm good," I whimpered. My hand tried to stop the blood from pouring out of the wound in my side.

His eyes flared when he saw the damage.

A warrior came around to finish me off. I parried his sword and slashed at his forearm, but missed. Braylor rotated his massive body, slicing hard across the man's jaw. Half of the warrior's head fell backward, remaining attached, as the body collapsed.

"Off to the gods with ya!" shouted Braylor.

I slid down the wall. Bright white lights flashed in my eyes. My head was spinning.

Pherric dragged me between Braylor and Temurr. He ripped off a section of his loincloth and placed it against the bleeding hole in my side.

"Not sure that's the cleanest thing to put on an open wound," I said.

"Quiet, Finley," he soothed. "Rest now."

"Oh, it's just a scrape. Put me back in, coach..."

Pherric's hands, arm, and shoulder had been sliced up. He had defended himself, but still wouldn't raise a weapon against them. Gunnr would have mocked him, but I gave him the best smile I could muster.

He still had that stupid hydra tooth tucked into the top of his loincloth. I was going to ask but got distracted by the pain. My hands were soaked in my own blood.

A chorus of boos rained down. And if they were booing, that was a good thing.

I watched Braylor and Temurr battle away, shoulder to shoulder. They swung their swords. Parried attacks. And the bodies piled up. Sweat, blood, gore and sand covered their half-naked bodies. They were actually laughing at one point. They had taken their anger, their grief, and they turned it against their hapless attackers.

My own anger still stirred. But I grew weaker by the second.

The audience hissed and howled, pissed off that they weren't getting the show they wanted. I glanced at Malek who shook with rage, pacing like a pissed off puppy dog. Kane stared directly at me—a distressed look plastered to his face.

He knew I was dying.

Standing on mangled corpses, Temurr towered over his foes. They slashed at the ape-man. They tried attacking him high and low in unison. One even threw his sword. But he fended them off, cleaving through their bodies with the strength of five men.

Braylor used the dead to create a wall and cut any gladiator who dared get too close. His long, dark hair had fallen free. The whites of his wild eyes stood out against the dark red blood that stained his face. He roared at the men, gnashing his teeth. He was a savage protecting his young.

After only a short time, forty or so warriors laid dead at our feet. We were severely cutting into the king's supply of quality men. Malek pouted on his platform, with his fists resting on the stone railing. He had heard the crowd jeering and moaning around him. He was tired of losing.

He held his hand in the air. At the gate, a new set of warriors stopped in their tracks.

"Archers!" the king screamed.

The men all around us on the first tier raised their bows. Notched arrows.

"End this!" he bellowed at the bowmen.

Most of the audience groaned. Then they booed. Fresh food was thrown onto the sand. Malek, Kane, and the other royals looked around the arena in shock. In fear.

The protests got louder. More intense. Fists were raised. Did they want our deaths to be in battle? I seriously doubted that they wanted us to live. But Malek had definitely lost the people.

Kane leaned over, whispered in Malek's ear.

Malek raised his hand again, quieting the raucous crowd.

"Stay that order!" he cried. "This contest has turned out to be worthy of... a Continuation!"

Malek got a mixed reaction from the people. Some wanted us dead. Most cheered. A noisy hum filled the stadium. Like my grandfather used to say—always leave them wanting more.

The king waved to the crowd, smiling through gritted teeth, and left his viewing terrace.

Kane gave me one last look before following Malek away from the arena.

I passed out from the loss of blood.

Chapter 61

I have a vague recollection of Braylor scooping me off the sand and running me across the arena. Pain racked my side so he slowed to a quick walk until we disappeared through the dark tunnel.

Braylor stopped when he came to a gladiator. "You! Do you have healers here?!"

The man shrugged. "No. We expect no survivors."

Braylor snarled at the man, causing him to take a step back.

Guards led us deep into the catacombs, down the stairs. Braylor laid me on the floor of our cell.

Panting hard, Pherric rushed in behind us, with Temurr in tow. The click of a key in the gate meant we were locked in.

Braylor sprang to Pherric, gripping him by the shoulders. "Save her, wizard!"

Pherric stood there, bewildered, looking from me to the giant. "I cannot do much of anything. I–I'm not a healer."

"Well, then... use your magic!"

"I do not have my bag. My potions. They took everything from me. And even then..."

He squatted by my side on the floor. "I'm sorry, Finley." He pushed the wet hair from my eyes.

"Ah, it's okay. Couple bandages and an aspirin. I'll be... good as new." More lightheaded than ever, I had to puke. So I did. All over myself.

Pherric pointed at Temurr. "Get some kind of bandage! Rags, water..."

Temurr leapt to the cell door, shouting at a guard standing watch.

Unsure of what to do, the man fled down the hall.

As Pherric pressed on my wound, I shivered uncontrollably. With the battle over, my adrenaline gone, the throbbing pain hit me hard.

When the guard returned, Temurr snatched his armful of rags. Braylor grabbed the pitcher of water from our cell and brought it over.

Pherric slowly poured water into my achingly dry mouth.

"Put pressure on her side," Pherric instructed Temurr. The strong ape-man pushed way too hard.

I squealed in pain. "Not that hard!"

"Apologies," said Temurr.

I shook my head to let him know I was fine. Big mistake. I grew even more dizzy, nauseous.

I heard the shuffling of boots in the dark hallway. The guards out there vanished.

Pherric felt my neck. "Her heart is erratic. And she turns blue. She has lost too much blood."

"Do something!" cried Braylor, hovering over us.

"What would you have me do?!"

Braylor stormed off to pace the cell.

Temurr grabbed a new rag, inspecting the damage under the bloody towel. He winced. I did not need to see that wince.

I heard a voice. One I recognized.

"You there!"

When I looked, Kane stood outside the iron bars.

He summoned Pherric. "Come here!"

Pherric looked at me. I squeezed his hand. "Trust him. Go."

Rolling his eyes in exasperation, he marched over to our cage door.

"I have a healer on the way," Kane told him.

Pherric looked at me as he nodded.

"Will she live?"

Pherric never looked away. "A healer will likely... not be enough."

"You. You are an Alchemancer, right? Can you help her?" pleaded Kane.

"I may be able to.... to do something. But I-I need my bag. My leather bag that was taken when I was arrested. Can you get that?"

"I doubt it," Kane exhaled. "Perhaps..."

"I saw Nerus. Next to Malek. In the arena. He must have my bag."

Kane nodded. "I shall return." He disappeared into the blackness.

I hated that they had dragged me down in the dungeon. Into a dank, dark hole. I didn't want to die there. I didn't want to die anywhere, really, but what are you going to do?

Pherric returned to my side, so I grabbed his arm. "Hey, do *not* blame yourself for this, okay? For *all* this. For bringing me here. Greatest adventure I've ever had, you know?" A bolt of pain ripped through me. "It was... a blast."

"Quiet now. Save your strength."

"Oh, my strength flew out the window halfway through the battle."

Temurr tried to keep steady pressure on the wound. "Do not die on me, Finley. I have lost enough already. I will not lose you as well."

"Not like..." I took a deep, painful breath. "I have a choice."

Pherric dipped a rag in dirty water, dabbing my forehead.

"I wish we could get you into a bed, to make you more comfortable."

"No way!" I exclaimed. "Most people die in a bed."

"Not on our world..."

I started to laugh but coughed violently, doubling over from the aching in my side.

Pherric wiped blood from my mouth, blood that I had coughed up. Fear washed over me. I began to shake, my lips quivering. I could feel my heart speeding up, then slowing down. I was slipping away.

I held onto Pherric's hand as tight as I could.

Braylor noticed. He brought me the biggest piece of cloth we had and laid it across me.

"Remain calm, Finley. We are here for you," Pherric told me as his eyes darted to the cell door.

"I know. I know. But... I'm scared," I cried.

Braylor went back to pacing. He knew how to fight but not how to comfort.

Pherric leaned in close.

I raised my eyebrows. "If you ask me if I've accepted Jesus Christ as my lord and personal savior… I will hit you so hard."

That made him smile. But the smile faded as I coughed up more blood.

"Finley, hear my words. We do not have much time," whispered Pherric. "Try not to talk."

"Okay, I'm… done… talking," I rasped.

"You are beyond the help of a healer."

I gave him a stern look.

"I know, I'm not very inspirational. But if Kane returns with my bag… in time. And if I have everything I need… I may have a way of saving your life."

Chapter 62

"What?" Pherric whispered. "According to the Scholomance texts I have studied, there is an elixir that can grant immortality to those who drink it. The formula for the potion is found in the *Arcanum Libellum*, the book I keep in my bag."

Braylor huddled down to listen in.

"The one you used to teach me your language?"

"And the one that you risked your life to save when I dropped it in Elysium."

I gave Braylor an arched eyebrow. "Who's the stupid one now?"

Braylor grunted.

Pherric went on like he always did. "I can try to fabricate this potion, but please understand that I have no actual experience. This alchemic practice is known only to those at the Preceptor level. I have studied the book and... and I should be able to duplicate the potion, but—"

"But you can... save me?" I asked. "Wait. Did you say immortality?!"

Pherric paused as I coughed up more blood. Braylor poured water into my mouth when I stopped hacking up a lung.

"That is the dilemma. This is not something to be taken lightly," admitted Pherric.

"But... you can... save me? That's all... that matters."

"Save her, Pherric!" Braylor said.

"I will try!" Pherric scolded Braylor. "If I do not do this correctly, it could be a fate worse than death. I need you to understand this. We haven't much time but please... consider the consequences."

I tried to talk but weakness overcame me. Of course I wanted to live. And be immortal? Hell, yeah. Who wouldn't want that? But then I remembered all those zombie movies I had seen. I did not want to be some freaky undead hag—with my skin falling off—trying to eat everyone's brains. I wanted to ask about the consequences, but I knew he had no idea. And I doubted I wanted to hear them.

All I could do was nod.

"You wish to go through with it?" Pherric double-checked.

I nodded again.

"Of course she wants you to do it! Make it happen, wizard!" Braylor shook Pherric's shoulder.

We heard the shuffling of boots on the stone floor. Pherric rushed to the cell door. Kane slid to a halt outside our cage, the leather bag in his hand.

"Here. Take this... Do what you can," whispered Kane.

Pherric pulled it through the bars, inspected the contents, nodded to Kane.

"You have my gratitude."

"Be quick!" Kane growled. "They will return soon. And they will find it."

Kane stared at me for a brief second, knowing he'd likely never see me again. Alive anyway. Then he disappeared.

They say you can feel your life slipping away. Mine was speeding down a water slide at a hundred miles an hour.

Pherric pulled out his ancient book, setting aside items from his bag. He plucked out the broken hydra tooth he had taken from the arena, inspected it, then quickly flipped to the back of the book.

"Hurry, Pherric! Hurry!" persisted Braylor.

Temurr exchanged the bloody rag he had held to my side for a cleaner one.

"What is in the elixir?" asked Temurr.

"A variety of metals, which I always keep on hand—the most important being gold." He held up a small nugget.

Pherric read from his book. He took out a small tin cup and set it on the floor. He measured out the correct amounts from several vials of metal flakes and poured them in the cup.

"That is all?! Metals?" said Braylor.

"No, but what is most vital is the ramidreju. This is the one that attacked Finley, near the Godsribbon keep," said Pherric.

He pulled out the snake-like skin from the ramidreju that Braylor had killed.

"By the gods!" Temurr stated, reverently. "That rare beast attacked her. On that very day, in the forest! And now she is being saved by it! Do you not see? She *is* the chosen one!"

Braylor remained skeptical. "I've eaten a few of those things. I am not immortal."

"The powers lie not in the meat but the fur." He showed Braylor the green fur. "When it is combined with other important ingredients." He held up the Hydra tooth. "Including this."

"A tooth from a hydra! I did not think of that!" cried Temurr. "Another testament from the gods!"

"What good is a hydra tooth?" asked Braylor.

I could barely keep my eyes open. Gunnr's notion of *neardeath* suddenly made complete sense to me. I was there.

Pherric pulled chunks of fur from the ramidreju hide. He checked the book. More powders were poured. He ground up the concoction, inside the tin cup, with his knuckle. Checked the book again. He used a fingernail to dig away some of the hydra tooth and placed it in the cup. Finally, he added water from the pitcher, only a small amount, and swished it around. Back to the book again. He turned the page. A look of confusion. He turned the page back, read the text again, and then flipped the page.

"Something is wrong," said Pherric.

Braylor scrunched his face up. "What?!"

"The text. There is a page missing," said Pherric. He held up the side of the book for a closer look. He then opened the book. All the way open.

"See? A page has been cut out, at some point, down near the binding. I don't know if I have the entire formula for the elixir!"

I coughed hard. The cold pricked at me like a thousand needles, all at once, over my entire body. Breathing was difficult. My vision blurred.

I needed to sleep.

"We are losing her!" cried Temurr.

"Give her the magic potion! At once!" Braylor demanded.

"I do not know if it is complete!" Pherric replied.

I closed my eyes for good.

"Before she is gone... give it to her," said Braylor, his voice no longer menacing. "I beg of you."

They lifted me up, sending pain shooting through my abdomen. I cried out.

"Finley, listen to me. Drink this. Drink it all," said Pherric's voice.

His voice was so far away.

The tin cup pushed against my dried, bloodied lips.

"Swallow."

I wanted to make a snarky 'That's what he said' comment but I was too far gone. I had shut down.

My throat instinctively swallowed Pherric's potion.

They laid me back down. Silence fell across the room.

I think I heard someone say, "Why isn't it working?"

And then I died.

Chapter 63

What's it like to die?

That would be great to ask someone who had died. But you can't do that. Because they're dead.

Death for me was... nothing. And that doesn't even do it justice. It was not black. Or silent. Certainly, time passed but I had zero awareness of any time ticking along. I didn't float above my body or see the proverbial *light at the end of the tunnel.* I simply no longer was.

Returning from death would be just as hard to explain. I didn't wake up, snap out of it, or come to. What I did was inhale nonstop for a half minute and then—opened my eyes.

The hot sun beat down on me. I was laying on my stomach, my legs bent awkwardly underneath me. An angry stench filled my nose. I turned my head to the side. A dead gladiator, half his face cut off, stared back at me. I turned the other way to see a wood wall.

When I lifted my head, I realized I had been put inside a wagon filled with bodies.

Behind me stood a solid white wall that towered straight up into the air—my death cart was parked outside of the arena. The sun still burned bright overhead, so I knew I had not been dead for long... unless that was a different day.

I wanted to scream at the top of my newly-filled lungs and take off running down the streets of the Black City. But I knew I had to climb out of the wagon, go back inside, and help my friends. I quietly crawled over the dead and slipped off the back.

I peeked around the side to see a frail old man shuffling toward the back of the wagon.

Before I got too close, I jumped out. "Boo!"

The color drained from the poor guy's face. He screamed and ran off as fast as his bony little getaway sticks would carry him.

That was fun. But then I stopped to feel my face—was I horrid; a scary zombie? All oozing pus and dead skin flapping about? My face felt normal, so I shrugged and headed through an open gate.

Inside the stadium, two tall guards, in the king's black and blue, stood farther along the dark hallway. Leaning against the wall, they whispered to each other. I tip-toed toward the one with his back to me, staying close to the wall.

Staying low, I slid silently up behind the soldier, ripping his sword from the scabbard and shoving it hard into his back.

"Sorry!" I whispered to his falling body.

The other soldier grabbed for his sword. I pushed forward, slashing down hard. The sharp blade easily cut his forearm. Startled, he backed away and I pushed the blade into the base of his neck, above the chainmail.

"Sorry," I said again.

"Not sorry."

I inspected my new sword, stepped over their bodies, and turned down a hallway to my left.

As I lifted my arm to grab a wall torch, I felt a sharp pain in my shoulder. Blood still flowed from the gash. I pulled my chest armor aside, tested the skin—the puncture from the spear, the one that had killed me, was gone. But I still had my other wounds from the battle.

"Your immortality potion kinda sucks, Pherric," I told the dark hallway.

I took the torch from the wall and raced down the corridor.

I slipped quietly up to the iron gate of their cell.

Pherric and Braylor sat hunched over on the stone benches. Temurr had slid down against the damp wall, staring at the floor between his hairy legs.

"Miss me?" I asked.

They leapt to their feet—standing there in shock.

"Well?"

Temurr cocked his head. "Finley?"

I held out my arm for a hug through the bars. "Yep!"

Smiling from ear-to-ear, Braylor and Pherric rushed the gate and tried holding on to me through the bars.

"Finley! You live!"

"The elixir worked!"

Temurr hung back, a fearful look on his face. I slid over so he could see me.

"Temurr, it's me. I'm okay."

He crossed and then un-crossed his arms, shifting his weight back and forth on his feet.

I waved my hand to him. "Please?"

"But... you are dead. I saw you die... They carried your lifeless body from this cell."

Pherric turned to the superstitious ape man. "My magic worked, Temurr. She lives. She is not a spirit. You can touch her. Come!"

He guided Temurr to the bars. I let him reluctantly tap my skin. I was solid. Real. A smile crept across this face. He placed both hands on me and jumped up and down.

Pherric held up his hand and whispered. "Listen!"

We heard sandals plodding on the stone floor toward us.

I slipped back into the darkness.

The short, dumpy guard carried his bucket of gray slop and a few bowls. There was a clinking of keys at his belt. He walked up to the cell, set the bucket down, and began ladling his foul stew into bowls.

I placed my sword at the back of his neck. "Keys!"

His hands shook as he pulled the keys from his belt. I snatched them from his filthy fingers.

The fat man looked around nervously. His mouth opened; he was going to cry out for the guards.

I pulled back my sword to strike the guard.

"Finley," Pherric scolded me.

I gave him a look. "What? No killing, right?"

"Well, that and... I need a clean tunic."

Using the handle on my sword, I struck the guard on the side of the head. He fell to the floor, but he was only dazed. I didn't have the strength.

I unlocked the cell and Pherric rushed out. He yanked the tunic over the guy's head.

Braylor plucked the sword from my hand.

"Hey!" I said. "That's mine!"

Braylor examined the Irkallan blade. "No."

I crossed my arms, pouted. "I still hate you."

He laughed as he strode down the hall.

Pherric slipped on the jailer's tunic. "Do you know how to get us out of here?"

"Yeah, but... I'm not ready to leave yet."

"What do you mean?! Finley, we have to go! This moment!"

I held up the keys and jangled them on the ring.

"I'm not leaving until I free every other prisoner stuck in this hell hole. No one should have to go through what we did!"

Pherric started to protest. I held a finger up to his face. He opened his mouth again. I waggled my finger.

"Then we must hurry!" he said.

Temurr stepped cautiously from the dungeon cell. I hugged him hard. He hesitated at first, then gripped me tightly.

I held his shoulders. "Find some clothes. Some weapons. And keep Braylor out of trouble, okay?"

He nodded.

"Go. And be safe! We'll see you in a bit."

Temurr gave me a slight grin and chased after Braylor.

Chapter 64

Pherric and I crept down the dim dungeon corridors, stopping at every cell we passed. We peered into the shadows, squinting for signs of life, and when we found prisoners, we wasted no time unlocking their doors.

"Leave quietly and quickly," I whispered to them. "Disappear into the city. Don't look back."

Some stared in disbelief before bolting out. Others, weakened and dazed, needed a shove to get moving. One by one, we freed them, urging them toward their fleeting chance at freedom. By the time we reached the last of the cells, we had opened at least twenty, if not more.

When we emerged on the ground level, the air was fresher, but the scene before us froze me in my tracks. We stood in a colossal corridor, three stories high, open to the outside. The exposed outer wall faced the city streets, letting in flickers of torchlight that danced on the iron bars of the rows upon rows of massive cells. But these weren't ordinary holding chambers.

They housed impossible creatures.

I scanned the surreal menagerie. Baby dinosaurs prowled restlessly, their scales shimmering under the faint light. A hydra coiled lethargically in its corner, its heads swaying in restless unison. Huge feline creatures with saber-like fangs growled low, their yellow eyes following our every move. A hulking wolf-like beast, nearly half my height, stood silently in its cage, its gray fur bristling.

Further down, furry pigs rooted at the ground, and woolly mammoths stomped, their tusks gleaming. I caught sight of slender, scaled lizards that stretched impossibly long and snakes coiled ominously in tight knots. But the worst were the black hellhounds. Their red eyes burned like coals in the dim light, their growls low and menacing.

Pherric pulled me aside. "We're done here, Finley! We cannot release these beasts into the city."

"But what about that poor hydra in the arena?! You said it was basically harmless."

"We must leave! If word gets out prisoners have escaped, Malek's troops will swarm the arena. We will surely die."

I look at the array of animals huddled in their stalls. They had been beaten and starved. Incapable of fending for themselves. Many were weighed down with heavy chains.

"Pherric, please?!"

"You have saved so many, Finley. We cannot save everyone," he said. "Or every creature."

I stared at the ground.

"Come! Let us run from here!"

I nodded my head, giving a last look at the creatures.

As he ran down the wide-open hall, toward the main tunnel leading out of the arena, I quickly unlocked every dungeon iron gate. Pherric stopped because I had fallen far behind.

Behind me, the animals pushed their way out the cages, nudging open the doors.

"Finley..." If looks could kill, I'd be back in that morgue wagon.

I ran up to him, stopping before the last cage.

"I know. I know! I couldn't help it!"

He stared over my shoulder. Creatures raced away from the arena. A few screams echoed out in the alleyways and along city avenues.

I glanced into the big cage to my right. "Um. What the hell?"

My hand trembled as I raised a finger to point at the largest of all the cages.

Pherric stepped back, his face pale. "By the gods..."

We stared, barely able to comprehend what we were seeing. In the dim light of the cell lay a dragon. Not a statue, not a skeleton, but a real, living dragon.

Its scales gleamed black, like polished obsidian. Sharp teeth projected out from the sides of its long, menacing snout. Two massive, white horns curved majestically from the top of its head. Its wings, bat-like and immense, were folded tightly against its body, attached to the muscular front legs in a way that reminded me of Kasuma's.

I couldn't move. My eyes widened as chills prickled my spine, and even the matted, bloodied hair on my arms stood on end. A thick iron chain circled its mouth like a brutal muzzle, and an even heavier one hung around its neck, securing it to the wall. The dragon's wings wrapped protectively around its body, shielding its blackened scales, while its spiked tail curled around it like a coiled spring.

Then it moved.

The faint sound of our footsteps must have disturbed it. One enormous, dark red eye slowly opened, its vertical pupil contracting into a slit. A pool of molten red and gold surrounded that inky black center, glowing faintly in the low light as it fixed its gaze on us.

I forgot to breathe. My chest ached as I stood there, utterly powerless under that alien, piercing stare. Time seemed to stand still as the creature's eye studied us—its intelligence, its danger, its sheer power unmistakable.

"Pherric…" I whispered, unable to tear my gaze away.

"Finley, whatever you are thinking, put it from your mind!"

Thinking was not an option. I needed to release that spectacular specimen. I unlocked the cage door.

"No! Finley, no!"

The dragon remained still. He snarfled but did not rise up. Or threaten me in any way. His eye followed me as I crept up to his long neck. I fumbled with the keys, trying a few different ones, trying to find the right one.

"Get out of there!"

"I will not allow Malek to keep him as a pet! No way!"

I found the key, unlocked the huge chain strapped to his neck. I stepped back but the dragon remained there, staring at me with contempt. As though I was an insect to him.

"By the gods, you are determined to die on this day!" Pherric was getting on my nerves.

"I already did..." I cautiously approached his head. Trying the same key, I released the chain circling his mouth.

"You have done enough! Run!" he screamed.

I backed away. The black dragon lifted his head from the floor.

As I bolted from the cage, I pushed the gate wide open.

Pherric snatched me, dragging me around the corner. We raced down the hallway. Toward the stadium exit. The dead guards were still there, blood flowing across the stone floor.

Several prisoners ran past us into the city streets.

At the tunnel entrance, I slid to a stop and pulled Pherric to the side. "I think I have a way out of here. Out of the city. But first, I need to find a clean tunic."

"Then what?"

I looked behind me, at the wagon full of dead bodies, then smiled from ear to ear at Pherric. "Braylor and Temurr are not gonna like it."

Chapter 65

Pherric held the reins to the two meaty karkadanns harnessed to our wagon.

Sitting on the front seat, I looked back at the pile of corpses. "Are you ready back there?"

Temurr and Braylor had hid underneath a few bloody bodies. I could make out Braylor's eye staring up at me. He actually growled at me.

I patted the sword that hung from my new belt.

We heard the sounds of boots on the cobblestones—the troops were descending on the arena. Pherric and I exchanged a harried look. He quickly snapped the reins. And we sped off, rounding a corner as fast as possible.

I kept turning back, looking over my shoulder, expecting to see the dragon fly up and away from the arena. But there was no sign of him.

I had a million questions swirling around in my head.

"Pherric, you seemed genuinely surprised that I'm alive. Did your potion, um, mess me up?"

"Well, not exactly," he said. "You died. The elixir was supposed to prevent that."

"So, I did... die. Huh." I swallowed hard. "How long was I, like, dead for?"

"You were only gone for a short time before the guards came to our cage. They took my bag and carried your body out. We had only started to treat our wounds from the battle when you returned."

Pherric steered our wagon through the city on the smaller streets and narrow alleyways.

"Where are you taking us?" Braylor whispered from underneath the corpses.

"We are headed for the nearest city gate. I highly doubt they dump their dead within the city walls."

"There are seven entrances to Biringan! How do you know which is the right one?!" Braylor asked.

"We are going to have hope that the gods favor us, yet again, on this day," said Pherric, as he winked at me.

"By all means! Leave it all up to your gods," harrumphed Braylor. "As if they know we exist!"

The white city wall loomed higher and higher over the rooftops as we rode on.

"So, when you left the Scholomance thingy, you stole the big book of doom... but why did you also take that little tin cup?" I asked. "To use with your elixir?"

"Ah, that cup is an ancient relic and is always kept with the *Arcanum Libellum.* It is to be used during official ceremonies that require healing. I really only took the cup because it is part of the tradition."

"Holy shit! I knew it!" I cried. "It's the Holy Grail!"

"The what?"

"One of the gods on my world drank from a cup, at his last meal, and supposedly this grail was used to collect his blood after he was crucified. People have been looking for that thing forever!"

"Why?" asked Pherric. "The cup is merely a symbol. A tradition."

"They say if you drink from the grail, you'll have eternal youth or live forever."

"Well, the cup has no healing powers. It is the alchemic ingredients that—"

"Shit! I drank from the freakin' Holy Grail," I said. "Which means Malek has already had the potion by now, too."

"How do you know this?"

"When I went to his chambers? To try to kill him? He was there, talking with Nerus. Malek asked him when they would perform the ceremony and the greasy weasel said he could do it at any time, since *he had the book*. Malek said something like 'immortality awaits', I think."

Pherric threw his head back, his eyes pleading to his gods in the sky. "Then there is no hope of ever assassinating Malek."

"This means we finally go with my plan to form an army then, does it?" asked a muffled Temurr.

"We no longer have a choice, Temurr."

Our wagon rolled up to a gate cut into the outer wall. A soldier held up his hand to stop our corpse wagon. Finishing with a merchant wagon coming into the city, he waved us forward.

Pherric looked worried.

The soldier, wearing the black and blue tunic over his mail, rubbed his blond beard and eyed us suspiciously.

"What is the meaning of this?!" he shouted.

"Begging your pardon, good sir!" said Pherric. "We were asked to—"

He walked past us, swinging open the back gate of the wagon. The hot sun had done its job—the stench from the bodies overwhelmed the man. He slammed the gate closed.

"Uh, we were instructed to dump the bodies from the games and—"

"Why did you not take this stinking pile through Penghou gate?!" demanded the soldier.

"I was not told which—"

"Oh, you were not told! Do you not work in the Arena District?! Any fool knows the carcasses go out Penghou!"

The soldier placed a thick hand on his sword hilt.

Braylor, from under the bodies, slowly slid the sword from my belt.

Not wanting to find out if I was immortal, I grabbed Pherric's arm. "I told you! You spineless, gutless, worthless... chupacabra!"

Pherric stared at me, shocked. Standing up, I stabbed my finger hard into his chest. "I said we had to go through Penghou, but did you listen?! Noooo!" I cried out, with overly dramatic humiliation. "Don't believe me! Your mate! What could *I* possibly know?! Huh? Wait until my mother hears about this!"

I went on berating poor Pherric until the soldier smirked, lowering his head.

"Enough!" bellowed the soldier.

I plopped back down on the wagon seat. Crossed my arms. Scowled, for effect.

"I will allow it... this time! I catch you coming through here with the dead again and I shall slit your throat. For *her* sake!"

He laughed and waved us through the small gate.

Braylor chuckled from under the pile. "Heh. She called you a chupacabra..."

"Hold your tongue, Braylor." But he broke into a sly grin, giving me a nod. He liked my little performance.

We rode away from the gate. From the Black City.

Pherric opened his mouth, but a loud *screech* cut him off.

We spun back to the city walls—but the city had disappeared.

Another haunting shriek echoed out.

"The dragon," said Pherric.

He cracked the reins hard, forcing the karkadanns to gallop.

I watched the empty sky, waiting. After a few moments, the dragon gained enough altitude and distance to emerge from the cloaked city. He snapped his wings and soared slightly higher. The dragon struggled with each beat. Years of captivity had weakened him. But he was determined. Still strong. With effort, he sailed up and away from the Black City.

Pherric veered our wagon over toward the evergreen forest, getting us out of the dragon's line of sight.

I cracked a smile as I watched him soar higher. Will he turn and attack the city as payback for his captivity? We had both gained an unlikely freedom. But we had been hurt by the ordeal. We needed time to regroup, lick our wounds, before we could think about getting our revenge. The faces of Frip, Cira, and Gunnr, in their remaining minutes, and their last words flooded my mind. The fate of their world depends on me. Their fear of an imminent death was surpassed only by a determination for me to succeed. Even though I had done nothing but fail and let them down. My smile faded away.

I watched the black dragon, as his wings caught the wind and he flew higher in the sky. I watched him until he disappeared in the thick clouds and we rolled under the cover of the trees.

Our time will come, dragon. Our time will come.

Chapter 66

"You were wise to release the other prisoners," Braylor admitted, his tone grudging but measured. "With Malek's soldiers scrambling to recapture them, they may think we are still hiding in the city."

After our escape, we continued deeper into the forest, a grim silence settling over us. A few minutes passed into the woods and we released Temurr and Braylor from under the bodies and disposed of them behind tall grasses. The weight of fear pressed on us like the shadows of the towering trees. The Irkallans could be on our trail, so we pushed through the night, the wagon's wheels creaking in protest. There was no sign of Kasuma—she had flown the coop.

By morning, the forest lightened, and we stopped by a narrow creek winding through the woods. Its cool, clear water shimmered like salvation. Exhaustion dissolved into eagerness as we waded in, letting the current wash away the grime and blood of the previous day.

"But releasing the dragon was reckless," Braylor said, his voice cutting into the fragile peace, after he dunked his head underwater. "That creature will only bring chaos and death—"

"I don't care," I snapped, the sharpness in my voice echoing my own uncertainty. I sank beneath the water, letting its cold embrace drown out his words and his doubts.

The dragon was free. For better or worse, the die had been cast. And maybe, just maybe, that chaos was exactly what we needed.

The people of Tir Na had every reason to fear dragons. They'd lost so much—loved ones, homes, entire livelihoods. And if they hadn't experienced the devastation firsthand, they'd heard the harrowing stories passed down from family or friends. Dragons weren't just creatures of legend to them; they were living nightmares. That fear ran deep, ingrained in nearly everyone on the planet.

I got it. I really did. But to me, dragons were something else entirely. They were wonders, the stuff of fairy tales I'd devoured as a child. The kind of magic you dreamed about, not ran from.

Of course, I've never claimed to be the sharpest knife in the drawer. Maybe I should've been more afraid. Maybe a little fear would've kept me grounded. But instead, all I saw was their beauty, their raw power—and a glimmer of something I couldn't quite put into words.

At the water's edge, Temurr found a weed called *sapon*, which acted like a natural soap. We cleaned ourselves and the clothing we had. While soaping my tunic, I realized how rarely I thought about my life back on Earth. I had completely transitioned to a new life on Tir Na. Sure, I missed luxuries and conveniences... like being able to live past my twenties. But throughout my life, I always had to be moving, doing something. Being on Tir Na opened my eyes, showed me that I had just been running in place. Not going anywhere. And the more I ran, the deeper a hole I dug. For the first time ever, I was truly alive. Living a wild and crazy adventure. One that got me killed... but, damn, it was fun.

We traveled west, staying hidden beneath the thick canopy of the woodlands whenever we could. Our destination was Kunlun, Temurr's kingdom. The wagon had been left behind at the creek, and we rode in pairs on the two karkadanns, their heavy steps muffled by the forest floor. Days passed in near silence.

Grief clung to us like a shadow, its weight unbearable, but it hit Temurr the hardest. He rarely spoke—just a handful of words since our escape from the Black City. In the mornings, I'd catch glimpses of tear streaks matted into the coarse hair of his somber face. His sorrow was unspoken but unmistakable, a reflection of all we had lost.

It wasn't just grief that haunted us. We were being followed—I was certain of it. Kasuma had drilled the skills into me: how to listen, how to watch for the subtle shifts in the forest, how to taste the air for unfamiliar scents. I couldn't see them or hear them, but something was off. The balance of the woods felt weird to me, like a thread pulled too tight.

Pherric would've had some lofty explanation, claiming I was sensing a mindform or some such nonsense. Which, of course, was why I kept my suspicions to myself. I wasn't in the mood for one of his lectures. He could be such a priss.

"I suppose now is a good time to discuss a plan of action." Braylor broke the silence.

After setting up camp for the night, he hunted down a moose-like beast. Pherric foraged a decent selection of berries and edible leaves. When we gathered around the fire that night, Temurr used a blade edge to whittle some arrows and fabricate bows.

"We ride west, to Kunlun, but what we do next… I have no notion."

We were still in no mood to talk.

I was happy we were talking again. "What can we do?"

"Very little, I fear," Braylor held forth as he chewed on meat.

"Well… what about raising an army? Isn't that an option?"

"It is the only option," said Temurr, without looking up from his bow.

"You saw the size of his army encamped outside of the Black City," said Braylor. "We are too late, fool!"

Pherric held up a finger, deep in thought. "If we can present a united front… seek an audience with the leaders of each nation, we might be able to garner their support."

"You are talking about a handful of outcasts trying to appeal to the rulers as if we had something to offer, wizard! The situation is beyond us now. We have done our part."

Pherric stood up. "The massacre at Agartha will have resonated with everyone on the continent! Each must be fearing they are the next to fall. That is why we head to Kunlun first! The Prominans know they are likely to be Malek's next target."

Temurr leapt to his feet. "And we will be ready for them!"

Waving a hand dismissively at Temurr, Baylor focused on Pherric. "I will give you that they are a target. But, what then? They are vastly outnumbered by the Irkallan army. I doubt that my people have trouble sleeping this night knowing the Bànshēn rén have been wiped out. The other hominan nations have no blood in this fight. I do not see—"

"Enough!" I shouted. My turn to jump to my feet. "Knock off the whole *Negative Nancy* routine, Braylor! What's your solution? Rather than just disparaging everyone's ideas, why don't you throw out a few helpful suggestions instead?!"

Braylor pointed at me, nodding to Temurr. "This one dies and suddenly she has stones of steel!"

"Stop deflecting!" I stabbed a finger way up at his chest. "What do you think we should do?"

"You had a chance to kill Malek," he snarled. "The only chance, mind you. But you were smitten by the Knight Commander and failed in your attempt..."

Pherric had had enough. "That is not fair, Braylor."

"Smitten?! I am alive today—*all* of us are alive—because of him!"

The giant crossed his arms. "And so is the king..."

His words cut me. I screamed in frustration, balled my fists, and stomped away to the edge of our camp.

"Braylor, she did everything she could have done. Had she tried to kill Malek, she not only would have fallen short—she would be dead," Pherric defended.

"She is dead..."

Staring into the dark woods, I heard a noise.

"Sir Kane manipulated her," added Braylor.

"To what end?!" objected Temurr.

I slipped away as they continued arguing. Stopping at a tree, I let my eyes adjust to the dark. I dragged my fingers through the ground and applied mud to my forehead and cheeks to cover my skin. Then I listened. If a spy were following us, he would use the sounds of our argument to get closer. To hear our plans.

Taking my time, I dropped low and advanced deeper into the gloomy forest. I took measured steps, on the balls of my feet. Waiting for my weight to sink into the dirt before stepping again. I paused, listening. The fading sounds of our camp echoed off the trees. A slight breeze wafted by me. The smell of blood. I slowed my heart, quieted my breathing.

When I was far enough away, I circled around to where I could come up on the sound I had heard from behind. I saw the silhouette of a man, created by the bright fire in our camp. Leaning against a tree. He was watching the boys. But I had no weapon.

I inched closer and closer. On slow, delicate steps. Adrenaline kept firing off from my brain. And the fight-or-flight was hard to overcome. When I was near enough, I reached for his neck.

The blade of a knife was placed against my throat.

"You did well," a voice told me. In that high-pitched, lyrical Australian-sounding accent.

The man leaning against the tree did not move.

"Do not concern yourself. He is dead," said Kasuma.

Spinning around, I embraced her... and got a mouthful of feathers in return. Her lilting laugh was music to my ears.

Chapter 67

We dragged the body of the spy into our campsite, dropped him next to the fire.

Braylor, Temurr and Pherric rushed to greet Kasuma.

"Thank the gods!" cried Temurr.

"You survived!" said Pherric.

Braylor patted her head, pointed to the dead guy. "Who might this be?"

The dead man wore a black tunic with brown leather straps. A sword was attached to his back. He was lean and strong, with a few old scars around his face and hands.

"A spy," she said. "He has tracked you since you left the Black City."

"You have been out there all this time? Why did you not join us?" asked Pherric.

"To ensure you were not being followed—you were," she said. "Malek knew you escaped. Or, he let you go."

Braylor scoffed. "Malek would not let us go!"

"Then perhaps it was Kane," suggested Kasuma.

"Kane would not send a spy after us," I said. "Seriously, guys. I trust him."

"She is infatuated, remember?" I punched Braylor hard in the shoulder.

"Braylor, there is more going on here than we realize," warned Pherric. He turned to me, placing a hand on my arm. "Finely, why is Kane helping us?"

"He doesn't believe in what Malek is doing any more than we do! He hates the genocide of the other species! Hates his grand plan to become emperor! All of it! He wasn't even there when the Bànshēn rén were killed—he had no idea what Malek was up to!"

Braylor dismissed me. "Then why not kill the king himself?"

"His father was loyal to Queen Dirvilia. He made Kane swear to carry on his legacy. To protect the crown and kingdom, but—"

"But he cannot execute Malek by his own hand? That is convenient..." said Braylor.

"Look, I don't know..." Anger welled in me. "I heard what he had to say and I trust him. He did everything he could to help me kill Malek! It almost worked! Can't it just be that simple?!"

"It is not wise to trust so easily, Finley," admonished Pherric.

"Especially the Knight Commander of the Irkallan army!" Braylor added.

"Well, I trusted all of you! And you assholes kidnapped me!"

"That is different, Finley. You are the Chosen One," said Temurr. "And our good fortune is only further proof that you are going to lead us to victory—"

"I am not the Chosen One!" I screamed. "I'm so sick of this! There is no such thing! Do you hear me?"

Temurr grimaced, a pitying look in his eyes.

Kasuma cleared her throat. "Enough talk of plots and destinies!"

She stepped between us. Carefully removed a pack she had strapped to her back. She took out a wood cask of wine.

"Gods bless you, Kasuma," exhaled Temurr. Of all of us, he needed a drink most.

She pulled out five small metal cups.

"I robbed a merchant's caravan on my journey here. So, tonight... we drink and celebrate our companions."

I held out my cup as she poured.

"First, we pour one out. For them."

I turned my cup over, spilling out the contents.

Braylor blinked. "Wha—?! Pour out good wine? On the ground?"

"Yes. Where I'm from, this is a sign of reverence for friends we've lost.

My grandfather and his buddies did this at funerals, whenever they lost one of their own in the line of duty. This is the drink the dead would have had... if they were still with us."

We stared at one another, then they poured out their cups. Except for Braylor. I gave him a stern look and he emptied his as well.

"Aye, that is now settled. Give me more wine!" demanded Braylor, holding out his cup.

Everyone laughed. For the first time in a while.

We drank and they shared their stories. I even slipped in a few of my more memorable moments from my time in Malek's castle. And as soon as a hush would fall over the group, someone would propose a toast.

In the morning, Kasuma stood before us. She flexed her wings in preparation for flight.

"From the direction you have been traveling, might I assume you are heading for Kunlun?"

Temurr nodded. "We can seek refuge there and I am hoping we can convince King Kwong to begin assembling a Prominan army."

I laughed and they stared at me.

"Wait. The king of Kunlun is called Kwong? King *Kwong*?"

"Yes," said Temurr in earnest.

Oh, my God. The jokes just wrote themselves.

"Nothing." I tried hard not to laugh. "I've got nothing."

Temurr gave me a cold stare.

Kasuma, pointing to the dead guy at the edge of our clearing, whispered, "That spy is not the one who started out from the Black City. The original has likely reported back to the king. They know where you are headed."

"And?" Braylor chimed in.

"Malek might send troops from garrisons between here and the Kunlun mountains. To intercept you."

"What do you suggest?" asked Pherric.

"Well... you could come to Nibiru, as my guests."

Eyes opened wide and Pherric took a half step back—I gathered that this was a big deal.

"Are you sure?" said Temurr.

"All of us?" questioned Pherric.

"Yes. These are dangerous times. Kunlun has certainly begun preparing for an Irkallan invasion. I believe we should try to convince the Tenguan leadership to do the same."

"If we do, would we be able to convince representatives from your land to venture out and advise the other kingdoms?" said Pherric.

"Even better. I imagine the Tenguans could invite the leaders to come to Nibiru," Kasuma said.

Braylor, Temurr, and Pherric exchanged looks of astonishment.

"That would be... monumental. Every sovereign state would understand the importance of such a request!"

She looked to each one of us. "I know. That is my plan. You are all brave and loyal friends. I trust you with my life."

"Our most sincere gratitude to you, Kasuma," said Temurr, with mad respect.

"So... what should we do?" Pherric asked.

"I will fly north to the city of Relna Thune, in Hyperborea. Secure passage for you. Do you know of it?"

"Vaguely," admitted Temurr.

Kasuma gave Temurr detailed directions.

She lifted off, soaring high into the morning sky.

The others grumbled, more than a bit hungover from our night, as they gathered the weapons stolen from the stadium. I really wanted to jog instead of ride, but only had the cheap flat sandals they had given me for the fight. I climbed onto the karkadann behind Braylor.

"We are in desperate need of supplies," said Braylor. He inspected his sword. "And better weapons."

"We have no coin," Pherric reminded.

"Ah, let me guess. The wizard is against thievery, as well?" Braylor teased.

"That... I have no issue with," he smirked.

Braylor laughed. We galloped from our camp, riding out of the evergreen forest and continuing on a new path toward the northwest.

I tapped Braylor's shoulder.

"Yes, child?"

"What's the big deal about going to Kasuma's kingdom? You all acted like it was the greatest thing ever."

"You know Kasuma is Tenguan. Her people are native to the isle of Oceantis, far out to sea in the west. Their species has always been an isolated one and they remain protective of their territory. Not much is known of Oceantis or their capital of Nibiru, other than what is whispered in taverns by drunken sailors claiming to have seen it. Those who talk in private of Oceantis invariably refer to it as the Forbidden Kingdom. Simply traveling there is a dangerous undertaking, and it is said that the city itself is impenetrable."

"Very intriguing," I whispered.

"Aye. For us to be allowed to visit there? Very *big deal* indeed."

"And if we have any hope of uniting everyone against Malek, getting a red-carpet invitation to go there means... other rulers might show up, right?"

"That seems to be Kasuma's design. She is a wise bird, that one. Never underestimate her!"

"I would never. She kinda scares me," I admitted.

"She should."

Chapter 68

For over a week, we rode our karkadanns toward Relna Thune, supposedly a bustling port city in Hyperborea. The journey was long and tense, but things only got more complicated when Braylor insisted we stop for "essential supplies." His tone made it clear there would be no arguing.

Our target was a small, nondescript village a few axims outside of Nirvana. Yes, they had Nirvana here on Tir Na. And while the name might sound familiar, they warned me that Nirvana was anything like heaven. Temurr said it was a seedy cesspool of crime, where gangs ruled the streets, and trust was a commodity no one could afford. That the only thing guaranteed there was trouble. It wasn't a city—it was a predator, waiting for its next victim.

So, we settled on raiding the nearby village.

Naturally, the big guy wanted to rush in and slice everyone up. But Pherric volunteered me for the job, claiming my "light-footedness" made me perfect for sneaking around. I couldn't exactly argue—they weren't wrong, and Kasuma's training in stealth had made me even better at slipping through the shadows unnoticed.

So, under the cover of darkness, I crept into the village. It was slow work, the kind that made my heart race with every creak of a floorboard or rustle of fabric. I spent hours sneaking into a few houses, quietly lifting food, weapons, and other provisions. Everything went smoothly—until it didn't.

One house, a farmer's, was my downfall. As I reached for a stash of dried meat hanging near the hearth, the man lunged out of the shadows with an ax. He must have been the lightest sleeper in the entire village—or just particularly protective of his food. Either way, my cover was blown, and suddenly, staying "light of foot" was no longer an option; I had to fight.

I wrestled away when he caught me, but years working the land made him quite strong. I had to hit and kick him a half dozen times before he finally went down. He did manage to elbow me hard in the side of the head, nearly knocking me out.

Pherric set my dislocated jaw once I returned to camp. The boys were happy I couldn't talk for a few days.

We traveled farther north, where the nights grew colder, and rain became a near-constant companion. The endless journey to Relna Thune gave me too much time to think, and my thoughts inevitably drifted to Kane. Those sharp, intelligent eyes of his, shadowed with sadness. That roguish smile, quick to disarm. His laugh, warm and inviting.

Kane wasn't just a warrior; he was a contradiction—a man shaped by loyalty and pain yet unafraid to be playful, funny, even vulnerable. He carried his burdens with an openness that felt raw and real, and somehow, despite his mystery, he seemed completely honest. I couldn't deny it anymore—I'd fallen for him, though I couldn't admit it to myself. It drove me crazy. How could I explain these feelings without sounding like a naive schoolgirl swooning over her knight in shining armor? I had to forget him. I knew I'd never see him again.

The final leg of our journey brought us to the dark, turbulent waters of the Triton Sea. Emerging from a scraggly forest of thin evergreens and resilient reeds sprouting from scorched soil, we found ourselves standing on a low cliff. There, overlooking the sea, loomed a castle—a fortress rather.

This wasn't a fairytale structure of bright spires and gleaming walls. It was a hulking monstrosity of squat, square towers and harsh battlements, encircled by a thick stone wall. Fire barriers covered every structure within. But the fort had been ravaged—its stones blackened by fire, its defenses abandoned to time. The ruins stood as a grim monument to a violent past, the smell of charred earth still lingering faintly in the air.

"Where's the damn port?!" Braylor grunted. "Temurr?"

Temurr spun his karkadann around in a circle. He stopped when he saw a range of tall, thin mountain peaks to the north along the shore. The peaks poked up through the ground like spears stabbing at the sky, each covered with splotchy sea-green moss and angry little evergreen trees.

He pointed at the mountains. "Ah, I believe I missed the target, it would seem." He looked up and down the coastline. "Frip was always better with direction. But... if this is Castle Leviathan, which I am assuming it is, then... we head north."

"What happened here?" I nodded toward the scorched castle.

Pherric exhaled. "Dragons happened here."

Braylor gave a final look at the castle. And shivered. "So, we head north then."

"Aye," said Temurr, rubbing the thick hair on his chin. "Off by only *one* axim, I was! Not bad. Not bad at all."

The fact that people could travel anywhere without an app amazed me. I would have puttered us around in circles for a month before realizing I was hopefully lost.

I took my own last look at Castle Leviathan. Instead of invoking fear, the blackened castle intrigued me for some reason.

We trekked up the rugged coastline, the sharp, salty wind whipping against us like it had a grudge. Towering peaks loomed ahead, their harsh edges stabbing into the clouds like nature's middle finger. As we rounded the base of the mountains, the landscape shifted, and when we turned inland, it was like stepping into a different world.

A massive gap split the peaks—a natural gateway carved over centuries by a slow, winding river. The water gleamed in the fading light, wide and unhurried, like it had all the time in the world. A road, well-worn and impressively straight, hugged its bank, clearly the result of relentless foot traffic and karkadann power.

The river itself was alive with activity. Flat barges, piled high with crates and barrels, moved against the current, dragged upstream by teams of karkadanns. Their handlers barked sharp commands, voices cutting through the creak of wood and rush of water. Downstream, empty barges drifted lazily toward the sea, their only cargo exhausted beasts catching a break. The river's rhythm was hypnotic—an endless back-and-forth feeding trade between the Triton Sea and the inland kingdoms.

As the sun sank behind the peaks, the shadows stretched long and dramatic, painting everything in deep golds and violets. Ahead, the glow of lanterns pierced the growing darkness, the first signs of a city tucked snugly where the river met the mountains.

The port town was a patchwork of stone buildings stacked in uneven clusters, functional yet stubbornly charming. The air buzzed with movement—merchants unloading goods, dockworkers shouting directions, and distant music adding an almost cinematic backdrop. Smoke curled from chimneys, blending with the salty breeze and the damp, earthy scent of the river. It wasn't glamorous, but it was alive—a gritty gateway to something bigger.

This was Relna Thune.

Chapter 69

No walls or iron gates blocked our entry. We dismounted and led our karkadanns through the pass into Relna Thune. The river split the city in two, flowing steadily to the sea.

From a small rise, we took in the view. Long wooden docks shot into the water, where a dozen ships were moored. Larger vessels anchored farther out, their sails swaying gently in the dark blue sea. Tall, narrow rock formations pierced the surface like sharp teeth, calming the waters around the port. A wooden lighthouse stood guard, while a new stone version was being built up within some scaffolding nearby.

The city sprawled nearly an axim wide, divided equally by the river. Warehouses lined the bustling port, while merchant shops, modest houses, grand manors, and ramshackle shacks clustered along wide streets and countless narrow alleys. The buildings stretched up the hills behind us, their silhouettes sharp against the twilight.

As night fell, torches flickered to life. Workers bustled between wagons stacked with barrels and crates. Beggars lingered on street corners, while drunks weaved unsteadily down the main avenue. Life thrummed through the city, exotic and determined.

I could see four wide bridges arched over the river, connecting the two halves of Relna Thune. The air was thick with the scent of salt, wood, and smoke. We exchanged uncertain glances, the question lingering between us: what now?

"Um, where are we supposed to go?" I asked.

Braylor shrugged and looked at Temurr. He shrugged.

Pherric shook his head. "We did not discuss this."

"Just like men—to not ask for directions."

Temurr took the reins of our two karkadanns. "I need ale. I'll see what I can get for these old ladies," he said.

He started to walk away with them.

I held up my hand. "Wait! What if we go somewhere and—"

"I have a feeling you will be here when I get back, you will."

I gave him my best glare. He headed down a dark alleyway.

Inspection time: I eyed the main roads on both sides of the river. Merchants hawked their wares. Prostitutes did the same. There were a lot of Prominans and Hominans, but no Bànshēn rén or any of Braylor's species. Most of the city dwellers ignored Pherric and I but more than a few cast glances at Braylor. He noticed, too. He pulled up the hood of his cloak, only there was no mistaking his hulking Fomorian frame.

"This is a test," I said. Out loud.

"A test?" asked Pherric.

"Kasuma always tells me to be aware of my surroundings. She says I need to know my escape routes, possible threats, and potential weapons. She didn't give you specific direction because… she thinks I can find them."

"Very astute," he said. "You impress me more and more each day."

That made me feel good. I smiled, for a brief second, then went to work. I retraced our steps into the city, looking for clues or signs she might have left. When I saw nothing, I worked my way back. Pherric leaned back, propping up a shed, with his arms crossed and a smirk on his face. Braylor sat on the ground, leaning against the wood wall, and closed his eyes.

"Okay, she knew we would come in this way, head down the main street and… stop at some point."

I walked along the worn road, every structure around me bearing the scars of time. Weather had taken its toll—wind, rain, saltwater, and sun had rotted wood, bleached stone, and dulled every surface. My eyes scanned walls, signs, and doors, searching for anything that seemed new or out of place.

Crossing the first bridge, I climbed for a better vantage point. From there, I stared down the main street, but the dim torchlight and deep shadows of the night made it hard to make out details. Frustrated, I glanced down at my feet—and then at the bridge itself.

Heart racing, I bolted to the side of the bridge, inspecting its edges. There had to be a clue, something to show me which half of the city to search. Unable to see clearly, I yanked a torch from the wall of a nearby food shop. Its flickering light cast shifting shadows over the wood as I leaned closer.

The first side revealed nothing. I sprinted to the opposite edge and held the torch high. There, faint but unmistakable, two small letters painted in black: LT.

I sprinted up to Pherric and Braylor.

"I know where to go!" I shouted.

"Where would that be?" Pherric said, amused. Braylor grunted.

"Well, not where exactly, but I know we need to be on that side of the river!" I pointed.

"Lead on."

Temurr arrived, coins in his hand, as we headed for the bridge. We crossed over and I showed them the two letters hand-painted on the side.

"See that?! The letters *L* and *T*!"

Temurr looked at me like I had lost my mind. "I see..."

"That's a *message*! From Kasuma!"

"And how do you know this?" he asked.

"LT! Lex Talionis! It has to be her!"

The boys exchanged an approving look.

We marched through the muddy streets in search of more clues. I found another LT high on the side of a kark barn. And another etched into a wooden post. We headed toward the sea and farther to the northern end of the Relna Thune.

One of Kasuma's markings led us down an alley full of shadows. Candlelight from broken windows and open doors lit our path. Her last LT, above a doorway, put us in front of a shady bar near the docks. Several wasted Prominans staggered out as we arrived.

"This is our final destination?" asked Temurr.

"Don't say it like that… but, yeah. I'm pretty sure."

Loud laughter, fists pounding on tables, and drunken sailing songs echoed out of the tavern. No doors meant the bar never closed. Probably not a good sign.

Pherric and Temurr went in.

As I followed, Braylor tapped my shoulder. "I will take a walk. To the docks."

That surprised me. I thought he could use a stiff drink. And I wanted him strutting through the place, right behind me, for backup.

"Why?"

"I doubt I would be welcome in there," Braylor said. Enough people had given him the stink eye—he had become an outcast.

I nodded. "Don't go too far away, big boy. This place gives me the creeps."

"Then go, and give back to this place even more of the… creeps." His big paw patted my shoulder and he walked off.

I stepped cautiously through the doorway, immediately hit by a wave of thick, choking smoke. The air reeked—a nauseating mix of cheap ale, sweat, urine, and the unmistakable briny stench of the seaport's fish markets. The dim light from scattered candles on the tables and a few wall-mounted lanterns barely kept the shadows at bay, leaving the corners of the tavern hidden in darkness.

The room was a chaotic blend of voices and movement. Rough-looking locals, mercenaries, and sailors packed the tables, drinking, shouting, and arguing over games or past offenses. Women in low-cut blouses and tattered skirts weaved between the crowds, balancing wooden trays loaded with mugs of ale. Their practiced smiles masked their irritation as they dodged and deflected wandering hands with swift, graceful movements, never spilling a drop.

It was a place that reeked of desperation and danger, alive with an energy that both warned me to stay on guard and dared me to hang around.

I tried to catch up with Pherric and Temurr. But a pair of hands grabbed me at the waist, pulling me onto the lap of a stocky Prominan goon. His thick black fur, filled with streaks of white, covered a multitude of scars.

"C'mere, you!" he bellowed. His rancid breath, wafting over all five of his black teeth, stung my eyes.

The other sailors at the table cheered him. I struggled to push off his gorilla-like paws.

I glanced around for my friends. Temurr's hand gripped Pherric's shoulder, preventing him from coming to my rescue. He flashed Temurr a worried look. But Temurr closed his eyes, shook his head. I was on my own... apparently.

The gorilla-man looked like a pirate who'd lost a fight with a Halloween costume store. His green jacket was way too tight. A gray knit cap sat awkwardly on his head, as he thought it gave him some mysterious edge. It, however, did not. Beneath the jacket, a dirty-white, baggy shirt hung loose, its fabric rumpled and stained with what might have been ale, grease, or worse. The combination gave him the look of a seasoned sailor— an ape who had seen hundreds of ports, survived countless brawls, and carried the grit and grime like it was a badge of honor.

"Let go, asshole!" I shouted.

"Oh, a feisty one! I likes 'em feisty!" said the pirate.

With his other hand, he grabbed a boob and squeezed hard.

"Hey!"

I kicked my heel hard into his shin bone. He twitched but didn't let go. I kicked again, causing him to grip both my arms to hold me away as he tried to stand. I tipped myself forward, trying to slide away from his grip, but he held on.

He flung me around to face him, spit drooling from his lustful grin. When I tried to knee his groin, he crossed his leg over to block it. I was too predictable.

With my arms pinned, I jumped up. Both of my feet kicked him in the stomach. Keeping one foot on him, I drove my sandal in his face. He released me and I hit the hard wooden floor, the wind knocked out of me.

Struggling to breathe, he pounced on me, punching my nose. Hard. His arm went back up, then his fist hurtled toward my face. I rolled my head to the side. He struck the floor, cracking the worn wooden boards. I pulled my knife from my belt, but he pinned my arm again. I managed to flick my wrist—slitting his thigh. The pirate gorilla leapt back, laughing at me.

"Feisty indeed!" he growled, holding a paw to the cut on his leg.

I sprang to my feet, holding out my knife. Panting hard.

"Oh, the little warrior wants to play!"

I cast a quick glance at Pherric. I needed one of his mindforms. If he could fake a tap to the jerk's shoulder... it would distract him. But Pherric stared straight ahead, not looking at me.

"So... let's play!"

He lunged at me. Both arms out. I sliced at his forearm and missed. Diving to the floor at his side, slashing at his calf, I drew more blood.

The gorilla pirate yelped with fury. He crouched in pain, then readied himself to pounce again. I hopped to my feet and we circled each other. At least his buddies stayed out of the fray.

I mentally pleaded to Pherric for a diverting mindform. I wiped away blood dripping from my nose with the back of my hand. *Come on, Pherric! Help me!*

The pirate's eyes gave him away—he was focused on my knife. I lifted the blade up and back, but threw the heel of my palm into his chin with a stiff jab. He rocked backward, briefly stunned.

He growled, pulling out his sword. The crowd murmured, backing away. Shit just got real. Death was now on the table. And I brought a small dagger to a sword fight.

Pirate ape stomped toward me, aiming his blade back to run me through. *Help me, Pherric,* my mind screamed. I backed up a step. But the tavern crowd had me fenced in. Before he could skewer me... a blurry hand of a man appeared over his shoulder. The hand seemed almost invisible, an outlined apparition. And that hand reached out, tapping the ape pirate on the shoulder.

He turned his head to see who had tapped him. I smirked.

Leaping forward, I slashed my knife at his head.

One of his friends shouted, "Ha! The little warrior missed!"

The pirate grinned, standing up straight.

"Can we kill 'er now, captain!" another screamed.

He gurgled. Like a massive tree falling, the pirate crashed to the floorboards. Blood poured from the slit in his neck.

I stood there gawking. My mouth dangling. Eyes wide. I stepped back as blood rolled toward my sandals. I had no idea I had hit the pirate, much less killed him. There was an inch of blood on the tip of my dagger.

Reality caught up with me. I inhaled deeply, after forgetting to breathe. I crouched down, pointing my knife at the pirate's friends. But they stood there. In stunned silence. Staring down at their dead captain.

"Excellent work, Finley Maguire," said Kasuma.

I had almost gotten used to her sneaking up behind me.

Like a mother disappointed in the actions of her child, she gave me her most stern look... with arms crossed.

"You just killed the captain of the ship that was to take us to Nibiru."

Chapter 70

The pirate captain's sailor buddies unsheathed their swords in one synchronized, overly dramatic motion. Shhhiiinngg. Seriously, it was like they'd rehearsed it.

The tavern exploded into disarray, the crowd scattering like cockroaches when the lights turn on. Chairs overturned, drinks spilled, and within seconds, only the sailors, my friends, and the tension of impending nastiness remained.

Temurr nudged Pherric, his expression saying: *It's about time we actually do something.*

The sailors weren't much to look at—grimy, sneering, and proudly displaying their collection of missing teeth. Or worse, the teeth they did have.

The boys slid into position on either side of me.

Kasuma was the picture of calm menace. She stood defiantly, her dagger spinning effortlessly between her fingers before she shifted her grip.

"You gotta teach me how to do that."

"Quiet, Finley," she hissed, eyes not leaving the sailors.

Then, a new voice cut through the air. "Let me correct you there, love."

The sailors parted as a dark-skinned woman with long, twisted dreadlocks pushed her way through. Only slightly taller than me, she wore a black leather jumpsuit that gleamed in the low light, and silver piercings ran across the skin of her cheeks in sharp, horizontal lines, making her grin even more intimidating.

"Ya see, little bird," she said, her smile cold and sharp as glass. "I aim to be the *new* captain of the *Jaculus*."

She withdrew her gaze from Kasuma and stepped to me, her nose an inch from mine.

"But, seein' as how you *challenged* the captain, and was the victor…"

I had killed her captain. And that's likely how you moved up the chain of command on their ship. So she would have to kill me to take *my* place. I stepped back into a fighting position, body to the side and dagger pointed toward her.

She lowered her head, then flashed a look at her mates and threw a darker one at me.

"I doubt she's wantin' the job though," she sniffed me. "With her not bein' of the sea, and suchlike. Therebies, the captainin' duties fall ta me. Me bein' second in command. Any got objections to my stated claim?!"

She placed hands on hips and glared at the sailors. No one objected.

"You got an objection, firehair?!" Her hand went to her sword hilt, resting there.

"Um, nope. It's all yours."

"Good on ya!" she smirked, patting my face. "Let it be known—Melcente is now official captain of the *Jaculus*!"

Melcente finally removed her sword, whipping around to her crew. "And if any of you Hibagons stab me in the back?! I'll ghoul ya for eternity! May the gods be damned!"

Kasuma grabbed my shoulder, easing me out of my fighting position.

She took her place in front of the new captain.

"What of the arrangement I had with… your previous captain?" said Kasuma.

Melcente sheathed her sword. "About that. I wudn't too keen on the terms of his arrangement there. Thought it bit light on your end, considerin' my crew had to sail to the Forbidden Kingdom and suchlike."

"The terms were *more* than fair," barked Kasuma.

"Them was his terms!" Melcente pointed to the body on the floor. "My terms… are twenty thousand plats."

"Twenty? You said my arrangement was a *bit* light. We agreed to ten," said Kasuma.

"That's my number. Pay or walk away," said Melcente.

"I could buy any ship in that harbor for fifteen!" countered Kasuma.

"But not with a crew willin' to take you to that accursed island, there!" She looked down and away, then back at Kasuma. "Eighteen thousand. Final proffer."

Kasuma crossed her arms, stared through the captain, then nodded.

"But we sail immediately," Kasuma stated.

"We sail tomorrow, before dusk, at high tide. Storm's a comin' in the wee hours. I'm already riskin' my crew castin' off for the Forbiddens. Be there and ready... *with* ya coin."

Melcente coaxed her sailors to the bar. "Ale for my crew, barman!"

I wiped at the blood on my face. Pherric checked me out, then pushed both thumbs in hard and, without warning, set the break in my nose.

"Oww! You could warn a person!" I yelped in pain.

"Would it have hurt any less?"

"With friends like you, who needs an evil emperor?"

The tavern din grew loud again as the drunken dirt bags returned to their partying.

I patted Pherric's chest. "Oh, and thanks for that mindform."

"What do you mean?"

"The mindform! You cast one of those things. I saw a fuzzy hand pop up over the captain's shoulder. It tapped him, he turned around, and it gave me my opportunity to strike."

"Finley, I did not project a mindform—I would not help you kill."

Confusion set in. "Well, who the hell did?"

Pherric looked around the room of boozy brawlers and then flashed a smile. "Your lessons are providing returns, Fin. That was *your* mindform."

III

Part Three

Chapter 71

By late afternoon the next day, gray clouds churned above the port, casting a dull, foggy sheen over the bustling docks.

Kasuma led the way, her confident stride guiding us in search of the *Jaculus.* Behind her, Braylor and Temurr struggled under the weight of our travel cases, each lumbering step accompanied by the metallic clink of their contents.

After leaving the tavern, Kasuma had vanished into the night, putting her stealth skills to work. Later that night, she returned, pockets lined with the wealth of a few unfortunate rich merchants. With funds secured, we crashed in the small room she'd rented. The next morning, we hit the garment district—*my* time to shine. Because shopping!

We ditched our ragged tunics for proper everyday attire and even splurged on some fancy outfits. I personally ensured Pherric and Temurr were decked out in coordinated looks made from the finest materials, much to their embarrassment. One tailor, after a hefty payment, managed to whip up two outfits for Braylor on short notice. We grabbed new cloaks, stocked up on weapons, and finally collected the travel cases before heading to the docks.

Braylor met up with me as I outfitted the other boys. He had gone to purchase a new sword for me. A kath sword.

"This is your new sword. The only one you will ever need. Correct?"

"Nice," I said, examining the weight and balance. "So this is... Sword Two?"

"This is *Other Sword.*"

We passed a dozen stunning ships, each more impressive than the last—sleek hulls, grand stern cabins, towering masts. And then we saw it: the *Jaculus*.

It sat low in the water, its hull barely ten feet above the surface. Compared to the others, it was painfully plain, almost laughable. The stern was bare, with no cabins in sight, and its two skinny masts seemed like afterthoughts compared to the triple-masted beauties around it. The ship's narrow, pencil-like frame leaned slightly to one side, as though it couldn't quite handle its own weight. Flakes of paint peeled from its hull, and rotting planks jutted awkwardly from the sides.

This was our ship.

"Is that thing seaworthy?" I asked Temurr. He shrugged.

"Watch your tongue, love!" shouted Melcente from the poop deck. "The Jaculus is the lightest, fastest ship sailing these here seas! We'll get ya there in half the time... before the sea serpents know you passed overhead!"

"If it doesn't fall apart first," I whispered to Temurr.

"What say you, firehair?!" she screamed.

"Permission to come aboard, captain!" I replied.

"Aye," she murmured. She squinted her eyes at me as we climbed onto her rickety boat.

We shoved off an hour later as her seedy crew hustled to and fro securing ropes, lowering sails, and unmooring from the dock.

Melcente shouted a flurry of orders as we pulled away. "Crank the warp line! Faster! And shift that spinnaker by twenty! There ya go, love! Let's not lose this high tide!"

We slipped away from the dock. One sail dropped down to catch the breeze. Melcente steered our floating disaster into the harbor and we sailed toward the tall rock peaks sticking up from the ocean. At the last moment, she rolled the wheel, cutting the ship hard to the right.

"Lower the mainsail full!" she bellowed.

The big sail unfolded as the ropes released. Wind drove into the sails, sending them billowing out like balloons. She had been right about one thing—this ship could fly. We shot away from the mainland. As the sun set, firelight from Relna Thune twinkled in the distance.

Our sleeping situation was laughable. With no passenger cabins, we tied makeshift hammocks up to wood posts below the deck. Braylor required two hammocks, one for each cheek, to suspend him above the rocking floor of the ship. I couldn't sleep that first night—something about the previous night still bothered me—so I tapped Pherric.

"Psst!" I whispered. "Are you awake?" He wasn't.

I kept poking him with my finger.

"Pherric. Psst!"

"Yes, Finley?" I knew he was awake.

"So, you really think I cast that mindform back in the tavern?"

"You must have done so."

"How?"

He rolled over in his hammock. "Do you remember being afraid during that confrontation?"

"Um, no," I said. "Not really. Maybe at first. I was kinda pissed."

"That is how you were able to do it. Your mind was calm even though you fought for your life. Heightened emotions cloud the ability. You were angry, but not angry... enough."

"Yeah, but... making a shadow—a vision—appear... that's one thing. But I physically touched him! How is that possible?"

"You are a learner. You listened and remembered all that I taught you. Just as your fighting skills have improved, your lessons in mindforms have been equally as effective. A little less killing would be nice, but... I am quite impressed with you."

The waves rocked the ship as we swung gently back and forth.

"So... I'm not the chosen one. But I'm becoming a *decent* one instead?" I said.

"You are quite good, Finley," he murmured. "Now, find sleep. And let me do the same."

I had no chance of that. Excitement coursed through me. What seemed like magic when I first arrived on Tir Na seemed more like an exact science.

Mindforms worked. And all my late-night training finally paid off. I tried to read Pherric's thoughts as I listened to him fall back asleep, but I got nothing. Trying too hard never seemed to work, so I let it go.

After I eventually fell asleep, a strange dream came to me. Two young girls were playing with me. They were big for their age and had Fomorian features. We were all playing in a fruit tree orchard. An old Fomorian woman watched over everyone intently. The girls hid from me behind trees, popping their heads out, throwing pieces of fruit, laughing. I chased them among the trees. We wrestled with each other. Climbed the trees. Warm, soft, happy memories. Then I jumped in my dream to three bodies being burned on a funeral pyre. Wind whipped the flames as I watched the bodies being slowly consumed.

I woke with a start, gasping for breath. My heart pounded. That was not a dream—it was a memory.

I squinted in the dark, peering across the cargo hold of the ship. Braylor snored loudly. He restlessly fidgeted, then rolled over in his double-hammock bed.

I think that somehow, I had managed to tap into his mind.

Chapter 72

My hammock lurched violently, swinging me awake. Gray light from the morning barely filtered through the cracks, but below deck was eerily empty.

I leapt down, but the ship rolled sharply, sending me sliding hard into the hull wall. Confused, I scrambled to my feet and staggered to the wooden stairs, gripping anything I could for balance. Climbing up, I was met with a deluge of icy seawater crashing down the steps, drenching me to the core.

On deck, mayhem reigned. Sheets of rain lashed my face, the wind a piercing scream. Captain Melcente gripped the ship's wheel with white-knuckled intensity, spinning it hard to steer us away from the monstrous waves breaking in every direction. Her crew shouted over the roar of the storm, wrestling ropes and sails.

The boom swung wildly across the deck, forcing everyone to duck or risk being knocked into the sea. Smaller sails were hoisted amidst the chaos, their ropes tied to the rails in desperation.

"Shake the reef! Tighten that jib sail!" Melcente bellowed, her voice cutting through the storm like a whip.

Another wave slammed the ship, water flooding the deck. I lost my footing and slid straight into the railing, my arms clinging to it for dear life.

"Hold tight, girlie!" Melcente barked at me, laughing—laughing!—as if this was her idea of fun. She fought the wheel, pointing commands. "Snug the vang and trim the mainsul, loves! This here's but a squall!"

Her words chilled me as much as the sea spray. *Just a squall?* My mind reeled at the thought that after surviving countless battles, this random storm would be the end of us.

"Let's ride this kelpie out!" she squealed with glee, her cackling eerie against the rage of the storm.

Another wave crashed over the deck, knocking Braylor loose. He skidded toward me, grabbed me with one arm, and tossed me into the rocking dinghy. "Hold on!" he shouted before dashing off to grab Temurr, hauling him in beside me.

Pherric caught on and sprinted over, barely managing to leap into the lifeboat. Kasuma, wings dripping and folded tight around her, huddled below the poop deck, her usual defiance dulled by the storm.

The ship groaned and tilted precariously, each wave threatening to swallow us whole. I clutched the edge of the dinghy, hoping the storm would break before we did.

The Jaculus rocked violently. Unable to see the horizon, I felt seasick. I had spent enough time on my father's yacht to know how to overcome it. I lifted my head up and stared at the rocking horizon. Giving my brain a faraway fixed point of reference alleviated sea sickness. I glanced at Pherric. He was feeling it, too. His skin was pale and he gulped for air.

"Get your sea legs, Pherric! Watch that horizon!" I pulled his chin up into the harsh spray.

"For what purpose?!"

"Staring at a point in the distance helps your mind process the movement of the ship!"

He tried his best as the rain assaulted us and the wind tossed the ship about.

We eventually sailed ahead of the squall. The seas returned to almost normal, with the rain subsiding to a light mist.

By dusk, sunshine broke through the clouds. The seas calmed. And the wind carried us further west. I stood at the bow of the ship, staring at the dark blue waters. Pherric staggered to the bow railing and sat near me, his face pale in the setting sun.

"Still seasick?"

"Unsteady and nauseous, yes. However, nothing remains in my belly to return on me."

"Well, unfortunately, it doesn't look like we're out of it just yet," I said.

"Another storm?" He panicked.

"Look." I pointed to the west.

A wide, dark gray cloud swirled ahead of us, roiling on the water surface.

Captain Melcente marched up, her face grim. "A foul tempest's coming for us."

"Can you go around it?" I glanced at Pherric.

"Efforts were made, love! The cloud... it follows us. Black magic's at play..."

Pherric shook his head—he could sense nothing.

The captain returned to the wheel, desperation in her movements as she tried to steer us away. But no matter which way she turned, that massive storm cloud followed, its dark shape unnatural, like it was hunting us.

We pressed on to the west for at least an hour, the air growing thick with despair. The crew worked silently, their glances flicking nervously to the mist creeping toward us. A few snapped at each other, but mostly we watched and waited.

After a while, the *Jaculus* slipped into the mist. The wind died instantly. The waves calmed. Our sails sagged, and the ship drifted, swallowed by an eerie fog.

It felt wrong. Dead wrong. The air grew thick and damp, like the sea was holding its breath. I couldn't see more than ten feet ahead, the ocean around us a blurry void. No one spoke. No sound seemed to come from the world outside.

Braylor, Temurr, and a few others drew their swords, their eyes scanning the fog with mounting fear. They moved cautiously, as though any second something—anything—might pounce.

Then we heard it. A sound. A woman's voice. Low, haunting, singing.

"What is that?" I whispered.

Pherric shrugged as his eyes darted around.

The singing was in a language I did not know. But it was beautiful.

Another melodic voice joined in.

I heard the ruffling of feathers, and Kasuma took off. She launched into the air, disappearing into the thick vapor.

The tension broke. Everyone on board stood up straight, listening. I tried to locate the source of that magnificent voice. Everyone walked to the railings.

"Sea sirens," mumbled Melcente from her ship wheel. "Sea sirens!"

I might have heard her run off the poop deck, down the stairs. But I was so completely drawn to the singing. That voice. The glorious song.

From the corner of my eye, I saw movement. A shape. Out on the sea, a gorgeous naked woman swam towards the ship. Her round green eyes looked up to me, her lips parted, and she sang out another beautiful chorus.

I wanted to... no, I *needed* to go to her. Girls were not my thing but I had to be with her, wanted to touch her, kiss those full red lips.

I put a boot on the railing. The lady in the water called, begging me to join her.

Melcente spun me around. But I strained to look over my shoulder at the hottest woman I had ever seen.

"Put this in your ears!" Melcente might have said. Her voice was distant, muddy.

I tried to climb the railing. "But... I-I need her."

The captain twisted my head around. Face to face. She had a white gunk stuck in her ears. A long fingernail scraped a thick, white candle. She stuffed wax in one ear.

I tried to push her away, to get back to my love in the water.

She crammed a chunk of wax in my other ear.

The epic song faded. My hands went to the railing; I searched for the beautiful girl. But she was gone. So, I tried to flick the wax out of my ears—Melcente smacked my hands.

"Sea siren!" she screamed, trying to be heard through the wax.

The spell had been broken. I scanned the deck. Everyone was affected.

Only Braylor hunched over, with hands covering his ears, and fought off the lovely voices.

The captain broke the candle in half, shoved it in my chest.

"Fill their ears!" she bellowed. "Quiet them voices!"

I scrambled to Pherric, drawing him away from the railing, and scratched off chunks of wax, pushing it in his ears.

One of Melcente's crew dove into the water.

I only heard the pounding of my heart. I tore a chunk off my candle, gave it to Pherric.

"Plug their ears!" I shouted in his face. "Block out the singing!"

Pherric, still dazed, blinked a few times before the urgency hit him. He stumbled off to help.

I turned to the nearest crewman, shoving a piece of wax into his ear. But before I could block the other one, he shoved me away and jumped overboard into the churning sea.

Nearby, Pherric worked with Braylor, who lunged to catch Temurr midair just as he was about to leap. Braylor pinned the struggling ape-man to the deck, his massive strength keeping Temurr still long enough to insert the wax.

We scrambled across the deck, jamming candle bits into ears wherever we could. The haunting voices continued, relentless and eerie, pulling men toward the edge. Despite our efforts, three of the twelve crew members succumbed to the siren call, vanishing into the fog and waves below.

Once the last crewman was secured, everyone dropped to a knee or onto their backs. We were all breathing hard and holding back our pounding hearts, the unnatural song still echoing faintly in our minds.

Melcente barked orders, her voice useless against deafened ears. Frustrated, she resorted to wild hand gestures, pointing emphatically. The crew, shaken but determined, snapped into action, raising sails and releasing ropes to catch what little wind there was.

A breeze finally stirred the air, cool against my sweat-soaked skin. Slowly, the sails filled, and the ship began to move.

I glanced back at the fog, now thinning into a harmless mist. The sea lay eerily empty.

Melcente, steady at the wheel, gave me a curt nod before steering the *Jaculus* away from that cursed fog.

Chapter 73

"Remove yer wax, loves!"

A soft purple glow from the setting sun bathed the deck as the ship sliced through the dark sea.

"We're outta danger now!"

We plucked the wax from our ears. The boys sat on the railing as I paced the poop deck. After the captain shouted orders at the crew, she returned to steering her ship.

"Okay, I guess I'll ask. Who was that woman in the water?"

Melcente heard the flapping of wings. She waited until Kasuma landed on the deck.

"That was a sea siren, love," said the captain. "I'd heard of 'em... but never laid eyes on nary a one. Before today."

"But her... voice. And she was—"

"Aye, a real beauty. She seemed... But that were no real female," she said. "That was a flesh-eatin' fish! Many a sailor been led to their death gettin' to that voice, them faces."

Pherric engaged the captain. "Thank you for acting so quickly. You saved all of us."

"Well, you owes me now," said Melcente. "We be short on crew cuzza dose fish-bitches. I need youse all ta take up da slack. Try not to get killed."

And work we did. By morning, Braylor and Temurr were patching up the storm damage, their strength perfect for all that hauling and hammering. Kasuma, of course, made it look easy, flying replacement ropes to the tops of the sails like it was her morning yoga. Meanwhile, Pherric and I got stuck with the glamorous job of hauling buckets to bail out the water below deck. Oh, and yes, I had to swab the deck—because apparently, that *isn't* just a pirate movie cliché. Turns out, sailors scrub the deck to keep the wood wet with saltwater. Why? To prevent fungus and make the planks swell, sealing gaps. Who knew I'd be learning *boat maintenance 101* on this adventure? It was exhausting, but it kept my mind off everything—for a little while.

The following day, Kasuma took off from the deck and flew ahead of our ship. She returned several hours later.

"Captain, the *Jaculus* is off course," Kasuma informed her.

Melcente checked her maps. "No. We're angled directly at da sunset. Oceantis is due west from Relna Thune."

"You need to correct course by fifteen degrees to the north of the setting sun," Kasuma told her confidently.

"This here map is less than a year out!"

"Few charts of our island are ever correct, Captain."

"We paid good coin for this!" Melcente shook the weather-worn map.

Kasuma shook her head. "My people secretly created many of the maps available on the continent. The more silver charged, the more inaccurate they are."

The captain turned the wheel to the right a quarter turn while glaring at Kasuma. The two worked closely after that, but Kasuma never let her sketch out anything on paper.

When we weren't working or sleeping, Braylor made it his mission to critique—and by critique, I mean tear apart—everything I did wrong in the arena fight. Apparently, there was a lot. What he called "training" was really just me dodging his massive broadsword as he chased me around the narrow deck, up and down stairs, and even into the hold. It wasn't exactly fun, especially when he almost chopped down one of the smaller masts—Melcente was not amused.

For three days, we sailed slightly northwest through the Triton Sea, the waves rocking us steadily toward Oceantis. It was exhausting, frustrating, and a little terrifying, but at least I wasn't bored.

"Land!" screamed the sailor from the top of the mast.

I stood at the bow, my eyes fixed on the horizon. What began as a tiny speck in the distance gradually transformed into an imposing island mountain range rising sharply from the pale blue tropical waters. The peaks loomed like a towering green fortress, their sheer height and density seeming to guard whatever secrets lay beyond from prying eyes.

Despite the waves lapping against the ship, I heard Kasuma's approach. For the first time ever.

"I did not startle you," she said. "You are improving."

"So that's Oceantis?"

Temurr, Pherric, and Braylor joined us.

"That is my home. I am happy to return."

"I'm sure. Where is Nibiru?"

Kasuma smirked. "The other side of the island. It is the most majestic city in the world."

I shared her excitement. "All right, guys! This is going to be fun!"

Turning to the boys, I held my hand up in the air. They stared at it.

"Smack my hand! This is called a high-five!"

Nothing.

"Come on! Whenever something good happens, you put your hand up and..."

Temurr got on board. He smiled and slapped his palm against mine.

"Yes! Pherric?"

The mage nodded and high-fived me.

"Braylor?"

Braylor threw his meaty hand against mine, nearly throwing my arm out of the socket.

"All right! Let's go!" I screamed. "Release the Kraken!"

And everyone freaked out.

I mean every single person on the deck flipped their lids. Temurr and Pherric ducked down. Braylor withdrew his sword, growling. A sailor screamed. Another dropped to the deck, his fearful eyes darting all around.

"Where is the Kraken?!" shouted Melcente, from the wheel.

"What?! Oh, no! I'm sorry!" I stammered.

"The Kraken! Where is it?!" Temurr screamed.

I stumbled across the deck, holding my hands out and trying to calm everyone.

"No! There is no—! I-I was kidding! It's just... It's a phrase!"

Melcente raced from the poop deck to the bow. Braylor held out his arm, keeping her from cat-scratching me.

"You do not joke about the Kraken, love!" she bellowed. "Ever!"

"That's a real thing here?!" I asked, knowing the answer as I said it. "Of course the Kraken is a real thing here..."

Deep sighs of relief from everyone on *Jaculus*. Braylor slid his sword in the sheath. The captain frowned at me, marching back to the wheel.

"Finley, you cannot say such things in jest," scolded Pherric.

"I know. I know! I totally didn't mean it. Honestly, it's a myth on my world. And it's a stupid phrase from a movie or something."

"What is a... moo-vie?" asked Temurr.

"Never mind. I'm sorry. Really."

My knees weakened. My face burned from embarrassment. I perched on the bow railing. Pherric and Braylor laughed at me as I stared at the island, humiliated.

Braylor leaned in over my shoulder, pointed at the water.

"Wait... is that the Kraken?" he whispered.

"Stop it!"

"No, that is a log floating in the water. Oh! Wait! Is *that* the Kraken?"

"Shut up, you big oaf!"

He howled. "Come, girl! You should be able to laugh at yourself! If not, I am more than happy to laugh at you!"

"No!" I cried, squirming away from his attempts to tickle me.

The captain steered the *Jaculus* toward the northern side of the island, the ship cutting smoothly through the turquoise waters. As we sailed past the towering mountain range, the city of Nibiru came into view—a breathtaking sight unlike anything I had ever imagined.

Perched atop a mountain, the city sparkled in the sunlight, its white towers rounded and wrapped in green vines that cascaded like flowing ribbons. The roofs resembled intricate Chinese pagodas, adorned with gleaming metal finials at their peaks. The architectural beauty was mesmerizing, and we couldn't look away.

Melcente's crew stood in awe, gasping and pointing, as the radiant city unfolded. Nibiru sprawled across the entire mountain summit, its structures built daringly close to the edges, as if defying gravity itself. No walls guarded it, yet it radiated an air of impregnable majesty. Swirling around the city like bees around a hive, Tenguans soared gracefully, their wings glinting in the light as they flew to and from the fortress.

But as the wind carried us beyond the southern mountain range, the true wonder of Nibiru revealed itself.

Standing on the deck, we froze, our breaths caught in our throats. Some crew members cried out in shock; others covered their mouths in disbelief. A few, visibly shaken, backed away. The fearless Kasuma grinned with excitement, her eyes alight with wonder.

Nibiru wasn't perched on a mountain at all—it sat atop an enormous monolith, a massive stone rising hundreds of feet into the air. And that wasn't all. The monolith floated, suspended in midair, hovering twenty feet above the ground.

The city wasn't just a fortress—it was a marvel, a levitating rock in the sky. Nibiru, like almost everything in this world, was a place where the impossible had become real.

"Oh. My. God." My jaw dropped open like a car glove box.

"And my gods, as well," whispered Temurr.

Everyone's eyes were as round as moons.

"It is impressive," admitted Braylor.

It looked as though the entire city had been built atop a mountain and then plucked from the earth, suspended effortlessly in midair. The sight was almost too much to process.

"That is the most unbelievable thing I have ever seen," I said, my voice barely above a whisper.

Pherric rubbed the stubble on his chin, his brow furrowed. "That is... quite amazing."

Kasuma smiled faintly, her gaze fixed on the floating city. "That is Nibiru," she said. "My home."

I squinted, scanning the base beneath the monolith for any sign of what kept it suspended. Surely, there had to be something—jet engines blasting away, massive propellers, *something.* But all I saw were roots dangling like veins and jagged rocks clinging to the underside of the massive stone. Below it, the monolith hovered silently above a smooth, square slab of stone on the island.

"Wait," I turned to Kasuma, grasping for logic. "Is there some kind of cloaking magic? Like what hides the Black City or the Godsribbon? Are there invisible poles or giant metal supports holding it up that we just can't see?"

She shook her head, her expression calm but resolute. "Nothing supports Nibiru. It is simply... there."

Her words sent a chill down my spine. Floating mountains were the stuff of legends or dreams—yet here it was, defying every law of nature, hovering as though the world had no claim to it.

The gods—the aliens—had worked their magic, eons ago.

Chapter 74

Our ship sliced through the choppy water toward a small harbor near the floating city.

As I stared in wonder at Nibiru, I noticed lots of bubbles surfacing just off the side of the ship. And then a bunch of fish swarmed to the top.

The guys walked to my railing and set down our travel cases, ready to depart the ship.

Kasuma appeared behind them. "I shall fly ahead and prepare my people for your arrival."

She spread her wings and launched, letting a strong breeze lift her high in the sky. I watched her glide towards the island. With a side glance, I caught more movement in the water—as a long pinkish-brown arm lifted up from the ocean.

A crewman screamed, pointing to the mast.

Another brown arm, as thick as a tree, towered high above the deck and descended toward our biggest billowing sail.

"Kraken!" I screamed.

Pherric turned to me. "Finley, not again—"

It was my turn to point. He whipped his head around—two more long tentacles reached over the railing, crashed down on the deck.

A tentacle grabbed a sailor, squeezed him tight, snatched him away from the ship. His terrible screams resonated off the deck.

"Kraken!" the captain shouted.

Braylor drew his sword as he sprinted to the nearest tentacle, hacking away at the thick rubbery flesh.

The first arm pulled down on the mast, snapping the wood in half. The pole and the rigging were dragged overboard.

"Abandon ship!" one crewman bellowed.

Melcente sprinted in with sword drawn. "Belay that! Fight back, cowards!"

She slashed her blade into the skin of a tentacle, blue blood splattering her as she cut at it again and again.

Two sailors dove off the ship, screaming as they hit the water.

"She did it!" a sailor shouted, pointing at me. "The flamehair cursed us!"

"Throw her to the Kraken!" another yelled. His beady black eyes locked on me, as he held up his sword.

Three of the crewmen came after me. My sword came out and I assumed a fighting pose. Before they could reach me, the *Jaculus* tilted to the side. We slipped on the wet deck, slamming up against the railing.

As Melcente sliced away at one tentacle, another wriggled over the railing from the opposite side.

I tried to warn her. "Captain!"

The arm curled around her and she spun about. Gashing at the tip, she cut into the round suckers. The tentacle snapped back, shoved her hard. Melcente went flying backwards on the deck.

A sailor grabbed at me and I pushed him away. I slipped my way over to help Braylor. He had nearly cut the arm in half. The Kraken slammed the remaining stub into him; he fell into me and we went flying on the wet wood. The tentacle slithered back to the sea.

Temurr fired arrow after arrow into every arm that shot up from the water.

Melcente jumped in front of another sailor trying to leave the ship. "Stay and fight, ya mucky bunyip!"

The Kraken had taken enough abuse. Its massive, bulbous head rose from the water, and two furious eyes, each as tall as me. Tentacles wrapped tightly around the ship, crushing the narrow frame with a sickening crack. The *Jaculus* split in two like a twig, sending everyone hurtling into the water.

The Kraken wasted no time. Both halves of the shattered ship were dragged beneath the waves, disappearing into the depths. Spouts of water erupted where it sank, and air pockets gurgled to the surface.

I hit the warm water hard, gasping as the salty fluid filled my mouth. Instinct kicked in, and I began swimming toward the distant shore. But we were a half axim out, the coastline a daunting blur. As I kicked and pulled myself forward, I couldn't help but glance back, scanning for tentacles slicing through the waves.

The Kraken resurfaced. My heart sank as I saw it lunge, snatching a flailing sailor and dragging him down into the darkness. I pushed forward, but my thoughts weren't on the shore.

To my right, Pherric was hauling Temurr, both of them struggling but moving steadily. Relief hit me, but it was fleeting.

"Braylor," I muttered, searching the waves. He was nowhere.

I stopped, treading water, spinning frantically.

"Finley! Keep going!" Pherric shouted, his voice sharp and urgent.

"Not without Braylor!" I yelled back, my chest tightening. There was no way I was leaving him behind.

I eventually spotted his huge frame plowing through the choppy seawater. He had been tossed farther away from shore than we had been— and he wasn't a fast swimmer.

"He can... take care... of himself!" Temurr advised, trying to keep his mouth out of the sea.

I dog-paddled toward Braylor, my limbs aching as the others swam on ahead. "I don't think he can make it!"

Braylor's strokes were slow, each movement looking heavier than the last. I urged him forward with my eyes, willing him to push harder. Then a sharp grunt from Temurr tore my attention away.

I spun just in time to hear a loud splash. Fear gripped me as I scanned the water for Temurr going under. But instead of a tentacle, two Tenguan males had descended from the sky, their long white wings beating furiously as they plucked him from the water and carried him into the air. Relief was brief; the craziness wasn't over.

I whipped back toward Braylor. His progress was painfully slow, the waves working against him. Behind him, the Kraken surged forward, its tentacles dragging yet another sailor into the depths. My heart pounded as I realized the horrible truth—there was no way the Tenguans could lift Braylor. Not him, not his size. Not even with a flock of them.

I made a split-second decision. Instead of closing the gap between us, I veered away, swimming parallel to the shore. I slapped the surface of the water, kicking hard, screaming at the top of my lungs.

"Hey, Kraken! Over here!" I yelled, flailing my arms wildly.

Two more Tenguans swooped down, this time grabbing Pherric and lifting him skyward. The Kraken shifted its focus, the water around it darkening as its massive bulk altered course.

"No, Finley!" Braylor's deep voice boomed over the chaos, raw with panic. "Save yourself!"

But I wasn't going anywhere—not without him. My screaming grew louder as the Kraken closed in.

"Yo! Kraken! Come get me!" I splashed the water as fast as I could.

As the beast closed in, I turned and bolted for the shore. My arms and legs burned with every stroke, but I didn't dare stop. I finally glanced back, but the water was eerily calm—the Kraken had disappeared. My stomach twisted. It had gone under.

"Ah, shit..." I muttered, forcing myself to breathe deeply.

My adrenaline surged, propelling me forward. Long, powerful strokes, legs kicking furiously, I swam as if my life depended on it—because it did. No time to look back now. I figured I had a minute, maybe two, before the Kraken turned me into an hors d'oeuvre.

The faint brush of rough, slimy skin against my leg shattered my focus. My heart plummeted as I gasped for air, my only hope now that Braylor would reach the shore. I kept going, stroke after stroke, determined to buy him every second I could.

Then it came—a tentacle coiling around my thigh, sliding to my ankle, and pulling tight. My head plunged beneath the waves. I thrashed, water filling my mouth, when suddenly strong fingers gripped my wrists and yanked me back up.

The Tenguans were above me, their wings beating furiously as they tried to lift me from the Kraken's grasp. The tentacle tightened, dragging me back under. It was a vicious tug-of-war.

I kicked at another tentacle, my boots landing solid hits. One Tenguan lost his grip as the Kraken's new tentacle coiled around my waist. I freed my knife and stabbed wildly, blue blood spraying as I hacked at the suckers. Each strike sent the creature retreating slightly, but it fought to pull me under again.

The Tenguans regrouped, their wings flapping in alternating rhythm. With one final heave, they wrenched me free. The Kraken released me, its tentacles retreating as it submerged and turned back toward the wreckage of the ship.

Dangling by my arms, I scanned the waves desperately. Then I saw him—Braylor, still swimming hard, safely ahead of the Kraken. Relief washed over me, and a weary smile spread across my face.

He survived.

Chapter 75

"That was madness!"

The two Tenguan males had flown me to the beach and dropped me on the sand near Pherric and Temurr. They were just catching their breath as they wrung out tunic shirts and dumped water from their boots. I fell to the black sand, gasping for air, utterly exhausted. When I finally sat up, my body shivered and teeth rattled. But not from the seawater.

Braylor slogged his way out of the ocean and marched straight up to me. "You should not have lured the Kraken towards you, foolish girl?!"

"How about a simple thank-you? Geez."

"You could have been killed!" he gasped.

"Yeah. Been there, done that. I'm good."

Despite the swim, Braylor had enough energy in reserve to pace the beach.

"I can take care of myself, Finley!"

Fatigue had overwhelmed me. Unable to contain my anger, I got in his face. "I saved you, dumbass! You couldn't swim for shit and I distracted the—"

"This body was not meant to *run*, Finley! It was meant to stand and fight! I *wanted* the creature to attack me!"

Whatever was left of my emotional filter flew out the window. Tears streamed as I stormed after him, poking my finger into his chest.

"I had no idea what you wanted! You never say anything! I can't read your mind, Braylor. The only thing I've ever known is that you hate my guts! You always wanted me gone and you've been nothing but cruel to me since I was dragged here kicking and screaming! Against my will! I never asked for any of this shit! Do you hear me?!"

He kept backing away from me. "Finley, I—"

"I was trying to protect you! And my friends! Protect the only people I have left in this world! I just lost *half* of them! Or, almost half, or... whatever! Do you think I want to lose you guys, too?! Do you? I have been straight-up scared for over half a year. And I'll be damned if I'm gonna end up alone here! So, you're right... I was stupid. I *am* stupid. For caring about you... and him and him!" I pointed at a startled Temurr and Pherric. "Deal with it, asshole!"

In a fit, I charged away from them. But it's hard to look angry when you're wet and trying to trudge through sand. Still, my face was red and my fists were balled up and I was angry. Dammit.

I stopped in my tracks when I heard wings in the air above.

Kasuma swooped down, landing on the beach in front of me. "Are you injured, Finley Maguire? I apologize deeply. We had no warning. The Kraken has never hunted anywhere near our island."

I crossed my arms. "I'm fine. We're... fine."

Still seething, I turned and sat myself down on the black sand, staring out at the waves.

Kasuma, confused, stood behind me for a moment before joining the others.

I heard Pherric call out to her. "As far as we know, we are all well. Our travel cases, however, are another matter."

He pointed to the sea—at our luggage floating aimlessly on the waves.

"I shall have your belongings salvaged... once the area is clear."

"Did the captain or any of her crew survive?"

I turned to hear her answer.

"The captain and one sailor were pulled from the water in time."

Great. She'll more than likely be mad at me, too. I was the *cursed* one.

Kasuma leaned in to whisper with Pherric.

Temurr picked himself off the ground, ambling over to me. "The gods have given you a remarkable gift, they have. How did you know the Kraken would attack? You can see the future as well?"

"I swear I had no idea, Temurr. That Kraken remark used to be a common phrase where I'm from. When that thing *pounced* on us? That was a coincidence. Nothing more."

"Well, dear," he said, uttering the loving term that Frip always used. "There are no coincidences. You have magic in you, you do. A strong magic."

Pherric watched Kasuma fly away. He shouted loud enough for Temurr and I to hear. "Everyone! We must journey on foot to the base of Nibiru!"

Temurr groaned.

"It will do us good to stretch out our legs after many days aboard ship."

Temurr flipped Pherric off, but used the wrong finger. I pushed down the one closest to his pinkie and pulled up his ring finger.

Pherric continued. "Our greatest challenge will be getting Braylor up to the city."

Braylor grunted. "What are you going on about?"

"Well, in order to reach the city, we must be flown up there... with the help of the Tengu and—"

"And those little insects cannot pick me up, correct?!" Braylor growled. "Then... what is their plan?!"

Temurr and I stood on a wooden loading dock overhanging the edge of the massive floating monolith that was Nibiru. The dock looked about as sturdy as a lollipop stick, holding up an iron derrick with pulleys and ropes that creaked ominously under the strain. Five Tenguan guys, wings tucked and muscles straining, were hauling on a thick rope.

We leaned over the edge, staring down into the dizzying three-hundred-foot drop. At the other end of the rope was a large, rectangular wooden box inching its way upward. And in that box? None other than Braylor, sprawled on his back like he was sunbathing. His massive arms were crossed in pure defiance, his big feet dangling off the sides, and he was grumbling under his breath like a kid who'd been told he couldn't have dessert.

Temurr and I exchanged a glance. We tried—really tried—not to laugh, but it was hopeless. A snort escaped, then a chuckle, and before we knew it, we were doubled over, barely holding it together.

When his royal grumpiness finally reached the top, we completely lost it. Tears streamed down our faces as we laughed so hard we couldn't breathe. Braylor, of course, was not amused. His glare could've curdled milk, but that just made it worse. We pretended to compose ourselves, wiping our eyes, but one look at his face and we were right back at it, hooting and high-fiving like idiots.

"This is not funny!" he bellowed, climbing out of the box with all the dignity of a cat falling off a couch.

Then, before we could escape, he grabbed us both, hoisting us off the ground like we weighed nothing. Our feet dangled helplessly as he marched toward the edge of the cliff.

"Braylor! Wait! We were just kidding!" I squealed between fits of laughter.

He paused, his expression somewhere between I'll kill you and I'll regret this forever. For one terrifying second, I was sure he was about to chuck us into the abyss.

"Who laughs now?!" Braylor seethed.

Temurr and I glanced at each other. He tried too hard not to smile, causing both of us to start laughing uncontrollably. Again.

Exasperated, the big guy flung us to the ground and stomped off in a huff.

Braylor bewildered me. I could not figure him out. Which made the brooding and bad-tempered enigma even more appealing to me—much to my regret. My relationship with him seemed to have gotten worse after my encounter with Kane. Mostly because Kane was the complete opposite—attentive, charming, and funny. Someone who listened and emotionally connected with me. And he didn't hate me, which was nice.

I knew that I wasn't being fair to Braylor. If the giant caveman truly didn't care, he would have completely ignored me. He wanted me out of his way—out of his life—but he also wanted me to stay alive. That realization made me feel guilty. I was probably too harsh with him on the beach. And I didn't help matters by laughing at him as he was hauled up to the city.

"We will show you to your quarters," one of the Tenguans said, his voice calm and polite.

Temurr and I nodded, noting how remarkably courteous they were. All of the Tengu had the same striking white hair as Kasuma, though their wings varied greatly. Some were cream-colored with streaks of white or tan, while others bore darker shades of brown or gray. The males were taller, broader, with massive wingspans suited for strength rather than endurance. Unlike Kasuma, who could soar for hours, the males who rescued us earlier had barely made it back before needing rest. Interestingly, none of the Tengu in the floating city carried weapons—not that I saw, anyway.

Despite their hospitality, there was a certain attitude about them. It wasn't overtly rude, but there was a subtle air of superiority—something I recognized from the elite kids and their too-important parents back on Earth. It was that smug assurance that they were inherently better, their status earned by nothing more than genetics and a long-dead ancestor's success. Honestly, if I could fly and if I lived on a giant floating city, I might be a little stuck up too.

They led me to a room in one of the round, white towers. The chamber was breezy and elegant, with vibrant red curtains swirling around every arched window as ocean winds rushed through. From here, the Triton Sea sparkled in the distance, a shimmering expanse of blue.

After I settled in, a female Tenguan brought me food, followed by chambermaids with pitchers of steaming hot water. After a much-needed bath, I found a perfectly tailored outfit waiting for me: a white canvas blouse with long bell sleeves and black linen pants. The fit was uncanny, but my boots were still wet, so I reluctantly slipped them on and strapped my sword scabbard to my waist.

I wandered to one of the arched windows and froze, the view stealing my breath. South of Nibiru, the landscape unfurled like a painted masterpiece. Thousands of fruit trees, planted in perfect rows, stretched across Oceantis, blanketing the island from the floating city to the southern mountains. A single wide cobblestone road wound through hills and valleys, connecting neat farms and small villages to a bustling port city at its end.

That was the secret to their survival. Cloaked in mystery, Nibiru thrived, its island providing the continent with rare, exotic food. It was isolation wrapped in elegance—and I couldn't deny, it was impressive.

I turned to glance out another window, but a flicker of movement caught my eye. Instinctively, my hand went to my sword. My pulse quickened—until I realized I wasn't staring at a threat but at my own reflection.

I stepped closer to the mirror, startled by the stranger looking back at me. Her red hair was cut short. Her skin was weathered and dry, yet tanned—a surprising contrast for someone with such light skin. The freckles across her face had deepened under the relentless sun.

But it was her eyes that stopped me. They were steady, confident, carrying a quiet strength I hadn't noticed before. Her posture was upright, shoulders back in a way I'd never dared because I hated looking too tall. Now, though, there was no hesitation, no attempt to shrink herself.

She was lean, strong, with muscle carved from hard work and survival. Sure, she had some scars and bluish-yellow bruises here and there. But her head was held high, her expression calm but determined.

I had the same feeling after seeing myself done up like an Atlantean back at Lady Anisha's manor. But this was the real me. And I truly didn't recognize this version of myself.

But I liked her.

She looked capable. Fierce. Like she'd face down anything the world threw at her and walked away stronger.

She looked like... a badass.

I heard a familiar grunt echo off the towers outside a window. Then another. I looked down to see a square lawn. Braylor was running through training drills with his sword.

By the time I made it to the yard, sweat bathed him and he panted hard from the effort. He stabbed his sword into the grass, pulling off his shirt to wipe himself down.

"Hey, you."

"What do you want?" he asked, throwing the shirt aside.

"Well, I wanted to apologize for yelling at you, on the beach."

He held up his long sword. "You see... that is your problem."

"What?"

"Why would you apologize? You were angry and... you *were* correct. I have been hard on you. And I do wish you away from all of this. Because you are not meant for this life. You are weak."

Braylor managed to get my Irish up again. "What?! That's crazy and you know it!"

"Your physical skills have improved," he said. Then he tapped his head. "But you are not capable... up here. Your mind must be as strong as the strongest kath sword. And this is why you will never be a warrior."

"God, why are you such a dick?!"

"Also, you are filled with fear."

"Well, of course I've been frightened! That's what I was talking about on the beach. The whole time I've been here people have been trying to kill me! Who wouldn't be scared?"

"No, Finley. That fear has been with you your whole life," he said, staring down at me with a look of pity. "In every conversation you have ever had. In every decision you have ever made. Fear occupies your mind, prevents you from doing what needs to be done, holds you back."

The badass from the mirror was gone. "But... but what about the Kraken?! I distracted it! Trying to save your sorry ass. I was scared then and still did it! What about that?"

"Aye, you did, rather foolishly, try to save me. And that is another reason why you will never be a warrior."

I tried to put on a tough front by crossing my arms, then placing hands on hips.

"Oh, please enlighten me."

"You do not believe in your own worth. You were willing to die to protect me out on the sea because you think I am more deserving to live. In your mind, you are but a puppet. A mere tool to be used as inspiration for us, as Pherric has suggested. However, I know you have always felt this way. You have no faith in your ideas, your skills, or yourself."

"Geez. You'd make a great therapist." I wiped away tears.

"This world is not for the faint of heart or mind. Alchemy helped you survive once but you will not be so fortunate the next time. Go find a small, quiet village and settle down. Bond with a respectable farmer and bear his children. Teach them to think decisively, talk with pride, and live without fear. Perhaps your young ones will become the heroes in your story."

His words stung, cutting deeper than I wanted to admit. But I'd heard variations of them my whole life—most often from my father. I was never good enough, never up to the task. Always doing things the wrong way, always making the worst decisions. The weight of it all crushed me, and I covered my face, letting the sobs spill out.

Braylor turned away, his broad shoulders stiff. He couldn't—or wouldn't—watch me fall apart. Humiliation burned through me, and every part of me wanted to run, to escape his gaze, to hide from the shame.

But then something shifted.

I balled my fists, nails digging into my palms, and felt the strength in my arms, the tension in my muscles. My mind flickered to the woman in the mirror—the badass I didn't recognize but who *was* me. The girl who always ran was gone. Fury roared to life inside me, a storm that I couldn't and wouldn't suppress.

I wasn't sure if it was because I'd died in that arena or because I'd simply reached my limit, but something snapped. It was as though a switch had been flipped, shutting off all fear, all doubt. In its place stood *me*—the real me. The woman who had hidden behind an anxious little girl straightened her spine, lifted her chin, and stepped forward.

I drew my sword with a sharp hiss of steel.

Braylor arched one eyebrow in surprise.

I strode toward him, grabbed his long sword from where it lay in the grass, and raised the pointed end. With a deliberate motion, I flipped it and offered him the handle.

"Finley?" he asked, confusion flickering across his face.

I dropped into a fighting stance, my blade steady.

"This is silly," he muttered.

"Maybe," I said, my voice firm, "but I am not."

I slashed down at him with my blade. He reacted in an instant, casually knocking my strike to the side. I circled him as he turned where he stood, his eyes rolling.

"This does not prove a thing, girl. You squander your time."

Without letting my anger take over—and my anger *really* wanted to be in charge—I attacked again with two quick blows. He parried one and side-stepped another.

But he dropped into his own defensive pose.

As I lunged at him, he fended me off, then raised his sword high. He came down at me with all of his might.

Rather than trying to deflect him, I jumped away. I turned sideways in midair, so he couldn't catch my leg.

"Good!" He elbowed me in the chest, sending my flying to the stone tiles. "But you must strike back *during* the leap!"

I returned to my feet. He charged and I parried a blow. He slashed at me and I ducked, rolling to the side. I leapt into the air, slicing at his torso. His sword caught mine and he flung me backwards.

"I am longer and stronger—as are nearly all your opponents! Take away my advantage. Fight close!"

I attacked again, hitting his blade away as I shuffled in tight. I pulled my sword up from below. He blocked my blade, so I hit him in the nose with the hilt. Then slashed at his shoulder. His arm pushed mine away, because I was so close. I slashed at him and he parried, but he backed up a step—on the defensive.

Dropping low, I swung my sword at his legs. Braylor hopped back again. I struck his blade three times in succession. He defended himself well but kept retreating. Blood flowed from his nose. Ignoring my training, I fought on instinct alone. Our swords clanged together as I advanced. I refused to give him room to extend his arms. I slashed, lunged, parried. His feet were heavy, slow. Mine quick and nimble.

Beads of sweat replaced the tear stains on my cheeks.

The base of his blade cut through my blouse, drawing blood. But I was relentless, deflecting his broadsword and using my legs to kick him backwards. A look of surprise on his face, his boots stepped off the lawn. I thrust my blade at him and he lost his balance. Braylor fell to the ground.

Rolling over, he staved off my blade edge as I swung at his head. I reared my sword back, drove the tip at his face. He tilted his head to the side to avoid being cut.

I leapt over him, slashing down at his head again. He blocked my sword with his own, as he rolled to his knees.

"Another mistake!" He panted hard. "You went for the head again but my legs were exposed!"

I rushed in, feigned a strike from my right side and twisted my body. I swung at him from my left. He deflected me but staggered back. I took two more quick slashes across his chest, jumped in the air, drove down with my tip. He tried to counter but was off balance. My sword dug into his collar bone, drawing blood.

"Agh!" He held his hand over the wound.

I backed off, breathing heavily—every muscle in my body screaming in agony. But I stayed in my fighting pose, taking a second to wipe my sweaty hands on my pants and then gripping my sword for another round.

Braylor looked at the blood on his hands, turned to me. Rage burned in his eyes.

If I died by his hand that day, so be it. I was ready.

But he lowered his sword, then tossed it on the ground. He chuckled as his hand went back to the cut near his neck.

"Well done."

"What?"

"I said... well done, child."

I grabbed his shirt from the lawn and rushed to him.

"I did not expect that of you. Not in the least."

I held the shirt on his collar bone, trying to stem the flow. Both of us stood so close, bathed in sweat, breathing hard.

"Are you okay?"

He snuck a peek at the wound. "A mere scratch, little one."

I moved closer to push harder against his shoulder. When I looked up, the smile in his eyes matched the smirk on his mouth. I felt a new heat rising up. Braylor's big hand pulled me in. I stared at his lips. And I saw a hunger in his eyes, an overwhelming need. His mouth parted. My other hand touched his tight bare chest. I stared up at him. A fire had been kindled.

I pressed against him. My leg moving closer to his.

We heard a voice from across the courtyard.

"There you are!"

I pushed away from Braylor.

Temurr raced over to our patch of lawn.

"Kasuma and Pherric are meeting with her king!"

I looked back at Braylor. He had turned away, standing over the short wall that overlooked the pale sea.

"What does that have to do with us?" I was unable to take my eyes off Braylor.

"Oh... did I... interrupt something?" Temurr asked tentatively.

I looked to Temurr, who seemed confused. "What? No. Nothing." Braylor gave me a look. "Nothing at all."

I threw the bloody shirt to the grass.

"Take me to their king."

Chapter 76

Temurr guided me to the low, white palace of the King of Oceantis, weaving through a maze of stucco hallways lined with arched windows and open doorways. The walls were alive with life—pots brimming with ferns and vivid flowers, their petals almost glowing in the sunlight, while wild, brightly-colored birds squawked and fluttered from their perches, occasionally throwing us a disapproving look as we passed.

We came to a halt on the cool, polished marble floors outside the king's great hall. The hall stretched long and open, with a row of elegant arches framing a breathtaking view of the dark blue ocean far below. Gusts of fresh, salty air swept through the space, ruffling stray feathers and making the room feel alive with movement.

At the far end of the hall, Kasuma and Pherric stood near the arches, speaking to the Tenguan court. There was no throne, but a simple, raised stone platform held a long wooden table, its surface carved with intricate patterns. Six Tenguans sat behind it in ornate chairs, the oldest positioned at the end near an arch, his white hair rippling faintly in the breeze.

"Shall we go in?" Temurr asked, looking at me expectantly.

I glanced down at myself and groaned. My clothes were a sweaty, blood-soaked disaster—not exactly the look you want for meeting royalty.

I shot him a glare. "Are you serious right now? Look at me!"

He chuckled, his amusement infuriatingly unbothered. "You are... quite a sight."

I rolled my eyes. "Let's just hang back for a bit."

Pherric stood before the Tenguan court, his voice steady but laced with urgency as he pleaded for their aid. He directed his words toward the oldest Tengu, who sat with an unnerving stillness in his plain wooden chair. The elder rested his elbows on the armrests, his long fingers pressed lightly together in contemplation.

When he finally spoke, his black, unblinking eyes seemed to bore straight into the back of your mind, pulling at every hidden thought. He listened with the same intensity, his gaze fixed on the tabletop as if to weigh and measure each word with precision. Every movement he made was deliberate, calculated, as though a single misplaced gesture might upset the delicate balance of the moment.

The only thing about him that wasn't restrained was his wispy gray hair, which fluttered lightly in the ocean breeze, a stark contrast to his otherwise immovable presence. His air of calm authority made even silence feel heavy.

"Sire, we desperately need to create an alliance that will bring down Malek. At the very least, we are asking for you to host a meeting—here on Nibiru—and invite every ruler from every kingdom and country."

The king took a moment to collect his thoughts. He started to speak but withdrew for further contemplation.

He looked up at Pherric. Then to Kasuma.

"Your wish to bring representation here is... denied," said the king in a sharp, clear voice. He sounded similar to Kasuma, with her Australian-ish accent.

Pherric deflated. "But, your majesty, I—"

"The Tengu have avoided all political... complications throughout our history." He held up his winged hand. "Thereby allowing us to remain impartial. If I invite any leaders to Nibiru, we would be choosing a side... even if our people do not participate in any future military endeavors."

Kasuma chimed in. "The time has come for us to choose a side, sire. We have seen the death and destruction that Malek has wreaked upon several nations. He has invaded their kingdoms, stolen resources, starved their peoples, and has wiped out nearly all of the Bànshēn rén."

"While I have not seen his atrocities with my own eyes, I do not consider my ears to be unreliable witnesses."

"Forgive me, sire," Kasuma sighed. "I understand that you are well-informed, but we have seen the evil in his heart. Firsthand. Watched as he slayed our companions by his own hand as theirs were tied behind their backs. He hates all who are not Hominan and plans to destroy every last one of us."

"I am also aware of what he is capable of, Kasuma. While I have not seen the blood of your friends running through the floorboards of his castle, I do know of his plot to create an empire... cleansed of other races."

"Then you know that we must act now! We must make a stand!" She instantly regretted her outburst, lowering her head and taking a step back.

He ignored her. "What you may not know is that the Irkallan army has already begun their invasion of Kunlun."

That caught Temurr's attention. "Wh-what?"

He raced across the hall to stand next to Pherric. "Forgive me, your majesty, but what news do you have of Kunlun?"

The king nodded slowly, allowing the intrusion. "According to my spies, Malek ordered nearly fifty thousand warriors to begin their march. Likely around the time you escaped Biringan City. They are likely near," he paused for a mental calculation. "the Kunlun border."

"Damn the gods," Temurr whispered as he lowered his head.

"Malek's new campaign has not been as swift or decisive as their... efforts in Agartha with the Bànshēn rén. And the mountainous terrain will slow them down. Resistance from the Prominans is fierce."

Temurr perked up. "We will fight them to the death."

"Of that... I have no doubt."

"We thank you for sharing this knowledge, sire," said Pherric. "But is that not all the more reason for every nation to unite and take up arms against this tyrant?"

The king shook his head. "Malek will not make a move against the Tengu. Not here. We are isolated enough. I have been assured by Malek's ambassador that he has no plans to make Oceantis part of his empire. But only... if we remain impartial. I cannot subject my people to a fight that will not involve us and, definitively, not be won."

I had heard enough. After staying on the sidelines, unsure of what to say during all the other conversations that I had been a part of, I had to speak up. I marched across the floor, hot mess and all. Two Tengu guards started towards me.

"She is with us," Kasuma informed the king.

He held up a winged hand—the guards relaxed.

Kasuma's eyes launched missiles at me. "Finley, allow me to introduce... Longzhe the Seventh, King of Oceantis. Your majesty, this is Finley Maguire."

"Ah, yes, the amateur assassin," the king recalled. "You have something to add? I am assuming."

"Um, okay. First let me say, I'm not good at speeches and public speaking is a nightmare for me."

The king squinted slightly, amused at my sorry state.

"Um, all right, here goes. I'm not any kind of diplomat or politician or even a military expert, but I have studied a *lot* of history. And where I am from—"

"Which is... where?" The king inquired from Kasuma.

"She is from... Mu," she replied. "The distant lands far to the west."

Longzhe sat up in his chair. "The Land of Mu? Interesting. Please go on, child."

"Well, we have a lot of history in... Mu. A long time of recorded history. And there have been a lot of dictators who have tried desperately hard to conquer all of... Mu. Men called Hannibal, Genghis Khan, Alexander, Caesar, Attila, Napoleon, and Hitler. And they have never been satisfied with just a few kingdoms or even a continent. They wanted every kingdom, every island... no matter how small. They tried to control everything. And some wanted to wipe out entire races."

"Ah, I see where you go with this narrative. However... Malek has made promises—"

"And all those men broke their promises, too! They made treaties and tore them up. They lied to get what they wanted. They knew it was smarter to take on one kingdom at a time, rather than face an allied set of nations all at once. The last tyrant made promises after invading the first country. And he nearly conquered the entire world."

"Who was this tyrant? Why have I never heard of his triumphs?"

"Um, you see... His name was Hitler and... And this was all taking place on another continent. A long time ago. Away from your known kingdoms. Now, I don't know all the details, but... I do remember a quote that came from that last great war. It really hit me when I read it. It was from a priest, who was actually from the kingdom where the dictator lived. You see this ruler selected a group of people who were different, used them as a scapegoat. People they could blame for everything wrong in their country. He knew that if his citizens had someone to hate, that needed to be wiped out, that this would focus them, enrage them, and make them start a war. When you give people a cause, driven by hate, you can get them to do the most unspeakable of horrors."

"I see."

I racked my brain. I couldn't remember the exact quote from that priest. I decided to wing it out of embarrassment.

"Okay, so the priest said something, like, um... He basically spoke out and they locked him in a dungeon for it. Because he saw the cruelty being committed on those people. And he was shocked that no one spoke up or tried to defend those who were different."

"What did he say?"

I exhaled. Everyone leaned forward to listen. Pherric and Temurr stared at me. Kasuma kept her head down.

The quote finally popped into my head. But I couldn't remember the details. So, I adjusted them for this world.

"He said... 'First, they came for the... Bànshēn rén. But I did not speak out. Because I was not Bànshēn rén. Then, they came for the Prominans, and I did not speak out. Because I was not a Prominan. Then they came for the Fomorians, and I did not speak out. Because I was not a Fomorian. But then... they came for me. And there was no one left to speak for me.'"

I took a deep breath. I knew I should have stopped there but my nervousness would not let me.

"So, that's exactly what happened. The dictator took out different nations, one by one, and nobody did *anything*. Because they might have hated those other races, too, and wanted them gone. But the dictator was just heating the water so slowly that none of the others jumped out of the pot where he made his stew. Eventually, all of the kingdoms around Mu came together to defeat this asshole. But, let me tell you this, while the rest of the world waited and did nothing, millions of people were executed just because they were different. *Millions.* My own kingdom? We waited far too long—until *we* were attacked—to join the fight. And so many people could have been saved... if only we had acted earlier. If only we had chosen a side. If only we had spoken up, so to speak. And—"

Pherric put a hand on my shoulder. His way of telling me to wrap it up. I bowed my head and stepped back in line.

King Longzhe the Seventh sat silent for a minute. He looked at me and smirked. "For someone who is not a politician, you speak quite well. I must... consider this matter further."

I nodded then awkwardly bowed to the king. Kasuma followed us out of the hall.

Chapter 77

"When will he decide?" I asked, my voice tighter than I intended.

We adjourned to a rooftop patio atop a tall white tower, open to the breeze and overlooking the vast ocean below.

"I do not know," Kasuma replied. "It could be minutes... or days."

We settled around a wooden table as several Tenguans brought mugs of ale. Kasuma and Temurr quickly excused themselves, murmuring about the news from Kunlun and disappearing down a spiral staircase.

Pherric and I sat in silence, sipping our ales. But something felt off. A wave of anxiousness swept over me, hitting like a rogue tide. My chest tightened, and my hands trembled slightly as I clutched the mug. This wasn't just unease—it was sharp, invasive, like claws scratching at the edges of my mind.

I didn't panic—this was something else. A pull. A calling. The overwhelming urge to *go*. To *act*. To be somewhere else.

"Finley, there's something I need to tell you—" Pherric started, but I was already on my feet, pacing in tight circles on the patio's wooden floor.

"Are you well?" he asked, standing now, his tone steady but concerned.

"I... I don't know," I stammered, pressing my palms to my temples as my mind raced. Thoughts fired off like fireworks, chaotic and uncontrollable. "It feels like... like I'm being pulled. I need to *go*. Like there's somewhere I need to *be*. Does that make sense? Probably not. I don't even know what I'm saying!"

Pherric guided me to sit on the white stone wall surrounding the patio.

"I think I understand," he said, his voice low and calming. "But you need to remember your mindform lessons. Breathe, Fin. Focus on inhaling and exhaling."

The pull didn't stop, but his words cut through the haze like a thread of sanity. I closed my eyes, trying to anchor myself in the rhythm of my breath. Inhale. Exhale. But even as I tried to calm myself, the pull lingered—insistent, unrelenting, like it wouldn't be ignored.

"God, I am so sick of breathing. Focusing my breath. In. Out. Blah-blah-blah. I get it. This is... new. I've never felt this before. And it's scary as hell."

Pherric gripped my shoulders. Closed his eyes. I think he was trying to read my mind. After a moment, he released me. Shook his head.

"That is odd."

"What?"

"I believe you are experiencing a... mindform. One directed at you. As if someone were trying to communicate. But I could interpret nothing."

"Someone is hacking my brain?"

Pherric gave me a bewildered look.

"No, I mean... is it an attack? On my mind? Could it be Nerus... Malek's mage? Trying to read my thoughts?"

"I sensed a benevolence, only this mindform was faint. As if sent from a great distance or... from a time long ago. Maybe from one who is deceased?"

"Oh, great. I got a dead guy trying to send me messages? How did that happen?"

My heart pounded in my chest. As though a dozen people were standing next to me, screaming at me all at once. And I heard nothing but a dull roar.

Pherric exhaled, rubbed his temples. "We are dealing with the unknown here, Fin. The fact is that you have been training in mindforms for some time now and... well, you—"

"Died. It's because I died, isn't it?" I exclaimed in fear.

"We have ventured into uncharted territory."

I started pacing the rooftop patio again. Just sitting was excruciating. Being in motion calmed me somehow. But I stopped and turned back to Pherric. "Wait. Didn't you have something to tell me?"

He stared out at the Triton Sea. "It can wait."

I barely slept that night. My mind churned with too much noise—too many emotions to untangle.

The next day, I dedicated myself to meditating, trying to quiet the storm in my head. I focused on slowing my heart rate until it beat only a few times per minute, filtering out the clamor of my thoughts. But one thing I couldn't filter out—one person, really—was Braylor.

So I avoided him. Completely. Thinking about him didn't slow my heart down at all. If anything, it did the opposite. My attraction to him had always simmered under the surface, but his attitude had kept me at arm's length. After... whatever that moment was in the yard, I didn't know what to think. Was there something real between us? Or was it just a fleeting spark of passion, ignited by rage and adrenaline?

And then there was Kane, living rent-free in the back of my mind. He was still part of this tangled mess of a story. Maybe. If I ever saw him again. I kept him there—at the edge of my thoughts—to protect myself. To avoid the heartbreak of uncertainty. It was maddening.

To escape the pandemonium of my feelings, I turned my focus to the one person who mattered most in the moment—King Longzhe. Using every rudimentary mindform skill I had, I worked to sway his decision. I didn't care if it was cheating. I needed him on our side.

I bombarded his mind with images: the king greeting rulers from every kingdom, standing as a unifier. I layered those visions with waves of positive emotion, hoping it would influence his thoughts without being too obvious.

And it maybe worked?

Several days later, Kasuma interrupted our late dinner on the rooftop patio, her expression triumphant.

"The king has agreed," she announced, her voice ringing with excitement. "He will invite the leaders of every kingdom to Nibiru."

It wasn't just good news—it was a huge victory. And for once, the furor in my mind quieted.

Pherric and I cheered. Braylor harrumphed. Temurr gave up a smile and clapped his hairy paws together once. Even though his heart was with his people in Kunlun.

"He will send out word to the heads of state in every nation. In one month's time, there will be a summit—"

"One month?!" I shouted. "That's way too long! Kunlun could be overrun in that time!"

Temurr furiously nodded his head.

"We should be thankful he has allowed this to occur, Finley. He admitted that he struggled mightily with the decision. But... your speech had a decisive impact."

She wanted to put me off from confronting him.

"I guess it's better than nothing," I admitted.

"My worry is that hardly anyone will accept the invitation. Or worse... no one will."

Chapter 78

That evening, the relentless bombardment of voices in my mind finally died down. At first, the silence was a relief, a chance to breathe without the constant assault of maddening mindforms. But as the hours passed, the quiet became unsettling—too quiet. My mind felt empty, haunted by an eerie void.

When I finally drifted off to sleep, there was no rest. Instead, my dreams were invaded by something far stranger than my usual nightmares of falling. This time, I wasn't falling—I was flying. I soared through clouds, the harsh wind biting at my face and blasting my eyes. The weightlessness felt so real, as if I was actually suspended in the sky.

I jolted awake, drenched in sweat, gasping for air. My heart raced as the vivid memory of squeezing through two jagged mountain peaks lingered in my mind. When I finally fell asleep again, the dreams grew darker. I swooped down on a cow-like beast, my jaws opening and then snapping shut around it. Its terrified screams echoed in my ears, and I woke up panting, wiping the spit from my lips.

Unable to calm myself, I poured water from a nearby pitcher, gulping it down as I slumped into a chair. But before the first light of dawn, a haunting shriek pierced the silence—a sound I recognized instantly.

The cry of a dragon.

I spun around, my heart hammering. The room was empty. I ran to the window, scanning the starlit skies. Nothing. The cry came again, louder this time. I checked the hallway, another window—still nothing.

Then, it hit me.

The sound wasn't coming from outside. It was inside my head.

My breaths quickened as realization set in. I wasn't dreaming of flying—I was *seeing* through the eyes of a dragon. The call wasn't just a noise. It was a connection, and it wasn't letting go.

As the first rays of sunlight rose over the Triton Sea, I suited up in my recovered clothes from Relna Thune, the ones I'd carefully chosen before the voyage. Other Sword hung at my side, a bow and quiver of arrows strapped to my back, and a knife sheathed at my hip.

Tiptoeing down the spiral stairs of the tower, I slipped into a pantry where dry goods were stored. A female Tenguan was already inside, gathering ingredients. She glanced at me briefly, her expression neutral. I gave her a small nod, acting like I had every right to be there, and she went back to her work.

I grabbed what I needed: dried meats, fresh fruit, and a burlap bag from a hook. Quickly, I slipped back out, moving through an open-air corridor as quietly as possible. I couldn't afford to run into anyone—not now. I didn't want the questions, the arguments, or the inevitable forbidding.

For once, I was listening to the voice in my head, and while that was usually a bad idea, this time felt different. The pull was undeniable, like invisible hands tugging at my thoughts, begging me to act. I had to leave Nibiru. Now.

No plan. No money. No map. Just the overwhelming need to get back to the mainland.

Then I saw it—a door swinging open up ahead. There was nowhere to hide. I was busted.

Temurr stepped out, fully dressed for travel, weapons in hand.

"Finley? What are you doing?" he asked, his brow furrowed.

"Going with you!" I blurted without thinking.

His eyes narrowed. "But... how did you know I was leaving?"

I grinned, tapping my temple

"Ahh," said Temurr, as if I could read his mind. "But you cannot come with me to Kunlun, Finley. It is... far too dangerous."

"Oh, um... I wouldn't think of it! I am merely your escort and will return here when we get you there."

He eyed me. "That is not your plan."

"Look, I can't sit here for a whole month, okay?" I pleaded. "Just let me go with you! Please?"

Temurr considered carefully before nodding.

"Thank you! You will not regret this."

"Really?" he said, smirking at me. "I assume you have not told the others?" He answered his own question. "Of course not..."

We worked our way out to a wide platform. Temurr sent a young Tenguan girl to fetch several of the males to fly us down to the surface of the island.

"So, uh, how are we getting off Oceantis?"

"You truly had no plan, did you?" surmised Temurr.

I exhaled, taking in the view from high up on Nibiru. "No. I have no plan. For anything! I never plan! I'm not a planner!"

He chuckled to himself. "You are one of those."

"Those what?"

"You are charmed, for sure. Always be where you need to be, when you are needed."

I pondered his words. "Isn't that serendipity?"

"No, there is no serendipity. There are no coincidences. The gods are at work. And they are guiding you."

I winked at him. "Then... that *is* my plan."

Four burly Tenguan males emerged from the city, their forms bathed in the soft blue haze of morning light. Their expressions carried a mix of irritation—clearly annoyed they had to help us—but with some smug satisfaction at having an excuse to take to the skies. Without so much as a word, they grabbed hold of our arms and launched into the air.

The rush of flight hit me immediately, the wind whipping past my face and pulling at my clothes. It wasn't just exhilarating—it was familiar. The sensation tugged at memories of my vivid dreams, of soaring through the clouds as a dragon, weightless and free.

For a brief moment, I hoped they'd carry us out over the island, letting us take in the vast expanse of Oceantis from above. But the Tenguans had no intention of indulging my fantasies. They swooped straight down, their wings slicing through the air with precision, and unceremoniously dropped us at the base of the monolith before zooming back up to the floating city without a look back.

It was over in seconds, but the feeling lingered, a mix of longing and unease. The dreams of flying weren't just dreams—they were echoes of something deeper, something that refused to leave me alone.

"Thanks for doing the bare minimum!" I shouted to our escorts. "I'm giving you like a two-star driver rating!"

"Finley," chided Temurr.

I elbowed him in the side. "Okay, where to now?"

"It has been said that the only other major city on the island is the port of Dimian. There we will find a ship."

"A ship, huh?" I wondered. "Well, sailing on ships has worked well for us so far! I guess we, uh, better get... crackin'"

Temurr side-eyed me.

We started off on the cobblestone path cut in the tropical forest.

"Should I stop crackin' jokes? We don't want the Pun Police crackin' down on me. I'm just crackin' myself up—"

Temurr elbowed *me* in the side, knocking me straight into a giant flower bush.

Chapter 79

emurr and I trudged along the main road that snaked across the island, the journey consuming the entire day as we covered at least ten axims. The road wound through endless fruit farms, their fields worked by Tenguans with small or damaged wings. Their movements were slow and methodical, their expressions dour as they harvested the crops. They barely glanced in our direction, their disinterest as thick as the humid jungle air that clung to us.

Short bursts of rain pelted us intermittently, soaking us through before the oppressive heat returned, turning the downpours into a sticky, sweltering mist. By the time we finally staggered into Dimian, I was runway-ready—for a zombie apocalypse.

Dimian was nothing like the bustling Relna Thune. It was smaller, poorer, and looked like it had been cobbled together from whatever scraps could be found. The tiny harbor hosted a ragtag fleet of mismatched ships, their sails patched and hulls weathered, bobbing in the murky water. Along the dock, rickety warehouses leaned precariously, their wood warped from years of rain and salt air.

The city itself sprawled like an afterthought, a jumble of bamboo shacks and wooden lean-tos with corrugated metal roofs. The structures were haphazard, thrown together without care for planning or structure, giving Dimian the feel of a desperate, worn shantytown barely holding itself together.

As we strolled toward the dock, the workers were hard at it—mostly Tenguans, their wings clipped or damaged or genetically too small, with a few Prominans mixed in. Temurr exchanged looks or brief nods with his kind, a quiet acknowledgment that felt weighted with meaning in a place like this.

"What's the deal with this city?" I asked. "It's such a slum. And it's so close to paradise."

I looked over my shoulder. Nibiru stared back from its perch on the giant rock.

"From what I am told, those living here are the outcasts—those born without wings or those with wings too small for flight. As well as some who were found guilty of crimes and had their wings clipped. Dimian means ground, by the way, in their language. These people are referred to as the Bunungfei... the Mud Walkers."

"Shit, that's a bit harsh. It's not like they chose to be born with little wings."

"No society is perfect. Frip and I were outcasts because of our love. I did not choose to love him... I simply did."

"I know. I get it. Where I come from, we deal with fear and hatred of those who are different, too. But it makes me sad. Why can't everyone just... be, you know?"

"Because fewer and fewer Prominans are being born, our king wants those like us exiled. Since we cannot bring children into our society. They have the same issue in Nibiru. As their population diminishes, they are trying to prevent those without the ability to fly from breeding with those who can. They fear they will lose their gift."

"Still... that doesn't make it fair. And it's going to happen anyway."

Temurr stopped on the street, a curious look on his face. "What do you mean?"

"Where I'm from, there used to be a variety of species. But that was many thousands of years ago. Now there are only Hominans."

"Did your people wipe out the others... like Malek?"

"I don't know. There are no written records. Some were probably killed. But not all. I think most were assimilated?"

"What does that mean?"

"Well, we have a powerful magic that allows us to look closely at blood, to see what it is made of. And my ancestors came from another continent than the one I was born on. In their blood, the Hominans from that land have traces of the race of people who looked a lot like Braylor. So, some of our Hominans must have hooked up with some of their Fomorians."

"There was hybridization in your world."

"Yes."

I saw fear in Temurr's eyes. "Oh, that is a serious offense among many species here on Tir Na."

"It is? Why?"

Temurr pulled me off the main drag through Dimian, so he wouldn't be heard.

"The gods warned our ancestors to not mate with other species. Most kingdoms have laws against hybridization. It does happen, but—"

"But that makes no sense!" I whispered loudly. "What if a Hominan falls in love with a... Fomorian? Hypothetically," Braylor popped into my mind. "Let's just say..."

Temurr smirked—he saw right through me.

"Ah, well... the only laws against love, that I am aware of, are the ones aimed at Frip and I. But breeding is another story."

"That's so not cool!"

"And yet, it is the way of life."

I gave him a smile. "Frip said the same thing to me when I first got here."

"Frip was wise."

I couldn't shake the feeling that what the Tengu were doing to their own people was too close to the mindset of what Malek wanted to do to the whole world. Of course, they were not killing off the deformed or disabled but isolating them on the same island. But those people could still look up to see paradise. Seemed excessively cruel.

The setting sun cast a bright, dazzling orange glow over the makeshift rooftops. But a dark melancholy hovered on Dimian like a fog. No one acknowledged us. The streets were eerily quiet, despite people going about their business. Laughter would have seemed out of place echoing off the tattered walls of the rundown shacks. As we passed by those souls with damaged wings, sadness and grief and regret flooded my mind.

Temurr must have seen my look of despair. He grabbed my hand and pulled me along.

"Come. We will find passage to Kunlun, we will."

He booked us on a ship leaving at high tide, with a cargo hold full of fresh fruit.

Several Tenguan sailors rowed us out to the *Alkonost*, a wide-bodied ship with three thick masts. I took one last look back at the sad, dark city as it laid in a lump across the black beach like the bones of a dragon.

As in Dimian, the ship's crew were mostly Prominans and Tenguans.

One of them screamed at us. "Oh, no! Not them! 'Specially not the firehair!"

Melcente marched by us, right up to the captain of the ship, pointing at us the whole way.

"Captain! Them's a bad potion! We'll sink surely if we carry them through!"

The captain, a severely thin Prominan who was nearly twice Temurr's age, stroked his white beard. He stared out at the sea, over her head.

"They paid."

"She brought the Kraken down on muh ship, she did! Sunk us straight away! I will not sail with that girl on board!"

She moved in close, wanting to intimidate him. But he refused eye contact.

"I recall you been paid, anont. Return the wage and you be free to swim back to shore."

Melcente couldn't afford to lose the gig. She turned to glare at me with narrowed black eyes and bared teeth.

"Back to work then," said the captain, still stroking his beard and staring at the sea.

Temurr strongly advised we stay below deck and out of Melcente's way for as much of the voyage as possible. A little seasickness, he said, was a small price to pay to avoid her temper.

The journey back to the mainland was uneventful, the seas calm and the skies clear. Most of my time was spent listening to Temurr share stories of his adventures with Frip. Each tale revealed a different side of their bond, but my favorite was the one about how they met. Temurr, then a soldier in the Kunlun army, had gone to Frip, a tailor, complaining that his tunic was too tight. Frip, ever blunt, told him to lose weight—then proceeded to alter the tunic anyway. And just like that, true love was born.

Every night on the voyage, my dreams were consumed by visions of flying as a dragon. The pull, that persistent tug in my mind, never left me. It followed me through the days, unrelenting, like someone knocking on a door I was already rushing to answer. No matter how far we traveled, it felt like I wasn't moving fast enough.

On the final night of the voyage, I was jolted awake by an intense dream. Climbing out of my hammock, I sat cross-legged on the wooden floor, trying to meditate away the anxiety clawing at my chest. These mindforms weren't from a dragon, I realized—they felt different. Faint, weak, but insistent, like whispers growing louder the longer I ignored them.

The message was clear: *Find the terrifying beast.*

Whoever was sending it wasn't strong enough to speak louder, but their urgency was undeniable. And as much as it unnerved me, I couldn't ignore the call.

In the morning, a sailor's voice rang out from above deck. "Land!"

I barely registered the call. My focus was locked on the chaotic images swirling in my mind. *Why would someone want me to find a dragon?* The mindforms were scattered, fragmented—a confusing jumble of thoughts that refused to align. I was a fortune teller staring at a deck of Tarot cards, desperate to make sense of my own cryptic future.

Suddenly, the ship veered hard, throwing me on my side. Pain shot through me as shouts erupted from above, followed by the pounding of boots on the deck. The turmoil outside collided with the storm in my head.

I forced myself to focus, gripping the thrumming energy pulsing through my mind. One wave stood out—strong, insistent, demanding attention. I latched onto it, the fragmented mindform sharpening with startling clarity.

Find the dragon. The dragon released from the Black City.

Why? I had no idea. But for the first time, the fragments in my head carried a purpose. A mission.

The ship groaned ominously, pulling me back to the present. Wood cracked and splintered around me, the sound ridiculously loud in the dim space below deck.

Then the Alkonost tilted sharply.

Something was wrong. Very wrong.

I gasped as the front of another ship tore into our hull like a spear through skin. Wood exploded inward, shards flying as water surged in, cold and ongoing. My stomach dropped as I scrambled to my feet, panic gripping me.

We were under attack.

Chapter 80

Temurr scrambled down the stairs from the deck. The intruding bow began to recede. Even more seawater poured through the new hole in our hull.

"What the hell?!"

"A ship rammed us! We must go!"

"Go where?!" I scooped up my sack and scabbard.

Temurr grabbed gear from his hammock, then grabbed my wrist. Water gushed in, filling the hold to our knees. We raced up the stairs. The *Alkonost* creaked and moaned from the mortal wound in her side.

Through the thick morning mist, we could see the other ship. Flying the Irkallan flag. Soldiers stood there, waiting to board us.

The Irkallans had T-boned the *Alkonost*. Sailors on the other ship ran about, pulling ropes and adjusting sails. They were trying to pull away so they could come alongside.

Nerus, King Malek's beady-eyed little wizard, stood on the poop deck, barking orders at the sailors and the ship's captain.

"We must jump ship!" screamed Temurr.

I looked at him like he was crazy. "And do what?! Go where?"

He pointed toward the bow of the *Alkonost*. Through the fog, trees at the edge of the shoreline were visible. We were close enough to land to swim—but still a long way out.

Melcente released her rope, ran to the captain of our ship.

She pointed a finger at me. "I told ya, Captain! I told ya! She a cursed one, that firehair!"

I turned to Temurr. "Can we make it that far?!"

"If we want to live…"

"No! You fools!" bellowed Nerus from the ship. He dashed across the deck to the bow, hiking up his black robes and waving his hands. "No!"

I tried to summon my courage, preparing myself for the swim ahead. I exhaled slowly, my eyes fixed on the faraway shore, vivid memories of my desperate struggle with the Kraken flashing through my mind. But then I noticed something—a large wooden pole drifting slowly across our deck.

My breath caught as I followed the pole with my eyes, its length leading back to yet another ship. An Irkallan ship.

"Stop!" Nerus' voice rang out in a desperate scream, but it was too late.

The new ship rammed us hard on the opposite side, slamming into the Alkonost with a thunderous crash. The impact threw us violently to the deck, the hull groaning under the new assault. Above the chaos of shouts and screams, I heard the sharp, sickening crack of one of our masts snapping.

The force of the collision shoved us against the first Irkallan ship, pinning the Alkonost in a crushing grip between the two larger vessels. Even Nerus, usually so composed, was on his knees at the bow, waving his arms helplessly as the havoc unfolded.

All three ships were locked together now, the Alkonost trapped in the middle like a battered prisoner. Our ship should have sunk instantly, but the crushing weight of the Irkallan vessels kept us afloat. The sails on all three ships caught the wind, pulling against each other and sending the tangled mess spinning aimlessly back out into the ocean.

The deck tilted wildly beneath me as the world turned into a chaotic whirl of broken wood, flapping sails, and panicked cries. *We were trapped, and the ocean wasn't letting us go.*

"Kill her!" commanded Nerus as he rose to his feet.

The Irkallan soldiers advanced to their bow, their short swords gleaming, while archers stepped into formation behind them. Without hesitation, they fired a volley of arrows aimed right for us.

"Go! Go!" Temurr bellowed.

Grabbing my bag and scabbard, I flung them over my shoulder and sprinted for the bow. With no time to think, we leapt over the side, plunging into the cool morning water as the arrows rained down.

Desperate to throw off the archers, we swam alongside their ship, keeping as close as possible to the hull. Temurr motioned for us to dive, and we submerged, kicking hard to pass underneath. The darkness of the water closed around me, the sounds of grinding ships above muted into an eerie calm.

We surfaced briefly for a gasp of air before diving again, every stroke and kick a battle against the pounding of my heart and the ache in my lungs. When I surfaced again, Temurr was nowhere in sight. Panic threatened to break my rhythm, but I forced myself to focus. *Just keep swimming. Stay calm.*

I dove again, stretching my endurance to its limits. When I emerged next, the ship was behind me, its shadow fading into the dense fog. A few stray arrows splashed harmlessly nearby. My strokes became steadier, my breathing more controlled, as I found a rhythm: stroke after stroke, kick after kick.

After an eternity, I could see the pebbles on the rocky beach. Gasping, I staggered to my feet in the shallow water and collapsed onto the hard, unforgiving rocks. My chest heaved as I sat up, straining to hear any sign of pursuit. Distant shouts echoed faintly from the mist, but no Irkallans appeared.

Moments later, Temurr emerged from the water, gasping for breath. He stumbled onto the shore, his massive strength no match for his terrible swimming skills. He collapsed into the lapping waves, utterly spent, his arms too heavy to pull himself onto dry land.

"Not your thing, huh?" I said between breaths, trying to grin through my exhaustion.

He just groaned, flopping onto the rocks like a fish out of water.

"Oh, I cannot tell you... how much... I hate the water, I do."

I scanned the heavy fog, waiting for our pursuers. As Temurr recovered, I heard splashing up the shoreline.

"Someone is coming. We have to go," I whispered, helping him off the beach.

He groaned, pushing himself up. From the haze, I saw a shadow striding toward us. I pulled my sword from the scabbard on my back.

Through the mist, Melcente emerged. A murderous look plastered on her face. She panted for air as water drained off her.

"Once again! *You* live... while others die!"

Temurr put himself between me and the crazy woman. "And if you wish to keep breathing, you will follow us..."

She doubled over, placing hands on her knees.

Temurr glanced at the sea. "Now."

The air filled with the unmistakable sound of wings—large, deliberate, and powerful. Each slow, heavy flap seemed to reverberate through the misty stillness. I swallowed the fat lump in my throat as I squinted into the low clouds, straining to catch a glimpse of what was above.

A faint shadow emerged, circling high overhead, its movements graceful yet commanding. Then, with a sudden burst of energy, it flapped hard and disappeared into the haze.

My breath caught. Was that a dragon? It *had* to be.

"Awright," Melcente exhaled deeply, waving a hand in surrender. "Awright! I be goin' with youse..."

Without waiting, Temurr grabbed my hand and yanked me into the forest. We were in his element now. He vaulted over fallen tree trunks, dodged low limbs, and easily scaled rock outcroppings. He stole quick glances back, stopping only to help the two of us to keep up. We raced along a shallow stream for half an axim, then ran back to the thick forest. Temurr kept us on this pace for almost an hour.

He finally picked a small hill, deep in the woods, to let us rest. He stood on the crest, sniffing the air, as we gasped for breath. Melcente dropped into the wet grass, rubbing her sore ankles.

"Why does everything want you dead, missy? The sirens, the Kraken and them Irkallans?"

"I think all the troubles we've had are related."

Temurr stopped sniffing the air. "What are you saying?"

"Well, spies followed us all the way to Kunlun. When we changed course and headed for Nibiru, the sirens followed our ship through the ocean. Then the Kraken suddenly attacks us before we reach our destination? Kasuma told me that giant squid has never been seen near their island before. And then Malek's mage, Nerus, just appears out of nowhere, directing two ships to try to take us out? There are—"

"No coincidences," Temurr finished, nodding. "So, Nerus used his magic to send the Kraken after us, he did?"

"I'm sure of it. Maybe even the sirens, too! He's been trained in mindforms for far longer than Pherric ever was. He might have that ability. And he either had spies on Oceantis, or he was able to sense that I was leaving the island. He wanted to kill me before we landed. Malek must really want me out of the picture."

"I still say you is cursed." Melcente was such a treasure.

"Maybe. Which means neither of you are safe being anywhere near me."

"That be the truth, right there." She shook a finger at me.

Temurr exhaled. "All the more reason I should stay with you."

I patted his furry jaw. "What I've got to do, I need to do on my own."

"But—"

"Shh. It's okay, Temurr. I'm a big girl now. I can take care of myself. Besides, you won't like where I'm going..."

He sighed, then flashed me a grin and nodded. Temurr removed his bow and quiver full of arrows and handed them to me.

"As is my custom, I give you a bow... for your journey."

"No, you'll need those!"

"Worry not, child. This is my kingdom. Shangri-La lies but a few axims inland. And, as you say, if I do not like where you are going, then I suspect you will need these more than me."

I slung his bow over my shoulder and grabbed the quiver.

Temurr reached into the pouch tied to his belt. He placed several coins in my hand.

"And I give you coins, to enrich you for your journey."

He held up a piece of flint.

"Finally, I give you flint, to light the way for your journey…"

I slid the flint in my boot.

He threw both of his long ape-man arms around me, pulling me in and hugging me tight.

"Be careful, Finley Maguire. You are on your way to becoming a warrior, but you're *still* a novice. Remember your training and… stay alive."

"I haven't managed to stay alive *yet*! Why the hell would I start now?"

He smirked at me, patted my face.

I turned my attention to Melcente. "I'm very sorry for all you've gone through and everything you've lost. I may be cursed, I don't know. But you're hard as nails—you'll bounce back."

"That ya can be sure of, love. May dem gods go with ya, sistah."

She grabbed hard on my forearm. I returned the gesture.

"Oh, hey! Do either of you know where I could find a dead dragon?"

Chapter 81

Temurr and Melcente had no clue where I might find dragon bones, but I knew I needed one of their dead bodies. Pherric had once mentioned that dragons return for their own. It was a long shot—my only shot—but if they really did retrieve the bones of their fallen, then perhaps I could find a skeleton. What would I do if I actually encountered a dragon? No idea. That was my stupid plan.

Run, I told myself.

With a forced smile, I waved goodbye and dashed into the dense forest of Kunlun. For most of the day, I tackled hills, skirting the mountains. Temurr had said that Shangri-La lay to the east. I looked up at the sun, like the group had taught me and headed south instead.

Finding food became my first priority. My answer? A massive, fur-covered pig-like thing that stood up to my chest—and was seriously hard to kill. My first arrow just made it mad. It charged, forcing me up a tree, and I emptied my quiver into the beast before it finally collapsed. Butchering it wasn't pleasant, but I prepped as much meat as I could carry. After slicing it into thin strips, I dried it in the sun and used salt extracted from plants Pherric had shown me to preserve it. The whole ordeal took days.

Heading farther south, I veered inland and left the dense evergreens for Kunlun's grassy plains. The golden expanse was encircled by towering bronze mountains capped with glistening white snow. Sparkling lakes connected by a winding river dotted the land, but the farms I passed, once full of a wheat-type plant, were abandoned and rotting—likely because their farmers had gone to fight the Irkallan invasion.

At first, I avoided the small towns, wary of what I might find. But I realized I needed information. Summoning my courage, I entered each village along my path.

In one town, I found a blacksmith and used Temurr's coins to buy a chainmail shirt and shield. Most of the Prominans I met were cautious but not hostile, though some glared or outright told me to leave. Others, however, were surprisingly kind, helping where they could—until I started asking about dragons.

I inquired about recently deceased dragons, bones, or the mysterious Valley of the Black Bones. But no one knew anything. More often than not, my strange questions left them frightened or retreating. For now, my search led only to dead ends.

One night, while camped on a small hill, I heard distant groans and some seriously heavy stomping. My heart leapt into my throat. I grabbed my bow, scrambling behind a boulder.

A family of Torodans stood grazing in the tall grass of the plain. They had long spiky tails, a big thick ridge of plates along their backs, and tiny heads. The dinosaurs were similar to the stegosaurus that had lived on my world, but these creatures had several sharp horns on their foreheads. One of the young ones kept trying to go off on his own and a parent kept corralling it back into the fold. I felt that little one's pain. Being on my own for the first time since I came to Tir Na still sent shivers down my spine. Mostly because my little quest was batshit crazy. But every night, when I'd climb into a tree or under a rock ledge to sleep, a smile would drift across my silly face. I was on a strange and dangerous new world. All by myself. Call it bravery or whatever you want, but I had changed. And I was happy with the new me.

Well, not the zombie me but the warrior me. I remained convinced my skin would soon start falling off. I even left the brain of the boar that I had killed behind. No sense taking chances that I would develop a taste. But as I walked the flatland or passed through a town, I felt capable. Dressed in my chainmail, a new shield strapped to my back, a sword at my side, I was a warrior. Yeah, I was still a novice, but a warrior nonetheless.

Once I set out on my own, however, the visions I was having stopped. Which worried me. Was I doing the right thing? Or had the person sending me those mindforms stopped because they realized I was an idiot? Probably the latter. But I kept going anyway because, well, I was an idiot.

Late one afternoon, I wandered into what seemed to be a deserted farm town. As I prepared to leave, I spotted a battered, round yurt and decided to check behind it for any leftover fruits or vegetables.

There, slumped in the dirt with his back against the yurt's wall, was an old Prominan man. His wispy orange hair, streaked with white, was matted and caked with grime. A once-royal blue robe hung on his frail frame, now faded by the sun, stained, and riddled with holes. He rocked side to side, arms crossed tightly over his chest, laughing and muttering to himself as if caught in a private conversation.

I approached cautiously, hands raised to show I meant no harm. Kneeling before him, I noticed his face: one eye clouded white with blindness, an old scar cutting from his forehead to his cheek—a silent testament to a life of battle. His good eye darted around wildly before settling on me.

"Hey there," I said softly.

He cackled, a high-pitched sound that sent a chill down my spine.

Then, from beyond the yurt, I heard shrill cries of playful laughter. Leaning out, I saw three Prominan children playing a spirited game of Keep Away—or maybe Monkey in the Middle was more fitting. Their joy stood in stark contrast to the somber figure before me.

I turned back to the old man, trying to connect. "Are those your grandchildren over there?"

"Yes, yes, yes," he mumbled, rocking more vigorously. "Yes."

The way he swayed, half-lost in his own world, left me wondering how much of him was still tethered to this one.

"Can you help me? I'm on a very important mission. I need to find... dragon bones. Have you seen a dead dragon anywhere near here? Or...

heard of one?"

"Dragons. Dragons!" he repeated. "Red dragons, blue dragons! Dragons everywhere!"

He laughed some more. I exhaled, staring down at the weeds beneath my boots. The old timer wouldn't be able to help.

"He cannot help you," said a boy's voice.

One of the children had run over to the yurt, retrieving the cloth ball that had rolled away.

"No, I don't suppose he can." I stood up and inspected the kid. He wore tattered, gray baggy trousers and a leather vest, with a wood sword held in place by a rope around his waist. "What about you? Can you help me find some dragon bones?"

The boy's eyes narrowed, wondering if he could trust me. He looked around us. So I looked around, too. The area was secure.

"Um, I... well, I have not seen one. But my grand uncle said he heard from a hunter returning from Penglai that she saw a dead dragon. Somewhere near Penglai."

"Really? Is your grand uncle here? Could I ask him?"

The boy looked down at the ground. "No. He was forced to fight against the Mad King. Week before last. All the males are gone now. I wanted to go fight alongside him, but... he said I was too young. And he is very, very wrong. I can fight."

"I bet you're a great fighter. Someday, you will have your chance."

He whipped out his wood sword, nodding to me, and slashed hard at the air—*damn straight, girl.*

"So, Penglai? Is that far from here?"

The boy pointed to a chain of gray hills being smothered by white clouds.

"About twenty axims south, beyond the Azel range, and maybe two axims west of the city."

With only a single platinum coin left in my pouch, I paid my new friend handsomely. Without thanking me or saying goodbye, he dashed off to show his friends how he had recently come into a fortune.

I smiled after the boy and slipped some meat to the old Prominan.

"Dragons!" he shouted. "Red dragons. Red. Red ones!"
I took off running toward the low gray mountains.

Chapter 82

I found the dragon's body farther away than the boy had described, by at least an axim or more. I might have missed it completely if not for the thunderstorm that crept up on me as night fell.

Seeking shelter, I stumbled into an ancient forest of dead, gnarled trees. Their trunks twisted unnaturally, curving upward into sharp, claw-like tips that seemed to cut into the black sky. Lightning lit up the spiked branches, casting eerie shadows that danced and shifted with every flash. The exposed, tangled roots clawed at the rocky ground, making each step hazardous.

This forest hadn't been burned by dragon fire—it bore the scars of a lava flow long cooled. For hundreds, maybe thousands of years, the trees had stood here, lifeless and ominous. At the edges of the wasteland, new evergreens and tall grass had begun to creep in, as if nature were slowly reclaiming the land.

Rain pelted down as I searched for cover, my soaked boots slipping on the slick rocks. The wind howled, relentless, driving cold rain at my face. Lightning struck again, illuminating the desolation around me. There was no shelter to be found.

Determined, I climbed a steep hill to escape the forest. Halfway up, a sudden, powerful tremor shook the ground beneath me. I froze, crouching low as the vibrations rattled my bones. This wasn't just thunder. It wasn't random.

The quaking wasn't chaotic—it moved deliberately, a ripple that surged down the hill and back toward the forest. My breath caught. *This isn't natural.*

The minor earthquake was a message, deliberate and purposeful. The fierce wind drove me forward, pushing me back to the dead trees. I turned, picking my way carefully down the rocky slope, back over the charred remains of a long-dead lava flow.

And then I saw it.

Lightning illuminated the base of the hill, and there, sprawled among the twisted roots, lay a dragon's skeleton. The massive black bones glistened in the storm, their sheer size enough to send a shiver down my spine.

I whipped my head toward the skies, scanning the storm clouds for any sign of a living dragon, but saw only the endless darkness. Thick, cold raindrops splattered against my face, and the wind howled louder, as if daring me to stay.

Every instinct screamed at me to get the hell away, but the storm had soaked me to my core, and there was no escaping it now. Against my better judgment, I crawled into the dragon's massive skull, its hollow eye sockets framing the chaotic flashes of lightning outside.

I curled up, shivering, as the storm raged on, my shelter both terrifying and oddly comforting. The dead dragon's presence loomed heavy around me as I waited out the storm.

I camped in the eerie, lifeless forest for nearly a week, the twisted trees and blackened ground my only company.

During the days, I poured my energy into training. My arms ached from countless hours spent firing arrows into the brittle trunks of dead trees, their surfaces scarred with the marks from my arrowheads. Sword drills consumed the rest of my time, each swing of my blade a test of endurance and precision. By the end of the week, nearly every tree carried the signs of my hard work.

At night, the forest fell silent except for the howling wind, and I turned my focus inward, practicing my mindforms. I concentrated on the dragon that had haunted my dreams, sending out deliberate waves of thought. I focused on my location in the forest, the towering black bones of the dragon, and the endless pull I couldn't ignore. Each pulse of energy was an invitation—a challenge—to the creature. But in truth, I had no idea what I'd do if it actually accepted.

The nights weren't without danger. One evening, a pack of black feline beasts emerged from the shadows, their glowing eyes fixed on me and their long fangs bared in hunger. They were scavengers, feral and vicious, but disorganized. They came at me one by one, a fatal mistake. I managed to kill two of them and sent the rest scampering off to find an easier meal. The ordeal gave me a few scrapes, a nasty bite on my leg, but also some much-needed food.

Still, even with the immediate threats dealt with, the forest felt heavy, as though it too were waiting for the dragon's arrival.

Late one evening, as the sun bled into the distant hills, I heard it—the unmistakable sound of wings beating the air. Heavy. Powerful. Close.

From behind and above me.

My heart slammed in my chest as I kicked dirt onto the fire, smothering its glow. My hand closed around my bow, fingers trembling.

My guest had arrived.

Grabbing my shield, I turned to face the shadow circling overhead. The dragon glided effortlessly through the darkening sky, his black scales catching the gold hues of the setting sun, glinting like molten metal. His shriek ripped through the quiet, sharp and commanding—a declaration of dominance that echoed through the forest and hills.

My arms prickled with goosebumps. But I focused on my breath. My heart did not race as much as it should have.

It was him. The black dragon I had set free.

I had no plan, no strategy. I only knew that I was entirely out of my depth. My sword felt impossibly small as I drew it, clutching my shield close to my chest.

Why the hell was I even here?!

The dragon banked lower, his massive wings casting long shadows over the skeletal remains below. He wasn't just circling anymore—he was watching. Assessing.

And I had no idea what to do next.

I waited for him to land on the grassy hill and stepped away from a petrified tree, showing myself to the dragon.

He had the higher ground. I backed up several paces, trying to not trip over twisted roots. He advanced down the hill, snarling and lowering his head. Panic finally hit me and my heart raced—forgetting once again to even inhale.

The dragon's yellow eyes locked on me, the same piercing gaze that he had burned into my soul when caged back at the arena. He reared his head, the glow in his throat intensifying, and unleashed a wall of fire.

I dove behind a rotting tree as the flames streaked past, the heat searing the skin on my sword arm. The air crackled with energy as the fire ignited the dead branches around me, turning part of the ancient forest into an inferno.

Stealing a glance, I saw the dragon roar at the sky, his massive form shifting to the right as he moved along the base of the hill, angling for a better shot. When his head reared back again, I bolted left, my boots scrambling over the uneven ground. I jumped over a root but tripped on another, slamming hard into the rocky dirt.

His fire came again, blasting past me, singeing the air. I fumbled for my bow, firing two arrows—one missed entirely, and the other ricocheted harmlessly off his black scales.

The dragon's eyes flared a terrifying reddish-orange, his fury boiling over.

Grabbing my shield, I ducked behind another tree, its thick ancient trunk catching fire instantly. The heat sucked the air from my lungs, blackening my hair and blistering my exposed skin.

I squeezed my eyes shut, focusing my mind as the pain surged behind my temples. My breaths came fast and shallow as I imagined myself running, weaving through the forest. The effort sent sharp pain slicing through my skull, but then I felt it—a connection.

Another shriek split the night as the dragon's flames lit up the forest again. But this time, they didn't come for me.

Peeking out, I saw the flames chase a shadowy figure—a mindform I had sent out. My phantom ran farther, effortlessly over the gnarly roots, drawing his fire harmlessly away.

Frustrated, the dragon turned back to me, but I sent out another image—a version of myself, bow drawn and arrow notched—stepping out from a nearby tree. The dragon lunged at it, unleashing more fire, his snarls echoing across the burning valley.

Through the haze of pain in my head, I conjured another shadow, this one armed with a sword. The dragon's eyes darted wildly, scanning for the real me. His fury erupted as he roared and scorched most of the forest floor, flames spreading in a sweeping arc.

I crouched behind the burning tree, holding my shield close as his fire engulfed everything. The heat was unbearable, blistering my skin, burning my legs and arms. Smoke filled my lungs and stung my eyes as the forest turned into a blazing hellscape.

The dragon's patience had run out. With flames licking the ground, he began his descent, each thunderous step shaking the earth. His wings, attached to his massive forelegs, folded tightly as he marched in to finish me.

Whatever I'd hoped to achieve from this confrontation? It didn't matter anymore. There would be no miracle, no salvation. This was it.

I stepped out from behind the tree, trembling but determined.

"All right, dragon," I said, my voice raw and hoarse. "Let's get this over with."

My head high, feet spread apart defiantly. Staring up at the towering creature. My lip quivered and my arms shook, but I wanted to go out with an attitude. A fighting spirit.

The dragon snorted. His mouth opened as he sucked in all the air around me. Fire burned in his angry eyes as he prepped to set me ablaze.

I tried to read his thoughts but sensed no specific intelligence. There was sentience, but no words that I could read. I felt only his anger. An overwhelming hatred, boiling over in his mind. And fear. The terrifying and ominous creature of death was himself afraid. I could also feel his sadness. His mind held onto the image of the black bones, lying at the bottom of the hill. Another of his own kind had died. Fear of isolation, loneliness. The end of dragons on this world. He was in mourning.

The black one released his fire on me. I dropped to my knees. My head down. I held up the shield up with both hands. The force of the blast shoved me back, dragging my knees through the dirt. Flames swarmed around the edges of my shield, but the fire was not as intense as before. The heat still burned my hands but I held on. There was no air to breathe. I stayed in place, bearing the brunt of his hostility. Pain raced through me as I died slowly from the outside in.

The stream of flame ended.

"Ow! Ow! Goddammit!" I leapt up, dropping the glowing hot shield. I slapped at the small fires burning my blouse. Whacked at the hot embers in my hair.

Panting hard, I inspected a huge burn on my forearm. My shield still glowed a bright orange in the dirt at my boots. I was exposed.

I wiped at the sweat streaming into my eyes. "Go on! Do it!"

The dragon cocked his head and then opened his mouth wide, his sharp teeth glowing in the firelight.

"Finish me!"

I winced, waiting for the final flame.

But nothing came out. The black dragon exhaled again. And there was no fire. He had no more dragonfire left. He sneered at me.

I exhaled.

The black dragon turned away from me. And I blinked hard.

My head snapped as two horns shot through my back. Stuck out of my chest and belly.

Searing, sharp pain. My eyes and mouth open. Blood gurgled in my throat.

My body was thrown forward, but stayed attached to the spikes on the dragon's tail.

I gasped but nothing would come. Blood gushed down my body, soaking my legs and filling my boots.

The tail whipped around again, tossing me through the air like a rag doll. I held my hands to the gaping wounds—but that was pointless.

The dragon roared in triumph.

I watched as he marched over to the skeleton. He nudged the black skull with his forehead. Gingerly, he used his teeth to grasp the skull and lifted it in his mouth.

He took a final look at me. Orange fire still burning in his eyes. The dragon flapped his wings once, then twice. And he lurched into the dark sky as the clouds opened up and let the rain fall.

As my body bled out, I was fixated on the raindrops that ran down my cheeks. They felt so cool on my blistered skin.

Then... I died for the second time.

Chapter 83

Life surged back into me like a jolt of electricity.

I rolled onto my side in the black, sooty dirt, gasping for air as if I'd been underwater for hours. Shivers coursed through my body, the faint warmth radiating from my chest doing little to shake the bone-deep chill. My stomach churned violently, and I tried to puke, but nothing came up.

On my knees, trembling, I reached under my scorched blouse and chainmail, fingers fumbling to assess the damage. My skin was sticky with thickened blood, but there was no pain where the dragon's spikes had torn into me. I yanked the mail up for a better look—and froze. The wounds on my chest and stomach were gone.

I slumped back against a charred tree root, lungs heaving as if I'd run a marathon. My head pounded, each throb like a hammer striking bone, and the nausea twisted in my gut, relentless and cruel.

Overhead, Tir Na's metallic moon hung high in the clearing night sky, its light glinting off the gray, wet trees. The storm had passed, and judging by the blood still fresh on my skin, I hadn't been dead long—an hour or two at most. But that was a longer time than when I had died at the Irkallan arena.

I couldn't help the grin that tugged at my lips. Whatever Pherric's twisted potion had done to me, it still worked. I didn't need him there to revive me anymore.

But the victory was fleeting. A crushing wave of exhaustion slammed into me, heavier than the dragon's fire. I felt like I hadn't slept in days, every joint and muscle screaming in protest.

So much for "I'll sleep when I'm dead." That turned out to be complete bullshit.

I was startled awake the next morning by several large black birds trying to pick at my burnt body. I swiped them away. They scattered, angrily cawing at me for having the audacity to not be dead.

I sat up, shuddering from the cold. I must have slept through the day and into the following morning. I staggered to my little camp. With my mouth as dry as one of my mother's martinis, I downed the contents of the waterskin. Still nauseous, I forced down leftover feline meat. My eyes turned to the bones of the dead dragon. He had taken the skull, but even more bones were missing. He had come back to collect more at some point.

An inkling of an idea formed. Even though I was covered in ash, soot, and blood, I did not clean up. Instead, I spent my time stacking up the large dragon bones into neat piles. When I heard the black dragon return, I threw myself on the ground in the spot where I had died. I slowed my breathing, pretending to be dead, as he collected bones. He flew back five times over two days. And each time I would lay there without moving.

Early one morning, his mission was complete. The dragon had cleared the base of the hill, and with a powerful sweep of his wings, he flew away. It was likely the last time I'd ever see him.

I wasn't sure what I had been expecting. Something... magical, maybe? But as I lay there, very much un-broiled, it hit me: this whole adventure had been utterly useless.

Later that day, while chewing through the last of my meat rations, I heard it again—the unmistakable sound of wings.

Even though the bones were gone, *he'd returned.*

I raced to the spot where he had killed me before and threw myself to the ground.

The dragon landed heavily nearby, his immense weight shaking the earth beneath me. Kasuma's voice echoed in my head, her training crystal clear: *Adarna-gakur—no fear, no movement, no reaction. You are stone.*

So, I became stone.

The dragon moved through the scorched clearing, his claws sinking into the dirt with each deliberate step. His breath came in low, growling snorts, heavy and unnerving. He paused, pawing at the ground, his massive frame radiating suspicion.

And then he sniffed me.

I felt his hot, sulfurous breath wash over me, stinging my nose and eyes. But I didn't flinch. Not even as he nudged me with his snout, testing for signs of life.

I stayed rigid.

Ten seconds passed. Then twenty. Every fiber of my being begged me to peek, to see what he was doing, but I fought the urge. Silent. Still.

I was stone.

The dragon drove his teeth into my body. I squinted in pain but did not open my eyes. Did not scream out. He bit down harder, his jaws locked on me. I bit my tongue hard enough to make it bleed. Fresh, hot blood cascaded down my skin, soaking me. I could hear it dripping down on the dirt. Tears ran from my closed eyes.

But I was made of stone.

As I bled out, I heard him snap his wings. Wind rushed over me as he launched into the afternoon sky. He carried me away, clenched between his sharp teeth.

Death. Nombre. Trois.

My chest expanded as I involuntarily inhaled air. I was alive again.

My heart beat furiously, making up for lost time. I pounded my fists against the ground. I panted hard, laying there with my eyes closed. It was time for my post-death checklist: acute pain all over my body (worse than the last time.) Check. Sick to my stomach. Check. Massive headache and weariness. Check and check. But I added a second affliction—painful dry skin. I scratched at my forearm, sending more sharp pain signals to my brain.

Panic surged through me as I opened my eyes and inspected my arms.

For a moment, I thought my worst fear had come true—that I had finally become a rotting zombie. But no. It was just a vicious sunburn. My arms were bright red, blistered in spots, the skin tight and raw. *How long had I been lying there, exposed to the relentless sun?*

I rolled onto one elbow, groaning as a new pain shot through me. Looking down, I saw small, sharp black glass crystals digging into my skin. I was lying on a bed of obsidian. My surroundings came into focus—a long, narrow valley running slightly downhill. The air was thin and sharp in my lungs, a sure sign I was high up in the mountains.

Walk. The word pressed into my mind, not quite a voice but an insistent thought.

I staggered to my feet, swaying like a drunk. My legs wobbled, and my arms hung uselessly at my sides. I felt utterly vulnerable. No shield. No sword—my stomach sank. Braylor was going to kill me for losing my sword.

Walk.

I took a long, shaky breath of the thin air and began to move.

The steep canyon floor stretched out before me, littered with dragon bones. Most were black, but others had been bleached pale gray or white, weathered by years under the blazing sun. Scattered throughout were stacked piles of massive bones, as if brought in by other dragons. Whole skeletons rested undisturbed, their colossal forms curled in final repose, as if they had come here to die from old age or fatal wounds.

I stopped in my tracks, the realization hitting me like a blow to the chest.

I was standing in the Valley of the Black Bones.

Despite the pain and exhaustion, despite the coagulated blood that filled my boots, squishing with every step, and despite severe thirst, I walked.

There were more than just bones in that canyon. I passed by a number of large eggs. Some taller than me. Most had cracks or large chunks of shell missing, with thin black bones visible inside. The dragons had lost a lot of their young.

Movement above caught my eye. Two green dragons—males—trudged to the edges of the valley. Pherric's voice echoed in my memory: *The ones with larger eyes and shorter horns are the females.* I swallowed hard. Their beady yellow eyes locked onto me, unblinking, calculating.

As I kept walking, I caught sight of a red female dragon farther ahead. Her massive form shifted as she snarled, baring rows of pointed teeth that glinted even in the muted light. She gnashed them together, a sharp, deliberate sound that sent a chill down my spine. But I did not cower—not in the slightest.

At the far end of the boneyard, the black dragon waited. Perched high on a ledge, he glared down at me, his piercing gaze filled with a strange mix of annoyance and curiosity. When I veered closer, he cocked his head to the side, as if surprised I was still alive.

Walk.

"All right, I'm walking!" I hissed under my breath at the persistent voice in my head.

Straightening myself, I threw my shoulders back and held my head high. Each step crunched on the obsidian glass beneath my boots, the sound echoing off the steep canyon walls like the rhythm of a death march. I forced myself to keep my pace steady, showing no fear, even as my pulse thundered in my ears.

When I finally exited the Valley of Black Bones, the landscape shifted. A white cloud drifted lazily across the green grass blanketing the mountain slope. I glanced back. The black dragon stayed perched on his ledge, watching me with an intensity that made my skin crawl.

I kept expecting to hear the whoosh of wings behind me, to feel the heat of dragonfire searing my back. But the only sounds were my own footsteps and the whisper of the wind.

The valley was embedded into the side of a mountain, or what was really the remains of an ancient volcano. And that made sense—the dragons, creatures of fire, had chosen a place steeped in molten death to rest in their final moments.

A shriek split the air, sharp and shrill. I spun around. The red dragon spread her massive wings, her fiery gaze locked on me, her body poised to strike. Now that I had stepped beyond her sacred burial ground, I was fair game.

She leapt from the ridge and took flight, her wings stirring the air into a frenzy as she bore down on me. My heart clenched. *So, this is it. Another death.*

But then, a flash of black tore across the sky. The black dragon intercepted her, slicing through the air and putting himself between me and Big Red. His massive wings beat the air in her face, a wall of defiance.

Big Red screamed, a furious, grating sound that made my ears ring, but the black dragon wasn't budging. He snarled, shrieking back at her, his cries full of warning. After a tense standoff, Red relented, flapping back to her perch on the ridge, her scowls still burning holes into me.

The black dragon lingered, hovering for a moment before returning to his ledge at the entrance to the Valley of Black Bones. His eyes tracked me as I descended the mountain, his head tilted ever so slightly, as if he were studying me—or judging me.

I disappeared into the clouds below, his gaze never wavering until I was gone.

Chapter 84

Since the black dragon had stopped Big Red from charbroiling me, I had no choice but to make my way down the mountainside. The voice in my head had instructed me to walk, so I walked.

Still, I couldn't shake the worry that this whole thing might be some twisted trap. Maybe Nerus was behind the voice, manipulating me to wander away from the dragons so he could take me out. But no, the mind-form wasn't laced with his arrogance or malice. It felt... compassionate. There was empathy in the voice echoing through my head, like someone genuinely trying to help me.

Unfortunately, my body had other opinions about starting a journey so soon. After what I assumed to be a week of being dead, I was a total wreck. Every step sent daggers of pain through my legs. My head spun, my stomach growled like a feral dog, and my dry, cracked lips were sandpaper against my useless tongue. I was the very definition of a catastrophe.

Stumbling through the thick mist, I distracted myself by dissecting the grim logic of my deaths. The first time, in the arena dungeon, Pherric said I'd been gone for ten minutes. The second, when the black dragon impaled me with his tail, seemed to be an hour or so. But when he bit me and carried me to the Valley of Black Bones? I'd been dead for *days*. The sunburn alone was proof of that.

So many creative ways to die on Tir Na—fangs, claws, swords. And now... skin cancer.

My theory was simple, if morbid: I wasn't truly immortal. More like... immortal-ish. Every time I died, it took longer and longer to come back.

What if one day I died, and it was a thousand years before I regenerated? Ouch. That kind of gap would *not* look good on a resume.

The dizziness worsened, but I forced myself to keep slogging forward. I needed distance. Distance from the cranky dragons, their burial ground, and whatever else this cursed mountain had in store for me.

"What the hell am I supposed to do next?" I muttered, glancing up at the sky like it might hold the answers.

Nothing. Just silence. And my own, increasingly frustrated thoughts.

I made it about half an axim before I had to rest. I melted into the tall grass on the slope. My stomach rumbled even harder. A wool sweater had seemingly been stuffed into my mouth. But I was too tired to hunt. Or search for water. Too tired to think anymore. My body demanded sleep. My eyelids grew so heavy. Maybe just a quick nap.

No. I needed to keep going. I had every reason to suspect that I would die—again—if I closed my eyes.

I groaned as I forced myself to stand again. Every part of me ached. My heart sank when I realized it might take me hours just to get off the volcano.

"Thanks for your help!" I shouted deliriously. But no one was there to hear. "Great. Now I'm talking to myself."

As I stood there, swaying back and forth, I heard the beating of wings high above. One of the dragons had followed me. I scanned the thick clouds drifting overhead but saw nothing.

Since my brain was moving at a slower pace than my aching legs, it dawned on me that I didn't know where I was—on an island or in some distant kingdom? I thought Pherric said the valley might be somewhere in Kunlun, but I couldn't remember. How long had it taken for the dragon to return and collect more bones? He had returned repeatedly, over short periods of time, to collect the bones. Maybe I was—

The wings flapped overhead again. Closer this time.

I could feel my heartbeat slowing. I took a few wild steps, stumbled, and fell to the ground—*neardeath* was close at hand.

My fingers clawed at the grass, attempting to drag myself down the mountain.

But my battery was too low. And I passed out.

A loud thump startled me awake.

In a daze, I blinked a dozen times and peered ahead of me to see—a long branch. It had been torn from a tree and dropped in the grass. The limb contained four fat lime-colored melons, each about the size of a fist, still attached at the stems.

I quietly looked around and listened for signs that someone was close by, but the slope was deserted.

I tore a melon from the branch, digging with fingers to crack open the tough skin. No luck. After a dozen bites, I broke through the outer layer, pried open a hole, and drank the beautiful, sour juice inside. Then I split it open and ate the fruit; it tasted like a salty apple combined with a lemon.

When I had finished the melons, I resumed my journey and descended below the fog that surrounded the old volcano. I entered a sparse forest of trees, with trunks growing out horizontally from the side of the mountain. Thick patches of green leaves hovered at the ends of each tree, pointing to the gray clouds above. Beyond the volcano stood range after range of steep and rocky mountains—which meant I might still be in Kunlun.

The scent of a fire drifted over me. Meat was being cooked. Perhaps there was a camp nearby. And they were the ones who left the melons for me. I reached for my missing sword and shook my head. I hated being without a weapon. But I had energy again. I could still fight. I picked up a rock, broke off a sturdy tree branch, and continued deeper into the woods.

Another half-axim down the mountain and my hunger pangs came back with a vengeance. Because I could finally smell the food being prepared— like a juicy ribeye steak being roasted on an open flame. I might have started salivating, I don't remember. Beyond a few trees, I saw smoke rising up from a row of reeds.

Being all stealthy, I carefully crawled up to the yellow stalks to see a freshly burned-out clearing, with dying embers floating up in the breeze.

Lying in the middle of the burn spot was the upper half of a bicorn.

Ragged pieces of smoking hide fluttered at the edges of the remains. I heard the beating wings in the clouds above. A dragon must have torn off a chunk of the animal and cooked it for me. Black smoke drifted up from the charred beast and flames flared as the fat burned.

I smiled. I had been given a gift.

Tearing into the meat, I ate until I could barely stand. I ripped off sections and stored them inside my mail shirt, not knowing when I'd have a chance to eat again. As I was without any decent weapon.

I heard a distant cry from the dragon flying. Hundreds of feet above me.

"Thank you!" I screamed as loud as I could.

I couldn't wipe the smile from my face. My body was happy again. The pain faded. And I took off running through the reeds and down the mountain as fast as my legs would carry me.

After hours of staggering down the mountainside, I reached a dense evergreen forest at the volcano's base just as the sun dipped low on the horizon. The fading light cast long shadows across the pines, and I paused, orienting myself. *If the Valley of the Black Bones was south of Shangri-La, I* thought, turning toward the setting sun, *then north should be this way.*

I plunged deeper into the forest, pushing past the thick, needled branches. My steps quickened until I came upon a small creek cutting through the trees. The sound of the bubbling water was almost soothing—until I saw him.

Crouched on all fours on the opposite bank was the black dragon.

His orange eyes bore into me, his snarl revealing teeth that had already tasted my flesh.

My breath hitched, and instinct screamed for me to run, but I didn't. I planted my hands on my hips and met his glare head-on. Defiantly, I stared into those burning orange eyes, my gaze following the thin black slits of his pupils. I reached out with my mind, feeling for the vibrations of his thoughts. Fear and anger simmered beneath the surface, as expected— but there was something else.

Curiosity.

He was bewildered by me. Confused. After all, he'd killed me. Twice. Yet here I was, standing before him, alive and unbroken.

I couldn't afford to show fear.

I took a deliberate step forward. The crunch of my boot on the river rocks broke the tense silence.

The dragon lifted his head, his eyes narrowing.

I stepped again. And again.

His growl deepened, a low rumble in his chest, as he inhaled sharply through his massive nostrils. I stopped. The threat of dragonfire hung in the air, and I knew all too well that this death might be permanent.

Summoning every ounce of courage I had, I walked to the creek's edge.

The dragon rose, his massive talons emerging from his paws with a scrape similar to fingernails on a chalkboard.

I leapt onto the first round stone in the water, arms outstretched for balance. My heart pounded, but I looked up, refusing to cower.

The dragon screamed, his roar splitting the forest. His teeth bared in fury, and his massive frame seemed to vibrate with raw power.

But it wasn't just rage.

He was demanding respect. I had challenged him and lost, and he was reminding me of my place beneath him. He wanted my deference.

I held my arms wide, standing tall despite the precarious footing. Slowly, I lowered my gaze, then my head.

The dragon snarled again, his head turning skyward as he let loose a bone-rattling howl.

Kneel. The command came sharp and clear in my mind.

"Seriously?" I muttered to the voice.

The dragon screeched, his eyes narrowing further.

"Okay! Okay!" I snapped, lowering myself to one knee on the slick rock. I bowed my head, showing him my empty hands.

His growling subsided, though his massive claws dug into the river rocks like stakes. He snorted, shaking his head as if trying to decide whether to tolerate me or finish the job.

For now, he seemed calm. But only barely.

I rose up and slowly, gently stepped to the next stone. Then another. I crossed over the creek and kneeled again. Close enough that he could have easily bitten my head off. But I averted my eyes and held out my open hands.

He sniffed me, which had to be so nasty—I couldn't even stand the smell of me.

The dragon unleashed one final imperious roar. He threw open his mouth and dropped his jaws over my head. But I remained perfectly still. I was a stone once again. If he bit down, I would have died. At least his sulfurous breath made me feel a bit better about the stink I had going on.

But he did not bite me in half. He ended his show of force, having established his dominance. The quintessential male.

I finally exhaled. I reached my shaky hand up and slowly stroked the hard scales on the side of his face. He recoiled at first, like a cat who hates to be touched. But he lowered his head and nudged me. I leaned into him and he knocked me over. He was playing.

I stood up, but kept my head down. His sharp eyes examined me, took in every line and pore on my dirty face. I slowly removed the leftover meat from inside my mail shirt, held it up for the dragon to sniff, and placed the strip on his pointy tongue. He threw back his long head and swallowed it. He thanked me by using his snout to slam me hard in the chest—knocking me flat on my back.

I pushed myself up on my elbows. "You're welcome. Douchebag."

The black dragon watched me as I got to my feet. I had no idea if our relationship allowed me to ask for favors, but fortune favors the bold.

"Hey," I said, trying to summon the calmest, most soothing tone I could manage. "I really need to get back to my people. And I was wondering... if you could help me out?"

The dragon cocked his massive head, his bright orange eyes narrowing, his scaly brow furrowing in what could only be described as skeptical curiosity.

I inhaled deeply, steadying myself, and began to walk slowly along his side. When I moved out of his line of sight, he shifted his powerful back legs, his claws scraping against the ground. Still, I didn't retreat. I stepped closer, my hands carefully pressing against his side.

He grunted, low and rumbling, and unsheathed his claws again.

"Would you take me there? Back to my home? To the island?" I asked softly, keeping my voice steady.

Reaching up, I ran my hand along his side. His scales were cool and smooth, like polished steel, sending a shiver through me. When he didn't pull away, I smiled. Slowly, I placed a boot on the back of his leg and gripped the edge of his wing.

"Considering you've already killed me. Twice. It's the least you could do, right?"

Taking my time, I pulled myself up, my fingers clutching tightly to the edges of his scales as I climbed onto his back. Once there, I rubbed his sides, letting my hands move gently over him. Then I laid my face against his cool, armored skin.

He tossed his head back and let out a piercing roar, a declaration of dominance that echoed across the valley. His wings unfurled with a whoosh, and he gave them a powerful flap. The ground trembled as his massive front claws lifted off the earth. Another beat, then another, and we hovered just above the rocky terrain.

I clung tightly to the sharp ridges of his scales, holding on with everything I had as he pumped his wings harder. The air beneath us rippled, sending waves through the stream below.

And then he rose, higher and higher, his mighty wings carving through the air with each thunderous beat.

The valley fell away beneath us as he leveled out, his body straightening into a streamlined glide. We soared up into the clouds, the wind roaring in my ears, and headed toward the setting sun.

Chapter 85

What's it like trying to steer a flying dragon?

My grandpa would have said, "It's like trying to nail pudding to a tree."

He would be pretty proud if he could have seen me up on the dragon's back, at least trying to make it work. I talked to the black beast, but that yielded nothing. I patted his sides, hoping he would turn one way or another. I even attempted a *mindform*... to no avail. Just getting a response from the dragon required slamming both boot heels into his sides. Even then, he would whip his head back and snarl menacingly. So rather than have him buck me off and send me plummeting to the ground, I just laid there holding on for dear life.

On my journey to find the Valley of Black Bones, I had traveled deep into southeastern Kunlun. I had hoped he would fly northwest, but he headed due west until we reached the Triton Sea. I attempted to get him to fly out toward Nibiru, but he ignored me. No matter how many times I kicked his sides. Instead we soared up the coastline.

Flying on the back of a dragon is not a fun thrill ride. While exhilarating at first, it was a bloody nightmare after only fifteen minutes. I had to sit on several rows of bony plates that were as hard as stones and sharp as axe blades. The wind dried my eyes and burned my skin. I nearly fell off a dozen times trying to hold onto his slippery scales.

During the night, the dragon got hungry. He dove down and scooped up a keresh grazing on a mountain. And that keresh, which is basically a giant deer with a single horn on top of his head, never saw us coming. He bit into the poor animal and we soared back up into the cool night air. I was reminded of all those dreams I had while on Nibiru. Dreams where I was flying with a dragon. A connection began to form in my weary brain. Those dreams must have been associated with the voice that had told me to walk away from the valley and kneel before the black dragon—a voice I didn't hear... until I died for the second or third time.

When he landed in a field to eat his catch, I was able to rest. Momentarily. Because he ripped through the deer in minutes and started to take off. I groaned in agony, leapt onto his back, and laid my head down between the sharp plates. Too afraid to close my eyes—because I'd probably fall asleep and then fall to death number four.

As the sun crept over the horizon, the dragon glided just above the clouds, keeping us concealed from prying eyes below. The world beneath us began to stir with the sounds of life: birds scavenging for fish, the rhythmic clang of bells, boots thudding on creaky docks, and sharp voices barking orders. It was the unmistakable clamor of a fishing village waking up.

Peering over the dragon's side, I caught glimpses of a small port town through the breaks in the mist. For a moment, I thought it might be Relna Thune, but the absence of towering mountains and the modest size of the settlement quickly proved me wrong.

As we veered slightly out to sea, the clouds thinned, and through a break, I spotted something that made my stomach lurch—the wreckage of the Alkonost, partially submerged in the shallow waters. The two Irkallan ships that had rammed us were nowhere to be seen, likely long gone.

That port below must have been the Alkonost's destination. And if that were true, then Oceantis had to be out in the sea to the west.

I leaned forward and dug my heel into the dragon's side, hoping to steer him in the direction of the port.

He let out a low, guttural growl, his massive head snapping around to glare at me. His orange eyes flared with irritation, and I froze. Determined to make his point, he twisted slightly, making sure I knew I'd get no control over him.

Irritated but resigned, I stopped kicking, gripping his scales tighter as he continued his steady flight.

"Take me to Nibiru!" I shouted, wanting to call him by a name... but he didn't have one.

"Hey, I need to call you something," I screamed over the roar of the wind. "Bob?! Bob's a good name. Can I call you Bob?!"

He might have shivered a little. But that could have been my imagination.

"No, you don't look like a Bob..."

He was a proud, noble creature who demanded respect. He needed a distinguished... dragony name. Draco popped into my brain, which was Latin for dragon. Drake? No, this dragon was too cool for a name like Drake. Draco Rex was Latin for *dragon king*.

"Rex! I'm going to call you Rex!"

When I got no response, the matter was settled. He had a name now. Even though he most likely couldn't even tell I was there, I stroked the hard scales and wrapped my arms tight around his neck. And for the first time since I had come to this world, I knew I had finally done something right.

Once out over the Triton Sea, I was completely lost. I took a quick look behind us to see we were headed away from the rising sun, so we *were* going west. I don't know how, but Rex seemed to know where he was headed. He had to flap hard to fight the strong wind currents. He would fly up high for a bit and then would drop lower in the air, trying to find the least resistance. The dragon had to be exhausted, but he was determined to get me to the island.

By the late afternoon, Oceantis appeared on the horizon.

"Welcome to Oceantis, my friend!"

I patted the dragon, pointed toward land, and urged him on with both my boot heels.

I had been away on my deadly adventure for at least a month. Maybe more. Excitement grew as we approached the island. I missed having

Pherric by my side, teaching me as much as he could. Kasuma sneaking up on me. And I really missed Braylor's big handsome face. But how mad were they going to be at me for running off like that?

My excitement was nearly unbearable as the realization hit me—*all the rulers of the kingdoms might be on Nibiru.* Meeting with King Longzhe. The thought ignited a vivid daydream: flying up on Rex, my magnificent black dragon, to the lawn outside the King's meeting hall. I could almost feel the weightlessness as I leapt off his back, landing in front of the gathered rulers with all the swagger I could muster.

Imagine their faces!

I'd stride into the center of the proceedings, delivering the ultimate surprise. *We had Rex on our side!* Pherric would probably nod approvingly, maybe even let slip one of his rare, smug smiles. Kasuma would give me that subtle look, like she knew this was exactly what I'd been born to do. And Braylor? Oh, he'd find something to complain about—probably that the dragon wasn't blue.

As Rex and I circled the floating city, he scanned for threats, his massive head swiveling with each beat of his wings.

"Stop flying around, Rex! You're going to ruin the big reveal!" I called out, kicking his sides in a futile attempt to get him to climb above the clouds for a stealthier entrance.

He ignored me completely. Of course.

Satisfied there were no archers lurking about, Rex swept under the floating city and along the monolith that supported it. Then, with a mighty burst of his wings, he rose and landed gracefully on the narrow lawn outside the long white hall with open arches.

I slid off his back, adrenaline surging. But as soon as my feet hit the grass, Rex reared back, spreading his wings to take off again.

"No! Don't go!" I shouted, leaping after him and grabbing hold of his neck. My hands clung to his smooth, steel-like scales. "I want to show you off!"

Rex responded with a deafening howl, his wings stretching wide as he shook me off. I landed on the lawn in an ungraceful heap.

Taking a deep breath, I pushed myself up, brushing off the dirt with a confident grin. I was still determined to make my grand entrance.

Turning away from Rex, I marched toward the nearest archway, my heart pounding with anticipation.

I did *not* anticipate the flat-out panic that ensued.

Screams echoed out from inside the hall. A throng of people scrambled away, slipping and sliding on the shiny floor as they pushed others out of the way.

"Whoa! It's okay!" I yelled. "He's with me!"

I held up my hands as several Tenguan soldiers rushed onto the lawn with spears and bows in hand.

"No, no, no!"

People fled from the nearby buildings, swarmed out of the towers, rushed further into the cloud city.

Pherric emerged from an arch, his arms reaching out to me. "Run, Finley!"

Braylor stormed out, a sword gripped in his huge hand and a battle cry on his lips.

I turned and bolted back to Rex. "Go! Fly away! Go!"

The dragon, fearing for me, dropped his head low and bared his teeth. He snarled at those brave enough to approach.

"Fly now, Rex! Get out of here!"

I ran to him, pushing hard against the scales on his chest. With another piercing scream, he arched back and flapped his wings. Several spears and a few arrows bounced off as he took flight. The rushing wind knocked me back.

Pherric rushed to my side, helping me to my feet. "Finley! Are you hurt?!"

Several Tenguans took flight, firing arrows as they chased after Rex. I even saw old King Longzhe the Seventh come rushing out from the hall with a kath spear shaking in his weathered hands.

"No!" I yelled at them, as Pherric held me back. "Leave him alone!"

"What are you doing, girl?!" a panting Braylor barked at me.

I watched until the dragon had flown clear and the Tenguans returned to the city.

A hundred archers emerged from every structure and spread out along the edges of Nibiru, prepared to battle the black beast. But the dragon flew up into the bright sky.

My heart broke for Rex. Tears ran down my filthy cheeks, as exhaustion and emotion bombarded me all at once.

As I fell, Braylor reached out for me. He pulled me in close, hesitantly patting my back.

"Fin! You have returned," he whispered. "You are here. I never thought I would see you again."

I looked way up at the big brute. "You're... actually happy to see me?"

There was warmth in those dark brown eyes. He wasn't crying but there was maybe some moisture there.

Braylor laughed off his caring look and held me at arm's length. To my shock, he lifted me off the ground and above his head. He spun me, set me down, and hugged me tight to his chest.

"I am not... unhappy to see you, girl."

"You ruin everything, Braylor."

"This is a well-known fact," he declared.

He held on to me as I sobbed, smiling at the same time.

Chapter 86

Oh, I knew the lectures were coming. And holy *hell*, did they bring the full TED Talk series.

Once the dragon flew off, everyone managed to calm down *just* enough to drag me into the hall for my interrogation. I gave them the full story—how I'd been dead twice, revived in the Valley of the Black Bones, and then somehow convinced a dragon to fly me to Oceantis. Instead of being impressed, they let me know *exactly* how idiotic it was to track down a dragon and lead it to their precious hidden sanctuary.

The Tenguans were furious. Apparently, I'd compromised their super-secret lair. I hit back with the obvious: *Rex already knew where it was! He didn't need my help to find it!*

Pherric, in full dramatic mode, reminded me that dragons had killed most of their ancestors and loved ones. Yeah, *thanks for the reminder,* buddy—I've also been on the wrong end of a dragon attack. Twice.

Kasuma came at me with a series of sanity-check questions that, honestly, I couldn't even argue with. She thought I was nuts, and she might've been right.

Braylor, though—classic Braylor—refused to say anything coherent. He'd stomp up, his face bright red, point a giant finger at me, start mumbling incoherently like some angry dad who forgot his line, and storm off.

After about an hour of nonstop scolding, they finally let me clean up. I scrubbed off every last speck of gore, soaked until I pruned, and crashed for a solid twelve hours.

When I finally woke up, I was at least 30% less of a disaster. Progress.

Late in the morning, I threw on an off-white blouse and black cloth leggings—simple and functional. My old boots were beyond saving, but a Tenguan butler managed to scrounge up a pair of knee-high leather boots. They were a bit snug, but they worked. At least I'd had the presence of mind to rescue Temurr's flint from my old boots before they got tossed.

Standing on a terrace overlooking the small Nibiru harbor, I counted over a dozen large ships moored in the calm, light blue sea. After scarfing down some fruit, I wandered toward the hall, curious to eavesdrop on the diplomatic talks.

Kasuma helped me navigate past the newly installed security detail—because apparently, the sudden arrival of a dragon had everyone on edge. For some reason.

Inside, the Tenguan king sat in his usual spot at the long table by the open arches, but this time his court had been replaced by leaders from the various kingdoms and nations.

One stood out immediately—a Fomorian who wasn't Braylor. He was taller by a head, with a more prominent brow and a wide nose. A heavy, dull-metal crown rested on his bluish-black mane, and his finely groomed beard draped over his sizable, round belly. His chair had been replaced with a bench to hold his weight, so he fidgeted on the hard wood surface.

Next to him, the Valhallan chieftain was the embodiment of Viking lore—broad-shouldered and imposing, with a silver helmet resting on the table beside him. His other hand stroked his long, braided white beard as he leaned heavily to one side in his chair, sighing loudly in protest of whatever discussion was unfolding. Every exaggerated breath practically screamed, *Can we get this over with already?* Diplomacy, it seemed, was not a universal skill.

I leaned over to Kasuma. "Who's the Valhallan?"

"That is Jarl Trym Baldrson of Vanaheimr."

"Gunnr killed his son, right?"

"I believe so."

I felt someone bump into me from behind. I turned to look up at Braylor.

He ignored me, instead staring straight ahead.

Also at the table were several Hominan rulers. A dark-skinned woman, in a colorful poncho and a crown made from bones, lounged regally in her chair with a finger poised on her lower lip.

I whispered to Kasuma again. "Who is she? She seems fierce." She reminded me of Genevieve.

She nodded. "Urraca. Queen of Ogun." Then added, "To the far south and east."

A curly-haired brute drank from a wood stein like an Irishman at an open bar wedding, holding out his empty cup every few minutes for a minion to refill.

A very young, astoundingly handsome Spanish-looking man struggled to keep his eyes open as he slid further down into his chair. If I had to guess, he was from Cíbola. He looked a lot like Pherric.

The Atlanteans were noticeably absent. Again.

At the center of the room stood a thick wooden table bearing a massive map of the known world. Strategically placed carved figurines of warriors and ships marked the positions of troops, a grim visual of the conflict raging across the continent.

Beside the table stood the Prominan King, supported by both the table's edge and sheer willpower. His tall frame, even larger than Temurr's, seemed diminished under the weight of exhaustion and war. His once-glossy gray fur was dull and matted, his sunken eyes rimmed with fatigue.

"That must be King Kwong," I murmured, a faint smile tugging at my lips.

Kwong looked like he hadn't slept in days, yet his determination shone through his wearied face. As he turned toward the gathered rulers, his gaze briefly flicked to me, sharp and assessing, before returning to the matter at hand.

"Now is our chance!" he declared, his deep voice carrying across the hall. "I have reports that Malek is personally overseeing his troops in the invasion of our land. He is no longer hiding behind the hidden walls of the Black City."

The room buzzed with murmurs and exchanged glances. Even in his battered state, Kwong's words struck a chord—a rare opportunity, but also a monumental risk.

The king pointed to a spot on the map, at a wood warrior statue standing on the east side of Kunlun.

"Like a coward, he is not fighting among his troops, but has set up a command post at the rear guard. Here, at the Gods' Eyes." Kwong tapped the map with a bony finger. "If we strike him down now—while he is exposed—we may be able to end this terror!"

The black queen with the bone crown leaned forward. "You must appreciate our position, your majesty. I need to protect my land and my people."

Kwong bowed his head. "And by 'your people', I take that to mean—"

"Take no meaning from that!" Urraca said, slapping her hand on the table. "My kingdom! My people!"

The primate king stood as tall as he could, composed himself, and stepped around from behind the table.

"Then I implore you to help us. I will drop to my knees and beg, if that is what you require. For *my* people," he said, his gravelly voice barely above a whisper.

The Valhallan king leaned forward in his chair. "But, what you ask of us—"

"I ask for life! For survival! Nothing more... Malek aims to put an end to my entire race! He has already wiped out nearly all the Bànshēn rén, and knows that if he attacks us one by one, he will encounter minimal resistance!"

The old Prominan fell into a coughing fit, shuffling back to the table for support. All the rulers looked away from him.

King Longzhe thumped the table several times for attention, giving the Prominan a chance to recover. "I have already committed my army to your defense, King Kwong. And I ask that the others do the same. Malek is building an empire. Of that there is no doubt. And I know you all fear the eventual ramifications of his actions."

The Fomorian king laughed. "We fear nothing! Let Malek try to take our land!"

"Your bravado aside, King Dagda, he has at least fifty thousand troops at his disposal," Longzhe told him. "His troops are well-trained and fortified. Malek is organized, funded, and motivated. He is not the fool we believed him to be. And once he has conquered the Prominans, he will surely turn on every other nation. While the fighting skills of the Fomorians are renowned, quantity will eventually overcome quality, Dagda. And then you will be in the same situation as the Prominans."

"Well, if that were the case, I would never drag my tail into this hall to beg for help. Never!" bellowed the Fomorian.

Some in the gathered crowd gasped. The primate king was enraged. He snarled, crouched low as if ready to leap on the massive king.

Longzhe pounded the table. "Silence! Silence!"

The murmuring subsided, but King Dagda kept his thick hands on the sides of his bench, ready to leap over the table at his old foe.

Kwong's guards held him back, but eventually relented.

I made my way closer to the table. Braylor followed behind me, keeping me within arm's reach.

"This is neither the time nor the place for infighting and bickering!" The Tenguan king snapped, trying to regain control. "This is exactly what Malek desires!"

Dagda leaned back on his uncomfortable bench, crossing his arms and nodding to Longzhe; the closest he could come to an apology.

The drunken ruler of Elysium, with the curly red hair, cleared his throat. "Our host is correct. Malek is not quite the idiot we thought him to be. We have fought so hard to survive—all of us—for so long. Our people have sacrificed greatly to be where we are now. But because we were focused on protecting ourselves, the clever bastard is striking out now before we have a chance to unite and create coalitions. Our people are weary and, to be quite honest, ready to be conquered. There is little fight left in them."

"So you are suggesting we yield?" asked the dark-skinned queen Urraca. "Let Malek play the role of emperor?!"

"Ah, so there does seem to be a little fight left in *you*!" teased the red-haired king. "And, no, I do not suggest we accede to Irkallan rule. I am merely stating the obvious."

"What is your suggestion, King Ferghas?" asked Longzhe.

Ferghas, the curly-haired king, exhaled and took another long drink. He wiped his mouth on his sleeve. "All species in our world have the right to survive. As such, we have an obligation to protect each other. As the Fomorians need our help now, I know that King Dagda will surely acknowledge—"

"Do not put words in my mouth, Ferghas!"

Ferghas showed all his teeth with an odd smile. "The Fomorians would appreciate our combined support when Malek attacks their kingdom. As sure as the sun rises every morning, he will come for all of our lands. Our resources. And our people. Once he has us under his control, he will be too strong for us to rise up against and overthrow. I have heard tell that the Irkallan king is now immortal. Meaning he could rule over us... for a thousand years or more."

Urraca nodded but remained unconvinced. "Continue."

I was unsure where this was headed. I looked back at Braylor and whispered. "Here it comes..."

Braylor grunted. "Do not say a word, Fin."

Kasuma placed her winged hand over my hand.

"But as everyone has pointed out—Malek is no fool. Since he knows we are all meeting here, he would suspect that some or all of us will band forces. And he would realize that if we come to the aid of the Prominans, our lands will be left defenseless," said King Ferghas. "So, I propose we commit... a percentage of our troops to this cause. While some might feel this is a compromise, we will be making a concerted effort to end Malek's reign."

Kwong turned to his map table, pointing at Kunlun. "This is madness! Malek is camped right here! Out in the open, at the Gods' Eyes! Are we to ignore this opportunity!"

Every ruler stayed silent. Some lowered their heads, avoiding eye contact with the heartbroken Prominan.

The queen beamed, turning to Longzhe, her voice smooth and commanding. "Yes, I agree with King Ferghas' proposal. We will request volunteers from our soldiers and send those troops to aid the Prominans, with the goal of pushing Malek back into his territory—"

"*Volunteers?!*" My outrage erupted before I could stop myself.

"Finley…" Braylor warned, his voice low and sharp.

Kasuma closed her eyes, a pained expression crossing her face as she lowered her head.

"Are you *crazy?!*" I shouted, loud enough for the entire hall to hear.

The room went dead silent. King Dagda's glare could have melted steel, and Jarl Trym's fists clenched so tightly I thought he might shatter the table. Even Longzhe, the unshakable Tenguan king, looked away, avoiding my eyes.

Queen Urraca, however, slowly straightened in her chair, her sharp gaze locking onto me like a hawk spotting prey. "Does the… *dragonwitch* have something to add?" she said, her words dripping with venom.

The air shifted, heavy with tension. Gasps rippled through the hall, and every single person except Kasuma and Braylor took a step back from me.

"Ignore her!" growled Ferghas, his voice like a rumble of distant thunder.

"I *do* have something to—"

Before I could finish, a massive hand clamped over my mouth—actually, my entire face.

"She has nothing to add," Braylor announced, his deep voice cutting through the silence.

I struggled against him, clawing at his fingers, but he was unyielding. Lifting me effortlessly, he turned and carried me from the hall like I weighed nothing.

The crowd parted in a stunned hush, making way for the hulking Fomorian as I kicked and screamed muffled protests into his palm.

It was pointless.

I had officially been removed from the meeting.

Chapter 87

"What did you expect?" grumbled Braylor. He had to drag me out of the hall, down the cobblestone street, and into a nearby tavern.

I fought him every step of the way, kicking and flailing, but he was unmoved.

When we finally reached the tavern, Pherric was waiting for us at a corner table. Braylor unceremoniously dropped me onto a bench and planted himself firmly between me and the door, ensuring I couldn't make an escape. With a grunt, he waved to an elderly Tenguan woman serving drinks.

The tavern was a world away from the dank hole in Relna Thune. Clean, well-lit, and surprisingly welcoming, it bustled with a noon crowd mostly made up of foreign aides and a smattering of guards. Thankfully, no one seemed to recognize *the dragonwitch.* Small miracles.

"I don't know what I expected," I finally muttered, throwing my arms up. "But they're *completely* dodging the problem!"

Pherric barely glanced up, his gaze fixed on the cup of wine he hadn't touched. "Permit me to hazard a guess," he said dryly. "They each vowed to send a token number of their forces to placate the Prominans... and, more importantly, to ease their own consciences."

"Yeah! Exactly! How did you know?" I asked, exasperated.

He sighed. "Because they are, quite simply, avoiding risk."

The server returned, setting two cups of wine on the table. Without hesitation, I grabbed one and downed half in a single gulp, letting the burn settle in my chest.

That meeting had gone about as well as everything else in my life.

"They are punk-ass bitches, if you ask me."

"Despite that, it is a smart tactic," said Pherric, staring at and spinning his wine cup. "I encountered a similar aversion to risk when trying to recruit our team."

"Don't they understand what's at stake?!" I implored, finishing my wine and waving my empty cup at the server.

"They know the consequences. Nearly all of the kingdoms have lost an entire generation of warriors, who fought against the dragons and torodans, trying to make the world a safer place for their next generations. Malek's ascendancy was aided by the fact that we have been beaten down by those creatures for so long, there is little will left to fight."

"In other words, the little idiot's timing is perfect." The cup was so tiny in Braylor's hand.

Pherric nodded. "Aye. If these rulers commit all their forces to fighting against him and he wins, their people will be judged harshly by this upstart emperor. They will also be left without an army to protect their kingdom."

I slammed my fist on the wood surface, rattling our cups and garnering looks from all those busy whispering at their tables.

"But if we don't fully commit, the plan *will* fail! He'll topple every kingdom one by one. Everyone loses no matter what..."

"That is why I had hoped we might be successful in our attempt to assassinate Malek. I knew every other course of action, short of a full-scale war, would be in vain."

"You could have shared that with us, you know," snorted Braylor.

"And add more pressure to our tenuous endeavor? Not wise, I would think."

Braylor pointed his big finger in my face. "But you... You!"

"What?"

"Why did you run off, only to bring back a *dragon* of all the horrid beasts?! What madness infected your mind, girl?"

"Are you still on that? I thought we'd moved on." I sulked on my stool.

That fiasco certainly didn't have the intended effect. "I have no idea. I really don't know."

"I believe you do, actually."

"What do you mean?"

"You had a calling, did you not?"

I thought about it for half a second. "Yeah, I... I think I kinda did. I was pulled to seek out that dragon. A voice even spoke to me."

Braylor grabbed my chin, inspected my eyes. I slapped his hand away. "You see? Her mind is infected. She is demented." With that, I took his cup of wine away and downed it.

"You heard a voice? In a mindform?" asked Pherric, slightly stunned.

"Y-yes. Is that a, um... is that bad?"

"I do not know. Honesty. Remember that we are—"

"We're in uncharted territory. Yeah. That's what has me worried." I wanted to lay my head on the table and cry. Why couldn't someone just tell me what the hell was going on?

"You have died. *Three* times now, correct?"

"Yes. In the arena and twice by... the dragon."

Braylor gave me that look my father would give after seeing my bad grades—for the seventh straight semester.

"From what I have read, those who take the immortality potion never actually die. You have died and returned several times because... I did not administer the true potion. You may be more in tune with people. Or..."

That freaked me out. "Or what?"

"You may even be able to sense those who have drawn their last breath. Accessed the energy—in their realm—that envelopes our world."

"Great. So now I'm a psychic who talks to the dead?! I just need candles and a crystal ball and I'll hold seances. You can chat with your Aunt Myrtle and find out where she buried the cash in the backyard!"

Kasuma appeared at our table, setting down a bottle of green liquor.

"To celebrate." She pulled up a stool.

"Celebrate what?" queried Braylor, raising a big eyebrow up at her. "Their compromise to send volunteer troops seems an empty gesture, at best."

Ignoring him, Kasuma placed both hands on my forearm. "You managed to get those rulers to commit soldiers!"

"Yeah. Volunteer soldiers," I said.

"That is more than I expected. I thought they would laugh and return to their realms and wait to be attacked. But the leaders know these are dark times indeed. Something is better than nothing."

"How long before their troops can arrive to help the Prominans? Months?" asked Braylor.

"Ah, my king was clever on that point!" Kasuma lit up. "Rather than wait for the rulers to return to their lands, he had them issue their orders on parchment. Tenguans will fly off this evening to personally deliver the requests directly to the commanders in each kingdom. Whoever volunteers will be dispatched immediately!"

I leaned in close. "What are we talking? A couple thousand soldiers?"

"If that," said Braylor. "And the quality of soldiers will be in question."

"What?! This is crazy? We just have to *hope* people show up to fight!?"

"It is in the hands of the makers now," Kasuma sighed.

Chapter 88

The false metallic moon of Tir Na bathed Nibiru in its cold, ethereal blue light, casting long shadows across the floating city's pristine white towers. Braylor and I stumbled out of the tavern, the quiet streets oddly peaceful compared to the frustration of the day.

Kasuma had disappeared hours earlier, dashing off to ensure the Tengu messengers were prepared for their journeys to the other kingdoms. Pherric, ever the pragmatist, gave up on us after we polished off Kasuma's bottle of revolting green booze and ordered more drinks. I couldn't blame him for bailing. The two of us had closed the place down, much to the chagrin of the elderly server who'd been sweeping the floors around our table.

"Should've paced myself," I muttered, my head spinning slightly as we staggered along the flagstone path toward our tower.

Braylor chuckled, a low rumble that sounded more amused than drunk. His massive hand rested on my shoulder, steadying me as my arm looped around his waist for support. Despite his sheer size, even he wasn't walking straight, his heavy boots scuffing the stones with every step.

Shadows shifted as we passed under arched walkways and low-hanging terraces, the faint smell of seawater carried on the breeze.

We laughed at some dumb joke I told, loud and unsteady, the sound echoing off the white stone walls. Somewhere in the distance, a pair of Tengu wings flapped, the sound fading into the night.

By the time we reached the tower, both of us were leaning on each other more than we probably cared to admit.

"Oh, I'm gonna regret this in the morning," I slurred.

"Regret nothing, little one! Memories have been made this day!"

"Um, I don't think you know how drinking works, Braylor. I won't remember shit."

His boot slipped and he started to fall. I tried to catch him, but wisely let go. He smashed hard on the smooth stone walkway.

"Ach! That stings," he said, rubbing his sore nose. "Thank you for your sad attempt to save me."

"Hey, no sense both of us going down! Tryin' to stop you is like tryin' to stop a falling boulder."

I guided him to his feet.

"Hmm. Nibiru not only floats..." He belched. "It also spins in circles!"

"I, uh, think that might just be us."

We laughed till we snorted. Well, I snorted. He shook his head to clear the cobwebs, pulling me over to sit on the white stone wall that lined our path.

"Wait, wait, wait!" he roared. "Where is *Other Sword*?!"

"What other sword?"

"The one I bought for you? In Thelna Ru—in Relna Thune?"

"I, uh.... left it behind. When the dragon carried me off to the Valley of Black Bones."

"So, you have lost *Sword* and *Other Sword*? Fin, that is unacceptable!" He slapped his knee, shaking his head in mock disappointment.

"We'll just have to get me another sword!" I said, feeling myself sway back and forth as if fighting a strong breeze.

"*Other Other* Sword?"

"Yes."

"You may not be worthy if you cannot hold on to your weapons..."

I exhaled deeply.

"What bothers you, Finley?"

"I feel helpless. Again. All those kings and queens gathered here and decided to do very little. Practically nothing!"

"What do you want to do?"

I had no idea. Opening my mouth, I found no words. Then I had an incredibly dumb thought. "Why don't we—you and me—sneak off and kill Malek ourselves!"

He laughed. "You are a strange one, Fin."

"I'm serious! We know where he is! He's in Kunlun! The god-eye thingy they were talking about!" As drunk as I was, the idea seemed to make sense. "We could sneak into their camp and kill Malek! Then... boom! It's all over! No more emperor wannabe!"

"Simply sneak in and execute him? Sounds easy enough..."

I heard none of his sarcasm. "You're right. He's immortal now. It won't be easy. But you! You're Braylor! You could kill him!"

"And you are a drunken halfwit. I cannot believe you are serious!" He held up my chin, inspecting my eyes. "Ah, you have the warlust now."

"Warlust? Yeah, that's not a thing. You just made that up."

"You have tasted battle. You have killed. And now you crave that feeling, that excitement. I will say that you have done well. Surprisingly well."

"Would you, um, say that I'm a *warrior* now?" I giggled, fishing for a compliment.

"Now? You have always been a warrior, little one."

That shocked me. "What? But you said I was a small, *podgy* child who—in no way—could ever help our cause!"

He gave me a wink, only... both of his eyes closed. The blue moonlight cast such a beautiful glow on his thick features and black hair.

"I expected Pherric to seek out a classic soldier, trained for battle. But, instead, he brought us... a warrior."

I blushed as he tapped his finger on my forehead.

"Up here," he added. "Here... you are stronger than ten. You have a determination I have rarely seen before. A drive to learn, grow, improve, and never stop fighting. We need to fight to stay alive, but you.... you want to win. I have never seen such optimism. With a hundred of you, I could rule the world!"

"I have never thought of myself as someone who could be a warrior, you know? Never..."

"Everyone alive today has the potential. It is in our blood!" he shouted.

His mouth was ridiculously kissable. And those adorable lips.

"What do you mean?"

"We come from warriors, Fin. You exist today because everyone in your line was a strong and brave survivor."

I thought back to the story Pherric had told me of my ancient ancestor, Fionn mac Cumhaill. How he had been taught to not only survive, but thrive. And shine. To be a warrior.

"And your courage?!" Braylor chuckled to himself. "You sought out a *dragon*! On your own. That is most impressive. Stupid... but impressive."

"There's a fine line between bravery and stupidity."

"People never change, Fin. It is impossible. Only what may be hidden deep inside is ever revealed. But there is no change."

I gave a knowing nod, with a memory surfacing that felt oddly fitting. There was a sign that hung in my grandfather's police station, one I used to see every time I visited him. He told me it had been there since September 2001, and that the words came from a poem by Mary Anne Radmacher.

The banner read: *Courage doesn't always roar. Sometimes courage is the quiet voice at the end of the day saying, 'I will try again tomorrow.'*

Those words had always lingered in the back of my mind, but now they struck me differently. I understood them. Courage wasn't about being fearless or invincible—it was about showing up, no matter how scared or broken you felt.

I might get scared, my heart pounding like a drum, but I couldn't let fear, or anyone, or *anything,* hold me back. Not anymore.

I would try again. And again. Because now I knew—I could never not try.

"Well, the whole dragon thing was a mistake. It seemed to make things worse."

"No. Not a mistake. Your act was indeed dangerous. But, by doing so, you revealed your true self to me."

He turned to me and I fell into those deep, dark eyes of his.

"I am sorry for doubting you."

I stood up, swaying on my feet until he grabbed my forearm. I climbed up on the stone wall, face-to-face with my massive Fomorian.

"Promise me we will go find Malek? And kill him…"

"You know that would not be wise, Fin."

"I need you by my side. One more time."

I stared at his lips.

"Says the one who does not die."

I pressed against him, wrapping my arms around his neck. He stayed close.

"I—"

"Shh! Shh. Just kiss me, idiot."

And kiss me he did. I melted into him, holding his face in my hands.

He pulled away, trying to control himself. I smiled at him and he kissed my eyelid, then my cheek. But my lips found his and drew him back in. His moan filled my ears as he kissed me.

On that stone path, as I stood on the white wall under the false moon, and as his strong hands explored my body and then his lips found my neck, I was his for the taking.

Early in the morning, with the sun still hiding below the Triton Sea, I woke in Braylor's bed. Still slightly drunk from our night out. A chilly breeze blew through his tower apartment, so I reached for him, wanting him to warm me. But Braylor was not in bed. I pulled a silk sheet around my body and padded across the room.

He stood on the balcony, his huge arm resting on the stone arch, silhouetted by the fading moonlight. I could hear waves crashing well below us on the black sandy beach. He glanced over his shoulder as I wrapped my arms around his waist.

"Did I wake you?" he asked.

I kissed the rough skin on his back. My fingers traced along the old scars that I had felt for the first time only a few hours earlier.

"Only by not being in bed," I purred.

He spun around to face me, but looked away when he saw my smile.

"What?" I asked, worried. "What's wrong?"

"Last night," he murmured. "Last night was a mistake."

I reached up and pulled his chin so he could face me. "I don't understand. Last night was great!"

"We were drunk and it was foolish and... and I took advantage of our friendship, but it will not happen again—"

"Whoa! Wait a minute. In vino veritas, big boy! In wine, there is truth. We didn't do anything we both didn't want to do. This isn't about that... what's going on?"

He backed away to avoid my eyes, leaning on the balcony railing.

"It is... it is simply not right... for us to be... together."

My hands went straight to my head. "Oh, is this about that hybridization shit? *You should only mate with your own species* or whatever? Let me guess—your people, the Fomorians, forbid it?! You're too good for me, dude? Is that it?"

He shook his head, staring down at the island.

"I am not too good for anyone, Fin."

I turned him to face me, pointing a finger in his face. "Bullshit! You are the most amazing person I have ever met. You can be a dick sometimes... but you are smart and strong and fearless! Everything I wish I could be!"

He gave me a pity smile, laying his big hand gently against my cheek. The hurt in his eyes crushed my soul.

"Why—what's going on in that thick skull of yours?"

"Finley... I have never told anyone this, not in our group especially. But... I am a hybrid. And I have lived with that shame my entire life."

"A hybrid of what?"

"My mother was Fomorian. My father... a Hominan," he said, exhaling deeply. "Other species usually do not realize this, but Fomorians do."

"So what? What does it matter?"

"It matters a great deal. I am an outcast. A mongrel. An embarrassment to my kind."

The giant Fomorian slave at the mines of Hell called him a mongrel.

And Braylor was smaller than every other Fomorian I had seen so far. He truly was persona non grata among his people.

"Again... so what?! Just because they don't like you, it doesn't mean—"

"They are my people, Fin. If I have any hope of ever being accepted by them, then..."

Anger rushed through me. "Then you can't be with me?! Yeah, I see. You really are too good for me, aren't you?"

"That is not what I am saying—"

"Yes, it is, Braylor! That's exactly what you're saying! Because what you really need is to find yourself a nice Fomorian female and have little Fomorian babies and then maybe they'll welcome you home with open arms! That's your plan and I don't fit into it. Doesn't matter that I care for you! A great deal! I was just a good time for a night!"

"I told you... this was a mistake."

"You're damn right, it was!" I burned hot as dragonfire.

He reached for me, but I pulled away. "I care for you, Finley. More than you will know."

"Just not enough! If you cared enough, then none of this shit would matter!"

"Family, community, our culture. It is very important to my people. I know that family is not as important to you, so you do not understand—"

"No! Wrong. Well, I mean... my family—the people who gave birth to me—are not important to me! They made me feel worthless and left me alone to fend for myself because I was too much of a bother. What they really wanted was a trophy to set on their mantle. Something to make them look good. But you guys... *you* are my family now." Queue the tears.

"But have you ever wanted something so much that it hurt? That you would give your life to attain it? And you—"

"Yes, Braylor. I have... I finally have a purpose in my stupid life. I now have all of you and I want to help so goddamn much that I would do anything! For Pherric, Temurr, Kasuma and... and especially you. And I have given my life trying to help! I have died—over and over—trying to save you and your people. I even brought a fucking dragon to help!"

I turned away, hiding my face as the tears streamed. I heard him step toward me, so I crossed my arms. He stopped in his tracks.

Braylor returned to the balcony railing. We stood there in silence, unsure of what to do or say. The tension filled the room like a thin layer of smoke, creating a barrier between us. One that we could have moved through... if we wanted.

He suddenly grew restless, pacing the balcony. He wanted out of the room. Away from me.

"None of this matters at all, you and I, in the end."

"What does that mean?"

"Because you will be who you are. You will take matters into your own hands. Yet again," he seethed.

"What are you talking about?" I stammered.

"You are going to sneak away and try to kill Malek. I know you, Fin. You cannot help yourself. And your foolishness will get you captured. Or worse... killed."

"But, I—"

"Yes, yes. I know. You do not stay dead. But if Malek burns your body, or has you quartered, I doubt you would return." His eyes closed as he envisioned my death in a raging fire.

"Where is all this coming from?"

I took a tentative step toward him, reaching out instinctively, wanting to touch his arm, to calm him. But Braylor moved back from the balcony, his massive frame stiff with tension. His hand shot out, pointing down toward the island below.

"He is still here..." His voice was low, a rumble filled with foreboding.

"Who?" I asked, my voice barely above a whisper.

I stepped closer to the railing, peering out into the darkness. The faint outlines of tropical trees swayed in the wind, hundreds of feet below.

"What are you talking—"

"There," he interrupted, his voice sharp, insistent.

I leaned out further, straining to see. At first, it was just shadows among the trees, the wind playing tricks with the shapes. But then my eyes caught it—a massive, curved form, nestled in a glade, its silhouette barely visible in the moonlight.

"He awaits," Braylor's words dripped with resignation.

My breath caught as I followed the line of his long finger, my gaze locking on the shape. A dark mass shifted slightly, the faintest ripple of movement in the stillness below.

"Rex..." I breathed, the name escaping my lips like a secret I wasn't sure I should say out loud. The black dragon laid silently in the grass.

So many questions crashed into me, my mind racing to make sense of what I was seeing.

But Braylor's voice snapped me back. He stepped further into the shadows, his expression unreadable. "You are frustrated with the leaders' refusal to commit, and you have the patience of a child. These traits will lead to your doom. I cannot stay to watch it happen."

Tears blurred my vision, but I wiped them away, my focus locked on the massive shape below.

I spun around, ready to demand answers, to plead if I had to—but Braylor was gone, swallowed by the darkness as if he'd never been there at all.

Chapter 89

G *o.*

The voice returned. Inside my head, waking me from a deep sleep.

After seeing the dragon sleeping on the forest floor, I curled up in a chair and recounted all the ways I screwed up my conversation with Braylor. I got angry when I should have been understanding. I made it about me when I needed to focus on his pain. So many things I could have said. Or just kept my fat mouth shut. And I fell asleep at some point.

Alone in his apartment, I let that vague whisper float around in my mind. My pulse fluttered as a cold chill ran down me.

Go.

"Go where?" I shouted at the white plaster ceiling.

I recalled the talks with all the kings and queens. They said Malek was exposed. And that he's in eastern Kunlun. At some place called the Gods' Eyes. Was that where I was supposed to go? Was that my mission?

"You want me to face Malek? Alone?" I asked.

Nothing.

As it always does, a panic set in. I slid off the chair, crumpled into a ball. Was I ready to fight Malek? My confidence swirled away, down a tiny drain at the bottom of my brain.

Go.

"No!" I yelled. Tears formed as I shrank into an even smaller ball on the floor. "No..."

You faced off with a goddamn dragon—it was my own voice this time, screaming back at me.

I shivered in fear. Ice water coursed through my veins. Death no longer scared me—been there and done that—but there was that fear of... failure. Fear of losing. Again. Of letting everyone down. Yet again. Almost all I had ever done since I got here was fail.

"I'll get Braylor to help me," I whimpered to the voice that was in my head and a thousand axims away at the same time.

Go.

I screamed so loud it rattled the walls. I pounded my fists on the floor. And I screamed again until my raw throat was ready to bleed. But I needed to listen. Needed to go. In a rage, I rushed into his bathing room, poured cold water on my face, and splashed myself clean. And hated myself for washing away the scent of Braylor from my body.

I began searching the room for my clothes from the day before... but they were missing. Across the apartment, stacked neatly on a sofa, I saw a new outfit. Clothes that were meant for me. I sifted through them. There was a padded top and a long-sleeve chainmail shirt, some black leggings, a set of mail stockings and gloves, and a pair of long leather boots... all in my size.

A silver kath helmet laid next to the clothes, with a metal strip to protect my nose and a black dragon hand-painted on the sides. I stared at everything, as the tears fell. There was a small kath shield, a new belt, and a scabbard. A small piece of parchment paper had been pinched between the scabbard and the hilt of a sword.

I pulled the sword from the scabbard. The note read: *Other Other Sword.*

Sobbing uncontrollably, I held up the blade. The handle had been wrapped with the finest leather and the pommel made to look like a black dragon, with yellow gemstones for eyes.

He knew. Braylor knew I would climb on Rex and fly off. And try to kill Malek.

I wiped away the stream of tears. Staring at myself in his mirror, I got dressed. My courage grew with each new piece I put on.

Maybe I would let them down. I probably would fail.

So fucking what?

I will try again... today.

The noon sun beat down as I gathered my gear, slipping the piece of flint Temurr had given me into my boot—my small, secret good luck charm. He probably wouldn't have approved, but he'd have sent me off with that teasing wink and smile of his, so I kept it close anyway.

The path from the tower to the loading dock was eerily quiet. A few Tenguans flitted about their day, but I saw no one from my group. No Pherric. No Kasuma. And certainly no Braylor.

The sound of heavy wings snapped me out of my thoughts.

I glanced up, then all around, searching for the source, until Rex emerged from the sky. My heart leapt at the sight of him, his black scales gleaming in the sunlight as he landed on the surface of Nibiru with a powerful screech, declaring his presence.

I bowed my head low, showing respect. Rex stomped toward me, lowering his massive forehead to mine. The brief touch was rough and grounding. Smiling, I scratched the hard scales of his cheek and gave him a playful pat. He shoved me back with a nudge so strong my boots slid across the wooden slats of the dock.

"Easy, big guy," I muttered. "I need to use a rope, okay? I gotta hang on somehow."

I held up the thick cord, showing him my intent. Rex recoiled slightly, snorting his displeasure, but I kept my head low, holding it out until he cautiously sniffed at it. With a reluctant grunt, he gave a slight nudge, begrudgingly permitting it.

Working quickly, I tossed the rope over his back, tying it securely and adjusting the knot between his tall spines. I strapped my shield tight, slipped on my helmet, and prepared for the flight.

Rex let out a nervous howl, his head twisting to survey the narrow streets. I followed his gaze, watching for guards or screaming Tenguans, but the area remained unsettlingly quiet.

Then I saw him.

Braylor, standing on a rooftop garden, arms crossed, scowling down at me like a parent watching their kid make a terrible decision.

For reasons I couldn't explain—and would probably regret—I waved.

He didn't wave back. He just looked down, his scowl deepening, and turned away.

Biting my lip, I fought back tears and kicked Rex hard in the sides. He growled but spread his massive wings, readying for flight.

As we rose above the dock, I kept my eyes fixed on Braylor. Was this the last time I'd see him? I wanted to hold him again. I wanted to kiss him.

Just as Rex leveled with the rooftop, Braylor turned toward us. His arms still crossed, his face still set in that stubborn, unreadable mask, but he nodded to me. Then, slowly, he lifted his hand in a small wave.

It wasn't much, but it was enough.

Smiling through my tears, I urged Rex higher into the clouds. Tenguan guards rushed onto the dock below, bows in hand, but none drew arrows.

Rex's wings beat the air as we soared through the white clouds, leaving Nibiru behind. Leaving the island. Flying across the endless Triton Sea, toward whatever awaited us.

Go.

Chapter 90

We spent hours flying east over the ocean, the salty air stinging my face and harsh wind blasting my eyes until tears stained my cheeks, and then soared over the lush landscape of Kunlun.

As we weaved between the mountains and darkness started to envelop us, I shivered, but not just from the cold—the shorter nights brought chillier air, sure, but my trembling came from something deeper: I had no plan. None. Déjà vu all over again.

Sure, I had my so-called mission—find Malek. But that was it. And it scared me senseless. I mean, I'm not exactly the queen of meticulous planning, but flying headlong into enemy territory to confront an immortal king, likely surrounded by his entire army? Even *I* could admit how insanely dumb that was.

If Pherric was right, Malek couldn't be killed now. And me? I might die. I might come back, but when? Six months? A year? Or worse, what if Braylor's grim warning came true, and they diced me into tiny pieces and flambéed me? My death clock wasn't exactly reliable, and this whole idea was a farce.

And yet... there I was.

My one advantage... I had a dragon.

The second we started out, I yelled at Rex to take us toward the Gods' Eyes in Eastern Kunlun. Did I know where that was? Absolutely not. But Rex flew like he had a GPS in his head. Maybe the same voice squatting rent-free in *my* brain was whispering directions in his too.

The truth? I wasn't sure if I was steering this mission or just along for the ride.

We soared over the breathtaking city of Shangri-La, nestled at the far end of a long valley flanked by two towering mountain ranges. The city sat precariously perched on a rocky precipice, its edges framed by a powerful river that surged through the valley, cascading off the cliff in a thunderous waterfall that disappeared into the abyss below. Shangri-La was both majestic and protected—there was only one way in and one way out, a capital city that was as much a fortress as it was a sanctuary.

Above us, dark storm clouds devoured the false moon of Tir Na, shrouding the city in an eerie gloom. Rain began to lash against us, each drop stinging like icy needles. Because the gods just had to make it interesting, didn't they? Lightning splintered the night sky, illuminating the city in fleeting bursts of brilliance. Each crash of thunder reverberated through my chest, as if it were pounding against my ribcage, a reminder of just how small I was against the elements.

The driving rain slicked the rope in my hands and soaked me to the bone. The wind tugged hard at the shield strapped to my back, as though desperately trying to rip me free. I gritted my teeth, ducked lower against Rex's powerful neck, and clung tighter. Every flap of his wings cut through the gale, but the storm fought us every step of the way.

Kane was the unknown variable in my mission. He was an ally. And he wanted the same result I did. But I knew I couldn't count on his help—especially not with Malek's army all around. He told me he had to stay neutral. Maybe he could help in some way… like keeping those Irkallan soldiers off my back.

As we flew deeper into Kunlun, the grim reality of the war unfolded beneath us. Thousands of Malek's troops were advancing relentlessly through the harsh terrain—marching over hills, winding through dense forests, and maneuvering steep ravines like an unstoppable tide. In their wake were the remains of smoldering villages, their charred husks littered with fallen Prominan bodies.

The sight made my stomach churn and my fists tighten on the rope.

If only I could've taken the rulers for a ride on Rex, let them see this devastation firsthand. Maybe then they'd stop bickering and half-committing, and finally send all their forces to stop this craziness.

The fury within me surged like a wildfire. My blood boiled at the thought of them reaching the gates of Shangri-La in just a few weeks, turning the Prominan capital into their next ruin. If I could somehow take out Malek—if I could just *end* this invasion once and for all—

"Come on, Rex! Let's barbecue those bastards!" I shouted, kicking his sides and pulling at the rope to steer him toward the marching troops.

Rex grunted, his massive body unfazed by my urgency, and continued on his course. He didn't even glance down, as if the slaughter below was in the past and no longer mattered.

My frustration burned hotter. He was right, of course. There was nothing I could do about what had happened. But charging in with no plan, no real allies, was suicide. But that didn't make seeing the destruction from above any easier.

We made a wide, sweeping turn and began heading back west. I couldn't tell if Rex was lost and trying to correct his course, or if he wanted me to see the devastation that Malek's army had done. I had no idea. Either way, I wasn't in control—he was.

Through the rain, with the faint help of silvery moonlight filtering through the clouds, I spotted a sprawling camp ahead. Thousands of tents stretched out in orderly rows across a massive clearing, a hive of activity as soldiers dismantled their makeshift city to march farther west—closer to Shangri-La.

A sharp bolt of lightning split the sky, flashing so close that it left me blinking spots into the stormy darkness. When my vision cleared, a faint bluish glow appeared at the far end of the Irkallan camp. It stood out like a beacon against the dark shadows below.

Rex didn't hesitate. He adjusted his wings, angling toward the mysterious light. As we closed in, he soared higher into the storm clouds, shrouding us in mist to avoid detection.

From above, I peered through the gray haze and saw them: two luminous orbs standing side by side, casting their eerie glow over the rain-soaked ground. At first, they seemed simple, unassuming—just two circles in the ground. But the longer I stared, the more they transformed in my mind's eye, forming the unmistakable shape of an infinity symbol: ∞

The Gods' Eyes.

The black dragon circled wide before diving down toward the clearing. As we approached, the Gods' Eyes came into sharper focus. They weren't two circles, but they were eerily reminiscent of Stonehenge: two towering, rectangular columns capped with rounded globes that shot a horizontal beam connecting them at the top. But unlike the ancient rocks on Earth, this monument was crafted from a smooth, gleaming metal that seemed alive in its own right. A faint, white light emanated from its surface, casting an otherworldly glow across the rain-soaked grass.

The sight tugged at my imagination. Had someone, centuries ago, seen these very structures here on Tir Na and tried to replicate them back on Earth with stone? The thought gave me chills. These monoliths didn't belong to any human world—they were far too advanced, too precise.

Rex adjusted his wings, gliding lower toward the ground. My attention shifted to a massive, ornately decorated tent pitched near the glowing monoliths. It dwarfed every other structure in the camp, its size and embellishments leaving no doubt in my mind.

That was Malek's tent.

The dragon leveled off, wings beating heavily to slow our descent. My heart pounded. This wasn't just an army encampment; it was the heart of enemy operations. And I was about to drop straight into it.

"Blast that tent, Rex! Hit it with your flame! Let's end this now!" I shouted, kicking at his sides and tugging on the rope around his neck.

Rex? Unbothered. He roared a deafening war cry that echoed through the storm, shaking the air around us.

"No! Don't make noise! Shush!" I hissed, panic rising as my dragon completely ruined my genius plan.

As we descended, several guards spilled out of the massive tent, their weapons drawn, scanning the skies. And then, Malek himself strode out. His expression shifted from annoyance to pure smugness as he caught sight of us. He crossed his arms and grinned, like he'd been expecting us.

Rex landed with a heavy thud outside the nearest monolith, the ground trembling beneath his weight. The faint glow of the Gods' Eyes lit up the clearing, mixing with the silvery rain and the occasional crackle of lightning. The storm seemed to pause, like it wanted to frame the moment perfectly, complete with thunder that rattled my bones. But it was wet. And I was already scared—I could have done without the added drama.

This was not how I'd imagined things going down. Rex had brought me straight into the lion's den, and Malek looked entirely too pleased about it. My heart raced as I slid off the dragon's back, retrieving my shield and pulling out my sword.

So much for the element of surprise.

"Well, well! What a wonderful treat!"

Malek swaggered toward us. I assumed a fighting stance. Rex roared at him but made no effort to help.

I whispered to Rex. "Thanks a lot, dickhead."

Kane stepped out of the tent, battle plans clutched in his hands, his face frozen in a mixture of shock and confusion. His eyes locked on me, then darted to Rex, disbelief flickering across his features.

Around us, a dozen of Malek's guards surged forward, their swords glinting in the eerie light of the Gods' Eyes. Dressed in their ominous blue and black tunics, they moved with precision, taking up positions in a loose circle.

But they hesitated. Their blades remained raised, their stances ready, yet none dared to step closer. Their wide eyes betrayed the fear beneath their practiced discipline. After all, they weren't just facing me—they were facing *a dragon*.

And Rex? He didn't even glance at them. His focus was entirely on Malek, a low growl rumbling deep in his chest.

"And you brought a friend! How lovely." Malek beamed at Rex, like a proud father.

Arrogantly, he kept his sword in his scabbard. That was a mistake. I slowly crept forward.

"Sir Kane! We have an unexpected guest!"

Malek looked back at Kane, holding his arm out toward me. I rushed in, slashing my blade down at his torso. Malek leapt back and my sword sliced uselessly through air—I had lunged too hard and lost my balance, tumbling into the muddy grass.

Scanning the area, his guards had stayed out of it. And Malek's sword remained in his scabbard. I smirked. Scrambling to my feet, I jumped back into a fighting stance.

"I would love to entertain you. Unfortunately, I'm famished."

He walked away.

"Guards.... kill her."

Crap.

The Irkallans let out their war cries, raised swords, and rushed toward me. Instead of waiting for their attack, I sprinted directly at Malek. With his back to me, he heard my squishy boots and drew his sword. I sliced at his head—he parried my strike. He slashed across my midsection and I deflected him. He was strong, but I was quick. I swung my sword at his legs, causing him to leap up, and then drove the tip at his chest. The flat of his blade diverted my thrust and he easily fell back on his heels, a stupid grin plastered to his stupid face.

"Wait!" Kane shouted at the oncoming soldiers. He *was* going to help me.

Unsure what to do next, Malek's guards formed a circle around us again.

"What is it now, Kane?!" Malek exhaled, his frustration showing. "Another attempt to delay the death of this poor, helpless mudlark?"

Malek backed from the reach of my blade as Kane inched closer. The heavy rain seemed to weigh me down. Breathe. I tried to refocus myself. My adrenaline was pumping and I had missed my chance (do you see the theme here?) I had forgotten my teachings. I let emotions get the better of me. I never should have lost my balance and fell in the mud.

"She provides useful information!" Kane seethed. "Your highness."

He was still on my side.

"We need nothing from this girl!"

"The fact she is here at all says we *do*."

Kane took a slight step closer, sliding between me and Malek.

"You came here," he said, his mind working overtime. "On your own? To kill Malek?"

"Well, yeah!" My eyes locked on the petulant king.

"Which means you think this attempt... to be your *only* hope of victory..."

Malek threw his hands up. "What of it, Kane?!"

Kane kept his eyes glued to mine. I measured my distance from the king, envisioning the steps and strikes I needed to end this fight.

"Our spies confirmed that many of the rulers on the continent convened on Oceantis. And this little one did not like what she heard," said Kane. A weird smile crept across his face.

"I'm hungry. Remember?" whined Malek.

"It is good news... your highness."

Why wasn't Kane letting me at least try to slice up the king?

"We will not be facing the full strength of their armies. The rulers met. And... most likely only committed the bare minimum of troops. *If...* they committed any at all."

Confusion set in. Kane wasn't stalling to help me; he wanted information.

"The plan has succeeded. Our conquest will be easier than we ever dared imagine."

Kane flicked a hand at the guards, waving them off. They hesitantly backed away.

He smirked again, in an eerie way, but gave me a slight nod and a wink. "Now is your one and only chance, Finley. Make the most of it."

Malek was as bewildered as I was. Kane turned away, headed toward the tent.

Not one to waste an opportunity, I ignored him and rushed at Malek. He stepped back and threw up his blade as I rained down several quick strikes.

His confusion faded. He jabbed his sword at my waist. I sidestepped him and swung my blade at an exposed shoulder. He expertly threw his arm up, deflecting me. He went on the offensive and I held up my shield, fending off the harsh blows. The king aimed down at my legs and I leapt away. He struck my shield again and then stabbed my arm. The tip cut through my mail shirt, dug deep in my elbow. I dropped the shield.

We both stepped back, circling each other. Our swords clashed repeatedly, as he tested me out. He was stronger and his long sword heavier. That dumb grin of his returned. Malek would wear me down, easily, and he knew it. Rain mixed with sweat, stinging my eyes.

I advanced again and sparks flew as our blades met. Lightning flashed directly above us. I jumped closer to him, where his long arms were a disadvantage. Thunder rattled us to our core as swords clanged together and slid to the hilts. We stood face-to-face, panting hard. I slipped the dagger from my belt—his eyes immediately found the blade. I feinted to stab, but kneed him in the groin. When I finally lunged out with the dagger, he leapt easily away and kicked it from my hand.

I had to stay out of his range or be in close. I gripped my sword with both hands, parried a strike, and launched myself in close. He swung across at me but I dropped low, kicking hard on his kneecap. As Cira had done to me in training, his leg buckled and he fell to the mud. I threw myself down at him, my knife directed at his chest. Malek rolled away, but I managed to cut into his shoulder... just not with a fatal blow.

He sprang to his feet, holding the wound. "You have been trained well, whelpling."

I lunged again—he parried me off, but I scrambled to keep near. Stabbing at his leg, I forced him to spin away but kept him from extending his blade. For every step he took backwards, I stepped forward.

A look of fear spread across his face. Blood stained his shirt. I slashed at him once, twice, and then again. He stumbled backward with each blow.

Lightning flashed. Rex roared back at the heavy thunderclap.

Both of us breathing hard, we parried blades. He shouted out in frustration because I would not go away. Feeling cocky, I swung too hard and missed his blade, briefly exposing myself. But he was moving back, off balance, and could not strike. In anger, he threw the pommel of his sword at my face. I spun, twisting my hips, and launched a strike down at his legs. Malek smartly hopped to the side—but his boots slipped in the mud.

I stabbed at his head but my sword only sank into the mud.

"Guards!" he screamed. "Help your king!"

Malek twisted on the wet grass as I yanked my weapon out of the ground. I dove onto his legs, holding him still, and threw the hilt of my blade across his jaw.

He dropped his weapon, grabbed my waist, trying to toss me off. I jacked my leg into the grass to keep my balance. I lifted *Other Other Sword* in the air—with a brutal yell erupting from deep within me—and drove the tip into his chest. Malek's eyes went wide.

Anger and fear poured out all at once as I screamed again. Using all my weight, I drove the blade deeper into the king... all the way through him and into the mud below. Malek coughed up blood. His body shook.

Panting hard, I released the sword. Fell back in the grass. Malek let out a final groan, his body fell limp, and he bled out in the rain.

Another flash of lightning lit up the darkness.

The black dragon roared yet again at storm clouds above.

The king was dead.

Chapter 91

Long live the king?

Malek was immortal! I leapt to my feet, grabbed the sword handle, yanked it from his chest. I quickly assumed my stance. Waiting for him to sit up, to attack me again.

He remained motionless, eyes blank and wide, staring up at the black night. His blood ran down my blade, but the rain battered me and rinsed the kath steel clean.

I stood there, unable to move. Should I cut his head off? Could I even do that? I took cautious steps toward the body.

Boots squelched through the muddy ground as grunting soldiers closed in around me, forming a tense circle.

I turned slowly, meeting each guard's gaze one by one. Their eyes burned with anger, but something else flickered beneath it—hesitation. Some looked down at the body of their king. They exchanged uncertain glances, their hands gripping their swords tightly, as if unsure whether to strike or step back.

Then Kane appeared in the entrance of the massive tent. His face was a mask of surprise, his brows knitting together as his gaze shifted from me to Rex. Two hulking soldiers flanked him, their presence more for show than protection against a dragon.

The rain lightened to a soft drizzle, each drop pattering against the ground like an impatient clock. Lightning flashed in the distance, illuminating the eerie scene for a moment, followed by the delayed, grumbling roar of thunder. The storm was trailing away.

No one moved. The guards held their ground, Kane froze mid-thought, and I stood at the center of it all, gripping my weapons and waiting for the storm—literal or otherwise—to break.

Sir Kane of the Black Bones clapped his hands. "Well done! I am impressed, Finley! You *have* come a long way."

"What... is going on?" I kept my sword pointed at the circle of guards.

He walked toward me but turned to the guards. "Leave us! Warn everyone that the king has been slain! By an outsider..."

The squad of men dispersed. The two large soldiers stayed with Kane, walking a few paces behind him.

"You have what you wanted, Finley. The evil king is gone!" He smirked, holding his hand out toward the body.

"Why do I get the feeling that was a bad thing?"

He walked up to me, my sword poised above his left shoulder. "No. No, Finley. You played your part to perfection."

I let down my guard, lowered my sword. My arms shook from the exertion.

"My part? This isn't some game I'm playing. I just killed the king. Your king!"

"That is what we both wanted, is it not?" he whispered. And his new grin made me feel nauseous.

"Something is... definitely not right here."

"Tie her up!" barked Kane.

Before I could react, his two hulking goons were on me. They grabbed my arms with tight grips, their strength overwhelming. I thrashed, kicking and twisting, but exhaustion hit me like a brick wall—the tank was on empty.

One of them stole the sword from my hands while the other shoved me forward. I stumbled, the slick mud beneath my boots offering no grip, as they dragged me toward one of the glowing, silvery monoliths.

The cold metal loomed ahead, its faint light casting distorted reflections of my captors, their faces blank and merciless. My pulse hammered in my ears as I struggled in vain, knowing this wasn't going to end well.

"I want to thank you for returning my pet," Kane announced.

He held up his hand—the black dragon slogged through the mud towards him. Rex roared at me.

I was stunned. "Your *pet*?!"

I flexed my arms, making them as big as possible, and pulled hard on the cord as his men tied me to the tall, rectangular monument. With me secured, they disappeared into the big tent.

"Yes, I raised him from a hatchling, when I was but a young boy myself. And, like you, he has done *nearly* everything I have asked of him."

The dragon lowered his head and Kane patted his hard cheek.

"All except for killing you on the beach in Kunlun. He did neglect that duty."

I struggled to remember what he was talking about. "The beach?"

I knew I was about to die. And I needed to stall him.

"Yes, yes. After the idiots rammed your ship. Ormrir here was tasked with killing you if you managed to escape."

I recalled hearing the beating of wings, up in the clouds, while I stood on the beach with Temurr as the *Alkonost* began to sink.

"He was tasked by... you?"

"Of course. While I had mistakenly thought you had served your purpose, you came through with even more valuable knowledge for me! I cannot thank you enough, Finley."

I figured Kane was going to have the dragon burn me alive. So that I would not be able to return from the dead. I strained to free my wrists from the tight knots.

"So, wait... if you raised him since you were a boy, does that mean—"

"That he is the dragon that killed Queen Dirvilia and Laran? Yes."

Kane stroked my cheek, turning to walk away.

"So, you didn't slay the dragon that killed them then?"

He sighed, looking back at me. "Oh, I went out and hunted down one of Ormrir's brethren. I needed something to show to the people."

He continued on toward the tent like he was on top of the world.

"Let me guess... this is the part where you reveal your evil plans?"

He laughed. "No. Why would I do that? You are about to die."

"Don't you... um, want me to know how incredibly smart you are?"

He pretended to consider it, mocking me, then shook his head.

"No."

"I thought you cared about me, Kane!"

"How sweet! I only feigned interest to find out more about you." He took a few more steps, then paused. "Have you developed feelings for me?"

"Oh, no," I said, gritting my teeth. "I made the mistake of falling for a different asshole. He wants nothing to do with me either..."

He laughed. I growled in anger, struggling against the cords and kicking the metal monument. To keep stalling Kane, I put my weary brain in overdrive and tried to connect the dots.

The black dragon backed up. His head low. His yellow eyes locked on me. Rex was preparing his flame.

"Okay! Okay! At least tell me if I figured out your master plan!"

He stopped, thought it over, and held up his hand, telling the dragon to wait.

"This... might be entertaining. But do be quick. I need to break camp this evening."

"All right. Um. So, you killed Malek's mother and oldest brother to—"

"Yes, we have gone over this."

"You did it to put Malek on the throne. And you purposely poisoned his mind with hatred for other species. You knew he would give you an opportunity to build an empire. Too many years of fighting off deadly predators had made the people weak."

"That is stating the obvious."

"Well, to you. And the people of this world. But... I'm not from here." Did he know I was from Earth? "And you knew I was coming, didn't you? Yes. You had heard that Pherric was gathering a team of warriors and... and you found out about the prophecy, didn't you?"

"Nerus informed me that the Preceptor had a wayward student who had stolen the *Arcanum Libellum.* And I learned of the prophecy from—"

"From Lord Diago! But... before that, you sent Malek to the Godsribbon keep to recover the book." I looked down at Malek's body in the mud. "Because *you* wanted to be immortal!

Malek stayed dead. "Looks like you never used it on him."

Kane smirked, a fire in his eyes. "If one is going to build an empire, it only makes sense to enjoy it for as long as possible."

"So, you let us stay in Quivira. Let them train me. And then let us travel to Irkalla. Because you... wanted to see what would happen? You wanted to know our plan? And... you were curious about me."

"Infinitely."

I started to slide around to the corner of the metal monolith, to give myself more slack in the cords.

"And you got your chance to meet me, at your homecoming feast, for slaughtering the Bànshēn rén!"

"Yes. They were the most formidable species and I needed them out of the way first. The beastly Fomorians still give me pause, but we vastly outnumber them."

"Did you let me into the castle?" I wondered.

"Yes. I made sure we turned away the others. I needed to see if you were resourceful enough to get in on your own."

"And once you met me, you realized I wasn't really a threat. Not the *Chosen One* you'd heard about in the prophecy." All the thoughts and clues raced through my mind at once. "But... you still helped me try to kill Malek? Why?"

"Well, I needed him out of the way. At some point."

"You knew you'd get more sympathy from your army and the Irkallans if he were assassinated. And with no heirs to take Malek's place, everyone would welcome in Sir Kane of the Black Bones, the Knight Commander of Irkalla, as their king!"

"Absolutely not. Why be king when I can be... emperor?"

"But... um, what I can't figure out is why you saved me? You didn't let Malek execute me and made him hold the coin lottery. And... when I was stabbed in the arena, you brought the book to Pherric! And he made me immortal. Well, sorta."

I could feel the piece of flint in my boot but had no way to reach it. I struggled hard on the rope—pulling, stretching, trying to free my hands.

"Ah, yes. I was curious to see if you had fortune on your side. You survived the... lottery, which was a matter of luck I suppose. But I wanted to see if your mage could save you. I had not taken the potion up to that point and Nerus could provide no proof that it worked."

"I was your guinea pig."

The rope binding me to the monolith cut deep into my wrists.

"But I was not about to give you the completed potion. I tore out a page and—"

"So that I wouldn't be a true immortal? Like you... probably are now."

"I will simply say that... I have never felt better!" He exhaled. "I have grown weary of this conversation. Congratulations on figuring it *all* out. And thank you for confirming the strength, or lack thereof, of the armies we shall be facing. Pity for them that you were not their chosen one."

Kane bowed his head, touched his finger tips together, and backed away from me.

"But why do you hate the other species so much?! Tell me! Why do you want to wipe them all out?!"

"Without dangerous predators to hunt down, we will prey on each other. I simply gave my people a new enemy, Finley. I turned them on the savage beasts of the world—"

"They're not beasts, Kane! They're not! And if you've proven anything, they're better than Hominans!"

Tired of me, he turned to his dragon. "Ormrir! Kill!"

I closed my eyes. The dragon snarled at me. An acrid brimstone smell washed over me. His hot air blasted my face—the fire was next.

As the dragon reared back his long neck to roast me alive, I quickly shuffled my feet. I slid back away, to the far corner of the steel monument. I kept my arm exposed. I got as far away as possible as he released his flame. I'd probably lose my arm in the blaze, but hoped to keep my core intact.

I threw my face against the cold, smooth metal and closed my eyes.

There was a bright orange flash, but fire did not engulf me. Flames didn't wrap around the monolith. My hand was on fire—and it hurt like hell.

With the rope severed; I fell to the tall grass. I rubbed my hand in the mud to extinguish the flame.

Rex had only released a small amount of his dragonfire—enough to burn the rope! My hand was scalded and several links on my mail shirt sleeve still glowed orange.

I turned to the black dragon. "Rex! Kill him!"

Dragons might not technically be able to smile, but Rex gave me something close—his version of a grin, toothy and terrifying.

Slowly, he turned his massive head toward Kane, who froze in the tent's entrance. For a second, Kane's shock gave way to panic. "Guards! Give me a bow!" he shouted, his voice cracking.

But the guards were too far away. Realizing he was on his own, Kane bolted back into the tent.

Rex arched his long neck, his scales gleaming in the silvery light of the Gods' Eyes. With a deafening roar, he unleashed a torrent of flame. The front of the tent ignited instantly, fire licking up the ornate fabric and turning it into an inferno.

Seizing the moment, I scooped up my sword and sprinted to Rex's side, mud splattering against my legs. Without hesitation, I grabbed hold of his scales and hauled myself onto his back.

"Go, Rex! Go!" I screamed, kicking his sides with all the strength I could muster.

Rex roared again, this time not in warning but in defiance. His massive wings spread wide, droplets of rain cascading off their edges. He beat the air once, then twice, the sheer force lifting us off the ground.

With a powerful leap, he launched us into the cold, stormy night, leaving behind the tent on fire and shouts as we soared into the darkness.

Kane launched himself through the opening of his burning tent. Rolling to his feet, he grabbed a longbow from one of his soldiers. Another handed him arrows from a quiver, but he selected just one.

"Hurry!" I screamed at Rex. "Fly hard!"

We rose up and up, but not quickly enough to be out of range. I turned as Kane fired his arrow—it bounced off of Rex's underbelly, falling harmlessly to the ground below.

Kane stole another arrow, took slow and careful aim, and let loose.

He knew a dragon's weak spot—and he hit Rex in that spot.

A deep, guttural sigh erupted from Rex's chest, a sound that made my stomach drop. It was the unmistakable gasp of someone wounded badly. We dipped sharply, and I gripped the rope with all my strength, struggling to keep from sliding off his back.

Rex let out a haunting wail, a cry of both pain and resistance that pierced the humid air.

Despite the injury, the dragon refused to surrender. His massive wings beat on, but there was a hesitation on his left side, each flap more deliberate and strained. The effort sent tremors through his body, but he kept us going.

I could feel his strength waning beneath me, the fiery energy that made him unstoppable now dimmed. But Rex wasn't done yet. He flapped harder, determined, his resolve as sharp as his talons.

With every ounce of willpower, he pushed us higher, away from the illuminated clearing. Rain pelted against his battered scales as we rose above the treetops, the black forest below swallowing the light behind us.

Even as he carried his pain, Rex flew on. And I held on, hoping his strength would last just long enough to take us somewhere safe.

Chapter 92

Rex carried us through the dark, moonlit expanse of Kunlun, his silhouette a shadow against the rounded mountains below. He glided wherever he could, seeking out pockets of warm air to ease the strain. Each flap was labored, a visible jolt of pain rippling through his massive body with every beat.

Tears streamed down my face, blending with the cold night rain. "Hang in there, Rex," I whispered, though my words felt small against his immense struggle.

I clung tightly to his neck, feeling the heat of his body even as the chill of the night bit at my skin.

But the pain was undeniable. And it was mine too. Every time I leaned over to grab him, I could see a thin stream of blood flowing from his belly and along his tail before the droplets scattered into the wind.

We both knew he had been mortally wounded. He seemed to only have one goal: make it to his home. To his burial ground.

I soothed him, telling him how proud I was of his heroic feats, and I sang to him (badly... but he didn't seem to mind.) My heart was broken. There weren't enough tears for him.

Rex gave everything he had on the final leg of his journey. His powerful body, once so invincible, now trembled with every beat of his wings as he fought to stay in the air. The silhouette of the ancient volcano loomed ahead, but the climb to the Valley of Black Bones seemed insurmountable.

We scraped through the tops of trees, branches snapping against his scales as he worked to maintain altitude. His one good wing flapped with desperate effort, tilting him unevenly to one side. He pushed forward, but his strength started to fade fast.

The valley was within reach, but Rex simply didn't have enough left to make it. With a final, valiant attempt, he clipped the slope and crashed into the grass. The impact shook my body as we skidded uphill, his massive frame carving a path through the mud.

When we came to a halt, Rex let out a deep, raspy groan—a sound that tore through my heart. It wasn't a roar of rage. It was a whimper, raw and full of pain, as if even this mighty creature knew his journey had come to an end.

Keeping my hands against his scaly hide, I slipped to the ground.

Rex tried to push himself up several times, but fell back hard on the thick grass. He pumped his back legs, trying to climb up toward the Valley. His claws gained no traction in the slick grass.

"It's okay, Rex!" I cried. "You've done it!"

More tears fell. I wanted so desperately to help him, to impel him up the hill, but knew any effort would be futile.

He grunted hard, sending warm air from his nostrils, and then sighed. The long, slow sigh of a life cut short. Blood trickled from the corners of his mouth.

I fell to the ground, staring deep into his sad eye, as I sobbed. "You're home, Rex. You made it. Rest now, my warrior. You did well..."

His eyes stayed shut longer with every blink, with the passing of every minute. The rise and fall of his chest slowed.

"You did really well. Sleep... Sleep. You've earned it..."

I held onto him as he let out his last breath.

A piercing screech from above jolted me awake.

I was lying in the damp grass beside Rex's massive, motionless form. Blinking into the cloudy sky, I saw them—Big Red and the two green dragons circling overhead, their wings slicing through the morning mist like knives. A shiver ran through me as I realized what was happening.

Instinctively, I scooted away from Rex, putting distance between myself and the fallen dragon. I had no plans to interfere with whatever ritual they were about to perform. This was their moment, not mine.

Big Red descended with a thunderous roar, her massive frame landing with a thud. Her fiery eyes locked onto mine, daring me to move.

I lowered my head immediately, keeping my gaze fixed on the ground as I slowly backpedaled further away. I forced myself to remain calm. Without Rex to shield me, I was exposed, vulnerable.

Still, walking away wasn't an option. Turning my back would show weakness—an insult in the presence of these mighty beasts. So, I stayed, rooted in place, my every move deliberate.

Would they take him to their sacred burial ground? I waited in silence, squatting low to the ground, my head bowed. The wind whispered faintly through the tall grass, carrying a heavy stillness with it. Even the distant birds seemed subdued, their calls soft and reverent, as though they understood the gravity of the moment.

Big Red crawled forward, her massive body moving with surprising grace. She nudged Rex gently with her snout, as if seeking confirmation that he was truly gone. The two green dragons followed suit, bowing their heads to press their foreheads against his still form. Their guttural groans filled the air, a raw and mournful sound. It was as if they were speaking a language I couldn't understand but felt deep in my chest—a language of loss.

Their grief struck me harder than I expected. Dragons were rare, their numbers dwindling by the day. The weight of losing one of their own seemed unbearable to them, and in their sorrow, I found my own grief magnified.

Tears spilled down my face, and not just for Rex. He had been my companion, my protector, for such a short time, yet his loss tore through me. But this pain wasn't just about him. It was for Frip, Cira, Gunnr—for everyone I had lost. Their deaths had been so sudden, so violent, I'd buried the pain just to survive. Now, on this mountainside, it all came crashing down.

And yet, I let myself smile faintly as memories surfaced—Frip's sharp wit, Cira's fierce loyalty, Gunnr's strength. They weren't just losses. They were gifts I had carried with me.

I spent the cloudy, somber day mourning alongside the dragons but away from their circle. Their heads stayed bowed in grief for hours. The air was heavy with their sorrow, a shared silence stretching between us as we waited for the sun to dip below the horizon.

As twilight fell, Big Red was the first to move. Her massive frame lumbered forward, and with a guttural snarl, she released a torrent of dragonfire onto Rex's body. The other dragons followed, one by one, their flames roaring to life and combining into an inferno. The heat from their firestorm pushed at my skin even from a distance, but I couldn't look away.

Rex's body finally ignited, consumed by the blaze, the flames climbing higher and higher into the night. Through the haze of my tears, I swore I saw something—an ethereal, blazing shadow of a dark dragon rising within the swirling smoke, as though his spirit was taking flight one last time.

The fire raged on, the glow casting long, flickering shadows across the hillside. The dragons resumed their circle, bowing their mighty heads in reverence as the flames roared in the center. The sight was both devastating and awe-inspiring, a raw, primal ritual of farewell that went beyond words.

I sat with them, feeling the weight of the loss we all shared.

When the black bones had cooled down, Big Red used her jaws to gently tug his skull from the spine. She soared into the night sky, carrying her precious cargo up to the Valley of Black Bones. The two green dragons joined in, carefully collecting more bones and flying them away.

I waited patiently until only smaller bones remained. I grabbed hold of a bone half as long as me and started my journey.

Big Red dove from the sky, her wings spreading wide as she landed with a deafening thud. She snarled, her sharp fangs bared, her fiery breath steaming in the cool air. Her rage rolled off her in waves, a primal warning that I was far too close to her grief, to her fury.

Slowly, deliberately, I set the black bone in the scorched grass. I dropped to one knee and lowered my head, my heart pounding so hard it echoed in my ears. The seconds dragged like hours. She stomped, growled, and filled the air with her harsh protests, but the fiery death I expected never came.

Her emotions flooded into me—fear, grief, and a raw hatred that was almost tangible. It wasn't just for me, but for all people. Her thoughts were chaotic, wild, a storm of vengeance and sorrow swirling in her mind. I stayed motionless, absorbing her pain while keeping my breathing steady.

Cautiously, I stood, keeping my eyes low. I reached for the black bone, fingers trembling, and held it firmly in my hands. The tension in the air was suffocating as I waited.

Then, without warning, Big Red shifted her massive body to the side, her burning gaze still fixed on me. She let out a low growl, a reluctant permission.

I stepped forward, carrying my treasure up the hill, each step feeling like a fragile truce between us.

As my boots crunched over the sharp obsidian, Big Red soared ahead, her massive wings slicing through the heavy air. She landed in the center of the Valley, waiting, her fiery eyes tracking my every move.

Ignoring the pain radiating through my arms from carrying the bone, I trudged forward to Rex's resting place. Gritting my teeth, I lowered it, placing it beside his spine. The weight wasn't just physical—it was the finality of it all shoving down on me. With a deep breath, I dropped to one knee and waited for her judgment.

Big Red's sharp gaze lingered, as if weighing the worth of my actions. Finally, she took to the skies, her massive form disappearing into the haze above the Valley. I followed her back downhill, my legs trembling but determined.

Long into the early morning hours, when the last of Rex's bones had been delivered, the dragons formed a half-circle around me at the mouth of the Valley. Their stares burned into me, filled with distrust and disdain. But they didn't kill me. I guessed that I had earned no alliance—only the privilege of walking away with my life.

Kane had raised Rex, which gave him a sliver of understanding toward humans. Big Red and her companions had no such connection. To them, I was a nuisance, a creature to be tolerated only briefly.

Without meeting their eyes, I gave a nod and backed away. They watched me with cold suspicion as I descended their mountain, each step reminding me of my isolation.

By the time I reached the bottom, dawn had painted the sky orange. There were no meals, no fruits to drink, no ride waiting for me. At noon, after sleeping fitfully up on a tree branch, I strapped my sword to my back and jogged off toward Shangri-La. Alone once again.

Chapter 93

With the towering mountain and the Valley of the Black Bones fading into the distance behind me, I pressed onward, heading north and slightly west toward Shangri-La. The Prominan capital was bound to be the gathering point for whatever reinforcements—if any—the other realms might send.

I ran for long stretches during the day, the miles adding up beneath my boots. Occasionally, I paused to scan the terrain and listen for any signs of Irkallan troops. Once, I spotted an advance force trudging west along a dry riverbed wedged between two shallow peaks. Avoiding them was easy enough. My knees ached, and my back screamed for rest, but there was no time to whine.

After ten days of grueling travel, I neared Shangri-La and began encountering spies making their way through the dense forests. They moved with a distinct lack of stealth, their boots crunching on leaves and twigs, alerting anyone within earshot.

Using Pherric's mindform training, I detected their presence before they ever saw me. Their thoughts betrayed them: two were bored, their minds drifting and idle. Keeping them distracted wasn't difficult. Another spy's mind bristled with anxiety, broadcasting a nervous energy that was almost palpable. His fear was justified. Kasuma would have been proud as I took my time, moved silently, sneaking up on two of them and slicing their throats. But I had trouble with the last one—he managed to slither away when my boot slipped on a wet tree root, trying to take him out. I doubt he got very far, with the deep gash I cut from his chest to his shoulder.

I evaded the few Prominan patrols I encountered, not wanting any of them to think I was an enemy. That might have been messy.

After several days of grueling hiking, I finally reached the valley of Shangri-La. The towering mountains flanked me on both sides, the icy wind sliding down their smooth surfaces and straight into me. Somewhere in the distance, the roar of the mighty river echoed. Despite the sun's presence that morning, its warmth was distant and indifferent. Each breath formed a soft plume of mist in the biting cold as I trudged through the dense grove of evergreens, rubbing my hands together for warmth. Winter was on its way.

Emerging from the forest, I found myself on a bluff overlooking a lush, breathtaking vale. At the far end stood Shangri-La, a vine-draped city precariously perched on the edge of a steep cliff. Beyond its walls, twin waterfalls cascaded from the mountains, their sheer power a stark contrast to the delicate beauty of the city. On the northern edge, a wide river surged before tumbling over another cliff in a magnificent display.

Only a single stone wall enclosed the inhabitants of Shangri-La. Two bridges spanned the river, one wide enough to let several wagons cross at the same time.

The city itself was compact but reached skyward, much like my home in Manhattan. Tall towers crowned with white domes pierced the morning mist, while trapezoidal buildings with pagoda-style roofs, moss clinging to their edges, rose imposingly above the single stone wall that encircled the city. Rope bridges crisscrossed between the towers, creating a web of connectivity. A sturdy keep sat proudly on a small hill at the heart of Shangri-La, dominating the skyline.

I was surprised to see a camp, with rows and rows of tents, set up in front of the big wall. Soldiers milled about under various banners from a few kingdoms. Based on their colors and appearance, if I had to guess, most seemed to be from Valhalla. I was happy that at least *some* people showed up, but I doubted there were more than three or four thousand souls starting to wake down there.

I descended from the bluff and marched along the sole road leading to the city.

As I approached the gates, a half-dozen Prominan guards leveled their weapons at me. Their sharp gazes darted from my worn clothes to the sword strapped to my back. A stocky commander limped forward, his scarred face barely concealing years of battle-hardened suspicion.

"State your business," he grumbled, his voice like gravel.

"I am..." My throat tightened. What the hell was I supposed to say? I cleared my throat. "I'm here to see my... friends."

Friends. Really? That was the best I could come up with? The words hung awkwardly in the air, and I winced.

The commander stepped uncomfortably close, glaring down at me. "You have no friends here... Hominan."

Oh, hell no. I squared my shoulders and thrust my chin up, putting my nose practically in his. "My name is Finley Maguire."

It sounded so stupid coming out of my mouth, but the reaction was instant. His eyes widened ever so slightly, and he took a step back. A flicker of recognition? Or maybe surprise? He nodded sharply to one of the guards—a man missing an arm. Without hesitation, the one-armed soldier took off running into the city.

The commander grunted, "Come with me."

I followed him through the towering gates and up a narrow boulevard that led toward a castle, sturdy and practical, like everything else Prominan. He handed me off to a pair of palace guards who flanked me without a word.

They led me through the inner walls of the keep and into a courtyard filled with weathered statues of ancient Prominan warriors. Their stone eyes seemed to follow me, their chiseled ape faces etched with the weight of battles long past. I wasn't sure whether to feel inspired or intimidated.

I paced the courtyard, shivering as the chill gnawed at my skin. My boots crunched against the gravel, the sound echoing off the weathered statues. Eventually, a small group of butlers appeared, their thin frames betraying hard times. They draped a worn cloak over my shoulders, handed me a plate of food, and offered water in a cracked ceramic jug.

I noticed the last butler linger as he passed me a piece of fresh fruit. His hollow cheeks and hesitant movements told me he hadn't had a full meal in days. I discreetly held the fruit back toward him, hoping he'd take it. He stared at it longingly, his hand twitching with the urge to grab it—but he shook his head and stepped back, bowing slightly before leaving. My heart ached for him, but there was no time to dwell on it.

The sound of heavy footfalls interrupted my thoughts. I turned just as Braylor stormed into the courtyard, with Pherric and Temurr right on his heels.

"By the gods, you survived!" Pherric shouted, relief and disbelief in his voice.

Before I could respond, Pherric grabbed my shoulders, his eyes scanning me for injuries like he always did. Once satisfied I was still in one piece, he pulled me into a tight embrace.

I smiled, leaning into the hug. I'd finally come home.

"You did it! You slayed the Irkallan king!" cried Temurr, hugging both Pherric and I together.

They stepped back and I looked up at Braylor. He stared down for a moment, his arms crossed, as though I had disappointed him and he wasn't sure how to break the bad news.

"Well?" I asked.

Finally, he stepped forward. I smiled. But rather than embracing me, Braylor held me at arm's length.

"Where is your shield?"

"My shield?! Well, I..."

Confused. I grabbed the hilt of my sword.

"That was a *good* shield."

"I still have *Other Other Sword*!"

"I paid a lot of coin for that shield," he grumbled.

"But I brought back the sword!"

"I liked that shield."

"I hate you..." I crossed my arms, pouted.

Braylor laughed and easily scooped me up. He spun me around high in the air and then pulled me in, squeezing me so tight I nearly passed out.

"Easy, big guy! I've got a poop I've been holding in for the past three days…"

He lowered me to the ground, with a disapproving look.

"Too much information?"

I grabbed his face and kissed him hard, but he pulled away.

He started to speak. "Finley, I—"

"Shh! I have decided I don't care about whatever it is you're dealing with! You are mine. And that's all there is to it, Braylor. You got me? Do you understand?"

He stepped back, opened his mouth. But I shut him down with a pointed finger and a shaking head.

Braylor smirked. "I have no choice in the matter?"

"No choice. You. Are. Mine."

"Aye… you really do hate me."

"So much that I love you." I was done messing around. Straight and to the point, from that moment forward.

This time, he kissed me. Long and hard. I melted into Braylor and forgot the world. It might have been an awkward moment for Temurr and Pherric but… I didn't care. I had the big man in my arms again.

Pherric cleared his throat.

Braylor held my face in his strong hands. "I hoped you would survive, but I could not believe it to be true."

"You taught me well." I pulled him down for another kiss.

"Come. Let us move indoors and warm you up," soothed Braylor.

"Oh, I'm plenty warm… now," I laughed, my arms locked around his neck.

Pherric cleared his throat again. "We shall discuss your epic adventure, Finley."

Damned Pherric.

We moved to a spacious, square hall within the castle, its stone walls lit by the flickering glow of sconces and the warmth of a roaring fire. The air smelled faintly of smoke and aged wood, a comforting contrast to the icy wind outside. Kasuma appeared moments later, taking a seat beside me at the heavy wooden table that dominated the center of the room.

Temurr busied himself pouring water into mismatched mugs. I leaned back in my chair, grateful for the fire blazing behind me. The heat seeped into me, chasing away the lingering chill from the courtyard and... all the dumb stuff I had done.

I stretched my hands toward the flames, letting their warmth ease the stiffness in my fingers.

"All praise to the victor!" cheered Kasuma, lifting her cup in the air.

"Aye!" added Temurr.

I tried to smile, but it looked more like a wince. They noticed.

"What's wrong, Finley?" asked Pherric.

"Well, I hate to break bad news to everyone. It's great that Malek's dead and all, but..."

"Sir Kane, the Knight Commander, is the one truly in charge of Irkalla," surmised Pherric. "And... he yet lives."

"That's right!" I pointed my cup at Pherric and nodded. "How did you know?! Never mind. You know everything... But he had me completely fooled! And I'm sorry for that, guys. I really am."

Braylor slammed his heavy palm on the table. "I knew Malek to be a fool. He was incapable of devising any such plan."

I turned to Pherric. "Okay. I have to know. How did you figure it out?"

"I had immediately sensed Kane's intelligence when we were in the grand hall—in Malek's keep. He was capable of deflecting my mindforms, but I knew he held on to a great number of secrets. And, after news of Malek's death, I realized that if Kane had been on your side, he most likely would have withdrawn his troops. Our spies tell us that the Irkallan forces are still marching on Shangri-La."

"So... nothing has changed. Once again, it was all for nothing!"

Pherric closed his eyes.

"What?"

"That... is not quite true. Fortunately."

"Wait! So you actually have good news?!" I practically jumped up and down in my seat.

"Good news, in a way, but you will not be happy with the origin of the news."

Braylor grunted. "What have you done, Pherric?"

Temurr seemed confused. "What does he speak of?"

Kasuma also let her head fall—she knew what was coming.

"Together, with King Longzhe of Oceantis, Kasuma and I devised a plan. We took advantage of your history of impatience and impulsiveness. When you ran off, on your own, in search of a dragon, we knew we could use your optimism and your, well... your lack of guile, for our benefit."

"What are you talking about?" Now I was confused. And a bit insulted.

"We decided to have you listen in on the talks in Nibiru. We had those rulers in attendance deceive you, as well. They agreed to announce they would only commit a handful of troops to fight against Malek. Which was not truthful."

"But why?"

"Because we also knew you would believe their efforts to be futile and that you would... rush off to try to kill the king yourself. As you did. If you were captured, which we assumed would happen, they might force you to talk and you would detail our seemingly limited tactics to fight back with only a small force. And if you managed to assassinate Malek, your connection with Sir Kane would provide access to spread the false story as well. If you were killed, it still helped our cause. Your desperate attempt would have shown them that you felt hopeless and that there was no alternative. No matter the outcome, they would know that our combined factions would offer little resistance."

"So you lied to her?! And—and what?!" Braylor was enraged. "You used her as a child's toy to send a message, knowing she might die out there?!"

Kasuma sat up straight, but avoided eye contact. "We had little choice, Braylor. Even with all the forces we have mustered, we are still vastly outnumbered! We need every advantage if we are going to defeat the Irkallans!"

I sat frozen in my chair, disbelief pinning me to the spot. My jaw hung slack, words failing me. The realization hit me like a sharp slap to the cheek—I was nothing more than a pawn. Expendable. A foolish, naive girl caught in a web of lies.

They had used me, just like Kane had. My chest tightened as the betrayal sank in. Hot tears spilled down my cheeks, blurring my vision. I wiped them away with trembling hands, but the ache inside didn't budge.

Braylor stood, pointing his finger at Pherric. "We should have been informed!"

"You knew she would leave, Braylor. You did. You even purchased her weapons and clothing. You—"

"I could not stop her! *Death* cannot stop her! But she never would have left if she knew most of the kingdoms were sending all their soldiers! So, you... you sacrificed her!"

Pherric rubbed his temples. "We are all replaceable, Braylor. All of us. And, yes, I did sacrifice her. But from the moment I stole her from her world, she has been dispensable. As have we all. I have done it all for the sake of preventing the creation of the Irkallan empire."

"Well, let us bake the sorcerer a cake and sculpt a statue in his honor!" bellowed Braylor, swinging his huge arms wide.

"I have sacrificed everything—just as you have! Gunnr gave her life so that Finley might live! We have already lost so much! Sending her off to face Malek was a risk we... I had to take. Do you not see?!"

Braylor waved Pherric away.

"Their deaths must mean something! We cannot have let them die in vain!" I had rarely seen Pherric angry. Veins popped out on his forehead and neck. "I would do it all again, if I had to, without a thought!"

The giant was unable to face Pherric. "We should have been told, sorcerer. We should have known."

"Would you have let her go? No. As you have stated, she might not have gone! Even if she had, Kane could have tortured her and our plot would have been exposed immediately! You know this!"

I gulped, remembering that I had told Kane about the thumb screws...

Pherric stood up and closed on Braylor. "She is fiercely optimistic... to a fault. You and I will never see someone transform from a gentle, fragile child to a hardened and menacing fighter as quickly as she has done. But trickery and court intrigue are not her strong suits. Kane easily manipulated her, and we had to... make use of her newfound confidence and her hopefulness."

"Um, you guys know I'm sitting right here? Right?" I said. "Look, I get it. I'm apparently just a tool to use and abuse. And I'm glad it worked out for you. But..."

I could not stop the tears from falling. I stared down at the surface of the wood table.

"Finley, listen, please. I was merely—"

"Doing what you had to. What you felt was right. Blah, blah, fucking blah. Like I said, I get it. But thanks for making me feel so worthless. Like... an idiot. A dumb, useless pushover."

I pushed away from the table. Stormed out of the room. I felt so small. And the tears made me look weak. I had to get out of that room.

Chapter 94

"Am I now the villain in your life story?" Pherric's words lingered and, despite everything, they made me crack a smile.

Wrapped in a heavy fur, I stormed out of King Kwong's castle—his name still hilarious to me—and trudged onto the patrol path along the outer wall. Below me, the camp bustled with activity, but I leaned against the parapet, resting between the squared stone wall, letting my emotions spill out into the cold air.

I cried—big, ugly tears. A mix of anger and self-pity poured out of me. I've always been great at justifying things, and honestly, Pherric's plan had worked. Kane had been misled about the strength of our armies. I had gotten lucky and taken out the evil king, which had to hurt Irkallan morale. Realistically, everything played out in our favor.

But knowing I'd been just a pawn in everyone's schemes—Kane's, Pherric's, maybe even their gods'—broke me. It wasn't just betrayal; it was the weight of being reduced to a tool. A means to an end.

I sniffled and wiped my face with my sleeve. "No, you're not the villain, Pherric," I muttered into the empty, gray day. "You're just better at this game than I am."

"I can live with that." He rolled up my charred sleeve and inspected the hand that Rex had burned. "Unfortunately, you have not heard my entire villainous tale."

"What do you mean?"

"I have deceived you on many levels," he said. He pulled a vial from his robe, applied ointment to my blackened skin. "If you are to hate me, I want you to know all the sordid details. The truth is... there never was a prophecy—"

"I knew it!" I shouted. "But, wait... if there was no prophecy, then I'm not—"

"The Chosen One? No. I purposely misled you. And everyone else."

"Why?" I asked. "Why would you lie to us?! To me?"

Unable to look me in the eye, he stared out at the troops running through drills on the grounds beyond the wall.

"I needed to give them something to believe in. I spent months wandering from kingdom to kingdom, desperately trying to convince every ruler to take up arms against Malek. But none would grant me an audience. When I returned and persisted, they sent out representatives who nodded and feigned worry and made lofty promises, but essentially ignored me. When I came back again, after promises remained unfulfilled, they shuffled me off to meet the members of our crew: Braylor, Temurr and Frip, Gunnr, Kasuma, and Cira."

"And that's when you picked me out... and brought me to Tir Na?"

"I had never been to your world. I had no idea where to go. Your world is... complicated. So full of life. I chose your city— and you—at random."

My mouth opened. Then closed. I figured I wasn't a Chosen One. But the attention was nice. I felt special. Unique. And for the first time in my life... needed. Turns out none of it was true. I just happened to be on the top of a building, in the wrong place, at the wrong time. Two minutes earlier, Pherric might have taken Genevieve. Or anyone else from that party.

"I am terribly sorry, Finley. I know you cannot forgive me. But I needed someone to be a symbol for our cause. I never wanted you to be hurt in any way. Only to be our standard-bearer."

"Yeah, well, the standard bearer is usually the one carrying the stupid banner, with no weapon in hand, and they're always the first to die..." Every rationale I had come up with, since being brought to Tir Na, faded from memory: the sights I had seen, the adventures, and having a purpose were just—*poof*—gone! I was suddenly homesick. And had an intense feeling of longing for my grandfather, for Genevieve, and even for New York. I missed my home. I missed my phone, school, and a decent conditioner for my hair—all the simple luxuries that had been stolen from me. And for no reason at all, other than being present on the night in question.

"I'm such a complete and total moron."

"You are no fool, Fin," he said. "I had little choice. However, by giving our circle of misfit warriors such a massive undertaking, along with a desire to fulfill an ancient prophecy, I was able to unite us all and we came within a hair's breadth of killing the dishonorable king! Do you understand how impossible our task was? And you nearly succeeded! The gods were smiling down on us. You especially."

"We got lucky, Pherric. That's all. And they certainly weren't smiling on all of us..."

"There may have been no prophecy. And you are not the chosen one. But we have accomplished so much. Including the death of Malek. We owe it all to you."

I wanted to crawl into a hole, fade from existence. "I was your plaything. Nothing more."

Pherric exhaled. "I am truly sorry, Finley. And I am not proud of what I have done."

The cold wind stung my cheeks where the tears fell.

"I know. And I know that, deep down, you're a good guy. Trying to do what's right and all that shit... but it still hurts. Really, really hurts."

"I understand. But given the chance, as I have said, I would make the same choices again. Just with a heavier heart. I want you to know that I am proud of you and all that you have accomplished. I will ask no more of you and will no longer deceive you. Your part in this is over..."

"Oh, so you've used me up and are just tossing me away now?! Nothing like being a means to an end, Pherric! Golly gee, it's fun!" I pumped my hands in the air.

He lowered his head. "You are so much more—"

I spun on him, balling my fist. I was so ready to knock him out. Or at least try.

"Don't start with that! I can't even deal with this—with you—right now! Just... just get out of my face with your 'I'm so sorry' and 'I feel so bad' bullshit!"

He nodded once and returned his gaze to the stone walkway.

"As you wish."

As I watched Pherric walk along the patrol path, the last bit of confidence drained away and my old friend *Panic* returned for a visit. My heart fluttered and throat closed. I felt completely alone. Isolated. There were no friends to comfort me and no voice whispered to my mind, telling me what to do next.

I shouted after him. "We still have to fight! Kane is marching on this city!"

Pherric placed his arms behind his back, slowly turning to me.

"Finley, you have done more than enough. I am not going to allow you to join in the upcoming battle."

"Yes. Please! Forbid me! Again!" I bristled. "You know how well that works, right?"

He shook his head. "I am beginning to think I should have told you everything up front and then forbade you from doing anything about it. But, we have done our part. Leave it to the rulers and their armies to do theirs."

As I leaned against the wall to watch soldiers and their drills, I caught Braylor marching up the stairs to the patrol path from the corner of my eye. He pushed Pherric aside. Temurr reluctantly chased behind him, pulling on Braylor's arm in a futile attempt to stop the giant.

"We must go! At once!" bellowed Braylor.

"Go where?" I asked.

"We need to leave this place," he said. His narrowed eyes glanced up and down the stone patrol path. Prominan guards had kept their distance, but they were near enough to hear Braylor's deep growl.

"You must trust me," he murmured.

"I do, but—"

Temurr peeked around Braylor's big arm. "He thinks Shangri-La is doomed."

The giant snarled at the ape man, who backed away with his hairy hands up.

"It is not safe here," Braylor said, keeping his eyes on Temurr.

"But we tricked Kane, right? They don't think he'll send as many troops here. We have a chance to win."

Braylor rolled his dark eyes at me.

Temurr bounded back up to Braylor. "She has not yet seen our army! Show her the army!"

"Where is this... army?" I asked.

The big man groaned. "We have amassed some troops. But not nearly enough to—"

"To the north! In Hyperborea! We can take you!" Temurr squealed with delight.

"I will see this army," I announced.

Braylor held up a thick finger, and started to speak. But he thought better and closed his eyes.

"I will not lose you, Finley."

"Then try to keep up," I said, patting his chin.

I put my arm around Temurr, walking him to the stone steps and back to the keep. I was tired of the cold. And tired of crying.

Chapter 95

As Temurr told one of his tasteless but undeniably hilarious jokes, we strolled into the Great Hall.

At the far end of the long table, Kasuma stood deep in conversation with a grizzled Prominan soldier. His silver hair gleamed under the torches, and an old scar slashed down the side of his weathered face.

When Braylor fell in behind us, Kasuma quickly replaced her concerned expression with a fake grin. She patted the old warrior's shoulder and called out, "Feeling better?"

"No," I admitted, crossing my arms. "But some wine might help."

Her fingers interlocked in mock sympathy. "Ah, but I fear we are completely out of—"

Heavy boots clomped on the stone floor, cutting her off mid-sentence.

I didn't bother turning toward the sound echoing from the hallway. My eyes stayed on Kasuma as she drew her wings around herself and disappeared behind a curtained wall, as though retreating from a brewing storm.

Two guards stormed into the hall, followed by the marshal of the keep and a half dozen Prominan soldiers in full gear. The urgency of their movements made the hairs on the back of my neck stand up.

My instinct screamed at me to follow Kasuma's lead, slip behind the curtain, and disappear into the shadows. But I remained.

Braylor and Pherric shifted behind me and Temurr, their shoulders squared and ready.

The marshal, draped in a flowing blue robe trimmed with red, strode forward, offering the group a polite but hollow smile. His gaze settled on me.

Pherric's arm shot out, pulling me back a step. For once, I didn't resist. "Yes?"

The marshal kept his eyes locked on me. "As guests of the king, we are here to escort you to your quarters."

"We know where the living quarters are, and we—"

The marshal cleared his throat. "This is by order of the king, Master Pherric."

"Surely you're not suggesting we are to be your... prisoners?"

He looked up at Pherric, then back to me. "You are certainly not prisoners. However, these are trying times. The Irkallans are but days away from Shangri-La. And the security of the capital is our utmost concern."

Braylor pushed Pherric aside, sticking a thick finger in the marshal's face. "What if we wish to leave? Are you going to stop us?!"

As the Marshal took a step back, a couple long spears and a sword were thrust in Braylor's face.

"Braylor... we are still allies, remember?" soothed Pherric. "Marshall Gorat, there must be a misunderstanding—we are not a security threat."

"His grace is not worried about *all* of you," said the marshal, then nodded at me. "But she... is not above suspicion."

"Me?!" I held my hands up in frustration. "What the hell did I do?"

He steepled his thick, hairy fingers as he thought out a delicate response. "Young woman, you are a known associate of Sir Kane, the newly uncrowned king of Irkalla. A man who has, by the by, been elevated to that position by you... with your assassination of Malek. As well, you managed to escape unharmed from within the heart of the Irkallan army. And—"

"Because I had a dragon!" My face burned red hot.

"And because you are a dragonwitch," he added.

He then exhaled deeply, turning a sympathetic eye to Pherric. "To be quite honest, this is a formality. The king and the other rulers, who are meeting as we speak, are simply concerned that their ruse—of our limited troop availability—will be exposed. Kane is upon us and we must take every precaution. You understand."

I started to open my big fat mouth.

"We do understand," said Pherric, stepping closer to me. "And we thank you for your hospitality."

"Pherric!" protested Braylor.

"This is temporary," Pherric said loudly. "Correct, marshal?"

"When the Irkallan horde arrives at our gate, we will need the help of everyone," agreed the marshal. He gave me a final look. "Everyone who is on our side."

"Then we shall retire to our rooms."

The marshal nodded graciously, knowing they would get no trouble from us. But then he held up a finger.

"Do you know where your Tenguan companion might be?"

Pherric shook his head. "I have no idea."

The marshal called it a formality, but it a punishment. They stripped me of every weapon I carried, locked me in a small room at the top of the keep's highest tower, and posted a guard at the door.

Braylor wasn't part of their plan, but he made himself one. He barged in behind me, crossed his arms, and glared at the soldiers until they gave up and let him stay.

I paced the cramped room, my frustration echoing in every step. How could they doubt my loyalty after everything I'd done? But, if I was being honest, the anger was a welcome reprieve. It kept me from drowning in the storm of betrayal and lies Pherric had left me with. It's hard to feel sorry for yourself when you're pissed off.

Braylor leaned against the door, arms still folded like a human barricade, his gaze tracking my back-and-forth path across the floor.

"Calm yourself, Finley," he said with a patience that only made me more mad.

I stopped mid-step and spun to face him, my glare sharper than any sword they'd taken from me.

"Rule number one, where I come from?! Never tell an angry woman to calm down!"

He chuckled and made his way to the bed. He sat slowly as the rickety slats creaked and moaned.

"Then at least come sit with—"

Snap! The strained wood gave way. The bed frame collapsed. Then a set of legs broke. Braylor rolled onto the floor.

"Puny, ignorant, confounded Prominan bed!"

I laughed out loud. He let a grin reach those strong lips.

"Sorry, B. You're getting no action on that thing tonight!"

He picked himself off the floor. "Would have been an excellent way to pass the time."

I fell into his arms and hugged him. Tight enough that I heard his air escape.

"Who says we need a bed?"

He lifted my chin and leaned down to kiss me. As I started to respond, I heard a fluttering sound. A breeze shot through the tall window at my back.

Shadows danced on the stone surrounding the window. A slender foot appeared on the sill. I saw her white hair first, as Kasuma poked her head in the room. She tucked her wings and slid through the narrow window.

"Kasuma! What are you doing?"

Braylor rushed up from behind me. "Kane and his army are coming and they believe she conspires with him!"

She nodded. "I was made aware before they came to collect you."

"Then you know you must get her out of the city! She is not safe here! These fools will blame her for every ill." He held on to my shoulders as if I were able to go anywhere.

"This will all pass. They must have discovered our plan to show you the assembled armies in Hyperborea. The rulers are meeting now in the temple of the keep, finalizing their strategy. If we were overheard, someone slipped in and whispered into their king or queen's ear. And they simply panicked."

"Well, I'd love to know what they're planning," I said.

"Then let us find out. My king holds sway still with this fragile alliance. Perhaps he has information he can share."

"They plan for battle and you are able to gain an audience with Longzhe?" Braylor scoffed.

Kasuma smirked. "My father would always grant me an audience..."

She turned to the window as Braylor and I stood there in stunned amazement.

Braylor gasped. "Your father—?"

"Is King Longzhe?!" I howled.

She looked down from the tower window. "Shall we go?"

Big Braylor marched forward and Kasuma laughed at him.

"Um, no. I am afraid not," she said. "I cannot even fly with her!"

He grumbled, stepping aside.

"Well, then how are we—?"

She held out her arms. "Just like we did over the River Styx. We will fall, but not as quickly as we would without wings. I will glide us to the ground. And it will be a hard landing. For you."

Kasuma and I inched through the window. Facing her, I grabbed her around the waist. She was feather-light and seemingly so fragile, but she was a killer, too. So...

"I never would've guessed you were a princess," I said, staring into her black eyes.

"And I never would have guessed you were a Chosen One."

I peeked over the edge—we were a hundred feet above the ground.

"Are you sure about this?"

"Yes. I will be fine... I can fly."

I nervously laughed. She was serious. I looked down again.

"Wait!"

She didn't wait.

We plummeted straight down, icy air slamming into us like a frozen fist. Kasuma stretched her wings, flapped once, then twice.

A sharp, stabbing pain split through my temples. My vision blurred, darkened. Distant voices murmured, clawing at the edges of my mind. I squeezed my eyes shut, trying to shake the agony loose.

When I opened them, the flat roof of a building was racing up to meet me.

Kasuma's wing caught a current, jerking us upright. We skimmed across the roof, the surface a blur beneath us.

"Now!" she commanded.

I let go, crashing onto the hard wood. Pain shot through my shoulder as I rolled to a stop against a low stone wall. Gasping, I lay still, staring at the stars above.

Kasuma swooped past, circling back to land beside me. She crouched low, her head swiveling like a hawk's, listening for the telltale clamor of boots or a warning bell.

But the night stayed quiet. No alarms. No rushing guards.

Kasuma gave a sharp nod. "Move!"

We stayed low, skimming over the roof like shadows. Dropping back into the keep, we slipped into the maze of halls, silent and invisible, hearts pounding in sync with the danger around us.

Food in the capital had grown scarce. The hallways were empty as most of the servants were eating their one meal of thin slop being served in the kitchen.

Kasuma guided me to the balcony entrance of the Prominan temple. The narrow space held two rows of wood benches. We were above the raised platform so this must have been for their choir.

Below us, on the altar, a hand-drawn map of the Shangri-La valley had been stretched out. All of the rulers contemplated the map as King Longzhe moved wood pieces about.

"They meet still? I assumed this would be over by now," Kasuma whispered.

We quietly slid up to the railing to peer over the side and listen in.

Jarl Trym stroked his white beard, pointing at the map. "My spies report that Kane's army is no more than three day's march from Shangri-La. We must advance our troops immediately, if we hope to save the capital."

"Arrive too early and we spoil the advantage of surprise," replied Urraca, the mysterious queen Ogun. Her long, dark fingers rubbed her temples as if she had already explained this to him.

"I have the most fighters camped outside this city! They are exposed and vulnerable! We cannot rely on perfect timing, where you swoop into the valley at the critical moment his army attacks!" argued the Valhallan. "Winter is upon us and delays are inevitable. I will not sacrifice my warriors."

Urraca watched the scarred finger of Trym tap the map. King Kwong sat in a dark corner, away from the altar.

"In good weather, the march from Hyperborea to Shangri-La requires less than two days," added Longzhe.

Ferghas waved his hand as he sipped from his cup. "See, Trym? You worry like an old hall mother! We have plenty of time! But if Kane discovers our army, he will pull back and mount a full-scale assault on us. You know this to be true! If our plan is to work, we must arrive at the latest moment possible!"

The burly king with curly hair did his own tapping on the map.

Pain shot through my skull again. I winced and Kasuma placed a hand on my shoulder.

"Are you unwell?"

I shook my head, not wanting to miss the meeting.

"We leave tomorrow. No sooner," Ferghas added.

Jarl Trym got face-to-face with Ferghas. "And I will dispatch a raver instructing my army to leave immediately!"

I leaned over to Kasuma. "What's a raver?"

"A large, white bird. Valhallans use them to send messages. They sometimes kill the person trying to retrieve the message."

"Huh. Where I'm from, the saying is 'don't kill the messenger'..."

As Ferghas and Trym continued with their dick-swinging contest, Longzhe cleared his throat.

"Let us run through our strategy. One final time?"

They returned to the map altar. Longzhe pushed a wood figure along the parchment.

"As we have discussed, this valley gives us the advantage. The only access to the city is through the east. And he will not be alerted to our presence or know of our surprise—my special guards are patrolling the forests between here and Hyperborea. None of his spies will escape. So, Kane will be wary. But if he wants to take this city he will have to lead his army between these mountains."

"Aye," said Trym. "The Prominans will meet Kane's army head on. And part of my army shall defend the wall."

Longzhe moved a wood piece to the mountains on the other side of the river. "My archers will launch an attack from these peaks."

"My spear men will strike from these northern slopes and across the bridges," said Ferghas, the Elysian king.

Urraca slid closer to the map, not wanting the boys to have all the fun. "And the fine warriors from Ogun will follow behind and ride against their cavalry."

I stood up, trying to get a closer look.

Longzhe stared at the map. "And what of the Fomorians."

Ferghas grunted. "We need them, but... cannot count on them. If they arrive in time, they have to attack from the rear and box his army in the canyon. If Kane is able to retreat and regroup, we are doomed."

"With the cavalry out of the way, we will advance on their swordsmen," confirmed Jarl Trym. "Hopefully, there will be enough Prominans remaining to aid my cause."

Two aides helped King Kwong off his chair at the edge of the dais. He hobbled to the map, resting on a cane.

"We will be leading the charge," he said, his voice breaking. "And I will be the one to remove the head of the immortal despot!"

Trym and Ferghas exchanged looks, likely sharing a knowing grin.

My headache intensified. A cloud, swirling and spinning, filled my vision. As if I were trapped in a tornado. Distant voices. Two of them. Male. I grabbed at my head, pushing hard against the pain.

I heard Kasuma whispering. "Fin? Finley?"

Where is she?

A male voice echoed in the back of my mind, faint but insistent. My vision plunged into darkness. I spun around, but there was nothing to see—only the void. Panic surged through me.

Real voices floated up from below, sharp and alert:

"What is that noise?"

"Someone is up there!"

"Spies! Guards!"

The balcony beneath me tilted—or maybe I did—and I lost my footing. My eyeballs throbbed like they wanted to burst. Kasuma shoved me onto my back.

What are their plans?!

Kane? Maybe. The voice was distant, fragmented, laced with pain.

Quiet! I must concentrate.

The sounds echoed in my skull, multiplying into unbearable agony. It hit me then—Nerus. That asshole mage was trying to rip through my mind.

I screamed, my boots kicking against the floor. The pressure was overwhelming. Breathing turned to shallow gasps as I tried to steady myself.

I conjured a wall in my imagination—a towering structure of stone. It rose higher, thicker. When cracks appeared, I reinforced it with steel.

She is fighting me!

Hands grabbed me, hauling me upright.

"It's the dragonwitch!" someone yelled, but their words barely registered.

Inside, I built. Taller, wider. The wall stretched to the sky, swallowing the landscape. But the pressure intensified. Steel buckled. Cracks split the surface. My mind boiled with rage.

I let out a primal mindscream, shaking the wall to its foundation. I pressed my hands against the cold steel, forcing it forward. Trees toppled as it dragged across the ground in my mental world.

I will not let you in!

I screamed again, shoving the wall until it collapsed, crashing into the void.

The voices faded to whispers. Darkness lifted into gray. Shapes formed. Faces swam into view.

I gasped, chest heaving. Then, everything went black.

Chapter 96

"Did she tell them our plans?"

"I do not believe so." Pherric's voice.

"How do you know?!" A woman. Probably Urraca.

A glass of wine splashed on my face woke me right up.

"Ferghas!" decried Longzhe.

"What? It was taking too long."

I licked the wine from my lips. "Nice vintage. Do you have any more?"

Pherric helped me sit up. I was on the dais near the altar. The rulers were huddled up on the other side of the map, giving me suspicious stares.

"Finley? How do you feel?" asked Pherric.

"Like... like a wall fell on me."

He guided me to my feet. "Can you stand?"

"Can I? Yep. Should I? Nope."

"We have some questions," he said as a defense.

The leaders gathered around. Kasuma stood back, whispering to Longzhe.

"What happened, dragonwitch?" asked Jarl Trym.

"Stop calling me that, please." He got my good glare. "Your... jarlship."

Urraca tried to muscle-in next to Pherric. "Was she spying on us?!"

"She was not spying," Pherric said. "Was Nerus able to discern your thoughts?"

"Then why was she in the temple?"

I shook my head and blinked repeatedly. "We were coming in to talk with Kasuma's... with King Longzhe... wanted to know what we could do... what was going on... how we could help."

"Did the mage read her thoughts, Pherric?" asked Longzhe.

Pherric locked eyes with me, his expression grim. Then he closed his own, steadying himself. His hands held my head firmly in place, and I forced myself to lower my defenses.

The gray smoke swirled through my vision, hypnotic and unsettling. I hesitated but then shut my eyes, bracing for the inevitable. A sensation like a physical force pushed relentlessly against my eyeballs, shoving its way into my mind.

The pain struck like a bolt of lightning searing through my temples from the inside. My hands clenched into fists as I fought the urge to cry out.

And then, with a sudden, silent whoosh that only I could perceive, the presence was thrown from my mind—it poured out in a rush, leaving an empty ache behind.

I gasped for air, doubling over as I pressed my hands hard against my ears, desperate to block out the lingering echoes of its invasion.

Pherric opened his eyes, his jaw tightening. "He did not," he said quietly, his voice cutting through the haze like a knife.

"How are you sure?" Longzhe asked, more for the others than himself.

"She sensed his presence and rebuffed him in time, it would seem," said Pherric. He turned to the wary rulers. "From the waves I am sensing, she formed a figurative wall inside her mind. As a way to prevent Nerus from stealing her thoughts. She has only been training in mindforms for a short time but she has a mental strength and certain abilities I have only read about."

Longzhe grabbed both of my hands. "Most impressive."

"Thank you, your majesty. I guess I... just got lucky."

He winked. "Good fortune seems to be your constant companion, my child. But this attack on you does bode well."

"How so?" asked Pherric.

Longzhe turned his head to make sure the others heard him and spoke loudly. "Kane enlisted his mage to determine our troop strength and location, I am quite sure. This means that he has not decided to commit his entire force to the taking of Shangri-La. We may yet have a chance."

Longzhe bowed his head slightly, placed his winged arms behind his back, and joined the others.

I leaned into Pherric. "Is he right?"

"You have, once again, improved our odds, Finley Maguire."

"And you're still a dick, Pherric," I said, patting his cheek. "Never forget that."

"You would never let me."

The next two days were the longest week of my life.

We all knew the Irkallan invaders were marching toward Shangri-La. The tension was a thick layer of smoke that made it hard to breathe. Everyone was on edge. And the harsh winter wind that blew across the valley brought a chilling reminder of the death that awaited most, if not all, of us.

People avoided me. I was either a spy to the foreign soldiers or a bad omen to the Prominans. So I forced Braylor to help me hone my sword fighting skills. We fought against each other for hours at a time and I wouldn't let him stop until I was utterly spent, too exhausted to think.

On the morning of the third day, our scouts reported that Kane and his army neared the entrance to the valley. Braylor, Temurr, and Pherric joined me on the wall to watch the Prominan troops march through the city gate and onto the frost-covered fields.

"I have a question," I said to both. "Why are we meeting them out there in the open instead of staying behind the wall?"

"Because we are not cowards," Temurr snorted.

"The city cannot survive a siege," added Braylor. "The Prominans were already low on food and supplies, and hosting these soldiers has depleted their reserves. Knowing Kane, he likely has a scheme in place to overcome a siege." Braylor gripped the ape man's shoulder. "And... because we are not cowards."

Temurr was all smiles at the big man.

"Gotcha," I said. It made more sense to me to fight from behind a tall wall. But what did I know?

I watched as a Valhallan commander barked orders, his voice cutting through the chill air. His warriors mounted their karkadanns, while the ground troops formed precise rows, shields and weapons glinting faintly in the early light. They moved with disciplined purpose, taking position on the north side of the field, close to the rushing river. Across the open expanse, the Prominan forces assembled on the south, their banners rippling in the wind.

High above, on the steep mountain plateau, Tenguan soldiers stood poised, their bows clutched tightly in their winged hands, ready to rain arrows down from the sky. Beyond them, hidden along the rugged peaks, were the combined forces of the Elysians, Oguns, and a significant Valhallan contingent, likely finalizing their strategies. Their presence was a faint but steady reassurance, even if they remained out of sight for now.

Notably absent were the Cíbolans, thanks to Lord Diago's chaotic new ruling family, and the Fomorians, from whom we had received no word at all.

The stage was set, but with so many missing pieces, the balance of power felt seriously thin.

As if reading my mind, Temurr nudged Braylor. "Speaking of cowards, where are your people?"

The big Fomorian growled and bared a few teeth at Temurr. "They will be here. I promise you this."

"Well, the surest way to die is being on time for a war..." mused Pherric.

"Mind your tongue, wizard," snarled Braylor. "Before I remove it from your head."

"Kinda seems like we have a lot of troops," I said. "From what I can see. Even without Braylor's people."

"We have almost thirty thousand troops. At least five thousand karkadanns," said Temurr confidently.

"That's good. And you say we're outnumbered?"

Braylor nodded. "Spies have reported Kane has over fifty thousand soldiers, with more than twice the number of our mounts. They even spotted a team of Behemoths."

I started to ask about Behemoths… but held my tongue, afraid that he might tell me.

"That's bad."

Braylor exhaled deeply. "We are indeed outnumbered. But… my people will arrive in time."

I felt so bad for him. I wanted nothing more than to hug him, hold his hand. But that was neither the time nor the place. There could be no love shown right before a big battle, I figured. So, I reached out and held on to his smallest finger as tight as I could.

"But what if he only sends half his troops?" I asked, hoping to cheer him up.

"I do not believe he will do that. I fear this Kane is too wise to fall for their scheme. He will send them all and make quick work of this city."

I leaned against the low wall and surveyed our army again, with Prominans lined up to my right and the small group of Valhallans to my left.

"Something is wrong," I mumbled.

Temurr rushed up next to me, looking frantically at the forces below. "What?! What is wrong?"

I turned to Pherric. "Can you take me to Longzhe?"

"Now?"

"Yes, now!" I shouted. "Immediately!"

He pointed up and across the river. "He is on that high plateau. With his people."

I pushed past them and ran to the stone stairs.

"We cannot get you there before the Irkallans arrive!" Braylor bellowed. "What is your concern?!"

I faced him. "We're going to lose this war if we don't do something!"

"What could possibly cause us to—?"

The distant beat of a drum cut him off. The guys rushed to the wall.

"What's going on?"

Another loud beat. Slightly closer.

"The Irkallans are here," Temurr intoned.

I stole a quick look up toward the Tenguans. "Dammit."

Pherric kept his eyes locked on the far end of the Shangri-La valley. "What is wrong, Finley? What have we forgotten?"

"Well, I think our strategy is all wrong."

Braylor snorted. "I thought you were no military commander, Fin?"

"You know I'm not," I said. "But from everything you guys taught me, we really shouldn't be all separated like this."

The line of drums beat louder, with a low morning mist obscuring the source. Small, white flakes of snow began to swirl through the valley.

"Separated?" asked Pherric.

"Yes! We should be fighting together?"

Temurr laughed. "That would be impossible!"

"Look, you all have trained me—Kasuma, Cira, and Gunnr included—and you showed me your specialties. Whenever our group fights, you all depended on your own skills. But... never on those around you. And this quote-unquote army looks like they're about to do the same damn thing. Prominans over here, Valhallans over there, Tenguans up there. If we work together and fight side-by-side we'll do a helluva lot better. Kane has worked very hard to separate the kingdoms and the species. We need to bring everyone together."

Along with the beating drums came the rumble on boots marching on the ground.

Braylor rolled his eyes. "So, you think we'd fight better if we... intermingled our troops? That is absurd."

"Okay, I'm not talking about mixing everybody up. But consider this—Prominans are great archers. But, well... you're not the best with a sword," I said. Temurr shrugged his acknowledgment. "Most of the Valhallans down there are armed with axes. Which are great for quick attacks but they wear you down, because all the weight is at the end. And you can't parry swords with them. So, you've got no swordsmen down here. I would think having a thick wall of spears up front would protect your archers, but Ferghas has his spears over there, across the river! The Tenguan could even be additional archers with the Prominans, but you've got them secluded on the peak. Do you see what I am saying?"

Temurr looked down and away. Braylor looked at me like I had lost my mind.

"This does make sense," Pherric said. "Very good sense, in fact."

"There's a saying on my world. United we stand, divided we fall. None of you have ever really had to unite before all this. But I've—"

"Finley," said Pherric, grabbing my shoulders. "I fear it is too late."

I turned to the wall, angry and dejected, as the first few rows of Irkallan soldiers emerged from the heavy mists.

Chapter 97

"Did you guys listen to anything I said?!" I screamed. "No, you did not!"

I parried an Irkallan sword and slashed hard through the soldier's jacket.

"We listened, Fin!" Braylor shouted over the din of battle. "We had no time to act!"

His broadsword sliced through the neck of a foot soldier holding a spear. Braylor grunted in anger, kicking away the body to release his sword—he hadn't cut cleanly through.

"We could've tried... *something*! Warned them somehow!" I stabbed an Irkallan in the chest and pulled my blade to block a blow from another.

Frustrated, I spun and let my blade slice under the swordsman's helmet, cutting halfway through his jaw.

Braylor shoved his thick sword through one soldier and into his friend. "I am a fighter, not a messenger!"

Ahead of us, two giant soldiers decided we were their next target.

Braylor nudged me hard. "I will take the big one."

"Thanks," I exhaled.

"You take the bigger one."

"Asshole," I whispered.

He laughed as he deflected the sword of one of the giants, but the blade of the other glanced the mail on Braylor's shoulder. He elbowed the guy in the nose, as I ran my sword through his gut.

"But what I said... made sense! They've gained... too much ground!" I had been swinging my sword for twenty minutes straight. My arms were about to fall off.

Behind us, Temurr jumped down from a stack of several bodies, firing arrows into two advancing Irkallans, and joined us. He put his back to mine, firing his bow again. "Stop chattering?! And start killing!"

"I am still warming up my bones!" Braylor crushed a man's forehead with the flat of his blade. "A gargoyle does not roast in minutes, Temurr." He cut into the breast of another with a quick slash. "It takes hours. It is a process!"

"Well, hours we do not have, my friend!" Temurr stabbed a soldier in the throat with an arrow, then fired it into the oncoming crowd.

The battle had started off rather slowly. Drums pounded away as Kane's army started to fill in the wide ravine leading up to the city. Snowflakes drifted down as the storm clouds darkened the sky. Troops with long pikes and shields formed a front line with archers behind them. Then the drums stopped. And nothing happened; the Irkallans simply waited.

Tension rippled through the ranks of the Valhallans and Prominans on the front line. Restless murmurs echoed across the field as nerves began to fray. Soldiers shifted uneasily, their hands tightening around weapons, their breaths visible in the cool air.

The Valhallan commander, a towering figure with a braided blond beard that reached his waist, sat motionless on his kark. He stroked his beard thoughtfully, his piercing gaze fixed on the opposing army. His unshakable calm radiated through his troops, keeping their growing agitation in check with sheer presence alone.

The Prominans, however, were not so soothed. Patience was clearly not their virtue. They snarled and growled, pacing like caged beasts desperate to strike. The waiting game was wearing thin, and it was only a matter of time before the tension broke.

Kwong, king of the Prominans, rode his way forward with a guard and his steward in tow.

He glared at the Valhallan. "Well?! What are you waiting for?!"

The commander looked the king up and down and returned his gaze to the Irkallans.

"Let us finish this!" Kwong roared.

Standing beside us, Temurr started to speak. He wanted to object, but knew it was not his place. His mouth drooped into a scowl.

Despite his haggard appearance, the king held his thin head high and stared confidently at the enemy.

Kwong coughed and spat on the ground. "It is time!"

His steward slid his karkadann up next to the king and reached out for his frail arm. "Sire, you are in no condition to—"

Kwong shrugged his servant's hand away. "Ah, but there is enough fire left in my belly to run you through, Baiha!"

The steward lowered his head, pulling on the reins, backing away.

"Onward," shouted the king. "To victory!"

The Prominan cavalry began their attack, riding hard across the vale.

The Valhallan leader shouted warnings, but was drowned out by the thundering of hooves.

Temurr took a step forward, his hand outstretched. He needed to help his king. Before he could take off running, Braylor hoisted Temurr into the air.

"Put me down, Braylor!"

"No. Follow him into this battle and you will die."

"We will all die on this day!" Temurr struggled to break himself free. "He is my king!"

Braylor pulled him in close.

"He is not your king. He banished you. And Frip. You no longer fight for Kwong—you fight for your people. Do not die in vain... for him," soothed Braylor. He turned Temurr to face the city. "If you are to die today, do it with purpose. For them."

The ape man went limp. Braylor dropped him to the snow.

We turned at the sound of a new drum beat. With the Prominan riders halfway to the enemy, the Irkallan archers drew their longbows and fired. A black cloud rose up and then their pointed shafts fell hard on the Prominans. Despite their raised shields, hundreds of bodies dropped to the field. The Prominans returned fire, but their short bows could not cover the distance. Another round of arrows rained down. And then another. So many Prominans were killed before they even reached the long spears of the Irkallans.

I looked up to the mountain across the river—no troops came riding down to the rescue.

"What are they waiting for?!" I shouted to Braylor.

"Kane is testing us," he grumbled. "He wants to see if we have forces in reserve."

The narrow canyon leading to the vale benefited us. Kane had to constrict his troops to get into the valley and lay siege to the city. But he was always two steps ahead of everyone. He would have figured out a way to turn such an exposed position, perfect for an ambush, to his advantage.

And the impatient Prominans were making his task easier. They howled their war cries as they rode toward the Irkallan pikemen. Their arrows decimated the Irkallan first line of spears, but another line of them pushed forward from behind. The Prominans were smart to continually fire their short bows, but they kept riding at them until the gap was closed. On either side, Kane's troops began to close around the Prominan offensive.

"They will be trapped! We must join the attack!" Temurr shouted as tears fell.

Braylor placed his hands on Temurr, to hold him back. And to comfort him.

We watched as the Prominan king was hit in the shoulder by an arrow. And we lowered our heads as a spear knocked him from the karkadann. We cried as the Irkallans pounced on the king and drove their swords into his thin body.

Temurr fell on his face and pounded his fists into the frozen ground. I placed my hand on his back.

After a fast but fierce clash, the remaining Prominans realized the futility of their unorganized assault. They had lost nearly half of their cavalrymen. But rather than turn and run, the ape-men were smart enough to veer toward the mountains and cut into the company flanking them to the south. They fought their way free, slowly backed off, and rejoined us at the wall.

Kane held his army in check. He was biding his time, testing us, waiting to see if reinforcements would finally emerge from the mountains.

The Prominan cavalry, battered, bloodied, and barely holding on, didn't have much fight left. Pherric darted into their group, tending to the wounded with frantic determination. Braylor heaved Temurr over his shoulder and hauled him toward the Valhallan commander's line of karkadanns.

The ominous thrum of Irkallan drums shattered the brief silence. The tempo quickened, signaling Kane's next move. His massive army began a deliberate, unrelenting march toward Shangri-La. Arrows rained down in waves, the air thick with their whistling flight.

The Valhallan commander stood like a stone sentinel, his broad shoulders taut as he assessed the enemy. His troops waited for the word, their hands tightening on reins and weapons. When the Prominans managed to regroup, arrows falling thick around them, the commander raised his massive axe high above his head, its blade gleaming in the gray light.

With a thunderous roar, the Valhallan cavalry surged forward, karkadanns bounding across the field. The Prominan cavalry, battered but unbroken, joined the charge, followed by the hearty ranks of foot soldiers from both peoples. The earth trembled beneath their assault, the battle for Shangri-La starting for real this time.

I've learned the hard way that trying to explain death is nearly impossible. And trying to explain the craziness of battle is just as hard. Charging headlong into people armed with sharp, pointy weapons, people who desperately want to use those weapons on you, is both terrifying and insane. It's everything your instincts scream against. But here's the thing—they don't tell you about the rush.

It's exhilarating, intoxicating even. My brain, dumb and reckless as ever, shoved the fear deep into a dark corner and replaced it with a tingling vibration that lit up my entire body—from my fingertips to my toes. It was beyond a runner's high; it was euphoria. For the first time, I understood the *warlust* Braylor talked about. That all-consuming surge of energy made the chaos feel like a thrilling dance.

And yet, twenty minutes in, the reality hit me like a collapsing wall. My body ached, my energy drained, and my arms screamed in protest every time I swung my sword. Just when I thought I couldn't take another step, let alone strike another blow, survival instincts kicked in. Something primal, raw, and unyielding kept me moving, kept me fighting, kept me alive.

Two Irkallan soldiers attacked in unison. I deflected their blades with my shield, but a sword penetrated my mail, cutting lightly into my hip. I drove the tip of my blade under the chin of one and Temurr ended the other with a knife.

Pain coursed through me as warm blood ran down my leg.

A worried look crossed Braylor's bloodstained face.

"Dammit!" I screamed. "Will you people stop stabbing me!"

Braylor laughed, shoving three soldiers back, then hacked away at them.

"Seriously! I'm practically just one big scar, at this point!"

The wound was not deadly. I could put weight on my leg—but no more high-slit dresses for this girl.

The snow fell in a steady stream as I pulled back my cloak, inspected the wound.

I searched for Pherric—he stood there with a worried look, but I shook my head. He reluctantly went back to treating a wounded Prominan.

An arrow thudded into the ground next to me.

Several soldiers yell out. "Shields!"

Everyone ducked down, shields over their heads. I grabbed mine and rolled onto my knees. Braylor squatted next to me, adjusted mine to a better angle. Thousands upon thousands of arrows rained down. *Thunk-thunk-thunk.* Soldiers all around me, on both sides, fell or screamed out as they were hit.

"Why are they shooting arrows with their own people in the way?!" I shouted at Braylor.

"This battle is taking too long—Kane wants to end this quickly!"

Someone far away screamed. "Attack!"

I started to stand, but Braylor pulled me back down. I crouched low as more arrows sank into the slushy ground. Prominan archers, from behind our front line, darkened the fake moon overhead with their own volley.

My knees sank into the frigid mud, my shield trembling under the relentless hail of arrows. I winced, cursing my earlier decision to tuck that shard of flint into my boot. Its jagged edge bit into my flesh, a cruel reminder of another bad idea. The pain was sharp, but it paled compared to the insanity erupting around me.

A Prominan commander's voice thundered over the battle. It was time to go on the offensive. With a surge of determination, we scrambled to our feet, joining the tidal wave of thousands of soldiers storming Kane's front lines. Their collective war cry tore through the air, a primeval sound that would freeze the blood in anyone's veins.

Beside me, Braylor let out his own feral howl, his glee an unsettling counterpoint to the carnage. We marched forward, driven by duty, desperation, and a flicker of hope.

Nothing would stop the grin that spread across my face as I cut an Irkallan's legs from under him.

We clashed for what seemed like an hour—but was likely less than half of that. I stole a quick glance around. The clean, white snow had been stained red. Bodies littered the vale. Cries from the wounded filled my ears. Many called in vain for healers, for family members, for loved ones, as they bled out.

Most of the Prominan karkadanns had been slaughtered. And we were still outnumbered. But we had done some damage.

When I looked back, we had been pushed back a lot closer to the wall than I thought. Ahead of us, beyond the piles of bodies, were their attacking foot soldiers. Beyond them, rows and rows of the black and blue helmet plumes. For every Irkallan I would kill, two more would take their place. The Prominans had taken heavy casualties, but they fought on. The Valhallan force had held up their end of the bargain. It was still morning, but the grayish black clouds made it seem as dark as night.

Leaders shouted orders to anyone who would listen. Soldiers yelled out to spur themselves on. Swords clanged together. And the screams of the dying filled my ears.

After the Irkallan troops had broken through our lines, pushing us back toward the wall, I expected our hidden troops would start their ambush. But they had not come yet. Where were they? Were they waiting for more of Kane's army to fill the valley?

I scurried to the top of a corpse pile, scanning the battlefield. I jumped to avoid a sword strike at my feet, then drove the point of my blade into the back of the guy's neck. Behind their front line, I spotted three chariots. The man standing on the middle one had his cloak hood pulled down, hiding his features. It wasn't Kane—the shoulders were too narrow. And the men on either side... were there for protection. That guy was important.

As I fought off a soldier's sharp spear, I turned to Braylor.

"That guy! There!"

Braylor nearly sliced a man's arm off. "What about him?!"

"I think we need to kill him!"

He laughed. "Aye, girl! We need to kill them all, do we not?!"

A horn sounded in the distance, from the northern mountain across the river. I looked up to see a line of mounted troops forming on the ridge. Valhallans, Oguns, Elysians, and a half dozen other kingdoms were poised to attack. In the dark skies above swarmed a thousand Tenguans, bows at the ready. Our horn sounded out again, rising above the thrum of battle.

"About damn time!" I shouted, mostly to myself.

I stole a glance at the cloaked figure standing on the chariot. When he pulled back his hood, my breath caught—it was Nerus. That oily, pallid face, framed by strands of greasy black hair I could never forget. With a sinister calm, he lifted his hands to the sky, closing his eyes as his lips shaped the words of an incantation. He was casting a mindform.

Our armies surged over the mountain ridge, descending the slope in a blurring wave of foot soldiers and mounted beasts. War cries sailed through the air, mingling with the pounding of hooves as the cavalry urged their karks to greater speeds.

But it was as if the Irkallans had anticipated our ambush. Their commanders bellowed precise orders, and a new drumbeat rippled through the valley like a heartbeat of war. In perfect formation, a third of the Irkallan forces broke away, their disciplined ranks marching north. They raced across the twin bridges, pivoting to scale the mountainside and meet them head-on.

From his chariot, Nerus' chant rose, sinister and unwavering. Panic prickled up my spine. I turned sharply, calling out to Pherric—but he was too far, lost in the melee. Desperation clawed at my throat as I screamed at a Prominan general to target the three chariots. My voice was swallowed by the deafening roar, my words carried away in the wind as the battle raged on.

I fought off several Irkallans, then glanced at the mountainside. Kane's troops scurried up the slope to take on our reinforcements. A swirling mist, farther to the east, caught my eye. *Thousands upon thousands* of Irkallan riders galloped out of the low, dark cloud. They charged on armored karkadanns along the ridge and the side of the mountain.

I stood there in stunned silence. *Where did that cavalry come from?*

More than half of our reinforcements halted their descent down the slope. They turned their attention to this new oncoming horde of Irkallan warriors.

One more look at Nerus told me everything I needed to know—those new troops were *not* real.

"It's a trick! They're fake!" I screamed at Braylor. "Those soldiers are not there!"

Braylor eyed the new massive force bearing down on our army. "What?!"

"Ignore them!" I shouted toward the mountain. "Keep riding down!" But no one could hear me.

Kane's soldiers took advantage of our troops breaking ranks. As many of our men focused on the new attackers, his army swarmed them.

"Keep coming down!"

I leapt off the mound, slashed through the foot soldiers, and worked my way toward Nerus—I had to end his mindform mirage. Before it was too late.

Chapter 98

"Finley! Wait!" Braylor shouted, struggling to catch up with me I ran low, slashed hard. I hit anyone nearby quickly—just enough to wound and distract as I rushed through. Then, I struck one soldier too hard. *Other Other sword* got stuck. Another blade came at me, so I fell backwards and let the body of the man I was stuck to take the blow. I kicked my sword free and quickly hit the attacker.

In a flurry, I swung wildly at everyone in my path—desperate to get to Nerus.

Kane must have feared he would be ambushed, so he placed Nerus in the middle of the battlefield to take away our element of surprise.

"What are you doing?!" Braylor bellowed as he caught up.

"Those Irkallans up there?! They aren't real!" I shouted, slamming my blade into another swordsman.

"They look real enough!" He drove his long sword through the chest of a soldier.

"Kane sent his mage out here!" I pointed at Nerus, parried away a blade and elbowed the guy's throat. "That's Nerus! He's using mindforms to create those soldiers!"

"Sorcery!" Braylor drove his blade into a man's collar bone.

"Kane planned for an ambush!"

"How did he know?!"

My mind struggled to put it together. Longzhe had told the other rulers that his special guards had cleared the forests, killing Kane's spies from Hyperborea to Shangri-La. And I had killed a number of spies... then it hit me.

"We killed his scouts!" I screamed. "Before the battle!"

Braylor hacked two Irkallan soldiers with one swing of his heavy sword. "So?!"

"If the Tenguans found all of his spies, and they *didn't* report back... then he knew!"

A swordsman was about to split my head open when an arrow struck him in the neck—Temurr had to be lurking somewhere behind us.

I turned toward him as he fired off another arrow, over my shoulder, hitting a soldier coming up on me. "Temurr! Aim for chariots! The guy in the middle!"

He nodded, notched an arrow. I fought off Irkallans as he released his bow. The arrow sailed over our heads. One of the chariot guards leapt in front of Nerus. Temurr's arrow sank deep in his chest.

"Again!" I screamed, fighting off more soldiers.

On the hill, our forces had completely divided—some fighting the real Irkallans, while most went after the fake troops.

Temurr launched an arrow. The other chariot guard leapt in front of the mage as the tip pierced his shoulder. Nerus kept his eyes closed, focusing his mind on creating the apparitions.

"Keep trying!"

With Braylor at my heels, I sprinted into a crowd of soldiers.

I heard warnings being shouted on the mountain—our troops began to realize the new attackers were not real. Confusion reigned as more of our soldiers charged at them. I wasn't getting to Nerus fast enough.

I grabbed Braylor. "Give me a boost!"

I guided him in front of me. He nodded, clasped his hands together. Running at him, I jumped and planted a boot on his big hands. He launched me high in the sky. I flew up in the air—exhaling and aiming—and threw my sword. The blade was on target, but I didn't balance it. The sword tipped down, rolled. The point didn't strike him, but the flat of the blade struck his chariot. Startled from his trance, he gasped and fell off to the ground.

On the mountainside, the ghost warriors disappeared. I jumped to my feet, charging forward. Braylor's huge boots clomped through the mud behind me.

Braylor grunted. "Another good sword... gone!"

"Shut up about the damn swords!"

I reached my hand behind my back—Braylor gave me a dagger. I used the short blade to deflect an attack and strike a soldier's thigh, dropping him to the ground.

I hopped on the empty chariot, looked around. Nerus was just lying there in the muddy grass. I dove down, driving the blade through his back—and he disappeared. It was a mindform! His apparition faded. I scanned the snowy field, spotted him running toward a crowd of archers.

Without thinking, I threw my dagger. The tip struck the back of his breeches, cutting into the muscle. He collapsed, unable to keep weight on that leg. I smiled—something *finally* went right for me.

I scooped up Other Other Sword from the mud and sprinted after Nerus. As the little weasel tried to crawl away, I pounced on him.

"No! Please! Spare me! I-I can help you!" he whimpered.

I plunged my sword into his gut as he squealed in pain.

"No, thanks!" I growled, twisting the blade.

I yanked his greasy black hair to expose his neck. I pulled out my sword and held it to his neck.

Then I heard a voice. But not from Nerus. The voice was inside my head.

Call to them.

I slit the mage's throat.

Braylor slid through the mud, stopping next to me. He took wide swings with his broadsword, clearing away the Irkallans. He grabbed my arm, dragging me back to safety.

Kane's mage was dead, but... the damage had been done. We had lost our element of surprise. The Irkallan forces had slowed down our advancing troops. Many stood on the side of the mountain, looking all around and wondering what had happened to the soldiers and karks that had disappeared. Commanders shouted orders, but our battle lines were in disarray.

If Kane had used Nerus to create a fake army, that meant he had not committed his entire force to attacking Shangri-La. From what I could see, our two armies seemed almost evenly matched. We had a chance. But a slim one. The armies from the individual kingdoms were disciplined but we were not working together. As I had feared. The newly-arrived Valhallans and the Elysians raced down the side of the mountain to fight alongside their countrymen. The Oguns took on the Irkallans that had advanced up the slope to block our surprise attack. There was still no sign of Braylor's Fomorians.

After he pulled me behind our lines, I turned to him. "We need to get organized!"

"A bit late in the day for that!" screamed Braylor.

A new drum beat echoed out. Kane's men formed two fronts, to counter our new forces as well as make a final push toward the city walls. Rows of pikemen, their spears held out as they hid behind shields, marched forward. Stout Irkallan knights on karkadanns backed them up. And swordsmen followed the cavalry.

What plodded along behind them stole the air from my lungs—the Behemoths. Towering giants, their hulking forms loomed thirty feet high, each step a seismic event that reverberated through the ground beneath my boots. Their coarse brown hides were streaked with scars. They were filthy, covered in layers of mud, as if they had crawled up from the ground itself.

Their heads were monstrous, grotesque hybrids of oxen and elephants, with wide, sloping foreheads and deep-set, glowing eyes that seemed to burn with an elemental rage. But it was the horns that held my gaze— massive, pointed spires of bone jutting from their foreheads, each one had been shaved to act as a spear.

As they moved, their muscles rippled under their thick, leathery skin, and the air filled with the sound of labored breathing, like bellows in a forge. Chains as thick as a man's arm connected them to their handlers, but it was clear these creatures were not controlled—they were barely contained.

I swallowed hard, my throat dry as I muttered the only words that came to mind. "We are so screwed."

"Aye! But who wants to live forever?!" shouted Braylor, slicing his bloodied sword through the cold day and into warm flesh.

I thought about my dream of being an old woman, lounging in a chair and sipping on a cocktail. Then I shrugged. "Well, living a little longer would've been nice."

"From your mouth to the gods' ears!" said Temurr, rushing up behind us and firing off his arrows. "If they have ears!"

Braylor laughed as he felled another hapless Irkallan.

"But I will say if the Irkallans force us to retreat into the city, we are indeed doomed," Temurr added.

"Well, then. Let us make sure that does not happen!" said Braylor as he let out a loud war cry and surged into a wide-eyed crowd of soldiers.

"Seriously?" The muscles in my arms and legs burned. And I desperately needed water. But I dug up a few extra ounces of resolve and followed him into the fray.

I scooped up the cleanest snow to be found, shoved it in my mouth, and chased after my burly barbarian. Grinning ear to ear. Fighting beside him was all that mattered.

"And here I was... having a perfect hair day!"

Chapter 99

Surviving a battle depends on a whole *truckload* of luck. Even the best warriors get killed by a random arrow or a sword slash from behind. On one occasion, I avoided death simply because I slipped in the mud and a sword I didn't see coming whizzed right by my neck.

Temurr caught up with Braylor and I as we hacked our way through the Irkallans. He managed to get a few troops to follow us as we drove deep into their ranks. Anger, and probably a lot of fear, propelled our little squad to make a stand. We held our own for quite some time, but... they just kept coming and coming.

I looked back at the city wall. Prominan archers fired aimlessly at any warriors who got too close.

I recalled my training with Frip and Temurr and raced to him, yelling in his ear. "Get your archers to form up behind us! Have them fire at everyone beyond us! Just over our heads, okay?!"

He nodded.

I grabbed him before he could race away. "Remember! Twenty arrows a minute!"

He winked, rushing off.

I ducked as a sword whooshed over my head, but the Irkallan struck me in the jaw with his elbow. I dropped to the bloody grass. My sword gashed his ankle and then stabbed into his side when he hit the ground.

A hand reached out to help me up. I pulled myself up to face Melcente.

The ship captain was dressed in mail, wearing a helmet, and holding a shield.

Covered in gore, she did not recognize me.

"Melcente!"

A second passed before she recognized me.

But then she shouted. "Down!"

I ducked as she rammed her sword into an approaching soldier.

"You!" she moaned, rolling her eyes after she recognized me.

As another Irkallan approached, I spun away. We fought shoulder to shoulder.

"What are you doing here?!"

"Fightin', love! These here baddies is the ones who sank my *Jaculus* and they sank the *Alkonost*. This here's my revenge!" she said, blocking a blow with her shield. "What kinda curse your throwin' at us on this here battle?!"

"Only the best kind!" I laughed. "But how did you end up fighting?"

I hacked my sword into a soldier's forearm and then his leg. I stepped on his throat to keep him down.

"Followed Temurr to dis city. Kept to me own on the odds them Irkallans was looking for me. When the battle come up, decided to fight with 'em."

"Well!" I parried a spear away. "Glad to have you on our side!"

"And now I know we be doomed..."

She got my best smirk. "May the gods be damned..."

I heard a volley of arrows whoosh by. Hundreds soared just over our heads and into the ranks of Irkallans. Then another volley. Over my shoulder, I saw Temurr leading his archers—most had jumped up on the piles of bodies and started clearing a path ahead of us.

"Leave no Irkallan standing!" shouted Braylor. He waved his huge broadsword into the air, setting off a wave of deafening war cries.

Melcente and I dashed through the mud behind him.

We started making a real push, putting the Irkallans on their heels. And that small turn of the tide gave me more stamina. My sword felt lighter. The gash on my hip stopped hurting... as bad. My legs were sturdier. We advanced more quickly as our arrows rained down.

Kane's commanders noticed our efforts.

As we battled on, I felt the ground shake. Then... a thunderous roar. Irkallan soldiers ahead parted. Armored men riding karkadanns stormed through the crowd, their swords hacking away at everyone in their path.

"Shields!" I cried out, then looked down—I had lost my shield chasing down Nerus.

Melcente threw her shield in front of me. "Get down, love!"

We dropped to the ground as heavy swords struck her shield. Hooves sank in the mud all around us. After the karkadanns blew by, I jumped to my feet. Braylor had cut down two of the beasts and was driving his sword through one of the riders. I turned behind us in time to see the Irkallans slaughter our archers. The Prominans had no shields.

Braylor and I bounded after their knights. He leapt on the back of the nearest kark, drove his sword through the rider's back, and tossed the body. I cut the leg of another rider, pulled him down, and ran after the next one. Braylor and I tracked down and attacked several more knights from behind.

Temurr crossed blades with two Irkallan cavalrymen, but his short sword was no match. But before the soldier could strike a deadly blow, the guy fell to the ground with an arrow to the eye. Then an arrow hit the other rider. He dropped off his kark. I looked up. Kasuma fluttered down to the mud. She fired another arrow and gave me a wink.

When the last Irkallan was dead, all of the Prominan archers had been killed. But we managed to save Temurr.

Braylor spun his karkadann back around, raised his sword, screamed a deep war cry, and bolted after the approaching foot soldiers.

I leaned over to Temurr. "You all right?"

"Aye. I will live. For a few moments more." He wiped blood away from his short sword on a sleeve.

Kasuma extended her wings, ready to take flight.

"Hey!" I shouted.

"I cannot stay on the ground!"

"I know. But... if you get a chance! Take out whoever is pounding those drums. I think it's how they communicate!"

Kasuma smirked, gave me a curt nod, and lifted up into the snowy gray sky.

The Irkallans came after us hard. With renewed energy. I could easily see their wide, white eyes inside those dark helmets. With our archers dead, their hope was renewed—and they regained the momentum. For every step forward, we took three back.

Fear itched the back of my brain. Where I had calmed my breathing when I fought, I now had to fight for air. My heart rate jumped back up. Other Other Sword got heavier with each swing. My legs were tree trunks. And the wound in my hip throbbed.

Call them.

The voice. Again. The same voice that had told me to go kill Malek.

I took on every soldier who came at me, but continued to listen for more instructions. For an explanation. None came. *Who should I call?*

As a spear nearly grazed my cheek, I realized I was too distracted from the fight—and that would get me killed. I shook off the *mindvoice* and attacked two Irkallans at once. My blade sliced into the belly of the first and across the thigh of the second.

I stole a quick look over to Braylor as he battled from atop the karkadann. I loved watching him work his blade. He slashed away at the Irkallans, seemingly growing more powerful with every stroke, with either a snarl or a grin plastered on his face. He instilled fear. And then backed it up with unbelievable strength. If only we had an army of *him*.

The drums sounded again—beating out a new pattern.

A soldier swung an axe down at my head. I stepped aside and slid my sword deep into his rib cage. As I pulled my blade free, movement from the top of the mountain caught my eye.

An arrow whizzed past my ear and I ducked down. As I rose up, I could make out thousands of mounted soldiers as they rode up to the ledge.

Whatever small amount of hope that I had left quickly disappeared. These new riders were wearing the Irkallan black and blue. And there were thousands upon thousands of them up on that slope overlooking the valley.

The drum beat again. The horde of Irkallan reinforcements began their hasty descent.

Kane had committed all his troops to the assault on Shangri-La. But he had held a lot of them back. Until now.

I whistled at Braylor. I nodded my head toward the top of the mountain.

"Eh... Good!" Braylor watched riders barreling down at us, shrugging at me. "More of them to kill!"

The leaders of our misfit army shouted out orders. But we were surrounded on both sides. Groups broke off or turned to face the reinforcements.

The Irkallans outflanked us.

I took a deep breath before diving back into the battle. Then the *mindvoice* returned.

Call to them.

"Call to who?!" I screamed up into the morning sky, my breath hanging in the cold air.

Silence.

That shout had burned the back of my dry throat. I tried to lift a boot out of the bloody mud but it wouldn't budge. Exhaustion and pain overwhelmed me.

The voice that called to me had never let me down. Even though I failed nearly every time, someone kept calling to me. Asking more of me.

Quickly.

I screamed in frustration at that point. I took several steps back, letting a few Valhallan warriors take on the foes in front of me. I focused my mind, trying to ignore the sounds of clashing steel and the screams of the dying.

I will call to them, I thought. *But tell me who to call? Our troops? The Fomorians? The—*

The voice said a single word, sending a viscous chill down my back.

Dragons.

Chapter 100

"The dragons?!" I shouted, my voice barely piercing the roar.

For the first time, the voice didn't echo inside my head—it came from somewhere. It resonated in the air around me, tangible, almost human. My heart rate quickened as the words lingered, as if whispered just behind my ear.

I spun around. The city wall loomed a few hundred feet away, its weathered stones a stark backdrop to the fighting. My eyes darted frantically, scanning every shadowy crevice for a figure, a face—anything that could explain the disembodied voice.

Then I saw something. Near the wall, a faint, shimmering outline began to take shape. It pulsed with a hazy white light, the kind that danced at the edge of perception, like the ghost of something not meant to exist. I swallowed hard, the metallic tang of fear bitter on my tongue.

I glanced over my shoulder. The battlefield churned on, but no one seemed to notice me—or the strange apparition. For a moment, I felt suspended, caught between two worlds.

Gripping the hilt of my sword, I took a tentative step forward, then another. My movements were slow, deliberate, every muscle tensed as I edged closer to the figure.

Temurr must have seen me wander off and raced after me.

"Finley! What are you doing! The battle is the other way!"

"I don't know. But... I think it might help us. Maybe?"

He exhaled. "Then I shall protect you."

Keeping his back to mine, he launched arrows at the enemy.

The torch fires atop the wall blinded me as I neared the base below. Even though I inched closer, the outline became less clear. I squinted, trying to bring the shimmering silhouette into focus.

I noticed Pherric further along the base of the wall. He kneeled over a wounded Valhallan, applied a powder, and rapidly bandaged the man's injured leg.

Call to the dragons.

The voice sounded female—it was a woman who had been calling to me! She still sounded close, but remained a swirling dark shape. I reached out to touch the shadow ahead and... she disappeared. Feeling like a fool, I stood there staring at a blank wall. Others were dying in battle and I was chasing a phantom.

A cold wind chilled me, my eyelashes capturing falling snowflakes.

Temurr gave me a worried look, but I could only shrug.

Further along the stone wall, the apparition appeared once more, its ethereal glow pulling me. I exhaled slowly, my breath misting in the frigid air. This time, I didn't hesitate. With renewed purpose, I marched toward her, my boots crunching against the frost-covered ground.

Her form wavered like a reflection on disturbed water, a glowing, murky shadow. It reminded me of the illusions Pherric had cast back at the Godsribbon castle, tricking the guards with images of us that weren't entirely solid. This was different, though. More... deliberate.

As I drew closer, the apparition shifted again, its shimmering edges blurring as if struggling against some unseen barrier. The air around her seemed to ripple, the boundary between her world and mine fragile and tenuous. For a moment, I wondered if she would dissolve completely, slipping away before I could uncover her truth.

But then, with a sudden clarity, she solidified. Her features sharpened, her form pulling itself into focus with an almost painful effort. And there she was.

Silvery hair framed her face, cascading like a waterfall of moonlight, and her sharp features carried an air of regal defiance. I froze, as recognition hit me. I had seen her before—not in life, but in the tall painting that hung outside the grand hall of the castle in the Black City.

The spirit floating before me was Queen Dirvilia.

Call to the dragons. Now.

"Oh, but I have so many questions..."

Her mouth did not move, but I heard her words. In my mind.

There is no time. They are your only hope. Summon them.

"Are you the one who's been helping me all this time?"

Her spirit wavered in and out of focus. A look of dread spread across her face.

"Okay. Okay. Um... I can do that. But they... the dragons kinda hate me."

Call to them.

I turned back toward the battle. Braylor hacked away with his massive sword. Melcente stood at his back, blocking attackers with her shield. Tenguans flew in and out, firing arrows into advancing Irkallans. And Temurr watched over me with his bow drawn.

Do this.

I nodded. Closed my eyes. I exhaled and worked to slow my heart. Focus. Breathe in for three seconds, out for three. Ignore the cries of the dying, the stench from the corpses, and the dull thuds of sharp metal tearing through flesh and bone. But nothing happened.

"I can't do it!" I kept my eyes closed, fearing she had disappeared.

Call the dragons to you.

Frustrated, I shouted, fists clenched tight. Rage, sadness, guilt, and fear churned inside me. I sucked in a deep breath, trying to push it all away. Snow landed on my cheek, melting into a cold streak down my face. I focused on that sensation, on the icy air slipping through my chainmail, and the beads of sweat trailing down my back.

My mind drifted, lifting away from my body. I saw myself below, just standing there, staring at the city wall. Irkallans were closing in, but Temurr held steady, firing arrows.

The dragons are alone, adrift. They are angry. Give them purpose.

A male Tenguan streaked through my vision, loosing arrows at the enemy. He didn't see me.

I let my mind float—over the wall, past Shangri-La's rooftops, beyond the roaring waterfalls, and across the stark peaks of Kunlun. I drifted effortlessly, untouched by cold or snow, soaring through gray clouds and down into a hidden valley.

There, in the Valley of the Black Bones, I found them. Three dragons, their massive forms coiled in restless slumber, perched above the remains of their ancestors. Big Red stirred first, sensing my presence. She lifted her head, nostrils flaring as I drifted closer.

I tried to speak, but no sound came. So I focused—on Shangri-La, on the army invading it, on the black dragon I'd lost, and on my hatred for the man who'd taken him from me. My mind reached out, merging with hers.

Her emotions hit me like a punch—raw rage, searing pain, and an aching longing for a life that had been ripped away. For a friend she would never find again. Tears blurred my vision, but I couldn't pull away. Her pain became mine, flooding every corner of my soul.

When I finally gasped for air, I was back, trembling in the cold, staring at Shangri-La's outer wall. My body felt heavy, my chest hollow. I wiped the tears from my face, but the weight of her sorrow lingered.

I heard the grunts of a man running up on me. I turned to see an Irkallan with his sword raised high. I reached for my blade, but it was too late.

He swung down on me.

Another sword shot out, deflecting the soldier's attack—and saving my life.

Pherric thrust his blade into the man's thigh. He growled in pain as he fell to the ground. I slashed his throat before he could hack at my leg.

"Pherric! You fought back!"

Ashamed, he threw the sword to the ground.

"Well, violence is occasionally necessary. At least... *I* did not kill him."

I looked beyond the body of the Irkallan. "Wait. Where's Temurr?!"

"I was not able to make it in time..."

I saw a lifeless shape lying in the field.

"No! Temurr!"

I rushed to him, turning him on his side. A long dagger stuck out from his chest. Blood covered his body. His eyes half-opened.

"Finley. You yet live. I am glad."

I scanned the field. "Healer! I need a healer! Pherric!"

He patted my hand. "I am beyond a healer now, child."

"No!" I held him tight. "We have to get you back to the city!"

"No, let me die here," he whispered. "On the field of battle. Fighting for a city that I loved... but did not love me back."

Tears streamed again. "You cannot give up, Temurr. We can save you."

His strong hand gripped mine.

"Please... please don't go," I sobbed. "Please?"

"Take out the knife, child."

I gripped the handle of the dagger. "But... but you'll bleed out. Y-you'll die."

"Oh, Fin..." His smirk turned to a wince. "I am already dead."

Reluctantly, I pulled out the knife. He refused to cry out, closing his eyes and fighting through the pain.

Temurr smiled up at me as I supported his head.

"The best part? I will be with Frip again, I will." He stared up at the gray sky. "I am coming home, dear."

I placed my head on his chest.

"Tell me, Finley Maguire of Mu... Did we win the war?"

I cried as I nodded. "Yes, Temurr of Kunlun. The war is won."

"This makes me happy..."

Over the din of the battle, I heard the air leave his lungs for the last time.

Pherric placed his hand on my shoulder.

"We must get you behind the wall..."

I sobbed as he pulled me to my feet.

"The Irkallans advanced rapidly while you were in the trance."

I fell into Pherric's chest as another round of grief chewed me up and spit me out.

"I can't do this anymore! I-I can't lose any more of you!"

He tried to make a joke. "Well, as someone who might live forever—"

"Stop." I turned to the battlefield. "And he sure as hell won't live forever..." I pointed to the front line. Certain of victory, Kane rode up on a massive karkadann, joining hundreds of his knights. Grinning, he made a remark to one of his commanders. I wanted nothing more than to wipe that smug smile off his face with the edge of my blade.

"He ends... today," I snarled. "Help the others."

I started running toward Kane. I heard heavy thuds on the ground behind me, but I sprinted all out toward the new Irkallan king.

A hand gripped my shirt.

Before I took another step, I was hoisted off the ground.

"Let me go!"

Braylor held me up by the chainmail.

"Put me down!"

"No." He turned me around to face the gates of Shangri-La. Our allies were racing through the main gate. "We are withdrawing."

"Help the others then! Get them to retreat!"

He nodded. "I will."

"He killed Temurr!" I screamed.

Braylor glanced back at the body near Pherric. He closed his eyes.

"I am sorry, Fin."

"Then let me go! I'm taking that son of a bitch down!"

An Irkallan rushed us—Braylor snarled and, while still holding me up, took the man's head clean off in one swing of his sword.

"You will have your chance, but... not now. We must retreat."

Waves of soldiers were bearing down. Our time was up.

Braylor set me on the ground. I was tempted to take off running again, but I knew I wouldn't outrun him.

"So... all is lost then?" I wiped at the tears freezing on my cheeks.

Ahead of us, two giant Behemoths plodded toward the city.

"It appears so."

He grabbed my arm, pulling me along. "Fall back! Everyone!"

Outside the gate, we turned around. As our troops raced by, we fought off the advancing Irkallans. A dozen Prominans joined us. And we held our ground as the rest ran for safety.

I noticed Melcente, a few feet away, stumble and fall in the mud.

An Irkallan swung his sword at her back. I rushed in and threw my blade across his, deflecting his blow. I slashed his leg, then up and cut his sword hand. I helped her to her feet as the soldier writhed in pain.

"Thanks to ya, love!"

"Now we're even!" I yelled.

She winked and shook her head. "No way, love! Save me twice more and... buy me a ship! Then we be even!"

I grinned as she limped through the gate.

We clashed with the enemy, taking steps backward with each attack, until the last stragglers were through.

Braylor turned to me. "Go!"

"Not without you!"

He laughed. "I shall be right behind you!"

With a furious roar, he swung his sword high overhead, the sound echoing like thunder. He stomped the ground, and a dozen Irkallans recoiled, their eyes dwindling to tiny specs.

I didn't wait—I sprinted for the gates. The Prominan guards were already pulling them shut. Braylor's heavy boots pounded close behind me, each step a drumbeat of urgency.

I dove through the black gates just in time. Braylor squeezed through right after, turning immediately to help shove them closed. The heavy doors groaned as they slammed shut, sealing us inside.

Chapter 101

A group of white-haired Prominan guards, too old and frail to fight, turned the massive iron gears with trembling hands, lowering the heavy bars to lock the gate behind us. With practiced precision, they sealed two thick wooden doors, the final barrier between us and the enemy.

Before I could catch my breath, Braylor hauled me to my feet, and we rushed through the stone hallway of the barbican. Emerging into the crowded courtyard beyond the city wall, I was met with a scene of utter desperation. Warriors who'd made it through the gate lay scattered across the cobblestones, too exhausted or wounded to stand.

Healers knelt beside the most gravely injured, their hands swift and steady. Older Prominan women and young children moved among the soldiers, offering cups of water and scraps of food. Despite the confusion, their quiet resolve made a world of difference.

As I gasped for air, a thin girl appeared at my side. Without a word, she pressed half-rotten fruit and a tin cup of melted snow into my hands. It was barely a meal, but at that moment, it was yet again the best I had ever eaten.

Pherric rushed up, his eyes scanning us for injuries. Without hesitation, he pulled vials from his leather bag. He poured a blue powder into the gash on my hip, and pain exploded all over, sharp enough to draw a scream from my throat.

"You fought valiantly, Fin!"

"Yeah. But... it wasn't enough." I stared at the main gate.

He tended to a deep cut on my elbow, then the one across my thigh.

With heartbroken eyes, Pherric gave me his best smile. "We all did what we were able."

As I finished off my water, I watched Braylor look up. Then all around.

He laid a huge paw on Pherric's shoulder. "This area is not safe. We must clear everyone from this yard."

"Why?"

In the cold air, I heard the distant buzz beyond the wall. As it grew louder, I quickly realized what he meant.

"Shields!" I bellowed.

Whistling through the cold air, thousands of Irkallan arrows fell all around us. Dozens of weary and injured soldiers were struck. Those with shields—and those who were lucky—raced from the courtyard to seek shelter inside buildings, under awnings, and behind wagons.

I pulled on a wounded soldier leaning against a wall, hauled him around the corner and into an alley.

My Irish temper flared, as it always does. I snatched a bow and quiver off the slushy cobblestones and bolted for the wall. Braylor and Pherric tried to warn me off, but I wasn't going to stop. With my shield over my head, I ran up the stairs to the patrol path along the outer wall. Braylor grumbled as he clomped along after me.

I raced by several Prominan archers as they fired at the troops below. One took an arrow to the shoulder and I helped ease him to the ground. Taking his open spot, I kicked his quiver closer to my boot and used the stone battlement for cover.

I snuck a quick look out at the battlefield. Thousands of corpses, and the gray lumps of dead karkadanns, littered the vale and the mountain slope. As snow fell to the ground, pools of crimson blood greedily consumed the fresh white flakes.

The ground shook as the invaders surged toward the city. Rows and rows of archers fired their bows, marching along as they reloaded. Dozens of men struggled to lead the two brown Behemoths along the icy main road.

I ducked as an arrow zipped past my head. With another quick glance, I spotted Kane as he rode forward with his knights. He sat tall and smug in his saddle, convinced of his inevitable victory.

I notched an arrow and pulled the bow string back. I waited for him to ride into my range. Despite his pompous attitude, he was smart enough to stay back as they slowed their beasts as the rest of the army slogged onward.

"Dammit, Kane. Play nice..."

I pulled my string again, but this time back a few inches and then arched the bow higher. I released my arrow. The harsh wind blew my bolt off course and the arrow landed in the brush ten feet from his karkadann.

But Kane heard the deadly point crunch into the frozen ground—his eyes scanned the wall until he spotted me. A big self-satisfied grin slithered across his face.

I ducked out of the way, then let my anger take over yet again. I notched another arrow and fired at his line of archers, striking a man in the face—not the one I was aiming for, but... I took the win.

Kane watched the archer ahead of him fall and laughed. At me. He pointed in my direction, shouting a command.

Arrows ricocheted off the barriers, sending me diving for cover. Beyond exhausted, I wanted to lay there on the stone path. But Braylor spoiled everything. He dragged me to my aching feet.

"We need archers up here!" I shouted along the path.

Braylor grabbed a handful of spears from a wood rack.

I raced to the short wall on the back of the barbican, shouting down to the soldiers hiding from the falling arrows. "Anyone who can fire a bow! Get on the wall! Now!"

At first, only a handful emerged. Then dozens popped out of every shop, warehouse, and home surrounding the courtyard. Some already had bows while others scooped up gear from the injured and dying. And they all met up on the patrol path—facing me *and* waiting for their orders.

I turned to Braylor, a look of shock plastered on my face.

He launched a spear between the battlements and flashed a grin. "Seems *you* are in charge now!"

"No! I–I don't want to be in charge!" Fear swept over me. I wasn't a leader. I knew nothing about *any* of this. "I could get people killed!"

He laughed, hurling another spear.

I looked around and then to the soldiers. "Fill in the gaps along the wall! Fire at anything that moves! No... wait. Aim for *their* archers!"

They rushed by me to take up positions.

"And kill anyone coming over the wall!" I added.

I shook my head, reloaded my bow, and began firing. With at least three newly placed soldiers shooting arrows through each opening along the wall, we launched round after round. Eventually, our attack slowed down their heavy volleys.

I shouted in both directions along the patrol path. "Concentrate on those Behemoths!"

Soldiers up and down the wall relayed my orders and we turned our bows on the massive beasts. But our arrows bounced off or merely stuck to the surface of their thick hides. And their march continued toward our front gate.

Kasuma flew down, landing next to me. Blood was splattered across her white suit. More than a few of her feathers were missing.

Breathing hard, she leaned in close. "Aim for the eyes and nose... Their ears. At every vulnerable spot."

Cupping my hands around my mouth, I shouted to my archers. "Aim for any weak point! Eyes, mouth, nose, ears and feet!"

Several Prominans nodded, relaying the message.

Before Kasuma could fly away, I grabbed her by the shoulders. "Can you take out Kane?!"

She shook her head. "I have tried. I cannot get close. His archers protect him."

Boom! The wall shook hard. We held onto each other for balance. I quickly looked over the edge of the wall. The two Behemoths had rammed the gates below.

I flashed her a look. "Then try to stop those damn things... or this will be over real fast!"

She nodded, took flight, and darted down at the monsters trying to break down our last line of defense.

Another loud crunch shook the wall. Stones shifted below my feet. Our front gate was not going to last long.

I peeked over the parapet to the snowy field below. The soldiers following behind the Behemoths parted as teams of Irkallans jogged past them, hauling long wooden ladders.

"I am out of spears!" announced Braylor.

He pulled out his long sword.

"What are you doing?"

He reached out to the stone wall, pulling himself into the opening. "Going down there!"

"Down where?!" I looked down at the large back of the closest Behemoth. "Oh, no! No way!"

He pointed out on the city. "Finley, when they break down the gates, then this will—"

"Then this turns into a slaughter. Yeah, I know. I know! But you can't go down there! You won't make it out alive!"

A Prominan soldier rushed up, out of breath. "Commander, we have a barrel of resin! Should I use that?!"

I turned to Braylor, confused.

"You have black pitch?!" He stepped off the wall. His eyes lit up as he pushed the soldier back down the path. "Yes! Bring it now! Quickly!"

"What is resin?"

"Flammable oil used to burn torches!"

Braylor ran after the Prominan.

Boom! The gates below groaned as the iron bent inward.

I grabbed a fiery torch from a sconce on the back wall, following Braylor.

As two Prominans pulled a wood barrel up the barbican stairs, Braylor plucked it from their arms and set it onto the cobblestones. He hefted it to his shoulder, walking it to the wall and spilling a few precious drops of the thick, black liquid. Once on the wall, Braylor ripped off the lid and tipped the barrel over.

The resin poured on the back of a Behemoth.

I held my flaming torch high, but he held his hand up to stop me.

Kasuma soared up, out of the way of the oil. She fired off a few more arrows as she hovered above.

I turned back to our archers along the wall. "Shoot the ones with the ladders!"

Braylor nodded—I tossed the torch over the wall.

Flames rose up in the dark sky as they engulfed the Behemoth. The heat pushed me back. A loud wail echoed off the mountains. The creature stomped the ground in pain as the Irkallans below screamed out commands to no avail. The smell of the charred, rough flesh roiled my stomach.

Braylor screamed at the Prominan. "You have more of that resin?!" The ape man nodded. "Get it up here! We will burn the other one!"

As he started to run off, I grabbed him. "And if you have any more bright ideas to stop these assholes?! Don't ask me—just do it!"

The soldier smirked, striking his fist to his chest, and sprinted down the stairs.

A fresh round of arrows rained down on us.

I grabbed the other Prominan. "Get half of our archers shooting at the men on those ladders and the other half on their archers! Got it?! Go!"

He pounded his breast, spun around, and ran along the path shouting orders.

I stole a quick look at Braylor. He was a bloody, gory, terrible mess and... I still wanted to kiss him. We had, at best, *maybe* an hour left to live. And I wanted to be at that man's side until the end. I placed my hand on his face and gave him a weak smile. He wrapped his giant hand around my forearm and smiled back.

"Let us kill these fools," he soothed.

"I just wanted to... I don't know... say that I—"

"I know." He gently held my face in his hands, kissed my forehead. "And I... just want to say... the same."

Damn. Even in the heat of battle, with death on our doorstep, I still couldn't get the guy to say he loves me out loud.

Another thunderous crash from below. While the burning Behemoth headed for the river, the other hammered away at the entrance.

Braylor grabbed my hand and we raced back toward the fighting at the wall.

Before I could notch an arrow, a Valhallan commander and his lackey cut us off.

His eyes landed on me. "I am told you are in charge here?"

"Unfortunately..." I sighed.

"You are the dragonwitch?" He looked me up and down, disappointed.

"Also... unfortunately."

His lieutenant, a taller woman, her helmet and mail covered in gore, scanned the wide deck of the tower.

"The Jarl wishes to inform you that we are leaving," said the commander, lowering his eyes.

"What?! You can't leave now!"

"The Valhallans and Oguns are making for the north mountain. Our fight is over. Nothing more can be done."

I pointed behind me as the Behemoth smashed into our gates again. "How will you get past that?!"

"There is another, smaller gate at the river's edge."

I turned to Braylor. He shrugged. There was a gate we didn't know about? Great.

"We have organized our retreat. But the Jarl thought it best to inform you. We will regroup and... this war will continue."

No, it wouldn't.

He shifted his weight, unable to maintain eye contact.

"But what about the bridges to the mountain?! They control the bridges!"

The Valhallan stared at the stone floor.

"To stay here is to die." Well, that was probably true.

"Coward!"

He had no taste for retreat. But my insult hit him hard. He gripped his sword, holding his tongue. Finally he raised his head and looked me in the eye. "May your gods be with you." They turned and raced down the staircase.

Another deep breath. I looked up to the sky, closing my eyes. For a few precious seconds, I calmed my mind. And concentrating on the cold snowflakes landing on my cheeks.

Thump! Thump-thump. Up and down the wall, Irkallan ladders fell against our parapet openings. Prominans fired arrows at their climbers, while others tried to push the ladders away. Soon, our swords clashed with the most nimble of their soldiers.

The invasion of the city had begun.

Chapter 102

I sprinted to the back wall overlooking the city, my boots skidding slightly on the frost-covered stone.

Below, the courtyard churned with activity. Those who could still fight—or at least stand—had gathered in tense formation, their weapons trembling in weary hands as the Behemoth assaulted the gates.

"We need soldiers up here! They're coming over the wall!" I screamed.

Prominans within earshot immediately sprang into action, racing up the stone stairs two at a time. Their faces pale but determined, eyes fixed on the battlements above.

Across the yard, I spotted Melcente, her black dreads barely visible beneath her battered helmet as she tugged it down firmly. Our eyes met for a brief moment, and I gave her a quick nod, even managing a strained smile.

Her expression was clear—equal parts exasperation and acknowledgment of the bad luck that always seemed to follow me. Yet she didn't say a word. With a sigh, she turned toward the gates, blade in hand, ready to face whatever came next.

Arrows fell on the patrol path as our soldiers fired back on the invading force. I shot an arrow into an Irkallan who had breached the wall—only hitting his leg—then drew my sword to hit a man crawling over the parapet.

"Let no one pass!" Braylor bellowed. He sliced his sword across an invader's waist, nearly cutting him in half.

The Behemoth struck the gate again. The impact shook the barbican beneath my feet, the vibrations traveling through my legs. A screeching wail of twisting, straining metal filled the air, followed by the sharp crack of stone splintering and tumbling to the ground below.

The beast had done its work. With one final, deafening groan, the gates gave way, crashing inward in a shower of debris.

I didn't wait. Spinning on my heel, I sprinted back to the wall, my voice rising above the din. "They're coming through!"

The Prominans were aware. They stared at the main gate, ready to die for their city. For their people.

The cold winter air stung me to my core. A chill so dark, so evil, ran down my back. Fear and doubt slithered into my brain and my hands shook uncontrollably. I somehow knew, in a flash, that I would be dead. Soon.

My gaze dropped to the Prominans below. The same fear etched across their faces mirrored my own. Their stances were hesitant, their weight leaning back, away from the fight. They weren't bracing for battle—they were bracing for the worst. Their terror seeped into me like poison, feeding my own despair.

I opened my mouth, ready to shout something—anything—to rally them, but the words stuck in my throat. Then, I felt it: an old, familiar thump in my chest. It wasn't my heartbeat but something deeper, a powerful rhythm resonating through the icy wind. My ears caught it next—a staggered whoosh that cut through the stillness.

Squinting against the driving snow, I peered across the city. The mist hanging over the waterfalls shifted, rising upward in great swirling columns.

And then, she appeared. The big red dragon emerged from the gorge, her massive wings unfurling as she climbed into the air. Each beat of her wings sent flurries scattering, clearing the storm's grip on the city.

My jaw dropped as I stood frozen, unable to believe what I was seeing. Behind her, two dark green dragons rose, their powerful forms cutting through the mist. They soared over Shangri-La's white domes and towering spires, their presence impossibly majestic and terrifying all at once.

They were here.

Someone in the crowd below: "Dragon! Dragon!"

The panicked screams snapped me out of my daze.

A Prominan soldier next to me pointed at the red dragon sailing over the city—toward our barbican. He started for the stairs.

"No. No! It's okay!" I yelled, first at him and then to the others as more frightened shouts echoed across the city.

The soldiers waiting below for the oncoming Irkallans fled the wide courtyard. Their worry and fear from before had been replaced by a primordial panic, a dread that was rooted deep in their souls.

"No! Wait!"

A crisp wind whipped around me as Big Red descended, her massive wings stirring the air. She landed heavily on the long rectangular roof of the barbican tower, the wood planks beneath her claws groaning under her weight. Overhead, the two green dragons circled in a slow, menacing rhythm, their watchful eyes scanning for threats.

Big Red threw her head back, her jaws splitting wide as a deafening bellow tore through the snowy sky. The sound rippled across Shangri-La, reverberating through the yard below. She shuffled toward the parapet, her claws scraping against the stone, and roared again, louder this time. It wasn't a warning—she was ready for war.

"No! No! Not them!" I shouted, frantically waving my arms to get her attention.

She paused, her massive head turning toward me. Her glowing yellow eyes narrowed, fixing me with a look of disdain. A sharp snort of hot air burst from her nostrils, ruffling my hair and filling the cold air with the smell of sulfur.

With my hands raised in a gesture of surrender, I edged closer. Slowly, I pointed past her, toward the wall on the far side of the barbican and the Irkallan army massing in the valley below.

"Not us! Them!" I said, my voice steady despite the tremor in my chest.

Big Red cocked her head, her sharp features cutting a stark silhouette against the stormy sky. She snarled again, a low, guttural sound that made the air vibrate around me. Her wings twitched, and for a heartbeat, I wasn't sure if she'd listen.

Braylor approached cautiously, his unease clear in the way his steps faltered. I could feel his instinct to grab me and bolt for the exit, but I didn't move. Behind me, the frightened Prominans clattered down the stone steps, retreating from the patrol path in a mad rush.

I closed my eyes, forcing myself to focus. Rage surged through me, burning like fire in my veins—the Irkallans and their endless campaign of slaughter and conquest. Kane and his obsession with dominion, his plan to twist this world into his own dark vision. The faces of the starving Prominans, the lifeless bodies of my friends, and the memory of the black dragon's death—all of it crashed over me in waves of fury and grief.

Tears welled, hot and uncontrollable, as I fixed my mind on the enemy. I pictured their black and blue banners rippling in the wind, their tunics and helmets bearing the same colors as the oppression they symbolized. I poured every ounce of my sorrow, my anger, my desire for vengeance into Big Red's mind, forcing it upon her with everything I had.

The release of the mindform left me gasping, as though I'd expelled a part of myself. My breath hitched, and the tears spilled freely, carving tracks through the mud and blood caked on my cheeks.

Big Red reeled, shaking her massive head violently as if trying to push away my intrusion. Her eyes narrowed to slits, glowing with fiery indignation. For a moment, I thought she might lash out, but then she stilled. Slowly, deliberately, she plodded to the edge of the wall, her towering form commanding the stunned Irkallan army below.

Braylor lingered behind me, still hesitant, his protective instincts fighting with his fear. But I stood rooted, my emotions laid bare, and watched as Big Red took in the battlefield.

"Yes," I said, sensing the fury within her build. "*They* are the ones who killed the black dragon..."

She leapt onto the parapet of the barbican and wailed to the dragons above—and then to the soldiers below.

I scanned the enemy forces, looking for Kane. His army stood there, paralyzed. Afraid. Kane struggled to control his bucking karkadann. His commanders tried to shout orders to the terrified troops, but even they couldn't take their eyes from the red dragon glaring down.

I growled. "Go get 'em, girl..."

She unleashed her wide wings. A host of arrows, fired weakly by a half dozen archers, bounced off her thick hide. Without hesitation, she threw her dragonfire at the foot soldiers cowering in the snow. Harsh screams echoed out as the Irkallans holding and climbing the ladders burst into flames.

I returned to the low wall overlooking the yard. "We need archers up here! Let's help her out!"

Only a handful of Prominans complied. Those who dared tentatively climbed the steps, giving her a wide berth, and scrambled along the path. But they took up their bows and fired on the retreating soldiers.

For a fleeting moment, concern flickered across Kane's face. But he quickly masked it, barking orders at his commanders. His sharp voice was swallowed by the terror spreading through his ranks.

Karkadanns reared and bucked, some spinning in confusion, others bolting in every direction. Foot soldiers broke formation, sprinting past their bewildered leaders in a frantic bid to escape. The archers didn't stand a chance, trampled under the stampede of fleeing men. The once-organized force was crumbling.

With a powerful thrust of her wings, Big Red launched from her perch on the wall, the air cracking under the force. She soared straight toward the heart of the Irkallan front line, her massive shadow spreading even more fear below.

The green dragons split off with precision, one veering toward the wide river, the other gliding south toward the silvery mountains. Their movements were fluid and deadly, each one claiming its part of the battlefield.

From my vantage point, I watched as the dragons unleashed their fury. Big Red roared, her jaws spewing torrents of flame that engulfed the enemy below. Fire streaked across the field, leaving nothing but scorched earth in its wake. The green dragons followed suit, their fiery breath carving destruction through enemy ranks, scattering soldiers like leaves in a storm.

Pherric gripped my arm and turned me around. "Did you call these dragons, Finley?"

"I did," I said, rather proud of myself. "I think."

"What have you done?" he moaned. I could see the fire reflected in his dark eyes. "We must take cover! Quickly!"

"What?! Why? They're here to help us!"

Braylor removed Pherric's hand from arm. "She has her way with dragons."

Confused and anxious, Pherric stumbled to the wall. The dragons drifted over the valley, lighting up huge sections of the Irkallan army.

He pointed to the battlefield, making his plea to Braylor. "You know what they will do, Braylor! When they are bored with the enemy—they will turn on us!"

Braylor exhaled. "You have not seen what they have done to us for generations, Fin. You have unleashed a mighty terror on—"

"Worse than Kane and his groupies? Seriously?! Look, I get you people have been burned in the past," I said, instantly regretting it. "Sorry... you know what I mean. But Queen Dirvilia *herself* told me to summon them!"

Pherric cocked his head.

"You are in communication with the dead? With the... the Irkallan queen?"

I turned back to the battlefield. "There's no time to explain!"

From my experience, the dragons were limited to how much fire they could breathe—I had seen this firsthand when Rex first attacked me. We couldn't rely on our new helpers to entirely wipe out Kane's troops.

I pushed Pherric away, sprinting to the parapets overlooking the city.

"Everyone! Hear me!"

Braylor appeared next to me, whistling loudly with his fingers. The Prominans still cowering in the doorways and around corners looked up.

"Listen! Now!" His deep voice echoed off the walls.

Even more appeared—the women, children, elderly—with bewildered looks plastered on their faces.

"I know you're all afraid of the dragons! But I know what I am doing!" I yelled, staring hard at Braylor. He nodded his approval.

More and more people made their way into the massive courtyard and main avenues into Shangri-La.

"Spread the word! We need to attack the invaders while we have the advantage!"

The crowd of soldiers murmured, exchanging worried looks.

"We will be burned alive!" someone shouted.

"By the gods, no!"

"I will not go out there!"

I held my hands in the air. "They are on our side! Trust me!"

As I paced back and forth, the crowd murmured and grumbled.

Braylor spun me around. "Let them know what is in... here." He laid his massive paw on my chest.

When I held my arms in the air, they quieted down.

"I am a stranger in your land. This is true. But I am your friend and I'm here to help you. We only have moments to act before it's too late. I summoned these creatures to come to your aid. And I am the only one who can command them! I am a powerful... *dragonwitch!*"

The people gasped and hushed whispers coursed through them.

"The dragons are mighty and, right now, they are slaying the Irkallans invading your land! But they cannot do it alone. They only have so much dragonfire in them. And if we do not attack, while they flee, they *will* regroup. And they will take this city! I am going out there to fight with the dragons. I am going to protect Shangri-La! Are you with me or will you hide like frightened little children?! Let us end this war together and... let us end it *now!*"

Like an idiot, I pulled out my sword and raised it in the air.

And the crowd was completely silent.

My face turned twelve shades of red in that excruciatingly long moment.

"I'm with ya!" I heard Melcente shout from below. I smiled at her. She winked back.

Braylor took a step away from me. "I am with you!"

He held up his sword.

Pherric stood next to me, nodded, and held up his hand. Then several of the Prominans who had fought alongside me on the wall stepped in, their swords raised.

"Let's save Shangri-La!" I yelled.

More and more swords began to rise up above the mass of people. Then more joined in. I soon saw hundreds of weapons waving in the air. They began to chant. And the chant escalated to a mighty chorus.

"Shangri-La! Shangri-La! Shangri-La!"

Braylor nudged me. "Not your best work, but... it will do."

"I hate you."

"I know..."

Chapter 103

"Gather any weapons you can find!" I screamed to the soldiers assembled in the courtyard below.

Braylor held up his sword "Show these invaders no mercy!"

Our soldiers shouted approval as they waited for the guards to open the broken city gate.

I turned to a Prominan soldier. "Get word to the Valhallans! I need them to ride out in advance of these foot soldiers! Got it? Go!"

He sprinted off down the patrol path toward the far side of the city wall.

Pherric hugged me hard. "Take care of yourself out there—give me your word?"

The emotions caught up with me. And tears fell far too easily. I hugged him tight. "I will."

A distant shriek sounded from the battlefield. I hurried to the front wall in time to see a group of Irkallan soldiers attacking one of the green dragons. He sat on the bank of the wide river, swatting his spiked tail at a dozen bold fighters. Spears and arrows were lodged in the side and neck of the dying beast.

"Dammit!"

"We must attack now," sneered Braylor. "While the dragons yet live."

We raced down the stone stairs, with a horde of eager Prominans following behind. Pushing our way past impatient soldiers; we waited for the main gate to be pried open.

The army standing before us hooted loudly and began a war chant—"Balo afan!"—repeating it over and over, louder and louder.

"What does that mean?" I whispered to Braylor.

"Balo afan! Balo afan!"

He nudged me, smirking. "I think... they are saying... you have nice cheekbones. Which is not an untruth."

Braylor got a sharp elbow in the side as I shook my head.

"It means..." I heard Melcente's voice. "Dragon witch."

She shoved through the throng of Prominan soldiers.

"Which is what you are... a witch."

I heard another blast of dragonfire outside the city gates, followed by the screams of burning men.

"Yeah... I'm starting to think that might be true, Melcente."

Several karkadanns rode up to the gate tower. I pushed my way back through our troops to greet them.

Queen Urraca of Ogun, Jarl Trym Baldrson of Valhalla, and King Ferghas of Elysium glared down at me from their mounts. Blood and mud from the battle covered them from helmet to boot.

"You summoned these dragons?" asked Queen Urraca.

Her face was calm but I could sense her fear. And her anger.

"You bet your ass, I summoned them," I said. "Your highness."

King Longzhe of Oceantis flew down from the gray sky. "Then you have delivered us a chance at victory."

"Aye," said Jarl Trym. "What is our next move? Dragonwitch?"

I nodded, accepting my new title. When I realized what he had asked, I held up my hands. "Hey! I am so not in charge here! You all are the warrior-kings."

"Warrior-kings... indeed," mused Trym. "This battle has been a catastrophe."

My heart stopped in my chest. I had no idea what to do next, other than get out there and fight.

"Certainly, you are not going to listen to this... this *demon* child?!" protested the queen. Not waiting for Trym's response, she turned to the other kings. "We must set up a defensive perimeter along the city wall and let the dragons—"

"That is the last thing we should do!" I chimed in. "Despite what you believe, the dragons cannot breathe fire forever! When they run out, the Irkallans will turn on us."

"If there are any left," she quipped.

I pleaded directly to Jarl Trym and Longzhe. "Right now, the enemy is disorganized and running scared. We need to go on the offensive! Maybe we should..." I struggled to think clearly. "We could lead a charge on the karkadanns, with all that we have left. And... and ride in an arrow formation—to drive a wedge between them, separate them. And right behind the karks, we'll have anyone with a spear to run through anyone who slips by! Then, we could put all the archers behind those foot soldiers, firing over the cavalry. The foot soldiers could follow those guys, providing support and for cleanup duty. And... and Tenguans can cover us from above!"

Trym grimaced. I shot a look at Longzhe—a barely perceptible smirk on his thin lips—and gave me a nod of approval.

"We split them up and drive some back against the mountain to the south and push the others into the river. We work *together*! As one."

Trym whistled to a soldier sitting on a karkadann behind him.

"Give her your ride!" ordered the Jarl.

Urraca was baffled. "You are going to do as she says?! Are you mad?!"

"At least she has a plan. A rather simple and amateurish plan, but with the dragons overhead... it stands a chance." He stroked his beard. "And it is possible that I am quite mad."

Jarl nodded again to his lieutenant. The man hopped down and handed me the reins. I stood there, dumbfounded.

"Lead the charge, girl," said Trym.

I opened my mouth, but Braylor lifted me up from behind and sat me on the beast.

The lieutenant rushed off, shouting orders and providing instructions... to follow *me*. I gulped hard but then nodded to the kings and queen. I was scared shitless but didn't want it to show.

Braylor marched up to another Valhallans and stared at him. Jarl Trym nodded and the man gave up his karkadann.

I yanked the reins of my ride until I faced the Prominans.

"There's an ancient saying in my land! Lex talionis! It means an eye for an eye. And so, we will retaliate against those who have killed our people! Your people!"

The legion of warriors before me shouted their agreement.

"Carry those they have taken from us in your heart! And let's give these bastards the death they deserve!" I screamed.

A new chant rose up from the soldiers. "Lex talionis!"

Even Melcente joined in the chorus.

"Lex talionis!"

When my gaze returned to the rulers, Urraca motioned to the city gates.

Prominans dragged open the bent and broken iron gate. Holding my head high, with a look of determination plastered on my face, I kicked my karkadann through the tunnel. I exhaled deeply as I heard the hooves of the rulers clomping through the mud behind me. I had no fear of the fight, but leading an army into the battle took my anxiety to a whole new level.

Over the crushed gates, we exited the city. I rode out as far as I could from the wall to give room for fifteen hundred karkadanns to line up behind me. The frightened, slightly-charred Behemoth had scurried off toward the mountains.

Braylor rode up. "Terror fills your heart."

I dropped my head. "Oh, god... you have no idea."

"Fear not, Fin. Your plan is sound. Our cavalry wedge might be cut off by the invaders, but—"

"I don't care," I growled. "The wedge gives me the quickest route to Kane. I *will* feel the final few beats of his heart, as it pumps a final time in my hand, before this day is over."

Braylor gave me a look of astonishment, followed by a hearty laugh.

"Your warlust is *legendary*, Finley Maguire! They will write songs of your valor on this day!"

Every able person in the city flooded through the broken gates of Shangri-La. Prominans stood in makeshift lines, shoulder to shoulder, with Elysians, Valhallans, and Oguns. As I had ordered, pikemen lined up behind our rows of karkadanns, with rows of archers beyond them. Tenguans landed on the top of the wall, bows at the ready. And the foot soldiers continued to pour from the city.

My hand shook as I reached for the hilt of my sword. I felt the carved dragon's head on the tip of the handle, trying to calm myself.

Braylor leaned over to whisper. "Give the command."

I nodded and inhaled as deeply as I could. "Let's do this—for Rex and for my friends."

Raising my sword above my head, I screamed at the top of my lungs. "Attack!"

Chapter 104

We drove our beasts hard across the wide valley and filled the cold morning air with war cries. Our karkadanns darted around and over the bodies littering the snowy field. Prominan and Tenguan arrows fell on the enemy ahead of our charge. We hacked and sliced a path through the Irkallans—some saw us coming, holding up their shields or trying to parry our blows with steel, while others had no idea they were about to die as they stared up at the sky in search of dragons. Quite a few were cut down in vain attempts to flee.

Massive fires roared all about us. The stench of burnt flesh and sulfur filled my nose and drifted over us like a thick fog.

The two remaining dragons swam through the smoky skies, occasionally diving down to douse a group of warriors in flame. I watched as the stiff, outstretched arms and blackened hands of their dead turned to ash as we rumbled past.

I slashed down again and again with my sword, cleaving helmets and slicing into bodies, as we rode deeper into their territory.

One brawny Irkallan soldier charged at me, swinging his axe toward my knee. I pulled my leg over the karkadann to avoid his strike, but slipped off the saddle as my mount bounded along the bumpy terrain. Holding tight to the pommel with both hands, I bounced against the side of the karkadann. As another soldier approached on my side, I pulled my boots up and planted them against his shield. He flew back and I was launched high enough to drag my butt back onto the saddle.

Irkallan commanders galloped around the battlefield, regrouping their forces. Their fear shifted from the flying dragons to our swift charge. As we drove deeper into their ranks, they began to fight back.

Both the green and red dragon bore the scars of the battle—spears and arrows jutted from their thick hides, and their wings were torn with ragged holes. Their strength was apparent, but even they were not invincible.

I motioned for Braylor to ride ahead, silently urging him to shield me as we slowed our advance. Ahead of us, Valhallan and Ogun troops surged forward, their weapons raised as they charged the enemy lines.

Tilting my head back, I focused on the gray sky where Big Red was carving a fiery path through the Irkallans below, her massive form veering south. I closed my eyes, letting the connection with her mind take shape once more.

Through the mindform, I poured my gratitude into her thoughts. *You are a mighty dragon,* I told her. *You have done well, avenging the death of the black dragon. We are forever in your debt. Fly away! You are free!*

For a moment, the connection held, heavy with shared understanding. But shouts from the Irkallan soldiers near the river jolted me back to reality. I turned in time to see the second green dragon falter, his reserves of fire exhausted. His once-commanding presence was diminished, his strength waning.

Big Red's shriek cut through the chaos like a blade. Banking sharply, she flew toward the green dragon, her cry sharp and commanding. He hesitated, his confusion evident, but he obeyed. With a powerful beat of his wings, he turned westward, retreating toward the distant waterfalls beyond the city.

Once she was certain he was safe, Big Red let out one final roar, then headed south, her silhouette disappearing over the steep mountains of Shangri-La.

The Irkallan troops erupted in cheers, emboldened by the dragons' departure. Their cries rang out, and their focus shifted back to us.

My heart sank as anxiety clawed at me. Had I called off the dragons too soon? "Dammit."

Scanning the valley, Kane and his knights were parked on a slight hill near the river. This was going to be my only chance to take him out. I snapped the reins hard, dug my boots into the flanks of my karkadann, and raced ahead to join Braylor.

Kane looked pissed. He snarled orders to a commander, who rode off to quell the revolt of a squad of pikemen near the front line. He struggled to calm his nervous karkadann. I could see the fury in his eyes—this wasn't going according to plan.

"We are in trouble!" shouted Braylor.

"What's wrong now?!"

Braylor pointed behind our wedge of karkadanns as he sliced the top of a man's head through the helmet. Our quick surge had spread us too thin. The invaders collapsed around us. We were surrounded.

"Well, you were right!"

"That should be the title of the song they sing about me!" he laughed. "'He was right! He was always right!'"

I glanced at Kane, judging the distance—he was within a half axim. I couldn't let him get away. But now that we were ringed in by the enemy, I needed to stick around and fight. I parried swords and sliced down at the Irkallans below me. My brain was a jumbled, dizzying mess. If we gained the upper hand, he might slip away. If things turned south for us, well... he'd be the least of my worries.

A deep, resonant horn echoed across the valley, its sound a rolling thunder through the frigid air.

Braylor's head snapped toward the northern mountains, his eyes widening in disbelief. "The gods must exist..." he murmured, his voice trembling.

"What is it?!" I shouted, swatting aside an incoming spear as I followed his gaze.

There, atop the northern mountain range, stood a line of massive, sinewy white horses—like real actual horses—their glossy coats glinting faintly in the dull winter light. But it wasn't the fact that there were horses standing there—it was the single, spiraled horns crowning their foreheads. Unicorns! Yeah. There were goddamn *unicorns* on Tir Na!

Hey... why not?

On top of the thousands of these beautiful beasts sat hulking Fomorian warriors, their ginormous frames draped in dark armor that glinted like obsidian.

The horn blared again, louder this time, reverberating through my chest. The Fomorians raised their weapons high, their guttural war cries tearing through the stillness. The sound wasn't just loud—it was alive, raw, and menacing.

As one, the mounted Fomorians surged forward, their unicorns galloping down the slope with terrifying precision, hooves thundering against the frozen earth as they barreled toward the bridges.

Then, from the opposite side of the valley, another similar horn bellowed—a call from the valley's entrance. A second horde emerged, this one of Fomorian foot soldiers. Their advance was slower but no less fearsome, their heavy strides seemingly shaking the ground as they marched toward Shangri-La.

I turned to Kane on his hill. He shifted his karkadann toward the approaching forces. He barked orders, but his troops were once again in disarray.

As the Fomorians ran forward, they chanted in a deep, steady voice that sounded like a drumbeat. I saw fear in the eyes of every Irkallan soldier.

Racing at them was an army of giants, each over eight feet tall and weighing more than three hundred pounds. Even the female Fomorians were larger than the largest Irkallan male. The fine hairs rose on the back of my neck. They were that intimidating—and they were on *our* side!

"Better late than never!" I shouted to Braylor.

My teasing had no effect on him. He had a grin that would not quit. He turned his newfound glee on the soldiers attacking all around us. With every swing of his broadsword, Braylor ended another life and moved swiftly to the next. He was back in his element.

Kane sent his knights and a company of foot soldiers to fight against the approaching Fomorian army. I stole looks in his direction whenever I could manage, not wanting him to run off.

King Dagda and several hundred of his finest Fomorians surged across a bridge and cut a swath through the Irkallans to join the other rulers near us in battle.

Trym pulled his axe from the shoulder of a soldier. "Finally you arrive, you bastard!"

Dagda laughed as his sword sliced across a soldier's neck. "Someone had to come to your aid! Might as well be me!"

Braylor pulled on his reins and rode alongside Dagda's unicorn. "I am glad you are here, clan chief!"

Dagda looked Braylor up and down, a mild look of disgust on his haggard face. He could tell Braylor was a mongrel.

As Queen Urraca joined their little get-together, Dagda turned away from Braylor. "And I am happy you saved a few hellhound pups for me!"

Queen Urraca slashed down with her sword, breaking an Irkallan spear, and then stabbed the man in the heart. "Why the delay, Dagda?! More pressing matters at home?!"

"Hardly! Seems the young dragonwitch here convinced the Irkallans they no longer needed all their soldiers on this front! Sir Kane sent eight thousand unlucky souls toward Mag Mell to slow our journey!"

King Longzhe landed next to Jarl's karkadann, breathing hard. "Enough of the idle talk—there is work yet to be done! And I am far too old to do this alone!"

The other rulers laughed as they spread out, riding off to rejoin their armies.

I pointed at Kane. "I must go now! He cannot get away."

"Then let us ride!" Braylor shouted.

I winked, then kicked my mount. Riding low and fast, I plowed through the crowd. Braylor and I cut down or trampled dozens of soldiers until we burst through their ranks.

My eyes locked on Kane, and nothing else mattered. Before Braylor could reach me, I spurred my karkadann straight toward him, my focus razor-sharp.

Kane spotted me, his gaze narrowing before he screamed orders to his closest knights. Without hesitation, they moved to intercept me. But the coward didn't stay to fight—he turned his beast and bolted, his cloak whipping behind him.

A snarl tore from my throat as I leaned low in the saddle, urging my karkadann faster. The ground blurred beneath us as we closed the distance. Two knights lunged at me, their blades slicing through the air, but I ducked low and shot past them, my kark weaving effortlessly around them.

Behind me, I caught a glimpse of Braylor clashing with the remaining knights, his sword flashing as he held them back. Only a handful broke free to chase me, but I didn't care. I would not be denied.

The chaos of the battlefield faded into the background, swallowed by the pounding of hooves and the fire in my chest. Kicking my ride again and again, I pushed us harder.

Kane was mine.

Chapter 105

The arrival of the Fomorian army, blocking the only way in or out of the valley, had sealed Kane's fate. He knew his troops were trapped.

The weight of that realization must have hit him hard. Without hesitation, he raced his karkadann into the forest to the southeast—the same one I had used to enter the Shangri-La valley. The rough terrain, dense with hills and vegetation, offered countless places to hide. The bastard had planned out his escape route.

I pushed my karkadann to keep pace, struggling to hold him in sight as he vanished into the trees. I got lucky when several of his panicked soldiers attacked him. Disoriented from the dragons' attack, they had run and were now turning their weapons on him. Kane swatted away their spears and blades with ease, cutting through the chaos. But as I passed through the gauntlet, those same soldiers came after me.

Their attacks were relentless. I parried blows, kicked one rider to the ground, and drove the others off. Each skirmish cost me precious seconds, but I refused to let him go.

But when I was free of them, Kane was gone.

I crashed into the forest, the crisp snow clinging to the pine branches breaking over my shoulders. Darkness swallowed me whole, the evergreens towering around me like silent sentinels. Though it was likely late morning or early afternoon, it seemed like night beneath the heavy canopy.

Slowing my mount, I strained to hear the sounds of Kane's karkadann ahead. My ride's labored breathing drowned out the faint noises of the forest, but soon I spotted fresh hoof prints in the snow. Snapping the reins, I pressed forward.

There—a shadow darted between the trunks, weaving through the trees. The evergreens. The trees that refused to shed their weight. My lips formed a grim smile. It was not lost on me that we were among the immortal trees that refused to die, even in the winter.

Kane's karkadann leapt over fallen logs, maneuvering through dense underbrush and snow-covered outcroppings. I followed, gripping the pommel of my sword, my breaths steady but shallow.

Something was off.

The knights chasing me had fallen behind, their pursuit suspiciously slow. A chill prickled down my spine—Kane was up to his old tricks.

As I rounded a tall rock formation, I caught a glimpse of a silhouette ahead moving through the forest. With renewed anger, I surged after him, ready for whatever trap he had laid.

And then I was not—a sword flew out from behind a massive boulder. The blade cut into the front legs of my karkadann. The beast tumbled forward, shrieking in pain.

I was thrown hard into the ground cover, my head striking a tree branch. I tried to stand upright, but fell back against the cold bark. I shook my head to clear away the cobwebs and aimed my unsteady blade at him.

Kane whistled, probably for his ride to return, and charged after me with a grin on his face.

I heard a rush of air, but kept my eyes on him.

Kane sliced down at me.

Kasuma landed in front of him, parrying his strike with her bow. The bow easily snapped in half. With the flat of his blade, he tossed her to the side. I heard the snapping of bones as she was struck—her wing out of commission.

Kane turned his attention to me. He jabbed hard with his sword and I fended him off. He swung his sword across and I dove down, rolling away. We clashed several more times, both of us breathing heavily.

"I must say, Finley, you are a remarkable girl!"

He swung down on me and I repelled his blade. I lunged at him, careful to keep my balance, but he easily side-stepped the tip.

"I resent the understatement."

Kane slashed his sword twice—I dodged the first, parried the second—and then shoved me hard to the ground.

His karkadann cantered into the clearing. He could hear his knights rumbling through the forest in the distance. He winked at me and turned to mount his ride.

But Kasuma was there. Her left wing hung loosely at her side, but her sharp dagger rose up in her right hand. Instead of stabbing Kane, she struck the point deep into the side of his karkadann. The beast cried out and bolted off.

Kane groaned in anger and struck her jaw with the back of his hand. More of her hollow bones cracked as she dropped hard to the snow.

Looking around, unsure of what to do next, the coward bolted deeper into the woods.

I dropped to Kasuma's side.

"Go," she whispered with a broken jaw.

I lifted her up off the ground. "Why didn't you stab him?!"

She grunted. "Because he is immortal. But his karkadann... is not. Leave me. Do not let him... escape..."

"But I need to—"

"Go, girl," she hissed. "Go!"

I worried for a moment that Kane's knights might find her... but then I reminded myself: Kasuma could handle her business. Gripping my sword, I set my focus back on the king of Irkalla and sprinted after him.

He was out of sight, far ahead, but his trail was clear. His boots had left deep imprints in the snow, and the long stride between them told me he was moving fast. I slowed my pace to a cautious jog. For once, I resisted the urge to rush—I knew Kane. He could easily be lying in wait, ready to strike from the shadows.

The chase dragged on, nearly a full axim, before I broke through the trees into a small clearing. My gut clenched with fear. The place was too open, too still. I dropped into a crouch behind a wide tree trunk, steadying my breath as quietly as I could. My ears strained for any hint of him, but all I heard were the rustling leaves and distant calls of the forest. Kane was here—I could feel it. Waiting.

Taking a slow, deliberate breath, I created a mindform. A shadowy copy. When I opened my eyes, the shimmering image of a red-haired woman in armor appeared before me—a ghostly imperfection. But it would do.

The mindform broke into a run, its movements slightly jerky but convincing enough as it charged into the clearing. Kane, clearly exhausted and on edge, fell for the trick. He sprang from behind a rock, his sword flashing as he slashed through the apparition.

The blade met only air, and the mindform dissolved. Kane roared in frustration, his voice echoing through the trees. His wild eyes darted around the clearing, his sword raised defensively as he began to circle, searching for me.

From my hiding spot, I tightened my grip on my blade, heart pounding in anticipation.

"Join with me, Fin! I shall name you the Knight Commander of the entire continent! Of all of Tir Na! We will rule this unruly world together!"

I turned my face away from him, letting my voice bounce around the woods. "Asking me to join you? Sounds like you're worried I might win."

He spun around, trying to locate me.

"You are a formidable foe, but I *will* be victorious!"

I made my way closer to him, slowly, silently.

"However... I do not want to lose your skills, child. I have never seen anyone with as much good fortune as you possess!"

I scooped up a small pebble. He stormed around the dark clearing, his blade pointing at every slight, perceived danger.

"Think of what we could do! Together!"

When he was close enough, I threw the pebble—he jumped at the noise.

As Kane shuffled backwards, towards me, I rose in silence and held out my sword.

When he was close enough, I rushed at him. And drove my blade through his back. He grunted in pain. Blood began to spread across his overcoat.

Then... Kane threw back his head. And laughed.

He snapped around, pulling the sword from my hands. As he moved in close to me, his dark eyes stared down.

"Have you forgotten?! I cannot die!"

I reached for the knife in my belt. He marched closer and closer. All I could do was back away—the point of my sword sticking out from his chest.

"You, on the other hand, *can* die... And you do not return right away. As I have seen with my own eyes. So, what I shall do then is slice you into small pieces and sprinkle you on a campfire. Hard to come back from a death such as this!"

My boots climbed the roots of a tree. I had no place to run. And he was on top of me.

"Ready to die, little one?"

I stood up as tall as I could. Looked him in the eye. Put on my bravest face. Tried to act all cool and menacing, but a snowflake landed on my eyelash. I tried to blink the snow away.

"Die for good?"

Another fat flake landed on my other lash. "Dammit! Hang on," I said. I stared up at the dark storm clouds. "Enough with all the damn snow!"

Confused, Kane looked up at the sky.

I aimed my knife at his neck, stabbing hard at him.

His strong hand caught my wrist. The knife twisted from my grasp.

The sound of hooves echoed off the clearing. Karkadanns were approaching in the distance—Kane's men had arrived.

"Your time is up. My men will escort me from here and I will build a new army. And I *will* rule all of Tir Na. But I do want your help. Will you serve your new emperor, Finley Maguire?"

"That'll be a hard *no* from me. Sorry."

With my back against the tree, he pressed the point of the sword sticking through the front of his overcoat into my gut.

So, I kneed him in the groin. Cira would've liked that. But he just laughed at me again.

I heard boots hit the ground as his soldiers dismounted. They ran through the woods in search of us.

"Such a pity to waste so much natural talent and drive. However, not all things are meant to be. Farewell, Finley."

Bright flames lit up the outskirts of our small clearing. We both squinted, covering our eyes. A wave of heat blasted us. We heard the screams of men.

Taking advantage of the distraction, I grabbed Kane by the shoulders. I pulled him hard against me. The sword in his back plunged into my stomach—the look of shock on his face was priceless.

I grabbed again, pulling harder still. The tip of the blade went through me and dug into the tree. He struggled to break free, but I kept driving the sword deeper and deeper into the bark, trapping him there against me.

The evergreens shuddered, and Big Red's massive head emerged through the trees, her glowing yellow eyes fixed on us. She had followed the chase, likely tracking us from above as we tore through the forest below. And she flew down and flame-broiled Kane's knights. Tears raced down my cheeks as blood from my stomach and back poured down my legs.

Kane twisted against the tree he was pinned to, his movements frantic as he struggled to free himself. His panicked glances darted between me and the red dragon, his breath coming in sharp, shallow gasps.

My grip tightened on his coat, my knuckles white with the strain.

"Light us up!" I screamed at Big Red, my voice raw with adrenaline and fury.

She tilted her head slightly, her sharp features cutting a menacing silhouette against the snowy backdrop. Slowly, deliberately, she pushed her long neck farther into the clearing, the trees groaning as her bulk forced them apart. Her fiery breath shimmered faintly in the cold air, a promise of the devastation she could unleash.

Kane slammed his fists down onto my shoulders. More pain shot through my body, but I held on. He had to be stopped, even if it meant my death. But I had lost a lot of blood. My head started to spin.

"Burn us with your fire!" I shouted.

Big Red cocked her head, unsure of what to do.

"Kill both of us! Now! I can't hold him... forever... I'm dying!"

My legs buckled.

The red dragon roared. I shook my head, focused my mind, and sent her a message.

Give us your dragonfire. Burn us both to death. This man cannot live. Kill him for the black dragon. Please.

Big Red rocked her head from side to side. She got my message, but she had formed a bond with me. She did not want to kill me.

My legs gave way and only the sword stuck in the tree held me upright. Kane shoved his boot against the tree and kicked us away. We fell to the ground, sending another wave of agonizing pain through my body.

"Seems as though your dragon is as unfaithful as my Ormrir!" seethed Kane.

I forced a smirk on my face. "Run away and she'll burn you to death!"

Horrified, he looked down at the sword and then back at me.

I begged Big Red one last time. *Please kill us...*

Big Red pulled her head back, her jaws parting as she prepared to unleash her fire. The air around me grew heavy with the heat.

I closed my eyes, gripping Kane's coat tighter. This would be my last death.

"No!" Kane shouted, his voice raw with desperation.

But the fire never came.

Instead, a searing, stinging liquid splattered over us. It burned like acid, hissing as it struck the ground. I gasped, my grip faltering as pain shot through my skin.

Kane, too, flinched at the initial spray, but his shock quickly turned to delight. He threw his head back and laughed, the sound hoarse and mocking. "Your dragon no longer has her flame!"

He pushed himself up and away from me. Which meant more torture as the sword slid from my gut.

"You might be right."

Rolling on my side, I grabbed my knife from the forest floor.

I pulled the flint from my boot. The flint Temurr had given me that was causing me pain all day.

"But I still have mine..."

I struck the flint on the flat of my blade—sparks shot off—and thrust it at him.

Kane's eyes filled with terror.

Sparks ignited the liquid that Big Red had drenched us with. Fire engulfed Kane. I rolled into the wet snow and as far away as I could across the clearing.

Kane flailed about wildly as he burned alive. His unnerving cries rang through my frozen ears. He tossed himself to the ground, tried to roll off the flames in the snow, but her dragonfire was too intense.

I dug my heels into the ground, shoving myself against a tree, and watched him die.

"Burn, baby... Burn."

I held my hands against my stomach in a useless attempt to stop the blood pouring from me—experience had taught me... I was too close to *neardeath*.

But we had won! And that's all that mattered.

Lex talionis, I thought to myself. An eye for an eye.

I shivered as I felt Frip, Cira, and Temurr there by my side, smiling and comforting me. Gunnr was there, too. But she was probably shaking her head that it took me so long to bring him down.

A massive grin spread across my goofy face. Kane was gone and our armies had the advantage back on the battlefield. Yeah, I would have liked to have ripped his beating heart from his chest and all that, but... you can't have everything.

I coughed up more blood. Then I died.

Chapter 106

Air forced itself into my lungs, sharp and unrelenting. I inhaled in ragged gasps, my chest straining as though it had forgotten how to breathe. And every breath was agony, a fire coursing through my body. Slowly, painfully, I became aware of my surroundings. I was lying on something soft—a bed. Sheets cradled my aching body.

Tears spilled down my cheeks as the realization struck me: I was alive.

"She... lives," a young voice whispered nearby. Then louder, jubilant, "She lives!"

I struggled to open my eyes, lids heavy as steel. When I finally succeeded, I glimpsed a blond boy in blue and black robes sprinting from the room. "She is alive!" his high-pitched cry echoed down the stone hallway, fading into the distance.

"That's debatable," I muttered to the empty room.

I took in my surroundings. I was on a four-poster bed, a heavy blanket draped over me. Across the room, a fire roared in the hearth, its warmth battling the cold lingering in my bones. Sunlight poured through four tall windows, framing a brilliant blue sky. Lush tapestries adorned the walls, their intricate designs catching the light. A silk sofa, finely carved tables, and elegant chairs completed the room.

I shifted slightly, pain firing through every muscle, ligament, and bone. Even my skin protested. Gritting my teeth, I forced myself upright, clutching the bedpost for support. I glanced down at the glossy light blue robe and white nightgown someone had dressed me in. My hand instinctively went to my stomach and back, searching for the sword wounds that had felled me. They were gone.

Minutes passed as I gathered the strength to stand. Leaning heavily on the bedpost, I took slow, deliberate steps. Each movement was focused, every breath controlled, as I crossed the room and staggered into the adjacent sitting area.

Recognition smacked me hard in the face. The dark wood timbers on the ceiling, the familiar furniture—a rectangular table, wooden chairs, a desk—were all exactly as I remembered. This place wasn't just luxurious; it was familiar.

Wherever I was, I had been here before.

The wood floors shook as Braylor hurried into the bed chamber. Then he rushed into the sitting room, scooping me up into his arms. He hugged me tight as we flailed around.

"Ow. Ow. Ow."

"You live!"

"Not for long!" I protested. "If you keep this up!"

His hearty laughter filled the room. Every room. Braylor placed me down as gently as he could, which was not very gentle.

He held my face in his big hands, gently kissing my forehead and cheeks. I smiled and pointed to my lips. He kissed me and I fell into him, holding him as tightly as my aching arms allowed.

"We feared the worst!"

"You and me both," I said. I teetered to the settee and plopped down. "I feel like I was run over by a team of karkadanns. And then they backed up and ran me over again."

When I was finally able to breathe normally again, I looked around the sitting room.

"Wait. Isn't this Malek's chambers? In the Black City?"

He looked around the room. "No."

"Huh. Sure looks like it."

"Come with me! I am sure you are famished. Let us get you food and drink. There is much to discuss." He paused. "And see..."

He held out his hand but I just wanted to crawl back into that soft bed and whine about the lingering effects of death.

"How long was I... gone?"

"You have been dead for over a month."

"A month?! Shit..."

He held out his hand. I took it and he dragged me up.

"My feet are freezing! I guess circulation takes a while when you've been deceased for a month..."

Braylor rushed away to the bedroom, returning with silk slippers.

"We did win the battle, right?"

He placed the slippers on me. "We won a mighty victory! Although, it seems you missed your chance to hold Kane's still-beating heart?"

"Don't kick me when I'm down, Braylor. Wait..." I yanked him close to me. "Please tell me... Kane is still dead."

He placed his hands on my shoulders. "Kane was burned to his bones. And then we fed his bones to a white boar to ensure he could not return."

I exhaled. A massive weight fell from my shoulders.

"Um, has anyone checked on that boar lately?"

He laughed, his deep voice echoing warmly, and draped his massive arm around me. Together, we stepped through the double doors of the sitting room and into a wide hallway. The right side was open to the air, and a crisp breeze brushed against my face.

I glanced toward the arches lining the corridor, their familiar curves framing the sprawling Black City beyond. Its dark rooftops and towering spires were now cloaked in a pristine layer of snow, the winter veil softening its usual sharpness. The sight was both foreign and familiar, a reminder of how much time—and how little—had passed.

"But... we're in Irkalla! This *is* the Black City."

Braylor laughed. "You are correct."

I looked back at the double wooden doors.

"This is the entrance to Malek's bedrooms! I remember it. I was here!"

"Those are no longer Malek's chambers, Fin."

I gave him a sour look. "Well, yeah. I get that. He's dead."

"Let me show you something..."

Braylor walked me to the doors of a massive stone balcony.

I grabbed his arm. "What about Kasuma? She was in the forest with me and—"

"I am well enough."

I turned. Kasuma was inches from my face. In shock, I nearly fell over but Braylor caught me.

"You got me again," I said.

With my heart beating out of my chest, I reached out to hug her. She backed away, bowing her head. I noticed that one of her wings was bent over to the side.

I nodded toward her damaged wing. "Are you well enough?"

"Enough. However, as is the custom of my people, I have been banished from Nibiru," she admitted and avoided eye contact. "Since I can no longer fly."

"What?!" I said. My fists balled up. "That's crazy! His own daughter? No. I will not accept that."

"It is... as it has always been, your—"

"He can't discriminate like that! Haven't any of you learned anything?! Staying isolated is what got us into this whole shit show! I'm going to have a little talk with King Longzhe."

"He will certainly take an audience with you. Now," she cryptically stated. And quickly changed the subject. "As I am not welcome in Dimian on Oceantis, I have humbly come to offer my services."

"What? Why me?"

Braylor stood beside me, grinning down at Kasuma. "She does not yet know."

"Know what? What the hell is going on, Braylor?"

He exhaled and spun me around again. "Another friend awaits you."

We continued toward the balcony doors, the crisp winter air seeping into the hallway ahead. A young female servant approached silently, her head bowed as she draped a thick fur coat over my shoulders. Before I could thank her, the blond boy from earlier rushed forward, swinging the doors open with practiced ease.

The icy wind bit at my cheeks as I stepped onto the balcony, shivering against the cold. I paused, glancing around. "Okay?" I asked hesitantly.

Braylor said nothing but pointed upward.

Following the line of his outstretched finger, my gaze landed on a stone bridge spanning two towering white spires. There she was—Big Red. Perched majestically on the bridge, her massive form framed by the brilliant blue sky, she fixed her glowing eyes on me.

As soon as she saw me, she threw her head back and roared, the sound reverberating across the castle and the city beyond. Then, with deliberate precision, she opened her jaws and unleashed a torrent of dragonfire.

Braylor pulled me close as the flames whooshed above us, a wave of intense heat melting the snow blanketing the balcony. The air warmed instantly, steam rising from the newly exposed stone.

"She visits the castle every few days," Braylor said, his voice softer now. "Waiting for your return."

A smile spread across my face, unexpected and utterly genuine. I waved at the dragon like an overexcited child, feeling a pang of joy as her head tilted, almost amused. She craned back to the bridge and clamped her jaws around a scorched bicorn carcass, hauling the steaming meat with her as she spread her massive wings.

With effortless grace, she descended toward us, dropping the still-smoking hunk onto the cobblestones below before soaring back into the bright sky.

A collective gasp rose from the courtyard below. Rushing to the edge of the balcony, I peered down at the Black City. A massive crowd had gathered at the inner wall of the castle, their sheer numbers growing by the moment as more people poured in.

The throng erupted into cheers. Their cries rang out, joyous and triumphant, as hands waved wildly in the air. They jumped and shouted, their collective elation reaching up to the balcony.

I turned to Braylor. "What is going on?"

His smile got even bigger.

"The people are glad to see... their queen is alive and well."

"Huh? Their... queen?!"

Braylor waved to the Irkallans below. They responded with another loud hurrah. I leaned over and gave a tentative wave—they screamed and shouted and waved back.

"What the fuck is going on?!"

"As Malek had no heirs, and neither did Kane, your official title is Queen Finley Maguire of Irkalla," he stated. "By defeating both, you were crowned while you were... away. You are the usurper."

"But... but I-I don't want to be queen!"

"Finley!" I heard Pherric shout.

He dashed onto the balcony and picked me off the ground—I grunted in pain.

"She does not like being picked up," mused Braylor. "For some reason."

"I worried you would not return to us! After one lunar cycle, I was so—"

"I know. I know. We're in *uncharted territory*."

He inspected me while I did the same. He looked crisp in his fresh dark green tunic and the white surcoat, with the red X on front and back.

"For someone who has been dead for thirty-six days, you are a vision of loveliness!"

"And you are looking quite tasty yourself! Let me guess—you're the new Preceptor of the Scholomance now?"

His grin was infectious. "By the gods, no! However, with Nerus gone, the new Preceptor has arranged for me to be Mage to the Queen of Irkalla!"

My hand went to my heart—he was talking about me! There was no way that was going to sink in any time soon. If ever...

"Although, with your incredible mindform abilities, your mage will be coming to *you* for advice. Your highness."

I eye-rolled him. "Okay, um... in that case, you be king and I'll be the Mage."

Pherric bowed slightly, smirking. "You will make an excellent queen."

I turned to Braylor. "Who am I forgetting? Did we lose anyone else?"

"The campaign was a smashing success. No other casualties of note," said Braylor.

"What about Melcente? Did she survive?"

Braylor shrugged. "I assume you are referring to your new Commander of the Irkallan Royal Navy?"

I laughed and clapped my hands. "Oh, is that what she calls herself?"

Pherric seemed confused. "She swore on her life that you had promised her this position. Is this not true?"

"How the hell would I know that I'd be in a position to promise her *anything*!" I cracked up at her boldness. "But I can't imagine anyone I'd rather have in that position."

"Then you have made your first proclamation as Queen," stated Braylor. "Now! Let us eat! Um... apologies... your highness."

"I will never get used to that."

He held out his arm and we walked off toward the great hall.

"What does that make you?"

"Uh, let me think... Royal consort?"

"Oh, I like that. Sounds kinda dirty. Is that dirty?"

"If it is not, we shall make it so..."

"Good boy," I purred.

I took one last look as the dragon flew up into the clouds and away from Irkalla. From my kingdom.

Epilogue

So, that's my story—or as much of it as I managed to write down. Turns out, I lived a whole week longer than Pherric predicted. But now, I'm officially out of time.

And I've managed to get myself killed a few times after this story. Because I'm an idiot. I died during the war with Atlantis and stayed dead for almost a year. Later, during that delightful skirmish with the Frost Giants north of Valhalla, I managed to be dead for nearly eight years. That little misadventure also cost me the crown. (Twist ending: the usurper got usurped. Justice, I guess?)

But this time? Pherric's math says I'll be gone for eighty to a hundred years. Poison is tricky like that. When I wake, maybe I'll write down those tales too. You know, for your great grandkids.

This manuscript will be placed in my tomb, so assuming you're the kind of person who skips straight to the end. If that's the case, let me reiterate: **DO NOT BURN MY BODY. DO NOT BURY ME.**

I *will* return.

Thanks for your cooperation...
Finley Maguire
Former Queen of Irkalla